William Gilmore Simms

Border Beagles

A Tale of Mississippi

William Gilmore Simms

Border Beagles
A Tale of Mississippi

ISBN/EAN: 9783337022815

Printed in Europe, USA, Canada, Australia, Japan

Cover: Foto ©Andreas Hilbeck / pixelio.de

More available books at **www.hansebooks.com**

A

TALE OF MISSISSIPPI

BY W. GILMORE SIMMS,

AUTHOR OF "RICHARD HURDIS," "THE PARTISAN," "MELLICHAMPE," "KATHARINE WALTON," "THE SCOUT," "WOODCRAFT," ETC

> "So, at length,
> The city, like a camp in mutiny,
> Saw nothing else to walk her streets unharmed
> But these, your free companions."
> VAN ARTEVELDE.

New and Revised Edition.

CHICAGO, NEW YORK AND SAN FRANCISCO:
BELFORD, CLARKE & CO.
1888.

BORDER BEAGLES.

CHAPTER I.

COURT SEASON.

> ——"I have got
> A seat to sit at ease here, in mine inn,
> To see the comedy; and laugh and chuck
> At the variety and throng of humors,
> And dispositions that come jostling in
> And out."—BEN JONSON.— *The New Inn.*

THE little town of Raymond, in the state of Mississippi, was in the utmost commotion. Court-day was at hand, and nothing was to be heard but the hum of preparation for that most important of all days in the history of a country-village—that of general muster alone excepted. Strange faces and strange dresses began to show themselves in the main street; lawyers were entering from all quarters—"saddlebag" and "sulky" lawyers—men who cumber themselves with no weight of law, unless it can be contained in moderately-sized heads, or valise, or saddle-bag, of equally moderate dimensions. Prowling sheriff's officers began to show their hands again, after a ten or twenty days' absence in the surrounding country, where they had gone to the great annoyance of simple farmers, who contract large debts to the shop-keeper on the strength of crops yet to be planted, which are thus wasted on changeable silks for the spouse, and whistle-handled whips for "Young Hopeful" the only son and heir to possessions, which, in no long time, will be heard best of under the auctioneer's hammer The population of the village was increasing rapidly; and what with the sharp militia colonel, in his new box coat, squab white hat, trim collar and high-heeled boots, seeking to find favor in the regiment against the next election for supplying the brigadier's vacancy; the swaggering planter to whom certain disquieting hints of foreclosure have been given, which he can evade no longer, and which he must settle as he may; the slashing over-seer, prime for cockfight or quarter-race, and not unwilling to try his own prowess upon his neighbor, should occasion serve and all other sports fail; the pleading and impleaded, prosecu-tor and prosecuted, witnesses and victims—Raymond never promised more than at present to swell beyond all reasonable boundaries, and make a noise in the little world round it.

Court-day is a day to remember in the West, either for the parts witnessed or the parts taken in the various performances; and whether the party be the loser of an eye or ear, or has merely helped another to the loss of both, the case is still the same; the event is not usually forgotten.

The inference was fair that there would be a great deal of this sort of prime brutality performed at the present time. Among the crowd might be seen certain men who had already distinguished themselves after this manner, and who strutted and swaggered from pillar to post, as if conscious that the eyes of many were upon them, either in scorn or admiration. No toriety is a sort of fame which the vulgar mind essentially enjoys beyond any other; and we are continually reminded, while among the crowd, of the fellow in the play, who says he "loves to be contemptible." Some of these creatures had lost an eye, some an ear; others had their faces scarred with the strokes of knives; and a close inspection of others might have shown certain tokens about their necks, which tes-tified to bloody ground fights, in which their gullets formed an acquaintance with the enemy's teeth, not over-well calculated to make them desire new terms of familiarity. Perhaps, in most cases, these wretches had only been saved from just pun-ishment by the humane intervention of the spectators—a hu-manity that is too often warmed into volition, only when the proprietor grows sated with the sport. All was crowd and con-fusion. At one moment the main street in Raymond was absolutely choked by the press of conflicting vehicles. Judge Bun kell's sulky hitched wheels with the carriage of Colonel Fish- hawk, and 'Squire Dickens' bran new barouche, brought up from Orleans only a week before, was "staved all to flinders" — so said our landlady — "agin the corner of Joe Richards' stable." The 'squire himself narrowly escaped the very last injury in the power of a fourfooted beast to inflict, that is dis- posed to use his hoofs heartily — and, bating an abrasion of the left nostril, which diminished the size, if it did not, as was the opinion of many, impair the beauty of the member, Dickens had good reason to congratulate himself at getting off with so little personal damage.

These, however, were not the only mishaps on this occasion. There were other stories of broken heads, maims, and injuries ; but whether they grew out of the unavoidable concussion of a large crowd in a small place, or from a great natural tendency to broken heads on the part of the owners, it scarcely falls within our present purpose to inquire. A jostle in a roomy region like the west, is anything but a jostle in the streets of New York. There you may tilt the wayfarer into the gutter, and the laugh is against the loser, it being a sufficient apology for taking such a liberty with your neighbor's person, that "business is business and must be attended to." Every man must take care of himself and learn to push with the rest, where all are in a hurry.

But he brooks the stab who jostles his neighbor where there is no such excuse ; and the stab is certain where he presumes so far with his neighbor's wife, or his wife's daughter, or his sister. There's no pleading that the city rule is to "take the right hand" — he will let you know that the proper rule is to give way to the weak and feeble — to women, to age, to infancy. This is the manly rule among the strong, and a violation of it brings due punishment in the west. Jostling there is a dan- gerous experiment, and for this very reason, it is frequently practised by those who love a row and fear no danger. It is one of the thousand modes resorted to for compelling the fight of fun — the conflict which the rowdy seeks from the mere love of tumult, and in the excess of overheated blood.

If there was a sensation among the "arrivals" at Raymond.

14 BORDER BEAGLES.

there was scarcely less among the residents. The private houses were soon full of visiters, and the public of guests Major Mandrake's tavern was crammed from top to bottom and this afflicting dispensation led to the strangest disruption of anciently adjusted beds and bedsteads. Miss Artemisia Mandrake, for example, was compelled to yield her cushions to a horse-drover from Tennessee, and content herself with such "sleeps" as she could find in an old arm-chair, that stood in immemorial dust in a sort of pigeon-roost garret. It was to this necessity, we may be permitted to say in this place, that she for ever after ascribed her rheumatism, and a certain awry contraction of the muscles of the neck, which, defeating her other personal charms, was not inaptly assumed, by the damsel herself, to have been the true cause of her remaining, up to the time of this writing, an unappropriated spinster. Major Mandrake has certainly had excellent reason to repent his cupidity.

The rival tavern of Captain Crumbaugh was in equally fortunate condition with that of the major. They were both filled to overflowing by midday, and after that you could get a bed in neither for love nor money. And yet the folks continued to arrive; folks of all conditions and from all quarters; in gig and sulky, or on horseback; some riding in pairs on the same donkey—and not a few short-petticoated damsels, led by curiosity, from the neighboring farms, and mounted in like manner, on battered jades, whose mouths, ossified by repeated jerks, now defied the strenuous efforts by which the riders would have set them forward with some show of life and spirit, as they emerged from the forests into the crowded thoroughfare.

"Well, there's a heap of folks still a-coming, and where in the world they'll find a place to lie down in to-night, is a'most past my reckoning. I'm sure the major ha'n't got another bed left, high nor low; and as for the captain, I heard him tell Joe Zeigler an hour ago, that all was full with him. Yet, do look, how they are a-coming. Can't you look, Jack Horsey, if it's only for a minute. You hav'n't got no more nateral curiosity than—"

"Shut up, Bess, you've got enough for both of us. What's it to me, and what's it to you, where the folks sleep? Let them sleep where they can; there'll be no want of beds where there's no want of money. If they have that, the captain and the major will take good care that they have every opportunity to spend it. As for you, go you and see after the poultry; court-time is a mighty bad season for chickens; they die off very sudden, and the owner is not always the wiser of the sort of death they die. Push, Bess, and see if you can forget for awhile the business of the two taverns."

The good wife was silent for a space, but this was the only acknowledgment which she condescended to yield her stubborn and incurious husband. She did not leave her place at the window, but continued to gaze with the satisfaction of a much younger person, at the throng in the thoroughfare, as it received additions momently from every new arrival. At length the stir appeared to cease — the carriages to disappear; horses vanished in the custody of bustling ostlers, and their riders, making amends for the day's abstinence, on a dry road, might be seen, in great part, at the bar-room of the major or the captain, washing away the dust from capacious throats by occasional draughts of whiskey or peach brandy.

The latter article seemed most in demand at the house of Captain Crumbaugh. He had the art of preparing it to perfection; and "Crumbaugh's peach" was, in my day, a sort of proverb with all who travelled in his parts. Major Mandrake took care to have the very best whiskey — of particular strength and peculiar flavor; and there was a class, and this no small one neither, that might readily be found to give it preference. I class myself among none of these. The oily excellence of the peach of Crumbaugh is still a flavor on "memory's waste;" (query, "taste?") and whiskey was never a favorite of mine, though I have partaken of it along with governors and judges, senators and saints.

But to return to the curious Mrs. Horsey. The dispersion of the crowd, as it ceased to furnish her with any new subjects of interest, necessarily left her somewhat more free to remember the injunctions of her husband; and she was about to turn from the window, with a long drawn sigh of weariness, or dissatisfaction that the show was over, when a smart-looking youth, whom she did not know, rode up to the door.

"Oh, Mr. Horsey — a gentleman — on a fine roan horse — he's at the door — I reckon he wants to see some of us, and maybe comes to look after a lodging for to-night. I knew the major was full, and the captain—"

"Now, the devil take the major and the captain, and all the taverns in the state, since they drive everything out of your brain that ought to be there," was the angry speech with which the stubborn husband interrupted the wandering soliloquy of his spouse. "Why don't you see what the stranger wants, woman? — you heard his knocking, and there you stand guessing about tavern business, and such matters as you've no need to think, much less to speak about."

"La! John Horsey — you're too positive and contrarious, not let a body think—"

"No! What the devil should you think for? that's my business, I tell you now, as I've told you a good hundred times before. But go to the door; don't stand there staring like a gray owl in a green bush; go and open the door and see what the man wants, unless you desire that I should get up with my lame leg and show him in. Won't you go, I ask you."

"Well, John, don't you see I'm going? You're always in such a fret."

"Enough cause too, with such a trouble as you are."

"Yes, sometimes I'm anything but a trouble; there's no word you have too good for me; and then agin—"

"There's none too bad," said the splenetic husband, finishing the speech as she had begun it; "but go to the door, as if you had some life in you, or the stranger will batter it down before you get there."

There was some reason, indeed, for the apprehension expressed by Horsey, as the applicant for admission, seeing that no heed was given to his first summons, yet hearing, without doubt, a buzzing of the sharp controversy going on within, had renewed his application with redoubled force, employing for the purpose the butt of a loaded whip, every stroke of which told like a hammer upon the plank. The dame started in compliance with the clamors from without, rather than the impatient commands within; for she still seemed panting for another word, and muttered between her teeth, as she slowly moved toward the door, something which, to the jealous authority of her liege lord, seemed to denote a resolution still to think as she pleased and when she pleased, in spite of his declarations against her right to do so.

"Look you, Bess, go to the door: and move a little more quickly, if you don't want to make me mighty angry. See what the stranger wants; and remember we don't keep a lodging-house any longer. We have no room; we want no company."

This was spoken in those subdued tones, and with that show of suppressed and striving feeling, which, perhaps, denote a greater degree of earnestness and resolution than any words might do. The effect upon the wife was instantaneous, and her hand was soon upon the lock.

"Remember, we have no lodging," murmured the husband, as the door opened. "I only wish I were a mile or two back in the woods, where I mightn't be worried as I am about board. There was a time when I might have been glad of a good stand on the road, but it's not so now. I can live like a gentleman, and why should I be bothered to get breakfasts, and see after strange horses, for people I shall never see but once, and don't want to see at all? I'll—"

The words of the stranger, spoken in bold, free, musical language, which reached the ears of the invalid at that moment, put an end to the soliloquy.

"Mrs. Horsey, ma'am?"

"He might swear to it, if he knew only half as much as I," exclaimed the invalid.

The stranger, a tall, well-made youth of twenty-five or thereabouts, meanwhile, drew up his steed, lifted his cap handsomely from his head, like one born a courtier, with a grace that found its way instantly to the lady's heart, and proceeded in his inquiries.

"I have been advised, Mrs. Horsey, by a particular friend, to seek lodgings at your house during my stay in Raymond. Can I have them?"

Before the good lady, prefacing her denial with a long apology and a pleasant smirk of the face, could bring out what she was preparing to say, the rough voice of the sultan from within, gave his answer to the stranger.

"Can't have 'em, my friend—this is no lodging-house—ne room to spare."

"Very sorry, indeed," said the old lady.

"Not sorry at all, stranger," said the truth-speaking Horsey; "for you see, if we wanted to lodge you, the thing might well enough be done. But we don't set out to keep company, and there are taverns enough in the village."

"Scarcely, if the story is true that they are all full," replied the stranger; "but let me alight and see you. I have a message to you, madam, and to your husband from my friend Carter, who tells me that he lodges with you, and that you could easily find me lodgings, also, for the little time I mean to stay in Raymond."

The effect of this speech was instantaneous upon the man of the house. He barely heard the youth through ere he replied,

"Eh! what's that you say, my friend? Did you say Carter—was it Ben Carter that sent the message?"

"The same," replied the youth while entering the house.

"And why the d—l, stranger, didn't you say so at first without any prevarications. What's the use of this cursed long palavar, when two words could have done the whole business. Of course we can give you lodgings. Ben Carter told you nothing but the truth. He has a habit of speaking the truth which would be very good for many other people to take up—not meaning you, stranger, for if you be a friend of Ben Carter, I reckon, it's like you are of the same sort of stuff."

"You speak only as my friend deserves, Mr. Horsey. Carter is the very man you describe him. True in all his words, and just in all his dealings with men, it is my pride in esteeming him one of the most valuable and closest friends I have. It is not amiss, Mr. Horsey, to add that he has an opinion of you no less favorable than yours of him."

"Tush, young man, soft soap don't tickle me at my time of life," replied Horsey with an Indian grunt of seeming indifference. "I am as I am, and it's no great matter what I am, seeing that I'm of little use in this world at present, and likely to be of less; yet it's not a bad thing to have the good words of them that's good. It sort o' reconciles a man to a great many evil things that might otherwise bring him a mighty deal of trouble. And Ben Carter is a good man — when did you see him last ?"

"Some ten days ago. He left me at Monticello, and was on his way to Jackson, from which place he promised to return directly to this. He was to meet me here to-night."

"Well, I reckon he'll be as good as his word, if there's nothing to stop him on the way. He's mighty punctual to his business, and when he says he'll do, you may count it done. True as steel, is Ben Carter, and it's no use to say farther. Bess let's have something. What'll you take, stranger ? — there's some mighty fine peach, some of Crumbaugh's peach, as they call it, which is pretty much the same as calling it the very best in Mississippi. I have some old Monongahela besides, which I can speak a good word for — sugar, Bess."

The beverage was soon prepared, and the two were about to drink, when Horsey reminded the other of a degree of inequality between them which needed to be reconciled before they could properly drink health together.

"You have all the advantage on your side, stranger; my name's John Horsey — that, it seems, you know already; but yours — what's your name ? There's no pleasure in calling a man 'stranger' every minute, when you're talking and drinking together all the while."

"True," replied the stranger; "but I never thought of that. My name, Mr. Horsey, is Vernon — Harry Vernon. It is not improbable that you have heard it before from my friend Carter."

"Don't recollect — don't think I ever did. Vernon, Vernon — it's a good name enough — comes smooth and easy to the tongue as a gentleman's name ought to do always; but Harry, Harry Vernon! You wasn't christened Harry, I reckon, Mr. Vernon? Must have been Henry, and they call you Harry for short."

"For short, say you? Well, it may be so," replied the stranger with a laugh, "but long or short, I was never called by any other since I have known myself; and never, until this moment thought of asking which of the two I had the clearest right to make use of."

"The old people living, Mr. Vernon? Your health, sir, is

the meantime. That's what I call peach brandy, sir—no make b'lieve—none of your whiskey run through peach timber such as they give you at Orleans. Old Crumbaugh warrants that stuff, and gets his price for it. Did I hear you, Mr. Vernon? the old people, you said they were living."

"Neither, sir."

"Try another sip, Mr. Vernon," said the other consolingly, "peach perfectly harmless; Crumbaugh keeps the temperance society house; warrants his peach; calls it sobriety peach; and so you've lost both parents, Mr. Vernon?"

"Both—all, sir. I may almost exclaim with the Indian, that there runs no drop of my blood in the veins of any human being."

"Don't say that, Mr. Vernon, don't say that. It's much more than any man can say, and be certain. Fathers, sir, are apt to leave children where they never look for them; there's something of that sort at my own door, Mr. Vernon, and so—"

"La, John, how you do talk."

"What, you're there, Bess, are you?" The chuckle of the veteran was arrested, and probably a long string of confessions, by the timely ejaculation of his wife, who happened to be busy in the closet—"these women, Mr. Vernon—but you're married?"

"No!"

"Be thankful, young master—it's a pleasure then to come, if it comes as a pleasure, which is something like Bazil Hunter's pea crop, 'a very doubtful up-coming.' You will run your race like the rest of us, and come up at the post as usual, but it won't be the starting-post, I tell you! You was saying something about the Indians, and that brought up some recollections of mine when I was among them. I've been among all the Southern Indians, except the Catawba. I've never been among them, and I reckon there's but few of them now left to see; but I've been among the Creeks and the Cherokees, the Choctaws and the Chickasaws, and there was another tribe, when I first came into these parts, that I hear nothing of now, called the Leaf River Indians; there was but few of them, and I think they belonged to the Chickasaws, but they were the handsomest Indians I ever did see in all my travelling, and I

begun early. I used to trade, when I was little, a mere sprout
of a boy, from Tennessee, through the mountains, into North
and South Carolina — then, after that, to the Mississippi; and
many's the time I've made out to carry a matter of five pack-
horses — I, and three other lads of Tennessee — through the
very heart of the 'nation,' without so much as losing a thimble,
and almost without having a scare. In one of these journeys
I saw my wife, then a mere bit of a girl.— What! not gone,
Bess! — It's gospel truth, Mr. Harry Vernon, from that day
there's been but one pack-horse in our family, and that's Jack
Horsey himself."

"La! now, John," cried the wife with uplifted hands, "the
stranger don't know your ways, and he'll take for true what
you're a-telling him. That's jist the way with him, stranger—"

"Stranger!—the gentleman's got a name, Bess. Mr. Vernon, Mr. Harry Vernon; remember, now, it's not Henry, but
Harry Vernon.— Mr. Vernon, this is my wife. You'd soon
enough find that out, if you lodged with us awhile. And now,
Bess, be off, and look after supper;—a silent wife, and a singing kettle — it's not always we can have 'em, Mr. Vernon, but
that only helps to make them the more desirable."

Mrs. Horsey was not to be sent off, however, in so conclusive
a manner. The complaints of Horsey, touching the constraints
upon him of his better half, were ludicrous enough; contrasted,
as they were, with the almost despotic sway which he exercised
at every instant. Perhaps a latent desire to show her guest
that her good lord did not have it altogether his own way, led
her on this occasion to dispute his commands.

"It's not time for supper, John Horsey. Now that you're
lame, you seem to think of nothing but eating and drinking."

"Did mortal husband ever hear to such a woman?" was the
exclamation of the sultan. The wife mistook for compliance a
mildness in the speech which was only due to the astonishment
of the speaker. She continued:—

"It's a good hour to supper yet. We have our hours, John
Horsey, jist the same as the major, and—"

"Now d—n the major, and d—n the captain, and d—n all
the taverns in Mississippi. Thus it is, Mr. Vernon, a wife
will make a man swear, sir, when there's nothing in the world

farther from his wish. You see, sir, my wife will do and say
just what she pleases, as I told you. She will always be
bringing up to me those cursed taverns; but I'll stop that, or
there's no snakes! Look you, Betsey!"

Here his finger guided her to the door, through which she
made her departure in the shortest possible space of time. A
look had done what, probably, no word in John Horsey's vo-
cabulary could have achieved half so soon.

"A good woman enough, Mr. Vernon; but women, sir, are
women; and the very best of them are incapable of serious
concerns: they are all triflers — mere children — a sort of gin-
gerbread creatures, the ginger of which lasts on the tongue a
deused sight longer than the molasses. But, as you were saying, Mr. Vernon, you are a lawyer."

"You have guessed rightly, sir, that is my profession indeed.
Your ears are something better than mine, I think, for I do not
recollect ever having told you the fact."

"Nor did you, my dear fellow," replied the old man with a
hearty laugh. "It was, as you say, a mere guess of mine, and
Jack Horsey's guess is seldom short of the mark. It's a way
with me to take for granted, just as if my neighbor had said it,
the thing which it appears to me reasonable to think he will
say; and I could ha' sworn, from a rakish, sharp, lively something about your face and eyes, and a little swing of your
shoulders, that you was a lawyer, or going soon to be one.
You practise in Monticello?"

"I came from Monticello last, but it is not my residence."

"Well, but you practise law somewhere in Mississippi."

"I shall in season, I doubt not, provided I get clients.
Young lawyers find in this their chief difficulty. They practise
with some such rule as governs a good angler — where the fish
bite best, there you are sure to find them. For my part, I am
but too lately admitted to determine where the best water lies
for my purposes; I have not yet thrown out my lines."

"And that you won't do till your hooks are well baited, for
that I believe is one of the first lessons which a lawyer learns.
I know'd if you had begun to practise, you hadn't done much
in that way; your chin is almost too smooth, though that's no
misfortune as times go, if so be your tongue proves smooth and

oily like your chin. But there, it seems to me, Mr. Vernon, that your difficulty lies. I'm afraid you ha'n't g .t the gift of the gab. I haven't heard you say much."

"And for a very excellent reason, Mr. Horsey : you haven't given me a chance. Your tongue has utterly outwagged mine, and I yield the palm to you, where my vanity, perhaps, would allow me to yield it to few other persons. But, it is now my turn, and if I do not prove myself quite your equal before I'm done with you, I will at least convince you that I am not entirely without my claims to take rank among the mouthing part of my profession."

"Spoken like a man, and a good fellow," cried Horsey with a hearty laugh, and with no sort of discomfiture at a retort as just as it was unexpected. "I have better hopes of you now, Mr. Harry Vernon. 'Ecod, you gave it me then—a raal dig in the side with a sharp elbow. The truth is, I am a leetle too much given to hearing myself talk, and what's worse, I can't easily be convinced that it is not my neighbor whose tongue all the while has been making the *hellabaloo*. Somehow or other, thinking of what the man ought to say, that I'm talking to, I come to think he says it, and half an hour after, could almost take my Bible oath to the fact. It's a strange infirmity, Mr. Vernon ; don't you think so ?"

"Very—very strange," said the other, smiling at the seem-ing seriousness of his companion.

"And so, you were telling me you practise law in Orleans.'

"No—"

"Ah, Mobile, yes—Mobile you said."

"Nay, nay, Mr. Horsey, I said neither," replied the youth laughing out aloud ; " this is only another sample of the infirm-ity you were telling me about—another of your guesses—and I will not tell you how far from the truth. But it is my turn now, and while I throw another stick upon your fire, and draw my chair a foot closer, I will prepare my thoughts for the cross-examination which I mean to give you in turn."

"Ah, well ; but 'wait a bit and take a bit,' first, as we say in Massissippi. We'll have it over after supper, when you may try your skill upon me, for a first witness, and see what you will get for going. I'm a tough colt to ride, when the bit hurts me; and he must be a skilful rider, indeed, if he saves himself a throw."

"We shall see, we shall see," said Vernon, confidently, and with a smile of good nature; while the old man, with whose humor the course which the youth had taken seemed admirably to tally, told him a dozen anecdotes of the young lawyers round about the country, with most of whom he had had sharp passes of wit, and in all cases, according to his own phrase and showing, had "come down uppermost."

CHAPTER II.

RETURN OF THE PRODIGAL.

"If you look in the maps of the 'orld, I warrant you shall find, in the comparisons between Macedon and Monmouth, that the situations, look you, is both alike. There is a river in Macedon, and there is also, moreover, a river at Monmouth; it is called Wye at Monmouth, but it is out of my praine what is the name of the other river; but 'tis all one, 'tis so like as my fingers is to my fingers, and there is salmons in both."

SHAKSPERE — *Fluellen.*

THE landlady spread her little board, on which a broiled chicken and sundry smoking slices of ham soon made their appearance. Chubby biscuits of fresh Pittsburgh flour, formed a pyramidal centre in the table arrangements, and a capacious bowl of milk stood beside them. Coffee, which is the *sine qua non* in a western supper, was of course not lacking; and appetite, that commends even the unflavored pulse and the dry roots, rendered necessary no idle solicitings to persuade our young traveller to do justice to a meal, in preparing which, the good hostess had spared nothing of her store.

"Fall to, Harry Vernon, and don't wait on me," was the frank command of Horsey, as, grunting and growling the while he worked his rocking chair, foot by foot, up to the side of the table, and drew from it one of the plates into his lap. Vernon had his good word for the hostess, and in a little time proved himself to be in possession of the best wisdom of the traveller whom experience teaches, that good humor and a cheerful spirit are the most valuable companions which he can take with him in a course of western travel. We recommend them to all your ill-favored bookworms who carry their stilts with them into our swamps and forests, and fancy all the while that they can see anything, who never cease looking on their own pedestals.

Vernon had been already something of a wayfarer. Necessities of one sort or another, had schooled him into a knowledge of men of every sort, and it was a rational boast which he was sometimes wont to make, in the glow of a youthful and pardonable vanity, that he could go from Tampa bay to the Rocky mountains, and win good usage and a smile with his supper every night. Such a brag may be made by few with safety. Invidious comparisons constantly rise to our minds as we think of the little and peculiar luxuries of our homes, and we lose our appetite for that which is before us, by suffering our feeble fancies to trouble us with the memories of what we can not have. Your Englishman is a traveller of this sort. From the first jump which he makes from Dover, or Liverpool, he begins to smell out novelties which are always offensive to self-conceit, simply because they are novelties. His sole business from that moment, seems to be to discover in what things his present differs from his past, and to find fault and grumble accordingly. He turns up his nose with such an inveterate effort from the beginning, that it remains in that inodorous position for ever after.

But we have nothing now to do with him. Vernon, as we have said, was of very different temper; lively, bold, frank, generous, he was just the sort of person to commend himself to the southern and western people. His dignity, never apprehensive of doubt and denial, was never on the watch to take offence at everything in the least degree equivocal. To avoid controversy, to avoid the crowd, to yield gracefully in argument, and to forbear pressing his advantage at the proper moment — were some few of the maxims by which, avoiding every prospect of offence, he gained the most substantial victories, as well over the hearts as the understandings of those with whom he contended. Fluent in speech, with a memory abounding in illus tration and anecdote, a fancy, lively and playful, an imagina

tion vigorous and bold, the profession which it seems he had
chosen, appeared to be that in which, above all others, he promised most to excel.   Such, we may add, was the opinion of his
friends, and such, were it proper for the narrator to predict, was
the appropriate event after the lapse of that usual period of
probation, to which it is natural and well that all ambitious
minds should be subjected.   Precocious greatness is generally
very short-lived.

There was that superiority in the mind of Harry Vernon,
which never suffered him to think himself above the occasion.
He could descend from the abstract to the practical with an
ease and rapidity at once singular and successful.   To rise
from the actual to the abstract is a far easier matter, and hence
it is that we have so many theoretical men, who always fail in
the attempt to carry out their own principles.   To accommodate himself to the understandings of those he addressed, without degrading his own, was another of those advantages — the
result of actual experience in the busy world, which, added to
the store of our young traveller, and supplied to him as it has
supplied to others, in many instances, the lack of money and
the aid of powerful friends.   Before supper was fairly ended
he had shown some of these possessions ; and Horsey, the rough,
garrulous, grumbling invalid, was not unwilling to hear another
voice than his own occupy those intervals in the progress of
the meal, which he had seldom failed to fill up hitherto from
his own resources, and to his own perfect satisfaction.   The
youth requited him with story for story, joke for joke, and
when, at the usual hour for retiring in the country, where folks
are very apt to go to bed with the fowls, the worthy dame intimated to Vernon that his bed was ready whenever he wished
" to lie down ;" her spouse blazed out like a splinter of fat lightwood — bade her begone and not send the young man to bed
at dark, to tumble about half the night in sleeplessness and
stupor.

" That's the way, Harry ; and by the Lord Harry, it's a
monstrous vexing way my wife has got.   She goes to bed at
dark, you see ; she's kept up a little longer to-night than's customary with her ; and before day-peep she's a-stirring, and
a 'ossing, and a-calling up the niggers.   Now, you see, I can't

sleep soon o' nights for the life of me. I never could ever since
I was a lad driving my pack-horses over the mountains. 'Twas
then I got a sort o' habit of sitting up late. When we'd come
to a running water, or a spring, or some such fine place for a
camp, why we'd drive stakes, cut bushes, make tents, and fasten
our horses. Then we'd feed 'em, git up a fire, and set to preparing our own feed. Well, we'd have to do all this mighty
slyly, I tell you, for fear of the Indians. We'd git away from
the main track, hide our horses pretty deep in the small woods,
and put our fire in a sort of hollow, so that nobody could see
the blaze. Then we'd git round it, put down a hoe and a grid-
dle, bake the biscuit and broil the venison. Ah! Vernon, it
was mighty sweet eating in that fashion. There's no meal I
ever ate that come up to them. And as we'd eat, we'd talk
about what happened to this one, and what happened to that;
and how many scares and dangers we'd had; and then we'd
steal off, taking turns at that business, to look after the horses,
and up and down the road, to see if all was right. And so we'd
pass the night, Mr. Vernon; and in the morning, betimes, we'd
brush up and gear the animals, and put on our packs, and be
ready for a start by dawn; and many's the time, Vernon, my
boy, in them days, that I've taken 'Sweetlips,' that ugly long-
shanked rifle you see there in the corner, and dropped a turkey
from his roost in the tree jist over the horses, so fat that his
breast-bone split open by the time he thumped the ground.
Ah! them days, Mr. Vernon, them blessed days, with all their
troubles, and all their dangers, I'd give all I'm worth, or ever
hope to be worth, if they only were to go over again. But it's
no use pining for what can't be got. We can't always be
young, Mr. Vernon, and if we could, pack-horses are gone out
of use, and there's no Indians to make us lie snug and suspicious, telling stories that helped to frighten us the more.
The Choctaws will soon be gone, and the Cherokees and Creeks,
I s'pose, though they're something farther off, and I don't know
so much about them. You can tell though, Mr. Vernon, seeing
you're jist from Mobile."

Horsey, with an inevitable tendency, had recurred to his old
practice. The youth replied good-humoredly:—

"I haven't seen Mobile for months, Mr. Horsey; but you

forget, it is my turn to question now, and lest you should start off, and throw me out again, I will begin at once. Have you had many visiters in Raymond — many strangers, I mean, until this time, within the last two weeks?"

"Psha, Harry Vernon, say what you want in plain terms. Is it a man, or a woman, you're in chase of? It's a man, I reckon; for Ben Carter an't the chap to encourage young lawyers to be running about the country after women. Am I right in my guess, Vernon?"

"Suppose I tell you, then, a woman?"

"Well, I've nothing to say; but I hardly think it. Are you sure it's a woman, now?"

"Nay, there's no certainty about it. A small man in woman's clothes, might very easily pass himself off for one," said Vernon, with an air of musing.

"Yes, nothing very strange in that, if he had to make a run for it, and had hope of outdoing his enemy's head sooner than his heels. Your chap has no such hope, I reckon, Mr. Vernon."

"It may be not; but man or woman, Mr. Horsey, have you had any strangers in the village lately?"

"Well, I'm the very last person in Raymond to see strangers, unless they come to me. I ha'n't walked out of the house for the last five weeks, and jist make out to hobble up to bed, when it's time to lie down. There's my wife, now — she can tell you more than I. She sees everything and everybody, I think, that comes into the village; I don't know but she sees whoever goes out of it. She's a most curious woman — my wife — likes to pry into everybody's business, and know all about them, but she means no harm; good woman — she's fast asleep now."

A hearty laugh of Vernon followed these praises of the wife, which she was no longer in a condition to hear; and drawing nigher to his companion, he renewed his inquiries, though with a slight change of topic.

"Your wounded limb disables you from seeing much of the world at present, Mr. Horsey, but it has not always disabled you, and there are some parts of it which I know you have seen, about which I would like to obtain some information — the 'Choctaw purchase' for example."

" How do you know I've been in the 'nation'?" demanded Horsey with some gravity.

" You told me so yourself."

" The d—l I did! Can it be possible! Well, it is strange how difficult it is, when a man's growing old, for him to keep his own secrets. Out he pops with everything he knows, and with the help of a long tongue, he will empty the longest head. Are you sure I told you I had been in the 'nation' Mr. Vernon?"

" I think so, sir."

" You are not certain, then. It is very probable you are mistaken, sir. I should wish to think so, for I look upon it as one of the last signs of dotage when a man can't keep his secrets."

" But this is no secret, surely. Can there be any harm in stating so simple a fact," demanded the youth, with curiosity mingled with amusement to discover in a man of so much good practical sense, an apprehension so ridiculous.

" So simple a fact has hung a man before to-day, as your law books should have told you. Not that I fear to be hung for anything I've done, whether among Creeks, Cherokees, or Choctaws. I've had something to do with all of them in my time, and can show some marks of my acquaintance with the red rascals; but then there's no sort of need to tell everything a man knows, even when it does him no harm to tell it; and when a man's brains become like a bottle of sassafras beer, ready to boil over when a little warm, I think he may as well cast up his accounts, and get his coffin made. But, sir, I have been in the 'purchase' and maybe can tell you what you want to know."

" To what portions do the people go who settle there now? Which are the portions most in demand?"

" Oh, there's a sprinkling of our people everywhere, there's no stopping them when they begin. When you think you've got to the eend of the settlements, there's still some farther on; and the business of the squatter always carries him over the line of the old settlements. But the quiet folks that have got something to go upon and something to lose, they stick a little behind. It does seem to me, that, if it's them you're asking for, you'll find a smart chance of them between the Yazoo and

the Big Black, mostly along the edges of the Big Black, and
not often west of the Yazoo. A heap of little towns are growing up along the Black. I could name to you a dozen, but it's
no more use naming little towns than little chickens, there's so
many of them, and they all look so much alike."

"And the gamblers, Mr. Horsey, where do they keep?"

"Nowhere in particular, and that's the same as saying everywhere. But—I needn't ask you, seeing you're Ben Carter's
friend—I was going to say I hope you wasn't looking after
company among them."

"No, no but they are numerous?" demanded the youth with
interest.

' As peas in a fair season."

"They are audacious, too?"

"D—d infernal impudent, if you let them. If you go up
in those parts it's my advice to you to keep finger on trigger
and use your pistol at a word. It's a'most always the quickest
hand that gets off with fewest scratches, and to stand palaver-
ing with a scoundrel, that you know to be a scoundrel, about
what's right, and what's not right, is, to my way of thinking,
little better than begging an ass not to kick you, while you
make a slow journey under his heels."

"But you're not always sure that it is a scoundrel—"

"Sure as a gun; there's no chance of a mistake if you keep
your senses about you. But that's the trouble. It's how to
keep your senses about you, Harry Vernon, that's the greatest question. Now, I'm clear to say, that it's only by getting
drunk, being put in a passion, or having soft soap poured down
their backs, that men lose their senses, and afterward lose everything beside. If they wouldn't listen to smooth words from
every stranger they meet; if they wouldn't stop to hug the
whiskey bottle, instead of taking a quiet kiss and walking on;
if they wouldn't get into a passion about every fool speech
they hear, then I'm clear, they'd never get cheated out of their
money, and knocked on the head, like a blind puppy in a dark
night. Now, Harry, you see the danger before you. So long
as a man keeps his senses, there's not so many dangers in life,
and they may be all got over by a quick head and bold heart.
But it won't do to believe in sweet-spoken strangers, and it

won't do to quarrel about a fool jest, and it won't do to get drunk. I wouldn't advise a lad to go up into the Yazoo, now, while it's unsettled, as I may say, and none but scatterers about: but if you must go, mind your own business, make no more friends than you can help, and keep sober as a judge. Come, sir, you've been talking long enough, let's have a toddy."

"Thank you—no more, Mr. Horsey; and let me correct your errors as we proceed. It is you and not I who have been doing the talking for the last half hour; and to say truth, I am so well pleased with your eloquence, that I'm for having more of it."

"No gammon, my lad, none of that. But I'm willing to tell you all I know, so long as you don't ask for it all. What's next?"

"What officers of the law may be found in those parts, in the event of my being in want of them?"

"Lord keep you from law officers in your own case, my lad, though as a lawyer, it's like enough, you'll be making them toil hard enough in the business of other people. But what makes you think of them—do you calculate on any trouble?"

"Nay, that matters not, my friend. Should I have any trouble, which a man of the world, who lives in the world, must always look for, I should like to know in how much I may depend upon the countenance and protection of the law in the places to which I'm going."

"Depend upon a hickory sapling and your own teeth rather Depend upon steel and bullet, Harry Vernon, when you're on the Yazoo. What the d—l would a man expect to find out, away on the very outskairts, as I may call it, of civilization? Would you have gentlemen and Christians in a part of the world where there's no timber cut, no lands cleared, no houses built, nothing done, but what's done by the squatters and that sort of people? No, no; your only chance is a keen eye, a quick hand, and a steady head. Trust to these in the Yazoo; there are few better friends anywhere."

"The counsel of one who has certainly done more by their help than most men," responded Vernon, with a compliment that was not displeasing to the veteran, and showed a degree of intimacy with his history on the part of his guest, which

proved him to have been no inattentive auditor of himself and
of his friend Carter; "but," continued the youth, "what can
you tell me of the ' Braxley settlement' ?"

"Not a syllable — I know nothing good of it, however;
though I couldn't say, more than from general report, anything
bad agin it."

" What of ' Ford's camp' ?"

" Nothing."

" Georgeville ?"

" That's sprung up into a village since my day. I believe
it's a poor affair : but two or three stores or thereabouts. I
never saw the place but once, and then there was but one; I
didn't stay in that longer than to take a sup of whiskey. If
there's nothing better in it than the whiskey, don't go there.
It's a place to shun, Mr. Vernon."

" What of Lexington ?"

" Don't know the place."

" Squab Meadow ?"

" Never heard of it."

" There's a little village called Lucchesa, that lies somewhere
upon Green Briar Creek in Carroll county. Do you know
anything about that ? it's a new village."

" New to me, yet I think I have heard the name; there are
several little villages grown up since I've been in those parts,
and, for that matter, they grow up every day. I know the
country well enough, but, bless your soul, Mr. Harry Vernon,
it's no sign of ignorance in Mississippi, not to know the towns
by their names. We can't find names for half of 'em."

This was said with some signs of impatience, and the youth,
though still seemingly desirous of pressing for information which
was yet desirable to obtain, was compelled to rest contented
with the imperfect statistics already gleaned, which, perhaps,
no continued examination of the old man would have rendered
more complete.

" I am afraid I have wearied and worried you, Mr. Horsey,
without much help to myself. What I get from you is to the
tail as satisfactory as the comparisons of that categorical personage, Captain Fluellen; 'There is,' says he, ' a river in
Macedon, and there is also, moreover, a river at Monmouth,' &c.'

The youth gave in full the passage which has been prefixed as an epigraph to this idle chapter, and which we care not to repeat again. Portions of the quotation, however, and the authority referred to, seemed to disquiet our landlord.

"Fluellen," said he; "where was he captain? There's Captain Fenelon, I know, that heads the 'Buck Swamp Rangers,' and that's the nearest name to it, I can think of. I know Fenelon, and a mighty clever fellow he is; a little too fond of the girls perhaps; but that only hurts himself. It isn't him, you mean."

"No, no—Fluellen is a captain far more famous, I think, than Fenelon will ever become. He is one of the honored names of Shakspere—the world renowned—"

"That d—d player-man!" cried the impatient landlord, interrupting the eulogy which our hero had begun, of the merits of the divine bard. "Look you, Mr. Vernon, if you want that we should keep friends, and part friends, say no more of that player-fellow and his cursed books; don't I beg you."

The youth was silent from wonder for a few moments, to behold such an earnest countenance as the speaker wore while he uttered this serious remonstrance. When he recovered breath it was to expostulate.

"In the name of wonder, and all the wonders, Mr. Horsey, but how is this? How is it that you are so hostile to a writer whom all the world joins to honor and applaud?"

"The world, Mr. Vernon, may honor as it pleases, and it frequently gives honor where very little is due. But it's the honor which the world gives to this same player-fellow, which has done more to make me an unhappy man, than anything in the world beside."

The wonder of the youth increased, and a single word conveyed his farther interrogation:—

"How?"

"I have a son, Mr. Vernon; you haven't seen him in my house; nor, till this minute, have you heard his name from my lips; nor, perhaps, from the lips of Ben Carter, though you may have got a good deal out of him. Well, sir, this son of mine, got in with some of these player fellows at Mobile or Orleans, and they carried him to their blasted stage-houses, where

2*

he got possession of these Shakspere books, and he's never been worth a picayune since that day. He took up with the stage-fellows, got to making a d—d fool of himself before the Mobile people, and had the impudence to send me a paper, a printed paper, with a great heading, and his name among the rest to play some pieces out of Shakspere. Sure enough, that very time my neighbor here, Major Mandrake, that keeps one of the taverns, being down on a visit to Mobile, saw Tom Horsey, with his own eyes, come out in front of the whole people, with a gold crown upon his head, and covered with spangles, and dressed up, in a most ridiculous way beside, jist for another chap, who come out afterward, to stick him with a sword. And there he rolled about over the floor, until he died, and the people shouted and clapped their hands, as if he had done some great thing, and it was jist that d—d stupid shouting and clapping, that led the fellow to make such a bloody fool of himself. But mind you, I don't mean to say that he died in airnest — it was all pretence — all make b'lieve; but, by the Eternal, Mr. Vernon, I'd rather a thousand times he had died in raal airnest, in a fair fight, than to have fallen into such a folly, and brought disgrace upon his family."

A playful commentary upon this speech rose to the lips of Vernon, as the old man concluded; but the youth saw that the grief was too serious and sacred, to suffer any light or irreverential remark. He contented himself with inquiring into the fate of a lad in whom he begun to take some interest, the rather, perhaps, because he saw the matter in a less severe light than the father, and possibly because he thought that the backwoods boy, wanting in all the advantages of education and city life, who could relish Shakspere to so great a degree, must be of something more than ordinary metal.

"And where is your son now, Mr. Horsey?"

"The saints know best, Mr. Vernon. Tom Horsey has not darkened these doors since March gone was a year."

"But you hear from him?"

"Ay, sir, and of him. I hear from him when he wants money, and of him when he has it. He makes me hear when he's out, and makes everybody else hear when his pockets are full. The misfortune is, that this Shakspere fellow never comes alone. He brings with him late hours and strong drink, and damned bad company, Mr. Vernon; and what with him and them, Tom Horsey is in the broad road to destruction."

"But do you provide him with money when he demands it for such indulgences."

"Fill your glass, Vernon; let us drink, and say no more. I'm a surly, crabbed sort of creature; they will all tell you so; and yet, they all wonder, and I wonder at it myself, that I have so little strength to do the things that I resolve upon. The boy's my only boy, bad as he is, Harry Vernon; and he gets more money from me than I ought to give him. But, what's that? Did you hear nothing, Mr. Vernon?—no voices—none —just below the window?"

The old man trembled with sudden agitation, while bending forward to listen, as indistinct accents fell upon his own and the ears of his guest.

In another instant, the room rang with a loud burst of declamation from without, in which Vernon detected some lines from the bard whom the old man had so terribly denounced, but which now seemed to awaken in his mind any other than hostile feelings. Meanwhile the voice proceeded, and the passages spoken seemed not inappropriate; and, perhaps, were chosen from their partial fitness, to those relations between father and son, which had formed the subject of the previous conversation. The passage was from the speech of Bolingbroke, third scene, fifth act, of Richard the Second:—

> "Can no man tell of my unthrifty son?
> 'Tis full three months since I did see him last:
> If any plague hang over us, 'tis he.
> I would to heaven, my lords, he might be found
> Inquire at London, 'mongst the taverns there,
> For there, they say, he daily doth frequent,
> With unrestrained, loose companions," &c.

The eye of the father caught the glance of his guest earnestly fixed upon him, and in that instant he recovered his composure.

"Now, out upon the scrub! he comes at last, with his player-verses in his mouth—"

"Ay; but how truly do they suit, Mr Horsey!" was the reply of Vernon.

"Yes, indeed, well enough; but will they cure the mischief that they tell of? No, sir; this graceless rascal thinks it handsome to swagger with a belly full of whiskey, and a brain full of Shakspere, at the lowest tavern in the city of New Orleans. By the Lord Harry, but he comes not in my door!"

A loud knocking from without answered this resolve; and, following the glance of the father's eye, Vernon rose quietly and opened the door to the son.

CHAPTER III.

FATHER AND SON.

"This fellow I remember
Since once he play'd a farmer's eldest son;
'Twas where you woo'd the gentlewoman so well;
I have forgot your name; but sure that part
Was aptly fitted, and naturally performed."—SHAKSPERE.

THE prodigal waited for no invitation to enter, but bounced in, the moment the door was opened. Seeing the stranger, he stopped short for an instant, his deportment bearing equal marks of confident assurance, and a reasonable consciousness of his own demerits. The habits of the player-men, however, got the better of his misgivings, and, without yielding any farther notice to Vernon, after the first glance, he advanced toward the father, prefacing his movement with a hearty salutation, of somewhat rowdy fashion, which made the old man wince in his seat, at the gross disregard of his dignity which it betrayed.

"Ha, dad! there you are, prime and hearty, as though you never had a son, to 'bring you cares for inconsiderate youth,'— and how's the old lady, 'our venerable mother, keeps she well?' gone to bed, I reckon, and fast; so I take it for granted she's as she should be, and you, sir, you and—"

Here his eyes wandered to the seat which Vernon had re-occupied.

"Puppy!" exclaimed the father, "can't you leave off your

cursed player nonsense, Tom Horsey, when you're in a gentleman's presence. That, sir, is my friend, Mr. Vernon, Mr. Harry Vernon, of Natchez, or New Orleans, or elsewhere."

"Sir, Mr. Vernon, of elsewhere, I am glad to know you 'If I mistake not, thou art Harry Monmouth,'" was the prompt address of the actor, extending his right hand, with an air of princely condescension.

"Monmouth, no!" cried the more literal father; ".Vernon, I said, Tom Horsey—Mr. Harry Vernon."

"The same—a good name, I think, sir, a very good name, and I'm glad to know you. Mr. Vernon, as I said before, 'there's matter in this;' and, some allowances must be made for the prejudices of age, and a hard school, sir, against the drama. It is only in the presence of gentlemen, sir,"—to his father—"let me tell you, that players should speak. The very element they live in, sir, is the applause of the gentle and the wise—their pursuits are 'caviare to the general;' and let me tell you, sir, that you risk not a little when you give way to this harsh and most unjust manner of speech, in respect to a profession, whose ill report while you live, it is said, will do you more harm than a bad epitaph when you die. You will find the passage in Hamlet—for the rest, sir—have you any-thing to drink?"

This speech was pretty evenly divided between the father and his guest. When it was concluded, he turned to the little table that stood between the elder Horsey and Vernon, filled a glass for himself, and drawing a chair from the corner of the apartment, placed himself, with a show of *sang froid*, which was not altogether felt, directly beside the father. The old man could no longer restrain his indignation.

"You d—d conceited squab, where have you been these eight months? Put down your glass, sir, until you answer me."

' Dry throats must needs make short speeches, sir—I have been at school."

"Do not mock me, Tom Horsey!—don't go too far, boy, in playing your d—d theatre stuff on me. I can't bear it much longer—you'll put me in a rousing passion."

"We'll have a rouse to-night, sir—Mr. Vernon, 'the king drinks to Hamlet.' Don't think, sir," addressing his father.

"don't think, I shall forget you, dad, but your glass remains unfilled. Shall I help you?"

"Help yourself and be d—d. Answer my question. Where have you been these eight months?"

"Egad, sir, that's the most puzzling of all questions, and the most correct answer that I can make you is that which I have made already. At school, sir! In the great school of the world, sir, I have been acquiring my humanities or getting rid of them. Don't you think me reasonably improved?"

"What have you done with the money I sent you?"

"Paid my schooling with it, sir."

"That is to say, you drank it out at taverns upon your roaring companions, your drunken actors, your bully gamblers, and all that strange sort of cattle that you herd with in Orleans."

"Alas! my father, revile not thus. Wherefore will you speak of things which you know not. Have more charity, I pray you. As for the poor sums of money which you sent me, they were as nothing to the good which they procured me. They brought me to a knowledge of the fine generous spirits, who are as much above the dirty wants and slavish necessities of common clay, as the divine Shakspere is beyond all the thousand priests and pretenders that officiate at the altar of the muse. Had you sent me ten times the sums you speak of, I had freely shared them all with the noble fellows whom your parsimony has chiefly compelled me to leave."

"Ay, and where would their generosity have carried you, you ridiculous spendthrift. To the calaboose, to the calaboose, you rascal. If it has not already carried you there. Pitiful sums indeed!—but you sha'n't impose on Mr. Vernon. You shall say what these pitiful sums are; you shall tell him what money I sent you, and let him say whether I have not been almost as great a spendthrift as yourself."

"No doubt, no doubt—I make no question. dad, but that your extravagance has always exceeded mine. I am but a chip—a small chip of the old block; and—"

"Why, you impudent rascal, my spendings have been altogether on you. If I have to reproach myself with any extravagance at all, it is only in having given you the means to make a fool of yourself."

"' Wisely, indeed, and worthily bestowed'—you do not re
pent, sir, of having provided for my subsistence ?"

" I have done more, sir. What amount did I send you by
Bill Perkins ?"

" Some fifty or a hundred dollars, as I think."

" As you think ! as you think ! Tom Horsey, will you lie
too ? Have your player-fellows taught you this among their
other accursed lessons. Speak, are you in earnest ?"

The old man's voice trembled, and passion seemed to be succeeded in his choking utterance by a fear that falsehood was to
be included among the other profligacies of one whom his own
tenderness had rendered somewhat incorrigible. Vernon
watched the scene with curious interest, and he remarked the
sudden flush which mounted up into the son's cheeks at the accusation, as if conscious innocence revolted within him at the
injustice. Such was the impression of the spectator, and it was
confirmed by the effect which it seemed to produce in the youth's
tone and general manner.

" You are a little too hard with me, sir," was his reply. " I
admit that you sent me some money by Perkins."

" Three hundred, not fifty, sir—not fifty or a hundred, but
three hundred dollars, Tom Horsey."

" Right, sir; Perkins brought me that sum, which I trust
you did not really think me base enough to deny. When I
said less I simply meant to compute it by the time it lasted
It was the very sum you name, sir, but it might just as well
have been the fifty—it was very short-lived."

" Very well, sir," said the father, glad to have an excuse to
forbear reproach and harsh language. " And had it been fifty
times as much, do you think it would have lasted much longer
with such company as you keep ? No, sir, they would have
spent my gains and your gettings, and counted my thousands
as you have learned to do by fifties and hundreds. But that's
not all. You got money from my factor in Orleans. What
sum got you ? for to this day I have never learned."

" I sent you two thousand dollars by Major Mandrake."

" I got it, but the crop sold for more, sir—cotton was
selling at sixteen; I had the price current of the week,
and have it now. What did my cotton bring ? You sent

money but no account of sales; what was done with
?"

" 'Gad, sir, I know not, unless we used it to make snow one
night at Caldwell's when the storm gave out. · I remember, we
were rather short of snow."

"Tom, Tom, don't rouse me—don't put me in a passion.
I'm sick—I can't bear it easily; and besides, I don't want Mr.
Harry Vernon to see what a d—d fool I am to let you treat me
as you do. What did you get from my factor in all? let me
know that. You sent me two thousand—what did you keep?"

" Well, sir, as nearly as I can remember, about seven hundred—"

" Seven hundred!"

" There may have been a forty or fifty tacked on to it; but
it certainly was not more than that. Suppose we call it seven
hundred and fifty dollars—'the very head and front of my offending, hath this extent, no more.' "

"And enough too, in God's name, to ruin any man that's got
so little to go upon as I," responded the father; "but there is
more, Tom Horsey—you took a hundred and seventy dollars
with you when you went; you collected ninety dollars from
Michael Hopper for so many bushels of corn; and what have
you done with Martin Groning's note for sixty-seven dollars?
If you got that, it makes—"

"But I haven't got that, dad. Groning's a great rascal;
'there must be lawings ere you get that gold'—we shall have
to set Master Phang upon him, dad, before he settles."

"No, let him go. It's but a poor sixty-seven dollars, and I
shouldn't miss so small a matter, if my own son didn't help me
to the loss of a great deal more. But now count up, count up,
Mr. Vernon, these moneys, as I call them out to you, and then
say whether I'm parsimonious, or whether there's a spendthrift
in my family, that'll let out at a thousand mouths what his father was compelled to take in at one."

"Nay, don't count up, I beg you, dad," cried the profligate;
" why will you bother Harry Monmouth with these 'small
chores.' To count up money that you have not, is to impov-
erish memory most cursedly. The very thought of my spendings is a misery, since it only the more forcibly reminds me of

the little that is left to spend. Wherefore have I left my company, 'my comates in exile,' but that the candle was at the last snuff—wherefore have I trudged homeward 'on weary legs—'"

"You don't mean to say that you walked from Orleans here, Tom Horsey?" cried the father, to whom the last fragment of a quotation uttered by his son suggested a new cause of apprehension.

"Not all the way. I had a cast in a steamboat as far as Monticello, and a fling in a wagon for some twelve or fourteen miles above; but, by the Lord Harry, the widow's mare did the rest."

"Why, where's your horse?"

"Gone—gone the way of all flesh."

"Dead—how was that—the botts?"

"Ay, botts enough to take off a dozen horses. The sheriff suspected I was out of money, and not able to keep him any longer; and so relieved me of the charge."

"Seized for debt!" exclaimed the father aghast; "a colt of my own raising—seized for debt!—eat his head off in a livery stable!—ah, Tom, Tom! you'll kill me yet!"

"At the suit of one Stubbs, a tailor; a fellow that helped me to fit up my wardrobe, and brought suit for all his suits. Thus was I nonsuited. But I punished the scoundrel, you may be sure. I basted him with his own yard-stick the night I left Orleans, till there wasn't a seam in his carcass that couldn't count stitches. You shall hear particulars some day, Harry Monmouth; a devilish good story—but—"

"Look you, Tom, this gentleman's name is Vernon, and not Monmouth. None of your tricks, I tell you."

"Vernon, is it? I ask pardon, but I thought it was Monmouth—Harry Monmouth—it was Harry you said—I'll swear to that."

"You've a free tongue to swear, Tom Horsey; but how would you like an oath of mine to cut you off with a shilling, and leave you to the miserable life you have so miserably begun. Answer me that, sir: what would you think of such an oath? and wouldn't it be justly deserved, Mr. Vernon?"

"Nay, father, do not bother Mr. Vernon any more in this matter, and above all matters eschew the sin of swearing.

Oath-taking is a bad business, and unless you take some such rash oath as that you speak of, I think I may promise you with safety to do nothing again rashly as long as I live. I am come home to be a sober fellow, follow the plough, drive the wagon, bleed horses, and cure bacon. In short, do just whatever is needful to make money, and keep it afterward."

"Can you keep to this?" cried the delighted father, who desired nothing more than such a concession on the part of his son, as should save his dignity, and obviate the necessity of more scolding.

"I think so — I'll try, sir."

" Ah, Tom, for awhile only, I'm afraid. You'll be reading in the newspaper about some new play-house or some new actor, and then, nothing will suit, but off you must go to see for yourself; as if the reading of it wouldn't do as well."

"It shall — it shall in future, dad. Don't be afraid of me. I think I shall keep my promises this time, for, do you see, whatever might be my own desires to go to Orleans, the drubbing I gave the tailor, Stubbs, will stand against me in the black books of the law, and I have too great a respect for that stately dwelling, the calaboose, to risk the chances of admission. As for the theatre itself, by my fears, I have just as little reason to venture near it. My chance is all up with the American, and my hopes with Caldwell; but for that, dad, it might have been, that you hadn't seen me home to-night."

"Well, whatever it was, I'm glad it happened so; but you don't mean, Tom, that you quarrelled with the actors."

"Ay, with the very chief of them — the manager."

" Well, the stars be thanked, I'm a great deal gladder than before. There's no fear of making up the matter, Tom, is there?"

"But little, unless you lend your help."

"God forbid! I lend my help! — I'd burn down all their establishments, if I could. But how was it, Tom — what was the quarrel? You didn't lick him, too, as well as the tailor?"

"Egad, no! The boot was on t'other leg! It was because I didn't lick him, that we quarrelled; it was, by my soul!"

"Come, come, Tom, don't, now; none of your d—d nonsense. We know it's all gammon that! No man would quarrel with another because he didn't lick him."

"True as gospel, dad, professionally speaking. An excellent adventure, by the way, Mr. Vernon, and I must tell it. Dad, fill your glass!—an excellent joke—fill, Mr. Vernon! You shall hear how I came over the manager—how I struck him, even when 'soaring in his pride of place.'"

"I thought you said you didn't strike him, Tom?" demanded the matter-of-fact father.

"You shall hear, sir. Understand, you are at the American Theatre in New Orleans, Caldwell, manager; and your humble servant doing third and fourth-rate characters at tenth-rate prices. Ten dollars a week is scarcely enough for gentlemen of my cloth♦ and just at this time Stubbs was writing to me in the very language of Master Shallow, 'I beseech you, Sir John, let me have five hundred of my thousand,' in other words, of less classical grace—'let me have but half of my bill.'"

"Drop the theatre talk, Tom," whispered the father; "drop it, d—n you, if you can."

"It was necessary to remit, to raise the wind. This was the difficulty. I had got rid of the seven hundred, and the three hundred, and the other odd hundred; and I had even drawn the week's salary in advance. I had the horse, it is true, but the colt was a favorite—I had helped to raise it; and, by Jupiter, I had much sooner have parted with my velvet plush breeches, than with Corporal."

The old man gave an approbatory chuckle as this show of proper feeling escaped his son in his narrative.

"But you should have gone to the factors, or wrote to me for the money, Tom, and redeemed the nag. I'd rather than **twice** his value that you had not lost him."

The son winked to Vernon, as he replied—

"Ah, dad, Stubbs is not the only tailor in Orleans; and one suit is not all that a poor devil actor has to suffer before his wardrobe's complete. As I was saying, I knew of no present mode of raising the wind, and I had but one mode left me. I went to the manager, implored him for a loan, on the strength of future services. He denied me; 'but was I to be denied?' You shall hear how I fixed him. That very night I was to play Richmond to his Richard. The manager had a **very strange** notion that he was a tragedian, and was, **therefore,** continually going out of his element, to try waters which were quite beyond his depth. He did well enough as a genteel comedian, but that did not satisfy his ambition; and among those who knew nothing better, he did monstrous well. I remember the first time I ever saw him was in tragedy. I went to Orleans, dad, if you remember, with uncle Wat Stevens, and he treated me to the show."

"Damn him for it," was the fervent ejaculation of the father The son proceeded without heeding the interruption.

"Like the rest of the gaping countrymen around, and the house was full of them, I thought him a wonderful man, though I soon learned other things when I looked a little more into the matter. But the opinion of the manager himself underwent no change. He was still ripe for tragedy and nothing else, and was that very night, when Stubbs sent me his impudent letter, to play Richard—I, Richmond. We went through the piece very well, till we got to the death scene. Then Richard tried his best, and I buckled to him. I had wounded him, and he had fallen; but that was nothing to a man determined to outdo Kean, and make the ghost of Garrick gape with astonishment, and shiver in his shroud. He rolled and writhed about the stage, keeping up the fight as he did so, and striving to show his skill of fence while in the death agony. It was then that the thought seized suddenly upon me to avail myself of the particular predicament in which he stood—lay rather—to bring him to an accommodation—to compel him to my own terms. What do you think I did, Harry Monmouth—Master Vernon, I mean—how do you think I fixed him? A thousand to one you can neither of you guess."

Vernon confessed his inability, and the father, now an attentive auditor, and a pleased one too, as he beheld the evident attention of his guest, and observed the more modest demeanor of his son, disclaimed with equal readiness any ability to conjecture the *ruse de guerre* made use of by the debtor to extort from the dying actor, the loan he found necessary to keep him from his tailor's clutches.

"I knew it—I knew it was beyond you both," was the chuckling response of Richmond to these admissions. "It was a thought of my own, and my own only; and what was it, you will ask. Hark ye then in your ears; it was simply to forbear killing him. I began to play slowly, to evade his strokes and avoid pursuit of him. You may imagine the predicament of Richard, half-dead, and inviting the fatal blow. He called to me in a hoarse whisper, while twisting and writhing after me, and sticking right and left, at moments when, in order to keep up appearances with the audience, I suffered our swords to mingle.—'Why the devil don't you play, Horsey?'"

"I answered him in a suppressed voice, speaking in the gorge of my throat, so that he could distinctly hear the emphasis which I employed, and supposed that it could not altogether escape the hearing of the audience. Yet, such was not the case. It is an art of speech which I possess, and of which, Mr. Vernon, you shall have a sample some day.

"'Look you, Richard,' said I, 'it was only to-day I asked you for a matter of seventy dollars to pay off a d—d tailor that was troubling me. You refused me; was that done like Richard?'

"'Strike on, you d—d fool,' said he, 'or I'll strike you off. What are you talking about? Strike!'

"'Never till you consent to let me have the money. You sha'n't die by my hands to-night, Richard. I'll leave you half-dead upon the stage, and for once there shall be no catastrophe. Will you let me have the money?'

"'Yes, yes, anything,' was his answer; 'but strike on, the pit is getting impatient. Strike! strike!'

"We tugged away quite heartily then for a few seconds, the house roared with applause, and some of the groundlings, after he had received the *coup de grace*, actually *encored* the performance, clearly signifying a desire that he should do the death over again. But, would you think it, the ungrateful tyrant refused to let me have the money the next morning, and added to the enormity of his conduct by giving me my walking ticket. Was it not shocking, Mr. Vernon? Did I not merit the money for the humor of the thing? But he had no soul to feel it—none, none!"

Before Vernon or the father could answer the question, or comment upon the transaction, another person entered the apartment and interrupted the dialogue. The introduction of the new comer must be reserved for another chapter.

CHAPTER IV.

THE WHY AND THE WHEREFORE.

> "It tastes
> Of rank injustice, and some other end
> Time will discover; and yet our grace is bound
> To hear his accusation confirmed,
> Or hunt this spotted panther to his ruin."—SHIRLEY

THE stranger was one of whom the reader has already heard
The quick eye of Vernon distinguished his friend at a glance,
nor was that of the other less observant.   The warmth of their
embrace, when they met, spoke for a deep mutual regard be
tween the two, not only superior to that which belongs to ordinary friendships, but something more than could be expected
to appear in the case of persons so unequal in years.   Mr. Carter could not have been less than forty-five; a tall, well-made
man, with a fine, full, but dark countenance; an eye, black and
lively, but of benevolent expression; and a look of amenity
and kindness which denoted a degree of soberness and subdued
thought, in which the buoyant spirits of the youth of twenty-
five, could scarcely find much that was congenial.   Vernon
could not have been much more than twenty-five; his temperament was evidently lively, if not rash; and good humor and a
playful spirit, seemed to predominate in his disposition.

The gravity, the almost sadness, of Carter's countenance, was
unreflected in his own; and yet, it may be added, the sympathy was quite as close between them, as could be hoped for
under any circumstances; and whatever might be the difference
of their moods and wishes, under the influence of unequal ages,
there was none of that exacting severity, on the part of Carter
or of that distaste to discipline, on the side of Vernon, which
might endanger the relation.   If Carter was grave, even to mel-

ancholy, he was, at the same time, benign and indulgent. He could make allowance for the impatience of youth, esteeming it, perhaps, a fault that was not without its virtues, in a country which calls more imperatively for boldness and adventure, than any other more sober qualities. If he smiled at the follies of youth, it was the smile of indulgence, or, at most, of pity and not the ascetic grin of scorn and malevolence.

Vernon, on the other hand, warm, impetuous, and lively, never once forgot the superior years of his patron—for such was Carter—nor suffered his veneration to undergo diminution because the latter sometimes encouraged him by the familiar freedoms of the companion. The utmost confidence prevailed between them, the result, possibly, of a mutual and perfect knowledge of their respective claims and character. The observation of Carter had taught him that his protegé was a man of the strictest honor, the nicest sensibility, the most fearless courage and the finest talent. Vernon was no less assured of the high virtues of one who had been to him a protecting and wisely indulgent parent, in the place of all others, from his very first moment of reflecting consciousness, to that in which they meet the reader.

The entrance of Carter was the signal for the flight of the *soi-disant* actor. His genius quailed before the eye of the new-comer, in whom he recognised a well-known monitor, who did not spare his rebuke, and whose influence upon the father, had tended in no small degree to restrain his eccentricities, by di-minishing the money, which the old man was but too ready to yield to his requisitions. Still, the deportment of Carter was kind and gentle to him, as to all the rest, and as it was, habit-ually, to everybody. His salutation differed not from his wont, when he shook the hand of the young man and bade him wel-come home, after so long an absence. But this forbearance in no wise encouraged the erring Master Tom. From a dashing, *nonchalant* personage, he became suddenly subdued to the awk-ward country lout, only anxious to know how best to effect his escape without challenging attention to his movements. This he was soon enabled to do, when he found the regards of Carter chiefly bestowed upon the youth, and his shoulder turned upon himself. He stole away, and was followed after a little while,

by old Horsey, whom a sturdy negro assisted to his chamber.
It was there that the father again found Young Hopeful, and
renewed the various dialogue, a sufficient sample of which the
reader has already had. We will not distress him by a repetition of the dramatic slang, with which Tom replied to, and annoyed the old man; whose chief objections to the quotations,
lay, perhaps, in the difficulty which he found to comprehend
them

Our present purpose carries us back to the apartment which
we left. There, the two, apparently resuming a subject already
partially considered, were earnestly engaged in the adjustment
of topics, the business of which will form no small portion of
the ensuing narration. It may serve us, therefore, who design
to trace its progress to the end, to give some heed to a conference which will, perhaps, the better enable us to understand
some of its objects, and of the histories of those who are most
conspicuous in its details.

"You are resolved then, my son; you know all the adventure — its troubles, its dangers and the numberless difficulties
that surround it. These, you see, at least, if nothing beside;
and with a perfect knowledge of these, and with the farther
prospect of incurring these risks and difficulties without effecting your purpose, you freely and voluntarily determine upon
the journey?"

"Freely, willingly, my dear sir, and with a satisfaction, not
easily expressed, that I find you willing to confide to me a
charge of such importance," was the unhesitating reply of the
youth.

The other squeezed his hand in silence for a few moments
ere he resumed.

' Perhaps, Harry, since such is your resolution, it is due to
you that I should unfold myself a little more. Your confidence
in me deserves it, and were it not so, the confidence which I
have in you leaves me without fear that I incur a risk in giving
you my nearest secrets. From this I can suffer no harm, now,
not even in feeling, by its revelation. But a few months, nay
a few weeks ago, it had been otherwise. I am now free to relieve myself from the accumulating pressure of a grief — a grief
of youth, that I have learned to silence, if not subdue — but

which at length breaks from all restraints when I am no longer young. You have seen this man?"

" I have, sir."

" Ay, but not to know him. He is my senior by five years, but he was my associate — my friend — when we were both young. Boyish friendships are of little value at any time, and in most cases they are of evil consequence. The name is perverted, the tie is not an enduring one, and, even if other harm does not come of it, the effect is evil in teaching us lessons of distrust, when genuine worth implores our confidence, and true friendship might be had by kindred worth. But I will deal in facts and not in maxims.

" William Maitland was my habitual associate from boyhood. We came to Mississippi together, and for several years I had no reason to regret my confidence in him. We lived together harmoniously, sought the same sports together, made the same journeys in company, and took pleasure in the same society. My labors grew prosperous, however, and his did not. This made him discontented. He left me and went down to Orleans, where he invested his capital in trade. Two years elapsed before I again saw him. I had in the meantime become acquainted with the family of Colonel Ralph Taylor, of Pearl River. He was a worthy old gentleman, but the chief attraction of his household in my eye, was his youngest daughter Ellen. I loved her, Harry, with all the· ardor of a heart as purely unselfish in its pursuit as belongs to mortal; but I told her not my love. I feared to do it, as I saw nothing in her deportment which, to my watchful eyes, held forth any encouragement to my hopes. Perhaps, it was, that, with all the doubts and timidity of a true affection, estimating its own claims at the humblest rate, as sincere affection is most always apt to do, I shrunk from pressing upon her those regards which I felt, and occasioned a kindred doubt in her mind of my real purposes. I had reason to think afterward that I deceived myself—that she really loved me — that — but this is needless. Enough, that at this moment I received a visit from Maitland. He came to borrow money, and finding me not at home, and his wants being pressing, he followed me to the residence of Colonel Taylor. There he saw Ellen; and, to shorten a story already quite too

long, there he won her. But not at this first visit. He came
back with me to my residence, which was then at Woodville,
and procured the money which he required. But while with
me, he artfully procured from me all necessary information
with regard to the Taylor family—its character, connections
and resources. I did not reveal to him my feeling for Ellen,
but he must have seen it. A short time after this, while on a
visit to Natchez, I was seized with the yellow fever, which
nearly brought me to the grave. For days I remained without
consciousness of what was going on around me; for weeks without strength to leave my chamber. In this time Maitland prosecuted opportunities which I had seemed to neglect. He pressed
his pretensions upon Ellen, and in a moment of wilfulness of
heart, such as seizes upon the best of us at times, she accepted
him. I had reason to know afterward that she had not been
insensible to my attentions, and that she was taught to believe
that I had trifled with her. William Maitland knew of my illness all the while, but studiously withheld the utterance of what
he knew. The first knowledge I had of my loss was the notice
of their marriage in one of the Orleans papers, to which city
he removed her a short time after the event. Since then I have
but once seen her, and then—"

Carter paused in his narrative as if struggling with the clima..
of those emotions with which he had evidently striven earnestly
for some time before. He rose from his chair and paced the
room a while, the eyes of Vernon in the meantime being fixed
upon the fireplace.

"I had thought myself too old and too strong for these weaknesses, Harry, but the affections which grow up in solitude seldom become obtuse. Were I a citizen, now, I could deliver
you this narrative with a smile; but, as I am, I almost regret
that I have begun it."

"Do not, then, pursue it, sir, I beg you—at least not on my
account," said Vernon.

"Nay, nay, Harry, it is begun, and the beginning is half the
battle always. I must now finish it, or never. I trust, having
opened my bosom to you, to be better able to preserve silence
on this subject for ever after. The affair staggered me in regard to Maitland's sincerity and faith. I was puzzled to deter

mine upon his conduct; and my chief suspicions arose, not so much from his having married, as from the studious secrecy which he had observed toward me on the subject. I got no letter from him; I heard of no inquiry or invitation — nothing, indeed, of him or of his business, until he had removed her to Orleans. He had need of me again. He became the candidate for an office of great trust, and applied to me to be his surety. It was then that I saw Ellen Taylor for the first, and, I may almost say, the last time, as the wife of another. She is in her grave now; but it will not disparage her memory, with you, my son, when I tell you, that it was from her but half-conscious lips, that I was taught to believe that I might have been the happy possessor of her hand, as, to the last, I was the real possessor of her heart. Do not attach blame to the pure spirit of her from whom this confession came. It was while her mind wandered in the delirium from which she never recovered, that her sweet lips told me this blessed truth. I kissed them, Harry, in a fond requital, when the angel had left the tenement in which it had been so troubled! I kissed them, Harry, when, colder than the marble which was so soon to cover her, I well knew that there was no danger that *his* lips would remove the sad and sacred seal which mine had set upon them!"

The struggling tear of Harry Vernon soon followed that of his patron. His silence was the best show of sympathy that his good sense suffered him to make. The other after a brief pause proceeded.

"The surety which I then gave for Maitland is the cause of our trouble now, as you may readily suppose. But for *her*, Harry, I had not given him my name, for I had sufficient reason then to distrust him; and, but for her — but that I still loved, fondly enough for any sacrifice — I had not been guilty of the greater folly of persuading our friend Gamage to a similar risk. The defalcation of Maitland will nearly ruin Gamage as well as myself. But this I can not suffer. As it was because of my entreaties that he consented to sign Maitland's bond with me, I must save him harmless as far as I can. To this point then, your commission extends. Let Maitland give up the money which he is known to have taken from the bank, and we will pledge ourselves not to prosecute, and I will secure

to his children—he has but two—the amount of twenty-five
thousand dollars, in any form of investment which he may pro-
scribe, so that it be under any disposal but his own. Nor shall
he be left otherwise unconsidered in the matter. I will give
him my bond, stipulating the annual payment while he lives of
three hundred and fifty dollars, being a sum quite sufficient for
his wants in that privacy to which he must, for his own and the
sake of his children, for ever after confine himself. He will
see from this, if he be not besotted and ripe for destruction, that
I have no disposition to pursue him with malice. But my forbearance is no tribute to my regard for him, any more than to
his worth. But he is the father of *her* children, and I would
wish to save them from that shame and sorrow which justice
might, without compunction, freely visit upon him. You now
understand, precisely, the relation between us, and will thus be
better able to exercise that discretionary power in any arrangement you may think advisable to make, which you could not
so well have done without this knowledge. I am guilty of no
ill-advised or idle flattery, my dear Harry, when I declare my
perfect willingness to rely upon your judgment and to abide
by any course which you may resolve upon. I have found you
always worthy; I doubt not that your ability will keep pace
with your worth. But you have no easy task, and your hope
of success will depend very much upon your being unknown to
Maitland.

"But for the risk of spoiling all, you should not go alone
upon this mission, nor, perhaps, should you have gone at
all. My appearance would alarm his fears and prompt his
flight, and indeed, the appearance of any stranger will have a
tendency to awaken his fears and compel his caution. He, no
doubt, wherever he may be, will have his creatures on the
watch, and be himself watchful. Your genius must contrive
its own modes for disarming his fears, and appearing in his
neighborhood as an ordinary character. I can give you but
little counsel that is not general. One rule is a good one always among strangers in our country, and that is to 'be secret,
yet have no secrets.' Utter yourself without reserve, yet say
nothing which had better be reserved. Have no mysteries to
your neighbor, though every thought be hidden. This is

enough; your own reflection must do the rest. I have wearied out your patience, Harry, but I have now finished."

"You spoke, sir, of his connection with gamblers: is this certain?"

"Yes; he is known to have lost a part of the property which came by his wife at faro in Orleans. He is also known to have frequented places of habitual resort by the blacklegs of that city. What connection he may have with them now, is simply conjectural, but there is great reason to fear that his separation from them will never be complete while he lives. He had a passion for play which has probably grown upon him, and which will no doubt lose him his ill-gotten spoils, unless he is very closely and suddenly pressed for them."

"May he not have lost these moneys already, sir — may not his defalcation and flight have resulted from his losses?"

"I hope not, and think not, for we happen to know that the particular parcels of gold and paper which he took, were in the bank up to within three hours of his flight."

"That may be, sir, yet he may have appropriated the sums taken to the payment of previous losses."

"This is probable in part. I make no doubt that he was compelled to appropriate in this manner, but it seems scarcely probable that he would have foreborne supplying himself with the means of future indulgence or support. That he did not appear at the tables after the robbery, we know from those whom the bank set as spies upon them. Suppose, however, that ten thousand dollars be already gone, which will be a liberal allowance, we can afford that — we must, indeed, and something more — but let us struggle for the rest. I make no secret to you, Harry, of the fact that my own responsibilities to the bank, and the resolve which I have taken that Gamage shall go harmless, will leave me destitute — utterly destitute — unless we recover something of this loss."

"My efforts shall not be wanting," was the simple assurance of the youth; "you have provided the necessary papers, sir?"

"I will do so, and expect the other documents from Orleans, by Friday next. You will be compelled to defer your departure until then. Meanwhile, it may be well if you attend upon the court. It will help to conceal your present object — which it is important that you should conceal here as elsewhere—if you should appear like the rest of your profession seeking its usual opportunities. I doubt whether you'll get business, but that lack is too general among beginners to occasion wonder; and it will be quite enough to show that you want, and would not refuse it, if it were to offer. But let us take a breathing spell — you have ridden far to-day, and so have I. A good night's sleep will freshen our minds, and probably help us to new ideas. You saw the youth—the son of Mr. Horsey—had he been long before me?"

"An hour, perhaps—not more."

"A thoughtless, improvident lad, with some capacity but little ballast. With his own turn of mind, and his father's indulgence, he will come to nothing. Caught young, and in other hands, he would have done well. It is too late now. I need not counsel you to say nothing that he should not hear; but, keep your papers close; make no memorandums that he may read. He is honest, I believe, but has a prying, curious disposition, as much the result of an idle, restless mood, as of anything else. Let him not feed it at our expense, when a little timely prudence may save us any risk. And now to bed, Harry, as Master Tom would phrase it, with what appetite we may."

CHAPTER V.

ALL THE WORLD A STAGE—VARIETY OF PLAYERS.

Clack.—But are there players among the apprehended?
Scentwell.—Yes, sir, and they were contriving to act a play among them-
selves just as we surprised them, and spoiled their sport.
Clack.—Players! I'll pay them above all the rest.
RICHARD BROOME, 1632.—*The Merry Beggars.*

WHEN Harry Vernon entered the hall the next morning, the
first person he met was Master Thomas Horsey, who encountered him, *selon les règles*, in the most approved fashion of the
theatrical world, with a fitting quotation, to provide himself
with which, he had, no doubt, groped half the night through
his pocket Shakspere.

"'My cousin Vernon! welcome, by my soul!' I've been waiting for you, sir, with the impatience of a thirsty throat, to which
anything like delay in the antifogmatic, is almost certain bron-
chitis. Here, sir, is garden mint—fresh, sir—I pulled it myself; or, if you prefer the animal julep, here is an egg—I did
not lay it myself, but will warrant it quite as fresh as the mint.
The whiskey is at your elbow, the peach at mine, and the sooner
we fall to, the better. 'A good sherris sack hath a two-fold
operation in it.' Which take you?—What! neither?"

Horsey put down his own glass in wonder. The idea of re-
fusing a morning dram had never entered his brain.

"You are not serious, Mr. Vernon?—you will surely take
one or t'other—the peach brandy?"

"Neither, Mr. Horsey. You must excuse me; it is not a
habit with me to drink in the morning."

"It is not, eh? Well, I'm sorry—sorry for your sake not
less than my own. The habit were not a bad one, Mr. Vernon, nevertheless; and I commend you to better example-

in this particular than it has been your fortune to fall upon. I drink, sir, to our better acquaintance. I should have relished much to have had some conversation with you last night, but that 'learned Theban,' Master Benjamin Carter, making his appearance, sent me off in a jiffy, and dammed up my ideas quite as effectually as if he had run the great raft of the Mississippi bend into my brain. He's a sober old boy, that, Harry Monmouth—likes not my merriment—'he loves no plays,' and still less players, 'and smiles in such a sort.' I tell you what, Master Vernon, though no man can think of Ben Carter more worthily than I do, yet, by the faith that is within me, I fear him something—that is 'I rather tell thee what is to be feared than what I fear.' He hath ever been a sort of curb upon me; he sees through my follies, when dad is about to reward them as virtues; and the tricks which would triumph over everybody else, he seems to unravel as easily, and trace home to the true author as certainly, as if he had a gift of divining. He's a relation of yours, Master Vernon?"

"No, sir—none—an acquaintance of my father, and friend of the family."

"You're from below?—left the old people?—'Egad I had almost asked if you had not left them with light heels and lighter heart. I've been so much used to doing that sort of business myself, that the suspicion was natural enough, though, seeing you with Ben Carter, such a conjecture would have been very foolish. You're a lawyer? Come to plead at Raymond? Got any business to go upon yet?" &c.

Young Horsey resembled his father in one respect: he had all his curiosity. We have thrown into the compass of one paragraph the hundred questions which he contrived to ask before the rest of the family made their appearance. In the sight of Carter his ardor was something restrained, though, in the mild benignant countenance of the latter, one would seek in vain for that sign of power to which the young actor ascribed so much potency. He finished his breakfast before the rest, and, as he left the room, catching the eye of Vernon, he put on the aspect and manner of an awkward clown, terrified at finding himself in so solemn presence, and striving to leave it with as little noise as necessary, by moving on tip-toe and backward to the entrance. Once there, he bounded from the steps, and by a single agile movement was in the middle of the road. The next moment he might be heard, spouting a favorite passage at the very top of his voice

"If Tom would only leave off that d—d player-book," began the father apologetically to Carter.

"It is a folly that will do no harm, my good friend, unless you stimulate it by hard usage. The book is innocent enough —it is not that, but the love of praise, which turns your son's head. Listen to his speeches patiently, and he will think you the best audience he ever had; and if you can sometimes contrive to clap your hands together in this manner when he has concluded his speech—"

"As they do at the theatre-houses?" demanded the father with some eagerness.

"Ay—even so."

"Well, Carter, what then—what'll be the good of it?"

"I think it not unlikely he will be content to stay at home with you and mind his business."

"But he promises to do so now, Ben Carter. He says he's done with Orleans and the play-houses. He has good reason for it, I can tell you. He's grazed upon the sheriff at Orleans, and had a queer bout with the head man of the theatre. He told us all about it last night—I didn't quite see into the fun of the thing, but Tom says it was deused funny, and Mr. Vernon was mightily tickled at the story. I think there is a change in Tom, and as he promises so fair—"

"Don't rely too much upon his promises. He can not so soon break away from his old habits, and must be allowed some little farther swing before he dismisses his levities sufficiently to suffer him to come home and go to work. Only do not by unnecessary harshness drive him into them. Notice his follies as little as may be, and tolerate his speeches even where you do not exactly understand them. The scorn of a father not unfrequently drives a son to defiance; when some little indulgence to his idle tastes, might leave him free to see into their absurdities himself. Let me warn you, however, to give him as little money as possible. He wants but little in the country, and where he asks for much, it is a sure sign of profligacy

Do not expect to see him sober on a sudden. I would rather he should not become so. I should suspect him of a worse offence still, than any you have against him—hypocrisy. The best sign in his favor, since his return, is that he still continues his spouting, knowing your hostility to the practice—though it may prove him wanting in proper reverence, it saves him at least from the suspicion of disingennousness. Give him employment as soon as you can, and let time do the rest. A sudden change is seldom to be relied on; and a transition from one extreme to another, is almost always the practice of a rogue."

" But Tom is honest—Tom's no rogue, Ben Carter."

" I believe it, Horsey. Do you take care that you do not make him one. It is not uncommon for you to denounce him as a rogue—to call him rascal, and scoundrel, and such abusive names as these. To give him the rogue's reputation, is to take from him one of the great inducements to be an honest man. Beware that you do not this."

Meanwhile, the subject of this discussion was pursuing his walk, with all the heedlessness of a wayward mind, through all the nooks and crannies of the village. He was busy seeking out old haunts and old associates. Tom Horsey was popular with everybody in Raymond but his father. His pompous declamations, his noisy humor, the readiness with which he joined in a joke, and the steadfastness with which he pursued it, commended him naturally to all the younger portions of the community; and now that he reappeared among them, there were salutations on every hand. Smiles and pleasant speeches, that inflated the vain heart of the youth to the utmost, encountered him at every corner, and he swaggered along the main street with the air of one conscious that his movements were witnessed by an audience far more indulgent than ever Richmond found at Orleans, even when he bestrid the tyrant, and commanded his own terms from the prostrate and ungenerous manager.

There was a miserable little rookery that stood at the western entrance of the village, where a still more miserable sort of business was carried on by a man named Hawkins. This man was an idle worthless creature, and his obvious pursuits were supposed by many persons to be only a sort of cover for other objects which were, possibly, far more profitable, though not so legitimate. In his shop might be seen a barrel of whiskey, a kitt of tobacco, a few knives, pipes, candles, and 'coonskins; seldom anything more; but there were shed-rooms to his dwelling, and upper chambers, which were asserted to be very well fitted up, in which no limited profits were made out of the ignorant and the unwary. Public Justice had her eye upon this establishment, but, up to the present time, nothing had transpired of sufficient importance to justify her in setting her hands upon the lintel. The proprietor kept a closer watch upon her movements, than her emissaries maintained over his; and whatever might have been the suspicions of the neighbors, Hawkins met them with a bold front, and challenged their inquiries.

To this house the actor drew nigh. His approach was watched by the proprietor and another man, who stood with him at the entrance.

"Here is the very chap himself," said Hawkins. "This is the younger Horsey — the crazy actor — who run away to Orleans, and paid the manager, it is said, for permission to appear and spend his father's picayunes as fast as they are made. Yet the old fool dotes upon him, and will leave himself bare to give the youngster his buff breeches. By a little management we may get out of him all that we want to know, or, at least, all that he is able to tell. He is vain of his abilities as an actor, and by feeding his swallow, we may easily pick his teeth."

"Is it he that struts so?" demanded the other.

"The same. This stranger, Vernon, lodges with his father. It is known that he inquired for Carter on his first arrival, and received directions to the house of Horsey."

"And what can this silly fellow know? If he be the man you speak him, would they be fools enough to trust him with any of their secrets?"

"Scarcely — I do not hope for that. But Tom Horsey is one of those restless, fidgetty sort of persons, who are continually meddling with the affairs of other people. He will glean from his father all that he knows of Carter and Vernon, and if they are not exceedingly sly, he will see into their concerns as far as themselves."

"It can do no harm to sound him. He draws nigh."

"Hawkins advanced from the doorway, and addressed the actor in a fashion of his own.

"'Horatio, or I do mistake myself.'"

"'The same,' Mr. Hawkins, 'and your good servant ever.' How does the world use you — still in the old stand, I see."

"Ay, Tom, and at a stand. But where have you been this year of Sundays. I haven't seen you 'since the gander's neck was last soaped.'"

"'No more of that, Hal, an thou lovest me,'" was the reply, followed by a hearty laugh from both, as the phrase, which may seem somewhat mysterious to any but southern readers, reminded them of one of those practical jokes, in which it was Tom Horsey's misfortune too frequently to indulge. "No more of that, Hawkins, I pray you — let that story be forgotten."

"Forgotten, indeed? — impossible ; the story's quite too good and I must tell it to my friend here. Saxon, Mr. Thomas Horsey ; Tom, my friend Ellis Saxon, a gentleman from the Yazoo — a glorious fellow like yourself, loves a joke from the bottom of his heart, and will die some day in a frolic—"

"In a ditch !" cried Horsey, concluding the sentence. "Pardon me, Mr. Saxon, the prediction is just as like and more like to fall upon me than upon you ; and it's an old rhyme of a song that the western boys sing when they're boating down to Orleans :" and he repeated the lines that follow : —

"Though we be not wise or rich,
  Yet what matter — touch the snag —
  We can frolic in a ditch,
  Fierce at poker, brave at brag."

"A good song — I've heard it a hundred times, though not lately. The boatmen are done up now. These steam-sturgeons have cut up as pretty a branch of business as ever needed a long pole, and deserved a glorious frolic. But what of that, Tom Horsey ? Is there to be no pleasure in the world because we can get to Orleans now in ten days in place of forty ? If the steam-sturgeon does up the 'broad horn,' there's a long horn that raises the steam. Come in, my son, and take a sup of whiskey while I tell Saxon about the goose's neck."

"No, no, Hawkins, let that dog sleep. I'll come in and join you with the whiskey, but no scratching old sores, say I."

"What, you're not afraid of consequences now—don't you know the old Squire's done up—gone to his long nap. He'll never trouble you about it, sonny."

"No matter, I've sworn off from these tricks, Bill Hawkins! —I've promised the old man to put on a straight coat, crop my hair and go to meeting o' Sundays—"

"And be at all the love-feasts!—what of all that, Tom?— do you think to keep your neighbor from being happy because you have grown sour. 'Because thou art virtuous, shall there be no more cakes and ale?' Come in, thou reluctant saint, who would put on two faces of tragedy and comedy at the same time —come in, and Saxon will tell you of the splendid blowout on the Georgiana steamboat, going up the river last month. They had a play on board, Tom Horsey—an amateur play—and played Julius Cæsar to more than four hundred persons, the part of Brutus by our old friend, Hugh Peters, the limping schoolmaster at Clinton."

"Hugh Peters play Brutus—the impudent pedagogue! You don't say so, Mr. Saxon; do tell me all the particulars. Hugh Peters, indeed! What could have put it into the leatherhead, to think that he could play Brutus?"

"What but hearing us spout the dialogue at school—'That you have wronged me,' &c. But, come in; the water's on the fire, and the whiskey on the stand."

The news of the amateur performance was quite enough for the mercurial Horsey. His good resolutions were forgotten in an instant, and in two minutes more he was sitting between Hawkins and Saxon, in a little cupboard-like apartment, back of the house, a kettle upon the fire, glasses upon the table, and everything in preparation for one of those regular rounds to which the young actor was already but too much accustomed.

"These steamboats have their advantages after all; and so, Mr. Saxon, the chaps on board the Georgiana got up a tolerable piece of work, did they?"

"Ay, on the upper deck, Mr. Horsey; and considering the short preparation they had, the thing was really well done. There was one chap, an actor from Orleans, named Tilton—"

"Tilton, I know him — a mere candle-snuffer — what the d—l did he pretend to do?" demanded Horsey, interrupting the speaker.

"He played Cæsar — played the ghost rather, and did it so well, that he scared the women half to death. His face was so pale — I can't conceive how he could have brought himself to so death-like a complexion."

"Psha, sir, the easiest thing in the world — a little chalk or magnesia does it — and as for the whiskers, the mustache, the imperial, and such small matters, they lie, sir, at the end of a burned cork, and may be had at a moment's warning."

"Ah, indeed!" was the response of Mr. Saxon, made with the utmost seeming simplicity.

The conceited Thespian continued :—

"These are the arts, sir, of the actor ; and, though not absolutely essential to the artist, yet you can not conceive how much they help the imagination of the spectator ; in the arousing of which lies, probably, the great secret of the good dramatist and perfect actor ; but what you tell me of 'Little Bowlegs' — so we used to call Hugh Peters — 'ye gods, it doth amaze me!' to. think that he should presume to play at all, and then to play Brutus — 'twas a test part — a fellow that talks through his nose, and swings his arms about like a windmill — that walks, for all the world, like a strutting gobler, and has a face like a squash. Ha! ha! it must have been very ridiculous, Mr. Saxon."

"Not at all," was the reply. "We were all too dull, and wanting something to enliven us, the thing did well enough ; and there were some present, who thought Cæsar was done quite as well as Caldwell himself could have done it."

"Caldwell be d—d!" was the irreverent response of Horsey to this opinion.

"Pardon me, Mr. Saxon ; I mean no offence, but it agitates my bile, when I hear Caldwell spoken of in tragedy. I should think better of Herr Cline, the rope-dancer. 'I'm a soused gurnet,' sir, if Caldwell is anything but a comedian — a devilish clever comedian, who spoils himself by attempting anything else ; and as for these folks in the steamboat, being pleased with such performers as Tilton and 'Little Bowlegs,' they must have been most cursedly tired of the boat, or must have had the smallest possible particle of good taste and good sense among them. 'Brutus, Hugh Peter,' 'Julius Cæsar, Jim Tilton'—candle-snuffers in extraordinary for the American theatre —it's very ridiculous. Hawkins, trouble you for that spoon, and the sugar."

A quiet smile of contempt played over the cold, dark features of Saxon, as he saw the importance which the youth attached to the matter, and beheld the swelling indignation with which he spoke of the despised amateurs. As if disposed to humor the folly and conceit of the youth, he continued the topic.

"But are you not exceedingly aristocratic in your notions, Mr. Horsey? Because a man has been forced to snuff candles, does it follow that he is incapable of something better?"

"Surely not, sir, surely not. The fates forbid that I should deal in such a pernicious doctrine. What was Shakspere himself, my masters; his early career is enough, without other authority, to prevent me from such sheer folly of opinion; but Tilton is no Shakspere, nor no Garrick; and, however he may have played the ghost of Cæsar, I tell you, he will be nothing but a miserable candle-snuffer all his life. Look you, I reason thus, Mr. Saxon. I have seen our friend, Hawkins, jump for a wager, and know his best pitch to a feather's width. Shall I not be able to say, 'Thus far can Bill Hawkins jump, and no farther?' Even thus do I tell you that Tilton was born to be a candle-snuffer, and nothing better—unless it be a call-boy on the stage."

"Yet was it said," remarked Saxon quietly, "that he was going to open the theatres at Vicksburg and Natchez."

"'Gods, grant us patience!' but it is scarce possible!"

"I heard as much myself," was the confirmatory statement of Hawkins.

"The d—d fool!—he's mad—utterly mad. On the word of a gentleman, Mr. Saxon, this fellow has no sort of rank—no reputation—no ability. Were I a manager, he should have no employment at my hands. The fellow is perfectly incapable."

"He is going to have a roaring company, nevertheless," said Hawkins. "He's engaged Peters for third-rate characters and is getting up recruits from every quarter."

"'I shall forget myself!' Was there ever such an insolent pretender?"

The amateur was almost furious. The moment had arrived when he could be best practised upon; and the game was continued.

"They say he has taken up actors even here in Raymond. Was not this young fellow Vernon, one of his men?" was the inquiry of Saxon, urged with a manner of the most perfect indifference.

"Yes, I think that was the name. He came into town last night," replied Hawkins.

"Who?—what? Harry—Harry Vernon! Psha, Hawkins, I know all about that. He's none of them—he's no actor —nothing but a lawyer riding the circuit. He's a sort of relation of sour Ben—so we call Ben Carter—and I s'pose the old boy's got him some cases. He stayed with us last night, and I took a julep with him this morning. Told me all about it himself."

"Indeed! He's a relation of Carter, and no actor, then?" demanded Saxon.

"No! he's no actor—has no notion of it. As for his being a relation of sour Ben, I don't know whether I'm right to say that—indeed, for that matter, I think he told me he was not— only an acquaintance. No, he's no actor, I assure you; and if all your information about Tilton and Bowlegs be no better founded than this, I wouldn't give much for the new theatre."

"You may be deceived even in this, Mr. Horsey," said Saxon. "This young man Vernon, they say, is going up into the Yazoo. Did he tell you that?"

"Lord, no! There's no truth in it, I'm certain, and sour Ben is too strict a chap to be very close with an actor. If he only once dreamed that Harry Vernon had such a notion, he'd throw up his hand in a minute. I know sour Ben too well: he'd cut loose from the young 'un, and leave him just rope enough to hang himself."

"What you say rather strengthens the report. If Vernon knows this of Carter, as without doubt he does, would not this be reason enough why he should keep his secret while under the old man's eye, particularly, if he has any favor to look for at Carter's hands—as it is said he has? Now, they de say, and I may as well tell you, I heard it from Tilton himself, on board the Georgiana, that Vernon was engaged secretly to play first characters."

"The devil! you say—first characters!" was the exclamation of the astounded amateur. "Who could have believed it —the fellow was so sly. But I needn't wonder at that. Egad, I played a shy game at first with Ben Carter myself. But, Harry Monmouth—well, to confess a truth, the chap played the sly one cleverly, if what you tell me be indeed the truth. But I am not certain yet."

"Look into it," said Hawkins carelessly; "and so sure am I that Saxon has good authority for what he says, I'll go a quart, and a dozen cabanas upon it."

"Soh! it's a bet," replied the amateur. "Our hands upon it, Trojan, and it will be a close tongue that can keep my worm from getting under it. I'll through Harry Monmouth's knapsack before he takes his crumbs out, or may I never look down upon the footlights again. Mr. Saxon"—drinking—"the stage, sir, though it be carried in a steamboat."

"Very good—devilish good, Tom," cried Hawkins, apparently delighted with the modest play upon words which the actor had attempted. "You were always clever at these things, but your frolic seems to have freshened and improved you. But what did the old man say, Tom, when you came back? The story was that you had made his factor hand over to the tune of three or four thousand dollars, which you lost at faro in one night."

"Not so bad as that, Hawkins, though bad enough still. I have worried the old man something too much, but I have promised him reformation, and—"

"Will keep your promise—if you can."

"Well said, Hawkins," responded the youth with a sigh; if I can. The task is a very difficult one; for this d—d stuff you've been telling me of Tilton and his floating theatre, has put me in a most inconceivable state of combustion. I should think well of the plan, if that wool-headed candle-snuffer had nothing to do with it. In good hands a theatre at Natchez—'

"Under the hill," said Hawkins with a sneer.

"No, no! there's too much hell-broth there; the gruel is slab, but not good enough in that quarter, unless in playing Tom and Jerry, to which I do not much incline; but for a respectable establishment, I doubt not that we should be able to keep it up, and put money in our pockets, at least four months in the year. We could then shift our quarters, as the old players did, from one barn to another. We could go to Vicksburg, Grand Gulf, Manchester, Port Gibson. and all about, and drive the prettiest and merriest gipsy business one could desire. ' By the Lord, our plot is a good plot as ever was laid !' but it would spoil the best plot, ay, and the best play too, to have such a botch as Tilton in the management."

"Tilton, or no Tilton, Tom, remember the bet. We must satisfy it before this youth, Vernon, leaves Raymond."

"My hand on't. But are you for court now — what's to be done — any murder cases. I like to listen to them; they are so many eggs for tragedy, which unborn Shaksperes may hatch. What say you, men — go along with me."

" Time enough ; the court won't open for an hour, and there are only a few cases of assault and battery ; nothing of interest. Stay awhile and sup your whiskey, and we'll go with you then. Saxon, your glass waits."

Let us leave the trio for awhile.

CHAPTER VI.

HUMORS OF A CLIENT—NEW MODE OF ARGUING A CASE OF ASSAULT AND BATTERY.

"See, where he lies, slaughter'd without the camp,
And by a simple swain, a mercenary,
Who bravely took the combat to himself."—Rob. Greene, 1560.

Vernon, meanwhile, accompanied by his friend and patron, proceeded to the court-house, in the area in front of which he encountered the curious gaze of all the natives to whom the face of a stranger is instantly obvious, and in the examination of whom they do not always content themselves with the keen scrutiny of the eye. "Whar' are you from, stranger?" and " whar' are you guine!" and " what's your business here?" and " what do you do there?" are the ordinary questions by which the forest-born contrive to obtain possession of that intelligence for which the Atlantic citizen has his morning gazette.

The crowd was fast assembling, and Vernon left alone by Mr. Carter, who was required to attend to some pressing business elsewhere, was, of course, compelled to go through his examination like all the rest, and bore it with the most becoming fortitude and good nature. Not that he answered his inquisitors with a strict regard to the truth; this might have exposed him to defeat in the purposes which he had in view; but with that ready adroitness which is the sign of keen and quick imagination, and which, by the way, is one of the very first requisites in a country circuit lawyer, he answered them in such a way as to reveal nothing, and yet satisfy them that he had nothing more to reveal. When asked about New Orleans, he could tell them a long story about the new big steamboat of which they had heard wonders; and by conversing freely with Tom, Dick, and Harry, about matters with which neither himself nor Tom, Dick, or Harry, had anything to do, convinced all around that he was no starched, stiff-necked upstart, so solicitous of his own birth, family, and fortune, as to dread the effect of their contact upon his nobility.

"A 'cute chap," said one, "that fellow, Vernon; knows all about that Orleans railroad and the big steamboat; says Madame Lalaurie, she that licked her poor niggers to death, and tied 'em week after week without hog or hominy, will get mightily smashed among the Orleans lawyers."

"He's an Orleans lawyer, then?" demanded another.

"I rether reckon so," was the reply, "though, by the powers, he didn't tell me that."

"Well, but now he's moved into Mississippi, or how could he come to plead here in Raymond."

"That's true — I'll go and ax him where he lives now; I rather like the chap," was the opinion and resolve of the baffled inquisitor, whom Vernon had contrived to lead from himself by freely enlarging upon other matters, which, for the moment, amply satisfied the hearer's curiosity.

But the youth had disappeared from the spot, and was then in the rear of the courthouse where he had been called by Carter who held him in close conference. Meanwhile, the court was convened, his honor had taken his seat, and the crowd, hurrying with that strange curiosity which is never so well satisfied as when it hears of the misdeeds of its own nature, and which is never so active and apprehensive as in a secluded country village, soon forgot all concern for the interesting stranger, and gave itself up, soul and body, to the clamors of officers, silencing clamor; the calls of jurymen and witnesses; the small wit of small lawyers, and the sapient wisdom of the judge, whose oracles, generally monosyllabic, are accompanied by a shake of the head, worse-wise than Burleigh's.

Carter, having concluded the relation of a matter which belonged to the expedition of his protegé was about to withdraw with him to the great moral bull-ring, when one of those little and most amusing incidents took place, which could only take place in a country such as ours, where a bold decisive character is formed by the adventurous life which it makes prominent, if not necessary; and where a free spirit and genuine humor seem absolutely to result from the absence of any of those educational restraints, which, in New England, graduate all intellects to an interesting level, making them as completely the creatures of mould and measure, as if God had decreed them, even in morals and expression, to the exquisite republican equality which they deny to none—who have a money qualification and are not Irish and Catholic

A broad-faced, brown-cheeked, good-humored looking farmer approached the two, and addressing Carter by name as an old acquaintance, turned from him to his companion, and slapping him upon the shoulder with all the familiarity of an old acquaintance, spoke to him in some such language as the following.

"Look ye, now, stranger, they tell me your name's Varnon, and that you're a lawyer, and I reckon it's true what they tell me. You're a friend of his, Ben Carter—eh?"

Carter answered by introducing Vernon more formally to the interrogator, whom Vernon himself satisfied on the subject of his other interrogatories.

"Well, Harry Varnon," said the old man in continuation, "I like your face—by the hokey but I do—and without meaning to praise you to your teeth, I tell you you're a d—d smart-looking fellow; and I want to give you some law business to do for me now, before the court's over here in Raymond."

"Your business is his, Mr. Shippen," said Carter, anticipating the reply of Vernon, "and I think that my friend will do justice to himself and you at the same time."

"Let the boy talk for himself, Carter. I want to hear him talk since I'm going to hire him, you see, to talk for me in the courthouse. By his face, he ought to have a mighty free speech, and that's the sort of thing you see that will best suit me at this present. What say you, Harry Varnon, are you willing to argify a little business for me in a mighty bad case."

The other professed his willingness to do what he could for his client to the best of his ability, and in such a style as to satisfy the old man that he was not likely to prove a bungler in his business.

"That's your sort," said he; "and now look ye, Varnon.
The law is agin me here for licking a d—d Yankee trader, that
said something sassy to my darter Nelly. She's only a child,
Master Varnon, a leetle over thirteen years old, and couldn't 'a
meant any harm in what she did; and if there was any harm
in it, d'ye see, why I was the only one to blame in the matter.
I gin her a five-dollar bill to go to Watson's store to buy some
little truck, and he said the bill was a false one and a counterfeit, and spoke so to the child as if she meant to cheat him —
and she a gal too — that I got angry as a buster, and went
straight off and mounted him. I pulled him out from his shop,
and it wasn't at all sheepish — nay, 'twas rether wolfish — the
way I handled him. I made his sides ache, I tell you. Well,
the long and short of the business, then, is this : instead of
coming out and making it a fight after his own fashion, with
any we'pons, jist as he might think best for himself, he goes
a-lawing me about for damages, and he's put down his bruises
and black spots at five thousand dollars; as if his laying up a
week, and putting a mush poultice on his shins, and a piece of
raw beef to his eyes, should have cost him so much money
Well, you're right to laugh, for that's the true state of the case,
and now what do you think you can do with it ?"

"You have counsel already ?" asked Vernon.

"Oh, yes; one Graham, here, that comes from Monticello; a
mealy-mouthed chap that don't please me at all; but he was
the best I could get to do the business when I wanted it. He
answered Perkins, who is Watson's lawyer, step by step, in the
law-papers he put in; and I s'pose did that part of the business
tolerable well; but then, he can't talk, Varnon; and he trim-
bles and looks afeard when the other lawyers talk, and that
vexes me, to have a lawyer that's afeard to open his mouth in
my business; and I wo'n't have him talk for me if I can help
it."

"But, Mr. Shippen, I can not think to supersede Mr. Graham
in this business; it is against the courtesy of the bar."

"There's no superseding at all. Graham's quite willing to
get somebody to help him; for, look you, he says that he knows
nothing that he can say to help me. He says they'll prove
everything agin me, and there's no sort of defence that he can

make. Now, he says, if I had only let Watson give me the first clip, he could defend me very well; but wouldn't I ha' been a blasted fool to ha' let him, when everybody knows that a first clip is half the battle? No—no! none of that stuff for me; it may be law, but I reckon there's no reason in it—none that'll sarve a man here in Mississippi."

" I don't know that I can do much more for you than Graham," said Vernon, modestly; "you, at least know, Mr. Shippen, that the law favors him most who suffers the first injury."

" You can talk, Varnon, and that's something more than Graham can do. You can tell the people what a darned skunk of a fellow that Watson is, to go and scandalize a child—and she a gal too—to call her a cheat and vilify her in front of his shop; and by the Etarnal, if that a'n't provocation and injury enough to justify any father for licking the rapscallion that does it, then I don't know any sense in our having laws at all. Well, then, all I want is that you should talk your mind freely to the people about these things. I know well enough, that by the law-books, a man's not to lick his neighbor for bad words, ginerally speaking; but then, you see, here's a case different. Here the bad words is spoken to a gal child, that has a character to lose, and there's no such thing as standing that; and it does seem to me that it's right to make a monstrous difference between blackguarding a man himself, and blackguarding his darter. Well, Varnon, you're just the man now, to hit the skunk hard on these p'ints. Do you score him now, up and down, hip and thigh, for half an hour—half an hour by the watch—and there's a clear fifty dollars in your pocket. Say the word—only half an hour now—I don't want a minute more; and it's a bargain."

Vernon laughed at the humor of the proposition, but seemed disposed to hesitate; when Carter, fearing that some nice point of objection might suggest itself to the youth, and knowing the importance to his present object of his appearing in Raymond only as a lawyer seeking practice, immediately closed with the offer on the part of the youth. The old farmer, however, was not so well satisfied.

" Let Varnon talk for himself, Ben Carter; he's got a tongue of his own, and it does me good to hear him use it. Come,

Varnon, my boy, say what you'll do. I've spoken to Graham
a'ready, and he says he's willing. It mought be that you think
he a'n't; but between us, he's mighty glad to get the trouble
on to some other body's shoulders, for he's plainly told me that
it's a darned black and blue case, all agin me, and he's r.o notion of any way to turn it about to my benefit. I'm candid you
see — I don't hide nothing from you. I expect to sweat a little
at my fingers' ends for this beating, but, by the hokey, five
thousand dollars will swallow me and all my substance, and you
must rub that down to a mere sarcumstance. I'm willing to
bleed five hundred, but the other is quite too digging. It'll
plough me out of the ground to raise it; and root and branch
must go along with it. A good talk now, that'll show what a
skunk Watson is, and what a shame it would be to let a child
— a gal child too — be abused by such a varment, and called a
cheat, and vilified as if she was a bad woman at the foot of
Natchy hill — will help me mightily, and I don't think the jury
will mind the law so much, when the reason and the right of
the thing is so clearly in my hand. Do your best, my chicken,
and the money's in your pocket."

"Did I understand you that Watson made no defence?"

"Took his beating like a holy martyr."

"What! did he not strike a blow?"

"Not the breath of one; he jist called upon the people to
see how I handled him, jist as if he had a liking for it. That's
the worst part of the business for me, so Graham says."

"I'll close with you, Mr. Shippen. I'll plead for half an
hour."

"Jist half an hour, Varnon; do it well and stick to him for
that time, my chicken, and by the hokey, I don't want a minute more."

"I will do it," repeated the youth, rather amused with the
aspect of the affair, and the requisition of the farmer; and not
so hopeless of his cause as Mr. Graham had been. From that
very feature, last related in the case, which Graham thought
the most unfavorable, the quickwitted Vernon argued the very
best results; and having appointed to meet Shippen within the
hour, to make the acquaintance of Graham and confer with
him on the business so far as it had gone, the stouthearted do

fendant left him for awhile, as fully satisfied with the proceed
ing, as if his case was already won. He was one of those worthy republicans who was not unwilling to pay for his liberties,
and the right to speak his mind, though it might be only through
the lips of another, was one of those rights which he esteemed
cheaply paid for with fifty dollars at any time.

When he had gone, Carter resumed his conference with Ver
non, which related, we need scarcely say, to the projected mission of the latter. Other items of intelligence had reached him
— which furnished additional clues to those already in possession — of the course taken i his flight by the faithless friend
and absconding debtor; but as these matters are destined to
have their distinct development in the regular progress of the
affair, they demand none of our attention now.

When Vernon entered the court-house he found his new client
awaiting him with the "mealy-mouthed" lawyer Graham. A
few moments sufficed to put Vernon in possession of all the facts
so far as their litigated character had become apparent to the
attorney on record. During the course of his narrative, Graham
did not scruple, though in the presence of Shippen, to declare
his utter hopelessness of his cause; a sort of sincerity which is
of very doubtful propriety, since it never yet discouraged a lit-
igant, and has often ruined a very worthy practitioner. It was
amusing enough to Vernon to survey the countenance of Shippen as these opinions fell from the lips of his lawyer. How he
would lift his eyebrows, and roll his tongue within his jaws,
and then turn away exclaiming—

"Never you mind, Charley Graham—never you mind.—
there are more eggs to be hatched this week, than was ever
laid by your mother's best hen; and some of the chickens, let
me tell you, will be long spurred before they chip the shell.
Only half an hour, Harry Varnon; only half an hour, my boy;
but let it be well talked."

At length, in its due place upon the docket, the long-expected
civil case of Watson v. Shippen, sounding in damages of assault
and battery, was called, and the several parties responded accordingly With the first sounds of his name, Shippen perched
himself behind Vernon, and renewed his exhortations and his

4

promises. The plaintiff, Watson, was also present — a huge mammoth-feeding sort of person, half as large again as Shippen and having the appearance of one, who, if he had not utterly lacked the spirit, could have annihilated, or at least, have swallowed his assailant. His downcast look, halting, hesitating but sly manner, sufficiently denoted the cold, calculating and cowardly wretch — such as Shippen had described him — who could wantonly insult the young girl, whose indignant father he dared not face, and could not contend with.

His attorney, Perkins, opened the case with considerable spirit, passed slightingly over the provocation by which Watson had drawn upon him the wrath of the defendant, and dwelt with proper details of law and fact, upon the enormity of the outrage which the latter had committed; described the cruel manner in which his client had been dragged from his dwelling into the public thoroughfare and beaten by the big-fisted pugilist, whom, in his passionate exaggeration, he made a giant, while the plaintiff was diminished to a feeble and delicate person, whose Christian forbearance, while receiving the injuries complained of, was the subject of most unbounded, and, it may be added, most unmerited eulogium. After this, it seemed something of an anti-climax to show that a physician's aid was called in to heal his hurts; particularly as the cross-examination determined the extent of this attendance to be little over three days; and the medicaments employed to be of little more cost than "eye of newt and toe of frog." A pea poultice was shown to be one of the most successful applications of Doctor Shinbone, and the application of the lancet, his most serious operation. With these proofs and the commentary which he made with so much unction upon them, Mr. Attorney Perkins, was willing to close his side of the case.

"You see," said Graham, in a half-whisper to Vernon; "it is as I have told you. He has proved everything, and our case is to be made out of his witnesses only."

The words, spoken however slightly, were audible to the keen ears of the defendant behind, who, smarting with the declamation of Perkins, retorted before Vernon could speak.

"And a good case, too, Charley Graham, if a man had it in him to bring out. Up and at him, Harry Vernon, and give him enough of it. By the hokey, Charley Graham, you talk as if your liver was all cream color."

A sly twinkle of Vernon's eyes was perceptible to the court, as, arising from his seat, he coolly took out his watch, and noted the precise minute before he commenced his operations. The bargain, meanwhile, which Shippen had made with the strange lawyer, to talk for him half an hour only, had got into considerable circulation, chiefly with the assistance of the defendant himself; and the curiosity was general, not less to hear the young and handsome stranger, than to see what he could make of his limits.

Vernon did not belie public expectation. Cool in temper rapid in reflection, and singularly fluent of speech, he commenced his task by reviewing briefly the evidence which had been given. He dwelt with much more emphasis than Perkins on the gross insult which had been offered to a young child, of good parents, and one of a sex, which needed, from the delicacy of its structure, the kindness and indulgence of man; and could not live either in his harshness or disesteem. This harshness, he proceeded to show, was quite hostile to that claim which had been so eloquently made by the opposite counsel, in behalf of the Christian meekness of his client; this meekness being the result of his cowardice, and not of his Christianity; since it was very visible in his encounter with the man, and was singularly wanting to his deportment in his interview with the child. "It is very well," proceeded Vernon, "to insist upon the integrity of the laws, to prevent the brutality of violence, to compel the strong arm to desist from strife, and refer to the authorities assigned by society for such purposes, to redress its wrongs; but there are some cases," he said, "where outraged Humanity becomes a rebel; and when, to wait for the dilatory process of the laws, might be to ruin her for ever. In all cases, where the reputation or the virtue of a woman — a wife, a sister, or a daughter — are at stake, the sudden blow of the outraged relative is a blow struck for Virtue herself, and in compliance with laws which are infinitely more sacred than any that can be framed by man. And, so universal," he continued, "are these laws, that I can not bring myself to believe that his honor, who now sits upon the bench, and you, gentlemen of the jury, or any man of proper spirit and feeling, could forbear, in like circumstances, to do as my client has done. Ay, gentlemen, even if the place of sanctuary which the ruffian had chosen for his retreat, had been the altar of God itself, rather than the counter behind which he sells his wares, it would not have shielded him from your honest anger, any more than the latter place has protected Watson from the just vengeance of a father.

"But I do not rely only on these points, gentlemen of the jury. There are others scarcely less important to be dwelt upon. Watson has come into court clamoring for justice. I should say he has already had it — that never was justice made so clearly manifest as when Shippen punished him for the defamation of his daughter. He founds his claim, as every man must, who comes into court, upon his strict compliance with the laws. But his eloquent counsel has not deemed it sufficient to confine himself to this modest claim. He not only asserts him to have borne the part of a good citizen, but of a most becoming Christian. 'Look at his meekness under stripes,' says Mr. Perkins, 'and you have the very deportment of the old apostles under like indignities.' Gentlemen of the jury, it is a new doctrine to be taught here — this meekness under blows — this calm, Christian toleration of injuries — this patient bending of the shoulders to any assault. But the counsel has himself proved quite too much for his case and client. He has shown you, by the evidence, that, so far from being meek under his suffering, he, at the very moment, called upon the bystanders to witness — not his courage in resenting injury — the courage of proper manhood, which always forbears insult, and always repels it — but the blows which he submitted to, that they might be counted down and paid for in money. This base creature, gentlemen, this pretended Christian, had no abhorrence of the shame to which he was subjected; had no consciousness of the disgrace and degradation; had, it seems, no actual feeling of the blows, while he consoled himself with the reflection that they were to be paid for; that he should get money for every stroke; that his blood was to be weighed in an opposite scale against five thousand dollars of my client. He comes into court not for justice, but for money. He comes not to sustain the

laws, for he himself violated them, when he slandered the innocent daughter of this old man ; but to speculate, like a miserable pedler, upon what may be made out of another's violation
of them. Does such a man come into court with clean hands?
Does he not come into court with the basest of all base feelings
in his soul? And would not such a man as this, who thus bar-
ters his blood for money as freely as another Judas, barter his
very God for a far less sum? I have no sort of doubt of this
myself. I believe, as conscientiously as I do that I now stand
before you, that neither your lives nor your honors could be
safe in such hands, were it profitable for him to dispose of them,
and were the danger not too great for one endowed with such a
dastard spirit.

"Let us go back to that chastisement of which he complains
the dishonor of which he thinks can be all removed by five
thousand of my client's dollars; and I, too, will pray you
to give as close attention to it, as was prayed for by my
worthy and eloquent opponent, though with a far different object. He called upon you to admire the meekness of this new
apostle come down upon earth. Your Christian feelings were
exhorted to take pattern after this blessed example of Christian
forbearance. Behold this lamb under the furious claws of this
lion going about seeking what he may devour. See how he
prays for his cruel assailant. Such was the picture of my able
brother. Let me pray you to give as much heed to one that I
shall draw. See, then, this miserable poltroon, submitting to
the assaults of one to whom, in physical capacity, he is a giant
—hear him how he shouts to the people. He calls upon all
around to see that he strikes no blow himself—he begs them to
take particular account of the number that he receives. When
jeered by the spectators for such tame and unbecoming submission, he grins, with a miserable delight, even while his foe
is kicking him. 'Never mind, he shall pay for this,' is the answer that he makes; 'for all these kicks I shall have coppers!'
His enemy wrings his nose—'Ah!' he cries with a miserable
chuckle, 'that shall cost him a thousand dollars. Let him kick,
he will have to pay for all!' And this, gentlemen, is the sort
of person, the Christian, of whom we hear a eulogy that would
rank him with any of the apostles that ever was flayed alive in

the cause of God and of mankind. To my thinking, so far from calling him a Christian, gentlemen of the jury, I can scarcely count him human. There is so much of cold insensibility about this creature—something so utterly bloodless, yet so malignant, that, were it not at the same time so very base, I should esteem it devilish, and worthy of Lucifer himself.

"But, gentlemen of the jury, I am not yet done with this part of my subject. I would like to place before you the evil effect of encouraging a prosecution, such as the present, sounding in individual damages; and the ground which I take for my objection is in the very fact upon which Mr. Perkins rests his strongest argument, namely, the patience with which this creature submitted to be beaten. This very patience under blows, I hold to be disgraceful to the manhood of the person, as it would be to the manhood of the nation that submitted to them tamely; and to pay him for thus submitting, will, gentlemen, be paying a bounty to the rankest cowardice that ever degraded man. Every dollar which you give to this mean creature for this affair, is neither more nor less than a bounty to the coward; the effect of which must be to raise a brood of cowards throughout the country. We want no cowards in this country. Our object should be to discourage them, to withdraw from them the countenance of the courts, and the approval, even indirectly, of all honest men. We punish the coward in the field, yet give a bounty to him in time of peace. What a monstrous contradiction—a contradiction not to be reconciled by any resort to common justice or common sense. Let us punish them alike in every case—refuse them countenance in ordinary life, and never trust them in the field. Do not suppose, gentlemen of the jury, that I am disposed by these remarks. to encourage the wrong-doer in his violence, and to drive the weak and unoffending from protection. Had this man, Watson, who is neither weak nor unoffending, made good fight, and been overcome after an honest struggle, by Shippen, I should have been among the first to say that he should have had a few hundred dollars damages; but, under existing circumstances, it is my firm conviction that you will give him only such damages as will carry the costs of prosecution, and dismiss him from the presence of the court with the unmitigated scorn of all who have listened to the dishonoring testimony, which he has this day, in his own case, produced against himself."

The half hour had elapsed, and Vernon sat down amidst a half-suppressed murmur of applause. Shippen, as soon as he had touched his seat, jumped up, clapped him upon his shoulder, and exclaimed, so as to be heard by all around—

"At him agin, Harry, only for a quarter more, and you shall have another fifty."

The tears were in the eyes of the old man, and the fervency of his expression, the frank, feeling tones of his voice, so opposite as he appeared in every respect to his opponent, Watson, moved the sympathy of the whole court in his favor. But Vernon declined his offer. He felt that he had made the proper impression, and that anything more would only tend to weaken and impair it. He was one of those fortunate men, of whom there are so few in our hemisphere, whether in the senate, the forum, or the pulpit, who know where to stop; and, though flattered by the obvious effect of his argument, so novel, and in some respects ingenious — of which we have given however, a very feeble report — he firmly resisted all the persuasions of Shippen to renew the speech.

This single fact was not without its effect upon the minds of those present. That a lawyer should refuse a fee for a matter seemingly so easy of execution, and that he should resist — a more difficult matter with young lawyers—the temptation still to talk when the auditors were willing to hear — were events to which our southwestern people are not habituated. The confidence which his refusal indicated in what had been already said, had its influence also. They jury retired from the box, but before the verdict was returned — which, *par parenthese,* gave only nominal damages as Vernon had suggested — Carter entered the court-room suddenly, and in a whisper summoned the young lawyer away.

"The governor is at Mrs. Baxter's, and would like to speak with you a while."

Shippen would have detained him, and released him only with a promise that he should go home and spend a night with him, and see his wife Susan, and Bella, the little girl who had been the innocent cause of the trial, and his plough oxen, and a

fine blood mare that he had just got from Georgia, and a thou
sand other matters, most of which, at that moment, Vernon
might have had for the asking.

CHAPTER VII.

POLITICIANS IN COUNCIL.— ESPIONAGE — GLIMPSES OF OUTLAWRY.

> "I do accuse thee here
> To be a man, factious and dangerous,
> A sower of sedition in the state,
> A turbulent and discontented spirit.
> Which I will prove."—*Sejanus*, BEN JONSON

LET us return to the shed-room in the shop of Hawkins,
where we left our quondam friend, the *soi-disant* actor, carousing
with his new companion, Saxon. Hawkins had left the two for
a while, and during his absence employed himself no less busily than did they, and possibly to more useful purpose. The
good liquor, aided by the arts of Saxon — who had his own
policy in it — had been productive of its customary effect upon
the erratic youth, who was now plainly in the seventh heaven
of theatrical hallucination. He treated his comrade to the
choicest selections of the old fathers of dramatic literature, and
mouthed in the becoming style of the best modern artists. Now
he gave imitations of Kean, excelling in the spasmodic hoarse-
ness of his utterance — in the fury of the Pythia without her
inspiration — now the lugubrious whinings of Cooper, when declining toward the fifth act; and now the guttural growl of
Forrest, when, with singular bad taste, he imitates even the
death-rattle in the throat of the obese Vitellius. With much
talent, and a good deal of taste for the profession to which he
so desperately inclined, the want of a proper education in
schools furnishing intrinsic standards, left Horsey entirely open
to that worst of all misfortunes to talent in any country — and
one which is the particular evil in ours — the formation of his

style and judgment upon models essentially erratic, and unregulated by any just principle. To make a point, rather than to act well the part, was too much his desire, as it seems the prevailing ambition with all our Daggerwoods; and in the course of a brief hour, Saxon was treated to a dozen different readings of all the disputed passages in Macbeth, Hamlet, Richard, and the rest.

It was curious to see with what industry the youth had accumulated authorities on Shakspere. He had Gifford, Malone, Steevens, Seymour, Rowe, Farmer, and some thirty or forty more at his finger-ends, and could we look at this moment into the little closet which was assigned him as a sleeping-room at his father's house, we should see the works of all these persons, accumulated on the table by his couch; he being also one of those erring persons who read by night in bed.

These books were all he had left to show for the thousands he had dissipated of his father's income; and whether his outlay had been a profitable one or not, would have been of no difficult decision, were the father chosen to resolve the question. To do the youth justice, however, it may be added, that he had learned something of good from the schools, however erring and even vicious, through which he had gone. A knowledge of books, and even of men, infinitely beyond that usually in the possession of persons in his secluded home, had been the result of his wanderings; and the roughness of the country clown had been fortunately exchanged for a manner, which, though it might be sometimes swaggering and obtrusive, was seldom rude, and never brutal or insolent. As a further set-off to his deficiencies, Tom Horsey was a good-natured, generous fellow, who readily forgave injuries, conciliated friends, and took the world always, as the world is required to take its wives, for better or worse. "It's a damned bad world," Tom was in the habit of saying over his cups, "that would not be content to take him too on the same terms."

He did the world injustice, however, as Saxon strove busily to convince him. The cool, wily outlaw, for such he was, listened patiently to all the youth's recitations, and even encouraged him to continue them by suggesting the quotations; but, at decent intervals, he would contrive to insinuate a side ques

tion touching other matters and in relation to persons, by which
he contrived, in the overflow of the youth's garrulity, to get
from him everything within his knowledge in regard to his
father's concerns, and those of Carter his lodger, and Vernon
his guest. Some particular interest seemed, in his mind, to
hang over the probable proceedings of the latter; and all his
remarks, even when he spoke of playing—the topic on which
Horsey could always be commanded—were calculated to fill
the latter with the persuasion that Vernon was about to go up
the country.

"If he does then, Saxon, by the pipers, I must pay for the
music; that is to say, I must treat according to the bet between
us—for then, I shall take it for granted it is as you say; and
he's going up to join that booby Tilton's company—though
he's but a poor codling if he does. That fellow, Tilton, is the
merest dolt and dunderhead, if you believe me, that ever bowed
to an audience. What the devil can he hope to play himself?
and as for his management—management indeed! 'A fico for
the phrase'—the thing can't answer, Mr. Saxon."

"Perhaps not, Mr. Horsey, yet what is the poor fellow to do?
'Young ravens must have food'—you know the quotation?"

"Ay, ay, 'mine ancient,' are you there? But let that humor
pass! It is my doubt that this chap Tilton is but a crow;—
and will never get his corn in this field. If he can, God speed
him, I say, and help him to a better mind and finer figure—
matters in which he needs all the help that God and man can
give him. As for the figure, I would not be his tailor for all
the cloth—there would be more cutting to be done on the mar.
than the stuff. What I chafe at is his chance of failure, which
is so great—for failure in a new scheme, throws back the
period and the prospect of success; and the thing, which in
good hands might, nay must, be successful, would, I am free to
take another bet, be sure to fail in his."

"But if he gets good actors to begin with, Mr. Horsey."

"Ay, that alters the case, but when did you ever know a fool
choose wise help? It is scarce a thing to be hoped for, however much desired."

"What of this young fellow, Vernon, if he be one of the
company?" insinuated Saxon.

"You know my thought on that point. Dad says he's a lawyer, and he as good as told me the same thing himself. I'll look into the business when I go home. But, let him be as you think, and still I can say nothing of Tilton's choice. Harry Vernon may be a smart chap enough, and certainly looks like one, but the stage requires something more than that. Is he a reader, say you; has he discretion of points; knows he his author; knows he his audience; and to sum up all in little, has he the divine gift, the born intelligence which makes the actor a born actor, as completely as the poet is a born poet, if one at all? These are the requisites, Master Brook, and a fellow may be smart at law and smart at physic, who would show but a dull ass upon the stage; as I have seen a chap make a fine speech at muster grounds from a stump, who sat a horse like a jackdaw. To speak plainly, though I would not have it reach Harry's ears, my best reason for doubting his being an actor is that I believe he has no turn, no talent for the stage. I like Harry so much already, that I should be sorry to see him fail."

"But why not join Tilton yourself?"

"Ah, Saxon, your question takes me all aback. If it were not this d—d fool Tilton, who will spoil everything, and, like others who are as great fools as himself, though probably better actors, he will be casting himself in all the first characters. If I could be sure—"

The sentence in which he was probably about to show the weakness of his heart in its yearnings toward the old vanities which he had so recently and solemnly renounced, was cut short by the sudden entrance of Hawkins.

"Horsey," he cried on entrance, "I am afraid we shall lose that bet with you. I have just got away from the courthouse, where I left your friend Vernon in full argument."

"The devil you did. Said I not, said I not! But what's the business — what's the case — murder, rape, burglary, battery?"

"Battery, battery! He defends old Shippen against Watson, whom he drubbed for insulting little Bella, his daughter. Watson got no more than he deserved, and your man Vernon's serving him like all the world. I think the jury will hardly singe Shippen's skirts, though Watson thought to smoke him to

the tune of two or three thousand dollars. Vernon's put a new
color on the colt, and people who thought him rather black
when he was first carried into court, now look upon him as
a rather pretty cream. He'll get off slick and easy; that Vernon's a smart fellow "

"By the ghost of Cæsar, but I must hear Harry, I must.
What say you, Mr. Saxon, will you go along? what say you,
Hawkins?"

An expressive glance of the eye, which the latter gave to
Saxon, led him to decline the invitation, and Hawkins pleading
business, the actor set off alone. He had scarcely taken his
departure when Hawkins, in a hurried and somewhat agitated
manner, taking Saxon farther into the apartment, and closing
the inner door, remarked —

"Would you believe it, Saxon; the governor has just got in
from below."

"Ah, indeed; he comes alone?"

"Yes, and has gone to Mother Baxter's. But you take it
very coolly. Will you not be off?"

"Why should I take it otherwise. I know not that I have
anything to fear from his coming," was the calm reply.

"How! said you not that you knew of advisers having gone
to him from Alabama of that d—d ugly business of Grafton;
and of your course from the Black Warrior, across to Mississippi."

"Yes! But this is no trouble to me here. These advisers
tell of my aiming for the Yazoo, but nothing of my being so
low as this. Raymond is the last place where he would think
to find me."

"What can he come for then?"

"That is a secret I should like to fathom. Can't we contrive
it, Hawkins. You have a room at this old woman's?"

"Yes: but it's monstrous dangerous. It is risking everything."

"True; and there are cases where everything must be risked,
if anything is to be saved; and this is one of them. It is important to find out how much of our secret they know. If they
have a list of names in Mississippi, the owners of them must
take tracks for Texas without more delay. There is no saving

them else, and I misdoubt that this fellow Vernon is employed on some business above against us, which, it is absolutely necessary that we should gain a knowledge of."

" But this pleading speaks against it. The youth seems really nothing more than a young beginner at the law on his first circuit."

" That may be, and there is no good reason why a young lawyer should not now and then try his hand at a more profit-able business. A governor's proclamation, with a reward of two or three thousand dollars, is no bad inducement to a con-fident youth to try the capture of an outlaw. I must see more of this youth and more of the governor before I leave them; and the long and the short of the matter is, that we go to your room at once. He is even now, you say, at Mother Baxter's."

" Even now—and more—another matter of which I forgot to speak—Carter has been with him ever since you came."

" And Vernon lodges with Carter! see you not; can you doubt, Hawkins? If I do, it is only the more resolutely to see how far they are linked together, and to ascertain their objects truly. We must see to it. I will leave you and take the right hand side of the way toward the courthouse. Send Jenkins round to the crooked oak with my horse, that he may be con-veniently in readiness. I may have to send on short notice That done, take your way to Baxter's, and meet me at the entrance. Perhaps it would be quite as well to send the old woman into the kitchen, or on some wild-goose errand, that the coast may be clear. See to it now, Hawkins, with all your eyes; for we are in no sort of danger *here ;* nobody *here* will suspect us, unless we blunder through stupidity or haste."

Saxon looked carefully to his pistols, which were well-con-cealed in the bosom of the overcoat he wore. Nobody would have suspected, under the calm, cool, dignified movement, the doomed outlaw, standing on the brink of danger, and thought-ful only on the means of extrication from perils that environed himself and comrades on every hand. His bowie-knife, that dreadful instrument of summary and sanguinary vengeance, whose edge, sharpened to a razor's keenness, was rendered still **more terrible by the** condensed weight of a sabre thrown into

its back, was adjusted in his breast so as to answer the first
movements of his hand; and, with the ·confidence of one who
has prepared himself at all points for the worst, the bold man,
who is probably already recognised by the reader of our
previous work (Richard Hurdis) as an old acquaintance, left
the shop of his comrade and emerged calmly into the thoroughfare.

Proceeding with corresponding boldness, he went forward
where the throng was. thickest, entered the courthouse, looked
on and listened for a brief space to the proceedings, then took
his way slowly to the house of Mrs. Baxter, where he had
appointed to meet with his comrade. Hawkins had so contrived it, as to keep the passage clear. He led him through it
with slow and cautious footsteps, up the narrow stairway, and
thence into his chamber, which lay on the left hand, being the
room opposite that which the governor occupied. The little
landing-course at the head of the stairs—a sort of platform,
some five feet wide, was the only space that separated the two
chambers. When Hawkins had closed his door, he gave Saxon
to understand that but a few moments had passed since Carter,
accompanied by Vernon, had gone into the governor's room,
and his intelligence quickened the anxiety of Saxon to inquire
into the purport of their business. Though scarcely governed
by so keen a motive as the outlaw, let us, however, go forward
more boldly than himself to procure the desired knowledge,
and at once enter the chamber in which the three are now assembled. We shall lose little by our delay, since the preliminaries of introduction—those little formalities without which
the world does no business civilly—occupied the brief space
between the entrance of Vernon to the conference, and the
beginning of our own and the outlaw's espionage upon its
progress.

"Our mutual friend, Mr. Carter, assures me, Mr. Vernon, of
your perfect capacity to do for me a certain business which is
important to the interests of the state, and which requires as
much secrecy and courage as intelligence. Can I hope for your
assistance?"

The youth answered him briefly, that any service not inconsistent with that upon which he was at present engaged would

be cheerful.y undertaken by him, which would subserve the
interests of the state, and oblige his excellency

"But your excellency is not aware, perhaps," he continued,
"that I am to leave Raymond, possibly to-morrow, for the
Yazoo neighborhood."

"It is that fact, in part," was the reply, "which prompts my
application. It is in that very neighborhood that your assistance will be required. I need not add, that, apart from the
state's commission which will be given you, an adequate compensation will be assigned for the time which may be consumed
in the service, and the degree of labor and peril to which you
may be subjected."

"It will give me pleasure, sir, to serve the state, even without
these considerations; but, I must remind your excellency of
one qualification with which I prefaced my first reply. If the
duties required at my hands, shall, in any way, affect the object
which I have in view, and which I must, under existing circumstances, esteem paramount to every other, I shall be compelled to decline the service, though I do so with extreme
reluctance, as a loss of opportunity for honorable employment.
Will you oblige me, sir, by suffering me to know the nature of
the business."

"Certainly. Briefly then: we have advices by express from
the authorities of Alabama, which inform us of a singular and
extensive plan of outlawry, which has its source either in that
state or in ours, and perhaps in both, and numbers no fewer
than fifteen hundred adherents in the two. This number has,
I doubt not, been grie ously exaggerated. If it be not, we are
in very sad condition. Of one thing these letters assure me,
that many of our citizens, hitherto held in good esteem, are
sworn confederates of these banditti, and in one disguise or
another trail through all parts of the state, and sometimes
operate in fixed places with even more effect, as they appear
under characters the more specious and imposing. Then we
have positive intelligence that some of our justices of the
peace belong to this band, and we are scarcely in doubt that a
militia officer, of whom the public has hitherto thought very
highly, is himself a leader among these outlaws. Their com-
mander-in-chief, one Clym or Clem Foster, made his escape

from certain citizens of Tuscaloosa county about three weeks
ago, and was reported to have crossed over by way of Cotton-
gin Port within the last ten days. A man answering to his
description was seen in that neighborhood about that time.
Thus, you have in brief the aspect of affairs. You see one of
the chief difficulties in our way. To move openly, and with a
force drawn from any other quarter of the state, to act upon
that in which these scoundrels congregate, would be only to
expel them temporarily, and we should fail probably in taking
a single prisoner. To place a special commission in the hands
of any person in that neighborhood, of whom we are not sure,
would be equally indiscreet, since it might be placing the whole
power of the state, for the time, in the control of one of the
very banditti whom we are striving to subdue. We want a
bold spirit, who will act vigorously when occasion serves; but
one who can keep his secret, work himself so adroitly as to
sound those with whom he mingles, sift the worthy from the
unworthy, and embody them in the proper moment for the
capture or destruction of these wretches."

Vernon heard the speaker with close attention. We have
summed up in short, what was only delivered in a dialogue of
some length, in which the questions of the former necessarily
led to the revelation of many facts, of which, it is quite probable, the governor spoke with some reluctance and with very
imperfect knowledge. When these facts had been obtained
the answer of Vernon was immediate.

"Your excellency shall judge for yourself of what service I
can be to you in this business, and how far it will prove consistent with my present objects to accept of your appointment.
While you will not deem my reluctance to arise from any lack
of desire to do my duty to the country which protects me, you
will, at the same time, hold me guiltless of the vanity which
would assume me to be possessed of those endowments which
you esteem, and correctly, to be necessary to the proper success
of the person you select. You are probably, in part, advised
of the mission upon which I go to the Yazoo. I am in pursuit
of one, also a criminal, who, for aught we know, may be one
of these very banditti. Will it be my policy to undertake this

trust, when its execution may lead me into conflicts and necessities which may defeat my present purpose?"

"Will it not?" replied the governor. "The capture of one
of the band, the discovery of the secrets of one, and that one
not the person whom you pursue — will these not be rather
more likely than not, to lead also to his detection?"

"I am afraid not, your excellency. Apart from the obvious
consequence of taking upon myself an additional employment,
which must be, to a certain extent, the diversion of my atten
tion from, and my pursuit of, the one object; these felons,
according to your own showing, are in possession of so complete
a system, that unless you strike them, by a simultaneous blow
upon every link of their operation, you endanger the success
of your whole project. No one man, setting out as I do, with
so little preparation, and without concert with any other opera-
tives, can possibly hope to effect anything in this double business. It would give me pride to act in this matter, as your
excellency desires; believe me, sir, I feel deeply this honorable
compliment; but I am perfectly convinced, that, unless it positively happened in my way, to act upon the information you
give, I should esteem it unwise to go aside from my path, and
jeopard the success of that other purpose, which, as it is of
vital importance to Mr. Carter, is, I assure you, of little less
importance to me."

The governor seemed much chagrined by this answer, and
strode the chamber with ill-concealed disquiet. Vernon resumed.

"When, however, I decline the assumption of this charge,
as a distinct and responsible appointment, your excellency, I
do not mean to say that I would not do anything, if called on
in a moment of emergency, to promote the welfare of the state
and secure its peace."

"You would confer on this subject with another, should I
send him to you—you would act with him if it took you not
off from your present business?" demanded the other eagerly

"More, sir; I acknowledge your right, in the state's emergency, to call upon me to risk my life should that be necessary."

"Enough—you shall have blank commissions to use at your
discretion, and I will give you--Stay! did you hear nothing,
Mr. Carter?" And as the governer put this question his finger

pointed to the inner door, leading to the stairway. **A slight**
rustling movement was evident at this moment, and· instantly
approaching it, his hand was extended to the latch, when it
partially unclosed without his aid, as if in consequence of the
sudden withdrawal of one's grasp from without. The dark
outline of a man was perceptible through the aperture.

"The outlaw himself, by heaven!" cried he, as he beheld
the indistinct outlines of the person without. "It is Foster—
it answers the description."

With these words the governor rushed to the door with the
intention of pursuing, but his purpose was defeated by a hand
from without, which, grasping the handle, drew it to, and held .
it firmly against all his efforts. Meanwhile, steps were heard
as of one descending the stairs. The moments were precious,
and with that promptness of movement which was a prime and
distinctive feature in the character of Vernon, and tallied well
with his keen intellect, no less than with his great personal
strength, he threw his weight with a bound against the obstruction, and bore it with a single effort from its hinges. The
frame-work was sustained only by the person from without
whose grasp had hitherto secured the door. In another moment
the arms of the youth were wrapped around him, and, in spite
of his exertions, he was hauled into the room to answer for his
essay at eavesdropping.

"What means this violence, gentlemen," demanded the eavesdropper, who was no other than Hawkins.

"Who are you?—what do you here, and where is the other
ruffian, your comrade, sirrah?"

"Hard words, sir, and you shall answer for them," was the
reply of the fellow. "I am here because I lodge here—that
is my chamber, and by these stairs I descend from it, and go to
it when it pleases me. Take your hand from my collar, young
one, or I will hurt you."

He accompanied these words with a threatening action, which
Vernon, to whom they were addressed, only answered by hurl-
ing him to the ground with as much ease as if he had been an
infant; setting his knee upon his bosom, and drawing thence
the bowie-knife, the possession of which he suspected, as he
saw the fellow unbuttoning his vest.

"But the greater villain must be secured. I saw his person —I have seen him before, and I am sure I can not be mistaken. It is Foster—you. heard him descending—he can not be far— let us take this fellow forward till we can deliver him to an officer, and set some in pursuit."

"You carry me not from this house," growled the fellow from beneath the knee of Vernon. "This is my house—my castle —and you shall answer for this, or there's no law for a poor man in Mississippi."

"You shall have law enough, my man," replied the governor. 'Ben Carter—since this fellow will give us the trouble to carry him—run to the sheriff, and bid him bring his posse. We shall provide him closer lodgings for a time, and he may then play eavesdropper to those who are more of his own com- plexion."

In due time Hawkins was delivered to the sheriff, and pur- suit commenced after the outlaw; but the hounds were soon at fault; the fox had baffled them, and was now out of reach— taking a zigzag course within five miles of Raymond, as coolly as if there were no sheriff within fifty. By night he was back again, and lingered long enough to hear from those who little suspected his interest in the narration, a long story of his own escape, and of Hawkins' commitment. The story went that he and the governor had grappled fairly—that the governor had got all the advantages, but that he had got—off. Which was pretty nearly the true state of the case.

CHAPTER VIII

—"I hope that I shall ride in the saddle. O, 'tis a brave thing for a man
to sit by himself! He may stretch himself in the stirrups, look about, and
see the whole compass of the hemisphere. You're now, my lord, i' the
saddle."—WEBSTER.—*The White Devil.*

THE necessary documents had come, court was over in Raymond, and on a cold, frosty morning, while yet the day only
glimmered with a faint redness through the eastern chinks,
Harry Vernon, booted and spurred, prepared to mount his good
steed, on his journey of adventure. Carter stood beside him,
having given his last instructions. He was visibly affected with
the thought of parting from one whom he regarded as warmly
as he could have done his own and only child; and this feeling
was much increased, as he beheld the unreluctant and prompt
determination of the youth to undertake and execute to the
best of his abilities, a labor which involved the prospect of so
much fatigue, and, possibly of so much peril. This last consideration, at the moment of separation, pleaded more strongly
in the old man's mind than any other.

"And yet, Harry, my son," said he, "when I hear of this
banditti, and behold the audacity with which they act, I am
afraid to let you go. God forbid that you should risk your life
that I might recover or save a few thousands, which I should
be suffered but a few years to enjoy, and which I need not now.
It is not too late—let William Maitland go, and prosper, if he
may, with his ill-gotten treasures—why should I send after
him, to possible loss, one that I value so much more? Why
should you undertake this toil, which takes you from a profes
sion which you have so honorably begun; and carries you
among the profligate and the dangerous?"

"Nay, nay, my more than father," replied the youth affectionately, "you make the risks too great, and the object less important than it is. There is but little danger, I trust, as I shall manage the pursuit; and it was only in order to avoid unnecessary encounters, that I declined accepting the governor's offers. On this point I shall be well guarded. I shall proceed slowly, moderately; neither seeking the crowd, nor yet avoiding it; and only penetrating into forbidden places, when there are probabilities of my finding William Maitland within. The loss is much greater than you think for, since, though you are liable only for the amount of your bond, yet, in a moral point of view, you are not free from responsibility for all the money over that amount, of which he has robbed the bank. Your readiness to answer for his honesty, implied in your guaranty for so much money, induced their trusts; and, though they may demand of you but thirty thousand dollars in law, in morals you owe it clearly to them to spare no exertions which shall, in addition, get them back the other sums for which they have no responsible guaranty. A moment's reflection, under your own convictions of what is right, must clearly establish to your mind this truth. As for my danger — set your heart at rest, as I shall certainly set mine. I have a cool, deliberate temper, which will not flare up at every fool's folly, and I am, I think, sufficiently under the guidance of prudent thought, to keep from the heels of any brute in his moment of anger. Give me your prayers, my dear sir, when I am gone, and I know not that I shall find or need any better protection."

"Yet it is needful, my son, that you have some of the more carnal engines. You have weapons?"

"Enough, if pistol and bowie-knife can ever be enough. I have a pair of pistols, and a small but heavy knife. I doubt if I shall need them."

"I have then only to repeat what I have said before, Harry : , have no desire to drive this man to utter destitution. He has children — the children of Ellen Taylor — and she in her grave. God forbid that I should do anything to make them destitute or wretched. Let him yield everything, and, as I have told you, I will secure to them the sum of twenty-five thousand dollars, under such restrictions as will keep it from his creditors, and from his own profligacy. I need not say to you, however, that he is one upon whom you can not rely; you must have him in your power; you must keep him in your power, and the money must be disgorged, before you sign papers. Avoid, I need scarcely tell you, all unnecessary exposure of his villany, for her sake, for the sake of her children, both of whom are females."

"You have written, sir, to Mason at Vicksburg?"

"Yes, and to Fleetwood at Benton, and Mercer at Lexington. They will provide you with funds when called upon."

"There is nothing more to be asked," said the youth, leaping to his saddle. "I will write to you at Natchez when necessary. God bless you, my dear sir, and keep you in health —farewell!"

He did not stop to hear the parting accents, tremblingly uttered, which the good man sent after him in blessings. In ten minutes the forest had shrouded him from sight, and the tearful eyes of Carter strained after him in vain.

Let us return to Saxon, otherwise Clement Foster, the outlaw of Alabama. Having satisfied himself, by personal inquiry, of the condition of Hawkins, his companion, in Raymond, he left the village at midnight, and, to verify the scripture phrase which denies all rest to the wicked, he rode nearly fifteen miles at that late hour of the night. His course lay somewhat across the country in the direction of Grand Gulf. He came at length to a little farmstead, which stood in a half-dilapidated condition at the head of a "turn-out," that was barely perceptible at any time from the road, and only obvious at night to one familiar with it. Here he routed up two men, who proved his confederates, and with whom he conferred for an hour before retiring to rest. This he did at length in a shed-room of the hovel, which, it would seem, from the tacit manner in which it was got in readiness for him, without orders, was reserved for him especially. Some portions of his conference with these men, as they may affect this narrative, should be given to the reader.

"Has Jones come up from Pontchartrain?" demanded the leader.

He was answered by one of the men in the negative.

"He will then be here to-morrow, but I shall not wait for

him. He must go on as fast as horseflesh will carry him, and meet me if he can at Brown Betsy's to-morrow night. You can counsel him to come sober, if he comes at all, for I wish him to skulk and follow, and play at point-hazard, perhaps, with as keen a lawyer as rides the Mississippi circuit. Be sure and tell him this, that he may drink his alkalis and purge himself of the whiskey-bottle. It is a day's purgation; but he must do it while he goes. He brings your share of the money from the Atchafalaya business; but, by the Lord Harry, Stanton, money seems to do you little good. You are even now in rags."

"That's because I don't get it by good means, I suppose" said the fellow spoken to, in half-sleepy, half-surly accents.

"What, do you preach too, sirrah? But—go to bed, and forget not when you waken what I tell you now. You will also remember it, Drake. The matter is of more consequence than you think for, and will swamp us all, if we keep not our eyes open and our heads clear. To sleep—to sleep."

At day-dawn, the outlaw was again in motion, visiting other haunts and dwellings of his fraternity, that lay in his way, while pursuing an upward course that carried him along the waters of the Loosa Chitto or Big Black river. It so happened that this very course was that taken by Vernon, though the latter, as his progress was straight-forward, was necessarily much in advance of the outlaw.

At the time of which we write, this region of country was very thinly settled. The traveller rode forty or fifty miles per day, very frequently without seeing sign of human habitation, and his road lay through swamps that seemed like vast rivers of mire, which his horse, with a feeling like his own, would approach with a footstep most mincing and deliberate. Travel in such a territory is travail, indeed; and to one accustomed only to the stage and steamboat facilities of the Atlantic states, it has the aspect of something even more afflicting. The swimming of creeks surcharged by freshets, and wading through the ooze of a cane-brake, each plunge into which makes the mire quiver around the very shoulders of your horse, would be something of a warning to young couples to stay at home the first month after marriage, in that neighborhood, and not go upon connubial expeditions of two or three hundred miles, just after the knot has been safely fastened. Its disruption might be no infrequent consequence of such a doubtful practice.

To one like Vernon, however, bold, and governed by a temperament that gloried in a dash of romance, the occasional perils of such a course were lost altogether in the novelty of the circumstances; and he dashed through the creek with a confident spur, without stopping like more wary adventurers to probe his footing with a pole, then drive his horse through the stream, while he " cooned a log" above it.

These little obstructions were not unfrequent in his route, but they offered no impediment to him. The duties of life and manhood, opening for the first time fairly upon his consciousness, were provocative of that stimulus only, which we are apt to see in the forward boy, to whom nothing gives so much delight as being permitted to flourish with the tools of full-grown men. He had neither father nor mother, with painful misgivings of himself, to awaken his own painful thoughts; and, unlike most young men of his age, his heart remained perfectly uncommitted to any one of the hundred damsels, who, in every civilized community, seem always to lie in waiting for fugitive hearts. In short, he had little to lose of positive possession, whether of wealth or affection; he had everything to gain in both respects. His income was yet limited, and for ties, he knew none nearer than that with the worthy Mr. Carter. His present object was calculated to serve himself no less than his patron, though the handsome reward offered by the bank for the recovery of the lost money, or the delivery of the felon, would never have moved the proud young lawyer from his chosen place at the bar, but that the interests of his friend — his preservation, in fact — absolutely required it. But this the reader already understands.

The turn of noon was at hand, and as yet our young traveller had eaten nothing. The thought of himself made him considerate of his horse, a noble animal, the gift of Carter some two years before. A pleasant rising-ground on his right, from the foot of which a little branch wandered prattling across the road, suggested all necessary conveniences for refreshment, the other appliances being forthcoming.

" We will ride, Sylvan, up this hill, which seems grassy enough to

give you a good hour's employment, and, in the meanwhile, Mrs. Horsey's biscuits and smoked beef shall answer my purposes. The good
old lady !—how she wondered to find her plate of biscuits missing,
and how she routed the cook, and Tom, the waiter, and the whole
household, except the true thief, touching their loss. I suppose,
by 'his time,· Carter has told her all about it—the why and the
wherefore. Good old man ! If I can only save him this money,
I shall feel that I have done something to deserve the favor which
he has always shown me. If mind and body can do this thing
such as I have shall be given without stint or hesitation to the task—so
Heaven prosper me in my own purposes hereafter."

This soliloquy was muttered as the youth rode his horse upon
the hill, and led him to a spot where he might graze freely without wandering. He stripped him of the saddle and valise, which he
placed beside a log, then seating himself, drew forth his little store
of provisions, the biscuits which had been appropriated by Carter
the night before, to the probable consternation of his worthy landlady. To have asked for them, would have been to declare the
purpose of travel which Vernon had in view, and this, once
known to the mother would have been soon known to the son Tom,
and through his communicative medium to every third person, at
least, in the little world of Raymond. The knife of our traveller
was already buried in the smoked beef, when his ear distinguished
a sound not unlike that of an approaching hor.eman. The ears of
his own steed pricked upward at the sound, and when it became more
distinct, the conscious animal whinnied as if with the joyful conviction that he was about to have a companion. Vernon started to
his feet as the horseman came in sight, and was absolutely dumb
with astonishment to recognize, at a single glance, the person of
our eccentric friend, Tom Horsey. His horse was well heated by
hard riding, and covered with foam ; and he himself, though chuckling mightily at having found the object of his search, alighted
from his steed with the air of one whose bones ached with his unwonted jolting.

"Ah, Harry, Harry ! What shall I say to thee, Harry ?
Shall I call thee a traitor to friendship—to heel it before day-
peep, and say no word to the fellow most after thy own heart ?

'That was the unkindest cut of all.' I did not think it of thee, Harry ! By the ghost of Garrick, I did not !"

Much annoyed at his pursuit and presence, Vernon was quite too much surprised at the event, and too curious to know the cause of the actor's pertinacity, to express himself as freely, and perhaps as harshly, as he might otherwise have done.

"Truly, Mr. Horsey, I know not what you mean, or what you have to complain of. I am surprised to see you here."

"You need be; you deserve no such love at my hands, Harry Monmouth. You should have spoken out like a man — though you said it in a whisper. Am I a man to blab? Can't I be trusted, think you? By Pluto, Harry Vernon, I can be as close as Ben Carter himself, and the dry cock should never have heard a syllable! Bah! I am monstrous tired. That rascally horse goes all one-sided — he has been ruined, by dad, and will never suit any but a lame man again. I do think he has dislocated my hip."

"Your father's horse, Mr. Horsey? How can the old man do without him? You will surely return with him immediately."

"Devil a bit, Harry, devil a bit. He deserves to lose him for not having a better in the stable, and I will trade him off the first chance, though I get one old as Methusaleh."

"But wherefore are you here, Mr. Horsey? You do not mean to travel, surely."

"Do I not? Look at the bags! Filled, sir — filled to the muzzle, with my best wardrobe. There's a Romeo and a Hamlet, two field-officers, and a Turk in that wallet, not to speak of certain inexpressibles, which will do for a dozen uncertain characters. But — this is dry work. What's in your flask?"

He did not wait to be answered, but clapped the bottle, which lay with the bread and beef at Vernon's feet, to his mouth, and long and fervent was the draught which he made therefrom.

"Good whiskey that, and whiskey's an honest beverage. And now, Harry, a bite of your biscuit. You will laugh, perhaps, but, of a truth, I look upon Falstaff's proportion of bread and sack, as decidedly the best for a traveller in winter. 'This is a nipping and an eager air,' and nothing blunts its edge so well as a good sup of Monongahela. This dough stuff makes one feel as dry and crusty as itself. But you do not eat, Vernon."

"Why, truly, sir, I am so surprised to see you here, that I had almost forgotten that I was hungry. But, perhaps, you bring me some message from Mr. Carter?"

"Carter, indeed! Oh, no! I was quite too sly for that. The moment Jim told me you were off—for it seems he saw you and Carter go to the stable by dawn, or, as he swears, be-fore it—I had just risen to take my antifogmatic; and at the word, I at once guessed what you were after!—"

"Indeed! And pray what was that?" demanded Vernon, with some curiosity, interrupting the garrulous speaker.

"Ah, ha! all in good season, my master. You thought to blink me, Harry, but you must know I had a hint of your true business two days before from some clever chaps in Raymond."

The wonder of Vernon increased, but the other suffered him as little time to indulge it as to make inquiries.

"I tipped Jim the wink—set him to saddle Gray Bowline, dad's old dot-and-go-one, and fasten him behind the stable, while I donned my first come-atables, and rammed the rest in dad's old saddle-bags, where I'll show them to you when you please. These I handed to the sooty scamp, who will do any-thing for my love—when paid in money—and he got the nag caparisoned in twenty minutes, and ready to my heel. Down stairs I went, and—plump!—met the old lady, my ever ven-erable mamma, in the passage-way. 'Tom,' says she, 'where are you going so soon?' 'Don't ask me, mother,' says I, look-ing monstrous hurried, and going fast ahead, 'don't ask me, I beg you;' and off I went. In two minutes I was on—and off. A few bounds brought me into the woods, and your track was fresh enough for the eyes of a young hunter. I heard of you once by the way, but—your nag goes monstrous fast, if he goes easy! Mine!—by the petticoats of Ophelia after her drowning—he has skinned me utterly all of one side. I have found you, however, my dear Harry, and I don't value the skinning. We shall never part again. Skin or no skin under my bends, I keep up with you though the devil's brimstone smokes under your horse's tail."

"Indeed, Mr. Horsey, but there go two words to that bar-gain," replied Vernon, with an air of resoluteness, and a face of but half-concealed chagrin.

"'Agreed' shall be one of them, Harry," replied the unembarrassed actor.

"But how, Mr. Horsey, if I tell you that our roads lie apart?"

"Impossible! they do not, Harry—by my soul they do not! I have the best information on that subject. As I said before, 'I know your secret, your whole plan of operations, and, by all the blessings of the foot-lights and a fine audience, if you do not suffer me to join with you in the business and share profits, I'll run against you. I'll take the morsel from your mouth,

> 'And pluck the golden-eyed success away
> From your young grasp.'"

"What can this witless fellow drive at?" was the unspoken soliloquy of Vernon, ere he replied to the speaker. "Can he really know anything?—it is scarcely possible. There is some mistake; and I must sound him cautiously." Aloud:—

"And what may be this goodly scheme of mine, Mr. Horsey, in which your mind is so resolutely bent to share. I am positively puzzled, and know not how it is possible that a purely private business—"

"Purely private, you call it. 'Egad, before I'm done with it, it shall be public enough. You thought yourself mighty secret in your schemings, and I confess you did blind me for awhile, and I took it for granted that you really had no other object in view than to run the dry course of a lean lawyer, and jog from court-house to court-house, circuit after circuit, picking up your pay in corn and bacon, and getting a bastard fame from speeches as full of words as Gratiano's, made in cases of trespass, pounding, black eyes, and bloody noses. I give you credit, now that I discover your purpose, for being something bolder, and for an ambition of a more enduring and ennobling sort. But I can hardly forgive you, Harry, for keeping a dumb side to me when you knew my passion. I can be trusted, as you shall see. You will find me a man after your own heart, if your heart be open; a fellow wise enough to speak only upon cues, though otherwise a born rattler; and one who, whatever his woolheaded neighbors may say, can always 'tell a hawk from a handsaw,' in whatever quarter the wind may blow."

"Puzzle on puzzle!" exclaimed Vernon, now more than ever convinced that his companion was mad. "What is it that you really mean, Mr. Horsey? speak plainly, or I shall suspect you to be a candidate for bedlam or the calaboose."

"Bedlam or the calaboose! Come! I don't like that so well, Harry Vernon. I take it as something unkind, sir, that you should speak in such fashion. But, I see how it is; I forgive you; it is natural enough that you should look on me as one likely to go between you and the public. But you shall find me generous. By the powers, Harry, I care not much where I come in, whether as one, two, or three, when a friend's fortune and desires are concerned. You shall go before, and I will follow, or we will enter side by side, on equal terms, marching to equal victory. Envious or jealous of rival merit, I never was and trust never to become, satisfied that success has twenty thousand hands, and one willing for every bold, worthy fellow that stands ready and dares to grasp it. Harry Vernon, I drink to our joint success."

The actor repeated his draught, but Vernon began to be seriously annoyed by the intrusion, and thought it high time to put an end t: it. Never dreaming of the conjecture which had taken such possession of his companion's brain, and ignorant, of course, of the stories which had been told him, he could form no positive idea of the subject of his ravings, and began seriously to consider him a fitting inmate for the calaboose or bedlam, as he had already suggested, to the other's momentary discomfiture. His first movement, therefore, was to restore his spirit-flask to the valise, then, assuming what calmness of manner he could, and taking especial care that while his words should be inoffensive, they should be to the point at least, he addressed him in a manner which was intended to bring his play at cross-purposes to a conclusion.

" You have said a great deal, Mr. Horsey, which for the life of me I can not understand. Pray tell me, without quotation or circumlocution, what it is you mean—what you intend— and above all what scheme it is, which you assume that we entertain in common. I am not peevish nor fretful in my disposition, yet I am not willing to suffer any trifling or merriment at my expense."

"Or, in more legitimate phrase, considering our purposes." repeated the actor—

"'Though I am not splenitive and rash,
    Yet have I in me something dangerous,
    Which let thy wisdom fear.'

Prithee, my good Hamlet, smooth thy looks, and dismiss that
cloud, full of lightning, that teems in threatening above thy
brows. I mean thee no harm, no hurt, no offence. I am a
fellow, as I tell thee, after thy own heart, and thou dost wrong
thyself no less than me, to be angry with me. Why wouldst
thou that I should tell thee in plain, point-blank matter, what
is thy business, and what should be mine?—as if thou wast
resolved not to know, and couldst deceive me any longer. Dost
thou not seek Tilton?"

"Tilton!" exclaimed Vernon in profound astonishment, mingled with something more of good humor than before, as it now
became obvious to him that Horsey had blundered upon the
wrong man, and knew nothing of his secret, of which he had
been in some little apprehension.

"Ay, Tilton, Tilton, the little lamplighter and candle-snuffer
and letter-carrier for so many years at Caldwell's. He, who has
now set up to be an actor, a manager, and what not; and is
going to open at Benton, where thou and I — if thy stomach be
not too proud, Harry Vernon, for such companionship, as I
greatly fear me it is — will star it together, to the confusion and
admiration of the natives. There! you have it; and might
have saved me all this trouble by owning to the truth before.
Deny me now if thou canst, my bully rook; thou art not aiming at Benton — thou dost not seek for Tilton — thou wouldst
not leave the dry bones of the law, for the wit of Mercutio and
the marrow of Falconbridge. In short, thy ambition leads
thee not to emulate the Garricks and the Keans, the Macreadys,
the Forrests, the Coopers, the —"

The unmitigated laughter of Vernon silenced the actor, whose
face of exultation it turned of a sudden into soberness.

"What do you laugh at, Mr. Vernon, I should like to know?"

"Who put this silly thought into your head, Mr. Horsey?
Who could have bedevilled you with this nonsense?"

"Bedevilled!—Silly thought! I see nothing silly about it,
Master Vernon, and wonder that you should. Do you deny it?"

"Every syllable."

" What, that you are about to appear on the stage ?"

" I do."

" You are not going to Benton to join the company ?"

" On my soul, I am not."

" Or wherever the company may act ? You go not to join Tilton ?"

" I know nothing of the man."

" It won't do—that cock won't fight, Harry Vernon," responded the other, after a pause. " I have the matter on good evidence. Deny it as you may, I believe it; begging your pardon for seeming to doubt you; but the truth is, that all the circumstances tell against you. I am sure you are going to join Tilton, and, my dear fellow, confess the truth; you will not trust me with your secret, for fear that I shall blab it to Ben Carter. But, on my honor—"

" Believe what you will, Mr. Horsey," replied the other with recovered gravity. " I have no sort of objection to any strange notion that you may take into your head; only, I pray that you may not bother me with the mare's nests that you may discover, nor challenge my admiration of the eggs."

" You're angry with me, Harry. Come, my dear boy, hand out your flask again, and we'll take a sup of reconciliation."

" No, sir; I will let you drink no more while you are with me. You have taken a mouthful too much already."

" How, sir, do you mean—"

The swagger of the worthy histrion, who was not apt to be a braggart, and was in truth a good-meaning fellow, was cut short by the sudden and angry interruption of his more solid and resolute companion :—

" Look you, Mr. Horsey, my road lies above, and yours is below, with your parents. Let us separate."

" Nay, nay, Harry Vernon; but you are quite too hard upon me. Don't be vexed with me, because I am a d—d good-natured fool, that loves good company too well to quarrel with it. I don't mean to vex you, but I am resolved, unless you put a bullet through my cranium, to keep up with you to Benton. I'd rather lose anything short of life than lose the chance of a good engagement. So, whither thou goest, thither will I go also—where thou leadest there will I follow—at least, until the manager gives out the casts, and then, Harry, as thou wilt, and the author pleases."

This resolution, though it annoyed Vernon, as it expressed a determination to keep with him whether he would or not, and might for a while operate against his objects, was yet expressed in terms and a manner so very conciliatory and the poor histrion seemed so completely to speak from his heart, that Vernon resolved to bear with him awhile, nothing doubting, that, when the other found, as he was like to do in another day, that his footsteps did not incline to the place where the actors had pitched their tents, he would be very willing to leave him without more words. He contented himself, therefore, with renewing his assertion that he had nothing to do with the players, and that Horsey deceived himself, or had been grossly misled on the subject of his inclining to the stage. But the reasseveration was of no avail. The faith was infixed too deeply, and with a chuckle, as he mounted his nag, the enthusiastic actor replied —

"Oh, what's the use, Harry, my boy, of keeping up that ball? It must come down sooner or later, and one would think you would be weary of such a sport. Let this humor cool — 'it is no good humors.' Look not coldly upon me, for, on my soul, if thou wilt have it so, thou shalt have the choice of the cast whatever it may be, and as for little Tilton, he shall learn, as a first lesson, that we shall neither of us do anything for him, unless we do it to our own liking. And now to horse — to horse —

'Wanton as youthful goats, wild as young bulls.'"

It was scarcely possible for Vernon to resist laughter; certainly, he found it impossible to keep anger with such a creature; a thing so light, so weak, so utterly wanting in all those timely calculations of propriety and good providence, as to make it seem a sort of brutality to visit upon his faults with harshness. They took horse together, and while they rode, the actor seasoned the way and dialogue with quotations,

"Thick as leaves in Valambrossa."

Vernon strove at every opportunity to disabuse his mind of the error which it had adopted in reference to himself: but his very earnestness seemed only the more to convince the other to the contrary. His answer to all such efforts consisted only of a half-laughing rebuke to his companion, who aimed at the monopoly of the best character, and was jealous of that inter-position and rivalship on his part, which he studiously assured Vernon, at the same time, should never annoy him. The latter gave up the effort which he found so perfectly unavailing, leaving it to time, the general rectifier of man's mistakes, to put a conclusion to this.

CHAPTER IX

SUPPER PROSPECTS — BROWN BESS — A COTTAGE HEROINE —
BLOOD AN' 'OUNDS.

"How indirectly all things are fallen out!
I can not choose but wonder what they were,
Rescued your rival . . . .
———— If I fit you not
With such a new and well-laid stratagem,
As never yet your ears did hear a finer,
Call me with Lilly, *Bos, Fur, Sus atque Sacerdos.*"
BEN JONSON — *Tale of a Tub.*

YOUTH is not the season for enduring enmities. That is a cold heart and a malignant spirit which preserves its bitterness and asperities through the summer, and in spite of all its sun-shine. Harry Vernon, besides being of a just and generous nature, was also of a cheerful and social one, and he soon discovered that there was no good reason for keeping up a cloudy front to the vacillating and wayward creature who rode beside him, and whom an erring judgment, and, probably, fine but misdirected endowments, were hurrying on to his own destruction. By degrees he resumed his kindly manner to the obtrusive but well-meaning actor, and as he found that he could not rid himself of his company, he resolved to make the most of it. This resolution once taken, it required but few words

on the part of Vernon to unlock all the stores of memory and
experience in Horsey's possession. The erratic creature, from
long wandering into forbidden places, had picked up a whole-
sale, if not wholesome, collection of anecdote and story. His
imitative faculties were good, and he illustrated his scenes by
taking off, with considerable humor, the various persons who
appeared in them. Shakspere, too, was at his fingers' ends,
and there was no lack of passages, to fill out his own remarks,
and enliven their deficiencies. The dog read well, too, with
the single reservation, that he had not yet learned that nice
and most necessary art of all — that art which scarcely one of
our artists possesses in a meritorious degree — of subduing his
utterance to the demands of the character, and the capacities
of his own voice. This evil results, in most cases, from the too
great size of the theatre, which, as it calls for great physical
powers of voice, must, except in the case of energies singularly
masculine, for ever defeat its nicer regulations.

Horsey had throat enough, and the very best of lungs, and
he was glad of any opportunity for using them. The woods
soon rang with his sonorous passages, and Vernon, with the
feeling of the cautious citizen, always alive to ridicule, could
not help now and then looking around him, as if apprehensive
that other ears were suffering from those clamors that seemed
almost to perforate his own anew.

These declamations, be it understood, however, were not
given with the reckless rapidity of one who has nothing beside
in store of his own; but the actor ingeniously contrived that
they should only occur in such places, in his own dissertations,
where they might enforce and illustrate what he said. This
was one of his arts additional, by which he contrived that his
masterpieces should be brought into play; and, like the fellow
who had a gun-story, and in order to introduce it fairly into
company, acquired the art of imitating the report of a pistol, so
Tom Horsey practised, when alone, those generalizing opinions
on a thousand subjects, under some one of which he could always
classify the fine things of Brutus and Cassius, Hamlet, Hotspur,
and Macbeth. When, with a generous consideration of his
companion, and a moderation which few great talkers are prone
to practise, he had tired himself fairly down, he came to a halt,

and declared aloud his resolution to pause in time, for fear he should also tire down his hearer.

" But, could you hear me, Harry, when the scene is filling, when the characters are by, the audience silent and watchful, and the curtain drawn—it would be something. You would say it were something, and that I were no insane fool, as some of dad's friends will have it, and Ben Carter among them. I feel that I have it in me, Harry Vernon, and, by the Lord Harry, but it shall come out. I have never had a fair chance yet, but the time must come. Hitherto, they have taken advantage of my necessity, and I have been compelled to walk through wooden parts, which I scorned to move in with any wasteful animation of my own. Nothing but the delight of being upon the boards, amid the blessed blaze of lights which are nowhere so lovely to my eyes as in a playhouse, could have made me endure the damnable persecution and miserable jealousies of those poor, incapable creatures, that were able to do nothing themselves, and hated the very sight of others who had it in them to do everything. I could tell you stories of the drudgery of the stage, of the malice and the meanness of the actors, of the mercenary baseness of managers, their impracticability and insolence when successful, and their d—d dishonesty when otherwise, which would shock you to hear, and which you could scarcely ever believe. But you will learn for yourself. One week with the little lamplighter—unless you make a hit—and then you can snap your fingers in his face, and kick him with your worst boots, and still have his thanks —one week with him, however, as a stock-player, and you will curse your stars that endowed you with faculties, yet left them at the mercy of such eternal skunks as your generality of managers are sure to be. But let us bully little Tilton, and play our own characters, work our way up the Mississippi, break out like little comets with a double length of tail in Louisville and Cincinnati, and, by-and-by touch the Park boards—the zenith of theatrical eminence in America, where Mr. Kean told us, with an equivocal sort of compliment, that the taste for the drama was periodical—and then, the devil take the hindmost —hey, for the crown and the triumph, the chariots and the horseman—

"'A kingdom for a stage — princes to act,
And monarchs to behold the swelling scene.'"

"Supper first," said Vernon, "or I shall never sufficiently ascend that highest heaven of invention, to behold with you so respectable an audience, or to regard it with any sort of satisfaction when I do so. Look ahead — see you nothing of a log house? There should be one on the left, a little in the woods. That must be our baiting-place to-night; and, if you will prick up your beast, Mr. Horsey, which, in your own industry, you have been indulging long enough, we shall probably avoid the prospect, of which there is some present danger, of being compelled to sleep in Big Black swamp to-night, with nothing but Shakspere to keep us warm or satisfy our hunger."

"And enough, too. He has kept me warm and been my only supper many a night. But, I do see something of an opening, and it is to the left. By the ghost of David, Harry Vernon, an' if it shall be a large one, we'll have a few passages — we'll make a rouse. 'Because thou art virtuous shall there be no more cakes and ale!' — it is a house — 'ay, and ginger shall be hot i' the mouth too.'"

"Hush!" said Vernon, with singular gravity. "Be still, if you do not want to lose every chance of supper. Chickens in these parts take to the woods whenever they hear or see a stranger — they know, poor devils, by a sort of instinct, the fate that awaits them."

"'Gad, if that be true, it is a very singular fact. Are you serious, Master Vernon?"

"Serious! Do you think I could jest about such a matter? But, see — there's the woman of the house. She must have heard you the last three miles. If not utterly out of voice from your late exertions, you will perhaps be the best spokesman here. See if we can get beds and bacon — the chickens, I suppose, unless she has them in coop already, can not be thought of."

"A very singular fact!" muttered Horsey, as giving spur to his steed, he led the way to the wigwam, leaving Vernon to follow at his leisure.

"Accommodations!" said the woman, who was a somewhat ill-favored person, probably forty years of age, having a face sober and grave even to sternness, and speaking in accents slow, harsh, and indifferent — have I accommodations for two for the night? Yes, sir, I have; but they are none of the best, and neither of you gentlemen would be much the better of them. Perhaps, you'd better ride farther, and you'll be suited better. The night's clear enough, though it be cool, and, if you're going to strike for the lower ferry, you'll get a place to lie at, ten miles ahead. The upper ferry-house is farther on, but not much, and the road's pretty clear in a starlight. You'd better ride on, I'm thinking."

"Nay, my good madam, that will hardly suit us," replied Vernon, riding up — " we have already ridden near forty miles to-day, having come from Raymond, and I am resolved, unless you positively deny us shelter, to go no farther to-night."

" I'm sure I don't deny you, sir; I only tell you how little we can do here to make you comfortable. We're mighty poor people in these parts, and have little to give strangers to make .hem satisfied. Now, ten miles beyond —"

"No more, my good madam," said Vernon, alighting from his horse; "we stop with you to-night; and the sooner you give us supper the better. In the meantime, you can tell my friend here what I have already told him, that your chickens have already taken to the woods."

" Chickens —"

The speech of the woman was cut short by Horsey, who had been steadily watching her features with an air of interest, and who now advanced, laid his hand on her shoulder, with a degree of familiarity that made her start and look disquieted, if not angry, as she strove to withdraw herself from so great a freedom. This, however, he would not suffer.

" By the cut of your teeth, as the cheese said to the mouse, 1 know you, my worthy professor of sassafras and gunja. Brown Bessy Clayton, as I live !"

" And who are you, young mister, that's so free with my name--my name that was, I mean — for though I'm Brown Bess, I'm no Clayton now? What's your name?"

" Why, Bess, you're getting old, my girl — your memory's failing you. Don't you remember me — don't you remember little Tom Horsey, that was your best customer when you sold

cakes and beer at Hogler's mill—that burst your bottles by
shaking, and punched your cakes out of the tray by a long pole
sharpened at the end?"

"Yes, and got punched for it himself," responded the woman,
as these reminiscences of Horsey awakened her own   "And is
it you, Tom—little Tom, indeed? Why, you ca., eat your
cakes now off my shoulder."

"Ay, Bess, and a bit of the shoulder with it when I happen
to be so hungry as I am just now. And so you're married—
and who did you marry, Bess?—I hav'n't heard of you for
these ten long years."

"But I've heard tell of you, Tom Horsey. They said you'd
gone crazy; and that didn't seem strange, for you always had
a little twist in your understanding, and couldn't do things jist
like other people."

"Did you ever hear such a defamation of genius?" exclaimed
Horsey to Vernon in a manner of affected misery. "But go on,
Bess. What did you hear?"

"Why, they said as how you had turned fair fool, and how
they'd got you down among the player people at Orleans, and
how they dressed you up in a jacket and breeches, full of colors
and spangles—"

"My Romeo, by the shade of Juliet!"

"And how," continued the woman, "they brought you out
before the company, and worried you, jist like so many curs
worrying a pig that had got into the 'tater patch—"

"Exquisite comparison, by my soul!"

"And how they all stuck at you with their swords, and how
you fell down and pretended to be dead, and then how they
dragged you out by the heels; while everybody, men and
women, little and big, laughed as if they would split. After
that I heard no more of you, and concluded you were dead for
good."

"For good, say you?" exclaimed the actor, as the woman
concluded. "Well, Vernon, only think now that this is the
representation of one of my best performances -- my debut in
Macbeth, for my benefit—when it so happened that a cargo of
Ishmaelites from Pearl river, that had crossed Ponchartrain
that day, came to the 'American,' with 'every particular hair

on end,' to see their 'old schoolfellow, Tom Horsey, son of
John Horsey, the lame man that kept tavern on the river-road :'
and this is the d—nable report which they carried back to the
country in their ignorance and envy. Is it not a most abominable trait in man, that he hates to see his neighbor's successes ?
Every whipster with whom he ever hunted 'possum in a dark
night, or shelled corn in husking-time, is ready to disparage
those talents which he can not rival, and to pull down that
merit in a companion which he thinks—and it is—a sarcasm
upon his own deficiencies. By Pompey's ghost, it is my own
people that have ever been the first to decry my performances,
and to wrest from me the just rewards of my labors."

"Well, don't you be running down the Pearl river people,
Tom Horsey; they're a mighty good sort of people, Tom, and
I only wish I was back ag'in among 'em," said the woman.

"Selling cakes and beer?" said Tom.

"Why, yes, sellin' cakes and beer; it's a mighty good business for the time it lasts."

"Five months at least, Bess—I remember all about it—from
May to September, and, if the season was very warm, a month
longer. 'Gad! my picayunes melted as rapidly in those months,
when I was a boy, as my Mexicans have continued to melt ever
since I was a man."

"There was another thing, Tom, that they told about you,"
said the woman.

"What was that?" quickly demanded the actor.

"Why, that you spent your father's money a deuced sight
faster than he could make it, and that you are a mighty great—"

"Say no more, Brown Bess; leave it where it is, at the
'mighty great.'"

"Riprobate, I was going to say," continued the matter-of-fact
woman; "and I reckon, Tom, it is not far from the right word"

"Perhaps not, Bess; but no more of that an' thou lovest me:
I am reformed now—grown quite sober—never drink unless
when the spirit moves, and I expect soon to confess a working
of mind as active as ever was your beer, whenever I can meet
with old brother Abrams—"

"Why he's dead!—dead five years ago!" exclaimed the
woman.

"Dead, you say! Who could have thought it. Why he was the last regular preacher that I ever heard. It makes me melancholy to think of it; so let's in to supper, Vernon, with what appetite we may. You're married, Bess? Where's your husband, and what is he—what's his name?"

A dark cloud rose and rested on the woman's brow as she heard this question, which she answered slowly and briefly.

"His name's Yarbers—he's a middle aged man, that'll be in, 1 reckon, directly. But I'm truly thinking, Tom, that you and the other gentleman had much better ride on to the other house It's a short ten miles, and an easy road."

"Can't think of it, Bess; by the soul and substance of the fat knight, I can not. We must partake of your hog and hominy to-night; and I'm surprised, Bess, that you seek to send us forward without supper. You were not wont to be so inhospitable. Marriage has changed you, Bess."

"I reckon it has, Tom," said the woman, "but I'm not wanting you to go without supper. I could get it ready for you in a short five minutes, and you might easily ride then."

"By the Lord Harry, Bess, but this is altogether too bad! What! pack us off the moment we've swallowed our coffee, on a long road in a dark night. I tell you, Bess, it won't do. We sleep in your house to-night by the peepers of that blessed saint Monajahadjee, of the Chickasaws, that slept every day in the week but the eighth, and never opened one eye, unless it was to see if the other was shut."

"Well, just as you will, Tom, but, perhaps, the other gentleman here?—"

"The other gentleman here is my Castor; we are Castor and Pollux, the inseparables. He never goes without me, and I never go without him, and so, strange as it may seem to you, we never go without one another. If we never go without one another, we also never stay without one another, and, Bess, 1 have drawn this proposition almost syllogistically to you, in order that you should understand that we shall sleep together in the same bed, provided you can not spare us one apiece."

"Ah, Tom, you're the same rattlepate that you ever was, and the older you grow, the wiser you don't grow. I can't understand the half you say."

"Not understand! Did ever one hear the like, when I stated the case with singular simplicity in order that you should understand."

'Well, well," responded the woman, "but let Mr. Castor speak for himself. He don't say much, and I reckon it'll be the easier for me to understand him. I was saying, sir," here she addressed herself to Vernon, "I was saying, Mr. Castor—'

"Ha! ha! ha!" was the ecstatic roar of Horsey, who made no attempt to correct the error.

"Vernon is my name," said his companion gravely. The old woman gave Horsey a single look of reproof, then turning to Vernon, proceeded to repeat what she had already said touch ing the propriety of his riding to the next tavern, which was at the lower ferry, and only ten miles off, for his night's lodging. Her reason for so singular a suggestion arose from the alleged poverty of her accommodations.

"There is something strange in all this; there is something secret here," was the unexpressed thought of Vernon, and he drew his conclusion as much from the earnest yet bewildered countenance of the woman, as from her words. His self-communion went farther : "I am on the borders of the Chittaloosa, and my labors should now properly begin. Every mystery may have mine in its keeping, and I must search it if I can. This woman, it is evident, would send me off rather than Horsey. I will stay."

He spoke this determination aloud.

"Mr. Horsey has spoken for both of us, Mrs. Yarbers, and we must stay with you to-night. Forty miles is rather more of a journey than a horse should be made to bear who is going to a swamp country, and I am almost as anxious for sleep as supper."

"Well, if you will," said the old woman ungraciously, as she ushered them into the hall, and summoned a negro-girl to take the horses to the stable. The saddle-bags, valise, and saddles, were carried into the house. The travellers drew chairs, rough, country-made, high-backed, and seated with untanned deer-skins stretched across and tacked beneath ; while the old lady, opening a wooden cupboard of plain pine that was fastened by pegs to the rear wall, drew forth a couple of common junk bottles.

one of which, as she said, contained Monongahela, and the other
honey, as a sweetener.

"A dram will comfort you after your ride, Tom, though if
you drink whiskey as freely as you used to drink the sassafras,
you'll have an enemy in your head that'll be sure soon to trip
your heels."

"I am commanded to love mine enemies, Bess, but I try to
weaken them a little, so that our wrestle shall be even; there's
no water here?"

"Mary's gone for some to the spring, Tom; my darter Mary,
she'll be here in a shake."

"You've a daughter, too, eh? What sort of a girl is she,
Bess? A good, smart, active, little creature, I suppose, a —"

The door opened, and the sudden appearance of the daughter in question, silenced the speech, and utterly confounded the
speaker for an instant, as he found himself confronted by as tall
and pretty an adversary in the shape of a damsel, as ever met
the eyes yet of an enthusiastic and self-assured young man.
He started to his feet, caught the vessel, which she bore, from
..er hands, a little clean white piggin with a gourd hanging
upon the handle, and setting it down upon the shelf which was
placed for it, exclaimed, all in a breath —

"This your daughter, Bess?—this your Mary?—by the
Capulets, but she is the very Juliet of the host. I must have
a kiss, Mrs. Yarbers—for auld lang syne, Bess—by all the
damask roses that ever tried to look like those cheeks, and
faded out of envy. I must, Mary—why, Mary, I am your
mother's old friend—I'm your great uncle, Mary, an innocent
old man—you need not fear me, I must—there's no use—I
must."

The girl, who was probably not more than sixteen, perhaps
not that, retreated with no less dignity than modesty, while,
between jest and earnest, her mother expostulated with the
bashaw; but it is probable that neither the reluctance and possible flight of the damsel, nor the expostulati·ns of the mother,
would have availed to protect her from the parental tenderness
of the venerable man, but for the sudden interposition of another
party, whose mode of proceeding was of a more summary and
imposing character. The door opened while the strife was at

the warmest, and the husband of the dame entered, followed by a sturdy youth of about twenty years of age. Horsey was too much interested by the game in hand to look behind him, and it was only when the youth, without a word, passed in front, and placed himself between him and the maiden, that he became conscious of the unexpected interruption of his desires. The intruder's presence seemed almost as much annoying to Mary as to the enamored actor. She shrunk back with quite as much promptness from her champion as from her assailant, and this movement probably encouraged Horsey with the idea that his chances were even better now than before.

"My worthy rustic," said he, "give me but a moment; another time I will acknowledge your presence, but just at this time—nay, stand aside, I pray you, that I may do grace to the lips of that little Juliet there—a moment—but a moment."

Suiting the action to the word, Horsey put forth his hand, intending, with the utmost gentleness, to put him aside from his path; but his hand had scarcely touched the shoulder of the other, when, putting forth all his strength, he planted a blow between the eyes of the actor, that gave him a very comical vision of two crossed rainbows, the ends of which were most singularly tied together. Down he fell like a bullock in the same instant, and his prompt enemy jumped upon him, and twining his little finger in the locks of the fallen man, prepared to thrust his thumb into his eyes.

"Touch my eyes, man, and I put you to death as sure as a catastrophe," exclaimed Horsey, characteristically, as the effort of the other had brought him to all his consciousness. The fellow would scarce have heeded his threats, but by this time the vigorous arm of Vernon had grasped him about the middle, and flung him to the other end of the room. We have omitted the screams of the women, which were as loud as usual, and as rightly timed. Nor have we deemed it necessary to say that old Yarbers—a fellow almost overcome with fat—offered sundry expostulations to the course of his companion, which, however, as he never hurried to enforce them, were as little heeded by the fierce young rustic as were the screams aforesaid.

The effect of Vernon's movement was more obvious. The youth glared now upon him and now upon Horsey, who had

taken advantage of the interval to recover his feet, as if doubtful which to attack. His hesitation resulted from no want of
hostile feeling, but simply from the consciousness that there
were two to contend with now; and one of them, however easy
he found it to trip the heels of the other, had convinced him that
the play in his case could never be all of one side. While he
stood glowering and glaring, Vernon, like a man satisfied that
he had done all that was required, resumed his seat, and with
the assistance of the woman of the house, made such an acquaintance with its master, as suited the relation of guest and
landlord. The good humor of Horsey did something to restore
the quiet of the rest.

"Young 'un," said he, "you've bloodied my nose, and done
it tolerably well, with some skill, but scarcely with sufficient
firmness. That up and down blow, though it would fell an ox
if hit squarely between the eyes, is a monstrous dangerous one
if the enemy is watchful. It leaves your whole side exposed,
all your ribs, not to speak of your diaphragm, a blow in
which would make a fat man uncomfortable for life. You,
sir," turning to Yarbers, "you would find a blow in your diaphragm a singular inconvenience."

"Ay, sir, or anywhere else," said the person addressed, with
a good-humored laugh, and scarcely knowing how to understand
the strange creature who confronted him.

"And now, Mary," continued the actor, stopping the blood
with his handkerchief, as it still continued to issue from his
nose, "you were the cause, though the innocent cause, of this
young rustic's incivility. You must help me to some water,
that I may remove 'this filthy witness from my hands'—and
nose. 'This is a sorry sight,' Harry. By the way,.I must not
forget to thank you, Harry, for taking that fellow's fingers from
my eyes."

"If you don't mind how you talk, stranger, I'll put 'em there
again," said the other, his wrath duly increasing with the seeming composure and good humor of Horsey.

"I hope not," replied the latter, "as well for your sake as
mine. Had you succeeded, my good fellow, in your first attempt, you'd have been, by this time, on the longest journey
that you have ever taken in your life. and doubtful whether

you'd have found easy ferriage across the river, unless your pocket is lined with more picayunes than I think it holds at present. What, my lovely Juliet, you have the water, have you?"

"There's the piggin, Mr. Horsey, and here's the towel, sir," said the damsel, whose sympathies for the hurts which he bore so good-humoredly, seemed to have made her less shy of him than she had shown herself at first.

"So you know my name already, Chuck—a good name, Juliet—and your mother knew it many days before you, though I must have known you once. There—there's a spot still, my Juliet!" he exclaimed, as, having wiped his face, he placed the towel upon her hand, and before she could be conscious of his design, threw his arm about her waist and inflicted upon her cheek as unequivocal a smack as ever came from the hasty application of lip to lip. The young gallant was again in arms, but Horsey was ready for him; and the father, probably dreading that the latter would use some weapon in the strife, as he had already intimated, interposed his authority with sufficient promptitude to prevent the encounter.

"If *we* don't get angry, Mr. Mabry, I wonder why should you? Besides, this gentleman's an old friend of Bess, and Mary's but a child to him."

"Not so fast—not so fast, old gentleman!" cried Horsey, who was considerably nettled at this imperfect sort of chronicling; "a child, indeed—a woman, a fine, lovely, ripe, bewitching damsel, this same Mary of yours. She's no more a child than I'm a grandfather. Now I come to think of it, there can't be much difference between us in age—not so much as to make a difference in any material respect. Let me see, she's about sixteen, and—egad, Mrs. Yarbers, it can't be more than fifteen years since I bought cakes from you at Hogler's, and I going to Hugh Peters's school. I was only ten then—sixteen and ten—why do you talk of her being but a child to me? Count for yourself—sixteen and ten are twenty-six all the world over, except Connecticut, where, they say, it counts more—and I'll take Bible oath I'm not a syllable older. What say you to that, sir? There's no young woman of sixteen in Mississippi, who, if she has any sense, will find fault with a man of twenty-six."

Vernon was amused at the pains which the actor took to
vindicate his youth; and the result of his calculations seemed
still farther to increase the annoyance of his rustic rival, who,
after a little while spent in a condition of fever-heat, got up and
left the room. He was followed out by old Yarbers. Meanwhile, Horsey continued a playful chat with the mother and
daughter—his philosophy under his bruises seeming to commend him to additional favor, and both listening to him with
pleased attention. But, catching the eye of Vernon, in the
midst of one his random speeches, he made him a sign, then
rising. declared his intention to see what sort of night it was,
and left the house. Vernon soon followed.

CHAPTER X.

CLOSING UP PEEPERS ACCORDING TO "THE SCIENCE"—HOW TO SQUARE OFF WITH A BULLY BOY.

Lycus. That spark jealousy falling into his dry melancholy brain, has
well near set the whole house on fire.

Tharsalio. No matter, let it work; I did but pay him in's own coin.-
GEO. CHAPMAN.

"I AM decidedly one of the best-natured mortals in existence," said Horsey, when Vernon joined him in the little area
in front of the cottage, "but there is something, Harry, in being knocked over, that would turn the sweet milk sour in the
best of bosoms. I bore with this thing as patiently as possible
while in the presence of the women folk, but my gall has been
rising for the last half hour, and I can stomach it no longer. It
must out, and nothing will help me, Harry, but a clip or two at
the muzzle of this same Master Mabry. You must stand by
and see fair play while I give him quits. Doubt not that I can
do it, Harry. 'I have the back trick simply as strong as any
man in Illyria.'"

"It will make matters worse, Horsey. You were wrong in

pressing upon the girl at first. She is something more than a child, and the customs of our country—"

"I know all that, Harry, and had I not been a sort of chicken under the wings, at one time, of the good old clucking hen, her mother, I had, perhaps, never thought of kissing the girl; though, by the divinity of Rosalind, there's justification enough in the lips themselves for the rashness of my pursuit. The guilt is equal between the tempter and the tempted. She who pouts a pretty mouth under one's nose can no more blame a body for snatching a civil kiss from the offender, than you can blame a hawk for stooping down upon a plump partridge that runs too freely from under the briers, and tempts the appetite it is yet unwilling to satisfy."

"You are supported. in this notion," said Vernon, with a smile, "by an authority no less moral than that of Dr. Johnson, who says that if you tempt a man you do him an injury, and if you overcome him you share his guilt. His view is also sustained by the decision of an English justice, who once committed the master to prison for laying money in the servant's way, and at the same time discharged the servant who stole it."

"'Gad, Harry, those were wise fellows. If I had known so much could be said in my favor, I had not stopped short at a single kiss. That man, Johnson, didn't he once write a play?"

"Yes—a tragedy—"

"I'll read it—a devilish clever sort of fellow. A fellow that knows so well how to justify a kiss, must have made a very amorous piece of business of it. Wasn't it so, Harry?"

"Nay—quite the contrary, I believe. The play was rather a cold performance—the author was a phlegmatic. It does not follow, you know, that a good judge is a good performer; and to kiss a pretty woman is a movement of one's blood rather than his thought—an instinct, not a reflection. But—to return to our subject. You can gain but a paltry satisfaction, Mr. Horsey, by punishing this young man; and I should say, judging from mere appearances, that he is too stout for you. He has more brawn and muscle, and though not so tall is a much heavier man."

"You shall see, Harry. I have what he has not. I have the trick of fence, and I have played long enough with muffles to venture a little upon the bare mutton. The stage is no bad school for acquiring agility of motion in foot and fist—a keen eye and sudden thrust makes me more than a match for this pudding-headed fellow, as I shall convince him no less than yourself, when I have laid eyes on him for awhile. Here is the path which I suppose will lead us on their route, part of which I saw through the window. They made for yonder thicket, where, I reckon, we shall find them."

"I will stand by you," said Vernon, with recovered gravity, "and see you through with this business, but while we keep together, Mr. Horsey, I trust, for my sake, you will provoke no more difficulties. I have some right to expostulate with you, I think, as you have constituted yourself my companion, not merely without my desire, but against my wish. My objects in this country are such as might suffer material detriment from any collision with the people."

"Pshaw, Harry, my dear boy, 'still harping on my daughter,' still at thy old 'humors;'" replied the unthinking fellow "It won't do, I tell you. Our objects are the same, though the range of character may be somewhat different; as I confess myself to be somewhat erratic, and a jump from Romeo to Dogberry has been a folly of mine more than once already. When you see me resolved, head and heels, to go on with you 'to the last gasp with truth and loyalty,' why, what the devil's the use of shamming any longer? You can't get rid of me, do what you will, unless, as I told you before, you put a bullet through my brains, and that were only to scatter them worse than ever, without doing me or yourself any great service. Be generous, man—do as I have done, make a clean bosom of it, confess—and we will down upon little Tilton with a concerted plan of operations which shall make the rascal stare. We can do as we please then with all the arrangements—get our own terms, declare our own casts, and—

    —— "'All furnish'd, all in arms,
    All plumed like estridges, that with the wind
    Bated like eagles having lately bathed:
    Glittering in golden coats——'"

By the way, Harry, you have not seen my dress in Hal. You shall see it to-morrow—you shall see me in it 'rise from the ground like feathered Mercury'—made a d—d ugly hole in dad's crop to pay for that dress, I tell you. What would the old fellow say, were I to count up to him the cost of stars and spangles, beaver, crosses, images and plumes, in cotton bags. Ha! ha! I think I see him now, his game leg in air, his sound one thundering on the floor, his eyes shooting out from their spheres, red and fiery, and his voice hoarse and choking, still resolute to roar the anathema, which sticks in his throat, at last, more rigidly than a better sentiment in that of Macbeth. Oh, Harry, what a scene!—But hold!—Here's our enemy."

A bright moon helped the progress of the several parties. Yarbers and young Mabry stood in a small open space among a clump of pines apparently in earnest conversation, as the two approached them. Mabry held his horse by the bridle, one foot already in the stirrup, as if—the important matters of which they spoke being fairly discussed—he lingered only for a parting word. That they were seriously engaged was likely enough, since they neither saw nor heard the approach of the two strangers, till they had already passed into the same open-ing with themselves. It was then that Mabry, as if apprehend-ing the object of his enemy, or, as was more probable, desiring an opportunity to renew a conflict in which his success had been so unequivocal already, withdrew his foot from the stirrup, and once more threw the bridle from his steed's neck over the stunted sapling which had before confined him. This done, he kept his place where the eyes of the two had first encountered him, while Yarbers, with some agitation of manner, advanced and addressed them

"A fine evening, gentlemen—fine for a walk, and—"

"Ay, or for any other purpose which needs a cool tempera-ture and a clear sky," was the ready answer of Horsey, who, at the same time passing by Yarbers, continued his speech to his companion—"I am glad this clear moon has helped me to find you, young un, since I should not have slept so comfortably with the thought of being your involuntary debtor. I bear, sir, some tokens of your favor on my cheek. I am not willing that you should go unrequited. Do you understand me, sir?"

This apostrophe did not seem at all ungrateful to the rustic, who had rather wished than expected so early an opportunity

to renew his punishment of an offence which he had shown
himself so unwilling to tolerate, and which had been repeated
so audaciously before his eyes. That he could punish the
impudent stranger, he had no sort of doubt. His own physical
prowess had been generally acknowledged among the young
Spartans of the neighborhood, and the sudden and easy over-
throw of Horsey by his single blow, but a little while before,
and the good-natured forbearance of the latter immediately
after, had given him but a mean idea as well of the courage as
of the strength of his opponent. That Horsey should, with
open eyes and cool deliberation, come once more within his
clutches, was no less satisfactory than surprising; and boldly
confronting him, he answered his salutation in language that
left little possibility of a reconciliation being effected by either
of the bystanders, both of whom attempted a consummation
which was so proper and desirable. Yarbers strove with
Mabry, and Vernon, though to a far more moderate extent,
with Horsey. He knew that the popular sentiment made the
course of Horsey one of retributive justice only, and his first
overtures being unsuccessful, he forebore renewing them, and
patiently waited in silence the progress of events. Yarbers,
also, after a while, gave up, as useless, the effort to mollify the
champion on his side of the hill, and the parties at length stood
fitted, both ready and anxious, to "feed fat the ancient grudge."
    Nothing surely could have been more curious than the dif-
ference of mood which the two exhibited while in this position.
Mabry, at first, like a young bull simply bent on mischief, approached his enemy with slow steps, his rising temper indicated
only by occasional sudden jerks of the head, and a slight fitful
stamping of the feet. A muttered growl escaped his lips at
intervals, and his fists were clenched and opened alternately —
his long fingers, the nails of which were quite as threatening as
any other premonitory symptom of danger, being sometimes
thrust upward, as if, of themselves, anxious to rend from their
sockets the eyes of all who beheld them with hostility.
    Vernon regarded this threat as so unequivocal that he inter-
posed, and insisted upon " an up-and-down, straight fight, fist,
head, and feet, but no gouging — no rough-and-tumble ;" but this
was to deprive the enemy of one of his most favorite weapons.

and that which he meditated to use with more malignant efficiency in this strife than any other.

"I fight as I please—according to my own fashion—and let him do the same," replied Mabry. "If he's afraid of my fingers let him say so, and I'll let him off."

"Afraid of your fingers, you catamount!" exclaimed the actor with contemptuous scorn, and a coolness that was really edifying; "use tooth and nail, my good fellow, if you please, or if you can. Don't trouble yourself, Harry, about me—'egad I'll swallow him, claws and all, though his scales were as rough and large as those of the biggest alligator that ever picked his teeth with a cypress on the banks of Pontchartrain."

"You will, will you?" cried the other, the foam gathering about his mouth, his teeth gnashing with rage, and his whole body in motion, like that of the bull, whose gradually accumulating fury, moves it from petty mischief to a destroying madness. He bounded from the earth, ran round his enemy, slapping his thighs with his hands the while, in the most savage fashion, and at length, with a whooping shriek, imitated from that of some wild beast of the forest, he threw a summerset. his feet aiming to strike the breast of the actor, who followed all his movements with eyes and hands in constant readiness.

The preliminaries of Mabry had warned Horsey of the mode in which his attack was likely to begin, and for which he prepared himself. It must not be forgotten that Horsey was Yorkshire too—that is to say, he was quite as well accomplished in the arts of the forest-fighter as was his opponent—with the additional advantage of knowing other arts which were even of more avail in such warfare as the present. The heels of Mabray were no sooner in the air, than the actor. sinking on his knees, removed the mark which they were meant to strike; but, rising the moment after, he sprang to the spot where the other had alighted, and dealt him a blow between the eyes which gave him an apparition of the four moons of Jupiter, with a very fine display of cross-fires playing in the centre, such as never yet blessed the vision of Herschel or Dick. This tumbled him over for an instant; but, nothing daunted, though confounded, he renewed his attack in a different form, and with a caution which had been more advantageously exercised in the first instance. The actor, no ways elated, but seeming to regard the proceeding, so far, as one which had been the result of the plainest calculation, calmly approached his enemy, speaking as he did so, apologetically, as it were, to the two spectators for continuing the fight.

"Blow for blow is quite enough in all ordinary cases; but this fellow tumbled me unawares, and in the presence of the women, and, by the valor of Orlando, he shall have another fall, ere our accounts balance. This I have sworn to, Harry— as firm an oath as if I had pressed my lips on the pocket Shakspere. I will give the lad a lesson which he will remember whenever he has occasion to take his measure by that of mother earth. Are you ready, young un?"

Once more they stood before each other—the language of superiority which Horsey employed, goading his rustic opponent to a degree of ferocity which made him forget his hurts; and conscious of his superior strength, he rushed in upon the actor, employing no art, and only seeking to come to the close hug—the grapple of sinews—in which lay his chief and only hope. But Horsey had no disposition to gratify him in this desire. He well knew the danger to him of such an issue. Once closed in with, his "cunning of fence" would avail him nothing; and once down, his eyes had no farther security against the long claws which had already been stretched out to pluck them forth.

It was fortunate, perhaps, that the rage of his enemy deprived him of his deliberation. His blind attack was not dangerous. His approach was met with cool, keen-eyed determination—a characteristic in which Vernon never could have conceived his companion to have been so strong. Talking all the while, and quoting as much Shakspere as ever, he parried the blows of the rustic, for a while utterly forbearing to put in any of his own. At length, as if he had yielded a sufficiently fair time to his opponent's play, he exclaimed—

"Now, sir, is my turn. I will close up your eyes, without putting you to sleep; though, let me tell you, it would be very easy for me to do that too."

"I don't fear you, d—n you—I'll down you yet!" roared the other in a rage of fury that increased with every failure of his own efforts.

"Your right eye first!" said the actor, answering this ebullition at the same moment with word and blow; "and now your left!"

Both blows took effect, in spite of the desperate efforts of the victim to defend himself, and he lay at the feet of his foe almost without motion. Yarbers assisted him to rise, but he was in no condition for farther conflict. Blinded and staggering he stood, and still his lips breathed nothing but defiance.

"The fellow's game," said Horsey. The voice, the words, roused the instinct of hate anew in the vanquished man, and he struggled in the arms of Yarbers to rush once more upon his foe. Restrained in this, his hand suddenly plucked a spring-knife from his bosom, the blade of which was instantly shot out, and, but for the timely grasp of Vernon, he had sheathed it in the body of the man who held him. The weapon, spite of his struggles, was taken from him, and a stupor which followed, seemed to possess his mind and body with equal apathy. He murmured incoherently while it lasted, his words consisting mostly of bitter denunciation, which, to the surprise of the two travellers, seemed chiefly to fall upon Yarbers.

"You're a villain, John Yarbers—you would shut my mouth up—wouldn't have me tell what I know—and have made your villains do this. But I will speak—I'll write it down—I'll declare your roguery to all Madison. They shall know who—"

"He raves!" exclaimed Yarbers in no little agitation; "you've beat all the sense out of him, Mr. Horsey, and he don't know what he says. But don't you mind him. Go home at once. Boss is waiting supper for you by this time, and there's no need that you should wait. I'll tend to him, and see him carried home."

"I'm truly sorry I had to thump him so hard, Harry," said Horsey apologetically to his companion, as they took their way back to the cottage, "but I had sworn it, you know, and couldn't so well get off. Besides, it's absolutely necessary now and then to make an example of these fellows. They rely on superior strength to be insolent, and nothing would have pleased this chap so much as carrying home my eyes as a trophy. Year hence he would have a history for Dick Jenkins, and Jim Dobbins and Peter Pinchback and a dozen others, of the danger

frɔm below that he met at Yarbers' house, and ' how he cotch'd '"
imitating the patois of the country, "' how he cotch'd the chap
mighty soptious with the gal, and how he gin him the cross-
buttock, and, before he could say Jack Robinson, had a finger
in his shock and a thumb in his eye, and sent him off with the
blind-staggers and two holes in his forehead that could make
no use of specks, though he was mighty glad to wear them ;'
and then, to prove the truth of what he said, he would bring
forth a bottle of eyes preserved in whiskey—my eyes with
fifty others, the Tom's, Dick's, and Harry's, the Ned's, Ben's,
and Peter's, the Billy's and Timothy's, that have been the
heroes of the barbecue and gin-shop from time immemorial—all
in attestation of the superior excellence of the claws that plucked
them out. The eyes of Tom Horsey preserved in whiskey !
Whew ! The thought makes me shudder again. Eyes, Harry
Vernon, are absolutely necessary to an actor."

"Keep yours about you as a traveller. You have made
an enemy of this youth, who will not forget you. We travel
in a wild region, and the securities are few for life and limb.
A man may be tumbled in these swamps, by the shot of the unseen assassin, and the wildcat alone will find out his hiding-
place. You, who have no sort of reason to be in this neighborhood, can not too soon take yourself out of it."

"To-morrow, Harry—you would not have me set off to-
night ?"

"No—to-morrow will be time enough. Return to Raymond,
set yourself in safety and your father's mind at rest."

"'Ha ! ha, boy ! Say'st thou so ? Art thou there, true-
penny ?' Now hear me, Harry Percy, I look on it that you
fear me—I hold thee jealous of my attributes, my attitudes,
my carriage, my certain something, which, being peculiar to
the individual man, is vulgarly called genius. I will outshine
thee before Jim Tilton—outdo thee—take the rag off the bush
in Benton ; and leave thee 'the mere lees to brag of.' You
give me counsel but no confidence—w'y should I keep terms
with thee ? Urge me again upon this matter, and I declare
against thee. Thou shalt know me as a rival rather than an
ally ; and I will foil all thy best points with my own. Look
to it, Harry—the gall rises within me."

Vernon regarded the speaker with mixed feelings of pity and vexation. But the monomania was too strong to be overcome by argument, or resisted by anything short of violence—a measure to which, as there was no present necessity to rid him-self of his companion, there was no occasion to resort. Sup-pressing, therefore, some stern expressions which had risen to his lips, he suffered the other to chuckle in the prospect of his theatrical superiority, inly consoling himself with the idea that before the close of another day he should be rid of his thought-less but well-intentioned tormentor; and he, disabused of the unhappy error which had probably, more than anything beside, seduced him from the home to which he had only just returned.

When they reached the house, the actor resumed his random and rhapsodical chit-chat with all around him, as if nothing had happened either within or without to discompose him for an in-stant. The hostess he reminded of old times, and of a thousand practical jokes which he had played, of which she herself had been more than once the victim. With a fresh memory he accompanied the vital requisites of narration, lively comment, and felicitous gesture; and, speaking with all the frank exube-rance of boyhood, which his playhouse habits had been rather calculated to increase than diminish, he had the satisfaction of seeing the blushing Mary watching and listening with an atten-tiveness scarcely less sweet and anxious than that of "the gen-tle lady wedded to the Moor"—her white neck stretched for-ward—her head bent toward him—her lips slightly parted, and in her eyes that glistening eagerness of gaze which betrays mingled pleasure and curiosity. It is more than probable that the likeness between his own situation and that of Othello, forced itself upon him when he made this discovery—for a moment after, without any preface, he began, half aloud, to mutter the fine description of the scene—

"These things to hear
Would Desdemona seriously incline," &c.

The summons to supper, twice, thrice repeated by the hostess herself, scarcely succeeded in diverting him from this theme and stopping him in the full swell and torrent of his declamation. But the old lady was already handling the coffee-pot, and there was no time to finish the quotation; yet, as if to revenge him self for the interruption, he seized the hands of the damsel, who still sat, almost as inattentive to ordinary matters as himself, and gently pressing them the while, he conducted her to the vacant seat beside his own at the table.

CHAPTER XI.

TREACHERY IN CAMP — POLITICIANS AMONG THE OUTLAWS.

Vol. You stand here, my lord, unseen, and hear all;
Do I deal now like a right friend with you!
Ans. Like a most faithful.—SECOND MAID'S TRAGEDY.

VERNON retired early to his couch, which stood, with that of Horsey, in an adjoining shed-room. He was pleased to find clean white homespun sheets allotted him; and, looking around the apartment, involuntarily congratulated himself that so tidy a damsel as Mary Clayton made up the beds and aired the chambers. Clear water in a clean white goblet stood on a chair—for there was no other washstand—on the back of which hung a couple of towels of coarse homespun, bleached by long use and good washing to a whiteness like that of the sheets. These little matters attested some larger degree of civilization than the externals of the mansion had prepared him to expect, and were the fruits, most probably, of better days and associations, which Mrs. Yarbers had brought with her from the lower country. Certainly they were only becoming features in one who had traded so long in cakes and beer to the common satisfaction. Yarbers himself appeared to be a slovenly, coarse creature, to whom the neatness of a household was not likely to be a subject of much consideration.

It was fully an hour after Vernon had retired before Horsey followed his example. He sat up talking with the hostess, to whom his sudden reappearance after so long an interval had brought back as many associations as her ancient features had awakened in him; and the ball of conversation, so busied were they mutually in asking and answering questions, was seldom suffered to fall for more than a single moment in all that space of time.

It would be difficult to say whether the old lady took any special pleasure in the chat of the individual in question. It is more than probable she would have found the same in that of any other young person who had presented himself at the close of day, and begged a shelter for the night. Age likes to enliven itself with the fires of youth, as the venerable monarch of Israel became conscious of a living warmth from the embraces of the young maidens who were placed beside him for that purpose. It seems like the pouring of new mountain-streams into exhausted channels, and impelling into consciousness and motion the choked and stagnant fountains of life. The heart grows young in the contemplation of youth, and a momentary forgetfulness of its own decay is the consequence of that revivification of memory which confounds the past with the present; or rather sends the mind back from the bleak eminence of age which it has reached, and where it stands stiff and frozen, to the green and flowery valleys below, from which it has risen at first, but to which, save by the aid of memory, it can never, never more return.

There may have been, indeed, some little occult policy in the gracious demeanor of Mrs. Yarbers to the dashing and good-natured actor. She was not without that social instinct which is called cunning, and did not fail to recollect that Tom Horsey's father was one of the stanchest proprietors in all Hindes county. It had not escaped her eye that her old customer for cakes and beer was really very much taken with the appearance of her lovely daughter, and here, to use the phrase of the sea-logician, was a "concatenation accordingly."

Perhaps, were it our cue to prosecute this inquiry still farther at this moment, it would not difficult to find strong sanction for the suspicion which is here presented to the mind of the reader; but this might be anticipating other passages. Enough to say, that Mrs. Yarbers was not pleased with her husband, with his relations, and her own position; and, as a mother, regarded the existing influences of the latter as highly detrimen tal to the fortunes of a child whom she loved, naturally and

necessarily, as a mother should; but to whom she gave additional regard, as, contemplating her through the medium of her
pride, she saw in her beauty a possession which lifted her
heart, and warmed her vanity, and made it a sorrow in her
mind when she reflected that such charms were destined to
ripen in the shade, and, like the fruits of the untrodden forest,
to ripen unprofitably, without eye to admire or lip to taste.

This was a subject upon which her mind was apt to brood,
and it need not occasion our wonder to be told that the instincts
of one brooding thus, would not be unlikely to result in practices
not very dissimilar to those of the professedly managing mother
in communities of more artifice and fashion. From the first
moment when Horsey declared himself and renewed his old
acquaintance with her, the fancy had floated in her mind that
his coming was a special providence; and this fancy, fixed
firmly at last, she resolved to lend all her powers to the consummation of the thing she wished.

With this resolution, Mary was suffered to sit up long beyond
the usual hour, listening to a conversation which, enlivened by
playful remarks and pleasant anecdotes on the part of the actor,
was very agreeable to a young creature who had as yet seen
nothing of the world; and the mother even assumed the performance of many of those tasks which, in ordinary periods,
were commonly allotted to her daughter, that there might be no
obstacle offered to the formation of an intimacy between the
two which promised to realize her desires, and which, so far,
had advanced with tolerable rapidity. The absence of her husband was favorable to her plans; and, it may be, that some im
pulse was derived for their provocation, from the fact that these
were calculated to interfere with his. He, too, had purposes in
view for the damsel — though not his daughter — which were
something less than agreeable to the mother; and the open
avowal of his preference in behalf of young Mabry had been
the signal for her declared hostility to his pretensions. Thus
matters stood at the period of which we write.

When Horsey retired from the hall, which he had not thought
to do until Mary disappeared, and certain admonitory yawns
from the mother denoted that condition of declining consciousness which could not long do full justice to his good stories and

choice quotations, Yarbers had not returned. But Horsey had been but few minutes in his chambers before the outer door of the dwelling was heard to unclose and his heavy tread sounded along the floor. Horsey had challenged his companion's atten tion the moment he entered the room, but the latter had discouraged him, by declaring a very carnal desire for sleep — an excuse which, at that moment, the buoyant actor was unwilling to regard as worthy a single consideration ; and he rattled on without intermission for a while, until, undressed and buried in the sheets, the animal obtained the ascendency, and his tongue, taking advantage of the circumstance, assigned the task of declaring his whereabouts to that distinguished member his nose, the extraordinary industry and capacity of which was soon a matter of general notoriety.

To this moment Vernon had not closed his eyes. His mind was just in that condition of quickening cogitation when, yet unpossessed of its definite purpose, it compares plans, analyzes its resources and dependencies, and from pregnant and critical doubts conceives and gathers hopes and resolutions.

There was much in the position of Vernon to keep him watchful, and the smallest unusual event was calculated to make his blood bound, and his fancy spring into activity. Thus, after Yarbers' return to the cottage, and while he meditated a thousand different courses of conduct for the better prosecution of his leading object, his ear, quickened by thought, under the influence of an imagination warmed and strengthened by the drowsy midnight horn that sounded throughout the world of silence, caught the sudden baying of a beagle, and a crowd of suspicious fancies thronged upon him

Once, twice, thrice, the loud, deep, prolonged note sounded faintly through the apartment, and then the footstep of Yarbers was again heard, slowly crossing the floor from the rear to the entrance of the house. The lifting of the latch followed, the door was opened, and again closed. Silence succeeded for a moment ; then arose a stunning bay from the hound, almost at the threshhold of the dwelling, a prolonged note like that which had awakened the attention of Vernon a few moments before.

This was singular enough. There were evidently no dogs

of any kind about the premises at the first coming of the travellers, and though they might afterward have come home with
the master of the house, yet it was highly improbable that such
had been the case, else wherefore had they heard nothing of
them when they sallied forth to the meeting already described
of Horsey with Mabry? Besides, it was scarcely possible that
a farmer on the outskirts of the then Mississippi border, should
so carefully exclude his dogs from the same apartment wit
himself.

Vernon was in the mood to conjecture a thousand strang
matters, and to convert into causes of suspicion many things
that might be innocent enough. To one in his situation, and
with his objects, this was sufficiently proper; and the occasion
for his excitation in the present instance was well founded.
The beagles that were in the wood then, run not on four legs;
and the last sound that reached his ears, issuing from the lungs
of Yarbers, was an annunciation to a companion that the coast
was clear. Under the shade of a spreading oak, a hundred
yards from his dwelling, he was joined by no less a person than
our old acquaintance, Saxon.

"You have lodgers, Jack?" demanded the outlaw in the first
moment of their meeting.

"Two chaps from below—one a quiet, sober, silent sort of
person; the other a fellow all tongue. His name's Horsey—
ne's—"

"No matter. I know them both. As for Horsey, it's a mis
fortune he's along. He may be in the way. Hawkins put
some nonsense in that fellow's head, and I fear has only thrust
him in our path. The other must be seen to."

"Ha! What is he?"

"A spy, I reckon. Such is our suspicion He's in with the
governor, and they have had some talk about an ugly business
which concerns us. The only good feature in the thing is, that
they do not know exactly which way to turn themselves, or who
to trust. What they know leads them to apprehend a great
deal of which they know nothing, and much more than is the
truth. What this youth knows is our question. We must
touch his wallet. You must manage that to-night"

"Has he money, think you?"

. 'Nay, that is no object now; besides, I doubt he has little. He is a poor young lawyer that the governor has tempted with promises of a great reward for every beagle that he can collar. Our object is to get hold of his papers, and see what names he has down. We know that certain papers of Mat Webber fell into their hands at that ugly business on the Black Warrior; and the confessions of that traitor, Eberly, if he made any, might give them clues enough to our most secret operations. That this fellow, Vernon, is employed by the state, I have no sort of doubt; but there's no telling to what extent — what are the powers given him, or what is the object he aims at. These we must learn. His papers we must handle, and you must contrive it if you can to-night, or the work will be more troublesome to-morrow. Have you found out what course he takes ?"

" To Beatie's Bluff, if he himself is to be believed; but the other lark told Betsy a different story, and said that they were both for the lower ford, on the route to Benton."

" And how's Bess now ? — has she got over her humors ? Does she still continue to suspect you ?"

" Worse than ever; and Mabry is also very troublesome."

" But have you not given him your daughter — will not that stop his mouth ?"

" It would, I make no doubt, could my giving be his having. But the old woman's stubborn as a mule, the girl herself dislikes him, and this evening there was a strange blow-out, that has made the chap furious as a wild beast — all tongue and wrath and no reason."

" Ha ! what was the matter ?"

" Well, you see, it so happened, that the old woman know'd this young man, Horsey, when he was only a little bit of a boy, somewhere down on Pearl river. Well, when they struck up the acquaintance between 'em, what should the fellow do, but, to make it fast, he ups and goes for kissing Mary, and for any· thing I know, the old woman too. Just at the time when he was about it, and pushing Mary, who was frightened enough, I warrant, all round the room, we came in, Mabry and myself; and before we could put in or say a word, Mabry jumps for· ward, and clips the stranger side of his head and tumbles him ever like a log. There was a great to-do after that. The old

woman set all the water in the house a-boiling, and it got quite
too hot for Ned. He started off and I followed him, and while
we were talking together under the trees, who should come up
but these two fellows. Horsey followed to get satisfaction for
the blow, which, it was surprising to me, he took so lightly at
first. He thought better of it afterward, however, and did better; for, I tell you, he handled poor Ned in two minutes in a
way that's a caution. He downed him, a fair stupid down—
Ned rolled about like a drunken bullock, and got mighty sick
with both eyes shut up, and a great retching at his stomach. I
had tight work to keep him steady on his nag and get him safely home. Since then. when he recovered, he's been in a mighty
crooked humor. He swears that I don't want he should have
the girl—that I'm only playing 'possum, and half believes that
I set this fellow, Horsey, on to beat him, though nobody could
have been more willing for the fight, at first, than Mabry himself."

"Does no threaten?"

"A little squinting that way, though he don't speak out
plainly. But he'd threaten and tell too, if so be he thought I
was only shamming in the business with Mary."

"You must run it through then, as fast as possible. He will
scarcely speak anything to your discredit, if he was once married to your daughter."

"No! But that's the worry. The old woman's hot ag'in
him. She thinks Mary meant for his master; and I do really
believe she fancies to marry her to a colonel or some great lawyer, or maybe to a member of Congress. She always rides a
high horse when she talks about Mary'

"But the girl herself?"

"Likes him no better than Bess. He stands but little chance
with either of them."

"But if Bess approved, would not that help his chance with
Mary?"

"Why, yes; but that's the swamp—worse than the Big
Black—which I can't manage to cross nohow."

"Why not make Mabry a colonel? The thing might very
easily be done. You can beat up and bring in stray votes
enough to turn the election, if the fellow could do anything for

himself. We must manage this matter hereafter. For this other fellow, now —"

"Vernon?"

"Yes—of course, you know which bed he sleeps in. Did you give an eye to his portmanteau?"

"It's in the room with him—I put it myself by the chimney. You don't mean to—"

Yarbers paused, and looked vacantly in the other's face leaving the sentence unfinished. Saxon smiled after a moment's hesitation, and replied—

"You are afraid to have more work on your hands than was stipulated for. Be under no concern. We shall avoid blood-spilling and violence, as a general good policy, which is the more important to observe now when we are under partial suspicion already. All that we ask of you is to find out what he carries. You must get his papers; and this you can do, I trust, without difficulty. You have the old trap in the floor by which to enter, and this key will open any portmanteau-lock that was ever sold in Mississippi. As for his life, that is the least consideration so long as we know his game. There is more chance of Mabry growing troublesome than he, and you may yet find it necessary to work with cold steel upon him. Make him a colonel, and if that doesn't bring Brown Bess to favor him, we must bribe him to good breeding in another way"

"It'll be hard work. I never seed a fellow that set such store on a ga'l in all my life. He can't bear to see another man look upon her, and he talks of nothing else."

"Unless it be of you; but his case needs no immediate attention. This of Vernon does. Did you note whether his saddle had pockets?"

"It has. I searched them already, but found nothing worth telling of. There was a newspaper, and some old accounts, take it—they looked like bills and calculations."

"You cared not what they looked like, Yarbers, when you found that they did not look like money. But I must see those papers. Where is the saddle?"

"In the stable. Shall I lead your horse round the old field? They may hear his footsteps if we take the path."

"Right—do so. I'll await you at the stall."

Yarbers had put a tolerably fair estimate upon the papers found in the saddle-pouches. An examination of them by torchlight resulted in no discovery such as Saxon sought for, and the attempt to arrive at farther knowledge was devolved for the present upon the adroit and prying industry of Yarbers

CHAPTER XII

TRAPS AND TOGGERY — THE RULING PASSION STRONG IN SLEEP — A STAGE SITUATION.

"It is in mine authority to command
The keys of all the posterns: please your highness
To take the urgent here: come, sir, away."
Winter's Tale.

BEFORE this long conference was ended, sleep had overcome the senses of Harry Vernon. The imagination which had so long kept him wakeful in spite of the day's fatigue, now busied itself only in his dreams, which were all of a kind natural to the young beginner on the weary paths of life. With a heart as yet unfettered, and a fancy free as that of the bird for the first time winging its way from the forests to the ocean, he was conscious only of that void and vacant region in his bosom, which is intended to be filled by love. The germ was there of the great empire over which the imperial master was yet to rear his wand, but the especial divinity had not bestowed a glance on the territory she was destined to inhabit. Warm and waiting for the advent, the heart of Harry Vernon did not yet repine in inconclusive fancies, hoping and sighing, and surrendering itself to imbecility. He suffered himself but little time to brood over the vague desires which he felt, but summoning to his side the thoughts which attend on duty, he addressed himself with ardor to the actual demands of existence, without yielding up more mind than was necessary to such as were eventual and prospective. It was only while he slept that his fancy gave itself up to the desires of his heart; and all the struggles before his pathway were thrust from sight, and all his duties and dangers forgotten, to give place to as lovely a vision as youthful bard ever conceived and young imagination ever desired.

A maiden conjured up in realms of faery, rose before his dreaming eye—just such a form as met and realized the ideal which his united taste and reason might have been disposed to create at a moment of particular inspiration. She was tall and graceful; her skin pure as marble and smooth as ivory; her eyes black and streaming with a melting light; her lips soft as the leaf and richer than the rose; her cheeks pale but radiant, almost transparent with a light like that which glistened from her eyes; and her forehead lofty, spiritually narrow, and shaded by the voluminous masses of silk-like hair, darker than that which shines on the shoulders of the raven.

She stood beside him—such was his dreaming fancy—in a vision of his sleep. He had sunk for shelter beneath the shadows of a group of mighty oaks that surmounted the brow of a hill, and was surrounded by a dense and untrodden forest. His horse drank the while and cropped the herbage upon the banks of a little stream that wandered down the hillside, and lost itself in the deep groves of a thicket which hid from sight the dark and gloomy recesses of an inland swamp. The midday sun shone above him in melting fervor, but the dense foliage shielded him from the oppressive heat, and but a few straying straggling gleams, trembling and retreating as if conscious of intrusion, stole in at intervals between the branches, as they slowly yielded to the capricious wind. A dark shadow, as if from an overhanging cloud, suddenly overspread the scene the moment ere she entered upon it, but at her approach the cloud disappeared, a glory like that of the moon enveloped him with its soft, fleecy edges, and his very soul seemed to melt within him as the entrancing vision drew nigh to his side.

Other forms followed and crowded upon the scene—strange events and mingling action disturbed its quiet, and his eye toiled in the survey of a thousand features, each changing at his glance and distracting his attention. But the lovely form which had fixed his eye and fastened upon his soul at first, was still to be seen amidst the crowd—now here, now there, nigh

and then remote, but still present, hallowing the scene to softness, mollifying the strife, stilling the clamor, and subduing the
turbulence, until — such was the strange fancy — the sudden
obtrusion of Horsey, and his fierce declamation, affrighted the
delicate and ethereal beauty from the spot; and he started from
his sleep with a harsher mood in his bosom toward his self-appointed companion than any which he had ever entertained
before.   It will be seen how far the random actor was answerable for the dispersion of his happy fancies.

Horsey was not without his visions also; but they were of a
very different character.   When he first fell asleep, his nose
performed such vigorous airs that Vernon was apprehensive
lest they might greatly interfere with his own desired rest.
But the mastery of this solemn member was disputed at frequent
periods by his tongue; which, as if never needing rest, continued at intervals to pour forth choice fragments from his favorite
Shakspere, growling at one moment in all the emphatic terrors
of the tragic muse; at another softening down to the most dulcet
parts of love, the sweet significant nothings with which every
hero regales his "Amaryllis in the shade."

These were long or short as the occasion seemed to require
them; and the prompt and well-versed memory of the actor appeared never to want the auxiliary help of a quotation.   Sometimes, the sentences would be broken, sometimes complete; at
first, they were usually short, consisting of two or three con-
secutive words of a single phrase; but Vernon, who listened to
him for a while with smiling curiosity, observed, as the night
advanced, that he rose from fragments to entire passages, and
when he himself was sinking into that sleep which yielded him
a vision so entrancing, he was conscious that the actor was gliding into the dialogue in which he personated the love-sick
Montague, and wooed the fair Capulet beneath the window
Something Vernon caught ere he himself slept, of—

"—— strides the lazy pacing clouds
And sails upon the bosom of the air,"

followed by an intense ebullition of the nostrils which probably
answered all the purposes of a reply from Juliet; when he himself, surrendering to the oppressive sleep, lost all farther apprehension of the dialogue.

But it was continued, nevertheless, by the actor, though so large a portion of his audience slept; and, perhaps, the interruptions from his nose allowed for, he never went through the part with more honest unction in his life. That he might have done better, or at least toiled for it, is unquestionable, if he could only have been told that at this moment his audience was increased.

So it was. Saxon, the outlaw, and his adjunct Yarbers, stood without the dwelling and beside the chimney of the shedroom in which slept the travellers. Their ears took in with readiness the earnest and pleading devotions of the amorous Romeo, and so greatly did the affair tend to the amusement of the former, that he could with difficulty restrain himself from taking the opposite part of the dialogue, and thus stimulating the enthusiastic actor to increased efforts. But the more timid Yarbers was opposed to this, and, speaking in whispers, scarcely audible to his immediate companion, dwelt earnestly on the danger of discovery.

"Pshaw, John Yarbers, the man sleeps—soundly too—no man sleeps more soundly than him who dreams of what he loves."

"But the other fellow—Vernon!"

"Ay—you have need of caution there; but I reckon he sleeps too. You must lift the trap cautiously and listen, before you do anything."

This trap was simply a square hole in the floor, made by sawing two of the flooring-boards across, fastening them together by a cross-piece below, and securing them with common hooks to the joist beneath. While, therefore, their ends rested upon the joists, they resisted any pressure from above, and it was easy for one under the house, by undoing the hooks, to raise the trap and make his way into it. The fabric stood upon raised blocks, from three to four feet from the ground, and, obeying the direction of the outlaw, Yarbers fell upon his knees, and soon disappeared beneath it.

It was easy to undo the hooks which secured the door, but the continued declamation of Horsey, in spite of all the assurances of Saxon that he slept, disturbed the nerves of the intruder, and he once more returned to the entrance to assure

his companion that it was certainly Vernon who snored **and**
Horsey who spoke; and that the speaking had none of the obstructions or hesitation of a sleeping man, and came most certainly from the throat of one as perfectly conscious as he ever
was in daylight. The impatient outlaw answered him with an
oath.

"Yarbers, you are but a dry bone after all. Stand aside,
and let me do it."

"Stay, sir—don't you hear steps? Don't you think he's
walking?"

"Pshaw, man! It's your own heart. It thumps hard enough
to scare you, I doubt not. Where does the portmanteau stand?"

"Right side of the chimney from the hall-door; and the saddle-bags on the left."

"But which is Vernon's?"

"Fegs! I don't know. I warn't home when they come, and
I s'pose they took 'em off the creatures themselves and brought
'em in. There's no telling which is which."   ·

"That's unfortunate. We must then examine both," said
Saxon, as he crawled under the house and made his way to the
still unopened trap-door. This he raised with sufficient care,
though not without some little noise—the hard, heavy pine, of
which the boards were made, requiring that degree of effort in
raising them which had been otherwise necessary to keep them
in equilibrium and prevent the edges from grazing against the
surrounding floor, to which they were made to correspond with
tolerable nicety. Once lifted, the intruder, still grasping the
door in his hand, raised himself and stood up within the opening, his head and shoulders being now within the apartment.
The door he laid down gently upon the floor beside the trap, so
that it might be drawn into its place on the first alarm.

To his confusion, however, while thus engaged, he discovered
that the conjecture of Yarbers was not unfounded. Horsey was
certainly out of bed, and striding the floor of the apartment.
His ruling passion had grown utterly ungovernable in his sleep,
and the somnambulist was now fairly in the highest realm of
hallucination. His movements were, however, slow enough at
this period; and Saxon succeeded, without noise or interruption, in stretching forth his hand to the fireplace and securing

the saddle-bags, which were the first that came within his reach. These he handed through the aperture to his comrade below, who proceeded to examine them in the moonlight without. His whispered words, as he looked at the contents, declared his own wonder, while they satisfied Saxon that he had fallen upon the wrong chattels.

"Jackets and breeches all covered with gold and spangles."

"Stuff 'em back," said Saxon, stooping down, and whispering; "stuff 'em back and hand me the bags. They are the actor's baggage. We must grope for the other's."

While this was doing, and at the moment when Saxon had received them in his hands, and was about raising them through the hole in which he stood, in order to replace them, the paroxysm came upon Romeo stronger and less controllable than ever. A rush of inspiration filled his veins, and to the great annoyance of the outlaw, he heard him growling and advancing. The play had made rapid progress in the sleep of the actor. He had reached the fifth act — he had got his poison from the apothecary — he had resolved upon his own death, and was hurrying on to give County Paris his.

"Give me that mattock!" he cried in low, hoarse accents to the supposed Balthazar beside him. His voice then subsided into a throng of pressing whispers, as if forced to speak, yet not desiring to be heard. This brought him within a few paces of the outlaw, who began seriously to feel the inconvenience of his situation. A few strides more would bring the actor upon his shoulders, and into the pit. To withdraw and let down the door at that moment, might be to arouse the sleeper, and defeat the object which he had in view; and no possible effort which he could make, short of rushing into the room itself, would enable him — this he discovered — to reach the opposite end of the fireplace where the valise of Vernon had been placed.

While he stood in a state of incertitude, which prevented him from doing anything, the passion of the actor had taken a new direction from the approach of Paris. He had gone through the paroxysms which made him beat down the gate of the monument; and here Saxon observed, with some surprise, that he now spoke the part of Paris as well as his own, to which, hitherto, he had entirely confined himself. The inference of the outlaw from this fact, was, that the pressure of sleep was passing off, the influence of imagination lessened, and that the actor's ear needed the absolute reality of sound, to continue any longer in his self-deception.

This added somewhat to the apprehensions of the intruder, who was not suffered very long to speculate upon the matter. The language of Paris was threatening—that of Romeo had assumed a tone of mildness, which, in reality, only disguised the laboring volcano in his bosom:—

> "'I beseech thee, youth,
> Pull not another sin upon my head,
> By urging me to fury.'"

Still he approaches, and his arm rises as if balancing the sword " Live," he says, in most soliciting tones—

> "'Live, and hereafter say,
> A madman's mercy bade thee run — away.'"

Here he availed himself of one of his own readings of the thousand unimportant distinctions in such matters, of which stage-struck citizens are so apt to make a fuss. Pausing at the word " run," which he had spoken along with the whole passage in the gentlest accents, he now made a tremendous transition, and the final word, " away," was thundered forth in tones to waken up the dead. This was a " point" upon which, in his waking moments, he was very apt to pride himself. The answer of Paris, which he also spoke, fell something short of this, but was still loud; and he had scarcely given himself time to finish it, before, reaching the acme of his paroxysm in the part of Romeo, he gave the torrent free vent, and leaped upon the shoulders of Saxon, while he cried aloud—

> "'Wilt thou provoke me!— then have at thee, boy!'"

The situation was awkward in the last degree, and the struggles of Romeo were such as to convince the outlaw that he was rapidly coming to his senses. Exerting his whole strength, therefore, he seized the half-prostrate actor by his shoulders, and flung him from him as far as he might while in the place in which he stood, not giving much heed whether the poor fellow was brought up by flint or feathers. Then, suddenly sink ing down with equal promptness and composure, he drew the trap into its place with a degree of ease which added but little to the bustle which the previous incident had occasioned.

The direction given to Horsey by the arms of Saxon, carried him upon the couch of Vernon, whom the struggling actor, now emerging into actual bodily consciousness, grappled with as he was rising up in alarm, and continued to contend with as if County Paris still remained to be slain.

But he met with no better treatment at the hands of Vernon than from those of Saxon, being tumbled, by a very unscrupulous movement, backward upon the floor, where he lay, for a moment, actually at a loss to determine where he was and what was his condition.

Vernon had been as roughly awakened from a pleasant dream as the actor, and, still in doubt as to whence the annoyance arose, he was soon out of bed and standing above Romeo, the moment he had flung him from him. What might have been his farther act had not Horsey spoken, though doubtful in character, would have been certainly decisive. The tongue of the latter, never for any length of time idle, happily resumed its offices in time to prevent more mischief.

"Why, Harry, my dear boy, is that you? Why, what the devil's the matter?"

"Matter, Mr. Horsey. That's the very question to be asked of you. How came you on my bed?"

"Your bed! Was that your bed, Harry? By all that's sacred in stage-lights, I took it for the tomb of Juliet; and Paris—you were Paris, my dear fellow."

"Do you walk in your sleep, Mr. Horsey?" asked Vernon, now beginning to conjecture the whole affair.

"Egad, it may be. I don't know, but, certainly, I have had a strangely exciting dream. It was our first night at Benton, Harry. I was Romeo, and that dear little Mary made her début in Juliet, under my instructions. If I ever play so well in reality, as I fancied I played this night—as I must have played in my sleep—I shall ask for nothing better. But," rising from the floor as he spoke, "my shin is cursedly bruised—the skin's off; I can hardly get up. I had some notion that I had got into a hole, but—"

The voice of Mrs. Yarbers at the chamber-door, demanding to know if anybody was sick, and asking the cause of the uproar, silenced the actor. After satisfying her, he was very glad to slink back into bed, as he found Vernon unwilling any longer to listen to his description of the scene, and the detail of points newly-made, which had broken in upon fancies of his own no less dear and exciting, though, possibly — it was his own reflection — not more real and stable than those of his companion.

Saxon was no less annoyed, and, perhaps, with more serious cause for annoyance, than those within. He waited long without the house, and near his place of secret ingress, in the hope of hearing those sounds from the sleepers which should assure him of an uninterrupted entrance. But he waited in vain.

Whether it was that the rough handling which Horsey had received had utterly expelled the nightmare, or whether he had become conscious of the unreasonableness of making any more disturbance in the house, and was willing to compensate for his excesses at one moment by an unusual degree of forbearance at another, he certainly did not snore again that night. Vernon's was a well-bred nose, that seldom violated the rules of decorum; and hopeless of the plan, the progress of which had been so forcibly interrupted in the first instance, the outlaw concluded to defer to another opportunity his intended purpose.

"We must do it on the roadside; and it may be necessary that we should even lay hands on him. These papers being of value he would most probably conceal them about his person. It is barely possible that they should be in the valise, and we should take no such risks as this on the strength of a bare possibility. We must keep your house in the reputation of being an honest one, Yarbers, as well to serve our purposes as to please your wife. Let her not know that I have been here to-night. I will go farther up, and be ready for our man at the fork."

"She'll guess fast enough though I don't tell her. She's mighty 'cute, and knows the bay of the beagle is not for nothing in these parts."

"So long as she can't see the beagle, and don't know whose name's on the collar, she knows nothing. But help me to my horse, while I ride. Jones will be here by daylight, I suppose. You can send him after me when he comes."

" And Mabry ?"

" If he ·blab, be must be silenced. If the mouth won't be sugared, it must be stopped. You will see him to-morrow when he is a little cooled off from the drubbing of this actor, and persuade him that you have nothing to do in the business. 'I his he will be the more apt to believe when he finds his enemy _gone ; and, perhaps, it might be just as well that you should see him at an early hour on the subject. Should nothing answer—should he grow troublesome—I will send a decoy-beagle, who will get him into Cane Castle, where he'll leave all his secrets before he comes forth."

" There was one here for you to-day from Cane Castle—. Stillyards."

" The hunchback ! well, what said he ?"

" He came from Monna."

" Ah ! she's impatient; but she must wait. She would fetter me, Yarbers, as Brown Bess fetters you, but that my blood is quite as quick and impatient as her own. Yet, she's a woman more to be feared than Bess She can't scold so well—nay, she seldom scolds; but she thinks and broods over her thoughts, which are sometimes fearful enough, and one day she may seek to act them She's secret, Yarbers ; and there she is unlike Bess, who would blab everything she knew to your hurt, if you once put her into a passion. Monna, if sometimes fearful as the grave, is at all times as secret. It would be twenty times our good, Yarbers, were your wife half as secret. But you took her for better or worse, and so must we. If you are satisfied with your bargain," speaking with a malicious smile, "·your friends have no reason to complain."

CHAPTER XIII.

THE RENTS IN "ROMEO"—BURNING ONE'S FINGERS — SPLENDID
ANTICIPATIONS.

"The confidence of youth our only art,
And Hope gay pilot of the bold design,
We saw the living landscapes . . . . .
Reach after reach salute us and depart."
WORDSWORTH.

The travellers prepared to set forth at an early hour on the
ensuing morning. The adventures of the night had tended
somewhat to sour the usually sweet temper of the actor. His
legs, which he displayed to the wonder and commiseration of
his companion, were skinned from knee to ankle, in a way perfectly mysterious to the sufferer, who could not conceive how
such an affliction could have arisen simply from his playing
Romeo to empty boxes.

"And yet it seemed to me, among other things, that it wasn't
Romeo, neither, but Hamlet. I was in the grave, grappling—
I'll be sworn upon it—with Laertes, with whom I 'fought a
long hour by Shrewsbury clock.' It must have been in the
grave that I got these bruises."

That imperfect state of mind which, in dreams, so happily
unites the fanciful with the actual, had, in fact, produced a rapid
transition in his thoughts from the one play to the other, while
his involuntary struggle in the hole with the outlaw suggested
a similitude of circumstances so favorable for a change of scene;
and the dawning of his right reason, which the struggle necessarily occasioned, forced upon him the partial conviction that
some other man, of considerable brawn and muscle, had, like
himself, been dreaming a part also, which had given the performance a termination so perfectly tragical. His inspection
of his saddle-bags contributed in some little degree to his confusion. The contents were in strange disorder.

"Could I have been so d—d stupid as to have dressed myself in costume ?   I don't recollect putting it back, and if I did,
I must have shown a singular indifference to Romeo's wardrobe
to have put it up without folding.   Look here, Harry Vernon,
what a bunch I've made of it in my sleep; a bag from a beg-
gar's press—and the garment perfectly new—a splendid garment, for which that skunk of a tailor amerced me in a greater
number of dad's dollars than I should be altogether willing to
count up in his hearing.   You shall see me put it on.   You
shall—you shall form an idea of the sort of chap that Caldwell
quarrelled with ; you shall see the figure, at least, of a Romeo
not to be met with every day."

This scene was going on in the chamber prior to their appearance before the family in the hall.   They had been already
summoned to an early breakfast, which Vernon, before retiring
for the night, had especially solicited.   He now ventured to
remind the actor that the family and breakfast waited upon
them.

"Only a moment !" exclaimed the actor hurriedly, as he proceeded to envelope himself in the glittering garment of the
amorous Montague—"only for a moment !   It's worth a glance
from a veteran stager.   Ha ! what's this ?—a hole ! a rent !"

The exclamation of the actor, distinguished by tones expressive not merely of surprise, but consternation and horror, drew
the attention of Vernon to the dress, in which an envious nail
—probably while old Yarbers was inspecting the glittering
sack beneath the house—had torn a finger's breadth.

"What the d—l shall I do ?—what a misfortune !" exclaimed
the actor, with a degree of concern infinitely greater than any
that his bruised shins had occasioned.

"It's but a small hole; it's easily mended," said Vernon.

"Small !" exclaimed the actor, with some indignation.   "Ay,
ay, not so deep as a well, nor so wide as a church door, but 'tis
enough to call for the instant succor of a darning needle.   Juliet,
that is to say, my little Mary, here, shall take it up off hand
She's a nice, handy body, that; would make, with training, an
admirable Juliet— gad, 'twould be a charity to give her lessons,
and I'll think of it.   But to the Romeo—she shall take up the
rent in the twinkling of an eye."

"Surely, Mr Horsey, you will not delay us for so small a matter."

"Small a matter, indeed! By St. David's best buckles, Harry, you have a strangely irreverent way about you! Such a rent in Romeo's body is no small matter. Let the audience see a hole in a hero's breeches, and d—me if it don't turn all his tragedy into farce. I once saw a chap named Barnes playing Lear, with his shirt—an ugly corner of it, I mean—depending, for all the world like a streamer, fully a quarter of a yard from his inexpressibles. The audience roared with admiration, which Barnes took for applause. Never did a fellow play so furiously fine—with so much earnestness and enthusiasm. But the more fire he put into his acting, the more it filled them with laughter; all of which he mistook, like an ass as he was, for pleasure at his performance. On a sudden, however, he happened to fling his left hand behind him in order to adjust his sword, and he grasped along with it the obtrusive garment. You never saw a fellow's comb cut so short off. He lost his voice in an instant—his head dropped, and when he came round to the wing, the sweat stood upon his brow like treacle. No, no! I am clear that no man should make his bow to the public with a hole in his breeches."

Vernon expostulated against the delay, but in vain. A new measure suggested itself to his companion.

"While her hand's in at one thing, she can do the other, or I'll do it myself. I'll get Mary to heat me an iron, and I'll smooth it before I start. It's ruined for ever if I put it back in this condition."

Vernon saw that expostulation and entreaty were alike vain. Horsey made a point of healing Romeo's hurts—the ruling passion rendering him equally obstinate to argument and entreaty; and with a complacency as enviable in the eye of a traveller as it is desirable in that of an actor, he sallied from his chamber with the fractured garment in his hand, and proceeded instantly and without circumlocution, to declare his requisitions to mother and daughter.

"Get your needle, my little Juliet, and show me what sort of a workman you are; but first put me an iron to warm; I must take out these wrinkles."

The girl willingly assumed the performance of task set her, and Horsey sat down the while to breakfast, but his eyes were upon her as she sewed, and more than once he started up to look at her progress.

"Well enough done, Mary. You are the girl after my own heart. Egad, if my wardrobe suffers much more injury in this fashion, I shall not be able to do without you. I shall have to come and steal you from mamma. A stitch or two more just there, Mary, if you please; and now that I look at it, just beneath the arm I see that a thread has dropped. The garment is rather tight over the shoulders, and it is only a timely precaution that would guard against the strain of any great action in that quarter. A man's blood gets up wondrously, Harry when he's in the fury of a fifth act—when he's warmed by opposition, and, more than all, by his own rising consciousness of what is called for by the character. At such a time his action increases accordingly, and it would be the most awkward thing in the world, if, extending his arm to convey the idea of command, to order Buckingham's head off, or any matter of equal tragic signification, he should discover to the inquisitive audience a rent under the arm, and a glimmer of a white cotton shirt beneath his buckram. It's the easiest thing in the world to upset the gravity of an audience in the deepest scenes. One fool makes many, and the first booby that laughs out, without any fear of shame, finds a hundred followers. I've seen it a thousand times, and know there is nothing so tragic as will frighten farce. Farce follows tragedy as naturally as the sparks fly upward. She stands beside her, ready to grin at the first opening; and let dignity forget herself for an instant, she claps her hands, and darts in, without any regard to decency, before all the spectators."

Thus rambling on, the actor ate his breakfast, and watched the progress of Mary with her needle. The bright eyes of the girl laughed the while, and her cheeks blushed, when he hung over her; his glances being equally shared between the semptress and the garment. The breakfast over, Vernon, with some consternation, beheld him proceeding to assist the mother and daughter in removing the plates and dishes, in order to convert the table into a tailor's board, on which he could perform the last-needled office of smoothing out the rumpled Romeo. Old

Yarbers looked on with a scarcely-suppressed smile, which was not lessened as the actor confessed to having disordered his wardrobe in his *night*-errant habits. *He* could have told a truer story, and have accounted more truly, if not more rationally, for the condition of the saddle-bags. But he was prudent enough to conceal his knowledge, and suppress, though with difficulty, his laughter.

The actor had made a clean breast, and declared the true cause of the uproar of last night to the family. There was nothing retentive in his nature, unless it might be in the one purpose of his mood; and, prattling ever, like the downward running fountain, his streams, the deeps and shallows alike, were equally open to the sunlight.

Harry Vernon, meanwhile, became impatient to the last degree. Not that he had any reason to wait for Horsey, beyond that of mere civility. He well knew that, before the day was out, they would reach the spot where diverging roads should prove convincingly to the actor that his course was other than that which he had so precipitately and erroneously assumed to be the same with his own. To hurry off before his companion was ready, in order that he might anticipate this truth, would at least seem rude, if it were not so in reality; and then the utter simplicity and good nature of the actor pleaded in his behalf, and made Vernon, who was generously and nobly constituted, reluctant to do anything which might inflict unnecessary pain, even though he well knew that a nature so mercurial as that of Horsey would not feel it long. Resolved, therefore, to await the actor's pleasure, he sat resigned to his fate, and beheld him removing the hominy, the remnants of the bacon and eggs—the mother, father, and daughter, equally, and in vain, striving to prevent him from performing duties so seemingly inconsistent with the dignity of a gentleman and the position of a guest. But his activity set their exertions at defiance. Plate followed plate, and dish dish, and cup cup, without stop or stay, until, striving to sweep up in one common effort the remaining odds and ends, he grappled them quite too unceremoniously together, and, to his own horror, and the great reddening of the hostess's cheeks, they came in undistinguishable ruin to the ground.

"Bless my soul, Mrs. Yarbers, but what have I done? I have broken all your cups and saucers."

"No! never mind, Mr. Horsey," stammered the old lady, half-angry with her old favorite, yet doing her utmost to conceal her annoyance.

"It's very unfortunate. I certainly had 'em fast, my dear madam. I could carry twice as many. I'll show you now, I'll bring back, in two turns, all that I have carried to the shelf;" and he actually proceeded to restore the plates and dishes to the table — "and if I break so much as a teacup, I'll give my head for a football. It was certainly the strangest misfortune."

Vernon interposed —

"Certainly it was, Mr. Horsey — a sort of fatality which can no more be accounted for than helped. All that you can do is to send Mrs. Yarbers a fine set from Vicksburg or Natchez, and take care to meddle with no more cups and saucers. The table is ready for you now — why not smooth the garment?"

"True, true, my cousin of Vernon, that is a good thought; and Bess — hold me your debtor for a set of china, the best that money can get in Natchez. Nay, nay, I will have no refusal — it must be so. You shall have the cups and saucers; I swear it by my Romeo, which stands waiting for smoothing. Let me have the iron, Mary nay, don't burn your pretty fingers with it — let me have it."

"It's hot, Mr. Horsey. Better take it up with the towel, sir," said the girl. But the rapid actor had already grasped the iron at the fire, with a rapidity only exceeded by the haste with which he dropped it again; and he now stood blowing his fingers, his face red as a lobster's with the sudden pain, and his mouth puffing and speaking alternately.

"Hot as — phew! phew! — the skin's off fingers as well as legs. Phew! Harry, my dear fellow, what an accident! Ay, do, Mary, that's a dear girl — do you iron it for me. Let your iron lie smoothly, Mary, my dear, and take care that it doesn't scorch Romeo as it has scorched me. That blue is very perishable — phew! — the misfortune of all things that are very beautiful. There, there — I think that will do. It must do. I won't worry you to work for me any longer, my sweet Juliet. Mrs. Yarbers, why didn't you call your daughter Juliet, instead of Mary?"

"As well might Mrs. Yarbers ask why you were not called Romeo, instead of Tom, Mr. Horsey. The one question might be answered just as readily as the other. But time presses on me, if not on you; and if you are disposed to stop until you have revised all the Christian names in the county, there is certainly no good reason why I should linger to assist you."

"Right, Harry; there's right and reason in what you say. Mrs. Yarbers, the best friends must part—you shall hear of me soon, and see me again when I have got through my business above. Mary, my dear, you shall be my Juliet—nay, don't look down; I tell you it shall be so. There shall go an oath to it that shall bind one of us, at least; and unless Mr. Mabry steps between us both—ha! so you turn away—you do not like that—well, I like you the better that you do not; and so good-by. 'It is a grief to part' so brief with thee. Come, Harry Vernon, I am ready now."

The actor had prolonged the parting words and moments to the last possible limits, and somewhat to the surprise of Vernon, he saw, or fancied he saw, an expression of seriousness and interest, rather beyond that of his ordinary manner, conspicuous in what he said and looked to the lovely forest damsel. Nor, on the other hand, did it seem to Vernon that the girl was entirely without some consciousness of the interest which she occasioned, and that which she felt, for her little rosy lips quivered as she spoke to them at parting, and the "good-by' trembled in imperfect expression upon her scarcely-opened mouth. Mrs. Yarbers was pleased to assure both the travellers that nothing would gladden her more than to see them often; a compliment which she then repeated to Horsey in particular; and one, in approbation of which, her lord and master growled out certain confirmatory, but scarcely intelligible sentences.

For a brief space after their departure from the hovel, the spirits of Horsey seemed considerably depressed. He said but little, and that little with the air of a man who speaks rather to avoid the imputation of sullenness, than with any desire to please. When he did speak more freely, and with the gradual assumption of his former mood, his expressions revealed the true source of his solemnity.

"There is something monstrous uncomfortable at parting

Harry, even with acquaintances of yesterday. I don't get
over it for an hour or two. It seems to me like rooting me up,
and tearing off some of my leaves and branches, when I am
compelled to grapple hands only to cast them loose again. It's
true it don't make me sick—for that matter, I shouldn't go to
bed, I believe, or lose stomach for a dinner, if I was to be separated for ever from the best friends in the world. I should
only, if that were the case, take a pine torch in my fingers, and
.go about looking after others; and a newer set might soon console me for the lost. But it seems to weigh me down; my limbs
grow weakish, and I lose all desire to make any exertions and
scarcely care to say or hear anything, though the best passage
offered itself for quotation jump to the moment, from Billy
Shakspere, that high treasurer of all manner of spoken
jewels. Now I feel just so in leaving these good people. It's
true Brown Bess is an old crony. I know nothing about her
husband, who seems but a curmudgeon; but that dear little
creature—that Mary—don't you think her devilish handsome,
Harry? What a forehead she has! what lips, eyes, hair! A
very collection of beauties! Celia, Rosalind, and Helen, melt-
id into one; and yet, Harry, she did not speak twenty words
to me the whole time she was present."

"How could she—who can, Mr. Horsey?" replied Vernon,
laughing, "you out-talked the whole family."

"The lawyer, also. By my faith, Harry, but that I heard
you made a long and good speech at Raymond, I should be inclined to say you had taken up the wrong profession. Now I
should have been the lawyer."

"You mistake. You would soon ruin yourself as a lawyer.
You would soon talk yourself away. A lawyer's words are the
materials he works with—you would soon dull them, or wear
them out. Your talking lawyer is a profligate who cheapens
his own wares by making them common. To talk in the right
place is his art, no less than to talk to the purpose. The where,
and the when, and the how much, are the three grand requisites
of public speaking."

"Egad, if that be the case, Harry, I should be soon swallowed up; for, as to stopping to think when I should speak and
what I should say, that would seem to be the most idle, as it would

certainly be, in my case, the most impracticable thing in the world
For that matter, I don't know half the time that I'm talking,
even when my tongue is most busy ' beating- all the chimes of
Westminster.' I catch myself, every now and then, speechifying
of my own head, or giving a reading from Shakspere to pine trees
and gray mosses, wasting myself, as the rose does its sweetness,
upon the desert air, when I can get no better audience.   Such,
I trust, will not be our fate at Benton, however, if Tilton has
any skill in management, and the Yazooians any taste.   By the
splinters, you shall see how I shall drive ; nay, there's no good
reason why I should not give you a sample now.   Here's a
quiet spot — looks for all the world as if it was meant for such
a purpose.   There is a space on the brow of the hill which
would accommodate a thousand people, and the pines rise, and
the oaks spread above and around it, and the vines link them
together and fill up the space between ; so that the amphitheatre
of the Romans was never so compact, and not half so well covered.   And, in the woods, with green leaves around me, my
voice seems to have a volume and a clearness that I can not always command in a building.   Ride up with me for a minute
and you shall see as good an imitation of Forrest — did you
ever meet with Forrest, Harry ?   A splendid, half-savage-look-
ing fellow — a sort of Mark Antony before dinner — who, by the
way, would make a figure in Dryden's Antony, perhaps superior to any who has yet tried it.   But I will show you Forrest
in Damon — you shall have the strangling scene — I'll choke a
pine sapling for Lucullus — I'll—"

He commenced riding up the hill as he spoke, but Vernon
stopped him.

"I ride on, Mr. Horsey. I would not now stop to see For
rest himself."

" The d—l you wouldn't."

" No, on my soul I wouldn't."

The actor stared.

" Harry Vernon, you are a bundle of mysteries. How can
it be that you love the stage ? — nay, how can you yourself
play with any hope of success unless you are willing to behold
the best models ?"

" Your remark reminds me of the error under which you have

labored so long and under which you still labor;" was the reply of Vernon expressed in looks equally grave with his language. "I will not ask, Mr. Horsey, by what means, or by whom, you became possessed of the idea that I entertained a passion for the stage and had resolved to go upon it. It is enough that such is your delusion, entertained in spite of my earnest and repeated assurances that such was not my intention—that I had no such passion, and that I was already earnestly and irre- vocably bound to the pursuit of another profession—one of the most jealous as the most absorbing—which will suffer neither rival nor interruption. With a most unbecoming resoluteness you refused credence to my own assurances to this effect, and have appointed yourself my travelling companion, without knowing how far I desired company, or whether your presence might not somewhat interfere with the object of my pursuit. It has not been through your forbearance, Mr. Horsey, that it has not done so, and I trust you will believe me when I tell you that it has been with me a serious fear that such might be its effect. Finding you possessed with this strange notion, and having exhausted all my forms of speech in seeking to convince you that I was no actor, and did not intend to become one, I forebore—in consideration of your parents, who have treated me so kindly, and with some reference to yourself, for I am not blind to your good qualities and natural parts—farther expos- tulation and complaint, and was contented that you should re- main in your error for a while, satisfied that it would not be very long before you would be disabused of it. That time is now at hand; a few miles farther will bring us to the forks, and you will then find that I will certainly take the upper road for Beattie's Bluff, while you, if your aim be Benton, will as certainly take that which crosses the river below. It only re- mains that I should again assure you, with all the solemnity of an oath, though I make none, that I am by profession a lawyer, that I have never dreamed of any other, and do not know, and have never thought to inquire, whether I have the most partial qualification for the stage. I admire good acting, am not defi- cient in a knowledge of the best dramatists, can quote Shak- spere almost as frequently, if not so felicitously as yourself, and, at another time than this—with less care upon my mind, and less business upon my hands—I should be particularly pleased to hear you in any, and all, of your favorite parts. Believe me, Mr. Horsey, from what I have already seen, I am prepared to believe that it is in your power, with study, industry, and *humility*, to rise to considerable distinction in your art."

"Say you so, Harry? Then I forgive you all the rest. I forgive you all that d—d dignity that makes me feel all over as if Carter himself had caught me playing tricks with my neighbors' sign-boards, and was scoring me hip and thigh with a most thorny morality. But, Harry, do you really think from what you have seen that I should become a proper actor?"

"I do, really, Mr. Horsey."

"That is to say with study and industry. But what do you mean by humility? I don't see any necessity for humility. Indeed, that's the last matter that a modern actor esteems as a requisite."

"The most necessary of all; for without humility one learns nothing. He will neither see in what he is himself defective, nor in what consists his rival's superiority. He can learn nothing who believes there is little left him to learn, and he alone learns all that man can teach, who is humble enough to doubt his own possessions, and hopeful enough to labor for their increase. I should have high hopes of you, Mr. Horsey, could you bring yourself to this conviction."

"God bless you, my dear fellow, these are devilish kind words of yours. Devilish kind! I'm d—nably unused to them. I've heard nothing all my life but censure; sneer and censure. Managers, and actors, and audience—no, d—me, I won't say anything about the audience—they have always treated me well enough whenever I had fair play before them —but, by my soul, I can't say the same for my brother actors, and still less favorably can I speak of managers. Had I believed them, I should have cut my throat, or turned in as a wagoner, or taken to some other villanous handicraft which only suffers a man to know that he is alive at meal-time. They have denied all my hopes and decried all my talents; and then came doubts to my mind—doubts, dark, dirty, earth-whelming, miserable doubts, Mr. Vernon—that made my soul sick, and made me feel as if I could steal away into some dark corner of the woods and die; satisfied, if out of human sight, that they spoke nothing but the truth—that I had deceived myself— that, in short, I had none of that genius, the fires of which I fancied to be blazing away proudly and inextinguishably in soul and brain. Oh, Harry Vernon, these were killing, crush ing doubts;—and when they came to me, as they always did when I was out of money, and the d—d tailors and tavern- keepers at my heels, I felt all over as the meanest of all possi- ble beings. But you cheer me; your words—for I believe you, Harry, to be a d—d smart fellow—your words reassure me. I feel my courage rise; I feel the fire blazing up within me, and by all that's resolute in man, it shall blaze out, ere many days, to the satisfaction of others. But, though you give me life, Harry, curse me but you crush me again when you tell me you are not one of us. I can hardly believe you even now. I heard it so solemnly asserted, and, indeed, lost and paid a bet on the matter."

"Something strange, at least, in all this business," said Ver- non, curiously. "Pray where did you hear this story?"

"In Raymond, while you were talking in the courthouse."

"My talking in the courthouse, alone, should have sufficed to prove my profession."

"Yes, it would; and it did, at first; but there was a d—d plausible story told me about the matter, which made me throw it all up as so much gammon."

"And who took so much interest in me, and so much pains to lead you astray in this matter, Mr. Horsey? Can you remem- ber?"

The actor, without hesitation, gave full details.of the confe- rence with Hawkins and Saxon in the village of Raymond, nar- rated such portions of the dialogue as had special reference to theatricals and his companion's probable connection with them, and from the succinctness of his statements, and the clearness with which he repeated the several parts taken by the two, he soon convinced Vernon that there must have been a sinister purpose in the minds of the men who made such seemingly gratuitous misstatements. The name of Hawkins strengthened this conviction

"Hawkins! Hawkins! That was the name of the man whom the governor arrested."

"The same," replied Horsey. "He's a strange sort of suspicious chap. Everybody thinks there's something wrong about him; but they can't tell what. He gambles, they all know; but he's so cunning, they can find nothing worse against him; though I've no doubt they're right in thinking him a great rascal."

"Indeed! and can it be that you value your character so little as to consort with a fellow whom you think a rascal?"

"Ah, Harry, there you have me. But, truth to speak, a poor devil like myself whom one set snarls at, and the other laughs at, is devilish well satisfied to get a companion who will do neither, without being particularly anxious to know whether he's as good a man as he should be, or even as he appears. Besides, let me tell you, Hawkins is a smart fellow. He has Shakspere at his fingers' ends, and I've seen him throw that into his face, while he's been going through a part of Iago, which would send a shiver through pit and gallery at a glance."

"Enough; these men have lied to you, Mr. Horsey, at least so far as I have been concerned. They have, I gather from your account of it, used you as a spy upon me."

"The devil you say?"

"Think over the matter yourself, my friend, and you can not escape this conviction. They have flattered your ruling passion, and have gleaned from you all the knowledge of me and my movements which might have been in your possession. Fortunately, you knew nothing, and could reveal nothing, nothing at least of very serious importance. Whether anything worse will grow out of it than this wild-goose chase upon which they have sent you, it is impossible now to say. It will be important, however, that we should both be cautious in our future progress."

"Spoken like a book, Harry. But why the d—l should these fellows want to know your movements—heh? So you *have* secrets, Harry—there is a mystery—there—"

"Professional and personal, purely, Mr. Horsey, and when I tell you this much, I trust, I secure myself against further inquiry. To convince you, however, that I regard you with interest and favor, I make free to counsel you to return to your friends and family. I do not believe this story of theatrical establishments at Benton and other places. The country is unfit for, and unable to support them. A circus, now, would be more reasonable; a place for ground and lofty tumbling; but, seriously, I look upon the dramatic art as utterly foreign to such regions as the Yazoo. There is, as yet no settled pop ulation. The country is uncleared, and thoroughly wild; set-tled by squatters chiefly — without means, tastes, education. or sensibility; rude, rough people; a people peculiarly fitted for the conquest of savages and savage lands, but utterly incapable of appreciating an art so exquisite and intellectual as that of the legitimate drama. Go back, and if it be your resolute de-termination to seek for fame in the prosecution of your present purpose — which I would not counsel — seek it, then, where only it is to be found. Go to the large cities — go to the largest. Where the ability exists to pay best, there will always the best talent assemble — there will the true standards of critical judg-ment be formed and rival powers will soon reduce each other to their just level, until which there can be no certain reputation. There is something very puny in the judgment of small commu-nities; and something very contemptible in being a little lion in a little plain. Go to the ring where all the challengers assemble, and strike the shield of the most insolent and bold. When you have done this, you will find your level, and what is of more importance to you still, you will have justly arrived at a knowledge of your own strength. Till then, you walk in vapor, and the stars which shine above you are far or near, according to the wind and the weather, your own caprice of mood, or the caprice of feeling and judgment of those with whom you mingle. Understand me, Mr. Horsey, I do not counsel you by what I have said, to pursue the stage. Far from it. I believe the glories of the profession to be very un-certain, and its golden rewards, half the time, to be visionary; besides, it is attended by a thousand defeats and humiliations which are gall and wormwood to the independent spirit. On this head, you know best what you will do, and to your calm, common sense reflection, I am willing to leave it. But if you are resolved to be an actor, then it is my advice that you break ground where the audience is large, and where the competitors are many; where you will be compelled to take pains to preserve rank and respectability, and where no petty management or petty clique can prevent your efforts, or do injustice to your performance. Go to the great city, if you must act, and throw yourself upon the waters. Remember the noble chorus in your own favorite play :—

> " 'A kingdom for a stage, princes to act,
> And monarchs to behold the swelling scene,
> Then should the warlike Harry, *like himself,*
> Assume the port of Mars —'

It is only, you perceive, where the field is large — commensurate to the greatness of the actor — that he can be *like himself*—that he can do justice to himself, or feel that ambitious spurring of the soul which is conscious always of her true occasions."

CHAPTER XIV.

RIFLE PRACTICE — WRONG CUSTOMER — ADDITION TO THE DRAMATIS PERSONÆ.

"You see this chase is hotly followed, friends."—KING HENRY V.

WE arrest the further dialogue which took place between the two before their separation. Horsey was gratified at the interest which Vernon seemed to take in his fortunes, for the simple but dignified manners of the young lawyer had impressed him with a respectful deference, which had the effect, not unfrequently, of restraining his exuberance of character, and compelling him to meditate awhile before speaking; a practice exceedingly novel to him, and one which kept him from sundry outbreaks of folly while they were in company together. He listened with unaccustomed patience to the exhortations of Vernon, and though he had not the courage to forbear the small game which he was even then pecking at, he acknowledged the generally beneficial tenor of the advice given him. He was not willing to believe that the forest world in which he was about to penetrate was unsusceptible of present dramatic improvement, and still less was he willing to tolerate the suspicion, which his companion threw out, that the story of Tilton's theatrical establishment at Benton was a falsehood — a hoax invented for the simple purpose of securing him as an instrument in the prosecution of some ulterior purpose as yet unaccountable to either party. His heart was set upon obtaining the plaudits of the Bentonians, and his ears already rang prospectively with their clapping and huzzas. These, he thought, would not be amiss, even though at some future period, he struck at the higher game of the great metropolis. Small triumphs are the forerunners of great ones; and he was one of those who thought it just as well to accept the wreath of myrtle, if the more enduring laurel could not be so easily procured. With this philosophy he was the more readily reconciled to a separation from the companion, in conjunction with whom, until the present hour, he fancied he was about to enter the green and verdurous fields of an actor's immortality. He had many regretful quotations to utter; many protestations of fidelity and friendship.

"And should you want help, Harry," he cried out as they rode asunder, "should you get into any spree and want a backer to see you safe, give me a sign, a signal — let me have the cue — and by the ghost of Garrick, I will need no prompter to tell me what my part should be in the business. I will be at your side in the twinkling of an eye, and they shall be Turks and Trojans of heavy metal, indeed — Syracusans of stamp and substance — who will hold their ground long before us twain — my Pythias and myself."

Long and heartily did the adhesive actor wring the hand of his companion, to whom, though not an ascetic, the scenic exuberance of his friend had become almost an annoyance; and he found it a relief to escape from that excruciating degree of affection to which he felt unable to make more than a very partial return. His escape was at length effected, though Horsey, like Prior's thief:—

"Now fitted the halter, now traversed the cart,
And often took leave, but seemed loath to depart."

It will somewhat confirm the truth of the assurances of sorrow which he expressed at parting with his friend, to say, that, for full twenty minutes after leaving him, he uttered no single quotation, unless we may except the fragment of a speech made to his horse, the renewal of whose irregular motion had revived all the peculiar sensibility of old sores made the day previous.

"Ah, Bowline, Bowline! Shakspere almost gave me warning against thee in particular; certainly I have the 'rubbers,' though I did not expect them. If you go on at this rate, you limping d—l, Romeo's quarters will be in no condition to climb balconies, or do the necessary action of a lover. I am parched and peeled, hip and thigh, literally scalded, as tender as a steamed potato, and as *raw* as a thoroughly done one. Well, well, it is to be expected. One should not complain where the end promises so much. These, I suppose, are the first pains which a man is expected to take in getting on in the world — the pains of immortality, the condition of greatness — a suffering in the flesh for the ambitious workings of the spirit, which should teach a man, among other lessons, to value the glory, when won, which he purchases at so much cost. Well, it is but a skin-deep suffering, after all, and there is some consolation in knowing, you limping rascal, that I can make you share it. My spurring shall equal your scalding, or there never yet went two words to a bargain."

While the actor communed after this manner with his uneasy steed, Harry Vernon, better mounted, was making his forward way with a speed rather greater than his wont, as it was his object to make up for the time lost in waiting upon Horsey's operations at the hut of Yarbers, and, subsequently, in that which had been consumed in their parting. He had ridden probably an hour after that event, and the motion of his horse had been suffered to relax into that ordinary walking trot to which most horses on long travel naturally incline. The thoughts of the rider, busied with other subjects, were now abstracted from the movements of his steed, and he was gradua'ly becoming indifferent to, and unobservant of, surrounding objects, when he was brought to his senses by the sudden and fast trampling of a horse's feet behind him.

Looking round, what was his surprise to behold Edward

Mabry, the lover of Mary Stinson, in the person of his pursuer Vernon drew up and awaited him — readily guessing the purpose of his pursuit, and really glad that Horsey had taken another course, and got so greatly the start of one whose desperate hostility was apparent in every glance of his eye, and in every motion of his malignant and now wretched countenance. The tokens of the combat of the preceding night were prominently offensive. His eyes were so swollen that the orbs were barely perceptible, and the sight must have been barely sufficient to enable him to ride. This condition of his face made . the rage which appeared its leading expression look monstrous and fiendish. His lips were tremulous though closed, the veins upon his forehead tensely corded ; and the skin around, affected by the injuries done to his eyes, had assumed in spots, a dark, dirty green color, which added to the general hideousness of his present aspect. He was armed with a rifle, which, perhaps, in the present situation of his eyes, would be found far less formidable than usual.

Glaring upon Vernon with an expression of hostility which almost left it doubtful in our hero's mind if he himself were not also the object of his pursuit, he demanded to know what had become of his companion. His words were few and passionate, and the disrespectful manner in which he spoke, and the brutal epithets which he applied at the same time to the person for whom he inquired, had the effect of producing a certain degree of irritation in the mind of Vernon, which kept his answer in suspense. The youth repeated his demand in a style of insolence more offensive than before.

"I have no desire to quarrel with you," said Vernon, "but still less am I disposed to satisfy the demands of any one who makes them disrespectfully. I will not answer your question. I will tell you nothing about Mr. Horsey or his movements."

"Ha! then you take his place. You shall answer for him yourself," cried the other, dropping his reins and grasping his rifle in both hands. The instinctive and natural movement of Vernon was to close with him at once, and thus defeat the contemplated employment of the deadly weapon with which he threatened him. He wheeled his horse instantly beside that of the assailant, and his left hand grasped the weapon also.

"What mean you, madman? What would you do?' demanded Vernon, sternly. "But that I pity you, your movement this instant would have prompted me to shoot you down
like a dog. If you are angry with Mr. Horsey, that is no business of mine. I am not answerable for his conduct nor his absence."

"Then tell me where he is," replied the other hoarsely, "or
stand in his shoes."

"Neither, sir. I will give you no assistance in your folly."

A scuffle followed this reply. Mabry strove to back his horse
in order that he might employ his rifle. Such at least seemed
his object to Vernon, whose efforts were directed to defeat this
purpose; and suffering the other to recede, he addressed all his
strength to obtaining possession of the weapon, which Mabry,
in the sudden backward movement of his horse, was compelled
to yield up, or suffer himself to be drawn with it between the
two animals. Furious at this disadvantage he leaped to the
ground and drawing a bowie knife, rushed forward. But a few
paces divided them, and the rapidity of his assailant's movement
was such that Vernon felt he could neither take aim, nor prepare
the weapon in time to anticipate his attack. With this conviction he put spurs to his horse and drew him up only after he
had put a space of fifty yards between them.

"Advance upon me a second time, young man, and I shoot
you without scruple. You are a madman to act in this manner
What have I done to you? Of what do you complain? Do
you think I will answer your questions, or the questions of anybody, who does not speak respectfully? Do you suppose I will
assist in guiding you to the commission of murder? You are
mistaken in me no less than in yourself. In a fair struggle.
were I so disposed, I should put you down as effectually as
you were put down last night; and were it not that I should
derive but little satisfaction from such a victory, your insolent
language might have provoked me to have done so before this.
Think a little before you move farther in this business. By
this time the person you seek is far beyond your reach; and as
for me, you gain nothing, I assure you, by annoying me. I will
return you your rifle if you will promise me that you will not
use it."

"I will make no promise," replied the other, leaping again upon his steed, "we shall soon be at closer quarters."

And with these words, with a fury even more blind than his hurt vision, the madman was preparing to urge his horse forward upon the speaker, heedless of warning, and in utter defiance of the lifted rifle.

"I warn you again — once, twice, thrice, I warn you," were the slow, deliberate tones of Vernon's voice, as, dropping the rifle in his left hand, he lifted the ranging sights before his eye, "approach me, Mr. Mabry, with bared weapon, and I will certainly shoot you."

"I defy you, I dare you. Shoot, and be d——d! I fear you not," said the fellow, as he put spurs to his horse.

"Hold!" cried the voice of one who darted before his path, emerging into the main road from a little Indian trail that crossed it at nearly equal distances between the contending parties. The interruption was seasonable enough. Vernon had already cocked the rifle, and the approach, by ten steps more, of his furious assailant, would have had the effect of drawing his fire. The entrance of the third personage relieved him from a dreadful necessity.

"Hold, you, Ned Mabry, you meal-headed fellow! What the deuce is it you're a-doing?"

The abrupt salutation arrested the rash onset of the youth, and probably saved his life. The stranger was a tall backwoodsman, fully six feet in height, and solid and massive like a tower. He rode a coal-black horse of proportions and strength of corresponding greatness with his own — a keen, fire-eyed animal, broad-chested, strongly quartered, slim in fetlock, small in hoof, long-necked, narrow-headed, and with a mane, which, though plaited and divided on either side, seemed scarcely less copious than that in the full possession of the one. The person of his rider was no less symmetrical and erect than it was large and powerful. His cheeks were of a fine sanguine hue, his eyes bright, blue, and lively, denoting good-nature, with an arch, lurking humor, that perhaps indicated a fondness for his jest in defiance of the broken bones which are sometimes apt to follow it. His nose was finely Roman, and his forehead though neither broad nor high, was yet full, suitably large, and contributed to that general expression of character, rather than talents, which belonged to his other features. He looked earnestly for a few minutes upon Vernon while addressing Mabry, to whom he spoke in the familiar language of an old acquaintance.

"Well, now you're a pretty lark to serve me in this way, Ned Mabry. Didn't you promise me you wouldn't do anything more with this business. Didn't you say you'd let the stranger get off, and say no more about it; and here, only two hours after, I find you, like a cursed maw-mouth that grows blind when he sees a worm wriggle, here you're mad after the bait though there's a hook in it. Don't you see the rifle — you a'n't bullet-proof, I reckon?"

"It's my own rifle, Walter," said the assailant, sullenly.

"The d—l it is!" cried the other with a laugh; "then it's a sign I haven't come a minute too soon. You've got another warning of the truth I told you. Look you, stranger," turning to Vernon, to whom the sudden arrival of a third person, who seemed an associate of his enemy, only cautioned to greater watchfulness; "look you, stranger, you mustn't take it hard that this mad fellow set upon you, seeing you've took his sweetheart from him, and put his two eyes in double-mourning. It's mighty hard to lose one's gal and get a beating all in the same night, and I reckon there's a mighty few of us that wouldn't be just as mad as Ned Mabry after it."

"But I've done neither," said Vernon; "I've neither beaten him, nor taken his sweetheart from him. I have done him no sort of injury, intentional or otherwise; and he has no more excuse to assail me than he has to assail the man in the moon."

"How! how the d—l's this, Ned? Didn't you tell me?"

"Not this one — the other — the man that was travelling with him."

"The splinters! and so you set upon the wrong man. Well, I say, that's being owl-blind, stone-blind, horse-blind; blind of three eyes, without even a smeller to go by. What the devil made you trouble him?"

This question was soon answered, and the cause of difference explained. The good-natured stranger proceeded to patch up the affair, and, if possible, reconcile the parties. On Vernon's side this was no great difficulty. The other, foiled on every hand, baffled so far in the pursuit of one who had humbled him so successfully, and suffering from his bruises of body no less than those of mind, was just in that state of stupid doggedness when conciliation was almost as much thrown away upon him as argument and explanation. More was done by the sheer influence of the stranger's wish, than by his reasoning. The rustic lover seemed to recognise in Wat or Walter Rawlins—for such was the name of the last-comer—a superior, before whom he stood irresolute and dependent. He confirmed the promise made in his behalf, by the latter, to Vernon, that he would offer him no farther injury or insult; and, at his solicitation, he returned the rifle to Mabry, though not until he had pushed the flint from the teeth of the cock, thus depriving him of the power of doing any immediate harm with the instrument, unless he went better provided than usual. He had performed this movement with so little effort, and so much adroitness, while the lock of the gun lay beneath his right hand, and on the opposite side of his horse to that where the other parties stood, that he had escaped observation; and, satisfied with the possession of his weapon, Mabry gave no glance to the condition in which it was returned to him.

"And now, Ned Mabry, go you home, and be quiet," said his companion. "You promised me before to do nothing in this business, and it's a dead weight on your credit now that you didn't keep your word. You ain't in any condition now to look up your enemies. With them eyes you could not see to hit a squirrel, though he sat on a bare stump grinning at you with all his grinders; and how should you look, going after a fellow who's got his own peepers wide awake. Go back, I say, and keep quiet till you see me again. As for this business of Yarbers, himself," continued the pacificator, drawing his companion away to some little distance from the place where Vernon stood, and lowering his voice to a whisper—"say nothing till you see me. There's something strange about it, and we've got some mighty strange neighbors. Don't whisper it to saint or sinner till we can tell whether it's a safe person that's to hear it, and this there's no telling jist at this time, when the whole country is in a real topsy-turvy, and strange men come about us hearing

what they can, and telling nothing in return. There's nothing
to do but to keep quiet, as I tell you, and out of harm's way.
I won't be gone longer than a week; in the meantime, get your
eyes open if you can, and keep 'em so. I'll keep on a while
with this stranger, and see what I can worm out of him. He
don't look and behave like a man who was one of Yarbers's
kidney, and I've a sort o' notion you're quite wrong in your
guess that they're in one and the same business. I'll worm it
out of him in no time, I reckon. If he's got the cunning of a
rogue, I've got cunning enough to see how deep it goes; and,
if he ain't a rogue, why, then, there will be one more honest
man found to help the rest."

Much more was said ere they separated, though the conference
occupied but little time. Vernon, meanwhile, bade them a cour-
teous "good-day," and was about to set forward, when the voice
of Rawlins arrested him.

"Stay a bit, stranger, if so be you like company. I'm driving on in the same track with you for a few miles farther, at
least; and, if you're like myself, you'll agree that it's no bad
thing to have somebody at your elbow, if it's only to answer
questions. When a man's by himself, he's apt to think strange
things; and the devil's more apt to be on the lookout for a single traveller than when they go in pairs to strengthen each other.
I am a ra'al joker when the humor suits, and I can sing, too,
when the weather ain't against it, and the frogs don't rise in the
throat. So you see—"

"Say no more," said Vernon; "it will please me to have
your company."

"Spoken like a man, and I'll be with you after a word more
with this unbroken colt. Now, Ned Mabry, you promise me to
give over the chase of this fellow?"

Such was the promise which Rawlins exacted from his companion, ere they separated—a promise reluctantly given, and
badly kept; since he had scarce reached the cross-roads in returning, ere his rage resumed full sway over him, and he struck
into the path which Horsey had taken, giving full rein to his
horse, in the hope to make up for that loss of time in the pursuit which had been occasioned by the events of the previous
hour. Vernon was joined by Rawlins, and in a few moments,

on the place which they had just occupied, stood the outlaw Saxon, who emerged from the woods on one hand, and was immediately after joined by a comrade namad Jones, who came to the spot from an opposite quarter.

"I would give something to know what Mabry and Rawlins had to talk about so long in secret," said Saxon. "Could you make out nothing?"

"Not a syllable," said Jones. "His coming was untimely."

"Yes; but for that we should have lost one who may become an enemy. Yarbers, certainly, would have been the gainer; and we should have had good reason for tying the arms of this fellow Vernon behind him. This, however, we **must do before** long." .

"**We must use Judge Nawls for that business, I reckon.**"

"Ay, none better," said Saxon; "but do you go ahead, and keep on the haunches of these fellows. Rawlins, I suppose, is on his way to the old methodist quarter. He and Vernon know each other for the first time, and they will probably separate at Brother Badger's turn-out. Do not lose him from sight. I will join you before midnight."

8

CHAPTER XV.

THE BEAGLES IN FULL CRY — PISTOL-PRACTICE — AN ADVEN TURE — A RESCUE, AND BLOODSHED.

'The noyse thereof cald forth that straunger knight,
To weet what dreadfull thing was there in hond ;
Where whenas two brave knights in bloody fight,
With deadly rancour he enraunged fond,
His sunbroad shield about his wrest he bond,
And shining blade unsheathed."—Spenser.

VERNON rode on with his new companion, Rawlins — whom he soon discovered to be quite a sociable, good-humored fellow — with a speed which was intended to make up for lost time. It was his desire to reach and cross the ferry over the Chitta-Loosa before sunset, in order that he might find lodgings on the opposite side at a conveniently early hour. But this purpose, when expressed, was discouraged by his companion.

" It will be quite dark before you can get across the ferry — which is more a ferry and a half than a ferry ; mighty bad crossing, and a strange up and down, in and out, turning and twisting contrivance as ever you did see — and then, when you're across, it's a chance if you find any place to stay at, that can be called a place at all, under seven or eight miles. But if you'll go with me to old Billy Badger's to-night — he's only two miles from the ferry — you can take an early start in the morning, and have a whole day before you. Billy Badger's a crumpy, stiff sort of a person — a raal, true-believing methodist, that preaches himself, when the parson don't come, and, to my way of thinking, makes a deuced sight the best prayer of any among them. He's rather strange in his ways, to be sure, but you'll be heartily welcome. He'll give you a good supper, but you must swallow the long grace that goes before it ; and, if one happens to be mighty hungry, it's a great trying of the patience. I've been a-bothered by it more than once before, but it's no use. Nothing can stop him when he once begins; and I do think if the house was a-fire, he'd sooner let it burn awhile than cut the prayer off in the middle. Now, I'm used to it myself, and don't mind it so much; but I think it only right, when I ax a man to another's house, that I should tell him what he's to look for."

"A good rule," said Vernon; "and without saying whether I will go with you or not, let me know whether Mr. Badger is in the habit of receiving company."

"Sure he is; he has 'em at all times and of all characters. Why, his house is something of a thoroughfare, you see; being so near the ferry, and folks a-travelling jist like you, and coming up late in the day, are mighty apt to go to old Billy's to spend the night."

"But that must give him a great deal of trouble, if he keeps no public house."

"Not a bit, or if it does, he don't mind it in consideration of the good company, and somebody to talk to. Though he's a gruff and grumpy sort of person, he's mighty fond of a confabulation, and so long as you'll listen, and even if you wont listen, he'll still talk on, exhorting, as it were, and mighty airnest. When he once gits hold of the flesh and the devil, there's no telling how long he'll hold on. It's no trifle that'll make him let go; and you'll see the blood git up into his face, and the veins grow big on his forehead, and the foam will come out and stand in his mouth-corners long before he'll think you've had enough. He never asks how you like the thing, for he always concludes that he knows best what's good for everybody; and as for disagreeing with him, when once you set eyes on him, you'll see for yourself that that's out of the question. I tell you, sir, Mr. Vernon, he looks like all the Laws and the Prophets; and he speaks as if he stood on a high place, and we were all put below to listen to him."

"A stern old man—a very judge in Israel—from your description."

"The very thing, Mr. Vernon; but then he's really kind as any man alive, though, for that matter, he hain't the knack of

showing it kindly. He'll help you up from the road with the
look of the same fellow that knocked you down; and bind up
your wounds with as sour a face all the while, as if his own
bowie-knife had made them. He'll talk to you as if he thought
you a rogue, just at the very time when he's lending you a cool
hundred; and when he's helping you to the best on his table,
he'll be grumbling something about the indulgences of the flesh,
and the profligacies of appetite, and all that sort of thing; so,
unless you set out to find a bundle of contradictions in everything he does and says, there's no telling how to take him."

"I've met with such a character before," said Vernon; "it
is neither unusual nor unnatural, and only indicates a predomi-
nating self-esteem, that asserts its superiority by eccentricities
of thought and manner. The eccentricities of men arise, mostly,
from an undue estimate of their own importance, which flatters
itself by the surprises it continually effects, by means of novelty
and strangeness, in the minds of the observers. So long as
these eccentricities hurt nobody, people are content to laugh or
wonder at them; when they exceed this limit, the owner ceases
to be a fool, and is locked up as a madman. Has this old gentleman a family."

"He has a son who is nothing like him—a sly, cautious fellow, that I don't know whether to like or dislike—he's neither
one thing nor t'other, and, to speak a truth, one reason against
my liking him may be that he don't seem to like me."

"A good and sufficient reason. There are some love-verses
which maintain this philosophy in strong and proper language:—

> "'What care I how fair she be,
> If she be not fair for me.'

Has the old gentleman no other family?"

"Yes," replied the other with a hesitating tone. "He's got
a niece—a mighty fine girl, named Rachel, out of the Scrip
tures; the young man his son is named out of the Scriptures,
too—they call him Gideon—though, I'm thinking that his
name is all that he ever got out of the Holy Book, or ever will
get. There's something wrong about him, I reckon."

"But Rachel, there nothing wrong about her—you don't
dislike Rachel, do you, Mr. Rawlins? for, if you do, I shall
begin to wonder why it is you visit the family."

" Ah, Mr. Vernon, you're a keen one. You must be a lawyer,
I'm thinking. But you say right, there's nothing wrong about
Rachel, and if the truth is to be told, I may as well tell it at once
—I do like Rachel. I think—though I don't count her so pretty
as some that I've seen and could mention—I think she is about
the finest and best. She's so sweet-tempered, and so modest
and good; and then, she has a great deal more sense, and a
power of l'arning, more than I ever expect to cram into this
bigger noddle of mine. I confess to you, Mr. Vernon, I do like
Rachel."

The frankness of the rustic lover, had already placed the
parties on the most friendly footing. His confession increased
the respect which the lawyer had begun to entertain for him.
He replied playfully :—

" And reasoning, Mr. Rawlins, from what you have said of
Gideon, I presume, one of your best arguments for liking Rachel
is found in her liking you. Is it not so ?—you love each other."

There is, perhaps, nothing so likely to win the heart of a
young lover, as to seek his confidence on the subject nearest to
his affections. The interest we betray in his passion saves him
from the fear of ridicule—an always prevalent fear with the
tribe of passionates ;—and that sinking fullness of heart which
distinguishes the lover, must find some friendly bosom into
which to pour its hopes, its fears, its tumultuous and joyous ex-
pectancies.

The words of Vernon unsealed the fountain, and took the
stone from its lips. After that, Rawlins had no further con-
cealments. He grasped the hand of his companion, and, warning him the while to secrecy—a caution which was rather insisted upon by the respect which he had for the maiden, than
because of any desire on his own part to maintain, as a secret,
a fact which was so full to him of triumph as well as joy—he
told him that he had been successful in persuading Rachel to
regard him as the properest man in the country. His court-
ship, from the beginning, underwent development in all its
details, with a more circumstantial distinctness than even that
of Othello, though it did not appear that the affections of Rachel
were secured for her lover through a like medium. The judgment of Rawlins deferred to that of the maiden of his heart.

He studiously insisted upon her mental superiority, and spoke in the becoming language of that humility which acknowledges the favor of fortune in his conquests, and assumes no share of the merit to himself.

"I will go with you to-night, Mr. Rawlins, and see this lady."

"Do, that's a friend, Mr. Vernon; it does me good when a man of sense and education talks with Rachel. She's mighty sweet-spoken and smart; has a whole closet-full of books; and sends to Natchy for more whenever she can get a chance. Now, other men would much rather have a wife to work and mend for them, and would count it mighty idle to see 'em poking over books; but I'm not that sort of man. I'd want my wife to talk respectably, jist the same as if she lived in a big city like Or- leans; for if a man's poor as Job's turkey to-day, it's no reason he should be poor to-morrow. In this country, a man may git rich in double quick time, if he's only constant and sober to his business; and if the Lord spares me, Mr. Vernon. I'm bent on making my children men of substance and education. If I had no l'arning myself—and, like most of our people, seven months time would cover every hour of schooling I ever had,—I know the good of l'arning, and my children will have enough to do them good, whether I live or die, if so be their mother's able to give it them; and I'd sooner have my wife teaching her chil- dren to read and write, than darning stockings, or mending breeches, or doing any of that sort of business, which a nigger girl can do that never had any education at all."

It amused Vernon to hear his companion counting his chickens with so much complacency, and making his arrangements how to train them, even before they were hatched. He smiled with an expression of that humor upon his countenance which formed no small portion of his character.

"Of course, Mr. Rawlins, you have consulted with Rachel on this subject; you have told her your plans at length."

"To be sure I have Do you think I'd keep such a matter from her? No, no, sir, as God's my judge there ain't anything in my bosom that I've kept from her ears, since that moment when she said 'yes' to my asking. It was only last week—I go to see her about once a-week, Mr. Vernon—it was only last week I tried to get her to say, if she had a son, which she would like best to have him, a lawyer or a doctor; and it was a great worry to me to get her to talk about the matter at all, and what she did say was as much as to say, 'Have your own way about it,' for it came to as little. Now, Mr. Vernon, I know that there's nothing so troublesome in families as a difference between man and wife about these things, and I wanted to put the matter out of all danger of dispute. It was strange to me that Rachel, who can talk so well about most matters, and give me so much good advice when I want it, shouldn't be willing to tell me her real notions."

"Perhaps she thought there was time enough a year or two hence for the consideration of the subject. You, on the other hand, I perceive, are for taking time by the forelock. You prefer being quick to being slow. She, too, might have been thinking of girl-children, only; who, of course, can neither be doctors nor lawyers."

"Well, that's true, there may be something in that, Mr. Vernon, but then, again, you know it's an even chance that we should have boys as well as girls. I was going to tell her that, but she broke off suddenly, because she thought she heard the old man calling her from the house."

The unsophisticated lover impressed Vernon favorably as regarded both himself and mistress, by the naturalness with which he detailed his own secret thoughts and desires, and the manners of the damsel. That Rachel was more thoughtful than her lover, and quite as good a tactician, he had no sort of doubt from the chapter of developments which had been made by the former. How long Rawlins would have gone on in a narrative which was too pleasing to his heart and fancies to suffer the obtrusion of other thoughts and objects on his mind, it would be difficult to say. He was checked by an abrupt inquiry of Vernon, and brought back to the more earthly objects of humanity, with some slowness and a little reluctance.

"Hear you those dogs? there are several beagles—do you hunt much in this neighborhood, Mr. Rawlins?"

"Beagles! I don't hear any, Mr. Vernon."

"I have heard them for the last twenty minutes; but the truth is, Mr. Rawlins, when a man's in love he hears nothing and sees little that does not concern his mistress. This is

your condition. For the last half hour we have talked of noth
ing else, and you have heard nothing that did not call for an
answer about *her*. Now I have heard the baying of these beagles beside and before us, as if scattered, and crossing on false
scents. Who keeps a pack about here?"

"A pack of beagles! I don't think there's such a thing in
the county, Mr. Vernon. There's one or two here and there in
different places—there's some two or three I know of, but no
more. John Herne—he's something of a hunter, and has several dogs, but only one hound, and that's but a poor affair.
Macartney, the Scotchman, that lives on the edge of Atala, he
has one, but he don't hunt. Ned Mabry, the chap that would
have mauled you this morning, if you had let him, he has two,
and both of them fine pups, but he's not the man to think of
deer-hunting to-day. Besides him, I can't call to mind another
man in our neighborhood that keeps a beagle."

"That is strange, for I have certainly heard several at different points of the compass within this hour. Hark! Hear
you not now?"

"Yes, that's a beagle, but it sounds mighty faint, and may
be, after all, from a tongue that you never hear close, and the
dog that own's it ain't so easy to be seen. You know there's a
story in these parts of a ghost-dog that haunts the woods about
the Big Black; they call him the white dog of Chitta-Loosa,
and old folks tell strange things about him; how he let his master be murdered, and now has nothing to do but to run through
the woods constantly looking after him. He is said to keep in
the swamp of the Big Black, and you hear him always just as
evening is coming on, as if he was calling to his master, and
was making moan that another night was near at hand, and he
hadn't yet found him. There's a-many sounds in these woods,
and sights too, I've heard them tell of, that you'll hear without
knowing where they come from, or who they belong to. People about here don't mind them much now, since they've got a
little used to them; but when I first came on the Big Black, it
made my heart beat mighty quick, I tell you, and made me
clap long spurs to my horse, to hear them; and even now, I
catch myself saying my prayers, without knowing when I begin, to find myself belated on the edge of the swamp, nobody

with me, and on a sudden hear a whisper close at my elbow, and may be a laugh and a clapping of the hands behind me."

"But why should you think this anything more than ordinary? This whispering, and laughing, and clapping—nay, this baying of dogs—may all be the work of men."

"No men, no men, Mr. Vernon!—I'm a man myself, and can answer that. I'm a stout man, sound in wind and limb, six feet in stocking foot, and able to swing a cotton bag, and that's a-much for anybody to do. Besides, I'm not afraid of any fellow that ever I saw yet, that had no better help than flesh and blood, broad shoulders, and solid muscle, can give him; and when I've turned and challenged them that made these noises, and put into the swamps after them—and I've a keen nose, and a quick eye among the bushes, Mr. Vernon—and after all could find nothing to lay a finger on, why, then it was time to think of saying one's prayers, and using one's spurs. Now, don't you go to think from what I'm saying that I'm easily frightened with ghosts and images. I'm frightened at nothing I can see and feel; but when a body can neither see nor feel—when eyes and hands fail, what's to be done? Am I to stand then, waiting what's to come? No, no, I'm clear for clean heels without waiting for orders. I asked Rachel if it was right for me to run in such cases, and she clearly agreed it was. Well, when our counts come to the same ending, there's nothing more to be said about it, and run's the word for me. A ghost that I can see, or a man that I can feel, will never make me stir my ankles faster than I choose; but I don't think it's any shame to use one's trotters when he can make no use of his other limbs."

"Give your horse a light spur now, Mr. Rawlins," said Vernon, gravely, "and let us ride on a little faster. These beagles seem to increase in number, and I can distinguish the baying of no less than three from several quarters. If there be so few in the county as you assert, then are these noises the more mysterious, and they must have some object Now, as I am one of those who will not easily believe in your white dog of the Chitta-Loosa, or in the ghost of a dog at all, I am persuaded that what we hear are the voices of real flesh and blood beings,

8*

whether of hounds or men. If they are the voices of men, they
imitate well, and must have some leading object for acquiring
the practice; if they are those of beagles, then may we get a
glimpse of a close chase, and, perhaps, join in a pursuit, which
I am very fond of. A pistol-bullet may bring down a deer at
a small distance, and I have known a man get a shot near
enough to enable him to do business with a pistol. I will have
mine in readiness."

"I will not fail you, Mr. Vernon," said the other, in suppressed accents, and bringing his horse more closely to the side
of his companion. "It's jist as well to have your pistols ready
if we are to seek for these hounds you speak of, for, to tell you
a truth, it has been for a long time my notion that there were
men at the bottom of some of these noises of dogs; not that there
are not other noises of the woods that could never have been
made by any man—that I'll swear for—and if you know'd
half as much of our country and the swamps as I do, you'd be
for thinking like myself. I could tell you of the strangest
things—"

"Not now ! not now !" exclaimed Vernon, impatiently, "but
get your pistols out, my good fellow ;. it may be a word and a
blow with us. I hear one sound responding to another, and the
last did not seem more than a short hundred yards distant, in
that thick branch. Let us ride apart; a rifle's sight could cover
us both."

Speaking thus, Vernon spurred his horse forward in a smart
canter, while Rawlins, obeying his suggestion, prepared his
weapons, and followed him at a horse's length behind. · They had
scarcely increased their motion, when a sudden clamor reached
their ears in front; a hoarse summons, the voice of a man in
anger, mingled with lower tones, as if in expostulation. These
were followed by a shriek—a repeated shriek, and the accents
of a woman—of woman in distress ! This put a life into the
limbs, and a fire into the hearts of the two young men, which
gave them no time for reflection, and left them in no doubt as
to the course which they should take, and the duty which lay
before them.

"Lord God !" was the somewhat irreverent exclamation of
Rawlins, "Lord God ! Mr. Vernon, if it should be Rachel !"

"It is a woman, Mr. Rawlins!—follow me close if you be a man. This is no time to loiter."

"You won't find me backward, by the powers! I'm at you, and after you. There's no scare in Wat Rawlins at the push. Lord help us! I'm afeard it's Rachel. She loves to walk in the woods so, every afternoon. Git up, you lazy b—h, or I'll knife your quarters!"

The last speech, warm from the blood, and breaking out in defiance of all restraint, was addressed to his horse, which, in his anger, it will be seen that he made feminine. The animal, though fleet, and now doing his best, yet lacked the speed of Vernon's, and the distance, small at first, was increasing fast between them. The fear that another should do for the safety of his sweetheart that which he alone aimed to accomplish, was wormwood to his spirit; and his apostrophe to his steed was coupled with the driving and constant application of the spur, until the flanks of the generous animal soon grew red under the infliction. The shrieks were renewed—fast, sharp, imploring—terminating, at length, in a long, piercing scream, which grew feeble, at last, as if from exhaustion; and when it closed, the thrilling words of Vernon, as he looked behind, and cried to Rawlins to follow, sent a creeping chill of terror to the heart of the rustic.

"Push, push, or we shall be too late!"

"I'm here—I'm close! This d——d beast! I hope it ain't Rachel! Get on, you brute!—Everything stands in the way; the trees, and bushes, and I never saw the creature so dull before. Get up, you clodhopping beast, or I'll kill you, by all that's certain! I've always told Rachel about walking out so far, but she wouldn't mind me, and said there was no danger; but I knew there was danger. and I said so. But these women—they won't mind anything—they're so obstinate if they're a little smart; and so—d—n the b—h, she'll stop full short before long, and want to take a roll in the road."

There was no good reason to justify this last apprehension of the excited woodman. The animal was covering ground with a rapidity which might have done some credit to Turpin's mare. But a few seconds had passed since the first alarm, and nothing but the impatience and the special apprehensions which had seized him on a sudden, in regard to the woman who was dearest to his heart, could have so utterly confounded his consciousness and judgment on all other subjects.

To be passed and left behind by the young lawyer—the citizen—one of a class for whom the forest-born of our country are very apt to entertain a very wholesome contempt as respects the exercise of all those qualities which require personal strength and agility, and more especially, in the management of a horse—also added to his affliction; which, however, was not destined to endure long.

Vernon had already entered upon the scene of action. The roads crossed—a large area was formed by the contact of the two paths—and here the strife was in progress, and hence the clamor.

A single glance at the objects before him, gave Vernon a correct notion of the affair. A travelling carriage crossed the road, the horses being checked and held by a man whose muffled face, cap drawn over his eyes, coarse garments, rude manner, not to speak of the pistol in his grasp, at once declared him to be a ruffian and an assailant. An old man, the proprietor of the vehicle, whose white locks and bald head were uncovered and exposed, lay on the ground beneath the knee of another ruffian, while a third was busied in rifling the carriage of its contents. Two females, one a tall maiden of seventeen or thereabouts, the other a child of twelve, were on their knees to the villain who held the old man down, imploring, seemingly, for mercy; the younger of the two, clinging to the arm of the assailant, seeking with a childish pertinacity, and in utter ignorance of any danger to herself, to push him from his position.

The screams which had alarmed the travellers arose from these; and they were continued by the younger of the damsels long after the elder had deemed it—the first alarm being over—an idle mode of remedying the misfortune, for the cure of which she probably meditated other means. Perhaps there were other apprehensions of womanhood more dreadful to the pure heart, which made her fearful to offend the insolence of those to whom neither herself nor parent—for such was the old man beneath the grasp of the ruffian—could oppose any

powers of defence. Her efforts were those of prayer, expostu
lation and entreaty, until the approach of Vernon, whom she
first beheld, suggested new hopes of rescue; and then her
screams were joined to those of her younger sister, and gave a
new impulse to the movements of our hero and his companion
who followed close upon his heels.

There was but little time for reflection — none for hesitation,
and the mood and character of Vernon were such as to require
neither. To assail the assailants, to rescue the victims, was an
instinct that sent him the nearest way to work; and coming, as
he did, somewhat suddenly upon the robbers, he was able to
effect that which, in a state of greater preparation on their
part, it would have been fatal for him even to attempt.

Their own interest in the prize, and the clamors of the young
women, had kept them from hearing the tread of the approaching horsemen; and as they came into the cross-roads from the
opposite track, they were totally unseen until within thirty
yards of the party. It was then too late to take any of those
precautions by which nothing would have been more easy than
to have shot them down at their approach, without risking an
exchange of bullets.

As it was, a single bay of the beagle—their accustomed
signal—was the only warning which the more busy robbers
received from the companion who held the horses, and who
occupied, with them and the carriage, the upper part of the road.
The ruffian who bestrid the prostrate gentleman turned about
at the signal, only to receive the bullet of Vernon, unerringly
aimed at his head. He fell prostrate upon the body of the old
man, and his blood and brains covered his face and garments.
In the next moment, the robber in possession of the carriage
fired at Vernon, and was about to leap with a second pistol
upon him, when the appearance of Rawlins, who made his
entrée with a shout which might have done credit to the lungs
of Stentor, determined the assailant to trust his heels rather
than his weapon; and without giving a look to his comrade, he
darted into the opposite woods, leaving the carriage between
himself and his foes. He who held the horses, kept his ground
until Rawlins had approached him within a few paces, when
lifting his weapon with as deliberate an aim as the circum-

stances of his position would allow, he fired, but ineffectually
at the sturdy woodman.

Could the latter have seen the bitter, nay, venomous expression of face which the fellow gave him ere he shot, he would
have congratulated himself, indeed, that it was not Rachel who
had fallen into his hands.

Vernon was the first to pursue the escaping ruffians, but he
had scarcely entered the wood ere he felt himself growing
sick and faint; and then, for the first time, he found himself
wounded in the thigh. He returned to the scene of action, and
with difficulty alighted from his horse. The old man and his
daughters, whom he had rescued, came about him to acknowledge and thank him for his services; but exhaustion, from loss
of blood, now overcame him, and he sunk to the ground with a
dim consciousness while he was falling, that the old man was
the very person whom he sought — the very William Maitland
who had defrauded the bank and involved Carter, to the loss
of so many thousands.

But this impression soon gave place to another, and it seemed
to the swooning youth that the features of the man were at
once absorbed in those of a lovely virgin — such a vision as
had filled his dreaming fancy the night he slept at the hovel of
Mrs. Yarbers ;—a form of chiselled symmetry, and a face, of
the exquisite beauty of which, the soul, alone, could feel the
perfection and the charm, in those vague and spiritual imagin-
ings which come to the youthful heart when it first dreams of
love — which come to it but once, and is believed by it for ever

CHAPTER XVI.

THE FUGITIVE FATHER — THE DAUGHTER — EVENTS GRADUALLY
DEVELOP — GLIMPSES BEYOND

> "Why do you strive so — whither would you fly
> You can not wrest yourself away from care,
> You may from counsel; you may shift your place,
> But not your person; and another clime
> Makes you no other."   FLETCHER.

THE woodman who had continued the pursuit of the ruffians
without being at all apprized of the malicious aim of one of
them upon him, from which he had been so fortunate as to
escape, soon found his efforts unavailing to overtake them.
They had made their way into a canebrake immediately contiguous, in whose thick, fostering glooms and secret abodes,
they could easily defy and baffle the search of any hundred
men. Ignorant of the hurt of Vernon, whom he had seen
enter the forest in pursuit, like himself, he shook his hand in
anger at the sheltering recesses in which the robbers were lost
from sight, and returned toward the scene of action, with a
degree of composure, which seemed to regard the fatigue of his
horse as superior to all other considerations.

His astonishment and concern, when he discovered the insensible condition of his companion, was worthy of a much longer
acquaintance, and a more social and equal relationship than
had existed between them. A few moments sufficed to convince him that his friend was not dead, nor, perhaps, badly
injured; and a few more enabled him to kick the dead robber
with a quiet conviction that he could do no more hurt. The
features of the ruffian he inspected carefully; but if he had
any knowledge of them before, he kept the matter to himself,
and having emptied the pockets of all that they contained of

value, and possessed himself of the pistols with which the fellow had been armed, but which the true and prompt shot of
Vernon had prevented him from using, he left the carcass in
the highway, with probably some such motive as that of the
woodman when he kills a snake—namely, the start and momentary terror which such a spectacle will provoke in the
spectator.

This business was the work of a few moments only; and he
now addressed himself seriously to the task of assisting his
wounded companion, and directing the further movements of the
party, all the members of which were laboring under more or
less excitement and apprehension. The whole scene was over
in a few minutes, but the full pressure of its terrors and dangers
had not passed entirely away. The old gentleman, who had
been rescued, was even then busy in cleansing his face and
bosom, as well as he might, from the blood and brains of the
slain robber which had spurted over them. He was a fine-
looking man, of very venerable aspect; but there was an incertitude in his looks, and a tremulousness of limb in his movements, which seemed to the mind of the woodman strangely in
consistent with the fine, manly mould in which nature had cast
his frame. It was also apparent to our forester that there was
a fidgety uneasiness in his manner, which denoted apprehensions no less active at the moment of his rescue and seeming·
safety, than when he lay under the weapon of the robber. He
spoke confusedly, yet not with rapidity; checked and interrupted himself repeatedly; caught up his speech before he had
completed his sentences; corrected, or strove to correct his expression; and increased his confusion, as folks are very apt to
do, by anticipating it. His determination on little matters
seemed to undergo alteration quite as often as his speech; and
in all that he said and did, he exhibited to the countryman,
who was not entirely obtuse, that purposeless, imbecile character, which is conscious of much to be done, yet is capable of
nothing, and despairs even while it undertakes, and falters before fatigue.

Yet, so far as the ordinary circumstances are involved, which
produce fear in the minds of men, the stranger had shown himself hardy enough. It is true, he did not offer resistance to the

robbers, though armed; but this arose as well from the manner in which he had been surprised by them, as from a proper conviction that he could not hope to resist them with any chance of success; and might, by doing so, have provoked their ill-treatment of his daughters, for whose safety he had shown all the solicitude of a father. He had not betrayed so much alarm for his own safety, while actually beneath the body of his assailant, as he did now, speaking of the event to the sturdy woodman, by whose assistance, in part, his rescue had been achieved. Indeed, his timidity, uneasiness, and downcast looks while he spoke, surprised the latter quite as much as they vexed him; and his words were spoken with the view to reassuring the courage which he could not but think—and this too with some feelings of contempt—had been quite too much cast down by the strife through which it had just gone.

"There's no sort of danger now, old gentleman, while we're so strong around you. It won't be any two robbers of the Chitta-Loosa that'll venture to lay thumb and fingers on the nose of Wat Rawlins, and he with his eyes open. So, since you're safe now, and don't seem to have lost anything, take your seat in your wagon, while I help Vernon into the bottom of it. You must make some room for him, young lady, and don't be frightened at a little blood. It is good blood, and spilt in your own behalf, so you may look on it with a sort of pleasure, if you ain't too faint-hearted—which I don't think so much your case as that of the old gentleman. He's mighty uneasy now, though for what there's no telling. Why don't you mount, old gentleman, and put yourself in readiness?"

In some agitation, the stranger turned to his daughter, and a brief conversation was carried on between the two in whispers. The woodman remarked that the fine eye of the maiden was kindled, her cheek flushed, and he could hear her distinctly exclaim, at the conclusion of a long and very earnest sentence: "Do not—do not think of such a thing, dear father; common humanity, alone, were there no other reasons, should require this; now, it is the due—gratitude—"

The rest of the words were lost to the listener, who, at the same time, busied himself in binding a handkerchief around the thigh of the youth, in the hope to arrest the bleeding.

While thus engaged, the traveller approached him, and asked how far they might be at that moment from the first ferry.

The question surprised the woodman, who looked up at the speaker with increased surprise. With a mind so utterly un-sophisticated as his own, he could conceive of no condition of things justifying the reluctance of the traveller to lend himself to the work of succoring one to whom he owed so great a ser-vice. His wonder, however, did not extend to the conduct of the elder maiden. She had stooped to assist him in his rude surgery, and had yielded the mantle from her shoulder to help in binding up the hurts of his patient. But his eye spoke to her father a different language from that which his lips ad-dressed to her. To him, he looked the surprise he felt, and something more. Scorn was mingled with his wonder, and anger rose no less upon his lips than upon his countenance.

" The ferry !" he exclaimed — " the ferry ! Why, what the diceans can you be after ? Ain't there time enough for that question to-morrow, or the next day, or the day after, or any day for the next six months to come ? We can give you house-room, stranger, as I told you before, and keep you in the dry, though it rains rivers. There's old Billy Badger, that'll give you something more than a supper — a sermon with it — and be glad that you eat heartily, if you can hear well. Come, old man, give us a lift, while we set the lad in your wagon. He won't oncommode the ladies much, and, if so be he does, it was all their own fault and yours, to git into difficulties, and he's hurt in gitting you out of them. Give us a lift, and look bet-ter pleased, and, by gimini ! I'll forget how little minded you seem to help the man that helped you."

" Do my father no injustice," interposed the elder maiden ; " he is not indifferent to the fate of your friend — of our friend — and will do what you require, and all that he can, for his succor and relief. Do not suppose, even had you not been nigh to urge it, that we should have needed any persuasion to move us to so necessary an act of duty. No, sir, believe me, had there been no better strength than that of my own feeble frame, that should have been given for the service of this gentleman ; and, though I sank beneath the burden, I should, at least, have lone my utmost to find succor for one who has been of the greatest succor to us."

"I believe you, my dear young lady, I believe you; there's no mistake in your face, by the powers! I believe you jist as much as if your words had come from the lips of Rachel herself; but the old gentleman—why don't he spunk up, and lend a hand?"

The keen eye of the woodman was fixed upon the traveller as he spoke these words. The latter became still more confused at the apostrophe; his glance sank to the ground, and he faltered out some only half-intelligible accents, about the necessity he was under of pursuing his journey, and the inconveniences which would arise to him, of any unexpected delay; and here he turned to his daughter, and proceeded to repeat what he had said to the woodman, touching the exigencies of his situation. The blunt language of Rawlins anticipated the maiden, and prevented her replying to a speech, which, though partially intelligible only, seemed greatly to distress her.

"By the powers! old gentleman, to my thinking you have been saying anything but the right thing. What are you talking about your journey for, at this time, when here's the man that saved your throats, and your money, and may be, God only knows! saved this handsome young lady, that's your own daughter, from something worse than all. Here he is, I say, lying on the ground, knocked over in helping you out of the hobble, and wanting help himself now to get him to a soft bed, and a quiet place to get well in. If it hadn't a-been for him, who knows what might have happened? It's true I was close behind, but my nag's not the creature that he rides. I'd ha' done as much for you as I could; but then he did it, and made no promises; so fall to, and give me a shoulder here, while I lift the lad into your wagon. The ladies can sit on one side, and we can lay him in the bottom; he's only swooned, and won't know anything about it, and it's only two miles we've got to go."

"Two miles!" exclaimed the traveller; "is it only two miles to the ferry?"

"Ferry! Why, what do you want with the ferry?" demanded Rawlins.

"I must cross the ferry to-night," returned the other.

"You can't—you shan't! by all the powers, you shan't! You shall carry the lad in your wagon to Billy Badger's, which is only two miles off, and it will be quite dark by the time we git there, for you'll have to go slow on account of the lad's hurts. After that, if you are so cursed hard-hearted, old gentleman, as to set off without waiting to know how the man is that resked his life to save yours and your daughter's, not to say nothing about your cash, which must be pretty considerable, to bring these robbers about you—"

"You mistake—you mistake, my friend!" was the hasty interruption of the traveller, "I have but little money with me—precious little—nothing to speak of."

"Tell that to the chickens—the old fowls won't believe you. But that's neither here nor there. As for your crossing the ferry this night, that's impossible. Where would you have been—or what, let me ask you, would you have had to cross with, if the lad hadn't put in to save you? If you don't choose to do the thing willingly, by the powers, I'll do it for you! I'll take possession of your carry-all, and fix the thing to my own liking."

"Oh! my father, why will you resist—why oppose any longer?" was the pleading inquiry of the elder maiden, whose own solicitations, though before chiefly whispered, as if in deference to her father's years and feelings, were as warm in expression, and as humane in their purport, as were those of the more abrupt and sturdy woodman. "The gentleman says rightly," continued the maiden; "we have all been saved by the valor of his companion, and we must see him carried safely to his dwelling. Nay, more, we can not leave him till he is out of danger."

"Virginia, my child, what is it that you say? You know not my reasons—my necessity," was the bewildered response of the father.

"Nothing, my father, but absolute danger can justify inhumanity." She laid down this just principle with due solemnity.

"I am in danger," whispered the father in her ear—"foes seek—evils beset—dangers follow me."

"God forbid! say not so!—your life—how?—from what?

—from whom!—speak to me, dear father! Tell me all—now, now. Let me know wherefore this journey—why have you left your home—our dear home—in this strange and sudden manner ?"

The anxiety of the maiden almost overturned her caution. Her whispers became full and perfect sounds at the close, and were silenced in much agitation by the father, who pointed to Rawlins, now approaching with the body of Vernon, which he had lifted upon his massive shoulders, and was bearing to the carriage. The groan of the father was insuppressible.

"Not now, my child, not now. We must submit to this. Take your seat; Ellen will sit on the front with me. The stranger speaks truly. It might have been, but for the youth's coming, that we had lost that which is of more value than life,"

The parties were soon seated, and the cushions of the vehicle were made to support, in tolerable ease, the form of the wounded man, from whom an occasional escaping groan announced the lingering presence of life within him. Having effected all the arrangements, to his own satisfaction at least, Rawlins took charge of Vernon's horse, which he led ; and congratulating the old man upon his slowly-recovered humanity, he proceeded to guide them to the dwelling which he had assigned for their temporary lodging-house, leaving the dead robber to the possible care of his comrades.

"By the powers! old gentleman," said he, with an air of great toleration, as he rode up beside the vehicle, and looked in upon the face of his companion, "it was only because of the young ladies that I let you off so easily. When you wanted to back out, and leave the lad in his blood, when he had just done getting you out of a mighty ugly scrape, I had it in my mind to make you walk your own trotters, and take the wagon to myself altogether; for, you see, it would have been mighty shameful in you to go off in safety, not asking and not caring what became of him that helped you. If you had seen him ride as I did, when he heard the screams of the ladies, and seen his face when he spoke, and heard his words when he cried to me that was riding close behind him, 'A woman's voice, Rawlins!' —Rawlins is my name, sir—you would say to yourself, 'By the powers! this is the very sort of man to wrap up in your

heart, and to love,' and I love him, stranger, by the powers!—
I love the lad for what I've seen him do to-day, jist the same as
if I know'd him for a hundred years, though I never set eyes
on him afore to-day."

"He is a stranger, then, in this neighborhood?' was the
inquiry of the old gentleman.

"A traveller, like yourself; he comes from below—I reckon
from some of the old states, for he's got a sight of l'arning,
knows everything, and talks jist like a book."

The eyes of the elder maiden were fixed for awhile with increasing interest upon the pale countenance of the wounded
man, and she now remarked the finely-formed and expressive
features—expressive even while overspread by a pallor such
as that of death—the softness and fineness of his skin, the
small, sweet mouth, and the flowing locks of hair, which escaped
in small, single ringlets from the confining cap which he wore,
but which had been displaced by the motion of the carriage.

The instincts of women are no less busy and prompt than
those of men; else why should the maiden blush when she beheld the eyes of the woodman suddenly cast upon her, as she
scanned the features of his unconscious companion? She had,
with equal suddenness, arrived at the conviction that the face
of the stranger youth was one of the most noble she had ever
seen, and distinguished by that delicacy of feature and expression which are conjectured to denote equally aristocratic birth
and natural genius. This conviction was, perhaps, strengthened
by the few words which Rawlins had spoken, and which represented the youth as a traveller like themselves. Imagination
soon busied itself to discover his objects, his pursuits, family,
and mental resources; and even when the searching glance of
the woodman compelled her to avert her eyes to the opposite
side of the carriage from the wounded man, the subject was too
interesting to suffer her to forego its consideration, which employed her young thoughts and virgin fancies in a manner
which did not please the less because they lacked all means for
arriving at any conclusion.

The carriage at length reached Zion's Hill—the name which
the strongly-assured methodist had conferred upon his habitation—and yet Virginia Wilson—for Wilson was the name

given by her father, as his own, in reply to the demand of Rawlins—with a tenacity which is probably rational enough among young ladies in all such cases, had not yet exhausted her subject.

CHAPTER XVII.

THE RIGHTEOUS ELDER—THE UNRIGHTEOUS SON—THE BEAGLES IN SWAMP.

> *Wolsey.* ———— Sir,
> For holy offices I have a time; a time
> To think upon the part of business which
> I bear i' the state.—*King Henry VIII.*

THE party was received very cordially, though with great solemnity, by the sober methodist. He descended from his steps to the carriage; freely welcomed the proprietor; commanded all care for the wounded man; bade his servants in attendance; had refreshments served, and though, in these respects, exhibiting the essentials of a most solid and earnest hospitality, he never yet unbent a muscle of his hard countenance, nor modulated to softness the harsh accents of a voice, stern, cold, slow, emphatic, and measuredly monotonous. He listened to the unusual narrative of their escape, with the same composure as he would have heard the complaints of his niece, Rachel, who had pricked her finger with a needle; and his congratulations of the party on 'heir escape, were uttered with very much like the manner which he employed when saying grace before the morning meal. A matter-of-fact face received every circumstance, and requited all the wonders which he heard; and nothing in the world could be more mortifying to the enthusiastic temperament, than the repulsive and chilling expression of a countenance that seemed to be set on high, as a sort of moral scarecrow, to rebuke the intrusive passions, the fervid temperament, the glowing and impatient zeal, that burns, and swells, and bounds, and is never so angry as when 't encounters the high fences which prudence sets up to restrain its roving and incursive propensities.

William Badger had no sympathy with the enthusiasm that dilates readily at every impulse. His enthusiasm was all religious; his zeal, deep, earnest, and perpetually glowing, was restrained by that decorum alone, which is the fruit of intense veneration. To speak fast, seemed to his mind to indulge in levity; to utter promptly his feelings, might be to do injustice to his own judgment, to the governing providence of God, or to the rights and interests of others. It may be added, that, with a temperament sanguine in the extreme; a mind free, full, and active; an intense self-esteem, and that disposition to sway which is, perhaps, a natural attribute of such a character, his impetuosity of disposition was simply methodized and more completely systematized and made equal from the external restraints put upon it.

"I have seen him in a roaring passion," said Rawlins to his companion, "when he didn't know what he said or did, and swore like a Mississippi boatman; and yet one word came out after another jist as slowly as if he was making his morning prayer. He's a most strange man, that same Billy Badger; but he means always to do right, even when he's most wrong; and if you'll let him alone, when he's most wrong, he'll come right after a season; but I do think he'd not suffer the angel Gabriel to set him right, or show him that he was wrong, one minute before he was willing to see it for himself."

The first care of all parties was to see into the condition and render assistance to the wounded man. He was conveyed into a quiet chamber, and Badger himself attended chiefly to his hurts. An inspection of them showed him to have been wounded by two balls, both of which had fortunately struck fleshy parts of the thigh, and the swooning had been occasioned by the loss of blood, and not in consequence of any serious causes of exhaustion.

When the venerable elder had satisfied himself of these facts, he made very light, in his solemn manner, of the danger. and assured the anxious Rawlins that the youth would scarcely feel his hurts in a day or two. The balls not having lodged, but having cut the flesh in two parallel spots, some two inches apart it was easy to dress the wounds, which had already ceased to pour forth those free streams which, at first, had threatened to exhaust the fountains of life within him, and might have done so, but for the timely bandaging that Rawlins had made both below and above the places which were hurt.

Badger, who asked no counsel of those around him, administered a sleeping draught to the patient, which silenced the groans, at moments escaping feebly from his lips, and set him to sleep so soundly that there was but little prospect—according to the woodman—of his hearing any of the long sermon that night.

To do Mr. Wilson all manner of justice, we may say, that he showed no lack of interest in the situation of the young man He watched beside him until Badger had declared his perfect conviction of his safety, and then left him only to quiet the becoming anxiety of another, whose solicitude in his fate, which might have seemed improper under other circumstances, found its sufficient justification in her gratitude.

Virginia Wilson felt a strange beating at her heart, and trembled with a new sentiment of pleasure, as she listened to these tidings. Was there anything singular in the fact that she retired that instant to the chamber which had been assigned herself and younger sister, and shed in secret those tears which it might have puzzled her to explain why she shed at all. Yet such was the case, and those tears, it may be added, were no less sweetly strange to her own heart, than they would have been surprising to any other not perfectly conscious of their source.

Meanwhile, Mr. Wilson and our friend Rawlins were compelled to undergo the protracted examination of the methodist, on the subject of the late adventure; the circumstances of which seemed to awaken in him no less curiosity than concern.

"Evil is abroad in the world," he said, beginning to sermonize at the conclusion of his examination; "there is no place altogether secure from the dominion of Satan; but that here, so nigh unto Zion, where I have, for the space of two blessed years, striven to uphold the work and the worship of our heavenly Father—that sin should so boldly demean herself, seems to be as passing strange, as it is sad. But, marvel ye not, Walter

Rawlins, at what I am about to say to you; and regard it not
as unbecoming in one who preaches peace on earth and good-
will to all men, if I declare to you that we must all arise and
put on the armor of strife, yea, the very armor of man, and gird
upon our thighs the carnal weapons of human wrath. The
traveller must not be stricken down upon the highway without
summons of eternity, without warning to prepare for death in
season. We must go forth in seeking for these bloody men;
we must put them to defiance; and as they have not hearkened
to our words of prayer and peace, neither have they given heed
to the forbearance of our own example, then must we use
against them the same weapons which they are so ready to use
against the wayfaring man, and we must smite them hip and
thigh to their utter undoing. If they will not hearken to the
imploring angel; if they will not heed the promise of the for-
giving angel; nor incline their hearts to the prayers of the
righteous, God will commission the destroying angel, even as
he has commissioned him against the Amalekite and the Assyr-
ian of old, until there be none left to tell the story of their un-
deserving, and their heaped-up bones alone shall remain to
declare their sudden punishment, in warning to the other tribes
of evildoers which shall follow them. Truly, it grieves me,
that here, within sight of the Hill of Zion, which I had
thought to set apart as a spot where evil should not have
foothold or countenance, such deeds should be done as shall
make the traveller tremble to approach, even when he comes
on the sabbath, seeking crumbs of comfort from the Lord. My
heart is full of shame within me, that I should have fought the
good fight with so feeble an arm, and should have gone into the
battle with a spirit waxing faint in the hour when there is most
need of performance. Here, Mr. Wilson, with the Lord's favor,
did I pitch my tent, at a time when the land around me was in
possession of the heathen, though even then decreed for the
heritage of the believing. Well may I declare that it was like
unto a desert, where the dews of heavenly bounty never fell, or
if they fell, which were drunk up without profit to earth or
heaven by the thirsty, but unimproving sands. Since that time,
the heathen hath sunk away from the broad possession of the
land, and hath given place to a people which, if they be not

yet holy, ware yet better favored of God with the true lights
of righteousness. Many, I am glad to declare, have had the
fountains of life to spring up within their hearts, with a strain-
ing which shall never fail; but as thou seest, there are many
still who grope in the way of darkness, and fight under the
banners of the mighty sinner who first made all to sin. These
robbers who have assailed, with design perchance to slay—"

The harangue which, temperately begun, promised to be of
interminable dimensions, was here cut short by the interruption
of one who had entered without being seen by the elder. This
was his only son, Gideon, a youth of twenty years or thereabouts, whom Rawlins had already described as a "sly fellow,
having something wrong about him," and one whom he did not
like. The youth was a proper-looking youth enough; but his
keen, quick eye, the lively play of temper about his mouth, the
sudden transition of expression in his glance, his studious methodism in garb and accent, so much at variance with the natural
characteristics of his countenance and manner, would have impressed a close spectator with a conviction of the perfect felicity of Rawlins's brief, but comprehensive description. He sat
demurely in the seat which he had taken at entrance, immediately behind his father; his hands were clasped upon his knees,
his legs drawn up, and half inclined beneath his chair, his eyes
cast down upon the floor even while he spoke. His interruption arose quite as much, if the truth was known, from his impatience at a sort of exhortation, in which, whatever might be
the case with the traveller, his experienced ears found little of
novelty; and though, in what he said, he fancied he should
gratify the *amour propre* of the veteran religionist, his aim was,
perhaps simply to suppress a discourse, of which the reader has
probably had quite as much as himself, and may thank him for
the interruption.

"It may be, sir, that you are doing some injustice to your
own labors, and to the character of the goodly neighborhood in
which we live. I am of the opinion, sir, that these robbers
must be strangers in these parts, the outcasts from other states
and cities, men of desperate hope and fortune, who rove the
country like raging lions seeking whom they shall devour, and
none of whom have ever hearkened to your voice, or to the

wholesome preaching of any of God's servants. I can not think that any of those whom we are accustomed to behold at Zion's Hill, hearkening to the word, will ever be found in the evil ways of these wretched robbers."

The lurking tribute to the old man's vanity which was contained in this speech, did not do away with the impertinence of the interruption. The father, slowly and without a word, when he first heard the voice of the son, wheeled his chair about so that he might face the speaker. He heard him patiently to the end, and then answered him in grave, stern accents.

"And what know you, Gideon Badger, of the hearts of men, even though they be neighbors unto Zion's Hill? And what know you of these robbers, of whom you speak so readily, that you should venture to hope—ay, sir, I say to hope—that all or even any of those who hearken to God's word in this place, are free from the damnable leprosy of sin? There is a great presumption in thy thoughts, Gideon Badger, which should be chastened by prayer, by the prayer of an anguished spirit, that knows its own presumption, and can find no check to chasten it but that which is the free gift of God himself. When thou speakest so freely of the goodness of thy neighbors, I greatly fear thou speakest a vain thing. There are many among them whom I fear lack overmuch the becoming humility of God's servants, and need the visitation of the Savior in their secret places, before they will hold up clean hands and pure hearts in the sight of their heavenly Maker. Nay, more, Gideon Badger, it is thy practice to seek and commune with some of those of whom but little that is good may be spoken. There is that idle man who lives by taking the innocent fish that swim to and fro in the Chitta-Loosa, which, though it bears a name of the heathen, is yet no less a river of the Lord—he whom they call Weston, whose blacksmith craft were of great profit to him would he pursue it, is another of whom it were well if thou hadst less knowledge—"

Here the old man experienced another interruption, but this time from no less a person than our friend Rawlins.

"He will have no more knowledge of Weston," said the woodman, "than he has already, and that I can give you now, since Weston was the very man who was shot down by Mr. Vernon :—he sat on top of the old gentleman, there, Mr. Wilson, with pistol out, and another loaded in his breast, when Vernon tumbled him. Here are the pistols which I took from him, here's his knife, and these knick-knacks also came out of his pocket. His carcass lies in the cross-roads at this moment, where anybody who wants, can have it for the carriage."

This revelation startled the methodist out of something of his equanimity. He half rose from his seat while Rawlins spoke, but instantly resuming it, as if conscious of improper precipitancy of movement, he sat quietly, without further motion, until the tale was finished; his eyes meanwhile wandering, with obvious anxiety in their glance, from the speaker to his son, and from him again to the speaker. When the latter had finished his statement, and thrown down upon a table the arms and other articles which he had taken from the slain robber, the old man spoke, but his voice and manner had resumed all their deliberateness.

"Walter Rawlins, this is a dreadful tale which thou tellest, and I tremble to hear it, as I can not doubt that thou tellest me the truth."

"True as gospel, Mr. Badger, if eyes don't cheat one in the business."

"Make no irreverent comparisons, young man, between such truth which thou tellest, on the authority of thy mortal sight, and that wondrous truth of the gospel which comes of the sight of God. Thy truth hath its use and its value, and I question it not, but the truth of eternity is another thing from the truth of time, and God strengthen the poor eyes that see but the one, that they be not blinded with the outer brightness and perfection of the other. Truly, I make no doubt that thou hast seen this wretched man, Weston, in the condition which thou describest, though it is a sinful scorn of God's best work on earth to leave the frame even of the wicked man to rot above the earth, a prey to the carrion birds and beasts who prowl by night for food. His burial must be seen to, his proper burial; and we shall commit him to his final resting-place, with a prayer for mercy, though cut off in the very acting of his miserable crime. Gideon Badger, Gideon Badger, my son, give thanks to God this night that my timely warning to thee against this man severed the association between ye, else it might have ripened into an intimacy with the same sins on thy part, and may have been followed by a death to thee no less sudden than it has been to him—a death without repentance and without hope. Truly, thy tidings, Walter Rawlins, are full of terror. This is an awful visitation. In the midst of life we are in death. We know not the hour, yet we must obey the summons, however sudden. This miserable creature —well that he hath no parent to sorrow for his sudden smiting, and his unatoned sins; he hath no hope of sympathy and sorrow from us—the law of God and the law of man command us otherwise. We are called upon to exult in the death of the evildoer, to rejoice in the downfall of sin—but we must put the dead out of our sight. Earth to earth, dust to dust; and it differs not though the earth be that of the sinner. We are all sinners, even when we are best; redeemed through grace and mercy, and not because of our own righteousness. Let us go forth and put our brother in sin into the grave, with a prayer for mercy to him and to ourselves. Order you the *hands* together, Gideon Badger, and bid them provide themselves with torches. Let Timothy and Ephraim bring pick and spade, that we may not waste precious time."

Gideon Badger went slowly to the performance of this duty, and some time elapsed before the party was in readiness. Leaving his guests in charge of his niece, Rachel, of whom the garrulous Walter Rawlins has permitted us to know something already, Mr. Badger mounted his steed, a heavy, English-built animal, sturdy, and slow, and solemn, like himself, and set forth with all the phlegmatic deliberation of manner which distinguished the ancient puritan going forth to battle. There were not wanting other matters to strengthen this similitude. He carried a pair of wide-mouthed iron horse-pistols at his saddle-bow, a pair which he had borne with him into battle when, in his younger days, he followed the banner of Andrew Jackson, among the mounted men of Coffee's brigade, and went down from Tennessee to the fierce and close combats on the Tallapoosa. Nor did he forget to take with him on this occasion the knotted hickory, a massive club, almost of the thickness of his wrist, which, as the supposed characteristic of a hero whom ne regarded with a large degree of veneration, he had made his own inseparable companion, not simply in times of danger, but on all occasions.

"And danger," said the old methodist, defending the propriety of this practice, "is even like sin, a thing of all occasions. The man of wisdom borrows his lessons from the Christian, and goes armed and ready at all times for the enemy There is no telling at what moment we may meet with him, nor in what shape; whether he shall appear as the wild beast of the wilderness, or as the wretched robber, seeking for your substance. Therefore, I say to you, be ye always ready."

He was attended by his son Gideon, and Walter Rawlins, both equally well-armed with himself, and followed by some six or eight negro men, his entire *force* of males, some of them bearing *lightwood* torches, and the rest, the necessary implements for breaking the mould, and preparing the place of interment. They traversed the path in silence and without interruption, but, to the astonishment of all, the dead robber was nowhere to be found. The traces of the conflict were numerous —the blood lay in clotted masses on the sand and leaves; but neither on the spot where he had been described as having fallen, nor in the immediately contiguous bushes of the forest, could they find traces of his mode of disappearance.

"How know you that his wounds were death-wounds, Walter Rawlins?" demanded the methodist. "May it not be that he hath feigned death while ye were present, having no serious hurt, and hath stolen away from the place of battle, the moment ye had all gone from sight?"

"If he did," replied Rawlins with a hearty laugh, "he was able to do with less brains than any man I ever heard tell of before. But there's no danger of that; his skull was crunched by the bullet, and a piece of it was wanting—clean blown off —as large as a table-spoon. Besides, I felt at his heart more than once, while I was searching his pockets, for I didn't want that a dead man even should open his eyes and catch me stripping him. The beat was all gone out of his breast, before I come up from chasing his brother rascals."

"Verily, Walter, thou couldst not have chased them to a

great distance, for they have surely returned to his assistance,
and it is by their help that he hath been taken away."

"Like enough, sir; but I did give 'em a chase, and a mighty
close one for the time I took about it. I wasn't going to run
'em fifty miles, when dark was coming on, and my company
was waiting for me in the open road. Besides, there was little
chance, if I didn't tree 'em at the first jump, that I should find
'em, me one only, in a close thicket like that. That canebrake
would hide a hundred rascals from the most honest nose among
us all."

"It needs not that we should speak longer in this idle fashion : thou hast too great a vanity of thy speech, Walter Rawlins. It is a sin in youth to multiply words, having neither experience nor thinking to make them stable and of fitting effect.
Thou shouldst better prefer to hear the language of wisdom, in
the counsels of age. Years must pass over thee, and thou must
clothe thyself in holiest meditation, even as with a shrouding
garment, which shall wrap thee in from all worldly shows and
affinities, before it will be thy right, or in any wise becoming in
thee, to speak freely in the presence of men, or confidently
among their counsels. I will speak more to thee of this subject on the way homeward. Turn thy horse, therefore, which
improperly crosseth the path, so that I may advance before
thee. It is, perhaps, well that we are not required to perform
this awful ceremony of committing dust to dust. Let the dead
bury the dead; these are the written words, which truly signify
that the wicked should take upon themselves the task of putting their fellow-sinners from sight. Yet, young men, the ceremony of human burial is not an unfitting spectacle for the
young and erring like yourselves; and had these wretched people left us the task of committing their slain comrade to the
earth, I should have striven to fill your minds with the goodly
workings of religious truth. Ye should have had ample premo-
nition of the fate of wickedness, so that your hearts might have
been touched in season, and your souls warned with a righteous
fear, which should have moved you in all haste to fly from the
wrath which is to come. Nay, there is yet time for this, and,
God willing, young men, this shall be the subject of our evening
exhortation, ere we seek our rest this night."

An audible groan burst from the lips of Gideon Badger, which the father ascribed naturally enough to the solemn and sad course of meditation which his words had inspired in the breast of the youth. The less rigid mind of Walter Rawlins referred it to a more simple, and perhaps equally natural cause — the terror which such a threat as that of the father was always calculated to awaken in his own bosom, seemed quite sufficient to justify the audibly-expressed tribulation of Gideon. If he suspected the latter of a little hypocrisy, he gave him credit, at least, for a certain degree of sympathy with himself in the unfavorable estimate which he had made of the elder's solemn outpourings — the chief objection to which, in his mind, consisted in the fact that they occupied .time which could be much more pleasantly disposed of, in communion with one whose discourse, if less saintly, was far more sweet, and whose periods were uttered with less elaborate lips, and closed sometimes with far more pleasant emphasis.

" But if the disappearance of this slain robber relieves us of one duty, Walter Rawlins," continued the old man in a differ ent strain of thought, " it seems to impress upon us the necessity of other duties, no less painful, and, perhaps, more full of trouble and danger. It is clear that the companions of this robber bear the name of legion — they are many, since they attack the traveller in troops and squadrons — they are bold, since they attack him in the broad daylight, and near unto the very foot of Zion's Hill — nor doth their boldness appear less remarkable from the fact that they have scarcely been driven from their prey, with the loss of one slain from their number, before they return to the spot and carry him away in safety. This conduct betokeneth the insolence of numbers. Doubtless, they came hither after your departure, with a force increased sufficiently to enable them to avenge their loss. The madness of wickedness would not stop even at the wanton and useless repetition of their crime. All this calleth loudly for exertion among the true peacemakers, the righteous, and well-wishing among mankind; and for the suppression of these evil-doers, the neighbors must be stirred up into activity and wrath. Rumors have reached me before this, of a gathering of evil men along this heathen river; and now, when it cometh so nearly to our own

9*

doors, it behooveth me as a magistrate under an earthly ruler no less than as one commissioned by the Most High, to search into this sin, with keen eyes and a sleepless spirit. Of this we must have speech and counsel to-morrow, giving our prayerful application to the Lord Jesus ere we lie down to-night, that the right wisdom may fill our understandings, so that we fall upon the fitting purpose, and take our way along the only path. Bid the *hands* follow, Gideon Badger—they loiter idly with their torches, and their voices swell into unruly sounds that are scarcely seemly in this solemn hour."

They had scarcely gone from sight, when three men, well armed, emerged from the edge of the swamp thicket.

" By the Dog Shadow of Loosa-Chitta," said one whose voice announced no other person than our old acquaintance, Saxon, " Badger deals in no small shot; he's a hundred pound parson, and I shall owe him large acknowledgments when next I find it needful to become ghostly and unctuous. That Gideon is a precious rascal; he groaned most piteously, as if no river could wash the salt savor and the true leaven out of him. Yet you tell me he scampered off rather fast, Burritt?"

"Ay, as fast as two slender shanks could carry a small body and a frightened heart. We put him at the easiest business— only to hold the horses while Weston grappled the old man, and I looked for the cash. With the first sound of the enemy, he was off."

"And had this old man any cash?"

" I'm afraid not, or he hid it too snugly for us to find it in a hurry. The watch was all I brought off, and that I pulled from the daughter's side almost without her knowing it."

" Well, say nothing reproachfully of Gideon; coward or not, he is of too much use to us, while his father lives, to suffer us to complain of his little deficiencies. The old man is no coward, that is clear, and would go as heartily into a fight as he goes into a sermon. He would fight like a bull-dog. The young man who gave Weston his quietus—you are sure you shot him?"

" If aim was ever good, mine was upon his breast-button."

" Well, it is, perhaps, quite as well that it is all over. If he's dead it's one out of the way that I suspect would have been very troublesome to us; if not, as old Badger would tell you, you have not the heavier sin to answer for.   But, dead or alive, it is still important that we should see what papers he carries; we must see what beagles are down in the governor's catalogue Gideon may get these papers without much risk; and when there's no danger, there need be little fear.   We must summon him to-night."

CHAPTER XVIII.

A GENUINE WOMAN AFTER A NATURAL FASHION — THE CONFERENCE BETWEEN BLACK AND WHITE.

> " A fair, young, modest damsel I did meet;
>   She seemed to all a dove, when I passed by,
>   And I to all a raven."—THOMAS DECKER.

THAT night, Gideon Badger encountered Rachel Morrison, his cousin, as she wandered forth into the shady grove of forest-trees, which were allowed to remain at the clearing, and conducted from the house into the garden.   The youth had evidently placed himself in waiting, as he sprang from the deep shadow of an oak at her approach, and presented himself before her.   She started at sight of him, with a feeling of mixed indignation and surprise.   Her form, rather inclining to be tall and masculine, seemed to rise in majesty beyond its wont, the moment she recovered from her partial surprise; and the tones of her voice, and the words she used, at once indicated a condition of *quasi* warfare between them.

" Why will you still pursue, still oppress me in this manner, Gideon Badger ?"

" Why will you still seek to avoid me in this manner, Rachel Morrison ?" was his reply.

" If it be true that I seek to avoid you, you, as a man, should scorn to pursue me.   Your own pride should preserve me from your persecution, even if your sense of generosity failed you. Will you not suffer me to pass ?"

"No! not yet—not for a while! I would speak further with you, Rachel, and you must bear with my persecutions a little longer, for a very good reason."

"Let me know the reason, Gideon Badger; and if it be a good one, rest assured that I will remain and hear you without reluctance. Until then, you must forgive me if I say I hear you with little pleasure."

"I doubt not that, Rachel," returned the young man gloomily, "there is another whose speech and presence have ever given you more pleasure than mine. It is reason enough why you should remain, that you can not so easily escape, and that I am resolved that you shall hear me; and yet, I would that you were more yielding to other reasons, which are enough, not only to persuade you to stay and hear, but to do so with pleasure and content."

"I know not these, Gideon—I would that I did! Heaven knows how willingly I should incline my ears to the words of one so dear to my uncle as yourself! But you well know what better reasons I have for distrusting your speech and avoiding your company."

"By heavens, Rachel, but you do me wrong! Because of one error—one crime, if it please you so to call it—am I to forfeit all your regard, all indulgence, all hope? You know that I have broken off from all intimacy with the man Furst. From that moment when you discovered our connection, and the offence of which we were guilty, I promised you, and my promise has been kept rigidly."

"And yet, Gideon, the fate of another of your intimates alarms me—this unhappy man, Weston!"

"Rachel, Rachel! can it be that you would couple me with that robber? Can you suppose me lost to all reason, as well as to all religion? Can it be that you hold me a confederate of this unhappy wretch, when you know that I have not been seen with him for months?"

"You have!" was her stern and startling reply, to the warm and earnest asseverations of the youth, given with all the seeming unaffectedness of truth. "You have been seen with him, Gideon, within three weeks."

"Ha! who says it?—how know you?"

" Mother Kerrison saw you with him at the ferry, three weeks ago."

" Pshaw ! Rachel, how anxious must you be to find out fault in me, when you fall upon such idle tales as these. For that matter, I have seen the man almost weekly every month in the past year, but we have had no intimacy, no communion 'ogether --we have been in no wise associated."

" Gideon, there again I must oppose the testimony of a third person to your own. Who caught those fish which you brought home with you last Saturday was a week ?"

A bitter scowl passed over the countenance of the youth as he replied :—

" Truly, Rachel, you are in no lack of spies upon my actions. I suppose it will be in vain to deny that they were caught by Weston."

" It will, indeed, be vain to deny it, Gideon, and my good reasons for seeking to avoid you, arise from your having done so already. Your father was under the persuasion that you caught them by your own hands."

" I never told him so," said the young man hastily.

" No ; but your words justified his belief that such was the case, and he spoke of your success in fishing to your own ears, and you did not seek to set him right."

" And I am successful in fishing, Rachel, and his compliments were just enough ; as for my statement misleading him, I can only say that I never intended it should. But you know, I see, that the fish were bought from Weston."

" I know that you got them from him, but I heard that they were given to you."

" Now, in the name of all that is precious in a spy, what old woman could have told you this ?—Mother Kerrison, again ?"

" It was, indeed, no other."

" That old hag ought to be carted through a cane-brake, and drawn through the bog. The fish were bought with money, Rachel Morrison, and I trust there's no more harm in buying fish from a man that turns out to be a rogue, than in buying them from the best citizen in the county. That you hate me, Rachel, is sufficiently clear from the collection of authorities and arguments which you have got together against me."

"Gideon, God knows, and you ought to know, that I have had, in the kindness of your father to the poor orphan of his brother's wife, every reason to make me try to love and to esteem you; and I know, however little you may be disposed to believe it, how much I have tried to love you. But you have not suffered me to do this. Your own wilfulness, your harshness—shall I say your cold, calculating artfulness of conduct in relation to your father, myself, and others—but your father chiefly—have baffled the desires of my heart. I can not love, I can not honor you—nay, I can not look on you without shrinking and shuddering—when I know how prone you have shown yourself to speak the thing which is not, and to do the thing which you are commanded by God and man not to do. But, if these reasons were not wanting, Gideon, to make me desirous to shun you, there were others, sufficient for my justification, in your caprice and violence of temper. You have striven to use me as your plaything; you have tried to abuse my ignorance—to take advantage of me as a child; and when you have failed in this, you have railed at me in ruffianly terms, as if I, too, were a ruffian. It were conclusive against your claim to manliness, that you have pursued this course of conduct, even while I have been in your father's house, protected by his favor, and almost dependent on his bounty. Be assured, Gideon Badger, that it was in my necessity, only, that I have remained and endured this treatment in silence. I could not have done so, had the dwelling of any other relative been open to my entrance, where I might have escaped such persecution."

"Ay, ay! Rachel Morrison, this is all very strong, and very emphatic," said the youth, with mocking bitterness; "it is, as the old man, my venerable father, would call it, a searching and soul-harrowing discourse; but it may be that you have still left unspoken some of the grounds which induced your hatred of Gideon Badger."

"I hate you not, Gideon," said the maiden, mournfully. "Alas! it is my great sorrow that you will not suffer me to love you."

"Nay, nay, Rachel! these sounds do not delude me. As I was saying, some of your reasons for rating me so humbly—so scornfully, should be the word—were unexpressed. You love another, Rachel Morrison; you love this swaggering fellow, Rawlins; deny it, if you can."

"I seek not to deny it, Gideon."

"It were in vain to do so. I have seen you together; your heads and hands mingling; your forms linked—ay, you may well shrink and blush while I say it, Rachel Morrison—your mutual lips glued to each other, as if they were never more destined to undergo separation."

The maiden did blush at the description of those scenes of secret tenderness which she had fancied utterly unseen by any eyes but those of Heaven, and which, in the purity of her heart and its emotions, she had neither shame nor scruple that Heaven should behold; but when her accuser spoke of her blushes, and counselled her to shame, her lofty spirit rose in majesty, her heart swelled with the pride of innocence, her form dilated in towering beauty, and she retorted the insolence of the speaker with well-deserved scorn.

"And if I blush, Gideon Badger, at these scenes, it is not because they have been witnessed, but that such as you should have witnessed them. You, without sympathy for truth or virtue, would only mock the sincere heart by your jest, or offend it by your presence. A noble witness had gone from the spot in silence, and in his secret soul had locked up the remembrance of what his eyes had beheld unwittingly. Certainly, he would never have labored as you have done, to make a woman regret that she had yielded herself to those feelings which, while they are pure in the sight of God, should be held no less sacred in the sight of man. To Walter Rawlins I am pledged —betrothed—it needs but the sanction of religion to make us one. We are already one in spirit and in truth—with God's blessing we shall soon be one in law."

"Never, never!" cried the youth impetuously, with choking accents, and the fierce gesticulation of one threatening an enemy. "Hear me, Rachel Morrison, you shall never wed this man. One or both of us shall first perish. I hate him now, as I have ever hated him, but with a hatred that will no longer brood and slumber over baffled hopes, and ineffectual purposes. If you resolve as you declare, then shall my equal resolution follow hard upon your declaration. Be sure that no peace which I can disturb shall dwell with you—no hope that I can banish shall warm your dwelling—no happiness follow your marriage with this man. Nay, there shall be no security. I will pursue you to the uttermost ends of the earth, but I will wrest you from his grasp; I will pursue him to the uttermost ends of the earth, but I will paralyze his embrace; and, if I can not triumph in love, at least I will do so in the exercise of the most despotic hate. You know what I can do—you know my powers and my passions. .Beware how you drive me to desperation—beware how you compel me to hate, when you know how heartily I can love."

"And know me also," replied the woman with tremulous but measured and subdued accents, "know, Gideon Badger, that you can no more terrify Rachel Morrison than you can terrify the man who is pledged to be her husband. In God is my trust, and with a proper confidence in his power to save, I bid defiance to all your powers to wrong and to destroy. He hath strengthened me to bear with many afflictions, with poverty, with evil tongues—even with dangers that might have stricken and destroyed—he will sustain me in flight, he will defend me against the pursuer, even if earthly powers should not avail for my protection. Yet, let me warn you, Gideon Badger, against this evil resolution. A word from me to Walter Rawlins, and his foot were upon your neck the instant after it was spoken."

"What! would you so soon threaten me with your bully, Rachel Morrison?—But I fear him not—"

"Enough!" she exclaimed, interrupting the further course of his insolent speech—"let us part, Gideon. You can say nothing more that can move me now."

"Nay, Rachel—you madden me. Why provoke me thus when you know my passions?"

"Your passions shall never be my tyrants, Gideon Badger; and you, who know so well how to conceal them in the presence of your father, exhibit but a poor sort of manliness when you refuse to restrain them in the presence of a woman. Let us separate, since it seems impossible for you to forbear language which it gives me pain to hear. Let us separate, but not in anger. I forgive you, Gideon; and if there be one thing more

productive than another of sorrow in my heart, it is that you
should so sinfully and perversely cast your good mind and better
nature beneath the trampling foot of passions which first degrade and afterward destroy. Why, Gideon, why—son of my
second father—why will you profligately cast away the noblest
gift of God, the noble reason, and madden thus in a hopeless
pursuit of that which it is beyond your power to procure?"

"Be not certain of that! It is *not* beyond my power, Rachel
Morrison—once more I tell you, you shall never wed this man."

"What mean you? Twice, Gideon, have you spoken in this
strange, wild manner. Do you threaten his life or mine? Can
it be that you mean to murder us?"

"Murder, indeed!" he responded with a hollow laugh. "Who
said that? Not I, Rachel, not I—your fancy is at work, and
upon this slender stock you will get up a pretty tale before
morning. No! no! I have no design to murder I have no
idea of shedding blood; but—ha!"

The bay of the beagle arose faintly from the forest, swelled
over the garden, and tremblingly fell upon their ears through
the umbrageous tree-tops that sheltered them in their conference.
A pause ensued, broken by neither for an instant. He then
continued :—

"Enough for warning, Rachel—enough. You will think
upon it and be wise. You know it is the wish of my father that
you should be my wife, and my own love should move you to
yield willingly to his wishes."

"Your love, Gideon Badger! Speak of the love of the storm
for the flower which it rends in its rude embrace; —speak of
the love of the ocean for the poor bark which it swallows up;
—speak of anything which makes a sport, a victim, of the object which it destroys, and you then speak of your love for me.
Your passions, not your love, are busy in all this. It is they
who would be my master, as they are your own. But they never
shall. I will convince you, Gideon, though I weep for you with
a sad sickness of heart all the while, that when you are most
ungovernable in your rage, I can be calm and unmoved by your
fury; when you are most angry, I shall be least moved; and
when, to others and to yourself, you seem most fearful, then
shall you behold the orphan of your father's bounty most fear-

less and secure. I praise God that he has given me a strength of soul, which enables me, whatever may be the terror and the danger, to keep in the way which my heart tells me is right. With this consciousness, you can not affright me, you can no more drive me from my resolution, than you can persuade me from the truth."

"You speak boldly, but you know me not. The time will come when you shall know more. But not yet—not now. Hark! I hear the whistle of your lover—he is summoning you to your old place of meeting. Make the most of your time, Rachel Morrison, for, by the dim lights that look down upon your endearments, they are destined not to last."

In another instant the maiden, stunned and oppressed with painful emotions and troubling fears, found herself utterly alone. Slowly she made her way to the garden, where, in a little time, she was joined by her lover. Gideon Badger, meanwhile, leaping the little worm-fence that ran along the lower limits of the enclosure, was lost from view in the forest, where his own voice, a moment after the woods had enshrouded him, might have been heard in responsive echoes to those mysterious bayings of the beagle which had summoned him to a meeting of his confederates.

CHAPTER XIX.

THE RIGID MAGISTRATE — HOW TO BADGER BEAGLES AND SNARE FOXES.

"Gentlemen have you provided me here half-a-dozen sufficient men!"
SHAKSPERE.

WITH the dawn of the day following, the traveller, Wilson, with his two daughters, prepared to resume their journey. The impatience of this gentleman seemed to grow with each moment of delay, and the protracted exhortations of the hospitable methodist, who proved no less liberal of his counsel than he had shown himself of his meat, contributed to heat his impatience into fever. Still, though perhaps rather from the promptings of his eldest daughter than the instigations of his own heart, he

took some pains to assure himself of the favorable condition of
the young man who had been wounded in succoring him; and
did not resolve upon his journey, or, at least, did not commence
his visible preparations for it, until he learned from the sober
report of Badger, and the no less credible but less solemn statements of Rawlins, that Vernon's hurts were not such as could
detain him more than a day in his chamber. This ascertained,
he bade adieu to Zion's Hill and his friendly entertainers, and
by the time the sun had fairly purpled the green tops of the
forest, he was speeding fast along the by-road which conducted
to Badger's, and which he had taken the night before with so
much unwillingness, and so little grace.

It was some hours after his departure, before Vernon awakened from the deep sleep into which he had been thrown by
the opiate which had been given him the night before. Nor
could he be said to have awakened to perfect consciousness
because he awakened to the light. The stupifying effect of the
laudanum benumbed his energies, and seemed to confuse his
faculties of thought and observation. A sort of dreamy consciousness of what had taken place, in which all things floated
incoherently and indistinctly before his mental vision, disturbed
the certainty of his conceptions; and it was only by the aid of
Rawlins, who sat beside his couch when his eyes opened, that
he recovered the knowledge of the events which had taken
place the afternoon before. The stiffness of his wounded limb,
and a trembling and slightly sore sensation about the spots
which were hurt, confirmed so much of the particulars as related
to his own interest in the conflict; and, gradually he was reminded of other circumstances, which it seemed to him no less
important that he should know.   . .

He had an indistinct recollection of a bright vision of beauty
which had hung for a few moments above his eyes—a vision
such as had been vouchsafed him more than once before, in a
dream no less sweet and inspiriting, though scarcely so distinct
as that which had been more recent. Then came the passing
consciousness that had possessed him in the moment when he
swooned away, of his having found the person of the escaping
criminal whom he sought on the part of his benefactor. With
this returning conviction, his faculties grew more assured and

industrious, and, cautiously concealing his great interest in the issue of his inquiry, he proceeded to examine his companion on the subject of the party rescued.

This examination tended somewhat to confirm the impression which he had received the evening before, that William Maitland actually stood before him, in the person of the man whom he had rescued; the description of his person, as given him by Rawlins, strengthened this belief. The mere difference of name was a small and trivial obstacle, and one readily overcome by a reference to the case with which a name might be changed, where the party was unknown; and the obvious policy of one flying from justice, to effect this change in order to avoid detection. The greater objection to his conviction lay in the two daughters, by whom Wilson was accompanied. The elder was already a woman grown — the other, nearly in her teens, and the description of Carter had led him to expect mere children in the daughters of Maitland.

This difficulty, however, upon reflection, seemed, to the sanguine mind of Vernon, scarcely less trivial than that of the name. Carter spoke of the children as he had known them, and probably with some reference to his own greater age; and as Vernon threw back his thoughts to the period when Maitland practised his treachery upon his friend, and married Ellen Taylor, the probabilities gained strength, as he found that, allowing them to have had children within a reasonable space of time after marriage, those children might very well be sixteen or seventeen, the apparent age of the eldest daughter of the traveller. But if this conclusion gave him pleasure in one respect, as it satisfied him that the means of retrieving the fortunes and the credit of his patron were almost in his grasp, he, singularly enough, felt some reluctance to pursue them, when he thought of the misery and disgrace which exposure of the father would bring upon the lovely woman, his daughter, whose first glance had so impressed itself upon his fancy.

The matter would have seemed easy enough to provide for the children, as such, who, at the tender years of childhood, could not well have been conscious of the shame which would necessarily follow the detection of the father. But the case became wonderfully different and difficult when the child was a woman

--and such a woman—having, without do.bt sensibilities
keen and quickening, such as are proper to her sex; and a
consciousness of shame corresponding with that intelligence,
which, without any other knowledge than lay in his own en-
dowing fancy, he assumed must belong to such lovely and
speaking features, as those which looked down upon him in his
moments of lapsing consciousness.   How could he pursue, without relenting, the father of such a woman? how could he, as
the stern minister of justice—in fact, the sheriff's agent, with a
special power to place fetters upon his limbs—how could he
drag that old man, felon though he was, from the presence of
that daughter?   He felt that she would rise between him and
his victim—the rebuking, the imploring, the preserving angel;
that her tears would be his reproach; her sorrows, his sentence
of condemnation; and he felt, even then, that her hate to the
oppressor of her father, would be a something beyond his best
ability to bear.   But when, on the other hand, he thought of
Carter—his patron, his only father—the sterner commands of
duty—the earnest voice of soliciting gratitude—spoke another
language to his better judgment.

"I must do my duty," he murmured to himself as he strove
feebly to rise from the couch; "it must be done. Rawlins, my
good fellow, help me to put myself in trim, for I feel very stiff
and stupid. I must get up: I must see this gentleman."

"What gentleman?" said Rawlins

"Mr. Wilson; the gentleman we helped yesterday. Did
you not tell me that he came with us—that he brought me
here?"

"Ay, but he cleared out by sunrise this morning. He was
in a monstrous hurry to be off, and would have gone before
daylight, if 'twasn't for that angel creature, his daughter. She·
told him mighty plain that 'twouldn't do for them to go till they
know'd that you were safe."

"Ha! Did she say that?"

"I heard her with my own ears, though she didn't know I
was nigh. I was coming in at the entry-door leading to the
shed, and her back was to me all the time. She said a good
deal more which I couldn't make out, but I understood enough
to see that she was blaming him for his hard-hearted way of

214 BORDER BEAGLES.

making thanks for the help he got from us—not to speak of
my help in the business, for it was mostly yours. Yet she didn't
leave me out, she spoke to me herself about it, and told me
how her father owed everything to us, and how I must tell you
this when you got better. Well, they waited, as she said they
must, till Billy Badger felt your pulse, and looked at your face
— and he looked long enough and felt long enough to have answered for all the sick men in Mississippi. When he told them
that you'd do well enough without any more doctoring, I never
saw a girl more relieved. She didn't say anything then, but tied
the bonnet on her sister, and went jist as the old gentleman told
her; but I saw a big drop in her eyes as she was going, and her
last words were to me, remembering me to tell you what she said,
and how sorry she was that her father's business made him
hurry away, so that he couldn't say for himself how much they
thanked you. She's a most notable fine girl, I'm thinking, as
ever I looked upon."

Vernon derived a greater degree of gratification from this detail of his companion, than the long, rambling sentences of Rawlins were usually apt to afford him. But though he lingered
over the narrative with a silent pleasure, he did not forego his
purpose of rising from his couch of inactivity, and of pursuing
the task which he had too deliberately and resolutely undertaken to forego without shame. The rapid haste of Wilson tended
to confirm him in the belief that it was Maitland that he pursued; and when he recollected the liberal and large extent of
the commission which had been entrusted to his hands, the discretion which it empowered him to exercise in the case of the
absconding criminal, and the ease with which, under its indulgent privileges, he might obtain his object without any public
exposure of the victim—nay, even without a revelation of the
crime to the innocent daughter of the criminal—he found himself strengthened for the duty, and eager once more for its resumption. But he rose with some increase of pain. The limb
which, in his quiescent state, was tolerably easy, now throbbed
painfully with the weight and pressure of his frame upon it;
and having, with the assistance of his friend Rawlins, reached
the hall where the family were assembled, he found himself compelled to appropriate the calico-covered sofa to its whole extent,

in the hope to regain that position of quiet which he had found before in his couch.

In this effort, and while enjoying the returning ease which it brought him, he was no doubt greatly strengthened and assisted by the consoling review of his situation, and the circumstances attending it, which his ghostly landlord, in his own measured manner, presented to his mind. According to this venerable cider, his hurt was a subject of self-congratulation, which should not be suffered to escape his own commentary. He was one of those who, regarding evils as masked benefits, looked upon Vernon as particularly fortunate in the favor of Providence, and rated the extent of his good by the degree of dissatisfaction and impatience which the victim displayed beneath it. Having exhausted all the proverbial forms of biblical and mere moral expression on the subject, he proceeded to a display of his own experience; and, if his judgment might have been regarded as equally valuable with his faith, it would have appeared convincing enough to his hearers that he had never yet suffered an affliction which had not in its ultimate consequences been a real blessing, infinitely beyond any other which, in its absence, might have fallen to his lot.

His voluminous history, fortunately for Vernon, had its own interest, apart from the savory Christian deductions which the narrator never failed to make from all its leading details; and if the youth was not greatly enlightened and strengthened in moral respects by what he heard, he was certainly edified, amused, and sometimes excited, by adventures on "field and flood," in forest and prairie, in which, like one half of the settlers of Mississippi, William Badger had proved the possession of a manly soul and strength, contending with savage beasts and forests, and not unfrequently with more savage men. But for these details, which gave action and vitality to the old man's prosing, Vernon might have made his retreat in utter desperation; but he bore it with becoming fortitude, until relieved by more exciting details, which put a stop to those of the methodist, and sent all parties to new subjects of cogitation and remark.

The dinner hour had arrived, and the family had already taken their places around the table; Rachel presiding, opposite to the uncle; on one hand, Rawlins, on the other, Gideon

Badger, as demure, while in the presence of the father, as the most worthy of the congregation. Vernon was indulged with a small table beside the sofa on which he lay, upon which was placed some thin soup and a few well-boiled fragments of chicken, such being thought the least hurtful diet for an invalid. William Badger had already commenced that interminable grace before meat, which Rawlins, after the fashion of his own wit, had styled "the dinner cooler," when a bustle was heard at the door, as of one about to enter, and the tones of a voice which Rawlins immediately recognised as that of Edward Mabry, the youth whose fight with, and pursuit of, young Horsey, has already been recorded.

"It's Edward Mabry," said Rawlins, looking up from his plate as he perceived from the pause which William Badger made in his grace, that the interruption had reached his ears. But, as if resolved that no intrusion ought to put a stop to the wholesome preliminary services in which he was engaged, with a devotedness which most persons of good appetite would have preferred paying to the dinner itself, he resumed his prayer just where it had been arrested :—

"—Thy divine countenance, O Lord Jesus Christ, and sanctify to us the food which is now before us—" and so he proceeded to the end, without further notice of the events going on around him, though, in the meanwhile, Edward Mabry, with more haste than was consistent, either with the solemn visage, rigid habits, or grave ceremony of the host, rushed into the apartment.

His audacity did not venture to go farther when he found in what manner the venerable elder was engaged ; and standing apart, with hat in hand, he waited, breathless and impatient, until the grace, which seemed to expand even beyond its ordinary limits, was brought to the conclusion. The "amen" was scarcely uttered before the torrent burst its barriers.

"Mr. Badger, Mr. Badger," said the young man, "I come for a warrant—take up a villain—enough to hang him—shall do it. Must grant a warrant, and send Harvey out this very evening. Only sorry I didn't come to you before. But it's not too late—never too late to hang a rascal, and a warrant this evening will answer—a warrant to Harvey. I'm ready to swear ag'in him any moment."

"A warrant, Ned!" exclaimed Rawlins.

"A warrant!" echoed Gideon Badger, with rather more ner vousness than the occasion seemed to call for; and even the usually-composed maiden, Rachel Morrison, could not forbear the like exclamation.

"A warrant!"

"Ay, a warrant!—a warrant against John Yarbers, Mr Badger—he's a villain, a thief—he's the man that helped to run Joe Watson's horse, and I can prove that he put him in the hands of Bill Munson, the fellow that got off last month from Deputy Nichols. I'm ready to take my affidavy to it."

The methodical lips of William Badger at length parted. His face put on new terrors, his words were stern, and the tone threatening.

"Young man," he said, regarding the disfigured visage of the intruder rather than the tale which he told, "young man, you have been fighting."

The youth muttered some hasty words, in which "honor"— "impudent fellow"—"had to fight," were strangely jumbled up with other less significant syllables, but the ascetic elder cut short the worthless pretext in a fashion of his own.

"Edward Mabry, have I not repeatedly counselled you against this brutal and blackguard practice? Have I not repeatedly told you that I care not to see you in my dwelling so long as you can not forbear the rending and gouging of your neighbors."

"I come about business, Mr. Badger," said the other, sulkily; "I come about business; I come to you as a justice, I don't come as a visiter."

"And I speak to you as a justice; and had I caught you, sir, in the brutal act, I should, as a justice, have had you taken and punished; though, to be sure, you seem to have had something more than your usual share of punishment already. God has seen fit to send you a foe who could imprint on you those marks which you are but too apt to put upon the faces of others; upon faces, Edward Mabry, made after God's own blessed image. It is his image that you tear, and bruise, and gouge, with a most miserable propensity to sin. But sit you down—why stand you in waiting when the meat is sanctified and ready? Sit you down and partake with us, young man, though it grieves and sickens me to behold you in this condition. Rachel, set a plate."

"I'm not hungry," replied the youth, with no abatement of his sullenness; for the reference which Badger had made to the superiority of his enemy, had irritated an old sore—"I'm not hungry, I thank God! Mr. Badger; since if I was, I could not sit down at a man's table when he don't wish to see me in his house."

"There is hope of you," was the cool reply of the methodist, "so long as you have the grace to thank God for anything. Sit you down, I say, whether hungry or not, and wait on those who are. As a magistrate, I will hear your statement, and take your oath, if need be, when you have dined; but I warn you Edward Mabry, that an oath is a serious and solemn invoca-'ion; the Lord is spiritually present when it is taken; it is an awful and soul-binding, and soul-responsible assurance. Beware, then, that you swear not against your neighbor, unless with a perfect certainty, so far as the blindness of human sense and judgment may admit of certainty, that what you say is the truth. But sit you down and eat. Gideon Badger, help Edward Mabry to some of the chicken which is before you. Eat, Walter Rawlins. And so, Edward Mabry, you are certain that it was Yarbers who run the horse?"

"Caught him a-doing it, sir. But that ain't all; there's another business more serious. I have a strong notion that I can prove he's been talking insurrection stuff among the niggers."

"That is a dreadful crime, Edward Mabry, and I could wish that you spoke not such suspicions aloud, until you have strong proof of their truth. If I remember rightly, it is now near a month since Joseph Watson recovered the horse which had been stolen."

"Yes, sir; about a month."

"Ah! and you knew the fact at the time. You knew when the robbery was committed?"

"'Twas I caught Yarbers with the animal, making tracks for Vicksburg."

"And wherefore have you kept this thing hidden so long, Edward Mabry? Why have you forborne to bring this **evil-**

doer to punishment before this? And why is it, that, having suppressed the truth so long, you now declare it in the unbecoming language of human passion? Answer me these questions, Edward Mabry, for something of my conduct will depend upon the explanation which you may now give of yours."

These were home questions, and the effort to answer them only involved the speaker in all the meshes of a seemingly inextricable confusion. It was only by piecemeal, and after the most Socratic examination, that the keen, searching, old methodist obtained all the facts, and came to the conclusion, that, but for a quarrel between the parties, the horse-stealing, and other offences of John Yarbers, might have been buried in utter oblivion, so far as the testimony of Edward Mabry was concerned. In brief, the party was soon apprized that Mabry, whose attachment to Mary Clayton was, like most attachments of country-lovers, known to all the neighborhood, had, after fruitlessly pursuing the actor to the river without overtaking him, returned with a double feeling of wrath and mortification to his own home. From thence he had gone, early the next morning, to the house of Yarbers, and there had pressed his claim, in the absence of the latter, to the hand of his daughter-in-law. He had done this quite as much in anger as in love, being resolved to bring the matter to a close, as he found himself unable to bear the continual anxiety and passionate strifes to which his position exposed him; and he did not, in fact, believe that he was entirely wanting in attraction to the eyes of the damsel.

But he made his application at the worst possible moment. The calculating mother and uncalculating daughter had but too recently parted with the gay and attractive actor, and he met with a flat rejection from both, the terms of which, on the part of Mrs. Yarbers, were uttered in a manner nowise complimentary to the pride and vanity of the suitor.

Burning with indignation, he rushed from the house, only to encounter John Yarbers at the entrance. To him he breathed, without stint or limit, the indignation which he felt; and his rage was complete when the husband simply and civilly confessed that he had no power to alter the decision of his wife. Yarbers was rather *nonchalant* in his treatment of Mabry, for he had just before had the assurance of the master-spirit, Saxon, that the thing should be settled in such a manner as to save him harmless; but he begged Mabry to wait awhile longer, and concluded—having a reference to some crude and half-digested plan of Saxon—by recommending that Mabry should contrive to get himself made colonel; a vacancy then existing in the regiment by the death of the late celebrated Colonel Quillinan. To the raging Mabry, this seemed little less than downright mockery; and, without further exchange of words, he put spurs to his horse, and took the road to the house of the justice of Zion's Hill. The progress of the visiter in this quarter has so far been narrated. Taking the magistrate apart, Walter Rawlins ventured to excuse Mabry's suppression of the facts so long, by taking upon himself a portion of the blame.

"As the thing's out, now, Mr. Badger, though to my think-ing it had been better in for a while longer, even though John Yarbers got quite off, why, I may as well up and tell you, sir, that I advised Ned Mabry to keep the matter quiet."

"And, pray, what may have been your reasons, Walter Rawlins, for thus seeking to screen the criminal from the hands of justice?"

"Only that the hands of justice might get a good gripe when she tried for it," was the prompt reply of the woodman. Then, proceeding with some rapidity, as he saw that his further treat-ment of the figure was regarded with a grave countenance by the methodist, he went on to give certain reasons and facts for the policy which he had pursued.

"You must know, Mr. Badger, that there are more persons than John Yarbers concerned in this trade of horse-stealing, and it isn't the one mare of Joe Watson that's been cleared out by 'em in my time. We happen to know of many horses that's been lost to their owners, that John Yarbers found a claim in; and we sort o' concluded—me, and Tom Coleman, Jack Andrews, and Ned Mabry, here—that, as we knew all that any did know, and as that wasn't enough to clinch any but John Yarbers, that we'd say nothing for a while, and only keep a sharp look-out, and be in readiness to find out the rest. We all considered Yarbers to be a poor shoat, that only did as others told him. We had suspicions of three other men that took the

horses, after Yarbers had run 'em to the river, and carried 'em
on from hand to hand, till they got 'em where they could sell
'em without danger of being known; and we thought, by keeping quiet about Yarbers, and watching him close, that we might
get on a trail that would lead us to the other rascals. Yarbers
don't dream, to this day, that anybody but Ned Mabry knows
about his rascality. Ned caught him with the horse hobbled;
and his liking for Yarbers' wife's daughter made him very
willing to say nothing, till now, about the dad. He told me
only because we were so friendly, and he knew I could keep a
close mouth over any secret."

"You have done wrong; you should have brought this man
to justice. The law is the terror to evil-doers, and they should
be made to feel it! And who, Walter Rawlins, are the men of
whom you have suspicions?"

"Well, squire, I can't tell you that, seeing that I've made a
promise not to do so until there's a good chance to clinch 'em,
and we get good witnesses. I'm sort of dubious it'll be a mighty
tough business whenever the time comes."

"And what, Walter Rawlins, may be the reason of this fear?"
said the magistrate, with increasing severity of tone and solemnity of look, his self-esteem being grievously disturbed by the
refusal of the woodman to confide to him the extent of his
knowledge.

"Because, squire, we've good reasons for thinking these rascals are backed by a great number that pass for honest men and
good Christians; and up to this time, squire, we're at a loss to
say which is which among our acquaintance and those that put
on religion, and talk very good things at meeting. Every now
and then there's a robbery, now on this, and now on the other
side of the Big Black, but at all times too mighty nigh us not
to make it very strange of the sort of folks that live about.
There was Dick Coby robbed of his watch and all he had, coming from Benton a week ago, by two men in disguise; and there
was the beating that Harvey got up by Doak's stand, about the
same time, by other men in disguise, while he was on his way
to sarve your warrant; then, again, this attack on the old gentleman, Mr. Wilson, here, as I may say, in sight of Zion's Hill
why, squire, you can't shut your eyes to the thing. It's clear

as noonday that there's a gang of rascals that stand by each
other, and ain't afraid of the worst that can be done to them.
Besides, I'm somehow thinking, squire, that there's nothing you
can do, or any magistrate, that they won't get wind of, in a
mighty short time after you do it."

Rawlins did not confine himself to this brief array of circumstances to establish the probability of the faith that was in him.
He proceeded to the detail of other events, some of which were
known to the magistrate and others new; but the accumulation
of facts had the effect of convincing and startling the methodist,
when, one by one, as they occurred, they would have made
little impression, and that of little duration, upon his mind.

"Verily, Walter Rawlins, thou hast shown me these things
in stronger lights than they have come to me before. It is a
shame and a discredit to me, as a magistrate under the appointment of man, and no less as an humble follower of Christ Jesus,
that these things should be suffered to go on around me. It
were well to get the young men together, and bestir ourselves
in the examination of this swamp which is beside us; for that,
according to my thought no less than thine, must be the place
in which these villains harbor. How many young men canst
thou muster at blowing of the horn?"

"Well, squire, I reckon there may be ten or thereabouts,"
returned the woodman, muttering their names over to himself,
and counting upon his fingers as he spoke.

"Ten!—ten only! Why, Walter, either I lose my arithme-
tic, or you have never yet found yours. By what rule can you
count? Instead of ten, there may be twenty, nay, thirty,
mustered by the horn blowing."

"Yes, squire, but it ain't by horn-blowing that I would bring
together the men for such a business as this. Some of the men
that would come at horn-blowing would be more likely to help
the rascals than to hurt them; and if I could tell you some of
the suspicionable names that I know on, you'd look green
again."

"I can not say, Walter Rawlins, that I altogether understand
you when you speak of my looking green again; but, at all
events, I will look farther and immediately into this business.
I will confer with this young man, Vernon, who speaks sensibly

on most subjects, and he hath shown himself bold enough to be
a leader in any strife that may follow, and is surely not to be
suspected of any connection with these outlaws of whom you
speak. If he will go forth with us, it were something; for thou
and thy ten men would go but a little way to compass all the
points of the swamp, and beleaguer those who harbor therein.
The canebrake were, alone, a sufficient protection. But let us
seek these other youths. We have already five in this dwelling, counting myself and Gideon Badger with the rest, and I
trust in God that when the hour of evil strife shall come, there
will be fifty rather than ten willing to gather together for the
good of the covenant."

CHAPTER XX

THE FOXES IN COUNCIL — TERRIBLE DISCOVERY — A WOMAN'S
STRENGTH.

"We are not grown so proud
As to disdain familiar conference."—MASSINGER

RAWLINS was not altogether satisfied that the methodist
should take the business so completely out of his hands, but he
well knew that there was no hope of successful resistance
against the usurpation. The self esteem of William Badger
was well-sustained by the firm rigidity of his character, and the
perfect unconsciousness of anything like presumption in the
lead which he was resolved to take. The woodman shrugged
his shoulders, therefore, and said nothing; congratulating himself that he had kept the suspected names to himself, and inly
determining to continue his own plans, which, though less dignified and imposing that those of the senior, yet promised to
be, for that very reason, far more effective. He followed the
squire into the *salle à manger*, where the young men had been
left, and where he found them busily engaged in the discussion
of sundry subjects, all of which were necessarily made to give
way to that which was always the most important to William

Badger—that, namely, which most interested himself.   The
latter proceeded, as if from his own knowledge and thought—
for he made no sort of reference to Rawlins in the progress of
his narrative—to give the substance of what he had heard, to
describe the evil condition of the neighborhood, and to expa-
tiate upon the necessity of gathering the young men together
for the purpose of routing the evildoers.

Vernon heard him with a degree of pleasure and interest
which he found it not so easy to suppress; but he regarded the
young Badger with eyes of too much keenness and suspicion
to suffer his real sentiments to be known.   Without hesitation,
he joined issue with the venerable elder, as well on the propriety as the necessity of the course he proposed to pursue;
deliberately questioning the correctness of the assumption, that
there was any number of men engaged in the outlawry which
had troubled the neighborhood; and insisting upon the strong
probability of all the detailed offences having been committed
by the same two or three individuals who had been conspicuous
in each.   Much of his argument was founded upon the broad,
patriotic text, that in a country like ours, where the means of
life are so readily and universally to be obtained, it was morally
impossible that any numerous set of men could be found, wilfully disregarding the laws and making themselves liable to
their penalties.

His views were supported at large, and with much more
earnestness, by Gideon Badger, who took especial care to wind
up his notions of the subject, by an elaborate eulogy upon the
moral and religious influences which had been exercised over
the neighborhood by the burning and shining light fixed upon
Zion's Hill.   .

But neither the well-tempered courtesy with which Vernon
had spoken, nor the closing and rather bald flattery of Gideon's
speech, saved them from the charge of vaingloriousness and
presumption from the venerable elder, who was never more full
of Christian texts than when he was following his own mind,
and resolved upon making others do so likewise.

Having adopted the notions of Rawlins as his own, he was
as rigid in their maintenance as he ever could have been in
that of a favorite text.   He went into a history of all the rob-

beries and murders in the county and in the neighboring coun-
ties for the ten previous years; connected them together by a
supposititious train of circumstances, ascribed them all to the
same set of men, and concluded by declaring, that "the time
was at length come for the punishment of the offenders; that
the vengeance of God was at length ripe; that the sword was
unsheathed to smite, and sharpened for destruction, and that
he"—though this was rather left to the implication of the
hearers—"was the appointed messenger of wrath, who was at
once to denounce the judgment and carry it into execution."
His resolution to obey the commission which had been given
him, was followed by a direct demand on Vernon's services, to
assist in carrying out his purposes, which he resolved to begin
forthwith.

"Impossible, Mr. Badger, impossible!" was the reply of
Vernon. "I am not the master of my own time, and can delay
no longer than is absolutely necessary. I must pursue my
journey to-morrow, and should have resumed it to-day, but that
my thigh felt too sore and stiff to justify the attempt to ride so
soon after my hurts."

"Young man, would you fly from your duty?" demanded the
other with solemnity.

"No, sir, it is in the performance of my duties that I would
fly so soon from your hospitable dwelling. I have occasions
which command my haste and attention elsewhere; and I propose to leave you, at the rise of to-morrow's dawn, with the
view to their performance."

The elder was not to be gainsayed, and he showed himself
as tenacious on the present, as upon most other occasions.

"There can be no call so urgent, young man, as that of our
country; no duty so clearly necessary as the detection and punishment of crime."

"You forget, Mr. Badger," replied Vernon, availing himself
of his own expressed opinions rather than those which he really
felt; "you forget, Mr. Badger, that I take a different view of
these facts from yourself; that I see not the same dangers, and
do not recognise the same necessity; but, even were it otherwise, I see not how I could assist you materially, and acknowledge the presence of other, and as you may think them, selfish

10*

obligations, which compel me elsewhere. Should it occur that
I may do anything to promote your wishes, I believe that I may
safely assure you that you should not find me wanting."

"We must even try to carry on the good work without you,"
replied the other stiffly; and with this the further conference
between the two ended. But the reluctance of Vernon rather
stimulated than discouraged the methodist, who was always
strengthened in purpose and performance by the increase of his
own personal responsibilities. Having despatched a servant to
summon his constable, Harvey, to his presence, he proceeded to
concoct his plans for taking the outlaws, or, at least, breaking
up their nest in the Loosa-Chitta swamp, with more earnestness
than secresy. The arrival of Harvey enabled him to issue the
warrant against Yarbers for horse-stealing, based upon the oath
of Edward Mabry.

"This knocks up your affair with Mary Clayton for ever,
Ned," was the consolatory remark whispered in the ears of the
lover by his friend Rawlins, as the warrant was given to the
constable.

"Well, I know it — I don't care a d—n ; I'll make him sweat
for his impudence, though it makes me lose everything."

Harvey, who was a stout fellow, of a bold heart and well-
tried honesty, was made a party to the further deliberations on
the subject of the outlaws of the neighborhood, and so much
time was consumed in the discussions of projects and difficulties,
that night came on ere he was permitted to depart for the purpose of arresting Yarbers. This duty was therefore deferred to
the ensuing morning; but that very night, a trusty messenger
conveyed the tidings of his danger to the horse-thief, who left a
warm nest but nothing in it, to reward the industry of the constable, who returned to the magistrate with another proof added
to the many commented on by Rawlins, that there was some
secret and sinister influence continually busy to find out his designs, and defeat his warrants. Yarbers, who was neither worse
nor better than a squatter, before daylight the next morning,
was speeding on with bag and baggage, wife and daughter, to
a place of hiding well known to all the beagles in the swamp.

But Vernon, though he refrained from yielding himself to the
importunities of Badger, had no such indifference to his project

nor did he entertain those doubts of the necessity of proceeding against the outlaws which he yet professed. In his chamber that night, alone with Rawlins, he declared himself more fully.

"I agree with you, Rawlins, in my doubts of the integrity of this youth, Gideon Badger, and I have as little faith in the judgment of his father. The one would wilfully and dishonestly betray—the other would commit the same fault through the mere love of display and authority. I am pleased at the reserve which you have shown, and will requite it by a degree of confidence which must move you to increased reserve. What I do and say to you, must, of all things, be most studiously kept from this old man and his son; and, indeed, whatever you propose to do in the case of these robbers, must be also withheld, if you hope to be successful in your projects. Your passionate friend, Mabry, too, should have none of your confidence in such matters, for, though honest enough, he lacks all discretion, and would blow us in the first gust of phrensy that happened to seize upon him. See to that door—I heard footsteps—I speak for your ears only."

This done, and assured that there was none to hear but Rawlins, Vernon proceeded to inform the astounded woodman of those facts in the history of the mystic brotherhood, and the flight of Clem Foster from Alabama, and his probable presence in the neighborhood, all of which had been gathered by him in his interview with the governor of Mississippi. We forbear the long detail, so unnecessary to us, and avoid repetition of the still longer conversation which ensued between the two in reference to the subject, and the proper course to be pursued by Rawlins in the management of the game before him. Vernon studiously counselled the other to forbear taking any active part in the affair, until events had more completely developed the persons, the aims, and the particular whereabouts of the outlaws. In all circumstances he especially counselled the sturdy woodman—who already regarded him as an oracle—while using the influence of William Badger, on no account to admit his privity to any plan which he might deem it advisable to pursue.

"It may be that I shall be able to assist you in person before many days. My present hope is to accomplish the urgent busi

ness upon which I shall set forth to-morrow, in time to fulfil the
partial promise which I made, on leaving Raymond, to the
governor. But, at all events, I will provide you with authority
for your own action, which will strengthen your power, and
confirm your influence over your neighbors. Here is a commission, with his excellency's signature, which makes you a
captain over such a body of men as you may gather together
willing to obey your command. Here, further, is a small list
of suspected persons. To none of these should you extend your
trust. Some of the persons, perhaps, may be among your acquaintance, and it would be advisable, however well you may
esteem them, to maintain toward them the utmost reserve re-
specting all your plans. I will write to his excellency to-night,
under an assumed name, and leave the letter with you, to despatch
from the nearest postoffice. The address will be one already
agreed upon between us, and he will give you further instructions—perhaps send to you a special messenger—as George
Jenkinson. You will answer to the name for a time, since it
would be unsafe to address you by your own. I will also give
you another letter to a friend, which you will oblige me by
despatching by the same post as that which takes my letter to
the governor. There are other matters upon which I will re-
flect before sleeping to-night, which will, perhaps, enable us to
correspond while apart, and play this difficult game with some
good prospects of success. For the present, let us separate, that
there may be no suspicions of the confidence between us."

That night Vernon prepared his letters for the governor, and
his friend and patron, Carter. To the former he detailed such
a portion of his adventures, and his brief experience at Zion's
Hill, as would enable him to form an idea of the material he
had to depend upon in the issue which, it was obvious enough,
was approaching fast between the outlaws and the government.
The merits of Walter Rawlins were set forth in proper language,
and a list of names, which had been furnished by the worthy
woodman, of persons to be relied on, was included in the letter.
To Carter he wrote a more comprehensive epistle, in which his
fortunes from the moment of their separation were described at
large. He did not fail to apprize him of the discovery, which
he thought himself to have made, of Maitland in the person of

the traveller whom he had rescued from the robbers. His hurt, slight as it was, was spoken of even more slightingly than it deserved; and he declared his ability and intention to renew his pursuit on the morning following. His language was full of hope and light-heartedness, his tone being studiously assumed to encourage his friend and patron. But it might have been remarked that though Vernon spoke freely and fully of all other matters, he yet found, on finishing the letter, that he had said not a word on the subject of the two daughters — or, rather, the one daughter of Maitland who accompanied him. He was reminded, on reperusing the epistle, to say something to supply this omission in the form of a postscript, but finding that he had not room to say much, he adopted the satisfactory determination to say nothing; and so his labors closed for the night.

While the conference was going on between Vernon and Rawlins, Gideon Badger was making his way to the woods, where he found Saxon, Jones, and another of the confederates. To them he narrated the discussion which had taken place, under his father's lead, between the assembled company at Zion's Hill.

"This fellow, Mabry," said Saxon, "will not sleep soundly until he's knocked on the head. We must send Yarbers off, for it won't do to kick up a bobbery on his account. Mack," he continued, addressing the confederate hitherto unnamed, "take horse instantly for Yarbers — tell him what's going on, and say from me, that we can do nothing for him just now. Let him make tracks for Bear Garden before day peeps."

To hear was to obey. The fellow was off in the twinkling of an eye, and Saxon continued thus :—

"What the devil shall we do to quiet your father, Gideon ? I am puzzled what to do with him."

"Knock him on the head, too," was the answer of Jones, "if it's only to help Gideon to a little that he ought to have, and rescue him from the strait jacket of methodism. Lord ! Saxon, it's the most funny thing in the world, to see the pompous old parson, his round, red face looking forth from his white neckcloth, and half fenced in by his high shoulders and black cape, like a terrapin on a wet log, meditating the ways and means for a Sunday dinner, and Gideon, meek as a mouse in the corner

of a trap that has baffled all his efforts at escape, patiently resigned to what is coming—an evening prayer and sermon three
hours long, church measure—cursing in his heart, all the while,
that sort of heavenly unction which keeps him in a stew worse
than any ever known in hell. I have peeped in once when I
went to look after Gideon, and once was enough. After that I
never went nigher than the garden fence, and there I gave the
signal. That sermon was quite enough to keep off any beagle
of any stomach, and sure am I, that the old man had better
begin to hunt us with a full mouth, such as he had that day,
than with a six-pounder. We could dodge the shot, but that
sermon would be sure to reach us wherever we might skulk.
For my part, let me be safe hidden in a hollow, and put Billy
Badger near by, well wound up for a long run, he'd be sure to
drive me out. I must stop my ears, or let my heels go, for
stand him ten minutes I neither could nor would, for all that
head or heels might be worth. I'm clear, the shortest and best
way for all parties is to knock him on the head with Mabry.
We have good reason for thinking that Gideon would never
take up preaching as a trade, certainly he can not give us such
prayers as his father; and so the sooner the old man is gathered,
the better for the goodly seed which he leaves behind him."

Gideon who was one of those goodly rogues that like to keep
up appearances even in situations where hypocrisy seems to
be the last thing necessary, growled out something in reply to
this, of an angry savor; but Jones knew his man and answered:—

"Tut, tut, Gideon, you waste breath. You know as well as
I, that were the Lord in his mercy—to use the goodly phrase-
ology of Zion's Hill—to summon to his keeping the blessed
head thereof, it would be a call more grateful to his devout and
affectionate son Gideon, than any his ears ever heard."

"Enough, Jones," said the more considerate Saxon, "this
talk, which Gideon may suppose you to utter earnestly, brings
us no nigher to our object. Of course you should never think
of doing hurt or harm to any of the family of one who belongs
to, and acts with us, unless it became absolutely necessary to
his and to our interests. The only course which seems clear to
me if the old man gets up his squad, which he will find it hard

work to do, is that we must skulk and run for it. That he can neither find nor trouble us, is sufficiently certain. Gideon, alone, as one of his band, will give us all intelligence; and there is Cotton, Saunders, Furst, Mason, Wilkes, and others, whom he will no doubt muster with him, and who will tell us just when and where the cat will jump, so that we may leave the nest empty. We must leave you, Jones, to receive notice from Gideon, whom you can see nightly, of anything that may be determined on, and this intelligence you must send by the quickest beagle you can call up, so that we may know at Cane Castle and Bear Garden what to look for and when. What you tell me of this young fellow, Vernon, is the most surprising of all. Can it be that I am mistaken in the man? Is it possible that he is only going for private business? But what business? It may be the location of Yazoo lands; he may be another of the mad fools who dream nothing but pre-emptions, and fancy they are playing the great game to themselves, while all the rest of the world is gaping and looking on. You say you searched his baggage and found no papers?"

"None. I emptied his portmanteau while he slept on the sofa in the hall, and found nothing but a few changes of linen, a vest, some handkerchiefs, and half a dozen stockings. There was neither letter nor writing."

"Did you open the stockings?"

"No! I didn't think of that."

"Ah! that was half doing the business only. But you say that he not only objected to going with your father, but doubted the truth of his conjectures."

"Made light of it—nay, laughed at it; and concluded by declaring his intention to resume his own journey upward by to-morrow's sun."

"I must meet with him. I must look into him myself," said Saxon. "I will join him on the road, to-morrow, and he will be a keen lawyer, indeed, if I do not probe his depth, and find out his secrets. It may be that I am deceived, yet the circumstances are all strong and strange. He may have laughed at the governor's fears as he laughed at Badger's; and yet, after all, it may have been a private speculation only. Would I could have heard that conversation; but regret is useless. We

must make up in skill the deficiencies of fortune, and make ingenuity do that which necessity requires to be done. If I do
not sound him thoroughly to-morrow we must call Justice
Nawls to our assistance."

Much of this was spoken soliloquizingly; and was, possibly,
beyond the immediate comprehension of his comrades. At its
close, Gideon Badger asked:—

" Did you suffer the old man, Wilson, to get off?"

" Yes:—your blundering the day before, and the death of
Weston, persuaded me that it was proper for us to do so, at least
in this neighborhood. I set a hound on his track, however, so
that we may know where he earths, and what course he takes.
If he has anything, we can easily cover him before he touches
the Tennessee line. But enough with you to-night, Gideon.
A dog will bark at the foot of the garden at noon to-morrow —
let him know what the old man has done, or is about to do.
Good night."

The confederates separated; Saxon and his companion, Jones,
sinking into the deep woods beyond the garden, and Gideon
Badger leaping the fence, and taking a shorter way to the house.

They had fully gone from sight and hearing — ten minutes
had been allowed to elapse after their absence — when Rachel
Morrison emerged from the cowering attitude in which she had
crouched and found concealment in a thick body of young plum
saplings, brier, and shrub shoots, that skirted the spot where
the conspirators had carried on their conference, and in which
she had heard every syllable that had been uttered. Her
cheeks were pale, very pale, when she came forth from her
place of concealment; her form trembled with the crowding and
conflicting emotions of her soul; but her resolution, which had
brought her to the spot, and had kept her firm, and above any
of those apprehensions which afflict most women, was still as
strong and unyielding as at first. Sick at heart, and sad, with
a bitter sadness, she was yet glad that she had so far conquered
her womanly fears—the scruples of a nice, and in ordinary
necessities, a proper delicacy — and had listened to that cold
calculating conference of villany, in which the fate of those to
whom she was linked by innumerable ties, was so intimately
interested.

"It is, then, true, all true," she exclaimed, "even as Mother Kerrison assured me, and as my own fears were most ready to believe. Gideon Badger is lost—lost for ever; and my poor old uncle—so proud in himself—so confident of all around him—with such hope in his only son—what will be the pang at his heart—what the crushing and humbling misery of his soul, when he shall hear of this! And hear of it he must. Even if my lips remain closed upon the subject, the truth will reach his ears at last. There must come the hour of discovery, when all will be known; and he—God strengthen and sustain him in that dreadful hour! For me, for me, what is left now? Shall I speak of what I have seen and heard? Shall my lips declare these dreadful tidings, and my hands offer him the bitter cup of desolation? No! no! I may not—I must not. I have not the strength—not the heart for this. I must contrive other means to prevent the utter ruin of the one, and the heart-wasting desolation of the other. God of heaven—eternal and preserving Father, be with me this blessed night, and counsel me in the fitting course, which shall defeat the danger, and disarm the sting of this threatening sorrow. To thy grace and saving mercy, Lord Jesus, I commend myself, in this moment of doubt and difficulty."

Never was prayer more humble and devout, and offered with a more becoming sense and spirit, than that of Rachel Morrison kneeling among the withered leaves, in the silence of the night on the edge of that deep, dim, and mournfully-sighing forest.

CHAPTER XXI.

KEEN ENCOUNTER OF WITS — THE ROGUES ARREST THE TRUE MAN — BATTLE OF RIVAL RACES.

"I. walking in the place where men's law-suits
Are heard and pleaded, not so much as dreaming
Of any such encounter; steps me forth
Their valiant foreman, with the words, 'I 'rest you.
I made no more ado, but laid these paws
Close on his shoulders, tumbling him to earth."
                                        GEORGE CHAPMAN.

THE hour was late when the strong-minded maiden, Rachel Morrison, reached her apartments. The family, guests and all, had retired to their several chambers for the night; and in the silent review which she made of the scene she had just witnessed, a most annoying conviction arose in her mind of the probable danger awaiting the young traveller, Vernon, who, she knew, had appointed to resume his journey on the morrow. She recollected the promise of one of the robbers (Saxon) to join him on the road; and this promise she naturally construed into a resolution to assail him.

To warn him of his danger was her first impulse, but how was this to be done? It was impossible that she should seek him then; it was scarcely proper, indeed, that she should seek him at any time; and to communicate her warning to Walter Rawlins—the most easy and natural mode—was to prompt his inquiries into other particulars within her knowledge, which she was not yet prepared to unfold. She dreaded the prying mind of her lover, and doubted her own strength to refuse him that information which was effectually to blast and destroy the son of her protector. The conflict in her mind kept her wakeful, and at the dawn of day she was dressed, and anxiously on the watch for that stir in the household which might denote the preparations of the traveller. To her great joy she heard footsteps in the adjoining passage, which she knew to be those of Rawlins. She went forth and joined him. "Walter," she said, "your friend Mr. Vernon must be on his guard while he rides. There is danger awaiting him —let him see to his arms, and be heedful of the company he meets."

"Ha! Rachel—but is this all ?—know you nothing more ?"

"Nothing that is of any service to him, and nothing more of his danger. The robbers are near us; they will be on the look-out for him. Counsel him to be well prepared; perhaps you may counsel him to defer his departure."

"I have tried that already, but he is bent on a push to-day. He's very restless to get off, though his thigh's mighty stiff and sore. But tell me, Rachel, how do you know all this ?"

"Another time I will tell you all, not now—Gideon is stir-ring. Beware of him."

"Ha! Gideon—say, Rachel, what of Gideon ?"

The person named, at this moment appeared in the passage-way, and the maiden was gone from sight in the next. The woodman instantly returned to the chamber of Vernon, and apprized him of what he had heard. The latter listened to him without emotion.

He looked to his pistols, felt the charge, renewed the priming, and this done, continued his preparations for departure as coolly as before. An early breakfast had been prepared, after which, and the unusually long grace which preceded it, Vernon bade adieu to his rigid, but hospitable host, and joined by Rawlins, rode forth upon his way. The latter escorted him to the river, and on their way to this point, Vernon suggested to him all those plans and precautions, by which the woodman was to conduct the contemplated operations against the robbers. The reasons for the exclusion of the old methodist and his son were necessarily increased by the significant warning of Rachel Morrison; and, counselled as well as he might be under the existing circumstances, Rawlins returned to Zion's Hill, leaving our hero to pursue his farther journey alone. The narrow, but deep and rapid stream was soon crossed, and now let us also leave him, for a brief space, while he struggles through the

rank ooze, and interminable ponds and sluices that skirt, at frequent intervals, and for continued miles on either side, the dead
level borders and drowned lands of the Loosa-Chitta.

The sun was slowly ascending through the branches of the
towering cottonwood and pine-trees, that seemed to throw themselves forward as barriers in opposition to his progress, along
the eastern elevation, when a small party of men, three in number, might have been seen in close consultation beneath their
concealing umbrage. One of these was no other than our old
acquaintance, Saxon. Their horses were in hand, as if made
ready for a journey; and that air of quickness, keenness, and
anxiety which mingled in their manner, and contrasted strongly
with the low, suppressed tones of their voices, plainly denoted
some new expedition. The robbers were evidently preparing
for business.

"Go you forward," said Saxon to his two companions as he
leaped to the saddle, "and let Nawls get the papers in readiness.
Meanwhile, I will take the road from the Benton turn-out, as
soon as I am sure that our man has passed it. I know his
course now, and can readily overtake him. Remember you are
to act as law officers, and you must do your duty with becoming gravity. None of your swaggering and swearing, Binks;
and do you, Davis, keep a dry throat. Be sure you cast no
discredit on the venerable authority you are supposed to represent. It is an honor no less imposing than new, that you
should be made officers of the law you have so often offended."

"Not the less worthy officers for all that," said one of the
fellows. " ' Set a a thief to catch a thief,' is a maxim which will
always give a thief employment."

"Ay, but you are to catch an honest man as usual, rascals;
so that you are only pursuing an old trade. But ride on; you
have no time to waste. In another hour our man will be within
reach, and you shall meet us ere we get to Lucchesa. Nawls is
better at running a horse than filling out a warrant, and you
will need to spur him to the task. Let him waste no minutes
that you can save — you, Binks, can fill up the blank and the
judge can sign it. That will shorten the business to his hand,
and by all calculations you should be able to tap your prisoner
on his shoulder ere we gain sight of the village. Away."

"It is done," said Binks, putting spurs to his horse and followed closely by his companion. Saxon, meanwhile, crossing the main road, sank into the opposite forests, and put himself in watch for the coming of his prey. He was not long in waiting. His calculations, the result of long experience of horse's speed and the road, were nearly correct. Before the hour was ended, the trampling of a steed was heard, and Vernon went by. Suffering some moments to elapse, the better to deceive the traveller as to his late proximity, Saxon at length followed and joined him a few hundred yards above.

With the first sound of approaching footsteps, Vernon prepared himself for an enemy, but the sight of the stranger somewhat disarmed his apprehensions. Saxon was seemingly without arms of any kind, and there was that in the frank and manly expression of his face, in the free, hearty salutation which he used, and the quiet and simple manner of his address, that Vernon, as a mere physiognomist—had he annexed any importance to this comparatively idle study — no *study* is wholly idle — would have been disposed rather to confide in the newcomer, than to regard him with distrust. He answered the salutation of the stranger with equal frankness, and it was agreed, as they both aimed for Lucchesa, that they should ride on their way together. This is not a matter of difficult arrangement in a country of such lonesome distances and long miles as ours; and where the parties are young, and where they have already had any experience in travelling, there is a very general flexibility of temper, which prompts them to great social compliances when upon the road. But, with the present parties, a mutual policy would alone have brought them together; and each aiming at concealment, the frank game was the only one to be played by those who had any occult objects in reserve. Something, too, in the really excellent capacities and good education of the two, may have contributed to bring them more readily together; and each perceiving in the other a nearer approximation to those standards of taste which were most agreeable to himself, and which were something above those presented by the ordinary intellects of forest life, the dialogue grew lively after a brief space of time, and soon became unflagging.

"A few years more, sir," said Saxon, in reply to a remark of Vernon, touching the sparse settlements along the Yazoo; "a few years more, and this country must become exceedingly populous. Its resources must be found out, as they are so greatly desirable to the poor settler everywhere. The wildness of the region will keep back the cold, the slow, the timid, and the wealthy. They will shrink from a too close neighborhood with the Indians, and, perhaps, be equally apprehensive of that wild class, the squatters, who, rude, rash, violent and reckless as they are, are yet the necessary men in all new countries. These will continue to be wild, until they have made some valuable acquisitions. It is the possession of something to lose, that makes your social and best citizen, and the robber himself, when his accumulations become valuable, will, I doubt not, settle down into the sober citizen, and grow grave and great among the first moralists of the land."

"If a more sudden elevation does not anticipate such slow results," said Vernon with a smile; "but," he continued, "I have no faith in half the monstrous robber-tales which are told of every new country. When you reach the scene of the story, the terrible and frequently bloody event is placed in a region yet farther off. The border is always beyond you; the country of the monsters—the anthropophagi—

"'Gorgons, and hydras, and chimeras dire'—

is still the country of the unknown. You approach, and the cloud disperses, and that which, 'afar off seen,' was terrible, not only becomes harmless when at hand, but lovely and inviting, perhaps, beyond all other prospects. A certain distance 'lends enchantment to the view,' while an uncertain distance clothes it with evil aspects, fills it with

———"'All prodigious things,
Abominable, unutterable and worse
Than fables yet have feigned, or fear conceived.'

In short, ignorance makes as many monsters as fear, nay, it makes fear;—and mankind for ages have shrunk from the possession of the garden spots of earth, through dread of those multiplied terrors which have been made to guard them, simply through the ministry of their own imaginations."

Saxon concurred with Vernon in his brief and natural view of the subject, and the conversation proceeded with a mutually increasing interest on both sides. The former spoke with fluency, and a considerable knowledge of the plain, the positive, and practical. Like qualities of mind were observable in his companion, but warmed and elevated by a quick and vigorous imagination, which heightened the color of his fancy, gave life to his delineations; and kindled his enthusiasm. This warmth suffered a check, and he himself received a warning, however, as he found the conversation, on the part of Saxon, gradually rising into a strain of complimentary remark, as the latter either felt, or affected to feel, the eloquence and wisdom of his companion's sentiments. The quick, sensitive mind of Vernon, which, like that of most ambitious men, had an instinctive dread of ridicule, was at once checked in its familiarity, and sunk back upon its caution and self-esteem for defence and protection. A cold, merely respectful and civil tone and form of expression, succeeded to the glow and energy of his previous manner; and Saxon, with that keen eye which belongs to the tactician, beheld the change, and readily comprehended its origin.

His own manner was also changed accordingly; his speech more qualified and cautious; and though he took care that in what he said the easy deference of his opinions should convey a no less flattering testimony to his companion's merits, he yet forbore any of those more open expressions of approval which he had imprudently administered *ad nauseam*.

But the nice sense of moral delicacy once startled, it was not so easy for him to overcome the reluctance of Vernon to engage in any new freedom of dialogue. Not that the conversation flagged between them; the frankness alone was gone; the playful indifference of expression had passed away; and though speech was no less ready than before, yet caution watched the utterance, and truth was content to show herself only at the staid and squared portals of opinion.

With some dexterity, Saxon contrived to reopen the topic which had suggested itself to them at their first meeting — that, namely, which arose naturally from the wild and equivocal character of the country, and its evil influence over the supposed physical resources of the soil. It was an easy transition, which the outlaw did not feel at all scrupulous to make, to the frequent robberies and misdemeanors in the neighborhood. He spoke of them, as all spoke of them, as frequent, and sometimes coupled with greater crimes; but, at the same time, seizing upon an expressed opinion of Vernon, he declared them to be infamously exaggerated, and deplored the evils to the country of such an unhappy notoriety as belonged to it.

"It is, in fact, in the absence of citizens that these things happen. Our population is guiltless, I am sure, of any participation in them; and these crimes are committed by those only who make our territory a stage for their villanous performances. Had we a community sufficiently dense to act with anything like unanimity—indeed, had we any one or two men, calculated by ability and energy to take a lead, and bring our men together, nothing, I am sure, would be more easy than to put a stop to these excesses. We might soon, by lynching a few, keep the rest in order, and in good time the want of means and money would compel labor, which is all that is wanting to good morals in any country."

This was all very fairly and frankly said; the truth of the latter opinion could not well be denied; but Vernon, though suppressing everything like apparent suspicion, was yet suspicious; and once startled, he was one of those keen, restless minds, that can not be quieted short of utter confirmation on one side or the other. The mistimed complimentary speeches of Saxon still occupied his thoughts, and were productive in him of some such musings as filled the mind of the Prince of Denmark under not dissimilar circumstances. The theatrical reference which his companion employed in one part of his speech, reminded him at the same moment of his quandam friend Horsey, and the phlegmatic and indecisive Dane. Why should he flatter so poor a man as Hamlet? Such applauses to one's beard were not in ordinary use in that time and country; and however grateful to such a man as Horsey, were scarcely pleasing to him, unless it were that his companion regarded him also as one of the players just "come hither."

At all events, the effect upon Vernon was to counsel him to more caution, but to no reserve; and with this policy in view he expressed himself very freely in accordance with the opinions of Saxon, which, indeed, happened to be precisely such as he had uttered at the council-board of old Badger—if that might be called a place of council where the chairman—as very often happens to venerable chairmen—was pretty much resolved from the beginning to have his own way. It occurred very naturally that he should relate his recent adventures on the other side of the river—so much, at least, as related to the attack of the robbers, and his own slight hurt in defence of the traveller.

"I then," he concluded, "in a conversation with a very worthy and respectable old gentleman—a Mr. Badger, with whom I remained a brief space, in consequence of my hurt—came to this very conclusion, though in direct opposition to himself. He was for turning out the trainbands at once, and searching the swamp—a labor which, I fear, will be utterly fruitless. The same scoundrels that assailed Mr. Wilson are, I doubt not, full fifty miles off before this time."

The keen eye of Saxon surveyed the speaker with a glance which seemed intended to penetrate his soul; but the calm, indifferent countenance of Vernon baffled the inquiry.

"This fellow," thought the outlaw, "is either a most admirable tactician, or I have taken a very unnecessary labor. But, let the game be played out. We are now, sir," speaking aloud, "we are now within sight of one of the prettiest little villages in this country. They call it Lucchesa—after some Italian city, I believe. We are all monstrous fond of going to Europe for names, which would be found more appropriate and quite as smooth and musical at home. But call Lucchesa by what name you will, you will admit when you see it that it is one of the sweetest spots that could be found anywhere for a village. It lies among gentle risings, which here may be called hills; and which so completely surround, as to leave it but a single opening for entrance, and that seems only to be scooped out for the purpose—a work not of nature but of art. The woods, you see, are thick—the old forests are barely trimmed to let in the daylight, as it were, and give room for the cottages. These are better built and more neatly decorated than is often the case in our country villages; washed with lime, which answers the

11

purpose of the best white lead for a season or more; and, peeping through the green openings here and there, they seem to be the pleasantest little temples that were ever yet raised by humility to happiness. I think I could spend my days in this little village, without ever desiring to look down on the outer side of the hills which surround it."

"You live here, then?" was the natural question of Vernon.

"Yes, I may say so," was the somewhat evasive answer; "I live here when not elsewhere. But it is not permitted us to choose our habitations any more than to choose our graves. No man can say, death shall seek me, here, however much he might pray for it."

Saxon was on the verge of Badgerism, as the two entered the little and lovely, but scattered village of Lucchesa. It seemed a settlement of some fifteen or twenty families — the cottages gleaming in a broken circle from among the trees, planted without much reference to each other, but amply gaining in picturesqueness what they might have lacked in regularity. Some of these were girdled and guarded by little low white palings, that followed the hill-slopes on which they stood; some were fenced by hedges of the wild rose or the box, and among the small trees and bushes, and the bush myrtles or spreading cedars that filled up the space between, the multiflora and the perpetual rose leaped and twined even around the topmost branches. A few pale sycamores rose up majestically amid the dwarf foliage that filled the valley, and ran down the slopes, giving a staid and solemn air to a scene that otherwise presented no other aspect than one of unqualified sweetness. But one object more than all gratified the eye of the observer, in the little stream that came stealing and whispering out from the hollow in which the village stood, by the only portal that led into it, with the sly, smiling glance of the truant boy, availing himself of the opportunity and open door, to steal away from the guarded circuit, and lose himself for a while among the thick groves that had beguiled him from a distance so often and so sweetly before.

While Vernon looked round admiringly upon a scene that seemed strangely placed on the very confines of savage life, he suddenly found himself confronted by two persons, who, with the air of men having a perfect right to his attention, demanded to know his name.

"My name, gentlemen!—my name is Vernon; but your demand is something singular. You will oblige me with your reason."

"Oh, yes, that's all fair enough; Harry, or Henry Vernon—that's right, a'n't it, sir?" said one of the men, drawing forth a paper.

- "It is, sir," was the reply of Vernon, with increasing surprise, and a slight increase of color in the cheek, and that dilation of the nostril which denotes the swelling choler. Saxon, meanwhile, looked on with well-affected astonishment.

"Then, sir, if you're the man, we are commanded to arrest you, in the name of the state, for murder."

"Murder!"

"Yes, murder!—the murder of one Thomas Horsey, a young gentleman from below that you travelled with a few days past."

"Horsey dead! Can it be possible? This is the strangest matter, sir, and—but show me your warrant."

"Let us go into the tavern, Mr. Vernon," said Saxon, sympathizingly, "and you can there look more calmly into this business."

Upon this hint the party went forward, Doe and Roe taking care to environ our hero in such a manner that escape, were he disposed to try it, would have been impossible. Here, with feelings of no enviable character, Vernon examined the instrument which had been issued for his taking. He found it to be a criminal warrant, proper in its forms, and issued by one William Nawls, a regularly-acting magistrate. Had an enemy confronted our hero with intent to kill, the absolute danger would have produced less disquiet and annoyance in his mind than did the simple instrument which he perused and reperused, absolutely bewildered and confounded for the moment. That Horsey should have been murdered, however sudden and unexpected this event, was certainly far from being improbable in a neighborhood where he himself, but a few days before, had a foretaste of a similar fate awaiting him. But that *he* should be made liable for the actor's fate, and arrested for his murder

was one of those contingencies which, a moment before, he
would have regarded as too remote and ridiculous a possibility
to occasion any other feeling than merriment in his mind.

"Gentlemen," he said to the constables, "I can scarce recover from my surprise at this strange accusation. Pray, on
whose oath was this warrant issued? What testimony furnished the grounds for this charge?"

"Well, I read the oath, too," said one of the officers, "but if
I was to be shot, I couldn't say if the man's name was Walker
or Wilkins. It was one or t'other, I could safely swear, but
which, there's no telling. Hows'ever, I don't reckon it makes
much difference now — you can see all about·it when you ge*
before the judge."

"True, true—Justice Nawls!" Turning to the landlord
and showing the signature of the warrant — "Is this name tha
of a gentleman acting as a magistrate here, sir?"

"Not here, sir, but a few miles off, on the Georgeville road,"
was the reply of the landlord.

"A mighty good man is Judge Nawls," said one of the bystanders. "It was only last week he prayed s'archingly at
Green Brier meeting, and the sperit worked in him so, that the
sweat stood round his eyes jist the same as he'd been a-plough-
ing."

"'Twan't the sperit, Dill, 'twas only the flesh that worked
so mightily," said another of the bystanders. "'Twas because
he had none of the sperit that the flesh had to do so much; and
I'm mighty sure Bill Nawls never found harder work at the
plough in all his life, than he did at that ar' very sarmon."

"Well, and worn't it a good one, John Richards?"

"A good one! Well, I can't say what you may think it, but
for myself I can say, such a sermon will never carry me very
far along the narrow track. There's no getting to heaven by
a preaching where there's no getting steam up; and it's a matter of small wonder that so many take the other road, and go
down to the big pit, when it depends upon the sweating of Bill
Nawls's flesh to keep 'em from it. But that's not to say, stran·
ger, that Nawls ain't a good judge. He's a most onbecoming
person, that'll see all sides of your case, and do you justice
enough —though, to be sure, he's mighty slow, and takes a par

ticular long time to get through any writing. I've seen him take jist as long a time, now, to get round the body of an '*o*,' or an '*c*,' as I would to put on the tire of a great wagon-wheel, drive the nails, and swing it on the body."

The merits of Judge or Justice Nawls as a man and preacher, thus made the subject of popular disputation around him, was very little edifying to our hero; and just at this point of the dispute his eye caught, on a sudden, the glimpse of an object which, for the moment, almost caused an entire forgetfulness of the predicament in which he stood. This was no other than the carriage of Wilson—otherwise Maitland—which he beheld, denuded of its trunks and the other paraphernalia of the travellers, yet evidently occupied, as if for an evening ride, by its proprietor and his family. A mere glimpse was afforded him of this vehicle, as it rapidly passed along the common highway, and a feeling of exulting satisfaction, which had its source in mingled emotions, sprang up in his bosom. Once more the object of his pursuit seemed to be within his grasp;—he did not, it may be added, fail to perceive that the daughter of Maitland was with him still, though it never entered his thoughts, at this early stage of their acquaintance, that she, too, had become an object of his pursuit. The desire to see the latter, had, without his own consciousness, quite as much influence over him, as the feeling of duty which prompted him to secure the former; and with these desires in his mind, uttering an exclamation, he was about to rush to the entrance of the tavern, when his arm was forcibly grappled by the officers.

"Not so fast, my lark. That cock won't fight, I can tell you," exclaimed one of the constables, while a brutal burst of laughter from both, reminded him of his predicament, which the sight of the carriage of Maitland had moved him momentarily to forget.

"Unhand me, fellows, for an instant. I would see and speak to the gentleman in that carriage;" and he almost shook himself free as he spoke, while his efforts were such as to render necessary all of theirs to secure him.

"Be quiet, man, before I put a spur into you," cried one of the fellows, taking him at the same time by the collar, and putting on a threatening and insolent look, that goaded Vernon to

a degree of forgetfulness and fury, to which the sudden arrest
of his previous movement had already greatly moved him.

"Dog!" he exclaimed, striking down the arm that grasped
his collar, and driving his clenched fist into the fellow's face in
the instant with a force that sent him to the floor, "do you
think I will suffer this?"

"Help! help!" cried the second officer, "an escape! Citizens, I command you, help, help!—stop the murderer!"

"Cease howling, fool!" exclaimed Vernon, "I seek not to
escape. I would speak but a moment with the owner of yon
carriage."

His words were disregarded; the constable clung to him with
the tenacity of a bull-dog, that clings still though it may not
conquer, and Vernon had already dragged him almost to the
entrance, when a short, stout Irishman, who lay upon a bench
in the room, and who, to this moment, had looked on the fray
with the most placid indifference, now sprang to his feet, and
lifting a bludgeon that had lain concealed behind him, felled
Vernon to the ground with a single blow. He would have repeated the stroke, when a stranger interposed—a young Alabamian who had also just arrived in the village—and catching
the lifted arm with a grasp that fixed it in its position, exclaimed:—

"Stick down, my lad! There go two hands to this bargain.
What the devil sort of soul do you think you have, d—n you,
to strike a man that is speechless?"

"T'under and turf, my honey! do you mane to make me your
inimy?" cried the Hibernian. "Would ye be after resaving a
tap on yer own pate, my honey?"

"Devil-may-care if I do, but you can't give it me, nor any
lad of your inches," cried the Alabamian, who in the same
moment lifted the astonished Irishman to his full height in the
air, in defiance of all his struggles, and then dropped him down
with as little reluctance as if he had been one of the most insensible "p'raties" of his fatherland.

"There, Patrick, what do you say to that, and be d—d to
you?"

A battle to the death was nearly the consequence of this display of prowess on the part of the Alabamian, who, nowise loath, prepared for it with the utmost *sang froid*, and answered the threats of Patrick with a swaggering and cool defiance, which denoted the most perfect confidence in himself. But it was not the policy of Saxon, who recognised a follower in Dennis O'Dougherty, to suffer it. He interposed to keep the peace, and used all the usual and effective arguments common to cases of such urgent necessity. The bar supplies the means of bringing about a pacification, quite as often as it promotes the strifes and vexations which lead to war, and the Alabamian expressed himself as clearly of opinion that the fun was quite as great to drink, as to fight, with a stout fellow.

"As for Patrick, here—"

"Dennis, if you plase — Dennis O'Dougherty, of the O'Doughertys of Ballyshannon by the pit of Ballany — a family of the ouldest — there's no telling, indade, when the O'Doughertys were not a family of the ouldest."

"That accounts for your loss of strength, Mr. O'Dougherty," said the Alabamian; "if you hadn't come from so old a family, I should not have tumbled you so easily. Your great-grandfather must have been rather a stout chap in his time, and it might have given me more trouble to spring him to the ceiling. But the blood gets mighty thin going through three, or five, or seven generations, unless the breed is crossed mighty often. Now, don't you see the advantage of being of a new family? In my state, all the men are of new families, and we've got the strength in us. Perhaps, the time will come that our children will grow weak and feeble like you, Dennis, and some chap, away from the Red River, or the Sabine — some new fellow from Texas or thereabouts — will swing the grandson of Dick Jamison just as easily as he can swing you, Dennis."

"Asily, do you say, Misther Dick Jemison!" exclaimed Dennis; "not so asy, my honey, if the thing is to be thried agin. You had the back of me, Mr. Dick Jemison, an' that's a rason why you should come to the front. But, shall it be for a quart, that we shall take a friendly gripe at the ribs, or will it be the shillelah, my honey?"

"Stick, fist, or hug, Dennis O'Dougherty, it's all the same to Dick Jamison. You're of too old a family, Dennis, to stand up with a young man from Alabam'; the stuff's net in you, my

lad, and I should swallow you at a mouthful and never ask after
the salt"

"Now, don't ye be after desaving yerself, my honey," replied
the Irishman, somewhat astounded at the cool impudence of the
Alabamian, not merely in disparaging his hitherto acknowledged
powers, but in the still more remarkable disparagement of the
greater merits of an old family, which, to the great horror and
surprise of Dennis, were now made to give way to the claims of
a young one. The almost contemptuous terms which the member of the new house employed in determining the proper prece-
dence of the latter, uttered with so much complacency, tended
still more to embitter the idea.

"Now, don't ye be after desaving yerself, Mr. Dick Jeemison,
saing it was behind my back that ye overkim Dennis O'Dougherty; and don't ye be after thinking that ye can overkim him
agin behind his back, when his face is turned upon ye. There's
a difference, my honey, between a jontleman's face and his back,
that ye'll be after belaving when ye've sane them together as
I will show you mine, with a shillelah in aitch hand, and a
- pistol in the other, and the spirit of univarsal liberty in the
sowl which will make a rivolution in your idees, Mr. Dick
Jeemison, and tache you a leetle abolition of doctrine, that ye
may take back with ye to Alabama."

"Abolition!" exclaimed one of the inmates of the bar.

"Abolition!" echoed another and another, and a dozen faces
were peering into the face of the Hibernian at the inauspicious
word.

"Who's talking abolition here?" said one.

"What blasted emissary of Arthur Tappan is it?"

"It's his own self, I do think," said a third; and the mur
murs began to close with the ominous inquiry after that venerable border magistrate, Judge Lynch.

"Jontlemen!" exclaimed the Hibernian, who began to feel
some misgivings that his position might be made a very awkward one, if the Alabamian should happen to take the lead
against him. "Jontlemen!" said he, turning from one to the other,
with an air of mingled apology and defiance, "don't be after desaving yourselves, and misconsaving Dennis O'Dougherty. I'm
a jontlemau by my mother's side — she was an O'Flaherty—"

"To be sure; don't you suppose, Dennis, that we know all that?" said the Alabamian; "look you, friends and fellow-citizens, we all know what Dennis means by abolition, but being an Irishman born, and of an old family that's nearly worn out, how should he be able to speak good English. He is a gentleman, as he says, by the mother's side—his mother being an O'Flaherty; and a lady by his father's side, the old gentleman being an O'Dougherty; and therefore he asks you all to join with him here in a sup of whiskey—regular Monongahela—that we may have a revolution of ideas and an abolition of distinctions. That's what Dennis means by abolition, only the poor fellow hasn't been long enough in America to speak good English. And, look you, my friends, it's not a bad notion now, I tell you, for a man whose family's almost worn out, to wish to abolish distinctions where our families are only just beginning. He'd be mighty willing to let that matter drop, and so you see he's for giving us a drop all round; so come Kitty, fill your quart and set out the sugar, and look you, friends, we'll drink to the health of Mr. Dennis O'Dougherty, who is a gentleman by his mother's side, and a lady by his father's; and may he soon recover his strength by getting into a new family."

This speech was received with loud huzzas. The explanation of the Alabamian, as it was only understood in part, was perfectly satisfactory to all parties; the countrymen around were satisfied with it, as its result was one easily swallowed and perfectly habitual; and the Hibernian, though there was much in the speech to confound his better judgment, and stagger his conception of the English he already knew, was also content to receive it without scruple as explanatory of his own ideas, simply as he found it so successful with all around, and as it relieved him from a predicament, which some recent examples had already convinced him, might have become an awkward, if not a dangerous one.

A more general diffusion of the peace principle was evident soon after the quart flagon was placed upon the counter of the publican, and the Alabamian, who was something of a wag, and no little of a democrat, was soon busy in laboring to convince Dennis that there was no greater misfortune on earth than to be the descendant of a very old family; as he proceeded to show by every analogous case, drawn from the history of bird, beast, and reptile, that the breed must degenerate, with every successive advance after the third generation; and the only hope of an old nation was to merge itself, as soon as possible after that period, in the body and bosom of a new. The final speech of Mr. Jamison, at the moment when we propose to leave the company, may be put on record as containing a proposition of quite as much political truth as theory.

"It's in America here, Dennis, my boy, that we will preserve the English, and the Irish, and the Scotch, when, in your own country, you'll all be worked down to a mere stump of what you were. It's here, I tell you, that the English people will get a new growth, a height and a depth, a breadth and a bottom, when the old families wouldn't have one fellow among 'em fit to carry guts to a bear. This is the country, after all, to make men out of your sticks, jist the same as taking a plant from one place where it's been growing so long that it's come to nothing, and putting it into a new field where it never was before. See the difference! how it shoots up—how it spreads, and what a fine crop you get from it for the first five years —may be seven—but after that you must carry it farther off to some new opening, and begin again. If I was to do anything for you, Dennis, I'd marry you off at once to Polly Whitesides—you all know Polly Whitesides, my boys!"—A general laugh attested the success of the reference.—"I'd marry you off to Polly Whitesides, of Beattie's Bluff, and make a new family out of an old one."

"It's a lady you spoke of, Mr. Dick Jeemison?"

"Ay, to be sure, a lady—what else? She's six feet in her stockings, with cheeks red as a gobbler's gills, and an arm, Dennis, that would put your thigh out of countenance!"

"J—s! and she's a lady, Mr. Jeemison?"

"And the very gal to make a new and rising family out of an old one on its last legs," was the reply.

Let us change the scene, and follow Vernon into the apartment into which he was carried at the moment when the blow from the shillelah of Dennis O'Dougherty had laid him senseless on the floor.

CHAPTER XXII.

PROGRESS OF DISCOVERY — A SNARL.

"Now we have argument
Of justice, and our very breath is law,
To speak thee dead at once."
SHIRLEY.

WHILE the uproarious controversy was in progress between the Alabamian and his Irish opponent in the tavern-hall, Vernon, through the considerateness and care of Saxon, was conveyed to an inner apartment in a state of insensibility. The outlaw had his unexpressed objects in this disposition of the youth, and his connection with the constables readily enabled him to make such arrangements as left him in his sole custody. A public assurance which he gave them in the bar-room, that he would be answerable for the forthcoming of the prisoner whenever they might demand him, not only satisfied the worthy emissaries of the law, but won golden opinions for the outlaw from the unreflecting spectators. They did not, with a single exception, remark the strangeness of such a proceeding; nor wonder, as well they might, how it was that a stranger's assurance, and one who appeared to have been the companion of the traveller, should be taken as good security for the temporary release of the same person charged with a crime so heinous.

The more acute Alabamian saw this matter in its true light, and was not the less curious though he said nothing on the subject. As for the constables, the reader, who knows already what they are, will not be surprised at the ready complaisance which they yielded to the will of the outlaw. They were very well satisfied to exchange the tedious watch over the prisoner for the livelier bustle of the tavern-hall. There they soon joined the revellers, and gave themselves up to that perfect

recklessness of good order and morality, which, in no little de
gree, tended to confirm the growing suspicion in the mind of
the Alabamian that there was something wrong in their proceedings.

A sudden regard for Vernon had been the fruit of the first
moment of their meeting; as he saw, or fancied he saw, even
through the reserve which is usually the accompaniment of superior endowments and education, a frankness of manner and
character in the youth, which, while resembling, was grateful to
his own.

These first loves, or favorable impressions, are very common
to a forest country such as ours, where no long time is allowed
for the formation of intimacies, and where the instincts of blood
are always more active than the slow and cautious approaches
of reason and philosophy.

He assisted, we may state, to carry the insensible form of the
youth into the chamber, and having ascertained that Lucchesa
was not without its physician, he despatched one of the urchins
that figured at the tavern-door, to require his assistance; a task
which the boy readily undertook with the tempting reward of a
fip-penny piece before him. This done, Jamison returned to
his controversy with the Irishman, which he made subservient
to the occult purposes of inquiry which lay at the bottom of his
mind. He plied the whiskey-flagon with an industry which
he took pains to make appear as a consequence of his own love
for the living beverage; and he soon had occasion to congratulate himself on the discovery of one or two facts which, though
subordinate in importance, were yet of a character to confirm
him in his suspicions.

He soon discovered, in the first place, that his Irish adversary, in one or two unwitting speeches, was an old acquaintance
of the constables; and, from the modes of speech and the sort
of anecdote in which the latter freely dealt, he was easily led to
infer that, however honest they might be at this writing, they
had certainly, at some past period not so very remote, been
very exemplary *picaroons.* That their morals were not such as
should entitle them to the selection of a devout magistrate such
as Judge Nawls had been described to be, was sufficiently clear
from the facility with which they threw aside that starched sem-

blance of decency which they had just before put on in the assumption of a character, and in the performance of duties, far
other than those to which they had been sworn. They soon
forgot the commands of their leader, who was too busy elsewhere to heed their behavior, and hear their riotous uproar, as,
in the person of Dennis O'Dougherty they recognised a well-
known Jack Pudding of their gang; and the renewal of sundry
old jokes at his expense, did more than anything besides to
convey to the mind of the acute and unsuspected Alabamian,
the extent and sort of intimacy which had before subsisted between them.

Their presence brought no little increase of merriment to
the carousing party. The fun had been about to decline till
their appearance. A renewal of mirth was the necessary consequence of the arrival of such old proficients, and the replen-
ishing of the flagon furnished an equal supply of the pabulum
so necessary for the fervor of village wit, and the otherwise cos-
tive humor of a country population.

Our friend Jamison, speaking from his soul, cried, "D—n the
expense," at every hearty summons to the company to refill —
a summons not less grateful than imperative, and one never to
be disputed among men no less social in character than docile
in obedience to the lawful authority. Leaving these good companions for a while, let us seek the chamber to which Verno1
had been carried.

This was a little low shed-room containing two beds, a single
chair, a broken mirror, and a couple of rude colored pictures,
such as good taste was willing to take, without scruple, during
the war of 1815, at the hands of patriotism. Never did native
genius effect a more rascally portraiture of humanity. One of
the pictures represented the battle of New Orleans; the other
a scalping-scene at the massacre of Firt Mimms, on the Tensaw.
In the former, Pakenham might have been seen going through
the air like one of his own congreves, as blazing red, certainly,
and describing pretty much the same sort of curve when at the
moment of declension. His head nearly touched his heels, and
the grapeshot might have been seen just about to bury their
hissing hot bodies in the gaping wounds, from which the blood
was already streaming, in pretty much the same volume as

would issue from the sudden opening of a water-plug in the
streets of Philadelphia. A complete display of pyrotechnics —
a shower of fire — encircled him, and formed the only light,
lurid and sulphurous still, which the artist permitted on the
British side of the business. In this he strove hard to accomplish the *clair obscur* with the utmost practical nicety. The
rest of the battle was a chaos of heads, legs, and arms; horses
kicking without bodies; men running without feet; and wheeling cannon just as busy advancing and receding, though never
a man was left standing at the drag-ropes. Here Imagination
had done much toward the achievement of that desideratum in
all her works, the vague, twilight, picturesque, and imperfect
dimness, which denotes everything that is not beheld, and
makes equivocal whatever is distinct.

But the amor patriæ was predominant in the display of the
American lines — there all was clear, effulgent, and imposing.
Still and stern, the Kentuckians and Tennesseans stood upon
the terraces. Never were attitudes more perfect. Even those
who knelt for the purpose of better aim, were drawn with wonderful exactitude and majesty. Here was truth. The eyes
ranged the tube with a mathematical exactness. Had you
taken the instruments in hand, and separated the lines between
the eyes, the drop, and the British, you would have seen in an
instant how certain was their defeat. Every muzzle covered
its man — every bullet had its special commission; and our
artist had made it a matter sufficiently clear, without reference
to any dull history, that the American victory arose from no
other cause than the excellent aim of the riflemen. The whole
story was told at a glance; and when you recollect that the
artillery was managed with similar nicety, you have no sort of
difficulty in accounting for all the havoc of that bloody field.
But the whole powers of the artist were concentrated around
the form of the hero of that day. General Jackson was surrounded with a thousand natural glories. The sun rose over
his left shoulder, and his epaulet, reflecting his light upon surrounding objects, was almost as bright, and quite as large, as
himself. "Bombs bursting in air" surrounded him with halos
of falling stars that became tributary, in like manner, to the
awful distinctness of his face and figure. There he stood,

"Fierce as ten furies, terrible as hell."

His portrait was true, as all the portraits of very great men must be true, even when most imperfect. There were the same thin pale cheeks, the raised cheek-bones, thin compressed lips, keen eyes, high narrow forehead, and raised hair — the head, for the greater perfection of the portrait, having been left un covered, in defiance of smoke and flame, bombs and rockets, crackers and carcasses.

But the terrors of expression in his face were the wonders of the performance. Even had the riflemen been utterly wanting to the battle, you would have seen that these were enough for the victory. There was not a wrinkle in the old warrior's brow that did not look like a two-edged sword. His mouth was pursed up to seem a *seam* — the lines forming to a common centre, the appearance of which led you to expect a sudden expansion, no less great than the undue contraction, from which triple hail and thunder were to issue. His beard, too — for the general, if the artist may be considered good authority in a particular so perfectly domestic, had not shaved for seven days — his very beard, too, like that of old Giaffar, "curled in ire," as he waved a sword twice his own length, and pointing to Pakenham's whizzing and whirling carcass, seemed disposed to thrust it — very unnecessarily, it would seem — into the aperture made so voluminously large already by the grapeshot aforesaid.

Language fails to do justice to this terrific picture — go to Lucchesa, reader, and see for yourself. We forbear that of the massacre at Fort Mimms, in order that nothing may be antici-pated. Like that of the battle, it is a painting *sui generis*. Never were scalps taken from skulls with more terrible felicity of execution than in this picture. At Raymond court-house you will see another, by the same artist, in which a muse more moral than she of history has been invoked ;--Justice with her scales very properly presides over the hall of justice. It is rather awkward, indeed, that one scale should be lower than the other, but this difference simply suggests a play of the fancy, and can not subject the painter to the imputation of any serious want of discrimination. Certainly, we shall venture to incur no risk, in this brief passage, of indulging in false and superficial analysis.

Strange to say, the merits of these pictures entirely escaped the notice of Saxon. Whether he had seen them before, or, as is quite probable, entertained no taste for the fine arts—a deficiency quite too general in our country, and quite too common among all people whose habits are wandering, to make it likely that any rebuke will be of service for a hundred years to come —one thing is certain, that he never gave so much as a glance to the panels in which these gorgeous performances had been set on high. His eye and thought were upon the young man alone, who lay insensible upon the couch; and, under the pretence of restoring him to consciousness, the outlaw, so soon as all other persons had retired from the chamber, very coolly proceeded to unbutton the vest and bosom of his patient, and explore the contents of a thin gauze-like handkerchief which encircled his waist, and which he untied with the dexterity of an old proficient in all such practices, without disturbing the position of, or removing the handkerchief from, the body. A few moments sufficed to enable him to disengage from the folds of the handkerchief a small packet which lay on the right side of the youth. This he transferred with all speed to his own bosom; and, folding a newspaper in like bulk and form, he deposited it in place of the papers appropriated, retied the handkerchief, rebuttoned the shirt and vest; and all this without disturbing the wounded man, and before the arrival of the physician;—an event, however, which occurred a moment after.

Dr. Saunders was rather a clever young man, who had re ceived a license to practise but a few months before, and was no less modest than well-informed. He examined the hurt of Vernon, with the assistance of the Alabamian, who, on the arrival of the physician, left the company without, and with the anxiety of an old friend, awaited the result. Vernon had overtasked himself. The wound in his thigh which had bled so copiously was irritated by the hard riding of the day. He had ridden rapidly in order to overtake the carriage of Wilson, and had overcome a distance of more than forty miles. The excitement following previous events, and the anticipation of those before him had also contributed to the irritation of his system; and, when arrested for so heinous an offence as that of murder, and the murder, too, of his late companion, it is not improbable that fever would have followed his mental suffering, even without the additional injury which he received from the unmeasured blow of the Irishman. The patient's consciousness returned while the examination of the physician was going on. He started, and with an instinctive movement which betrayed the deep interest which he had at stake, he threw off the intrusive hands about him, and his own were thrust into his bosom and not withdrawn until he assured himself of the safety of the secret deposite which he had bound around his body. With anxiety and agitation heightened by fever, he turned to the two attendants, and demanded what was meant by their familiarities. The matter was soon explained, the doctor announced himself, and coming slowly to a recollection of what had taken place in the tavern, Vernon quietly submitted himself to his hands.

Meanwhile, in the possession of his prize and anxious for its examination, Saxon availed himself of the coming of the physician to retire to another apartment. There, in secret, he unfolded the packet, the contents of which had the instant effect of clouding his brow with anger, and sending the blood into his cheeks.

"It is then true—it is as I thought and feared! This is, then, only another Hurdis—another spy, self-appointed, for our destruction. He has played his game admirably, but not perfectly. Not well enough for success, but so well as to make it necessary that we should silence, him for ever. It is needful for our own safety that we do this—we can spare no longer—his doom is written."

He conned the papers closely; one of which, a blank commission with the signature of Governor Runnels, he tore into fragments and flung into the fireplace. The others comprised a brief narration of his own doings as Clem Foster in Alabama; copies of affidavits sworn to in that state, and a list of names—a copy of which had been given to Rawlins by Vernon the night before—of suspected persons in Mississippi. These called for the more serious attention of the outlaw.

"These must fly," he muttered, as he looked over, and pencilled off, a portion of the list; "the neighborhood is closely settled and will soon be too hot to hold them; but they may

stave off danger here on the Big Black for a year or two more
Still it will be as well to warn off some of the more black and
crooked—fellows who can not even look honest, may well run
in advance of the danger. But Cane Castle will hide all their
vices, and that is as far as they need go for the present. This
agent of his excellency—would he had come himself—once
fairly salted, and we shall have no trouble for some time to
come. There are few in Mississippi prepared to take his place,
and manage his cards so cunningly as almost to blind so old a
stager as myself. His game's up—and there's an end of it.
Nawls will send him to Vicksburg, and the 'beagles' will take
him by the way. Then follows his execution, *in terrorem*, for
the benefit of our own doubtful and soft-hearted fellows in the
swamp. He will die by our laws—he has assumed the toils
of the spy—he incurs its dangers; and our own require that
we should show no mercy. And now for a little more hypocrisy. I would know why he seeks this traveller, Wilson—and
the hurry of Wilson to leave old Badger's is no less curious. I
must sound him on these subjects."

With exemplary composure he proceeded to the apartment
of Vernon, which was still occupied by the physician and the
Alabamian, and placing himself on one side of the patient, congratulated him on his improved looks and restoration. The
compliment was a very suspicious one, for, by this time, our
hero felt himself seriously ill—he could not mistake the heat
of his frame; the bounding quickness of his pulse; the parch-
ing thirst which assailed him; the soreness of his head; and
the painful throbbing of his wounded thigh. These were evi-
dences, even if the physician had been absent, sufficient to
make him aware of his true condition.

I thank you," he said, "but I am not better. I feel ill —,.
seriously ill; and this painful accusation, this troublesome ar
rest! So strange, so sudden and startling:— I trust, gentlemen"—looking round as he spoke—"I trust that you believe
me guiltless of this crime—nay, it must be so —the officers are
gone—they have been convinced of their mistake, I suppose."

"Mistake!" said Saxon, with an incredulous expression,
"what mistake, Mr. Vernon?"

"Why, sir, mistake of facts or of person. Did they not

arrest me for murder — the murder of Horsey, poor fellow ?"

"Yes, sir; but if be a mistake, it is one of those mistakes
that they continue obstinately to persist in. They are in the
adjoining hall. It was on my pledge that you should be forthcoming that they consented to leave you in privacy until you
might be recovered from your injuries."

"I thank you, sir, again I thank you," replied Vernon; "it
is due to the kindness of your interposition, and to the attention
of these gentlemen, that I should assure you that I am wholly
guiltless of the crime which is charged against me — that, so far
from seeking to harm the unfortunate young man, whose fate I
have heard of for the first time from this proceeding, I should
feel myself bound by every duty and feeling to succor and to
save him. He is a wild, hairbrained, but worthy youth, whose
family is good, and whose old father has treated me with kindness. That I may be suspected is, perhaps, not so strange : —
we travelled together, and separated suddenly — he taking the
lower road for Benton at the forks, and I the upper, which, with
some delays and interruptions, has led me here. That he may
have fallen a victim to some wanton assassin is, perhaps, little
surprising in a neighborhood in which crime is said to be so
frequent; but that I should be seriously held to answer for his
death, is a matter too idle to annoy me much or make me apprehensive of its consequences. I have no sort of doubt, gentlemen, that an examination before the magistrate will result in
my immediate discharge from arrest."

The company unanimously expressed the hope that such
might be the result; and Jamison loudly declared his conviction of it.

"The truth's in your face, Mr. Vernon — I saw it from the
first, and that made me so willing to give Paddy O'Rafferty or
O'Dougherty, or whatever O' it may be, an ugly hoist, for the
liberty he took with you, bringing you soon to an acquaintance,
all on one side, between your head and his shillelah. He'll not
do it again, I'm thinking, not while Dick Jamison is bystand-
ing. I know well enough you'll get out of this scrape, so cheer
up, Mr. Vernon. I'll see you out of the mire while I've got
any footing to stand on, and when I ha'n't, why I'll walk the

bog with you. D——c, but I like your face, and there's no telling what I'll do and say for a fellow I like. I'll run, ride, talk, and fight for my friend; and when he's a stranger like myself in a new place, that's the very time that I can't desert him. So count upon Dick Jamison while the breath's in him."

The expressive eye of Vernon made an acknowledgment to the hearty volunteer, which his lips did not articulate; and his hand freely returned the pressure which the latter gave him as he concluded his characteristic speech. The sympathies of the stranger, however rudely expressed, were grateful to the youth in the feeling of discontent and depression which was natural to his condition; and the unstudied frankness of his utterance was only an additional proof that his sentiments came from the fellow's heart. The reflections of Vernon's mind were nowise cheering at this moment. His course, upon which he had entered with so much confidence and hope, had been attended with disasters from the beginning, produced, not through his own measures or management, but by influences entirely foreign. Pursued by Horsey and annoyed by his prying curiosity —scarcely freed from him, before suffering in an encounter into which he was forced by a sense of duty which no honorable mind could shrink from; and now, arrested and suffering for the alleged murder of the man whose presence was so perfectly unsought and so undesirable:—these continuous events seemed to hold forth auguries the most inauspicious to that adventure which had been undertaken with so much hope. The voice of kindness came to him, therefore, at the moment of his despondency, with an influence to be remembered; and he felt that he was not altogether desolate while the sturdy Alabamian was beside his couch. The truth, which was declared by his frank utterance, and denoted in the manly and not-to-be-mistaken expression of his features, won instant confidence from our hero; and remembering one of his leading objects, he thought to himself, "Here is another ally—here i another to join with me in the strifes that may follow any pursuit of this banditti."

The wounds upon Vernon's thigh were re-dressed—the irratation of the part soothed by the application of external dressings; his head, which had suffered a severe contusion, was

properly bandaged, a nostrum given intended to lessen the
fever, in the attainment of which object, a vein was also opened.
This done, Doctor Saunders proceeded to silence the worthy
Alabamian, whose tongue was one of those habitually restless
ones, which, suspended in the roof of his mouth, rather than the
gap of his throat, are for ever wagging from side to side in the
fruitless hope of finding a place of rest.

"We must leave our patient in quiet, gentlemen—his fever
is high—his mind is not at ease, and the necessity of the case
must be my apology for insisting upon his being left to himself."

"I will but say to the officers that I yield him to their
custody," said Saxon, leading the way to the bar-room.

"They can not remove him," said the physician.

"That is for them to determine," was the reply of the outlaw.

"It will be an unnecessary and wanton cruelty if they do.
The young man can not escape if he would. He is really too
feeble. They may watch him, and be at hand, but must not
intrude upon him."

"I'll be d——d if they do?" was the asseveration of the Alabamian, glad of an opportunity to use the instrument upon
which, the interdict of the physician, while in the chamber of
the patient, sat with a very unpleasant weight. The keen eye
of Saxon surveyed him for an instant with no very pleasant
expression, but he said nothing; while the other proceeded to
declare that, law or no law, he would see that none but himself
should approach the sick man's chamber, and "As for taking
him out," he continued, "until he's willing to go himself, let me
see any one try it, and if he don't bear a hickory, his mother
never bore a fool."

The arrival of another party suggested, however, a new plan
of arrangements. This was no other than the traveller whom
Vernon had pursued—certainly, with no sort of apprehension
on the part of the former, that such had been the case. Old
Wilson entered with timid, trembling footsteps—a cautious
tread, as if walking upon eggs—and a furtive glance thrown from
side to side as the different groups of the bar-room met his eyes,
which denoted either a very suspicious temper, or one strangely
unused to the devil-may-care freedoms of a public tavern. As

he advanced he encountered the three persons who had just emerged from the passage-way into the public hall, and whose more respectable appearance, in garb and manner, than that of the persons generally by whom the tavern was filled, naturally prompted the visiter to address his inquiry to them.

"Gentlemen, I would like to know—sorry to stop you—but is there not a young gentleman here by the name of Vernon?"

"There is," answered Jamison, who already assumed the entire representation of his new friend.

"Can I be suffered to see and speak with him?" inquired Wilson.

"I am afraid not," replied the physician. "Mr. Vernon has suffered some serious hurts which have brought on fever. Even the noise of this bar-room is unfavorable to him in his present situation. His mind is very much excited, and inclines to wander. I would prefer that he should not be disturbed."

There was some eagerness in the expression of Wilson's face, and in his manner, as he replied:—

"I have heard of his hurts, sir, and as I partly know him, and believe him to be a worthy young man, I came to propose that he might be taken to my house, while his illness lasted. It will be more quiet than he can possibly find it here, and—"

"You, perhaps, have not heard of the accusation against him?" was the remark of Saxon.

"And what the d—l has that to do with the gentleman's offer, I'd like to know?" was the fierce demand of the Alabamian. "I'm sure nobody who knows Vernon would think him guilty of the thing after his own lips had told 'em he hadn't done it."

Jamison spoke for his new friend as sturdily as if they had been intimate a thousand years. His manner startled and somewhat aroused the outlaw. This might be seen in the kindling and flashing of his eye, and in the sudden glow that flushed his cheek; but however much he might have been moved to resent it, there were other considerations, much more strong, that counselled forbearance; and the reply of Mr. Wilson to his inquiry, interposed, as it were, between himself and the man who had shown himself so susceptible of provocation.

"I have heard of the charge to which you allude, and which, I think with the gentleman here, must be quite groundless. It was the rumor which reached me of his arrest, and of his illness, but a little time ago, by which I was informed that he was in my neighborhood; and the thought that he might be removed with advantage to my dwelling—"

"This is an offer not to be disregarded," said the physician interrupting him; "and if the officers would permit his removal—"

"Permit it—they must, and be d——d to them. Look you, men, this here prisoner of yours—he's in a d——d bad way, and will be worse, unless you let us carry him to the old gentleman's house. See you, I'll be bail for his coming whenever he's able to see the justice; or you can stay here and keep on the lookout for him, and for me too if you choose, for I won't budge till the lad gets better. What do you say, you man-catching rascals, to being civil for awhile—it'll be nothing out of your pockets, I can tell you, while Dick Jamison has anything in his."

The constables, at whose approach Mr. Wilson might have been seen to shrink with some trepidation, were not disposed to consent so readily. They hemmed and hawed awhile—muttered together as if in consultation—spoke aloud of their duties and the great risk and responsibility, and, from their delay and reluctance, were rousing up the choler of the irritable Alabamian to a new outbreak of ferocious friendship, when Saxon, to whom they looked entirely for their cue, quietly remarked:—

"It appears to me that the officers can not refuse so reasonable an arrangement. They can keep as close a watch over the prisoner at the house of Mr. Wilson as at the tavern, and the doctor's opinion that the young man can not fly in his present situation, and should be free from noise, ought to satisfy them without any other security; though, if they need any other, I'm ready to become bound in bail along with this gentleman."

"Will you?" said Jamison; "well, d—me, you're a better fellow than I thought you, after all—so give's a shake of your paw, and let there be peace between us. Well, what do you say, you sharks in fresh water, have you got your senses yet?"

"Faith, we must let the jontleman off the hook, since ye all says it," began the Irishman, when interrupted, no less by

the stern expressive looks of Saxon, than by the sudden burst
of his former opponent.

"Hillo! Dennis! and what the d—l have you got to do in
the business, my lad? Shut up, you little old fellow—you
have no right to speak at all until you are fairly married into
a new family. Get you gone to Polly Whitesides, and let her
give you a brush up before you dip your oar into another's
navigation."

And, with these words, the now good-humored rowdy clapped
his open hand as an effectual stopper on the widely-distended
jaws of the only half-sober son of St. Patrick, whose brain was
just in that condition of fermentation when he could understand
that he had blundered, though in what respect he did not hope
to divine, until he had taken an additional supply of the
"crather," or utterly freed himself from the control of thi*
which he had already swallowed.

CHAPTER XXIII.

THE FOREST REFUGE—GRIEFS OF GUILT—FEMININE DREAMS
—BUDDING FANCIES.

High-climbing rock—low sunless dale—
Sea—desert—what do these avail?—
Oh, take her anguish and her fears,
Into a deep recess of years."—WORDSWORTH

THE arrangement thus effected needed but the consent of the
principal party to its immediate operation; and Mr. Wilson
was ushered into Vernon's chamber by the ready aid of Dick
Jamison. Our hero, though confused by his application as
much as by certain medicines which had been administered by
Doctor Saunders, was yet not insensible to the advantages in
sundry respects which the contemplated removal might afford
him. As an invalid, with the possible prospect before him
of a protracted illness, it promised that repose and quiet
which he felt would be grateful, if not necessary to his condi

tion; and when he reflected on the probability of his being able to secure the main object of his journey, in a quiet pacific manner, and by degrees which would neither startle nor offend, he could not mistake the course which he should at once adopt. But still he hesitated, nay refused;—thanked the old gentle-man for his hospitality and consideration—made light of his own services previously rendered, and, though in faltering ac-cents, declared himself utterly unwilling to transfer the cares ˙of a sick bed, and that too of a stranger, to the household of his friendly visiter, and to the great interruption of its domestic privacy and quiet.

The nice and jealous sensibility of Harry Vernon was busy to produce this determination; and feelings which he did not then seek to analyze—which he might not at that moment have perceived—influenced his declared resolution when all the obvious reasons of his mind fought against it. He remem-bered the lovely daughter of the defaulter; and when he re-flected that it might become necessary to expose the crime of the father, he was unwilling to incur the reproaches—the prob-able and perhaps well-founded hostility—of one whose favora-ble opinion already grew in his mind the imbodied standard of a becoming excellence.

But the reluctance of our hero warmed the manner of the old man to something like persuasiveness—he urged many good reasons why the patient should consent—denied the inconveni-ence and annoyance—spoke of his own little household com-forts—and, to sum up all in brief, assured him that his consent alone would make easy the minds of himself and family, since the necessity under which they labored of attending to some pressing interests had compelled them to leave their preserver on a previous occasion, with a seeming indifference to his con-dition which might well expose them to the charge of coldness and ingratitude.

The objections of Vernon gradually vanished when he heard from the lips of the father that such was the argument of his daughter by which he had been moved to the offer; and it needed but the reasseveration of Dr. Saunders that the removal was full of promised benefit and might promote his more speedy restoration, to induce his full consent to the arrangement.

12

Behold our hero then, fairly admitted as a guest in the dwelling of the man whom he pursued as a fugitive.

Two days only had passed since Mr. Wilson and his family had become occupants of the same household. They had pursued their way to this secluded and lovely spot, with direct steps, from the moment when they left the hospitable dwelling of the rigid methodist. They had reached it late in the evening of the same day, and the night was too far advanced to enable them to behold the beauties of the locality. But the cottage, though small, was neat, and furnished with a larger attention to those things which are classed under the ordinary term "comforts," than was commonly the case in a region so remote from the demands of fashionable society. Virginia Wilson beheld on all sides those little items in the shape of carpet, chimney ornament, piano and guitar, which, if they do not of themselves secure the happiness of life, at least contribute somewhat to its good humor and content. But the circumstance which chiefly satisfied her on the night of their arrival, was the improved temper and cheerfulness of her father. While on the road, he had exhibited a degree of querulousness and impatience which she had never perceived in him before the commencement of their present journey; and this temper was coupled with an air of precipitance and apprehension — a seeming distrust of all he met — a shrinking that looked like fear from all he encountered — which filled her own mind with apprehension, and made her at moments doubtful whether there was not something like mental alienation in him — a suggestion of her fear which alone seemed sufficient to account for a course of conduct and manner such as he had never shown to her before.

These had worn away in great degree from the first moment after they had set their feet on their new threshold. The natural cheerfulness of the father seemed restored. He spoke soothingly and tenderly, as if desirous to compensate his children for what they had been made to suffer in their journey; and the fond, pliant hearts of both responded to his cares, and grew glad in the return of those smiles of the parent, which are the sweetest sunshine to the devoted and dutiful child.

"Virginia, Louisa, my dear children," he exclaimed, folding them in his arms as soon as the first cares and excitements of their arrival were over, and when they remained alone together in their little parlor, "we have reached our resting-place at last—henceforth, my dear children, this is to be your home. Lucchesa is one of the loveliest spots on the Mississippi, and I have chosen one of the sweetest spots that surround Lucchesa. Here, Virginia, your rambles will be unimpeded and always beautiful; the woods are thick and various, and filled with the sweetest flowers; and you may now pursue your study of botany with more perfect self-approbation, since you will find abundant varieties of subjects to justify your love. And you, Louisa—what will you say to these little hills when you shall see them? They will seem to your eyes, which have never seen any but the dead flats of the low country, to be little less than mountains Your feet will tire to ascend them at first, but after a little while you will grow wild as a kid in your rambles—there will be no keeping you in."

"But, father," said the child, drawing closer to the old man, "the woods are so wild and strange they frighten me—there's a strange noise among the big pines, and when I walk among them I hear sounds that seem like the voices of spirits."

"It is the wind, my child, that shakes the trees, and murmurs when it presses against them as if vexed at being arrested. You will grow used to that, until you learn to like it, as I doubt not your sister does already. What say you, Virginia?"

A melancholy, spiritual smile, which passed over the lips and lightened in the eyes of the elder maiden for an instant, was his sufficient answer, and the father proceeded.

"Our cottage is not one of the best in Lucchesa, but it was the best that I could buy. We will improve it as we can. You will see in the daylight that it lies on the side of a little depression that we low-country people may almost call a valley. It is so low that you can only see it from the top of the hills; and the houses of Lucchesa can scarcely be seen at all from the top of ours. We have a little garden, Louisa, and you shall tend the flowers, while I raise the squashes and the potatoes and the cucumbers. Our gallery [piazza] runs round three sides of the house, the north only excepted; and though we lie in the valley, we have a sweet and extended prospect of hill-slopes on every side. The woods seem naturally to open into vistas, and these I will improve, until the cottage shall be the centre from which a hundred avenues of sight shall diverge, and into which they shall gather from every point of the compass. But enough of plans for to-night. Louisa, your eyes grow heavy in spite of all I can tell you. Kiss me, my child, and then find out your chamber."

The child, drowsy, but still striving to be attentive, did as she was bidden. The elder sister was left alone with her father, whose mood grew less cheerful with the absence of the child, and whose manner became far less easy. For a few moments a silence that was painful to both succeeded her departure. Mr. Wilson rose from his seat and paced the room with emotions that were evidently oppressive. Twice, thrice, did his step falter and seem about to pause as he passed before his daughter, who, with head leaning upon her palm, seemed oppressed with emotions also, which, if not so exciting, were, perhaps, scarcely less oppressive than his. At length, as if overcoming a strong reluctance, the father stopped beside her, drew a chair, and taking her hand in his, addressed her as follows:—

"Virginia, my dear child, you have said nothing."

"Father, what should I say—what would you have me say?" replied the daughter, the cloudy sadness deepening on her lovely countenance.

"That you repine not—that you are satisfied—that you are happy. See you not, my child, that the same paternal love which has striven so much to make you happy before, has spared nothing here within the compass of the country's resources to supply what you may have left behind?"

"But wherefore are they left behind, my father? Wherefore have we left the home where the same pleasures, if you call them such, were already ours? Was there nothing in the old home to endear us to it—was it not endeared to us by the happy life we had led in it—was it not endeared to us by the very death of her—that beloved mother—who made so much of the happiness we have lost—whose loss made so much dearer the little we had left?"

"And was it not good reason that we should fly, my daughter, from a dwelling where we had known that loss?"

"Alas, my father, it could not have been for that reason that you left our home — our home which death itself had seemed to sanctify. Years have passed since that cruel hour of parting, and the pang had passed away in the bitter memory of joys felt without a pang, and the assuring hope which was so cheering to us all, that she who suffered was now sainted beyond suffering. Oh, no! dearest father, my heart will not hear this reason — my mind can not receive it. There must be another cause, and that cause, my father, is one which it doubly grieves me to believe, has made whiter than ever the hair upon your fore-head."

"Virginia, my child, why will you press me thus?" cried the father, striding hastily along the floor, with his hands clasped above his eyes, as if to shut from sight the mournful and in-quiring expression of her countenance.

"Because I am a child no longer," was her reply, as, darting from her seat, she rushed toward him, and, catching one of his hands in both of hers, sunk upon her knees with a passionate manner which well accompanied the earnest and emphatic lan-guage which she employed, and which, while clinging to him, she continued to pour forth.

"Because I am a child no longer — I am a grown woman — I can both think and feel. I can surely understand the sor-rows that I still must share, and if I understand, my father, may I not help to relieve them? Were my dear mother living, I should look to her for the truth when sorrow troubled and dan-ger followed your footsteps; but in her absence I must take her place, and I implore, nay, I claim it as my right, my father — to know what grief, what threatening danger, has driven us to this wilderness, where the forests are yet almost as wild as at their birth; where we have no society, and where we see no friends."

"And can it be for the absence of society — nay, can it be even for the loss of friends, when her father and her sister are still left her — that I hear these questions — that I witness this affliction of my daughter?" was the answer — an answer, the burden of which did not represent the real conviction in the father's mind, but which enabled him to evade the more search ing inquiries which the first portion of her speech had con-veyed.

"No!" she exclaimed, rising to her feet, "as Heaven is my help and hope, dear father, I answer 'No!' It is not the little circle which I have left, nor the few friends for whom I had sympathy and attachment, that gives me cause of sorrow, however their loss may at moments occasion feelings of regret; nor is the wilderness into which we have wandered so uncongenial to my tastes and habits as to provoke inquietude and annoyance. I think not of these in the conviction that you are unhappy — that a secret cause of dread and danger hangs about you which makes you so often heedless of my love and indifferent to my endearments. Nay, shake not your head, my father — that smile does not deceive me. You require me to be happy, to be at ease, and find satisfaction and pleasure in the dwelling which you have found in Lucchesa, and the comforts which your customary care has gathered about us. I answer you that I will, so soon as I find that you derive pleasure and content from the same sources. Let me see you at ease, and you shall find me so; but while your brow is clouded — while your air and movements denote a secret apprehension of evil, I can not but share the cloud upon your brow, and my apprehensions grow only the greater because I can neither see nor guard against the coming of the danger which you fear. Let me know all, my father. Give me the knowledge of this mystery — for there is mystery — and rely upon me to soothe your sorrows, though I may not avert their cause. Rely upon me to share those griefs with satisfaction which now bring me nothing but terror and despondency."

"You know not what you ask, my child!" cried the father, hoarsely. "What if I should answer? What if, foolishly persuaded by your entreaties, I should reveal the cause of my sorrows — nay, to silence you at once, what if my revelations brought you shame along with sorrow? Ha! do you shrink — do you tremble? — Would you still hear — Virginia, would you still listen to a narration of guilt, which would make your sorrow less endurable? Speak! shall I now relate what you have been so curious to hear?"

"Guilt!" exclaimed the daughter, with feeble accents and a shrinking, sinking pain. "No! no! It can not be — there is no guilt — there can be no shame. These are cruel words, my father ; do not again speak them, I implore you — forgive me, forgive me — but you were so serious just now, when you spoke, that I almost believed you. Tell me your afflictions, but tell me not that there is guilt and shame, which, indeed, I well know there can not be.

"Enough! Press me not further, Virginia," continued the father, recovering his calmness in some degree, and, with some effort, smoothing the excited expression of those features, which, almost convulsed a moment before, had nearly convinced his daughter of the truth of the general confession he had made. "I trust that you will never know that guilt or shame could be coupled with your father's memory and image—"

"And yet, my father, this change of name."

She spoke with tremulous accents, and a renewal of that look of shrinking apprehensiveness which denoted the bewildered state of her judgment, warring with her feelings and desires ; unwilling to believe aught that could degrade or lessen the worth of one whom she was no less bound to venerate than willing to love, and yet the mystery of whose conduct left her utterly doubtful in which direction to incline her faith.

"Policy, my daughter, need have no association with either guilt or shame," replied the father, evasively, and by a general remark, to which there could be no exception as such. "When I tell you," he continued, "that the assumption of another name is necessary to my present interests, you are not to imply anything dishonorable or unworthy in the change. There are motives which justify — there are reasons which make it neces sary."

"Ah, my father, but there are no reasons which should make you deny your confidence to your daughter," was the prompt reply. She, at once, seized upon the true and only point at issue between them, which she urged with as great a degree of earnestness as became the relationship between them.

"I believe you that there are motives which require you to do this ; but, surely, my dear father, you can neither deny my interest in a knowledge of these motives, nor my prudence in reserving them from exposure as carefully as yourself. Give to my love, dear father, that reliance which it has evermore given to you."

"You ask too much, Virginia; you are yet but a child to me. There are many things which are neither becoming nor necessary for a woman to know — which, indeed, she could not know — could not understand. It is enough that this is one of them — let me hear no more of this."

"Father!"

"Nay, my child, I mean not to be stern — I would not be angry — but this is a point upon which you are too earnest — too much disposed to insist — of which you speak too frequently."

"It is only because it is a constant thought, my father — a painful thought — a doubt — a fear."

"Let it be so no longer, my child. Do you not see that I have grown cheerful since I have reached Lucchesa? You do not see me apprehensive now that we are in a place of safety."

"Safety!" was the natural exclamation. "And was the danger then so near us?"

"Nay, how can you ask, Virginia, when but three days ago we all lay at the mercy of a gang of robbers?"

A deep sigh escaped from the lips of the serious maiden, but she said nothing. She saw that her father strove to deceive her, and she forbore any further reference to a topic which he was so anxious to exclude, even at the expense of truth. He saw her conjecture and sickened as he did so; but he could say little or nothing to remove it; and conscious of his feebleness in this respect, and of the inadequacy of any art or argument, short of a frank confession, to do away with her apprehensions, he resorted to the humbler policy of seeking to divert her mind by reference to other objects. With a general knowledge of the feminine nature, in certain minor respects, such as their love for petty pleasures, he strove to engage her mind in such matters as might amuse rather than employ it. But in this, he soon perceived, from the quiet indifference of her answers, that he must fail; and tired of his task, and dissatisfied with himself, he forbore all further effort, and the lateness of the hour soon furnished a sufficient reason for their separation for the evening.

Virginia Wilson retired to her couch, but sleep was slow to

visit her that night. Her heart was too much filled with the mysterious circumstances which hung around her father—her mind too much troubled with the apprehensions which had harassed him for several preceding weeks—to suffer the velvet-footed deity to approach her without warning, and to obtain facile possession, at an early hour, of his accustomed dominion. The night waned slowly, while a thousand thoughts and conjectures, chasing each other with as much rapidity, if not with as many startling transitions, as the images that flit over the magic glass of the wizard, made her mind a populous world, where all was commotion and much was strife. She thought, with unspeakable anguish, of the reserve of her father on those circumstances, evidently momentous, which had troubled him, and still troubled him, though, under their terrors, he had sought safety in a region still wild, and still the abode of so much that was barbarous.

What were those circumstances?—and had he indeed found the safety which he admitted had been the object of his aim? These were questions that did not cease to afflict her, because she lacked all means for their solution. She could only hope and pray—she could only resolve to assume a cheerfulness which she could not feel, and to drive from her mind, by the acquisition of an early interest in the strange world to which she had been brought, that more grateful region to which she had been accustomed. This was, perhaps, the least of the mental difficulties in the way of Virginia Wilson. Hers was one of those commanding intellects that depend little upon the mere externals of society for their comforts and enjoyments—that make place and fortune subordinate considerations in an estimate of life's resources and rewards; and require peace of mind and confidence of heart in their own, and the purity of those with whom their lot is cast, rather than the praise of man or the plenty and profusion, which, to so large a portion of mankind, constitute the "be all" and the "end all" of existence. The wilderness had no terrors, but many charms; and to one who has seen quite as much of the superficial worthlessness and empty vanity of society, as of its harmony and grace, it was no difficult matter to find a charm in solitude which more than atoned for the fleeting pleasures she had lost. Under the ca...

of such a mind as hers, and surveyed through the medium of
such sweet affections as ministered around the altars of her unselfish heart, the wilderness could soon be made to blossom as
the rose. But the dread of that nameless danger which followed the footsteps of her only living parent, haunted her
thoughts with a continual presence. She estimated the powers
of this danger from the terrors which had possessed her father'
mind, and the very failure of conjecture to answer the doubts
of her constant inquiry, was of itself a source of wo, which
made her misery the greater.

    Still, it had never possessed her mind until the evening of her
arrival in Lucchesa, and until the occurrence of that conversation with her father, a portion of which is briefly reported above,
that there could be any shame or disgrace in connection with
the necessity which had driven him from his home. It will be
remembered with what earnestness and pleading anguish she
had exclaimed against the brief and passing suggestion of her
father, that guilt and shame were coupled with his sorrows.
This hint—though afterward evaded and denied by Mr. Wilson, when he beheld the effects upon his child, to whom he did
not dare communicate the truth—yet took possession of her
mind, when the silence and secrecy of her chamber left her at
liberty to re-examine the subject; and when she recurred to
the secret and precautionary measures which her father had
taken for his flight from Orleans—the indirectness of his course
—the change of name—the constant apprehensions which
harassed him, making him as imbecile in resolution as they
made him acute in observation—her fears, faint and shadowy at
first, grew into distinctness, and acquired new bulk and body
with every additional moment of reflection.

    She could now, and for the first time, readily conceive the
motive for flight and fear, for that startling terror which at moments enfeebled his limbs and covered him with tremors—
which made his voice sound hollow in his throat—which made
his eye shrink to encounter even the fond and affectionate gaze of
hers; and which, in the dialogue already briefly given, had moved
him to those few but incoherent expressions, convulsively uttered, which could only have found their way to the lips of one
laboring under insanity or guilt. That he was not insane she

knew—that he was guilty, the fear was rapidly growing into a
faith within her. But of what was he guilty? Strange to say,
the difficulty became as great as ever when she reached this
stage of conjecture, or conviction; and, after a vain effort, by a
reconsideration of all the subjects attending his movements
from Orleans, to arrive at such hypotheses of the particular
crime for which he fled, as would seem reasonable to her
thought, she gave up the effort in sheer exhaustion, not without
a lurking dread that, in a moment of passion, he might have
stricken some enemy to the ground, and forfeited his own life
in atonement for that of his fellow. Not for a single instant
did she fancy that he had been faithless to his public trust—
that he had incurred the scorn of all good men through a miserable appetite for gold.

Still, though dismissing, as well as she might, the distresses
of her father's situation from her thoughts, she found it difficult
to win the slumbers that she wooed. Her mind had been too
much excited by events and scenes which were new to the even
and unbroken currents of her ordinary existence, to sink into
quiet and leave her to repose; and the new world in which she
found herself, and the circumstances, some of them exciting and
startling enough, which had occurred on their journey, called
for brief review. Some of these were like a dream—the flitting
shadow of a disordered image, such as gathers before the eye
of a drowsy fancy, and fills the mind with conflicting impressions. Yet there was one image that lay at the bottom of all
others—which rose last to her survey, and lingered long after
all the rest had departed—which was neither indistinct nor
imperfect—which stood proudly and nobly before the eye of
her imagination, and on the pure tablets of her memory—alone,
unmixed with any other form or fancy—a controlling, commanding, imperial presence. This was the image of Vernon.
She saw him once more as, bounding from the wood, he rushed
forward without fear to the rescue of her father. She heard
the clear, silvery accents of his voice, sweet, though stern, as
he shouted to his companion to follow, and to the robbers as he
pursued. She beheld the grace of all his movements, as, bending in the saddle, he passed the carriage at full speed in chase
of the assailants, though already wounded; and a sudden

tremor was renewed at her heart, as she remembered his faint accents when he returned, and when, sinking down before her in the road, he lay unconscious—until they reached the dwelling of the methodist—a noble specimen of manly grace and beauty. Not a single feature that her eye scanned at that moment, but rose to her memory with the distinctness of life; and, with a sentiment of fluttering pleasure at her heart, strangely mingled up with that sadness which is ever the companion of devoted love, she continued to muse upon the events connected with his presence, until thought subsided into sleep, and her dreams renewed, under various aspects of pain and pleasure, the images and events which she had been last reviewing.

CHAPTER XXIV.

AN INTERESTING GUEST—A LONG LETTER—OUR HERO WARMS TO NEW ADVENTURES.

" More particulars must justify my knowledge."—Cymbeline.

VIRGINIA rose the next morning with better spirits. Her "bosom's lord" sat somewhat lightlier upon its throne. Sleep had refreshed and strengthened her, and those dreams, those sweet, vague, twilight fancies that came so commended to her heart by their association with its own, as yet unexpressed desires, had given a warmer glow to her cheek than it wore on the preceding evening. How soon youth relieves itself from the pressure and weight of most afflictions—with what elasticity it springs from the earth, and shakes off the dew and the despondency, and laughs aloud in the consciousness of a new birth, as it prepares, like the swif arising sun, to set forth on the glorious race of life. Sorrow to the young is only one of those shadows that momentarily cloud the skies. Wait but the morrow—nay, wait but a single hour—and the cloud has passed away, the sun resumes his empire of light and laughter and universal dominion: the stars sing out a fresher song of rejoicing at the coming of the moon-browed night; and the recollection of storm passes away from the reviving spirit with the succeeding glories of every changing moment. True though it be, that memory may preserve the pain — nay, the pain it-self may still lurk within the heart — and yet, it is as a memory only — there is no venom in the wound. The pure of heart sooner than any other, relieve themselves from the heavier pressure of their burdens. Like Christian in Bunyan, every additional step, advancing up the hills of virtue, diminishes the weight of that bundle which the best of us are still compelled to carry.

The cheerfulness of the maiden was increased as she found an improvement in her father's mood and bearing. He had resumed the old smiles which he was accustomed to wear in those more palmy days of the heart to all parties, when fortune smiled upon his household, and indiscretion had not as yet prepared the way for guilt. The gloomy humors, which had made contact with him for the last few weeks unpleasant, even to a daughter so dutiful as Virginia, were seemingly all dissipated; and before breakfast was well over, the resumption of old aspects in the little family, gradually had the effect of softening what was strange, and providing what was deficient, in their place of forest retreat.

The cares of the new household — the work of order — occupied the morning, and employment is a choice morality, as it promotes content. The furniture was to be arranged; the pictures to be hung; the curtains raised; the carpets laid, and a thousand little matters to be attended to, which employed all parties, and prevented that brooding gnawing thought, which is quite as frequently the growth of the body's idleness as of the mind's activity. Then, there was the little garden to be looked at, and plans were to be hit upon for disposing of its solid squares, and cutting into angles, crescents, stars and circles, its dead and uniform levels. To survey the little farm in its whole extent, was the business of an hour, and dinner-time approached with a rapidity which was unaccountable to all. After dinner the carriage was prepared for a drive about the environs of Lucchesa; and in a better mood for appreciating the beauty of rural objects than she had been for weeks before, Virginia took her seat in the airy vehicle, from which the travelling top had been removed, and prepared, with the more easily delighted Louisa, to see all the charms of scenery of which her father's taste and previous knowledge of the region, made him a very able cicerone.

We have already afforded to the reader a brief and passing glimpse of Lucchesa, on the approach of Vernon to that lovely village. It will not surely be supposed necessary that we should endeavor to dilate upon this portion of our labors ; since, with a few small and partial exceptions, most country-villages have the same general outlines. Yet, as we have said before, Lucchesa was a village among a thousand, and stood almost alone in many respects among most of the little villages of Mississippi.

The general aspects of a social settlement in countries purely agricultural, are seldom very pleasing. The proprietors of the land are better pleased to centre around themselves, on their own plantations, their resources and attractions. These persons seldom dwell in communities, and villages are, accordingly, with few exceptions, given up to such only as ply the arts of trade, and subserve, in some central spot, the wants and wishes of a populous surrounding country. As this surrounding country is thickly or sparsely settled — as it is rich or poor — will be the moral and social characteristics of the village which looks to it for support. The occupants are usually such as need has driven. They are not often natives of the neighborhood for which they toil ; and until very lately, but few tradesmen were known in the southern country, who did not " hail from" New England or New York. The exceptions to this general rule were, perhaps, the blacksmith or the wheelwright. The Yankee adventurer is seldom a laborer. He is a trader, a tavernkeeper, a tailor, a pedler — he will do anything that will enable him to avoid those heavier toils that call for great muscular activity and power. He is a jobber, a contriver, a calculator, an inventor — one of that cunning class, which, like the fox, takes good care always to employ another's fingers to draw his nuts out of the fire.

It demanded brief time for our party to see the whole extent of the little settlement ; and this done, as the afternoon was only half spent, the ride was prolonged by a short ramble in the neighboring country. They had but a little while returned from this ride before they were apprized by a talkative African, who was employed as a sort of gardener, of the events which had taken place at the tavern—the arrest of Vernon—his supposed attempt to escape, and the injuries which he received from the officers in consequence.

The tale did not lose in the usual exaggerations, nor was it quite so briefly narrated as it appears in this passage. It might be easy for us to let Cudjo speak for himself, as it is so favorite a custom with so many of our authors to make the negro a conspicuous actor in their scenes; and we see no good reason why a negro who speaks better English, and wears breeches, should not be quite as decent a personage in a modern novel, as a naked Highlander. Besides, Cudjo was an actor, and his animated gestures and fitting action might be a very good lesson to many of more pretension and a less imposing color, who have greater rights, and make more use of them to the great annoyance of deliberative assemblies. He commenced his story with a serious bluster; something like the manner of a northwester in its first approaches. The restraints, self-imposed upon his manner at first, were only intended to heighten the Kean-like outbreaks toward the close. He was, according to the prevailing rules among the stage-stricken heroes, simply reserving his powers for the fifth act—and when he reached the part where he proceeded to show the conflict between Vernon and the officers—when he described their joint rush upon him, and the descending blow of the Irishman's shillelah—he did it with such terrific truth, that Virginia screamed aloud, and Mr. Wilson, grasping the arm of the negro, demanded to know if the youth was killed.

But to this question he could obtain no satisfactory answer. Cudjo knew, indeed, well enough, but like a prudent narrator, he drew the curtain over the scene at that point when the doubt was most oppressive. He knew no more—he would tell no more—but confined himself, when more particularly examined, to simple reiterations of the part into which he had studiously thrown his greatest powers; and the renewal of which no persuasion could move him to forego. He knew his strong ground, and was resolved to make the most of it ; the more particularly

when he found that he had acquired, as well from the burden
of his story as from his manner of telling it, a fearful interest
in the eyes of his young mistress.

The agitation and alarm of Virginia Wilson were great, but
natural enough ; and while her father stood looking with equal
surprise and indecision upon the reiterated gestures of the
slave, which were made to supply those breaks in his story
where his language was imperfect or incomprehensible, she
clasped her father's arm, motioned his dismissal of the negro,
and proceeded, though trembling with emotions of no ordinary
character, to remind him of the duties which lay before him.

" You must seek this gentleman, my father. He has saved
us in a moment of great danger, at the peril of his own life.
You can only atone for the seeming indifference with which
you left him, sick and wounded, at Mr. Badger's, by attending
to him now."

" How attending to him, Virginia ? I am no doctor."

" Oh, sir ! — Oh, my father !"

" Yes — I don't see, Virginia, what we are to do."

" Oh, sir, but you can not help seeing. He is at this tavern
— you know not in what condition. If he be seriously hurt,
you must provide the physician, and bring him to your
house."

" What ! here, my child ?"   .

" Yes, sir, here. What can the sick man expect of comfort
in a public tavern — in one where he can have no attendance ?"

" And what attendance can he have here, Virginia, more than
from a physician ?"

" Your attendance — mine — Louisa's — the attendance of a
private family having more comforts at command, and acknowl-
edging a debt of gratitude to this youth, whose weakness, and
sickness, and injuries may all arise from the very part which he
took in our rescue. He is charged with murder ; and what murder can it be but that of the man whom he killed in preserving
us ? It is your duty to preserve, and to succor, and to defend
him. Your evidence, alone, may save him from the punishment
of that deed, for the justification of which no one can offer better proof than yourself. Go to him, my father, bring him to
your own house, and see to his injuries. Our utmost pains

will scarcely acquit us of the deep debt of gratitude we owe him, and for which we could not even before bestow our thanks."

We have seen the result of this interview between the reluctant father, and the resolute and well-minded daughter. She gained her object, though not without finding considerable difficulty in the coldness and the fears of the conscious criminal. The very name of a sheriff's officer distressed him; the idea of absolute personal contact with them filled him with apprehensions; and, when Virginia suggested the probable importance of his testimony in the youth's defence, the image of the keen-eyed magistrate, looking into his own secret soul, reawakened the terrors which beset him on his flight.

But the maiden's mind was too firmly impressed with the conviction of what was due by her father for himself and his children to the daring stranger, and she was too happy, even in spite of the youth's sufferings, that the chance was afforded them to remove the impression from his mind, that *they*—perhaps, if the truth were properly written, it would read *she*—had been ungrateful, in so speedily flying from one who had done them such good service, without speaking their acknowledgments—nay, without ministering to those hurts which he had suffered in their defence.

And yet, when her father had departed on his mission of humanity, her heart began to tremble with some new misgivings. Had she not been too urgent in this business—had she not overstepped the nice boundaries of maidenly modesty in pressing for the admission of this young man into her father's dwelling? Might not the tavern be as good as any other place for his recovery—as full of aids and comforts? And, again, what if he were not a gentleman? A man might be brave and generous enough to risk his own life for the succor of a stranger, yet lack all those more estimable points of character, which would entitle him to the freedom of a family—to an *entrée* into its sacred retreats—to a seat beside its hearth—to the ministering cares of its daughters.

But such was not the case with Vernon. Her convictions fought earnestly against this suggestion. Her arguments were such as, naturally enough, rise uppermost in the mind of the young, the beautiful, the amiable, and true. He was himself

young, and his face, distinguished by the clear skin and features
of a nice symmetry, wore an expression too unequivocally noble
and manly, even while his eyes were closed in the swooning
fit which had overcome him during their brief ride to the house
of Badger, to suffer her to suppose him wanting in those advantages of birth, education, and a proper taste and character, with
which her hoping fancy had already endowed him. He, too,
must be true and amiable; and with this satisfactory conclusion
to her thoughts and doubts, it was still surprising to herself
why her heart should so flutter and beat, when she listened to
her father's narrative after his return, and when she knew that
the youth was already an inmate of the house.

But the agitation of her heart passed away when she was informed of his condition—when she learned that his hurt rendered it necessary that he should be kept in a state of the
utmost quiet, lest the delirium which had already shown itself
partially in his words and actions, should be increased to an
extent which might baffle the powers of medicine. It was then
that she became the woman—that she threw off the enfeebling
apprehensions and fancies of the girl, and, following her father
to the chamber of the patient, prepared to assist in the labors
of the nurse.

The position in which Virginia found herself was an intoxi-
cating one. The strong man, whose gallantry had saved her
father and herself, lay before her, an unconscious dependent.
To her feeble strength and whispered will, he could oppose
neither strength nor will. She could look upon his pale face,
and the subdued and silent features, without challenging a returning glance. She could hear the feeble moan and incoherent
sentence that fell from his lips, and without being startled by a
single consciousness of the exquisite delicacy of her own position. While he lay helpless and delirious, her emotions were
all of that serene order which belong to the undisturbed performance of a single duty. There was nothing to alarm her
sensibilities—nothing to make her look too narrowly into the
propriety of her position, or the seeming tenderness of that regard which, she persuaded herself, was the due of gratitude—
of humanity—anything, in short, but the ministrations of love.

The affections of women are usually unselfish. They love

the more profoundly, the more they serve. Their love grows with their labors — with their toil for the beloved — and, the idea of all injustice or oppression excluded, their passion is proportionately increased by their cares. To be allowed to serve is, with them, to love the object of their devotion. It is for man to show himself grateful for the service; this, perhaps, in the warmth of their devoted homage, is the utmost that they ask. Yet, even when this acknowledgment is withheld, the greater number of them will still continue the service. The service itself, to the dependent spirit, is a joy; and they will ask little more than the vine that only prays the privilege to be suffered to cling around the tree. Perhaps, the heart of the woman who has once loved, will only cease to love when it is denied to cling and to entwine itself. Even when there is no returning caress, the sufferance of love will still be a sweet privilege to the very dependent spirit. How many are there who enjoy no more than this — how many more are there who merit, much more than man, that unceasing homage which women are suffered only to bestow!

It might have been that Virginia Wilson would have soon forgotten Vernon, had they not a second time encountered. Love is not a thing of first sight, though first impressions, confirmed by a subsequent favorable knowledge of the object, will very commonly ripen into love. However favorable had been the impressions made upon Virginia by the appearance of the handsome stranger, changing scenes, objects, and circumstances, must soon have erased them, or subdued the vivid colors in which they were first made. But the cares of tendance upon the sick-bed of the youth — the deep and difficult respiration of his breast, laboring under the fever which assailed him — his languid but incoherent utterance — the occasional moan and whisper which escaped his lips, and those broken words which had a meaning she would have given worlds to understand — these were all circumstances which, as they denoted his dependence upon her, increased her interest in him; and no hours were more sweet, during the time of his illness, than those in which she was suffered to watch beside his couch.

But the crisis was soon over — a few days effected a favorable change — the returning consciousness of the patient, in freeing her from her attendance, deprived her of the sweet privilege which his situation had afforded ; and the languid eyes of Vernon looked round him vainly and impatiently for that lovely countenance of which he had some sweet and partial glimpses in the intervals of his disease.

In place of these, he encountered no forms more interesting · than those of Mr. Wilson, or the little Louisa, or the sturdy Alabamian, or the more wily Saxon, the outlaw — both of these last being necessarily admitted to visit at the house of Wilson, as *friends* of the invalid.

As Vernon grew better, his anxieties at his situation were renewed. He felt the difficulties increase of declaring his true character, as the agent of justice, to his hospitable entertainer ; and the annoying character of this feeling was not a little heightened as he looked upon the bewitching grace, and encountered the timid glances of his lovely daughter. There was another circumstance that also afflicted him. He could not mistake the interest with which the keen eyes of Saxon followed the movements of Virginia Wilson ; nor suppress the involuntary pang with which he listened to the language of the outlaw, subdued, conciliatory, yet free and graceful, which he held with her. Saxon, too, sometimes enjoyed a privilege, which, in Vernon's feeble state, was necessarily denied to him. He could attend her in those afternoon walks, when the sun, sinking behind the forests, left only a few glimmering tokens of his light to soften the scene, and beguile the musing and melancholy spirit into groves, which, shady, sweet and solitary, seemed, more than all other scenes beside, to harmonize kindred spirits, and bring them into a more near communion with each other. Vernon, he knew not why himself, felt uneasy at these rambles. Not that they were frequent. Had he been a just as well as a close observer, he would have discovered that, on those evenings when Saxon returned with the maiden from her walk, she always came back at a much earlier hour, and her reserve was no less obvious than the obtrusive attention of her companion. Could he have been permitted a glance at them in their rambles, he would have been as much struck with the cold courtesy of her tones in replying to her companion, and the evident unwillingness which she displayed to receive those thousand little attentions which are so apt, where the parties incline to each other, to sweeten the dull ramble, and shorten the prolonged paths of the forest.

But Vernon already watched all things with eyes readily disposed to see them through a false medium, and a spirit that conjectured the worst of all things which it is not permitted to see. His inability to share in the rambles of the maiden necessarily increased his apprehensions of the more fortunate person who happened to be her companion; and his distrust of the outlaw, which had been a sort of instinct, making him reluctant to assimilate with that person from the first, was now heightened to a feeling of positive dislike, as he contemplated the superior advantages which he possessed, and dreaded the events which might spring out of them.

Assuming that the attentions of Saxon were as grateful to Virginia as they seemed imposing in his own eyes, he suffered his annoyance to show itself, sometimes, in a cold glance and colder speech to the maiden herself, at moments when the jealous fit was particularly active in his bosom; and it was only by a strong and resolute exercise of that manly sense, which was the prevailing characteristic of his mind, that he could see, and seek to repair, by an immediate change of deportment, the brutality of which he felt himself guilty. On such occasions her eyes would sink to the floor—her voice, which had urged its inquiry in a tremulous tone, that might have conveyed a grateful meaning to the heart of any lover, not blinded and made obtuse by other and perverse feelings, would become silent; and she would seize an early opportunity to retire from the eyes of all, and in the solitude of her chamber pore over those mysterious emotions which oppressed her, without remedy; and wonder at the excitement in her heart, for which she felt unable to account. Why had the words of Vernon such power over her? Why did she shrink from his gentler glances —why did she suffer at his cold ones? Why was it such a pleasure to hear that voice, the sounds of which yet made her tremble? It was not long before circumstances provided her with a reply.

Meanwhile, Vernon improved hourly, and the attendance of the physician ceased to be necessary. The hour was ap-

proaching when the officers of the law would claim their pris
oner, though this conviction was productive of more disquietude
in his mind because of the pleasant communion which it was
destined to disturb, than because of any danger in which his
arrest promised to involve him. That he should be seriously
made to answer for the death of Horsey, he did not suffer himself to think for an instant; yet, he did not, because of his confidence in himself, neglect those duties, the performance of
which arose out of his present situation. He prepared letters
to his friend and patron, Carter, giving a succinct detail of his
wanderings and adventures, up to the very moment of his wri
ting, omitting no event which might be held worthy of commu
nication, excepting such details as belonged to the conferences
which he had had with Badger and Rawlins on the subject of
the banded robbers of the country. On this head he deemed it
prudent to forbear all remark in a letter which was to be in-
trusted to the ordinary post; particularly, indeed, as Carter
was not greatly interested in any such matters. With respect
to the fate of Horsey, he related all that had reached him and
all that he knew — detailed the chief particulars of their dia-
logues where they threw any light upon the purposes or course
of that erratic youth, described the circumstances under which
they parted, and, after relating the affair of young Mabry, and
the assault of the latter upon himself, suggested a surmise —
which he would yet have willingly forborne — that this young
man himself might have been the murderer; for the probabilities strongly inclined to this opinion.

"I know," he continued — "I know, my dear sir, that you
will not need my solemn assurance — which I yet make — that
my hands are utterly guiltless of this young man's death. I
trust to make this appear in my examination before the justice,
and I am scarcely less anxious that you should do your best to
convince his worthy old parents to the same effect. Next to
the pain of this most humiliating situation in which I find myself, is the deep sorrow which I should ever feel at incurring,
however unjustly, the suspicions of the good people whose
kindness to me was not the less grateful to my heart, because
it was comparatively unimportant to my interests. I must pray
you then to spare no effort, by an array of all the favorable

facts which you possess, and a careful display of those arguments which you understand as well as myself, and which conclusively establish the folly and impolicy of such a deed, to acquit me, in their eyes, of the cruel imputation. I write," he continued, "from the house of William Maitland, himself, with whose family I have been an inmate for the last five days. I am in part indebted to his hospitable care for my improved health and recovery from my hurts. As yet he knows nothing of me, of my connection with you, or of my objects. My development of the latter, in such a manner as to effect your generous intentions toward his children—both of whom are females —and to escape the reproach of requiting good with evil, shall be my study between this and the period, when, in compliance with the demands of the officers of justice, I shall be compelled to leave him. My position is one of considerable delicacy, and my course, therefore, must be the result of a calm and serious consideration."

Such was a portion of the elaborate letter which Vernon prepared for the perusal of his guardian. Could it be imputed as insincerity, or an improper suppression of necessary particulars, that the writer said not a word more on the subject of those children of Ellen Taylor, in whom Carter had such a prevailing interest, and to whom he was disposed to exhibit a degree of generosity no less novel than extreme? Vernon's own conscience smote him for the suppression of particulars which he knew must interest his patron to know; but he strove in vain to overcome a reluctance, the sources of which he was unwilling to examine.

He was yet writing, when he heard the fall of a light footstep passing through the gallery. He knew the step; and he hurried to the window with a movement, which, in his feeble state, it required some effort to make. His eyes followed the slowly moving form—the form of perfect symmetry—the movement of perfect grace. Her course lay through the garden to the shrouding woods beyond it. This was her accustomed walk. He forgot himself while he gazed—his thoughts were steeped in the dews of a most Elysian fancy—his worship was oblivious of all other objects than the one of its adoration. On sudden she looked behind her—she looked upward

—their eyes encountered, and then she fled—fled even as the young fawn, that, wandering forth from the forest for a single instant, and, for the first time, in that single instant, encounters the glance of the hunter.

CHAPTER XXV.

LOVE-PASSAGES UNDER AN EVIL EYE—ASSAULT—CUSTODY— A RIDE TO PRISON.

"Well, perform it,
The law is satisfied: they can but die."
THE OLD LAW

A NEW spirit rose in his bosom as he beheld this movement. Why should I not pursue?" was the involuntary self-inquiry of his mind. He grew stronger as he proposed it. The stiffness of his wounded limb seemed to lessen, and grasping the staff with which he had been wont to hobble across his chamber in the last two days, he moved forward with a degree of rapidity that was scarcely justified by prudence. Unseen, he passed through the gallery, descended the steps, followed the lightly-beaten foot-path which he had seen her take around the garden, and was soon hidden in the same forests which yet concealed her from his sight. A new thought entered his mind at this moment. A keen pang of jealousy thrilled through his heart.

"What if I intrude upon a sacred privacy? Goes she not to meet this smiling fellow—this Saxon—this pleasing word-monger? Walk they not together daily? Wherefore should I approach them?"

Had the question been answered by his reason merely, he would most probably have returned to the dwelling without farther search. But he remembered the backward glance which she gave him—her sudden flight—and that memory, which answered nothing and told nothing, had yet a signification of more effect upon his heart than all the arguments of his mind

to his understanding. He went forward, and she had neither
fled so far nor so fast, but that he was able to overtake her.
She sat upon a fallen pine—one that the hurricane had but
lately wrested from its foundation, the foliage yet green upon
its branches. The long leaves hung around, and half-shrouded
her from his sight. Him she saw not, but remained in her sitting posture, unconscious of his approach, until he was within a
few paces of her.

Then she started to her feet—then he beheld that face—
those eyes once more turned upon him, and he fancied they had
been glistening with tears. But this might have been a fancy
only—what need had she to weep? He saw no tears, and dismissed the suspicion from his mind; but he could not doubt
that her cheeks were more pale than usual, and the languid
brightness of her eyes—their dewy softness—could not be
mistaken.

There were certainly some keen sensibilities at work within
her bosom. He was moved instinctively by this conviction—
he felt that there were some weaknesses in his own, but he
strove to silence and put down that ever-ready consciousness
which is so apt, in every young man's bosom, to convert into
his special divinity the first passable damsel whom he sees.
Vernon was a youth of calm, good sense, and he was determined to keep his emotions of blood and fancy from having
their own way. He assumed a lightness and gayety of tone
when he addressed her, which called for an effort. He took
her hand, reconducted her to her seat, and placed himself beside her while he spoke.

"Give me joy, Miss Wilson, that I am at last able to find out
your favorite walks. I caught a glimpse of you from the window, and grew strong to pursue, as I beheld the ease of your
flight. I have long envied you these walks—let me make you
my acknowledgments, since it is, perhaps, owing to your friendly
cares that I am so soon able to enjoy them."

"Not to mine—not to mine," was her hasty reply. "I hav
done but little, Mr. Vernon; I am very happy that anything
that we could do should have been agreeable to one to whom
we owe so much. You—"

"Ah! you would remind me of a happy moment—but you

13

need not; I am too proud of having served you, however
slightly, to forget my own good deeds. I may not boast of
them. but I need no help to persuade me to remember them;
they will always form a part of that pleasant chronicle, Miss
Wilson, which the heart makes of its fortunate events. I shall
set them all down together with the five days enjoyed in your
cottage."

"Enjoyed, Mr. Vernon?" was the smiling question. "Endured, you mean."

"No, enjoyed," was the answer. "The pain of the illness is
soon forgotten in the cares of the nurse; and the kindness
which has soothed is always a pleasure to be remembered, even
when the pain is forgotten. Let me say, then, how sweet to
me is the obligation of gratitude which I feel to you and yours,
for the pleasant cares which have ministered to my feebleness
and need."

"Do not speak of it, Mr. Vernon. My father has only done
his duty. But for you, we know not what might have happened to us. You saved us at the hazard of your life, and what
we have done called for no hazard."

"But much trouble — much annoyance—"

"No, no! Mr. Vernon — it was a pleasure, sir — to—"

She paused — the jealousy of a nice maiden delicacy became
apprehensive that her gratitude might express itself too warmly.
Gratitude she knew was justified, but *that* had its own language, and the caution was only a proper one, lest she might
employ for its expression the language of a warmer sentiment.
Perhaps Vernon detected something of this consciousness, for
he put his hand upon hers with a gentle effort to detain it in
his grasp, as he said, hurriedly:—

• "Speak, Miss Wilson — go on."

She withdrew her hand — the flush was renewed upon her
face, but she said nothing. A moment followed of awkward
silence to them both, which was only broken by a strong and
decided effort on the part of Vernon. His lively manner had
utterly departed in the first few moments of their interview, and
it was with a gravity, natural on many accounts to his situation, that he renewed the conversation.

'Next," he said, "to my acknowledgments for your hospitality and kindness, Miss Wilson, is the desire which I feel to place myself in a right point of view before you. I would seek to assure and convince you that your kindness has not been bestowed upon a criminal, though I have no proof beyond my own asseveration, by which to convince you that I am utterly guiltless of this murder which is laid to my charge."

"Oh, think not, Mr. Vernon, that we believe—that we can believe this foolish charge—I am sure—I know that it is groundless."

"On my honor, you do me only justice. The shedding of blood—the taking of life—is an offence against humanity from which my soul would shrink, unless in a case of absolute necessity. The only deed of the kind of which I have ever been guilty is one that took place almost in your sight, and was strictly justifiable from the circumstances preceding it."

"Yes—yes!" faltered the maiden, with a shudder.

"The young man for whose death I have been summoned to answer, was one of whom I knew but little—nothing unfavorable—but on the contrary, much which commanded my indulgence and regard. I had neither quarrel to maintain against him, nor interest to pursue; and my own objects, Miss Wilson, were of a nature which made me particularly desirous to avoid all strife and difficulty with any and everybody. That I have not been able to avoid them, is due rather to my evil fortune than my desire. I know nothing of the grounds upon which this charge has been made against me, or of the parties making it, but I trust soon, Miss Wilson, to satisfy the judge of that innocence which you have so kindly declared yourself willing to believe."

"Oh, sir, we know—we hope it will be so. I am sure there can be no doubt of it. My father says he is certain you will be released, and Mr. Jamison told me but yesterday that you no more committed the crime than he did, and he will soon enough convince the justice to that effect. He is very friendly to you, sir, that Mr. Jamison."

"A good fellow—a strange fellow—whom I never saw before the evening of my arrival at Lucchesa; but, like the frank men of our western forests generally, he carries his heart in one hand and his weapon in the other, always and equally ready

whether for friend or foe. I hope he may not be too sanguine
in this matter — I rely rather on my own consciousness of innocence than upon any knowledge of the facts with which I am
acquainted. I know nothing of the circumstances upon which
the accusation is based."

"Nor does he, I imagine; at least, he could tell father nothing, who was very anxious to know. His convictions in your
favor seemed to arise from his prepossessions; you are fortunate, Mr. Vernon, in finding friends so readily — perhaps that
fact alone may be considered a presumption in your defence."

"I am afraid it would go but a little way toward my acquit-
tal; but then it can be nothing but a presumption against me,
and a presumption, unsupported by strong circumstances, can do
me little harm. And yet, Miss Wilson, there is something in
your opinion which carries to my mind a hope scarce less grateful than would be the assurance of my easy escape from this
cruel imputation."

"What is that, sir?" she asked, innocently. The question
would have been left unspoken had she looked up in his face
when she replied, and beheld the increasing brightness and
piercing regard embodied in his glance.

"That you found nothing strange or wonderful — nothing
unnatural or unexpected — in the supposed facility with which
I have secured the favoring prepossessions of others. May I
hope that he who has won the friendship of the rude countryman, will not be thought too presuming if he fancies that he has
also not vainly striven for that of the city maiden? Your
friendship, Miss Wilson, would be that of beauty, and youth,
and education — taste without artifice — opinion without rude-
ness, and intellectual strength mingled with grace and sentiment. May I hope for these — may I dream, in the vanity of a
too sanguine spirit, that in finding these qualities in you, and
estimating them at their true value when found, I have not
prayed in vain for the acquisition of your regards. Your friendship—"

He paused — the sentence remained unfinished, though its
purport was no less clear to her mind than it was in the mind
of him who yet withheld its utterance. It may be added, that
she felt how much more grateful it was, left unspoken, than *if*

it had been concluded. Vernon himself felt that it could not be concluded as it then stood. It was too cold a projected termination to matter that was naturally rising into warmth, and a manner already warm and beginning to be impassioned. He wisely stopped short—short where he was—and she breathed less freely under the pressure of a sentiment which was strangely sweet, though almost suffocating.

And he—the glow upon his cheek made itself felt—the .tremors at his heart grew almost to a murmur like the swift dropping of distant falling rain. Was it, indeed, friendship that he solicited from the favoring estimate of Virginia Wilson? At that moment neither of them thought of friendship,—they thought of anything besides. The sympathy was of a stronger sort which was stirring in the bosom of the two, and it found its proper utterance at last.

But let us abridge the scene. Love passages are rarely of interest to third parties; and either glide into the bright fantastics, such as glow in the ethereal world and season of a Romeo, or become, in the measured economy of the modern calculator, a question of portion, pin-money and proper establishment. In either case, the reader or speculator yawns in weariness or disgust, and is satisfied with those results which tend to a final dismissal of all the parties. We might hope—we certainly should pray—for a better interest with these. Vernon was no lovesick fantastic, though warmed by a temperament never subdued, not always measured, and sometimes endowed with no limited tongue for utterance; but his passions were perhaps more governable than those of most young men, and he had gone through a long course of severe self-study, by which they had not only been regulated to a certain movement, but his reason had also been advanced to a certain supremacy. This self-acquired power kept his utterance within the bounds of good taste and propriety—his love was that of the man and the gentleman—his passions were those of civilization. He had learned to know that *blood* frequently presumes in the language of affection, and becomes obtrusive because of a selfishness which it disguises by another name,—he also knew that the first lesson which true love has ever taught, is one of humility—but that humility which is always allied to hope.

Love is the religion of the passions, and its zeal, though warm and fiery, is still that of one officiating at high altars, where the first sign of the advent of the God is shown by the submission of the worshipper. By gradual transitions—by the one mystic key-note—the look, the word, which, here and there, suggests the stages by which two hearts, having the same journey to take, are gradually brought together—an interest grew up in the breast of each, leading to a just comprehension of the other; and ere the one spoke, the other felt. Vernon to his own surprise, discovered that he had won a heart long before he ever dreamed of looking for one; and Virginia Wilson—certainly, until she met with our hero, she had never thought it worth while to take any care of that, which she now discovered it to be so seriously sweet a business to surrender.

Though we have denied ourselves the pleasure of beholding the love scene and hearkening to the love dialogue between the parties, there was another who, "squat like a toad" in the cover of the neighboring foliage, had no such scruples as restrain us. He heard and witnessed all. This was the outlaw Saxon. He had followed their footsteps, and had penetrated to a spot which would enable him to arrive at a knowledge as vexing to his spirit as was the manner degrading by which it was obtained. He heard, with ill-suppressed fury, the whispered word, half doubt, half tenderness—he saw the smile which trembled in the eye it lightened—the gentle meeting of those mingling hands, which, under Love's slightest pressure, become instincts themselves and of the most sensitive character;—and no less new than bitter was the pang that went through his own breast, as he beheld the happiness he envied. He had only of late grown conscious of a passion such as he had never felt before. He had sought Virginia Wilson daily from the first hour that her presence had shone upon his sight; and under the pretence of an interest in his wounded fellow-traveller, he had obtained access to her dwelling with the purpose of pressing those attentions by which he hoped to secure an interest in her heart. He had joined her in her daily walks—was not without that easy dialogue and graceful manner which are of all things most essential to success with woman; and had striven with his best powers to commend himself to her regards.

Yet she had shrunk from his pursuit; had discouraged the intimacy at which he aimed—had responded coldly to his conversation, and shown herself more than commonly obtuse whenever he had striven to be more than commonly intelligible. Yet, here was one, who, almost without his own consciousness—certainly, without design—had succeeded in that which had .asked his utmost ability, even under the guidance of a settled purpose and a deliberate scheme. The mortification of his pride increased the pang of his disappointment, and the vindictive purpose, with which he had before regarded Vernon, now assumed a deeper character in his mind.

" It is well," was his thought, as he surveyed the pair—" but the hour of vengeance is at hand. You would bind the outlaw, Harry Vernon! We shall see. Artful, and strong, and sagacious, as you think yourself, you are in the toils. Deceived by one traitor, Clement Foster will scarcely suffer himself, hand and foot, to be manacled by another. Pliant once, he is now unyielding; and by all that is sacred in the love of the saint and the fear of the sinner, you shall pay the penalty of your presumption by your life. You would hunt the bear in his native brake, beware of his embrace."

He left the place of his concealment with a stealthy step, and without disturbing the lovers, who were now but too much absorbed with one another to have senses for the rustling branches, or the slight motion of a gliding form among the leaves. He proceeded to the tavern with all the impatience of hate, and summoned his confederates who played the part of the officers of justice. To them he issued his commands, and described the place in which the lovers were still to be found.

" Seek him there," said the vindictive outlaw; " and seize on him at once. Give him no indulgence—drag him away, though you find him in her arms. Hear none of his promises—hearken to none of her entreaties. The scoundrel is a spy upon us—another Hurdis; and he deserves no mercy at our hands. Away! you know the place."

He saw them depart in the same instant, and waited with malicious impatience, the result of his furious mandate. The lovers meanwhile had prepared to return to the cottage. They were already on their way—the hand of the maiden in that of Vernon's; her eyes cast upon the ground as she listened to those accents so dear to the young heart—those idle words and whispers, which, though they sound sillily enough in the ears of third persons, seem to the initiate more precious than manna in the wilderness. At this moment they were encountered by the ruffians who stood suddenly in the path before them. Virginia shrunk back in alarm, while a faint scream issued from her lips.

"How now, fellows! What mean you?" demanded Vernon, who did not at first recognise them.

"Fellows! indeed!" said one. "We'll see who's the better fellow when Judge Nawls sets eyes upon us. That's for being civil to you, I suppose, and letting you off when we had you. But there's an end to that. You must go along with us."

"Along with you! Who are you?"

"Oh, you've no memory of us! I shouldn't be surprised if you've forgotten yourself too. You're not Mr. Harry Vernon, that killed one Thomas Horsey, and we ain't the men that 'Squire Nawls sent to catch you! Come, come, young 'un, that's not doing the thing handsomely—that's not keeping to your promise. You must go along with us at once, so drop the young lady's arm, and here's our'n. It ain't quite so soft a one, it's true, but, by the hokey, it's better able to help you; and then you know, need must when the devil drives—so no grumbling."

The action of the ruffian corresponded with his words. His hand was already extended toward the collar of Vernon's coat, when, stepping back a pace, the indignant youth lifted his staff with a promptness and determination which drove the fellow back much faster than he had advanced. In another instant, however, a calmer mood filled the mind of Vernon.

"This is all idle. I certainly do not mean to resist these men—I have no reason to fear the magistrate." Such were his thoughts as he turned to Virginia.

"Miss Wilson, forgive me. I am giving a needless alarm. These are the officers of justice, and seeing me well enough to travel, they naturally enough seek to perform their duty Will you proceed to the house?—I will follow you. I would speak with them a while."

He led her forward until they had passed the officers, then left her to proceed alone while he returned to them.

"Gentlemen, I will be ready to go with you in an hour;—I will but return to the dwelling of Mr. Wilson, and at the end of that time I will meet you at the tavern."

"'Twon't do, my boy," was the answer, "you're too ready with your stick to be trusted. You must go with us now. We can't trust you out of our sight."

The youth would have expostulated, but while he spoke, one of the ruffians threw himself upon him, bore him to the earth, and, in spite of all his assurances that he would quietly accompany them, proceeded to bind his arms with a cord which the providence of Saxon had procured for the purpose, and which the assistance of his companion enabled him to use in spite of the angry but feeble resistance of the prisoner. When bound, they lifted him to his feet, and placing themselves, one on each hand, commanded him to move forward in the direction of the tavern.

He did so with as much quietness of temper as he could command under the reasonable anger which naturally followed the provocation. He tried to convince himself that they were doing nothing more than their duty—that they had yielded him all reasonable indulgence—and were bound, as soon as they discovered his ability to travel, to secure his person against the chances of escape. But the sedative effect of his own reasonings was very partial. He still could not resist the wish that his arms were once more free, and his staff once more in his hands. "My staff should make ye skip," thought he, in the language of the "Ancient Mariner." But he overcame a desire which he felt to be no less idle than hopeless, and tried to obtain his remedy in another way.

"A civil answer turneth away wrath," and he had long known that a civil tongue will carry a man unscotched through the whole western country. Assuming the men beside him to be no other than what they professed to be, he determined to reason with them as persons who could have no motive for re-

fusing any ii dulgence to a prisoner which was not inconsistent
with the security of their trust.

"You are unnecessarily hard with me, men," he said, quietly.
"You can have no reason for thinking I would run away, since,
if such had been my desire, I could have been off at daylight,
and none had been the wiser. Why then would you make an
enemy of a man who can be your friend—who is willing to reward you? Suffer me to go back to the dwelling of Mr. Wilson for an hour only. You, in the meantime, can watch the
dwelling on all sides. My horse is at the tavern—you can secure him—and without a horse I can not fly very far. I wish
but to make my acknowledgments to the family which has
treated me with so much kindness."

"You ought t'have done all that before, my lark—there's
no time for you now. So set forward. I tell you there's no
trusting you. You clipped me over my noddle already, the
first day I set hands on you, and my jaw isn't quite smooth yet;
and you forget, just a bit ago you'd have tried it again with
that stout hickory that helped you forward. Twice warned is
enough for me—I don't risk a third scuffle with any man if I
can help it. So, look you, give but a single flirt again, and
here's into you."

The fellow showed a monstrous bowie-knife as he spoke
these words, and by his reckless expression of countenance,
suited to his bold and unfeeling language, Vernon readily believed that his better policy was to obey quietly. He went
forward, and encountered the hardy Alabamian, Jamison, who
was just about setting out for Wilson's on his customary afternoon visit to his friend. Saxon was nowhere to be seen.

Nothing could exceed the rage of the Alabamian, as he wit
nessed the degrading situation in which his friend stood. He
was at once for fighting the officers, and nothing but the most
earnest appeals from Vernon kept him from violence. One
thing, however, he was resolved to do, and in this particular our
hero was satisfied he should have his own way—that was to
cut the cords which bound the arms of the prisoner. He drew
his knife for the purpose, and was advancing, when the constables both opposed him with like weapons. But he was not to
be intimidated by this show of valor.

"There's two of you," he said, "but I count myself good for three, at least, such slender chaps as you; so here goes at your kidneys, and one drive of my six-pounder will let more sins out of your carcasses than all the saints could ever put in virtues."

With an earnestness which left nothing to conjecture, the stout-heart Alabamian, wielding his knife in air — a huge, bright instrument, with a back-bone like that of a butcher's cleaver, so heavy that its own weight, if falling, must have made its wounds deadly — prepared to rush forward upon the constables. But these worthies were not willing to wait for such an encounter. Receding from their posts, they clamored to the bystanders for protection, crying out a "rescue" — a "rescue." Without heeding their clamor, or suffering anything to divert him from his purpose until it was finished, Jamison cut the cords of the prisoner, and seizing the moment when the officers were most noisy and most remote, he whispered in his ear :—

"Be off now, Harry Vernon — there's my own horse hitched close beside you, and I'll keep off the rascals while you're mounting. Show 'em clean heels, and I'll be after you with your own nag, and will join you at Buzzard's Roost in two hours. They're afraid of me, the niggers, and you see I ain't afraid of them. D—n 'em, I don't mind half a dozen of them, fair front and no dodging. So go ahead, my boy, and leave the scatteration to me. You're too weak to fight now, so there's no reason or right to expect it of you."

The Alabamian was astounded when Vernon thanked him, but declared he had no purpose of the kind.

"I am innocent of the charge, Mr. Jamison, and do not fear to meet it."

"Oh, well! That's right enough ; but guilty or innocent, you see, Harry, when they're for putting ropes on a freeman, that's a time to be off, or to fight with tiger's tusk. I'm all grinders after that, and a ridge-saw that works along the middle."

Meanwhile the clamors of the constables were gathering a crowd about them.

"He has cut the prisoner loose — the man that murdered Tom Horsey — help ! — seize ! — catch the murderer," &c. .

"Shut up, you yelping pugnose!" cried the indignant Ala

bamian; "none of your d——d lies about a business you can't understand. Look you, men, they had the gentleman corded up as if he had been a panther of the wilderness—roped his hands behind him—and he just out of a sick-bed, and making no resistance, and telling them all the while he was ready to go along with 'em. It's only they're sich blasted cowards, afraid of a sick man—afraid of any man. Dang my buttons, I'm almost ashamed I didn't borrow a pen-knife to do the business. This bowie-blade is a'most too big for such etarnal small souls as they've got."

"You hear him confess he drew his knife upon us?" said one of the officers to the crowd.

"Ay," said Ja'mison, "and how it scared the niggers white when they saw it."

"He rescued the prisoner from us."

"A lie, nigger—he's at your service—he says it himself—so bring out his horse; and I'll tell you another thing—I'm at your service too. I'll ride along with you and see fair play, and if you've got anything to say agin Dick Jamison, let it out as loud as you please when you stand before the judge."

The scene ended with the quiet departure of Vernon, accompanied by his friend Jamison, under the enforced escort of the officers.

CHAPTER XXVI.

THE STAGE-HERO AND THE INCUBUS — ROMEO APPROACHES THE FOOTLIGHTS UNDER A FAMOUS MANAGER.

Caliban. Lo, how he mocks me ! wilt thou let him, my lord ?
Trinculo. Lord I quoth he, that a monster should be such a natural !
The Tempest.

HAVING now fairly lodged Vernon for the murder of Horsey, it is high time that we should retrace our steps and look into the progress of the latter important personage. Though somewhat baffled in his hope of having a companion, in a kindred spirit, to the end of his journey, the stage-struck hero was not without his consolation in the moment of the parting from his friend. He was on his way to the scene of action ; another day would bring him to the place where the wandering tribe was to be found, for whose communion he panted even as the hart panteth after the water-brooks ; and visions of theatrical glory began to gather on his eyes. With that restlessness of imagination which betrayed itself in everything which he said and did, he was already fancying himself in the midst of such difficulties, arising from bad management and the labored rivalry of inferior persons, as were really grateful to a man of his temperament. His cogitations, which broke forth at moments into rabid soliloquy, were most generally of this description. Now he laughed at the idea of Jim Tilton and Hugh Peters, and the ridiculous figures which they must cut as Brutus and Julius Cæsar ; at the next moment, he was soliciting their applause for some new reading with which he contemplated to astound the natives and improve Shakspere. Anon he went back to the cottage of Yarbers, and his visions, then, were of Mary Clayton, as the most perfect Juliet that ever stimulated the

best capacities of a Montague; and as that fancy worked in his
mind, his voice grew more emphatic, and a spectator in the
bushes might have been no less surprised than amused to have
heard and seen him as he rode, declaiming at the full pitch of
his lungs to Juliet in the balcony; and, at moments, in the
earnestness of his action, almost flinging himself from the ungainly and venerable steed of his sire, whose neck he sometimes
embraced, by a very natural error of his imagination which con
founded it with the form of Juliet, or Mary Clayton rather, who
in such moments, seemed brought immediately within his reach.

In this manner, with a mind far away, in a province utterly
foreign to that through which his only half-conscious person
travelled, he went forward without interruption, and was only
brought back to the actual condition of things around him when
he reached the river, and the grim Charon of that Stygian
stream, leading his horse through bog and sluice, contrived,
with some difficulty, and after no little delay, to place the two
fairly in his boat. Some time was consumed in conveying
him across; for the river swamp, in the day of which we write,
was one of the most interminable intricacies that ever distressed
a good steed or vexed an impatient traveller. But the delay
did not so much affect the actor. He soon made a companion
of the boatman, a simple, stupid fellow, who scarcely comprehended five of all the words that were said to him, and answered none.

But Horsey needed no answer—his only object was an auditor, and he was sufficiently satisfied, if suffered to talk on without stint or limit, though the hearer made no response to any
of the questions which he asked. These were neither few nor
unimportant; but as the actor did not wait for an answer, why
should we? He was soon, comparatively speaking, set across
the river; but the thousand hollows of the swamp, filled wit
the waters of a recent freshet, were around his path, leaving ·
at moments doubtful in what direction he should pursue his
way.

But Tom Horsey was not the man to suffer himself to be bewildered long. His mind soon ran off in the direction of his
desires, and, looking rather to the end of his journey than to his
course, he gave himself not much concern about the way which

led to it. After a few moments of reluctant attention, in which it seemed to his eyes that all his efforts only led his hobbling horse from one sluice into another, he soon forgot everything but the one subject most at his heart; and if his allegiance wavered for an instant, it was, perhaps, in regard to an exception which might be considered, indeed, only as an auxiliar to the other — namely, the person of Mary Clayton, and she as Juliet.

With a mind thus directed, he had no attention to bestow upon the external world around him, and did not seem to heed, or be conscious of the fact, that the day was approaching to its close — and that, so far from nearing the cottage where he proposed to spend the night, he had, in fact, utterly departed from everything like a road, his horse slowly toiling forward through Indian footpaths that deepened occasionally into the cart or wagon-width, but only at places where the presence of bog or creek suggested the best of reasons why they should do so, and not because they had ever been employed by any such vehicles. But, utterly absorbed in his own speculations, none of these signs were perceptible to the actor, and night would have come upon and caught him in the swamp before he would have been conscious of his predicament, but for the sudden appearance upon his path of one, whose wild and uncouth exterior and abrupt *entrée* were of too startling a character to pass without regard.

The stranger was a chunky little imp, not more than four feet high, wearing a bunch upon his shoulder, which at first glance, suggested to Horsey the idea of a native-born Richard. His arms were long like those of an ape; his ears of corresponding dimensions; his lips, pursed into a point like two bits cf shrivelled coonskin, were covered with a thick furze, not unlike that of the hair upon the same animal; and with a short, pug-like nose, and little, quick, staring gray eyes, that peeped out from under a shaggy white pent-house of hair; he presented altogether the most comical appearance that could be imagined, and one that would have made the fortune of a cunning showman in any of the Atlantic cities. His legs, though short, were strangely bowed — indeed, the extreme curve which they described was one cause of their shortness. He might have risen to five fair feet, could they have been smoothed out symmetrically. As he went forward, which he did with a readiness that occasioned surprise in the spectator, the bow of the advanced leg would completely overlap the other, so that he would seem, to the passing glance, in possession of one only.

His garb contributed something to his comical appearance. He wore tights, as pantaloons, which showed to a nicety the attenuated size of the crooked limbs on which he depended for support. He seemed almost entirely without flesh. The lower limbs were not merely short and deformed, but slender to a degree, which made the spectator apprehensive that they might snap as readily as pipe-stems under the swollen and dropsical bulk of body which they carried. But this show was deceptive. The urchin had an elasticity of muscle, a capacity of stretch and endurance in his sinews, and a share of positive strength in his excessive breadth of shoulders, which made him little inferior in conflict to most ordinary men, and in speed he could have outwinded the best.

A little jacket of green bombasin, made on a plan quite as narrow and contracted as the breeches, rendered the hump singularly conspicuous upon his shoulders; and by contracting these somewhat too closely, served to throw the long and apish arms out from the body in such a manner as greatly to increase the similitude between the owner and the ungainly animal to which we have likened him. A coonskin cap, set rather jauntily on his cocoanut-shaped head, and tied under his chin with a green riband, completed this parody on man, who, leaping suddenly out of a green bush in the middle of a mud puddle, that lay beside the path, proved a more startling object of terror to the horse of the actor, than of surprise to himself.

The animal sunk back on its haunches with a snort of terror; and, with a greater show of muscle and spirit than he had deigned to vouchsafe since he had begun the journey from Raymond, he was for wheeling about in good earnest, and making fleeter back tracks than he had ever made before. But that Horsey was a born rider, like every other western man, he had been sonsed for a season in any one of the hundred miry habitations of frog, hog, and alligator, which so thickly garnished the low territory around him

Meanwhile the little urchin stood upright, or as nearly upright as he could, in the narrow pathway, never making the slightest movement to budge or assist the rider, but grinning with a smile of satisfaction at every wheel and flirt of the still frightened animal, which promised to fling his rider into the ditch. The unassisted efforts of Horsey, however, managed to evade these attempts, and, at length, finally succeeded in subduing the spirit—no difficult task—even if he did not so soon quiet the terrors of "Old-dot-and-go-one." Shaking his finger at the dwarf as he forced the horse forward, the actor exclaimed, with a degree of good nature which probably arose from the consciousness that his good horsemanship had not been without a spectator—and which, had he not been the conqueror in the strife, would not have been so apparent :—

"Ah, you comical little fellow! how you scared my horse!"

"And you too, if the truth was known, I reckon!" was the unhesitating reply of the urchin. "I'm a man mighty apt to scare people that's not used to me."

"Gad! there's reason in what you say!" exclaimed the actor. "But look you, my pretty little Jack of Clubs, suppose I had been a sour-tempered fellow instead of what I am, what would I be doing at this time, and what sort of speech would you be making? Wouldn't I be using a hickory upon your shoulders, my lad, for scaring my horse, and—"

"His rider!" The urchin finished the sentence after his own fashion. "Ha! ha! ha!" The woods rang with his yelling laughter—a peal more strange and unnatural than anything in his shape. "Ha! ha! ha! Mr. Traveller—more easy said than done. If the thing were tried, it might be your shoulders and my hickory; and if you think otherwise, why, you can only begin the business as soon as you please."

"Say you so, you little apology for a man—you little cock-a-doodle-doo!—I'm almost tempted to try odds with you for the fun of it, for riding by one's self makes one rather dull, and the fun that turns up by the roadside is always apt to be the funniest. Wait a bit, then, till I can cut a hickory."

And the actor made a show of dismounting as he spoke.

"Boo! boo!" cried the little urchin with a yell, as, leaping from the path, he ran along a fallen tree, slippery with mire,

that rose out of the ooze of the swamp and stretched away into
a canebrake, in the midst of whose tops the dwarf squatted
himself down, and grinned, and laughed, and pointed with his
finger at the assailant, confident that he could not so easily be
approached by an unpractised footman, and secure of a second
means of flight in the branches of a tupola hanging above him
into which a customary leap would easily carry him.

"Ah! ha!" exclaimed Horsey, "there you are; and you
think yourself safe, do you, but what do you think of that, my
little mannikin, eh?"

He pointed a pistol upward as he spoke, but the derisive
laugh of the dwarf mocked this exhibition, as he in turn produced from his breast a like weapon, the dimensions of which
would have swallowed up those of his assailant.

"Ha! ha! and what do you think of that?" said the urchin.
"It's snout for snout—and the advantage is all o' my side as
yet."

"How do you make that out, you pretty little deformity?"
demanded the actor, in good-natured accents, amused rather
than annoyed by the readiness of the urchin.

"Well, it's easy enough, and you might see for yourself," replied the other; "I'm rather the littlest man of the two, but
I have the biggest pistol—you're the biggest man with the
littlest pistol. Ain't my chance the best to hit, you big fellow
—ain't it now? Suppose we try—that's the best way to come
at it—you may bang away first, for all the good it's going to
do you."

"Come down, you small specimen of humanity—you youngest son of the little old gentleman in black," said the actor,
with a hearty good humor that satisfied the dwarf there was
nothing more to fear. "Come down, you queer little cox-
comb, and let's hear all about you. You are certainly the
strangest sniggering little scamp that I've seen in all my
travels. You'd make a most superb fellow on the stage—
a witch in Macbeth—no!—Gad, maybe you're one of us
already!"

"Maybe I am, maybe I'm not!" said the dwarf, with a grin,
as he descended. "Who are you—can you bite?'

"Bite!"

"Yes, bite; have you got teeth to bite, or are you nothing but a barking dog?"

"Teeth to bite—barking dog!—why, you talk as queerly as you look, my little Richard."

"Richard! Why, who told you my name?"

"What! your name is Richard, then?"

"Yes, with a pair of scales to the end of it—you couldn't guess that, I reckon!"

"No! I don't know what you mean."

"I'll tell you—my name is Richard Stillyards, or Dick Stillyards—sometimes they call me Dick Still, and sometimes Dick Yards, and then it's only when I'm in the humor that I answer them. I always answer gentlemen when they call me by my right name."

This was said with a manner which filled Horsey with merriment, and would have filled a wiser man with sadness. The swagger, the solemn strut with which it was accompanied, and the air of superiority with which the narrow and protrusive chin was perked forward, had in it so much of a rotund self-conceit, that never was that foible of humanity so completely be-mocked and be-devilled.

"Why, what is there to laugh at, I wonder," said the dwarf, in tones and with a manner of more real dignity, though with an equally-ludicrous effort.

"Hark ye, Stillyards, my dear fellow," cried the good-natured Horsey, "let us shake hands. You're a d——d comical little fellow, Stillyards, and we must jog on together. I'll make your fortune, Stillyards; by the powers, you shall grow famous—you shall. Don't you grin, my boy, I'm telling you nothing but the truth. You shall grow famous and make your fortune. You shall be one of us—and I'll undertake your tuition. By the ghost of David, Stillyards, I'll find you a dozen characters in Shakspere alone which could not be done by anybody half so well as yourself. You have read Shakspere, Stillyards, have you not?"

"Read!" said the dwarf, with something like a sinking of his dignity. "Well, stranger, to say the truth, reading ain't my business, though, I suppose, I could larn just as soon as anybody else. There's a nigger of Joe Smith's, named Peter—his young missis taught him to read in a short six months only, and he can now read write-hand 'most as good as print. I'm sure if I had any chance, I could larn as quick as Peter."

"Devil a doubt, Dicky, that you might, but who's to learn you, unless you could persuade the same young lady that taught Peter to give you a few lessons?"

"Why, didn't you say you'd larn me?" said Richard Still yards, with a grin of satisfaction that caused a considerable encroachment of his mouth upon the territory usually conceded to cheeks and ears.

"To speak and act, you terrapin, and not to read," was the reply.

"Look you, stranger, if it's the length of my teeth you want to know, call me out of my name," replied the urchin, with a grave air of offended dignity. "You're not the first man that's lost flesh between my jaws for making too free; so it's jist as well you should know it beforehand. I know I'm a little smaller than you, and maybe not quite so good looking, but that's neither here nor there, and I don't mind the difference of size no more, when I feel wolfish, no more than I'd mind a dog-bark in a seedy night. I axed you a question jist now, and didn't get an answer."

"What was that, Mr. Richard Stillyards?" demanded Horsey, with an air of respectful deference, exceedingly delighted with the strange monster he had encountered, and disposed, with a true actor's fondness for fun, to humor the weakness which betrayed itself so ludicrously.

"What was it, Mr. Richard?—speak again, and don't imagine for an instant that I am at all desirous to fill your jaws with my flesh, as I can not say with certainty that I have any to spare—certainly none to spare unless you are willing to take it just where I give you leave. I could give you a bite in one place or in another, and not miss it, perhaps, but it's likely you'd be choosing for yourself. Eh?"

The literal manner in which Horsey had chosen to accept the coarse figurative language which the urchin had employed was, in western parlance, "a huckleberry above his persimmon," and Mr. Richard Stillyards began to regard his companion as an animal no less strange to him than he appeared to

Horsey. After a brief space, which he devoted in silence to a jealous survey of those features which, by this time, the actor had schooled into inflexibility, he replied, as if satisfied with his examination :—

" I was a-thinking at first, stranger, that you was a-funning with me, but I believe it's only because you don't know no better. I'm a country gentleman in these parts, and have company camping out in the woods, here away, down by the corner of Little Bend in the Cane Prairie—every fellow's a man among 'em, all barking dogs—and so I axed you about your teeth."

" My teeth ?"

" Yes, your teeth," replied the deformed curiosity ; " ain't you got teeth ? Can't you bite ?"

The actor surveyed him with intentness, and the result of his examination, as he beheld the *bonafide* earnestness in the fellow's face, was to convince him that Richard Stillyards was an idiot—a conclusion which, no doubt, has been already reached by the reader. But let him not be mistaken. Dick was no idiot, but a cunning owl that hoots with a greater drawl of melancholy when most meditating mischief. He had his purposes in the question that seemed so excessively simple to his companion, and was answered satisfactorily when he received no answer.

" Dick, my lad, you're a strange fellow. To ask a man whose teeth have been opening upon you every moment since we have met, if he has any !"

" Oh, no harm, mister—I don't mean any harm—to be sure, I see you have got teeth, and I oughtn't to ask, but it's a way I've got; but you're a-travelling only ?" and here the urchin gave a keen, quick glance to the corpulent saddle-bags, filled to the brim with knight, prince, warrior, and tyrant, which hung across the saddle of the actor. In a second instant his eye was averted, as he beheld that of the traveller fixed upon him.

" Dick, my boy," said Horsey, " you're a nut for the devil to crack ; d—me if I can. To be sure I'm a traveller, just as certainly as I've got teeth ; and now that you remind me, I'd like to know where I'm travelling, and how far I may be from a place of lodging ?"

" Why, don't you know ?"

" Devil a bit !"

" What! you don't know where you're a-travelling? I reckon you knew when you begun ?"

" Why, yes! that I did; but look you, many a man sets out for the horse and finds the halter. I started for Benton."

" Benton ?"

" Yes, Benton. How far am I from the house of one Jenks Glover ?"

" Jenks Glover! Why, he's on the lower road — a matter of sixteen miles to the left of you. You've got on the wrong track."

" The devil you say !"

" No! I say the wrong track; it's you that said ' the devil,' three times, or maybe more, and it's no wonder you lost the road. You must have lost it after the first jump of the ferry."

" And it's how far to Benton ?"

" Mush! I can't tell you — it's on the other road, and a smart roundabout chance to get to it."

This news confounded our traveller. He shrugged his shoulders, and looked round him upon the dismal, dark, and seemingly impenetrable swamp, the pale cypresses of which shot up sparingly, with the tupola and the ash, to gigantic heights, interlaced between with a complete wall of matted canes, briers, and wild thorny vines, that promised to defy even the rude pressure of the grisly bear, or his more good-natured sable brother. The prospect made the actor shudder.

Dick, my boy," he said, " whose is the nearest house, and how far ?"

" There ain't no house on this road, that I knows of, and nobody."

" ' If that thy speech be sooth !' " the actor began, after the nature within him; but the dogged stare of the dwarf warned him that his companion suffered nothing equivocal, and he resumed in plain English : " No house, Richard — no house, my dear fellow ? — Why, what am I to do — where am I to sleep to-night ?"

A grin diffused itself from ear to ear upon the fellow's countenance, as he listened to the words and beheld the visible con sternation of the actor. He seemed disposed to amuse himself at the expense of the traveller.

"I reckon you ain't used to sleeping out of the dry. You were born, maybe, in a nice house, with a close roof to it?"

"Ay, to be sure, and in a devilish comfortable bed too, I reckon; but what then, Dicky, my darling?"

"It's a bad chance you'll have for a dry house here in Big Black Swamp; there's no better house than Cane Castle, and it's so large you can't see the walls, and it's so high you can't see the roof; and if you ain't used to the stars for candles, you'll have to go to bed in the dark. There's no house near by, and only one under ten miles, and that's 'Squire Nawls'—and he's a judge, and don't take in travellers."

"But he lives on the Benton road."

"No he don't. I reckon he's on the upper road, a smart distance from it. As for road—you're in no road at all here—you're in Big Black Swamp, and if your nose was long enough, you could smell the river at a short mile off, on your right. If you was used to the smell, you could smell it here without going much farther. I can, easy enough,"—snuffling, while he spoke, with consummate complaisance—"and a mighty sweet smell it has, too, just after the sun's gone down."

"You're an amateur, Mr. Richard."

"No, d——d if I am, and I tell you agin, stranger, 'twont do to call me by any nickname. I'm Mr. Richard Stillyards, or Dick Stillyards, and I won't go by any other, so I warn you before danger."

"Well, Dick, my dear fellow, I'll be civil—the fact is, I'm in no humor for making enemies. But tell me where I am to sleep to-night—where shall I get a bed?"

• "I licked Ike Laidler only a month ago, 'cause he called me a little sarcumstance," continued the deformed.

"And sufficient provocation too," said the actor; "but, Mr Stillyards, the bed—the bed—the house to sleep in."

"Well, now, stranger, you're mighty pushing. Ha'n't I told you there's no house under ten miles—"

"Then you told a whopper, Dick Toady," cried a third person, suddenly emerging from the bushes on the left, and interrupting the dwarf without any of that scrupulous consideration

upon which he was so much disposed to insist in his con
versation with Horsey. The stranger was a small man, with a
narrow sunburnt face, a hook nose, and lively twinkling gray
eyes, that seemed to cover a world of cunning. His voice was
good-humored, and at the first sound of it the dwarf started
with an air of dissatisfaction, which did not seem to justify
the free and familiar manner with which the new-comer had
addressed him.

"How should you tell the gentleman, Toady, that there's no
house nearer than Judge Nawls'?"

"Well, where's any?"

"Why, here, you blue-bottle, here in Cane Castle, hard by,
within a Choctaw's mile. When the stranger asks for a house,
what does he mean but a place where he can take his snooze
out without danger and disturbance. He don't mean wall of
clay and clapboards—he means nothing more than a good supper and an easy sleep. Am I right, stranger?"

Horsey, somewhat relieved of the annoying conviction that
he must sleep in a canebrake with the soft ooze of a rank
swamp in place of a mattress, was yet not utterly satisfied that
this description of his desire was altogether a correct one.
Still, there seemed little choice, and the free and easy manner
of the stranger was too much after his own heart not to reconcile him to things even more disagreeable than those he
feared. He was consoled to find that if he must sleep in the
swamp, he was to have a good bedfellow—a conviction which
had not soothed him for an instant during his whole protracted
conversation with Mr. Richard Stillyards. He expressed his
assent to the suggestion of the speaker, though in a qualified
measure, but this the other did not seem to perceive. He pro
ceeded in his speech in a manner still more agreeable to the
traveller.

"We are a few of us, stranger, almost playing gipsy in the
swamp to save expense. There's some six or eight of us,
Toady here not being counted, though he may be thrown in as
a sort of make-weight. We sleep pretty much in a huddle,
under pole and bush tents, and there's room for an odd one
when the river's foul and the swamp rises. We are players—
play-actors—perhaps you don't quite know what a player is!

—the people in these parts look on us with as much wonder as pleasure—we play plays—speak speeches—show tricks, dance and sing, for the public gratification and our own. We shall soon set out for Benton, Lexington, Lucchesa, and other villages—soon as the rest of the boys come in—and if you'll keep in the neighborhood till then, you'll see rare sport, I tell you"

The effect of this speech upon Horsey may readily be conjectured. His ejaculations of pleasure interrupted the speaker a dozen times before he had finished, and then he grasped his hand with a hearty tug that threatened to shake his arm off. He forgot his cares of bed and lodging and supper—all cares —all doubts—all apprehensions—in the one predominant pleasure that filled his soul; and a hundred questions and ejaculations followed each other too rapidly for correction or reply, as he gave free vent to those emotions which he had so long and so unwillingly restrained.

"And you belong to little Jim Tilton's company? And where's Jim?—I knew the little fellow in New Orleans, when he was—a-hem!" He was about to say candle-snuffer, but a little prudence came to his aid at the moment, and put an estopel on his tongue.

"Jim Tilton," said the other, "is no go. He's but a poor drab, and the less we say of him the better. He's not with us now, and I seriously doubt whether he'll ever show his face among us. It'll be a dark day for him when he does."

"Ha! how so? how so?"

"Well, he's a rogue—that's the long and short of it. We played at Manchester to a good smart chance of a house, and before the play was over, Jim was missing, and the treasury with him. We heard of him going down to the river to Vicksburg, and that's the last. He won't come back, unless he brings a double chance of picayunes to make up hush-money."

"The skunk! But it's like him," said Horsey. "He was a poor shote of a fellow at Orleans, a mere candle-snuffer for Caldwell, when I was playing second-rates at the American."

"You playing—you! Why, who are you?" said the new-comer, with a very natural expression of surprise.

14

'My name is Horsey," replied our traveller, with a modest dropping of the voice.

"Horsey!—Not the famous actor at Ludlow's in Mobile? It can't be possible. Tell me, stranger?"

The gusto with which this was spoken—the voluminous odor which it bore up into the mental nostrils of Horsey, was as good as a year's growth—a prize in the lottery—or a crowning benefit. His blood tingled in his veins from head to foot, yet never did mortal face struggle more hard to subdue the exulting smile—to assume and wear the pursed-up aspect of humility.

"I was at Ludlow's," he replied, modestly, "and I don't know that there was any actor there but myself of my name; but I was not famous—no, no! I did some good things—I think I did—but they passed without notice. I do not think I got much reputation in Mobile."

"My dear sir, you do the Mobilians injustice—great injustice. I have heard of you a thousand times in Mobile, and from the best authorities. Rea thought you a first-rate. Rea was an excellent judge in theatricals—my particular friend—a noble fellow, and there was—what's his name?—the editor of the Commercial—ah? devil take it, I have such a memory. But it matters not. I tell you, Horsey, never did dramatic reputation stand higher in Mobile than did yours. You were off for New Orleans when I reached the city, but everybody was asking after you, and on one occasion it was reported you had arrived but had no engagement, and then there was a hue and cry after the manager. It was asked in all the papers why you were not engaged, and he was compelled to assure the audience, under the terrors of an uproar, that you should be engaged as soon as your arrival was made known to him. I was present at the time, and know the stir it made."

"Is it possible? I wonder I never heard of it before."

"I reckon you didn't read the newspapers. It was all there —all put down as large as life. Nay, if you were in Orleans, you must have heard of it."

"No,—indeed I didn't. I never read the newspapers. I took a dislike to editors. I thought them all humbugs—they spoke very disrespectfully of me at my first beginning, and I was resolved never to read their stuff. But I was wrong, I suspect—"

" Wrong! Yes, that you were! You have shut your ears against some pleasant truths. If they treated you ill at first, they made you ample amends afterward, as I think I can show you. I have, I think, some of the Mobile Patriot of that time that'll open your eyes. Newspapers and editors, Mr. Horsey, should not be looked down upon with too much contempt. They are useful in their way. They may be made so at least; and, between us, it's best to treat the humblest profession with charity, since, if our managers continue this trick of running away with the strong box, there's no telling to what condition we may be reduced."

" Very true! But what could be expected of such a fellow as Tilton. I was astonished when I heard that he had presumed to set up for a manager."

" What! you heard of us then?"

" Yes—I heard of you down in Raymond, and my purpose was to join you."

" Join us! God bless you, Mr. Horsey. It'll be the making of us," said the stranger, grasping Horsey's hand and flaming out with the opening in Richard—

> " 'Now is the winter of our discontent
> Made glorious summer by the son of York.' "

" That was well spoken, Mr.—ah, pardon me!—but oblige me with your name."

" Jones! an humble one, sir, utterly unknown to fame!" replied the other with a great show of modesty.

" It may be, Mr. Jones," replied Horsey, warmly; " but those two lines which you have just now spoken were really well said—very prettily said—excellently well said. I shall look for good things from you. Indeed, I shall."

The flatteries of the stranger had seduced the judgment of Horsey into a corresponding flexibility, and, in a few moments, the apprehensions of the traveller were all forgotten in the exultations and resuscitated hopes of the actor. The anxieties natural to his situation, and which, but a moment before, had grown almost painful, were dismissed entirely from his mind, and in a moment he had resumed all the characteristics of manner and feeling, which he had shown to our readers on his first introduction. He now spoke, *ad libitum*, of plays and playing only. Every third word was a quotation; and it was only when the new-comer, who had kept up the ball with no little show of practice and ability, found his corresponding store of quotation utterly exhausted, that he was brought back to the more immediate necessities of his situation. It was now the turn of Jones to remind him of his lodgings for the night. But it was not so easy now to direct the attention of our actor, who, once aroused on his favorite theme, would wag a tongue in its honor so long as the member itself had a single working hinge to depend upon.

"But we forget, Mr. Horsey," said Jones, in prosecuting his often-baffled purpose—"we actors, who so love our profession, are very apt to forget other matters. Here we are, wasting car readings upon the desert air, when we should be thinking upon other matters. Supper now and a place to sleep in—I must crave your pardon for keeping you from these things so long."

"Nay, these are small matters. The toast and tankard can be got at any moment, but for the rest—what of my old prince of Hickories? What of Hugh Peters, and how are his timbers? He to make a Julius Cæsar? Ha! ha! ha! The thing's ridiculous, Jones; and he must be got rid of as well as Tilton—birds of a feather—no game—fellows that will disgrace us only. Crows, crows!"

"Very true, sir—I agree with you fully, but—"

"Oh, to be sure, I know there will be a difficulty about it; —it will be unkind to drive the fellow off and hurt his feelings; though, d—n his impudence, he deserves no better for presuming on such a vocation. Why, Jones, I remember even now the comical figure the old fool used to cut in giving us lessons in reading. Even then, when I was a mere brat of a boy, and knew little or nothing, I could scarce keep my face to see him mouthing out the golden verses of the great master. He'd get upon a box for a stage—his bow legs at a straddle, as if a ditch lay between 'em, for the better support of his bag-of-cotton body; and then he'd turn his little turnippy pugnose, fairly

affronting the heavens, and his lips sinking deep at every sentence that he spoke, in the hollows where his teeth were
knocked out just in front—he got it done one dark night as he
fell over a wash-tub, and composed himself among the stumps
of a new clearing. The hole was large enough for my finger
—and he to be an actor! Ha! ha! ha! It's ridiculous—we
must get rid of him; though, to be sure, as you say, we must
do it in such a way as not to hurt the poor devil's feelings
by the ghost of David, though I should remember Little Bowlegs only by his hickories, yet I'm for doing it tenderly. We
must smooth the track for him, so that he may walk off freely.
But go he must, if we hope to do anything. He'd be only in
the way — he can do nothing."

"Yes, to be sure—you're perfectly right, Mr. Horsey, and
the management might very well be put into your hands. I'm
sure we might make our monster Dick here do everything that
Peters might do; but, as I was saying—"

"What, Stillyards!" exclaimed Horsey, turning upon the
attentive dwarf, who stood, all the while the dialogue proceeded, wondering, with owlet eyes and broad-distended mouth,
swallowing the incomprehensible stuff that he never could di-
gest.

"Look you, Jones, that fellow's a host himself. I wouldn't
give my friend Dick here for all the Peters under the sun.
He's the most comical fellow! What a Caliban he'd make—
a natural-born Caliban! Egad! we had a scene between us
just before you came up—a scene for a melodrama—it was
worth a picayune to see it. He ran up that tree like an orang-
otang; drew out his barker, squatted on his haunches, with
the felicity and grace of a black bear at a honey-gum, and challenged me to a regular exchange of shots. The comical fellow
—he's worth a company himself; and in New York—look ye,
Jones, after all, New York's the place—on the Bowery, that
fellow, as Caliban, would be a sure card, and we must play him
when we play ourselves."

"We must talk of this to-morrow," exclaimed Jones, desperately; and seizing upon the only pause which Horsey had
made for an inconceivably long time—"I will send Dick forward to get things in readiness for us—supper and a bed. He

Dick! let the boys know that the great actor, Mr. Horsey, is coming with me. Away, by the gulleys, while we ride round We'll be with them in a half-hour."

The urchin prepared to obey.

"But why not go along with Caliban?" demanded Horsey.

"For the best of reasons. He can go where our horses can not. On a line we are but a poor quarter of a mile from our camp-ground; it will be a good half hour's ride to reach it the way we must travel, and night will swallow up the track before we are done. We must ride, therefore, to make up lost time. I was so pleasantly occupied, Mr. Horsey, in listening, for the last half-hour, that I never saw that the sun had left us. You must give our boys some lessons to-night as soon as supper's over."

"Ah, Jones, you flatter," said our friend, modestly; "I am no such man as you think me. You can do the thing quite as well as myself."

"No, no!" replied the other, with something of a mournful tone, as he rode forward — "No, no! that is not to be hoped for. Would to Heaven it were!"

Horsey followed with a new feeling of delight within his bosom. The tone of the cunning Jones, the words he employed, not to speak of the prospects and promises of ultimate and unqualified triumph before him, were all so much heavenly manna to the still hungering vanity of his heart; and never before, in all his career, when the possession of money, lavishly squandered, secured him the clamoring applauses of the profligate associates who misled him, had he received a more grateful tribute to his ruling desire than that afforded by an adroit outlaw of the Mississippi border. He followed his guide without suspicion, and was soon swallowed up from sight in the darkness that now environed the dense swamps of the Loosa Chitta.

CHAPTER XXVII.

RAW RECRUITS—AN AWKWARD SQUAD—MORE MYSTI-
FICATION.

Corb. I know thee honest.
Mosca. You do lie, sir.—VOLPONE.

IT was quite dark before Horsey and his companion came to
a halt; and when this was done, the former looked round him
with astonishment, as he could not well divine at first the reason for doing so. There was no more sign of habitation or
human comfort then, than had been seen at the moment when
he encountered the dwarf. Indeed, if possible, the *locale* looked
decidedly worse than ever. The very spot on which they
stopped was a perfect quagmire, to which the rising waters of
the contiguous river had access at every freshet; and, beheld
in the uncertain starlight, our actor could see that there were
ponds all around him, and little crossing brooklets that seemed
to struggle slowly through the thickening ooze, as if seeking to
regain the parent-stream, by whose subsiding torrents they had
been left. A dense wall of canes spread itself over the path in
front, and Horsey was about to give utterance to the doubt and
bewilderment which he felt, when his companion, who seemed
in nowise disconcerted, uttered a shrill whistle, which was immediately answered by the deep bay of a beagle at a little distance ahead.

"They will find us now in a twinkling," said Jones; "that
dog will soon tell them where to look, even if that crooked
scamp, Stillyards, should prove a sluggard by the way. You
will be relieved of your nag in a few moments, Mr. Horsey, and
we will coon a log for the rest of our journey. So much for

living in a swamp. These are difficulties which would scarcely trouble us in Natchez or New Orleans."

"Well, but why do you incur them? Why live in the swamp?" demanded Horsey, to whom the increasing difficulties and perplexities of the last twenty minutes of circuitous navigation had begun to suggest certain doubts of the policy of choosing places of abode for which there seemed no justifying necessity.

"Ha!" said the other, with a laugh, "there are troubles in the city which we have not here, and which we count a great deal worse. Here we should laugh at a sheriff's officer—there we should pull hat and bend knee to him in respectful deference; and if you ever blarneyed a tailor or bullied a landlord—"

"Say no more," said Horsey, to whom the references of Jones seemed to have almost a personal direction, and were therefore sufficiently conclusive—"say no more—I see the wisdom of your arrangements, and were I as near New Orleans as you are to Vicksburg and Benton, I should most probably have needed no explanation."

Some merry references to the artifices and annoyances of duns and dunnees followed this sally, in the relation of which the experience of the two seemed to be by no means unequal. If Jones had his story of sharps and flats in Vicksburg, Natchez, Manchester, and Benton, Horsey could tell tales quite as lively of Mobile and Orleans; and could these stories have been heard by the city sufferers, the consolation would have been of a sort to have induced a large addition to the sum total on the off side of the profit and loss account. Certainly, the most patient of all fashionable costumers would have cursed such customers.

Their merriment had not subsided, when the figure of a man plunging from a fallen tree that lay half covered and quite concealed in the dark by the canes which grew luxuriantly around it, presented himself in front, and immediately took charge of their horses. A word between Jones and the new-comer furnished sufficient explanation; and the former, telling Horsey to follow him closely, put aside the canes which concealed the fallen tree, and was, an instant after, hidden from sight. Horsey followed promptly, and found himself on a sort of natural bridge which carried him safely over a creek, of whose existence, though but ten feet from where he had been standing, he had not till that moment been aware. Though deep, and pursuing a direct course to the Loosa-Chitta, it kept so quiet a travel all the while that its murmurs were barely heard among the canes that grew out of it, even when Horsey stood directly above its bed; and the assurance of his companion only then certified him of its existence.

"Steady now, Mr. Horsey. The creek below you has a depth of ten feet, and a sudden souse at this moment would startle more alligators than a man could ride for a half-mile around us. There is some soft clay on the log that makes it slippery, and if you find it ticklish, you had better squat in time and coon it."

But Horsey was too good a Mississippian to need such cautious counsel, and he boldly followed his conductor after his own fashion, and in perfect safety. A few moments brought them to the end of the tree, when, leaping to the earth, after the example of his companion, our traveller once more, after a long interval, found himself upon *terra firma*.

"Here we are," exclaimed Jones, "in the immediate neighborhood of Cane Castle. Our way is clear enough, though it still seems thick to your eyes. We are in an Indian trail, which the Choctaws have used, I reckon, for a thousand years. I knew it was ready made to our hands—our feet, rather—and very good use we've made of it so far. Congratulate yourself, Mr. Horsey, that there's no hope for a sheriff here! We have security in the bog and liberty in the brake, for which I know one poor devil that would pray in vain were he in the swamp at Natchy. Here you may laugh as loud as you please, and sing as perverse, and no one to remind you of laws and judges—no one to say 'Shut up—you shall neither sing nor smoke.' There's no law here against tobacco."

These assurances, which promised so great a degree of liberty to the habitual swearer, singer, and smoker, and which, in brief, summed up the amount total of what are usually defined as the blessings of civil and religious liberty, did not, however, seem to awaken that degree of satisfaction in the mind of the actor, which was justified by the importance of the promised benefits. A word about the cast of characters, or the selection of pieces, or anything, however immaterial, in the business of staging, would have called for infinitely more of his regards. Receiving no answer to what he had spoken, Jones, with practised cunning, readily changed the subject to one more grateful; and mustering all that he could remember of the plays he had ever read and seen acted, he contrived, by some imperfect quotations, to divert the attention of Horsey from such subjects of speculation as would most probably have occurred to almost every ordinary traveller in his present situation. Naturally frank and unsuspicious, it was by no means difficult to deceive a person whose mind was so completely surrendered up to the one engrossing passion; and though exceedingly acute in his judgments, and active in his inquiries, on all subjects not actually swallowed up in the maelstrom of that mania which, at an instant, absorbed everything that came within its whirling vortex, yet nothing was more easy than to lead him off from the minor pursuit, by the suggestion of the smallest gleam from that greater object which was the all in all of his desires. But, on this head, the reader wants no new lights at this late moment. He, perhaps, unlike the deluded traveller of whom we write, is not so sure of the Thespian character of those performers whom the worthy Horsey is about to encounter in the swamp. He is not now to be told that — but why should we anticipate?

A few moments sufficed, following the little Indian footpath and his companion, to bring the actor into something like an opening in the forest, which consisted of mingled pines, cypresses, and ash-trees, closely set, and still more closely united — save in the opening mentioned — by the matted canes, which seemed to fill up all the intervals between them, and, in fact, formed a dense margin to every one of the hundred beds of watery ooze which skirted the river, the rank and festering deposite of a thousand years. Here the actor was encountered by gay gleams of firelight at a little distance, by the imperfect blaze of which, he discovered himself to be on the verge of a little area, or amphitheatre, in the swamp, high and dry, a sort of island, the circuit of which was probably a meagre quarter of a mile in extent. This, following his conductor, he rapidly overpassed, until they reached a sort of nook whence the fire met their eyes.

Here they found as merry a set of scamps at their revels as ever blessed the sight of a wayfarer on the edge of a gipsy encampment. There were about seven or eight persons, squat upon their haunches, and busily engaged in the adventurous business of *vingt-un ;* a sight that warmed the heart of our traveller even more than a smoking supper might have done, since, though not absolutely dramatic in itself, it suggested to his mind one of those leading associations of theatrical life, which brought back his fading memories with fresh colors, and greatly increased their vitality.

But if their present employment seemed natural enough to the heyday recklessness of the ordinary actor's life, there was little besides, in their air and appearance, to justify, in the mind of Horsey, their adoption of the business. He looked in vain for that happy ease, sometimes, in " mouths of wisest censure," esteemed impudence, which distinguishes so greatly the actor by profession. The dashing effrontery, the devil-may-care deportment of the sect, was lacking. There was none of the graceful swagger of the genteel comedian — none of the 'solemn emphasis of him who wears the image of fate, and looks habitual tragedy upon his brow — a Prometheus-like gloom and defiance which would have realized the ideal of an Æschylus, and filled the eyes of the poet with the figures that else had only had existence in his mind ; and as for the comedy of stare, and grin, and clatter — the broad fun, and ridiculous, reckless farce — never was pleasant company so utterly without its enlivening and mirth-compelling attributes. The very soul of every rascal in the group seemed set only upon the sixpences before him. Mammon, not Momus, was the god of the entertainment, and our traveller's anticipations were taken half aback, as he beheld an expression of care and intensity in every face, so utterly unlike that good-humored indifference to fate and fortune, which hitherto had been to him one of the chief attractions among his intimates of the lobby and the green-room.

" These chaps have greatly mistaken their profession," was the unexpressed thought of the idealist. " There is not a scamp among 'em who will ever do more than snuff a candle or shout at a pageant. They will give me no support — they will bungle most damnably 'Then came each actor on his ass.' Gad !

the ass will be uppermost here. But these are supernumeraries only. There must be others. I must wait. At least, I am sure of good foils, if I have no rivals; and if they can make play at all, they will give me all the chance I want. But they are mere Turks and Muscoghees—a sort of savages that will never stop till they scalp what they have murdered. Their parts are all in danger of a bloody death. But—buz! buz!"

The introduction of the stranger was rapidly gone through with — too rapidly to enable our traveller to witness any of those beauties of deportment which he still fancied might make their appearance in that nice performance — the reception of a guest for the first time — which so eminently calls for a pleasing and prompt gracefulness, without which reception is more properly repulsion, and an invitation to make oneself at home, looks very like a suggestion to depart. Jones seemed to conjecture what was passing in Horsey's mind, and took an opportunity, a few minutes after, to say to him, in a whisper, that the giants were yet to arrive — these were the pasteboard personages — that class of creatures which we use from necessity, and keep out of sight when we can.

"But they will improve, Mr. Horsey, under your tuition — under your example I mean. They have had no opportunities — have seen no shining lights, and are shy, sir, very shy — much can not be expected from them as yet; but when you have given us some readings, Mr. Horsey — then, &c."

It was not surprising after this appeal, that our vain actor beheld his companions with a look of greater indulgence and more charitable thoughts. The wily Jones knew all his soundings, and the tragedian was little more than a puppet in his hands.

Meanwhile, new fires were built, new combinations formed, and Horsey found himself as busy about the blaze as the rest, and, though with a less intense feeling than the rest, receiving his cards, and "planking" his shillings. His friend Jones sat beside him and assisted him as a partner to lose his money in the game. As the "stakes" disappeared, the good humor of the group seemed to increase, and the contagious mirth soon made Horsey as indulgent in his criticism as unmindful of his losses. He thought the scamps susceptible of improvement.

and, stimulated by the suggestions and applauses of Jones, his quotations became recitations; and his own language was at length limited to a few occasional comments which served to introduce and link together the choicest declamatory passages of Shakspere. The Toms, Dicks, and Harries, around him looked as grave and seemed as attentive as possible; but it might have been perceived by one more watchful than our amateur, that none of them forgot the game in the delight which he felt or affected to feel, and the stakes were always lifted as soon as won. They were men who had long since learned to combine the severest cares of business with the utmost relaxations of pleasure.

"That was superbly said, Mr. Horsey," remarked the attentive and respectful Jones, as the actor concluded the famous soliloquy in Hamlet, "to be," &c., "I can say with confidence that I have never heard that passage delivered before — never — though I have heard it a hundred times from other lips. You make us *feel* the poet, sir, and tremble at the philosophy. Ah, sir, how these reflections come to us, poor outcasts of fortune, like so many dreadful experiences. Who has not asked himself whether it was not better and nobler to make his own quietus with a bare bodkin, than to suffer the thousand cruel and crushing evils, such as the rest of the passage has described? Not that it is all evil, Mr. Horsey. I am disposed to think, so far as my experience goes, that that part of it about 'the law's delay' might very well be left out. The law's delay, sir, is one of the most agreeable features which the law ever shows to a poor debtor like myself, and as I have said before, but for the law's delay, and that of the deputy, many's the poor devil who would have lain at the mercy of tailor and tapster, without hope or redress, to the detriment of his genius, and to the great loss of the majority of mankind. I'm thinking, Mr. Horsey, that that half line might very well be left out of the passage."

"Impossible, Mr. Jones — there would be an ugly hiatus — the music of the line would be lost — utterly lost."

"But the passage might be altered — something might be supplied in its place. Supposing we were to read 'the play's delay' — now that would be such an improvement as would be grateful to every ambitious actor."

This suggestion grated on the ears of our amateur. He was one of those profound devotees of the great literary outlaw, who venerates his very faults, even as the antiquarian treasure up the rust and canker of the relic. To remove anything, in his eyes, would be to impair the value and take from the propriety of what remained; and his reply was uttered in tones more energetic than he had hitherto employed.

"Sacrilege! sacrilege, Mr. Jones—how can you think of it! No, sir, the passage must stand as it is—neither too little nor too much—nothing can be added, nothing taken away. It's true, as you say, the law's delay is a very agreeable thing to the debtor. Gad, sir, I have been indebted to it quite as often as yourself; but our notions would be greatly altered if we stood in the creditor's shoes; we should then hold the passage to be perfect as it is; as, indeed, I hold it now, having no debtors, and being still over shoes on the books of other men. No, no! sir—no liberties with Shakspere—remember the admirable counsel to this effect which he gives to our profession in partic ular on this very head—to 'speak no more than is set down for them'—I can forgive a fellow when he is out and the audience waiting, and the prompter asleep, if he fills out from his own head; but when he does it out of presumption, seeking to improve the work of the mighty master, 'that's villanous, and shows a most pitiful ambition in the fool' that does it."

"I don't know but you're right, sir."

"I am! I am right, Mr. Jones—I am positive in this matter. The more you think of it, sir, the more you'll have occasion to agree with me; and in the beginning of our campaign, sir, the thing can not be too much insisted upon for the benefit of the whole company."

"I was thinking, sir," said Jones, with some hesitation of manner, and a bow and look of particular deference almost amounting to veneration, "I was thinking, sir, that it might be of great service to our boys if you'd be so good as to give us your reading of that very part."

"What! the advice to the players?"

"Yes, sir; I'm sure there's not one present that would not be delighted to hear it from your lips. What say you, boys— what Ricks, Mason, Baker, Bull?"

"Ay, ay! let's have it!" was the lively cry from all, in tones far less full of solicitous deference, and a great deal more indifferent than those of Jones.   Meanwhile, however, the cards were shuffled, the stakes set down and lifted, and the game underwent no cessation, though, in the excitement of his declamation, our friend Horsey's cards remained upon the turf, from which, however, his stakes were always considerately withdrawn by the banker, as soon as laid before him.

" But it will interrupt the game," was the considerate suggestion of the actor.   "Our friends would rather play than listen to those dull recitations, of which they hear so much professionally."

" Devil a bit!" was the warm reply of Jones to the modest apprehension of Horsey.   "Devil a bit!   Dull recitations, indeed!   By ——! such luxuries are more than they are used to — more, perhaps, than they deserve.   Put up your hands, men, while Mr. Horsey gives us these passages; down with your pictures, take up your picayunes, and let us surrender our souls for a while to the scene.   By the way, Mr. Horsey, if you have no objection, the thing might be made more complete — the illusion rendered more striking and fascinating — in short, sir, if you would consent—"

He paused and looked in the actor's face with doubt and entreaty, equally mingled with respectful deference;—but he spoke not.

" What, Mr. Jones?" was the demand of Horsey, who was at that moment too well pleased to have refused the speaker anything in his power to bestow, and who felt assured, from the manner of Jones, that he was only about to solicit some further extension of that courtesy, the concession of which was, perhaps, far more gratifying to him than it could be to the hearers. The reply of Jones was uttered in the hesitating accents of one who still scrupled to give offence.

" If I remember — I think, Mr. Horsey — nay, you *did* tell me, that you had brought with you a portion of your wardrobe."

" You are right, sir — I have with me a Hamlet and a Romeo, Rolla, a Turk, and two field-officers, in my bags, but—"

" The very thing, my dear sir!" cried Jones, with an air of

inexpressible delight; "and now, sir," he continued, "if you
would only crown your favors and give us your readings in costume—give us the favorite passages in Hamlet, which, I should
think, from what you have suffered us to see, your best perform
ance, you would bind us to you eternally. It would make us
so happy—it would help us so greatly—we should all be so
much pleased, not to speak of the immense benefit—that—
that—"

Here the cunning dog stopped very judiciously, leaving unexpressed the superb climax which the imagination of the
hearer was better able to provide, than the flattery of the eulo-
gist. Soothed, seduced, perfectly overcome, in the weakness
of his heart, by the adroit management of the wily Jones, the
reluctance of the actor was very feeble. He said something
about his horse and saddle-bags not having come, and murmured
a fear that he might be tiresome. But these objections were
soon met and overruled by the other.

"Your horse is here in our stables. The bags you can get at
in a moment; and if you will go with me, we can put you at
once into a chamber where you can make all your changes without disturbance."

There was no resisting the pleasant importunities of his companion; and, following his guidance, Horsey was led through a
contiguous thicket into another smaller area, where he found
several huts of bushes and bark, in one of which his horse was
fastened, along with that of Jones; while the fellow who had
taken charge of them lay fast asleep before the door, using the
saddle-bags of the actor for his pillow. He was soon aroused,
and made to carry them into another of the huts, where Jones,
having studiously repeated his flatteries, left the delighted actoi
to prepare his toilet prior to his first rehearsal before his new
companions.

These, meanwhile, had their own thoughts on the subject of
the new-comer.

"Now, what the devil can Jones be after," was the muttered
speech of one surly fellow of the circle, "in bringing this conceited ass among us? He seems to have precious little money,
and he's not worth robbing; he's a fool and can't be trusted;
and why we are to pretend to be actors, and all that nonsense.

and listen to his stuff, is more than I can reckon up at a single tuning. What do you say, Baker—do you understand it?"

"No better than yourself, but I s'pose there's something in it, since Jones says that he's ordered by Saxon. Saxon's after some strange business, I reckon, and I s'pose he's got his reasons. What they are, I don't care to know, so long as the fellow has a Mexican to lose, and don't know when he loses."

"Nor when he wins, for that matter," said another. "Bull gathered up his stakes and winnings together, the first time in his life that ever his losses filled his pockets."

"The fellow's well enough," said Bull, with a growling chuckle—"so say no more. I'm for his playing cards, or anything he pleases, so long as the playing is profitable to us. But here's Jones coming back; let us know all about it from him."

"How now, growlers?" said this last-named person, as he returned among the group. "Can't you be satisfied with your gettings, when they come with so little trouble? This fellow's your pigeon, pluck him as you please; but look you that he does not guess what you're about. Take your counsel from me, and humor him awhile—it will give us quite as much sport as profit."

"But what's the upshot of the business—are we to stop his wind, or is he to be one of the family? He'll never make a beagle, so long as his head's full of play-stuff."

"Let that give you no trouble. It's enough that Saxon plans it. This fellow's nothing in himself, but we use him against another. There's one thing, let me tell you, before you go further. Weston is dead—shot through the head by a young lawyer going up to Lucchesa, on t'other side of the river by Big Ben's. There's a start below against us; and the old methodist, Badger, is beginning to growl aloud. So, lie close—there's no fear of the dad, while the son is a beagle. He'll give tongue enough when the hunt's a-foot. As for this chap, all that you have to do is to wink, look wise, talk what player nonsense you can, and praise him for his acting, whenever he asks questions that you can't answer. That will stop his tongue, and turn his thoughts, and that's all that you've to do. I'll manage all the rest of the business. Put up your cards now, and get the grog

in readiness, and let Girhan get our supper, while I'm gone for
the actor. You'll see him in his glory when he comes back,
but no grinning—nothing to frighten him. Hear him with
open mouths, and if you can throw in a bit of blarney, let it be
done. But do it neatly—nothing slippery—nothing stupid.
The fellow's no fool when he ain't flattered—it's soft soap only
that turns his head. Enough—you have the trail."

CHAPTER XXVIII.

SWAMP THEATRICALS — NO FUN IN TRAGEDY — A BULLDOG
AMONG THE BEAGLES — THE STAR UNDER A CLOUD —
STRIFE IN THE SIGN OF TAURUS.

Serv. My lord, you nod ; you do not mind the play.
Sly. Yes, by Saint Anne, I do. A good matter, surely. Comes there
any more of it !—*Taming of the Shrew.*

WHEN Jones returned to his comrades, accompanied by
Horsey in character, the scene had undergone a change. The
cards had disappeared—fires were lighted anew—a rude plank
table, with rude block seats, had risen in the midst, garnished
with sundry black bottles of strong waters, and everything
looked fair for a promising carouse. The men, too, had undergone some little change. The exhortations of Jones had not
been lost upon them, and, taking it for granted that their account lay, as it had always done before, in securing the desires
of their leaders, they were prepared to yield themselves, heart
and hand, to the game that was before them. A warm cheer,
thrice renewed, received the actor, who stalked before them in
all the mournful and philosophical dignity of the youthful Dane.
A buzz, a murmur of approbation, followed this outbreak, and,
whether sincere or affected, the result was everything that
might be desired. For the first time in his life, Horsey found
himself in the presence of actors who were not rivals—candi-
dates for popular favor, who had no jealousy of their neighbors
—and professors of an art that lives on popular applause, who
were yet no less prompt in bestowing it. Our traveller was the

last man in the world to mortify himself with any unnecessary doubts of that sincerity which spoke in the language of encomium. And yet, to do his understanding all justice, it must be added that Jones took infinite pains to avoid arousing his suspicions. His own applauses were all well-timed, judiciously expressed, and had the appearance of being urged with great hesitation and forbearance. A respectful deference distinguished even his solicitude; and his chief argument to Horsey, and one which he had insisted on in frequent whispers, was the necessity of a good model for his wretched creatures.

"These fellows have never played before, my dear Mr. Horsey. They have been picked up from all parts of the country. Some of them have never even looked upon a play, and none of them have any just idea of what a performance should be. I know the trouble it will give you to tutor them, but it is so important that we should make a good figure at first, and if, as I believe, you regard the drama as so important to the civilization of the people—to the improvement of popular taste, and—and—"

All this kind of stuff was very convincing to our stage-struck hero. His eye brightened while he looked around him, and surveyed the mute watchfulness and vague curiosity of stare that met his glance on every side.

"Something can be made of them, Jones," he said paternally, in a confidential whisper, "and, considering the great importance of the thing, I am not unwilling to undertake their tuition. You are right in regarding it as all-important that they should know something before they begin; though, really, it is surprising—very surprising—that they should have ever thought of the stage. It seems to me that any other vocation—"

The comment was answered by a conclusive whisper.

"Beggars, you know, Mr. Horsey, can not be choosers. We must make the most of them till a better bargain offers, and then I'm clear that we get rid of them. On this head we must confer together hereafter. We must take the management into our own hands, since Tilton's off, and there's no knowing where to set hands on Peters. It is a happy chance that sent you in our neighborhood. I was beginning to think matters desperate and had almost given up in despair, and gone off. Now, there's no danger. You will set us on our feet again. But there's time enough to talk of this hereafter. Now, the lads are waiting. Gentlemen, Mr. Horsey is ready — pray give your attention."

"Ay, ay," exclaimed the surly fellow, Bull, "and so are we. We've been ready this half-hour to hear him; but, Jones, s'pose, if it's not disagreeable to Mr. Horsey, let's take a swig all round to better acquaintance. It sort-o' makes a body easy to listen when the liquor's afloat; and sort-o' softens the ear and opens the understanding. I always feels a great deal easier to judge, when I'm in sperrits."

"Vulgar fellow!" muttered Horsey to himself, annoyed at an interruption at the very moment when, throwing himself into posture, he was about to begin. He concealed his chagrin as well as he could, while the vigilant Jones, calling to order, endeavored to keep down the moral scum which promised to rise up with quite as much pertinacity as ever, with the very next agitation of the atmosphere.

"A good idea of Bull's, that, Mr. Horsey," said the politician. "A glass to better acquaintance is not amiss; though I'm not so sure it makes one judge the better, in intellectual matters and things of art. What have you there, gentlemen?"

"Monongahela, fresh from Beattie's Bluff," was the reply of Bull. "There's a piggin of peach in the bushes, the last of the barrel — prehaps, the gentleman will take his pull from that?"

"Prehaps! Take his pull!" Horsey could scarce suppress his astonishment, and forbear repeating the offensive vulgarities aloud.

"Our Jack Pudding! — our fellow for broad grin and buffoonery!" whispered Jones in the ear of the amateur. "A very comical fellow when he's in the humor, Mr. Horsey — never saw so comical a dog as he can make himself. All this is put on — it's in character only. He is only disposed to let you see that there are other actors beside yourself."

' Indeed! Is that it? But he looks very serious for a funny fellow."

"That's the beauty of it, sir — that's the wonder — that's what makes him inimitable in his way. You'll hear him speak the dialect of the most ignorant backwoodsman, as if he was born to it, and look for all the world as if he never could have spoken any other. But, I can tell you, so far from that being the case, he's well educated—speaks Greek like a native, and is profound in mathematics, besides having an excellent taste in poetry."

"Is it possible?"

"True as Holy Writ; but he has his humors, sir—and one of them is to disparage himself. He will even lie, sir—lie like a Trojan—in order to make himself little. Ask him now about Greek; and if he happens to be in the humor for running his cross-rigs upon you, he'll swear he knows nothing of what you say, and will probably answer you in the coarsest lingo of Catahoula and the swamp."

"A strange perversity, indeed."

"It's the way with all geniuses, I believe; but—here he comes. Don't mind his extravagances. You'll see the fun of them, now that you know something of the fellow."

By this time Bull returned, bearing in his hands the piggin of peach-brandy, for which he had gone to the bushes where it had been concealed. His salutation as he placed the vessel on the table, was calculated to justify in some sort the description which had been just given of his eccentricities.

"Here, you b—hes," he cried aloud—"here's stuff enough, and sorts enough, if your stomach's not too swingy proud for an honest liquor. This peach is a beauty, and the whiskey's as lovely as a sinner alongside of it. If you don't like one, take the other, and if you don't like neither, mix 'em and swig both, and see which end'll come uppermost. Blast my buttons—what do you wait for, you—"

We omit the more decided expressions of blackguardism.

"You see," whispered Jones to the actor, "he's as full of Aristophanes as an egg's full of meat. Fond of all the old comic writers, and don't stand at calling things by plain names. You'll know more of him directly."

Horsey drew a long breath as he replied—

"'Gad! he is the strangest fellow—"

His speech and wonder were briefly cut short by the uproarious challenge of the eccentric Bull, who, having filled a tin mug of more than usual dimensions with one of the two potent beverages so highly eulogized, extended his gracious permission,

after a fashion of his own, to all others who might be disposed
to follow his example.

"I'm a man that has a notion that all sperrits loses that
stands too long open to the air. You must pour it down or cork
it up, one or t'other, and so, fellows, I drinks to you, and my
sentiments is — here's to the tongue that never sticks in the
way of the swallow — meaning no harm to them that stands off
talking, when they might be doing a better business."

And with these words, and a scornful leer at the actor and
his companion Jones, the Grecian humorist, turned the bottom
of the can to the north star, while the mouth of it clung for an
instant to his own with a sympathetic tenacity.

"Well said! Well hit!" exclaimed the ready Jones, with a
wink, to Horsey. "We certainly deserve the censure of all
good spirits, when we leave such good spirits untasted. Horsey, my dear fellow, shall I pour you out from the jug or the
piggin? I can answer for this peach — it's as good as any of
Crumbaugh's."

"The peach, I thank you," was the answer of Horsey, in
somewhat subdued accents. The fact is, his genius was confounded in the presence of that of Mr. Aristophanes Bull, of
whom, as yet, he could not exactly succeed in reconciling what
he saw with what he heard. A little time after, and he grew
more flexible; but let us not anticipate. His glass was filled,
and with the kindest condescension in the world, he bowed to
the company ere he drank, and uttered some commonplace
compliment, which was lost, like many better wishes, in the un-
heeding air.

"And now, gentlemen, give attention — now for the part of
Hamlet by Mr. Horsey, of whom you all have heard, and by
whose counsel and example, I trust we shall all improve. Mr.
Horsey, perhaps that part about actors and acting — I mean the
advice to the players — might be the best to begin with; unless, indeed, you should prefer to give us some more tragic parts.
I know that your forte lies in tragedy."

Such was the conciliatory preludium of the adroit Jones, and
its effect promised to be exceedingly happy upon the person to
whom it was addressed. A smile rose upon his lips, his eyes
sparkled, as he felt the convincing deference of the speaker,

and a ray of self-complaisance, such as the sun sheds over the western heavens, after he has done a good day's work of illumination, gave to our actor's face an inexpressible benignity of beam, which was most unhappily overcast, in another instant, by the intrusive comments of the eccentric genius, Bull.

"Tragedy be d———d," said he, striking his hand down upon the table, to which, in the next moment, he elevated his foot; "tragedy be d———d—that's all in my eye and Betty Martin. There's no fun in that, no more than in thunder and hoxy-doxy. Who want's to see a fellow get up and blow out his cheeks, and roll up his eyes, and growl and roar and choke, and shake all over as if he had an agy? None of your tragedy for me. There's no sense in it. Tain't raal. I was once down in Mobile when I saw them making tragedies, and, darken my peepers, but the bloody b—hes made me mad enough to swallow 'em, they were so cussed rediculous."

"But, my dear Bull," was the beginning, thrice begun, of our friend Jones, in the endeavor to stop the torrent of the humorist. In vain—Bull kept his ground and shook off the intruder with as much ease as a three-year-old colt would shake off a Connecticut cavalry officer.

"Oh, be d———d," said he, "don't I know? There was a tragedian that came in looking after his enemy. He had his sword out, and he made a show as if he was mighty angry, but, between you and me, he didn't want to find him, no how. The other fellow was hiding behind a tree, and this chap looked for him everywhere but there. So, as I wanted to see how they'd fight, I up and told him where to look for him—says I, bung up my peepers if you don't find him agin that rock, squat, jist hiding behind that tree. It was a scrub oak, or something like it—I never seed sich a tree before. Well, instead of thanking me, he dropped his jaws and his sword, looked at me as if he'd seed a ghost, mumbled something in his throat, nobody could tell what, and then there was a spree among the people, and some of the larks below cried out as if they were gwine to lick me. 'Lick and be d———d,' says I, ' lick if you can. Where's the first man?—let me look on him.' So up I stands, and devil the bit of a nigger among 'em to say another word. Well that was all bloody foolish. If the chap was in a'rnest, it was

the easiest thing to find the other. He had only to say I'm
ready, clap his hips and crow like a chicken, and if they was
ser'ous, what more ?   But tragedies ain't ser'ous things.   It's
all make-b'lieve.   They know there's nobody to be hurt,—nobody's in a'rnest ; for they'll stand and talk for a long quarter,
though the enemy's at the door, with bullet and bowie-knife;
and they pretending to be mighty scared all the time.   Then
they hide where its so easy to find 'em.   Grim ! only let a
nigger hide from me in Loosa-Chitta as them fellows hide from one
another in tragedies, and how soon I'd ride through his rig'lets.   I'd
be into 'em, and on 'em ; over 'em, and through 'em ; round 'em, and
about 'em ; front 'em, and a-back 'em ; in the twinkle of a musquito
—race lightning never could go quicker.   No ! no !   None of your
tragedies for me."

"But, Bull, my dear fellow !" expostulated Jones, with something more of anxiety in his accents and manner, as he saw the
almost pallid expression of discomfiture in the blank visage of
Horsey—"why should you go on so ?   Though you don't like
tragedy, that's no reason why other people should not, and we who
labor for the public, or propose to do so, must do that which will best
please the public.   Now there's no doubt that most people prefer
tradgedy—"

"The more fools they !" stoutly replied the obdurate Bull,
"They're not of my kidney, then, by hocus ; and I recon there's
none of the boys here that wouldn't prefer a sup of whiskey
at any time, and a frolic at Mother Surgick's, to all the tragedy
stuff."

"But, Bull, my dear fellow—" Jones resumed his expostulations, but in vain.   Bull had been supping whiskey for a good hour
before Horsey had reached the camp, and had grown too inflexible
to engage with readiness in any scheme so intricate as the one proposed.

"Butt Bull," he retorted, using the language of Jones, with a
grin, as if a good joke lay at the bottom—"Butt Bull, and get the
worst of it.   See whose head's the hardest, you b—h, and be off with
your mug broken.   Its a bad chance to butt any of my breed.   No,
blast my buttons ! hide and horns, head and tail, are all too much for
such as you, Jones ; so no rearing, unless you want to come down on
your haunches."

"A wit, you see," said Jones, in a whisper to the waiting
Hamlet—"a fellow of infinite humor;—and as he's a little
drunk he begins to show it. The true nature always comes up
permost with a man in liquor. A fellow of contradictions—
we must bear with him a while longer."

There was little or no consolation in all this for the actor.
He began to suspect that the organization of such an unruly
gang would task the best manager in the worst fashion. He
saw treason, uproar, and utter discomfiture in all the proceedings
of the green-room. But he said nothing in reply to Jones, and
before the latter could say more, the sarcastic Bull had resumed the subject of which he seemed as tenacious as the
grave.

"Now," he said, "if you're for acting at all, give me them
funny things, where they make all sorts of faces, and play
tricks, and tumble one another about, and jump on shoulders
and ride like monkeys, and run up the chimney, and hide behind the door. Give me the comedies and farces, and them
sort of things that make a fellow laugh to split. I'm for the
frolicking plays, and I reckon we're all for them. Ain't you,
Baker?"

"Ay, deuce take me, if I don't vote with Bull," was the
response of Mr. Baker.

"And I too," said another.

"And I," said a third.

And the majority sent up an assenting voice which put a
stop for an instant to all the expostulations of the indefatigable
Jones. Bull looked round him with an air of triumph and complacency, as much as to say,—there, you have our decision, so
let your tragedy be comedy—your fate, fun! He filled up
his can, as the difficult question was thus determined to his own
satisfaction; and, as if to reconcile the minority to a decision
which is always disagreeable to a minority, he proposed a bum-
per all round.

"Come Jones, come Doughty," so he named Horsey, "my
dogs, we'll begin the fun by a full swallow. I'm always for a
frolic when there's good stuff to go upon; and a comedy, says
I, because a comedy's always ser'ous a'rnest, and it's all my
eye when they makes tragedies. Tragedies is mighty foolish
15

and rediculous things. They ain't ser'ous. The killing ain't
ser'ous. I don't reckon a man was ever yet killed in a tragedy.
Now, I'm for killing in a'rnest when I set about it. I don't
leave off when I begin, and if I once put knife into a fellow's
ribs to make small meat of him, wouldn't I be a blasted fool to
go off, before I made sure that the thing was done in right
a'rnest? I'd git on him astraddle and feel at his kidneys; and
if there was only the littlest shaking of the flesh, d—me but
I'd give him another dig or two to make sure and put him out
of his misery. I would, d—me."

There was something exceedingly literal in the latter part of
Bull's speech, which our friend Horsey found it very difficult to
account for. It seemed to him that the witty fellow was con-
founding real events with theatrical illusion; and the idea of
his bestraddling his slain opponent, and giving him a thrust
extra seemed rather Choctaw-like and savage. Besides, he
could not understand how such a proceeding should ever be
tolerated by an audience. On this head he thought it important
to express his doubts. This he did, however, with less than his
usual fecund flow of language, and with a hesitancy of manner
which showed how greatly the eccentric genius of Bull had
cowed himself, no less than the rest of his companions.

"I am afraid, Mr. Bull, the spectators would not permit such
an unnecessary proceeding. The moment the man lies, apparently dead, the end of the performance is obtained. There is
surely no sort of necessity to repeat the blow; and I am afraid
that the dignity of tragedy would be utterly overthrown by bestraddling the slain man. I am also disposed to think—"

"Look you, Doughty, my boy," cried Bull, with an air of
most paternal superiority, clapping his open hand as he spoke
over the mouth of the tragedian—"you're but a young hand
at the hatchet, I see. Do you think," with an air of great
seeming circumspection, as he bent his mouth to the ear of the
hearer, and spoke in a half-whisper—"you talk of spectators,
but do you think I'd be such a blasted b—h of a fool as to let
anybody see me at the business?"

"How! how! the audience not see you?"

The actor was bewildered. Jones, with some consternation interposed. The game at cross-purposes, which he had

so cunningly introduced, was on the verge of a sudden termination.

"Ha, ha! A good joke—an excellent joke!" he exclaimed
aloud, laughing immoderately as he spoke—"Bull, you're a
born devil of a joker. He's trying to quiz you, Mr. Horsey—
I warned you how 'twould be—a very Momus, sir—all fun,
all mirth, all deviltry."

"Quiz me!" exclaimed the actor, with a genuine expression
of tragedy—a sublime indignation—in his countenance as he
spoke, which, in an instant after, changed to one of haughty defiance, as his eyes turned from Jones to the person of him to
whom had been ascribed the impertinent effort which promised
to be so offensive.

"Nay, take no offence, Mr. Horsey, don't you see the man's
drunk," said Jones, in a whisper. "But I'll mend his manners
—I'll lead him off for a while, and cool him. I'll say that
which will bring him to his senses."

"Tell him you'll discharge him!" said Horsey, with all the
terrors of a managerial countenance, as he whispered this severe
counsel in the ears of the other. "By the body of Polonius, it
would be impossible to keep such a fellow in order—all his
merits, were they twice what they are, could never reconcile
me to tolerate such presumption."

"You are right, perfectly right, sir, and I'll make him hear
to reason," said Jones—"meanwhile, sir, when I take him off,
do you occupy the rest. They are very anxious to hear you—
very good fellows, sir—a little tainted with Bull only. They
will keep order."

While this brief dialogue proceeded between the two in whispers, the eccentric Bull had glided, by a very natural transition,
from the proscenium into the orchestra, and was leading off, in
a dithyrambic, famous among the beagles of the borders, to the
air of the "Raccoon skinned"—a melody which only needs the
lyrical genius of General Morris, who quelled the rioters of New
York in 1834, to marry to universal song, and embalm, with
other "refrains," in the cedar oil of immortality. We shall
copy it out, when more at leisure, for the special benefit of that
gentleman; at present, a single verse must suffice, as well for
him, as for our amateur.

"Bish war ben it dan i' nee
Blif nel de mor ,
So ma nol, it cal a fo,   . .
   —Chi, cha, ch°, chow,
Tra la chin, et car .t lee,
   —Chi, cha, c'io, chow,
Blit nel de mo ;,"—etc.

"Bull, a word with you," said Jones, abruptly, as the up roarious ditty was ended.

"Well, out with it, and be d——d to you. If it's only one, the pain's soon over."

"Come with me."

"Why can't you out with it here? D—n my sixes! There's no use to get up while one's able, and there's any stuff left. See here."

"Let it rest! It'll wait till you come back."

"I don't know that," retorted the humorist—"and though it might, these d——d fellows won't—they swallow like a sand-hill after a long drought in August. I'm almost afraid to leave it. If I go now, it's like parting with a friend for ever."

"Pshaw, Bull—what nonsense. There's business, I tell you."

These words, coupled with a particular and significant move-ment of the hands which escaped Horsey's observation, at once had an effect upon the person addressed. He rose, grumbling all the while, and followed his companion, leaving the field to our actor, who, like long-pent-up torrents, glad of the moment of liberation, soon burst with all his thunders upon the remaining assembly, and strove to make up for lost time by redoubled efforts. He was beginning to forget his previous annoyances in the evident attention of his audience, when Jones and the refractory Bull reappeared.

The latter was somewhat sullen, but he remained silent for awhile, contenting himself with refilling his glass, and resuming his seat as before. He stuck his legs boldly upon the table, crossed his arms as if in contemplation, and, not deigning a glance at our actor, fixed his eyes upon the heavens, tracing Boötes, Orontes, and the rest, with a face of particular and philosophi-cal speculation, and, possibly, discoursing in fancy with that venerable old gentleman of nursery authority, the ancient and ever to be remembered man in the moon—his dog and his bush. Thus he sat for some time in dogged silence, while our actor, who needed but little encouragement to rouse every echo known to the tragic muse, having already gone through several passages, proceeded to Macbeth.

The soliloquy in the dagger-scene, being one upon which every witling labors to expend himself, was that which tasked all his powers; and whether he did well or ill, or whether it was because of some affinities in the passage which came home to the bosom and the business of Bull, it is certain that our actor's declamation in this part was honored with a greater share of his attention than he had condescended to bestow previously. This did not escape the notice of Horsey, and he was beginning to congratulate himself that the eccentricities of the genius were about to pass away, leaving his lights their accustomed brilliance, when the grateful anticipation was suddenly defeated by the latter's starting to his feet, and thrusting his mug, well filled with the generous potation, full in the face of the actor, exclaiming, while he did so, and cutting off entirely the closing lines of the part—

"Oh, d—n it, Thompson, take a drink and shut up. This tragedy stuff is too dry and dull—let's have no more of it. Here, drink, and let your tongue have a bit of a holyday."

The indignant actor could no longer restrain himself. His hand, which had been extended to grasp the imaginary dagger, was swept round in the twinkling of an eye, and the next moment the vessel was seen flying in the air, liberally bestowing its contents in its flight, upon the face and bosom of the circle, among which the portion of Mr. Bull was in no manner stinted. This proceeding was the signal for an uproar, and Bull's hand was already laid upon the collar of Macbeth, whose blood was still rising, when the sudden appearance of another personage upon the scene, produced an instantaneous change in its circumstances.

CHAPTER XXIX

THE SIDDONS OF THE SWAMP—PASSION AND CUNNING AT ODDS

"Ay, answer that,
The questioner hath need — where went he then !"
The Royal Fugitive.

THE effect upon the group of the sudden appearance of a single person was no less strange than instantaneous. And this
person was a woman. She emerged from the edge of the little
nook, near which the revel had been carried on, and stood, without speaking a syllable, for several seconds, looking upon the
circle with an expression of high-raised scorn in her countenance,
which, though beheld only by the ruddy blaze of firelight,
seemed to the eyes of our actor to be haughtily beautiful. Her
complexion was dark, but richly lustrous. Her hair black as
midnight, and glossy almost as its stars. Her eyes were large,
quick, and dazzling, of the same deep raven hue with her tresses, which hung down upon her shoulders, streaming from be
neath a sable network, which, covering her head, partially concealed her forehead also. Her person was rather masculine —
her carriage majestic — and the involuntary notion which rose
in the mind of Horsey, as he beheld her, was that she would
make a most magnificent Lady Macbeth.

Somewhat ashamed of being caught by a lady in a hand-to-
hand scuffle with a genius like Benjamin Bull, our actor drew
off from his opponent, who, to his surprise, exhibited an equal
degree of willingness with himself to bring the contest to a sudden conclusion. He slunk away, and, with an evolution no less
prompt than unlooked for, actually took shelter behind Horsey,
surveying the intruder with eyes of cat-like cunning, mingled
with some little apprehension, from over the shoulder of the actor. The effect upon the rest of the revellers was very nearly

the same. In a moment they had left the board; and one or two, who were nearest to the woods, might have been seen stealing out of sight into the shadow of the contiguous trees. Jones was the only one of all the assembly who maintained his former place, and exhibited neither apprehension nor confusion. He met the gaze of the lady with respectful firmness, and, as he passed our actor in approaching the spot where she stood, whispered in his ears : —

"Our prima donna—our heroine—a star of the first magnitude. But—mum !"

His finger touched his nose, and his air and gesture were that of one whose words, had they been supplied, would have been :—

"But a Tartar of the first degree."

Horsey fancied such to be the meaning of the other's gestures, and was half confirmed in this opinion, when the first accents fell from the lips of the intruder.

"Mr. Jones, I would speak with you a moment."

"Certainly, ma'am — I will but give some directions to the gentlemen, and follow you."

"Gentlemen !" was the half-subdued utterance of the lady, in tones of scornful irony. "Gentlemen, indeed !"

The words came faintly to the ears of Horsey, who stood, with Jones, somewhat in advance of the rest; and, however little complimentary to himself and his companions, he could forgive the sneer which they expressed, in consideration of the intense superiority of manner which accompanied their utterance, and which assured him that the company was not entirely without a redeeming measure of that talent for theatricals, the want of which had hitherto appeared painfully conspicuous in his eyes, in spite of the obvious genius of Mr. Benjamin Bull and the flattering judgment of Mr. Jones. The lady turned on her heel, without further word or look, disappearing in the recess of the woods, as suddenly as she came.

"So, Bull," said Jones, reproachfully, when she had gone, "it's just as I told you. Mark me — you haven't heard the end of it. I warned you, but you must be drinking; and all that I said by way of counsel has been wasted upon you. She's heard all the uproar, and seen it too, and she will tell *him* every syllable when he comes. She will forget nothing You know that."

"Ay, ay—blast it—she has the memory of a devil's dam Well, there's no help now—I must grin and and bear it," said the genius, sullenly.

"At least, it will be wise only to do no more mischief for the night. Away, all of you, to your nests; and no more uproar. There's no telling how soon *he* will be here, and if he finds you—"

The speech was finished in a whisper to the parties immediately interested, and lost accordingly to our amateur. He had heard enough, however, to perceive that there was some mystery connected with his companions, some matter of domestic history, which was yet withheld from him. Who was "*he*" of whom Jones had spoken so emphatically, yet left unnamed; and why should a woman, however great might be her merits as a player, maintain an influence over the company, of such seemingly tyrannical extent—a tyranny which, from their spontaneous recognition of its sway, would seem to have been of habitual and undisputed exercise? The approach of Jones arrested his cogitations.

"This path, Mr. Horsey, will lead you to your place of sleeping for the night. You will there find fire-light, and a boy waiting you. I will join you before you sleep."

"But, Mr. Jones—the lady—who is she?"

"Our great gun—our princess—a most royal heroine. You see what a magnificent carriage she has?—she is tremendously popular—wins applauses wherever she goes—our trump-card which always secures the game. But she knows it, sir—that's the misfortune. She knows her popularity too well, and she is capricious in consequence. We have to humor her, sir, in all her fancies, and some of them are strange enough. You have no idea how extravagant she can be at times. Exercises the most tyrannous authority, and we dare not offend her."

"I'd like to know her. Suppose I go with you? You can introduce me, and, by the ghost of Garrick, Mr. Jones, to have a chat with such a woman will only be a proper compensation for the annoyances I have had to undergo from that d——d comedian—that fellow Bull, of whom you think so highly."

"Not now—not for the world to-night. She's in her fit to-night, and would fly at you like a tigress. To-morrow, or the next day, Mr. Horsey, as soon as the fit passes off. I'll tell you when she's in the humor to be seen."

"Do, do—I long to know her. She looks as if she'd make a first-rate woman. But of whom did you speak when you threatened Bull with the anger of some person whom you did not name?"

"Oh, that was her husband—our chief musician. A bloody fellow, by the way, of whom Bull has a monstrous terror. He came nigh cutting Ben's throat once already, for some liberties he took with his wife, and since then we know how to keep him in order. We have only to say '*he* is coming'—meaning the husband—and the fellow's tail's down in an instant. He loses all his wit and humor, and skulks off, as he did to-night, out of sight and hearing, a most thorough-paced coward, as ever you saw. But I must leave you. Our princess is as jealous as her husband; and as I am acting manager at present, I must be careful how I offend her. Your path lies there. I will look in upon you as soon as I am dismissed from her presence."

Horsey, somewhat bewildered, followed the path which had been pointed out to him, while Jones proceeded to join the empress whose dictatorial summons he really did not dare to disobey. The spot in which she received him was not far distant from that which the revellers had occupied. It was more thickly garnished with trees and shrubbery—more closely encircled by the swamp-thicket, and, in place of a rude tent of bushes, such as served the rest of the company, a log-house was provided for her ladyship, rude and clumsy, it is true, but comparatively full of comforts, and not without its attractions. Deference, if not affection, seemed to have striven to gratify her pride, and commend itself to her consideration. A little arbor was raised before her door upon which the wild grape clambered; and rose-bushes had been planted along the path, which was neatly shorn of weeds and made free of all obstructions. Within the cottage the same care might have shown itself, in a hundred little particulars, but we need not waste our attention upon details.

15*

The lady met Jones at the entrance, and, without a word, led the way into the dwelling. Her manner betrayed no little impatience.

"You have been slow, Mr. Jones. I heard of your arrival some hours ago, and have been expecting your presence ever since."

"I had a particular charge ma'am, which kept me busy. We had a stranger to manage, and—"

"Ay, ay—some other hopeful scheme—but I care not to listen to the small details of some new villany. My desire is to know where you left Saxon. That you have seen him, I know —that you must have seen him within a day, I am convinced. What I desire to know is, where you saw him last, and when I am to expect him here."

"Really, ma'am, it would be very difficult—nay, almost impossible—for me to answer all these inquiries. You know, quite as well as I do, the danger that our captain incurs at this moment—nay, at every moment, and—"

"Pshaw, Mr. Jones—you speak as if you thought me a fool, or doubted my prudence and fidelity. Is it likely, do you think, that I shall prove a traitor to Edward Saxon? or is there any probability that I shall deal in the small tittle-tattle of my sex, and, with its usual vanity, reveal, with unconscious stupidity, what I know, to those who might do him hurt? You know me better—you would evade my inquiries."

"On my honor, ma'am—"

"None of that—none of that. Leave off your long preambles, and answer my question. When did you see your captain last, and where? I repeat, I know that you have seen him within the last two days—where was it, and what was the precise time?"

"Perhaps, ma'am, you have more knowledge at this moment of the captain's movements than myself. He has not confided to me any particulars but those which had connection with the tasks upon which he has set me, and which I was endeavoring to execute at the very moment when you came out upon the bayou."

The woman looked upon the speaker with a degree of intense earnestness in her glance which savored of a rising anger

Her dark eyes gleamed with the fires of a gathering thunder-storm, while a smile of ineffable scorn, that seemed like its softer lightnings, passed over her thin and ruddy lips.

"Mr. Jones, you look upon me as upon a child, with whom you may trifle at pleasure. Why do you talk to me of your duties, and of your efforts to execute them? I do not doubt your diligence, nor am I a miserable spy to watch your performance of them. I ask a simple answer in reference to the movements of another — your captain, sir!"

"Yes, ma'am, but you know my oath. I am forbidden—"

"What! to communicate with me? Has he then forbidden you? Ah! has it come to that—does he fear that I should know? Are his doings of such a character? An outlaw to society, is he faithless also to me?—and you—you, sir, know, and are forbidden to declare. It is well, sir—very well—it is exactly what I thought—exactly. You may go, sir—go! I ask you not to betray your leader, sir—keep his secrets—conceal his perjuries—cloak his excesses—you are both worthily employed—both. Fear not, I shall do you justice to your captain. You may go now. I have done with you. I have no more questions."

This speech was spoken with an impetuosity which defied all interruption. The torrent of passion convulsed the frame of the speaker—fired her eyes—made her cheeks glow with the tempestuous blood that coursed through her veins with the fierce rush of a stream that no longer knows its limits—but offered no interruption to her accents, while her feet traversed the little floor of the cabin, with every sentence which she uttered, arrested only at the close of each when she stopped to confront the hearer with her flashing eyes.

"Madam," said Jones, when her pause suggested to him an opportunity for reply, "what will you have me say or do? I am commanded to obey you."

"Yet forbidden to answer my questions."

"No, madam; only on such subjects as concern the movements of the beagles."

"Ay, that is the pretence. You know that I care to know nothing of your movements. or of any movements which merely affect your schemes of plunder, and when I would ask of *him*.

I am answered by a reference to your oath What has your oath to do with his movements?"

"He is one of us—his movements are those of the beagles.

"You will not answer me, Mr. Jones?"

"Madam, are you not already in possession of all the information which I can give you?" said Jones, significantly.

"What mean you, sir?"

"The dwarf—Stillyards."

"What of him? Has he returned?"

"He has, madam. He stood near the captain last night—so near that, had he been discovered, his life had been but little worth. Saxon would have put a bullet through his head had he known of his presence, and dreamed that he had been sent as a spy upon his actions."

"Ha! what mean you by calling him a spy—who sent him as a spy?"

"You, madam, should need no answer to that question. Enough, that I know that he was present—that he was present as a spy—and may reveal to you those matters which I dare not. Stillyards is already here, if you have not seen him; and has, probably, been so far successful that he is able to answer all your questions;.as he has no such scruples as myself, he probably will do so. But, let me counsel you, madam, for your own sake, no less than that of our leader, that you employ that crooked scoundrel no farther in such matters. If discovered, Saxon will kill him, and, if not, he may pick up some secret of the leader, upon which his own life and the lives of all of us might depend. You do not know the evil which may follow this evil practice, for which, if you will permit me to declare, there can be no sort of necessity. Saxon, let me assure you, is as faithful to you as he is to us; and if ever mortal man loved woman, it is certain that he loves you."

"Ah, Mr. Jones," responded the woman in milder accents, "could I be sure of this; but the feeling of my own unworthiness, is one that always produces a doubt of his fidelity; and, if he loves me, as you say, why is it that I am now so constantly deserted?"

"Believe me, madam, it could not well be otherwise."

"Would I could believe you, Jones; would I could—but—

but—no matter. You will keep my secret, Jones—you will say nothing of what you know?"

"Why should I, madam?—it were of no use, unless it became necessary to prevent a repetition of a practice which endangers the lives of all. Stillyards must not be again employed in this business."

"How, sir, do you command me?"

"No, madam, far be it from me to do so. But I take leave to counsel you; and to add, that my own knife should silence the dwarf for ever, should I again detect him in the position in which I encountered him last night."

"Enough, sir," replied the lady, proudly, "I shall take care that the lad encounters no such risks at your hands in future, and warn you, therefore, that I shall avenge any injury which your suspicions or your malice may prompt you to inflict upon him."

"Malice, madam! it would be malice were I to declare to our captain what has passed between us. But you mistake me, madam; I have no malice against you, if for no other reason, because I sincerely love our leader."

"Mr. Jones," said the lady, "I requested you to say nothing to Saxon of what you know. I now amend my request, simply to beg that you will merely give me an opportunity of anticipating your communication to him of every particular relating to the spy, as you have been pleased to call the dwarf, in my employ. It shall never be said that Florence Marbois, whatever may be her errors and her vices, dreaded to speak the truth herself in the ears of the man she loved. I may have wronged him by my suspicions—but I will not wrong him so greatly as to yield to an underling any confidence, however unimportant, which I yet withheld from him. You may leave me now, sir."

A faint smile passed over the features of Jones, as he left the apartment.

"Now, were I the malignant she has called me," he uttered in low soliloquy as he entered the woods, "I should not forgive — certainly never forget—this bitter and foolish speech. It were no difficult matter to ruin her with Saxon for ever. But what use? A woman, in all her pride and glory, is something like a soap-bubble after all. She glitters and floats in air for a while, is decked with all the colors of the rainbow, but you see through her all the time, and she bursts at last. I pity Florence—she has many excellent qualities, and, but for the convulsive jealousy of her temper, would be as amiable as she is lovely. She will break some day, and cover us with lather. It will be our care to see that she does not blind our eyes with the soap."

With this effort at small philosophy and smaller wit, the outlaw proceeded to the hut of the wandering actor. His place was supplied, in the presence of the lady, by the dwarf, Stillyards, who made his appearance the moment after the departure of the other. He had evidently continued his occupation of the spy, and had listened to the whole conference between them. With a grin, which had in it as much malice as delight, he prefaced his revelations to the lady by some natural remarks upon what he had heard; but was surprised at receiving a rebuke for his ill-timed impertinence.

"To your business, Stillyards! you saw the captain—he was well?"

This question answered to her satisfaction, she dismissed him without further inquiry, betraying, in the novel forbearance which she manifested, the influence had upon her mind by the serious caution which Jones had given her. The importance of the dwarf was in no small degree lessened by this course of proceeding.

"A fool's journey, indeed," he muttered to himself as he went, "if I'm not to use what I went for. But I'll pick a hole in both their coats when they're least a-thinking. I've a word to open madam's ears whenever I choose it, and I'll speak it too, sooner than lose my best business. The only good shares I gits comes from my lady, and if she stops hearing, she'll stop paying. Well, it'll cost 'em both a great deal more in the end; and if I don't git nothing by it, I'll git satisfaction. I'll show 'em that the broken back that makes 'em laugh, can make 'em cry too; and if I only gits my laugh for my pains — well, that's something.

CHAPTER XXX

TERRIBLE EVENTS — HAMLET BECOMES COMMON WEAR — THE
OUTLAW — THE HEROINE.

> "And he had learned to love — I know not why,
> For this, in such as him, seems strange of mood!"
> *   *   *   *   *   *
> "And there was one soft breast, as hath been said,
> Which unto his was bound in stronger ties
> Than the church binds withal."—*Childe Harold.*

JONES, when he returned to the woodland cover which had
been assigned to Horsey as his sleeping apartment, discovered
the worthy actor half undressed, squat upon the turf, and looking around him with a countenance in which consternation might
be said to be the prevailing expression.

"Why, what's the matter, Mr. Horsey?" demanded the
outlaw.

"Matter, sir," returned the other, "matter enough."

"How! you seem alarmed — you seem angry."

"Not alarmed, but cursedly astounded, and, as you say, a
little angry. Mr. Jones, I'm cursedly af.aid that this company
of yours will not exactly answer."

"How, sir?"

"They lack moral, sir," was the reply of Horsey, in lower
tones, and something more of caution in his manner.

"Indeed," said the other, "what leads you to this conclusion?"

"Nay, let me not do injustice to all, when the offence may
be that of one only. Would you believe it sir? — my clothes
are stolen!"

"Can it be possible?"

"Not only possible, but true. They are gone, sir — a tolerably new coat — blue cloth, gilt buttons, with velvet collar, and

silk lining—two shirts—pants, a sort of pepper-and-salt, very
fine though, with figured braid front and broad edging—vest,
fine satin, a little frayed at the right pocket, double buckles in
the back, no strings, and my name, written in India-ink on the
lining, 'Thomas Horsey, American Theatre, New Orleans,' all
in full.   In the vest, a silver pencil-case, ever-pointed, without
leads; in the pants, a penknife, toothpick, and comb; in the
coat, a handkerchief and pocket Shakspere, fine miniature,
Cadell's edition, London, much used, and with pencil-marks for
reading, under emphasized passages.   I would not take twenty
dollars for the Shakspere alone, to say nothing of the clothes."

"Truly a very serious loss, if they be lost," was the reply of
Jones; "but I'm in hopes, Mr. Horsey, that they are only mis-
laid.   Our profession, as you well know, calls for persons of
nice honor in particular, and I should prefer believing any mis-
chance sooner than the dishonesty of any of our men.   Have
you looked where you left them?"

"Everywhere."

"Let us look again.   It is too much to lose without some
effort, and you may have overlooked them in the darkness of
the night.   Where did you lay them?"

"Here,·on this very pole, and beneath these two trees; I
changed my dress behind them.   My saddlebags, you see, are
safe, and that is fortunate, for my favorite costume, and the most
costly, is within them.   I have a Romeo there, sir, a Richard,
two field-officers, a Mustapha, and other uncertain characters.
My Hamlet, you see, I have on, and, egad, 'motley's my only
wear' now, unless I can recover the missing matters.   The only
citizen's dress I had, is gone, and I should make a comical figure by daylight, in this dress of Denmark."

"A noble figure you mean, sir—you never looked half so
well in any dress in your life, Mr. Horsey, as in that," was the
reply, full of tones of admiration, which the outlaw made.   It
went consolingly to our actor's heart, through the medium of his
vanity; and the importance of his loss became a little lessened
in his eyes.

"Upon my soul, continued the outlaw, with a successful gravity of countenance, while he affected to look for the missing articles, "were I you, Mr. Horsey, I should never desire any

other dress than that which you wore to-night. Your figure and general air, sir, suit admirably the costume of Hamlet."

"Do you really think so, Jones?"

"Indeed I do; your carriage was particularly fine—the union of royal dignity and profound human thought, which you contrived—I know not how—to throw into the countenance of the melancholy prince, was inimitable. The habitual sense of royalty was there—present always to the sight; and yet every movement of the lips, every turn of the body, every glance of the eye, subdued while graceful, and full of signification while most easy, seemed to say, with the preacher, 'Vanity of vanities, all is vanity.' Your Hamlet, sir, seemed to denote, what he must have felt always, that he was the victim of the destinies."

"That is a good idea, Mr. Jones—a devilish good idea—a correct notion of the character. I must confess I never thought that before, though, certainly, I must have felt it, if my person ation was correct. I must read the play more closely—I must renew my studies. D—n the fellow for stealing the book—the breeches he may have—can't you make it known without offending the company, Mr. Jones?—Say that the thief may have vest and breeches, returning me my Shakspere and the coat?"

The result of the search, in spite of the liberal offer which Horsey had made, was unsatisfactory. The worthy actor was compelled to wear his professional costume in common, and the merriment which his appearance by daylight occasioned among the outlaws, whom he was still persuaded to regard as brethren—fellows of the sock and buskin—may be more easily conjec-tured than described. Not that he himself was suffered to be-come conscious of the fun which he inspired. Jones had his object in preserving order, and was successful in curbing the open expression of that mirth which was felt on every side as the actor strutted among them—perhaps not so much dissatis-fied with his losses, as pleased with the opportunity of appear-ing so often in character, to a person who, like Jones, seemed to behold his display with so much unction, and with such a laud-able desire to profit by his exhibitions. It would have been easy to have kept the actor some time longer in so pleasant a

captivity, had it been the object of the outlaws to have done so
It was only necessary on the part of their leader to hint a desire that the phlegmatic, yet fanciful Hamlet—a Jacques under
different aspects of fortune—should become the proud and passionate Moor for a season; and Horsey, whatever might have
been his rising suspicions of his companions, would have dismissed them on the instant that he put on the habit of Othello.
Vanity is one of the most unsuspicious of all moral objects. The
ear that is open only to praise seems to acquire its intense eagerness at the expense of the other perceptive faculties. The eye
is closed to the sneer that lurks about the lips of irony—and a
general obtuseness of the judgment, in all but the leading desire of the mind, distinguishes that moral gourmand, for whom
toiling Flattery—a creature that is base in proportion to the
folly which it feeds—ministers its spurious sweets, that, perhaps, only do not satiate, because they are so utterly unsubstantial. But let us not anticipate. It will not be necessary here
to say how long Horsey remained in the neighborhood of Cane
Castle, or what were the events that subsequently befell him.
Let us finish with the night in which he lost his inexpressibles,
and in which we have still something more to do, and some
other parties to produce.

After devoting considerable time, and a reasonable degree of
effort, for the recovery of the lost wardrobe, Jones left the actor
to his sylvan couch, while he returned to his own—a shelter of
twigs, bark, and bushes, some fifty yards distant. The actor
soon slept, to dream of parts and persons, in the assumption of
which the loss of his own garments could not have been seriously
felt. Sleep soon overcame the outlaw also; and it was only
after several shakes of the shoulder that the latter was awakened from his slumbers by a stranger at his side.

"Ha! captain—you!" he exclaimed, when fully aroused,
and starting to his feet as he distinguished the face and form of
his visiter in the dim starlight.

"Yes," was the answer in the tones of Saxon. "Have you
found your man?"

"He is here—we have played the game so far with tolerable
success."

"You have the clothes then?"

"Yes — coat, vest, and breeches."

"That is well. Let them be well blooded; put a knife and bullet hole in the breast and body, and send them off with the first peep of morning to Nawls. Keep up the game with this silly fellow a few days longer, and I will then give you orders what to do with him. He is unsuspicious of the truth?"

"Quite."

"That is well — keep him so — but do not suffer yourself to be deceived. He may play in characters more troublesome to a good beagle than Othello or Macbeth. You were careful to take him along the cross paths to the swamp?"

"Ay, sir — it would puzzle him to find his way out again without help; but he will not seek to do so while we hold to our theatrical purposes, and this we can safely do for a reasonable space longer. Do you leave the castle to-morrow?"

"To-night. I will but see Florence first, and excuse myself for another flight."

"That is only a proper caution, sir. She needs it."

"How! Have you seen her?" demanded Saxon with some anxiety.

"She came out upon us while we were drenching the boys in the very height of our play with the actor."

"Ha! — well! The old passion, I suppose?" inquired the outlaw, with some disquiet in his tones. "Would she were safely in Orleans again. What did she come for?"

"To summon me to the castle — to make inquiries after you — your whereabouts — your objects — the cause of your delay."

"Jealous, suspicious woman! — I must cure her of this; but the task is not so easy. She has a furnace in her veins that maddens her. Her brain is all fire and suspicion, and her heart — but I must forgive her all, since her madness grows out of a love, which is as little qualified and doubtful as her jealousy. And yet, Heaven keep me from such a passion as hers — to be its object even is a terror. It would consume while it worships — and still enslaves by the intensity of its regards. There is no tyranny like that which never suffers you from under its eye."

The conference between the two outlaws was continued for a brief space longer, but as it involved matters which have no connection with our narrative, it needs no record here. When they separated, Jones resumed his couch, while Saxon, passing through the narrow pathway already traversed by the reader, entered upon that densely-encircled area, on the edge of which stood the little cottage of his leman.

Florence Marbois—the young, the beautiful, the devoted—was a creole of Louisiana, whose parents were French, and who, dying of yellow fever in Orleans when she was yet a child, left her to the doubtful care of indifferent relatives, whose responsibility, however lightly it may have been felt, had been abruptly terminated by her clandestine flight to the arms of another guardian, from whose affection she had better hopes of those regards and that tenderness, which were so dear to one so adhesive as herself, and of which she had heretofore known so little. Edward Saxon—of whom she then knew nothing, but that he was noble in form, handsome in features, proud in spirit and intelligent in mind, far beyond the average of those intellects to which she had been accustomed—became her protector—her protector in that sense of the word which excludes her from all social consideration; and though it may most frequently have its origin in love, more certainly finds its termination in disgrace. She fled to his arms, and in the intoxication of a first dream of passion realized, she felt no rebukings of conscience—no compunctious visitings—no misgivings that the love which had prevailed over virtue would fail to survive its loss. But the heart which craved the affection which it has not often found, is of all others the most suspiciously watchful of that brief portion which fate allows it; and when, in process of time, the various employments of her lover, took him from her side, and kept him absent for days, and weeks, and sometimes months, Jealousy, that twin-passion of love, which, perhaps, must always be as active as its elder sister, particularly where the rights of the latter have been left unestablished by the legitimate authorities, grew no less violent than the flame of which it may be called the black and veiling smoke; and she who could dote, at one moment, with devotion, on the bosom of her seducer, soon showed him that she was not without the spirit to rise, at another, into rebellion and hostility. Her fits of passion annoyed and sometimes confounded him; and the first impulses having subsided, which had led him, as fiercely fond as herself, to assume the charge of one so wild and violent, he sighed with something of regret as he looked back to a condition of freedom, which he now craved, but which he found himself utterly unable to restore. Though outlawed, he was not utterly abandoned, and his soul shrunk from the suggestions, which had never been self-prompted before, to rid himself, by a single act of brutality, from ties which, however sweet at first, had now become an encumbrance. Now, for the first time, however, dark resolves were self-offered to his mind; and ere he emerged from the wood which separated the encampment of the robbers from the arena in which the cottage of his mistress stood, he paused under their influence, and his lips parted in murmured soliloquy :—

"And why should it be borne longer?" he exclaimed—"why should I be the victim of eternal jealousies—a suspicion that haunts my footsteps—that watches my actions—that hangs like an incubus upon my heart? Can there be any wisdom in such patience? Shall it be that I, who have shaken off the fear with the love of man—who have bidden defiance to his power no less than to that of God—that I should yield up life and freedom—the enjoyment of other society which might in part console me for the loss of those which the outlaw must ever forfeit, in a base homage to one for whom I have no love—for whose claims, even lust now fails to offer any argument? Beautiful once—beautiful still—loving me as I believe thou hast done—Florence Marbois, thou art yet nothing in my sight. Thy love is persecution; and it is pity—pity only—which has made me, at great effort, wear a face, when I approached thee, of regard which I can no longer feel. I remember what thou wast when I first saw thee—when I first took thee in my arms that fatal night, when, in a boat which might have been a coffin to us both, the winds bore us over the Pontchartrain together— I remember what thou wast, and what I promised to thee then, and the memory of that night rises up to save thee and to soften me. But, can I always spare—can I always endure the tyranny which thy vain jealousies inflict? Is there reason why it should be borne—nay, is there not good reason now, why it should cease soon and for ever. It must—it shall! There is

a bound beyond which passion must not go — a limit where
endurance stops, and forbearance becomes a shame as it has
long before become a weariness. That bound is reached — that
limit is overpassed; and the heart which now flows with all its
streams to another, must soon be freed from thee. But for this
I had borne with thee still longer — I had borne with thee in
pity for thy youth — for that love even, which thou still bearest
to one to whom it has been an annoyance for weary months,
and to whom, unless checked in season, it must become a curse!"

He paused and looked around him, as if struck by approaching footsteps, but no one approached him. As if reassured, his
words again broke forth in soliloquy — such soliloquy as denoted
the doubts and indecision of a spirit, for the first time approaching a purpose of excessive guilt and danger. What he said
tended to show that the woman whom his arts had betrayed,
was about to be cast from his least regards; and nothing seemed
to be wanting to the more fell and cruel resolution which would
thrust her from his path, but that frequent contemplation of the
subject, which reconciles the corrupted heart, step by step, to the
last degree of crime. That this stage of wickedness had not yet
been reached by the outlaw, was clear enough, by the frequent
recurrence, in what he said, to that period in the history of their
mutual fortunes, when the intercourse between them had been
productive of equal pleasure to them both. So long as the
memory may still look back with tenderness to the green gar-
den-spots of youth, the heart is not utterly corrupt — there is
still a part not yet ossified — a narrow, isolated spot, from which
the springs of relieving pity may well up and soften, though
they may not often heal, the rest

CHAPTER XXXI.

THE DEATH OF PASSION—NEW PASSION FROM ITS ASHES.

"Die all my fears,
And waking jealousies, which have so long
Been my tormentors; there's now no suspicion."—MASSINGER.

IT was midnight, but Florence Marbois did not sleep. She sat beside the window, looking forth upon the various shadows of the night and forest. The scene was unspeakably sweet and soft, but it was also sad and mysterious. A faint murmur, like the distant moanings of a spirit at watch over the desolate abodes of youth and happiness, came to her ears through the subdued silence hanging over the scene. The shadows drooped, as if in kindred affliction, beneath the grave and brooding star-light. The gray cypresses rose up like spectres amidst the green foliage that grew thickly along the edges of the swamp, and looming forward in the dewy haze of midnight, seemed to harmonize with the melancholy aspects of the region. Nor was the voice of the water, as it rose from a brooklet that gurgled under the upbulging roots of a tree which it had partially de-tached from its foothold, without a fitting tone of sadness for the scene.

The heart of Florence felt the mysterious sympathies accord-ed by the unintelligent nature at her feet. Her head rested upon her palms as she looked forth and listened—her eyes, as if satisfied, strove not to pierce the dense maze of forest all around her; and while her lips murmured a complaint of soli-tude, such as seemed to be the burden of all voices, her cheeks were glistening with those holy dews which such beauty as hers —had she been still alive to social vanities—should not have regretted, since they served to crown beauty with the more pre-vailing charm of sweetness, and to consecrate to love the very sorrows in which their origin is found.

The heart of Florence was softened, but not at ease. Tears had brought relief—a brief respite from the gnawing discontent which preyed upon her heart—but not a cure—not a remedy. If she felt more at ease, it was the ease of one who has just drank the soothing draught, and can only find relief while under its influence. Fancies, which are sometimes hopes in disguise, the ephemeras of the soul, had been with her in momentary visitation; and, though vague, unstable, and illusive, they had at least diverted the grief which might else have overborne. True, they fly at last, but so do the angels; and who would refuse the blessing of the visit, in which the very air blossoms, through which they come, because of the conviction that they must fly with the morning? The heart that has been full of sorrow, should be the last to speculate unnecessarily upon the always unprofitable future.

Unfortunately, the hopes of Florence had not been wise hopes, for they had not been good ones. She loved unworthily —she had sinned—she lacked the securities of virtue, and had no confidence in that of others. Her hopes, based upon the probable truth of her lover, were idly founded. They were made to rest upon his tastes, his passions, her own powers of pleasing, her frail and fading charms, and her undisguised attachment for him. They had not been placed where, to be secure, all affections must be placed—upon her own just claims to respect, and upon the inflexible principles of truth in the man to whom her affections had been given.

Her lover—so she once held him—had raised his hand in defiance to society, in the rigid exercise of whose laws the only security of woman may be found; and her appeal for justice now lay to his passions and caprices alone—to passions which constant provocation made active and imperious—to caprices that fluctuated with an appetite more peevish with every indulgence, and more recklessly resolved with every denial.

But Florence Marbois was a creature of impulses, not of thought; and, if there were moments in which she estimated correctly her miserable condition of dependence, such thoughts were soon driven away as intruders, by the gentle accent, the kindly solicitude—not often shown in the latter days of her heart's history—which the pity of her betrayer vouchsafed to

bestow, in return for that increasing homage and devoted love
—shown even in its most jealous frenzies—which she had
never ceased to feel for him from the first hour of their ill-
appointed union.

And, sitting beside the window of that rude hovel, alone, in
the deep mazes of an uncultivated forest—the savage almost at
her side—a band of outlaws at her feet—midnight gathering,
vague, wild, indistinct, and mysterious around her:—the play-
mates of youth—the friends of maturity—the social and kindly world in which she had lived—all banished from her sight
—all lost, and, probably, lost for ever:—still, she thought of
no privation—she knew of no loss—she dreamed of no evil—
no—no danger—nothing to make her doubt—nothing to make
her dread—she thought only of him! Where was he? When
would he come? Was he still true? Did he still love her as
before?

Could she have found a grateful answer to these questions,
her heart might have been pacified. She would have asked
no other questions—no other fortune from the hands of Fate.

Such is love—that thing of greatest dependence—of greatest strength and weakness. Strong above all powers for endurance—weak beyond all moral supports, when it knows not
where to confide, and can not command the sympathy which it
ever seeks, and without which it is little better than a flower
cast upon the unreturning waters, and borne with feeble struggles to the wide ocean, where it is swallowed up. Strong, vigorous, climbing, triumphant, and beautiful, like the vine, when
the gigantic tree suffers its embraces; but wretched, sinking,
and perishing, prostrate upon the earth, when, throwing out its
tendril-arms for the support to which it was destined, and without which it can not live, it grasps only the unsubstantial air,
and perishes at last in feeble despondency upon the damp and
noisome ground, from which it has ever sought to rise.

In the cold world how many affections spread forth their arms,
seeking, but in vain, to clasp themselves around the rugged nature which they would adorn and beautify—failing in this, that
perish upon the spot which gave them birth but denied them
sustenance—putting forth no fruits, bearing no flowers, yet
beautiful while they lived—so beautiful in promise, that the

16

heart can not help but weep, for its own sake, that they were denied all fruition.

The tears were yet on the cheeks of Florence, when Saxon entered the apartment. He entered it unobserved. Her face was yet turned upon the forest; her thoughts were far distant; and in the absence of her thoughts, her present senses had become obtuse, or heedless of their duty. He strode firmly, but not heavily, over the room, but she heard him not. He stood almost immediately behind her, and still she turned not.

He stood awhile surveying her in silence. Many and changing thoughts seemed passing through his mind. His brow darkened for an instant—his hand was lifted in the same time, and seemed searching in his bosom, while a glance of savage ferocity lightened in his eye. At that moment, a deep sigh escaped from her lips, and the expression passed from his face, his hand was withdrawn from his bosom, and, placing it upon her shoulder, he pronounced her name. She turned, almost with a scream—an exclamation, which had in it as much delight as surprise—and, rising from her seat, threw herself into his arms with all the abandonment of joy.

"Oh, Edward! dear Edward! it is you—you are come—you are come at last, and I am so happy! But you have been gone so long—so very long, Edward—that I feared you had forgotten me—that you had deserted me for ever; and my heart sank within me, and I have been so miserable, that I wished myself dead a thousand times—indeed, I did; for it seemed to me far better to be dead, and cease to feel, than to have such miserable feelings as have filled my heart. But you are come now—you will now stay with me a long time, and I shall be so happy."

While the poor heart-dependant hung upon the bosom of the outlaw, and poured forth these words in a stream that lacked emphasis as it lacked obstruction—for the sentences which she so rapidly uttered were spoken without the cessation of the smallest pauses—his looks were cold, his eye was aimless, his whole air and manner were those of a man who could no longer be moved by anything that she might say. His head was thrown back to avoid the flowing tresses of her hair which brushed his face, and his arms made a slight movement to put hor from him. This she felt – this she resisted, and clung to him with a firmer hold than before.

"Do not push me from you, Edward — not yet — not awhile —let me cling to you only a little longer. I have thought upon this dear embrace, and wept and prayed for it so long, that you must not deny it to me now. Yet I will not worry and vex you with it. I know you have grown colder and harsher than you were — that you are not so fond as you used to be when we first came to the woods. I feel that — I know it; forgive me that I press it upon you — but remember I am a woman, and believe me that I love you, O Edward, as warmly as ever, in spite of all the changes which I can not but see in you."

"It may be so, Florence — it may be so," replied the other coldly.

"It may be so, Edward — may be so! Can you doubt it — can you think otherwise for a single moment? Have you not seen it in all my looks — have you not felt it in all my actions — from the first to the last — from that sweet — perhaps, most unhappy hour, when I believed all your assurances of love, and gave you, oh, how entirely! all of mine — even to this, when you speak as if you believed me not, and look, as if you are indifferent whether it is truth or not which I speak? Do not force me to think this, dear Edward — do not, I implore you — unless you seek to discard me — to crush me quite — to trample me for ever in the dust! I can bear the world's scorn —nay, I do not see — I do not feel it! I can bear anything — all things — denial, privation, banishment from friends and family --burial in these swamps — anything, but the conviction that he, for whose sake I am thus desolate — thus dependent — now makes light of the sacrifice, and takes from me, all at once, that love which I found more than a recompense for every loss. Turn not from me, Edward — speak not — look not so again upon me; for, in truth, I am very, very wretched — I know not well why, unless it is that I see so little of you. And, unless you smile upon me — unless you are willing to let me love you when you come to me — I would rather far that I were dead — I would rather far that you would kill me with a sudden blow and end all my sufferings at once The pang of the blow, even from your hands, given in your anger, would not be half so great a pang as that which I should suffer, without mitigation and without cure, could I feel that you were indifferent to my love."

The imploring solicitude of this speech — the tender accents — all failed to move the now cold heart of the outlaw. He suffered her hand to rest upon his arm — but his eyes turned away from the large, tear-filled orbs, that implored more eloquently for his love, than any of her accents. He had not yet attained that recklessness of spirit and of conscience which could enable him to meet without shrinking, the glance of her whom he was not unwilling to destroy.

" Florence," he replied — " either I have, or I have not to go elsewhere, and be absent from you long. If such be the necessity, you have no reason to complain of me ; and, if there be no such necessity, then there is no policy in your complaint. In deed, you will only drive me away from you by such complainings. I hate such scenes."

" Edward," returned the other, reproachfully.

He proceeded with an air of dogged determination, to push his new-formed resolution to the utmost.

" The best regards in the world may become oppressive. There is a season for love as for other things. When a man has reached the age of thirty, life has other businesses besides love. It is surprising that you have not discovered this truth before — that you should need now to be informed, that, even with the most pliable men, there are certain moods and dispositions of the mind when love is an intruder, and the embrace of the most lovely woman, an annoyance. I do not profess to be of more tender stuff than other people, and I confess to you that I hate very much to be continually excruciated !"

And this was the end of passion ! — of a passion that had seemed more like frenzy than feeling — more like the outpourings of a heart convulsed by its emotions into madness, than the ebullitions of human hopes, fears, and fancies ! And this was the man who had persuaded Florence Marbois to give up all — hope, honor, society — friends and family, and fly with him into the wilderness — to share with him his shame and guilt, his exposure and isolation. Verily, there is no sting

—no sorrow—greater than the wrong of the beloved one—the desertion of him in whom we had put our bosom's trust!

This was the first time that the unhappy Florence had ever been compelled to listen to language so unequivocal from the lips of her betrayer. It has been said already that, up to the present moment, a sense of pity, rather than of justice, had prevented the outlaw from showing the indifference which he felt. Hitherto, he had made an effort to exhibit a fondness which he had long since ceased to feel. A new passion for another, made him anxious to cast off a connection which had become an encumbrance; and the desire, which had almost moved him to the commission of a more brutal, if not a worse crime than that of his first wrong to the unhappy woman—if insufficient as yet to reconcile him to her murder—was quite active enough to render him unscrupulous about the open declaration of those real feelings which he had only successfully disguised, because of her unwillingness to behold and to believe them.

His tones and language now, no longer to be mistaken, were instantaneous in their effects. She started from his side—her hand shrunk from the arm which it had grasped, as if there had been danger in the contact, and she retreated for a few paces, then stood with arms drooping at her side, and her head slightly bent toward him.

Her eyes, no longer suffused, became, on a sudden, keen, arid, and burning. They shot forth an intense glare—an expression of mingled consternation and inquiry; and, when they encountered only the cold, inflexible gaze of one from whom all motives to further deception were removed—who now, perhaps, rather sought an occasion to declare the indifference which a better feeling had once made him studious to conceal—it was then that they became fixed, as it were, with a death-like distension of orb, such as betokens the first bound to madness of an oppressed brain and overpowered reason. A brief space of time elapsed, in which she preserved this posture without speaking. Her intensity of stare was painful to the outlaw, even if he no longer felt it to be reproachful; and he advanced, speaking as he did so, toward his unhappy victim.

"Come, come, Florence, I must not suffer this. These arts must no longer be practised upon me. Let us understand each

other. Let us put an end to these follies. We have both of us
lived too long in the world, not to feel the wear and tear of such
passions as these; and the impolicy of indulging them should
be known to all who have discovered, as I have long since
done, that our affections and sympathies, to be grateful and
worth preserving, must not be suffered to become tyrannies.
Do you understand me, Florence?"

He approached her as he spoke—he made a show of taking
her hand, but she retreated, drawing her arms behind her as
she did so, but preserving, at the same time, the same searching
scrutiny of gaze which he had found so painfully oppressive.

"No! no! no!" she exclaimed, mutteringly, a moment after.
"It can not be. It was a dream. I could have heard no such
accents from his lips. It can not be that I am reserved for so
dreadful a punishment. I know that I have done wrong—that
I am guilty before man—guilty in the sight of Heaven—but
oh! not to him! He can not have spoken thus—I will not—
dare not—believe it!"

She paused, her eye still followed his, and, unwilling to endure its expression, he turned away to the window she had left.

A new resolve entered her mind—she darted rapidly toward
him—caught his wrist with a nervous grasp, and spoke in clear,
soft, untremulous accents—

"Edward—Edward Saxon—what was it that you said to
me but now—not a minute since?—Speak!—Speak aloud—
let me hear your words again, for I feel that I have not clearly
understood them—I hear badly, Edward, of late, and, unless
the words are spoken very distinctly, I am very apt to misun-
derstand them."

"Florence, why do you annoy me in this way when I come
to see you? You know that I hate these wild passions—these
tumults that produce no good, and are without any necessity.
They trouble—they oppress me—nay, more, I confess the
truth to you—they make me exceedingly reluctant to approach
you."

"It is true! It is all true!—my ears did not deceive me—
I heard it all—all!" she exclaimed, breathing deeply, after
several protracted moments in which her bosom seemed not to
heave—her lips gave forth not the slightest respiration. Her

eyes were fixed upon him with a gaze of mingled horror and surprise, and, more than once, as she gazed, her hands were passed over her brows, as if striving to put aside some obscuring tresses, which were yet not in the way. Well might she doubt her sight, when she could no longer withstand the evidence of her other senses. The now desolate and abandoned woman—abandoned by the man for whom she had long since abandoned virtue—had still a hope that there might be some smile on the lips of the speaker—some expression in his eyes, softening, subduing, qualifying, disarming the deadly accents which had reached her from his lips.

But no! In his cold, calm features, she beheld most truly the hopelessness of her heart. She saw that she was for ever banished from those affections, in which she deemed herself secure. The veil, with which pity had striven for awhile to hide from the eyes of passion the fatal truth, that love had for ever gone from the shrine where he had been worshipped, was ruthlessly torn away; and the mocking spectre alone remained, to grin over the devotee, who had for so long a season bent before its unholy and delusive features. The sin which had assumed the aspects of a power the most commanding of all others in the heart of woman, having secured its victim, beyond recall or recovery, no longer cared to preserve even its disguises, and she stood alone in the presence of the tempter, his veil uplighted, his scorn openly declared.

Florence Marbois, weak though she had been at first, and easy, like all her sex, to be overcome where she loved, and believed herself to be beloved, had yet her strength; and the strength of woman, defrauded of her hope, and despised in her affections, is no less immeasurable than fearful. The cold composure of the outlaw's glance moved her indignation, and a bitter smile of equal scorn flushed the face that a moment before had been of a deadly whiteness.

"I thank you, Edward Saxon—I thank you. Cruel as the truth is which you have at last spoken, it is some consolation that it is the truth. You have deceived me for a long time; and in this practice my own blind attachment has made the toil of artifice an easy one. But your looks tell me more than your language; and there are other truths, yet unspoken, which I

need not that you should declare. Edward Saxon, you love
another !

"I know it — I feel it — else why should you now forego the
deception, so long continued, and which you found so easy ?
Why should you teach me with such effort — so plainly — that
you had ceased to love me, when it cost so little effort to persuade me that you did, and when such a faith was so grateful
— so essential — to the poor heart that loved you ? You are
not naturally cruel, why then be guilty of so great a cruelty ?
why open my dreaming eyes to the loss of all for which I had
lived ?

"There could be but one reason — but a single motive. From
the moment that you fixed your eyes upon another, the task
had become irksome of continuing those shows of love to me
on which I have fed so long. There was no absolute need to
wear a mask any longer — you had nothing to hope, and, in the
excess of your power, you, perhaps, felt assured that there was
nothing which you had to fear.

"Perhaps not ! Edward Saxon, you are free. You shall hear
no further reproaches from Florence Marbois. Devote yourself
to the hapless woman whom you have selected to fill my place.
You may never discard her — she may never suffer my wrongs
— and yet, if she is unlike me, perhaps she may avenge them.
Enough — you are free to seek her. Though my heart withered, and my hope died, yet, I tell you, Edward Saxon, they
should do so, sooner than I would implore you for the delay of
a single instant ere you cast yourself into her arms; or for a
single accent of reluctant love, from lips which have been so
dishonored as yours."

"Florence, this is a sort of madness to which your constant
jealousies have long made you liable. They have annoyed me
long enough — they shall annoy me no longer — and since you
so boldly declare yourself — now learn from me, that your conjecture is true. There is another — a woman, loveliest among
the lovely — you shall see her — she shall even dwell with you
here for a season — though I say not that she shall take your
place."

"Wherefore not say it ? Think not you will offend me
further, Edward Saxon — think not you offend me at all. I

tell you, my heart has survived the possibility of offence at your hands. You have wronged me too deeply to offend me. I see not your scorn—I hear not your accents of coldness and cruelty—they are lost in the overwhelming conviction of the injury which you have done me. You are a bold man, Edward Saxon—a bold, brave, bad man. I am but a woman—a frail, feeble, desolate, abandoned woman—"

She paused.

"There is something more, Florence. Why do you stop? Surely the comparison demands an inference—a conclusion—a point. Shall it be a sting?"

She looked on the speaker, whose contemptuous smile showed how little he valued the feelings which he had so deeply outraged, with a grave countenance, expressing a singular degree of composure, which, but for the feelings that it really served to hide, must have been unnatural; and replied briefly—

"It may be so—bold, bad, reckless as you are, Edward Saxon—worthless as am I, and feeble—God will raise me up an avenger. I may be guilty in his sight, but it can not be that you, to whom I owe it all, should be suffered this double triumph over me. There will be an hour of retribution. There must be pangs for the betrayer as well as for the betrayed; and I will only pray that I may live long enough to know that you feel them."

"The prayer of the wicked, you know," was the sneering reply of the outlaw. "I could preach you a sermon from that text, Florence, were I in the mood, which would be unctuous enough for the orthodox in any congregation in Mississippi; but I spare you that, and my further presence. I must leave you for a while. I trust to find you in a better humor when I bring you a companion."

"Now, may I have strength for my vengeance against that day!" was the exclamation of the discarded woman, as the outlaw left her; and a wild, cruel resolution rose up in her mind, as, brooding without sleep through the remainder of that weary night, she thought only and ever of the woman—who was destined to take her place in the embraces of unlawful love—as of a victim!—the last sacrifice upon that altar of passion, on which her own virtue had been the first.

16*

CHAPTER XXXII.

> " I'll no more tender him,
> Than had a wolf stol'n to my tent in the night,
> And robbed me of my milk." — JOHN WEBSTER.

SAXON knew, in fact, but little of the nature of woman. Her heart was a fountain shut up, and a book sealed to him. He had the arts which could win—these, perhaps, are few and not difficult of attainment. They may be acquired by almost every youth of tolerable deportment and moderate common sense. But those finer arts which may secure the possession, and make the conquest permanent, he did not seem to possess, and, indeed, did not seem to value. Men who are rapid in their conquests, are not apt to value them. " Easy won, easy lost," is something of a proverb, which holds no less good in the affairs of the heart than in those of the purse. Had Saxon been a more thorough examiner of that various province—the heart of a woman who loves; could he have looked deeply into its hopes and fears—its tumultuous passions, and capricious fancies—its suspicions, which grow naturally out of a just feeling of its dependence upon that arbitrary lord whom it is born to serve and must suspect—and which make it a thing all watchfulness and jealousy; he would have known that there was no object in nature so sensitive—no object so perfectly fearful—when touched rudely by reproach, or mocked by indifference and scorn. Perhaps, had he not grown too indifferent to the possession, he would have been more considerate of the claims of that affection which he once sought with avidity, and which was never more truly and devotedly his than at the very moment when he encountered it with a contumely as reckless as it was undeserved.

He little knew the fierce and uncontrollable spirit which he roused in the bosom of Florence Marbois during the brief interview which has been just recorded. She might have forgiven the neglect which was only suspected — she might have forgotten the partial inattention of his regards, so long as he still returned, and while his lips still yielded, however unfaithfully, some vague assurances of his attachment. But when he boldly declared his defection — when the vain beauty was taught to know that there was a more highly esteemed beauty, set up as her rival; — when the devoted heart was rudely thrust from the altar, where its tendrils were still resolute to cling — when love could no longer doubt its desertion — it was then that another and a wilder nature, rose up, gloomy and terrible, within her soul.

Some glimpses of this nature had been shown the outlaw a moment ere their parting, but he had not seen them. These had been the outbreakings of a spirit which could not altogether be suppressed; but its language was beyond his comprehension. He had heard so many upbraidings from the lips of the neglected woman that his ear had grown obtuse to their true signification. He confounded the vindictive mutterings of a passion which was scorned, with the tender reproaches of a heart which was still allowed to hope. Having denied hope, having trampled upon love, having cast faith and feeling from his consideration — he should have known that Hate would be the deity most likely to be raised upon their ruins, by the spirit which he had so rudely driven from all communion with his own.

There is quite as little wisdom as virtue in injustice. Perhaps it may be affirmed, with equal truth and certainty, that it is also without cunning. The wholesomest moral prudence is truth and good faith. Good faith in all human relations. Had Saxon not been blinded by his resolution to do wrong, he must have seen, in the keen yet composed glance of the woman — in her deliberate accents — in her slow, cold, resolved manner — that a sudden and singular change had come over all her feelings in the moment when he made his open avowal of injustice.

Her temper, passionate and deep, earnest and gushing —

overflowing in its fullness, and always warm in its expression in all ordinary cases of excitement — was now, when the occasion became one, perhaps, of the greatest and most painful provocation suddenly subdued — almost frigid — an embodiment, in marble, of lofty elevation and dignified indifference. The change in character should have occasioned surprise; and reflection should have taught the outlaw, that the woman he had wronged had become an object of apprehension. But he had none. He was too glad of an occasion to shake off bonds which had become irksome, to see that, in doing so, he had incurred the resentment of a heart which could be as dangerous as it had been devoted. This sudden obtuseness of intellect may be accounted an essential part of that blindness and madness to which the gods deliver over those whom they have previously determined to destroy.

Florence Marbois watched at her window while the night faded away; yet she seemed utterly unconscious of its passing hours. She was unconscious of all things around her. Her heart was changed within her, and bitter thoughts and envenomed resolutions were growing up, and taking the place of those which, but a short time before, had been only those of tenderness and love. The cruel iron of desertion, and the sharp steel of scorn, had entered deeply into her soul, and left nothing but rankling irritation where they went. Desolation she had endured for him — but desertion by him was unendurable; and wild, vague, changing, but always hostile measures presented themselves to her mind, as she brooded, in the darkness and stillness of the night, over her wrongs, and the bitter-sweet hope which she indulged of redressing them.

"There are means," she murmured at intervals, "there must be means everywhere provided to humble the oppressor — to revenge the injured. I am weak — I am woman — but God has not left me utterly helpless, if he has made me destitute. I know that I can have my revenge — I know that I can strike — that I can triumph; — and here — here in the darkness of this hour, and in the presence of such spirits of evil or of good — I care not which — as travel the eternal realms of space, I swear tha', sleeping or waking, my prayer, my dream, my desire — my only study, as it is my only hope — shall be in what way to revenge my wrong—to bring this proud, insolent man to the dust—to deprive him of those joys of which he has for ever deprived me!"

By what means she hoped to effect her object, may not even be conjectured in this early stage of her resolution; but no one could have hearkened to the tone of her accents, or beheld the fixed expression of decision in her eyes, and reject the conviction that she was as solemnly sworn to her revenge, as if the demons of the air whom she invoked as witnesses, had received and registered the oath. They did so; and it may be that, ministers of justice, no less than of evil, they wrought in behalf of the deserted leman of the outlaw, when the ordinary powers of society would have failed, and the laws would still have been, as they had ever been before, objects of scorn and mockery to the reckless spirit who had so long held them in defiance. But let us not anticipate.

In leaving her that night, Saxon also left the encampment to which had been given the ambitious title of Cane Castle. Another brief conference with his coadjutor, Jones—that dexterous agent, who had so successfully entrapped and deceived the unwary actor—by which he was provided with final instructions for the future disposition of that unconscious worthy; and then the outlaw sped off to those other performances, which have been already narrated, and which ended in the arrest of Harry Vernon.

The next day rose upon Horsey, still as Hamlet. The grave habit of the prince of Denmark was that which, in all his wardrobe, came nearest to the guise of a simple citizen; and half reconciled to the costume in character, from a pleasant conviction which the flatteries of Jones encouraged, that he looked a marvellous proper man in it, the worthy actor renewed the search after his ordinary garments with something more of equanimity than he had shown on the preceding night. Still, he did not hesitate to speak of the robbery in proper terms.

"The mere loss of the clothes is nothing, Jones," said he "but that we have thieves in the company is most shocking. There must be a stir about it—the rogue must be found out, and we must purge ourselves of the connection as soon as possible. Our profession is one quite too noble for any such com munion."

Jones fully agreed with him that it was shocking indeed; but suggested the difficulty of finding out the thief, and the awkwardness of any direct inquiries. It was agreed upon. that their conduct was to be governed by circumstances; and, meanwhile, a sharp look-out was to be maintained upon the movements of all suspicious persons;—Jones confessing that there were some two or three of the *company* whom he really believed to be no better than they should be.

"Now, that bull-headed fellow, Bull, I take to be one of these suspicious persons," said the actor, remembering the annoyances of the previous night; "a fellow that gets drunk and makes a beast of himself, will be very apt to steal. Don't you think so, Jones?"

"I do," replied the other, very courteously. "As a general rule, Mr. Horsey, a drunkard is bad enough to be a thief; but there are exceptions to all general rules, and Bull is one of them He's a genius, Mr. Horsey, as I said before—an immense genius You may see nothing of it for some days; but he'll break out at last, and overwhelm you. He's the very impersonation of fun, farce, and frolic."

"But the heroine, Jones—sha'n't I have a talk with her today? It's strange that all your first-rates should be so eccentric."

"Natural enough—they all know their value. You would not think it strange, when you know them as I do, and know the extent of their popularity."

"And what do you call her—what's her name?"

"Her name?—oh, yes—her name's Clifford—Mrs. Clifford—Mrs. Ellen Clifford—she's married, you know I told you, and—another reason why you should be cautious in approaching her, and why she should be devilish shy of all third persons—her husband's worse than a Turk for jealousy. He flames up, like a rocket, on the smallest occasions. Nay, it is said he gave a poor fellow three inches of his bowie-knife in Natchy, for praising her beauty off the stage. You see she's **very** beautiful."

"What a d——d fool. Egad, I'd like no better fun than **just**

to plague such a fellow; and if you had no other reason than
his jealousy to keep me from looking her up, I'd be at her in
twenty minutes. Can't you get me a chance to talk with her.
I'd like to see what sort of stuff she's made of."

"Time enough to-morrow. Let us go now and see after the
boys. We have a boat here on the bayou—a little dug-out—
and, if you say so, we'll take our fishing tackle, and get some
fish. Fishing here is our most profitable idleness, as, indeed, it
is everywhere else; and, if you like it half so much as I do,
you will not think much of the manager's absence."

"But my Hamlet!" exclaimed the actor, looking at the costly
garment. "Such a dress as this, Jones, won't do for every day.
The d——d strange-looking green and yellow mud of this river
—the water, if I'm splashed—will play the very d—l with my
Hamlet."

"Won't splash you," said Jones, hurrying along. "I'm like
a bird in a boat—can't be said to dip a wing, even when I take
my fish. I handle a dugout, Mr. Horsey—not to compare low
things to high—with almost as much grace as you do the foils
in Hamlet. But come on—fear nothing, and if we get no fish,
why, you can give us the grave scene, which shall make our
time pass with less gravity."

The last suggestion was the finishing stroke, and Horsey followed without further opposition, though not without sundry
misgivings that his sables might suffer some hurts much too serious for any smoothing or stitching, even from hands so white
and dextrous as those of Mary Clayton. Many a compunctious
glance did he give to his inexpressibles as he went forward, following his cunning confederate through bog, bush, and brier,
until they reached the muddy mouth of the narrow creek where
lay the egg-like skiff which was to bear the twain to the main
trunk of the Chitta-Loosa.

Here they embarked in the trembling fabric, the heart of
Horsey rising to his throat, with every roll and reel of the frail
vessel; while his eyes, drawn by a natural attraction to the
banks, surveyed, with momently increasing disquiet, the yellow-
ish slime upon their surface; the soft miry ooze of which seemed
for all the world as if it were intended to receive with close
embrace and a most yielding compliance, the pressure of any

derelict body, the waif or tribute of the slow and turbid river
which had left it where it lay.

But that which disturbed the composure of the actor had no
effect upon his companion. His muscular arms sent the little
dug-out through the narrow passage with a dexterity no less
prompt than fearless, and Horsey had not drawn a second
breath before the boat quivered upon its centre, and hung suspended for a moment in its course, as, leaving the sluggish ca-
nal through which it had emerged, it felt the downward rush of
the main current, in its restless passage to the Mississippi.

Florence Marbois, as soon as she discovered that Jones had
left the island — a knowledge obtained without difficulty by one
who was so well served as the lady in question — immediately
went forth from her little habitation to a spot, the path to which
seemed familiar, where she found the dwarf Stillyards busy
mending his nets. He stood up as he beheld her, with an air
of deference in his manner which he was not wont to show to
all other persons.

"Richard," she said, "I have need of you again: are you
ready?"

"Soon will be, ma'am — have nothing to do but tie a few
threads, and lay a draw-cord through the end-loops of the net.
This hole here would let a dozen jacks through; and there's
not a suckfish in Big Black that wouldn't laugh at this for
gill-tackle."

"Richard," continued the lady, in tones at once of command
and entreaty, "put by your net for the present, I would speak
with you."

The foot of the dwarf turned the net over a low bush; his
hands would have done it more effectually, but his vanity was
unwilling that he should stoop, in the sight of a lady, to a
performance in which his physical deformities became only the
more conspicuous. His manner the while was that of the most
respectful deference. He declared himself ready at that instant
to obey her commands, and made some rude assurances of his
great willingness at all times to do her service.

"I know it, Richard — I know that you have always served
me faithfully — and believe that you will continue to do so in
this, probably the last task which I shall ever give you again."

"Ma'am! Heh — what?"

She did not seem to heed the interruption or the exclama
tion, but proceeded :—

"You have kept my secrets, Richard, and always made, I
have good reason to believe, a faithful report of what you saw.
Here is some money for you. It is more than I promised you,
but not more than you deserve, and not near so much as you
shall have when you have done for me another service, and, as
I said, most probably the last."

"The last, ma'am?"

"Yes, Richard, my fears will soon be at an end," replied the
lady; "she should surely cease to fear who has at length
ceased to hope."

The dwarf looked up, wondering more at the looks and
accents of the speaker, than at the words she uttered. She
continued :—

"Did you know that Saxon was here last night?"

He nodded assent.

"He went before daylight," continued the lady. "He went
from me for ever. We are no longer one — we are parted —
parted for ever."

The dwarf grinned, but not with any pleasure. The expression of his face was that of good-natured incredulity.

"You smile — you believe me not, Richard."

"Ah, Ma'am Florence, how can I believe you? you know
how often you've said the same thing — every time you've sent
me to look after him."

A faint smile passed over the lady's lips as she listened.

"You are only right to doubt, Richard. I have, indeed, too
often *spoken* only, when I should have performed. I will not
seek now, by any new assurances, to make you believe my present resolution. Whether you believe or not — whether *he* believes — is of little importance to either of us now. But there's
some difference of circumstances, Richard, of which you may
have no knowledge. Hitherto, I may have done him wrong
by my suspicions — now I can do him none. Last night he
told me that he loved another."

"He!"

"Ay, he! Edward Saxon, for whom I gave up all — friends,

family, good life, good name — hope, truth, and innocence! He has forgotten the sacrifice, which, indeed, I too had forgotten so long as he loved me. But that is over, and I am now lost to him as I have been so long lost to all. I have nothing now left me but to die."

"Nothing, Ma'am Florence, nothing! Sure—"

"Ay, there is something, Richard — there is something more. It is a woman's feeling Richard, to desire some knowledge of her rival — to desire to see her, to know if she is beautiful, to hear her speak, and hearken if her accents be sweet; and, perhaps — but I need not say more of this to you, Richard."

"Oh, yes, Ma'am Florence — I beg you do."

"No, no!" was the rather stern reply. "It needs not. It was only of another feeling — they call it a woman's feeling too — that I would have spoken — that I would gratify. But here it shall remain — secret from you — secret from all — doubly sweet to myself that it is so secret! — untill the blessed day which shall enable me to realize my last hope — the hope of—"

The word was unspoken, but the vindictive gleaming of the the eye, and the convulsive quiver of her lips while she shut them together, as if to prevent utterance, were sufficiently conclusive that "revenge" was the only word which could have properly finished the sentence. Her heart heaved with the suppressed secret — her hand was clenched, and for a moment she stood gazing on the dwarf with an expression of face which almost startled him with a feeling of personal apprehension.

"Richard, you must follow Saxon — once more you must follow him. Find out where he goes — whom he seeks. Look not on her — so that you may not be won by her beauty also to betray the poor Florence — then come to me — come back and get your reward. You shall have money and jewels — all the jewels and money that I have, Richard — they will almost make you rich; but you must be sure to tell me where he hides her, when he brings her here — and how soon I may look upon the woman whose feet have trodden upon my heart. Go! let me hear your horse's tread immediately. Away, Richard! Sleep not as you go — God be with me and strengthen me, for well I know I shall never sleep till you return — even if I sleep then. Away!"

CHAPTER XXXIII.

THE APE CHAFES THE TIGER — A SNARE AND A SURPRISE.

"I do pronounce him in that very shape
He shall appear in proof."—*Henry VIII.*

THE dwarf listened to the commands of his mistress, and prepared to obey them. He had been accustomed to do so; indeed, it may as well be stated in this place that Richard Stillyards, as he was called, was rather an attendant of Florence Marbois, than of the outlaw by whom she was betrayed. What were the particular circumstances by which he became bound to her service, may not here be known; but it has been seen that there were events and performances by which she had deserved his gratitude; and his devotion to her service showed that he was not unwilling to give it. He had been faithful to her for a long period; obeying her slightest and her strangest behest; ministering, perhaps harmfully at times, to her jealousies of the outlaw, though without seeking to encourage them; for Stillyards, so far, had been able to discover no single instance of a departure from his pledged faith to his leman on the part of Edward Saxon; and he now regarded the bitter rather than the angry mood of his mistress, by which she declared her renewed suspicions, as being equally without foundation with all which she had entertained before.

But though he assured her of this conviction, his assurances were made in vain; and he was sagacious enough to perceive that her present disquiet was of a character which she had not before exhibited. Hitherto, she had shown a vague jealousy —a general but uncertain suspicion — of the truth of one upon whom she felt she had none of those holds, which can alone be found in a compliance with the established laws of virtue and society. There was hostility now, and hate; mingled with her suspicions; and the very calmness which overspread her features, and 'which regulated and made deliberate the tremulous accents of her voice as she spoke, convinced him that, whether she had or had not occasion for her anger, it was yet of a kind to prove dangerous.

Stillyards was not so bound to Florence Marbois, as to lend himself to all her purposes; as to become the mere tool and agent of a rash and improvident vengeance; and while he prepared, without scruple, to set forth in obedience to her commands, he half-resolved that Saxon should have warning that his mistress was no longer to be trifled with. Still, with a partial curiosity, he resolved first to discover, if he could, whether the outlaw was really unfaithful to his vows — an assertion made with so much solemnity now, by the deserted woman as to impress itself upon his mind with some force, in spite of his constant conviction heretofore, that she had but little reason for complaint. His purpose was to counsel the outlaw, if such were the case, to greater prudence in his declarations and proceedings; and, tickling his own vanity with the patronizing idea of being an adviser to the master beagle of the band, he saw but little harm in practising a like unfaithfulness with his master toward the mistress whom he served.

These resolutions passed through his mind as he proceeded upon his mission. He soon got upon the track of the outlaw, and followed him to Lucchesa, where he arrived in time to become privy to the position of Vernon in the house of Mr. Wilson, and that of Saxon in reference to his daughter. He was soon convinced that the story of Florence was not without foundation. For the first time, he beheld the reckless outlaw in the character of a devoted, if not a sighing lover. He saw that the affair was rapidly advancing to a close, and on the afternoon of the day when Vernon was hurried from his mistress by the self-created officers of justice, he availed himself of an opportunity to emerge from his cover and present himself boldly before the outlaw.

The place chosen for this revelation, was a thick copse in the very wood in which the final scene had taken place between

Vernon and the maiden. To this copse Saxon had retired after he had witnessed the successful termination of one portion of his projects. Stillyards had been equally fortunate in beholding the events which we have already described, and he was, therefore, very well able to speak home upon the subject. While Saxon, seated upon a fallen poplar, was busy chewing the cud of various thought—thought no less perplexing in some respects than it was exulting in others; and while his eyes, fixed upon the ground, saw no image but that drawn by his amorous fancy upon the warm glass of his affections, he was suddenly and unpleasantly startled into a new sphere of existence by the abrupt appearance of the dwarf at his side.

"How now, sirrah!—What make you here?" he demanded in harshest accents, as he beheld the intruder. With a grin of equal consequence and humility the dwarf replied:—

"She sent me—she's heard it, sir—heard it all—knows all about it, sir, and it's only right, sir, you should know it won't do to vex her; she's angry as a tiger-cat—looks as if she could bite and do a great deal of mischief; and though she don't say, yet I can see, and I thought it only right to let you know, and to warn you, sir—there's danger—danger in her eye—"

"What the devil do you mean, fool?" demanded the outlaw, with an impatience momently increasing, as he beheld the air of self-esteem which now distinguished the manner of the speaker.

"Fool!" cried the other, with a vexatious diminution of his importance; "fool! Not so great a fool neither, if you knew all."

"All!—what all? What is it that your sagacious head carries, that it is fitting I should know? Speak out, booby, and leave off your damnable faces."

This startling, and most humiliating reception, effectually turned the sweet milk of the dwarf's disposition, and a burning sentiment of indignation in his bosom, made him wish he had left things to themselves, confined himself to the old system of espionage, and suffered the revengeful mood of his mistress to work its own way, without offering any obstructions to its progress. It was necessary, however, that he should now

speak, and to some purpose, in order to account for that obtrusion of his ungainly person, upon the secrecy of one who
seemed in such excellent temper to resent it. It may readily
be conjectured that what he did say, in the momentary confusion of his thoughts from such a reception, was scarcely satisfactory.

"You don't know, perhaps, sir, that she sent me."

"Pshaw! you are a spy upon my actions—you have long
been so, booby. Do you think me ignorant of that? Her folly
and your stupidity have taught me this long ago; and, but that
you could do me no harm, and that I care as little for your
cunning as for her jealousy, I had stretched you out straighter
with a bullet than you have ever been able to stretch yourself.
Begone, fool—she is no less a fool that sends you. Cross my
path—lurk about my footsteps—let me but catch a glance of
your monkey visage again where it should not be, and I silence
you for ever. Begone! — But — remember!"

With these words the outlaw rose, and seizing the dwarf by
the ears, sunk his finger-nail into the flesh until the blood oozed
out from the wound, then flung him from him with a force that
needed not the additional impetus given by his foot, which was
yet applied with no qualified energy.

The violence of the effort flung the deformed upon the
ground, from which he sprang to his feet with the agility of a
tiger. He turned upon his assailant—his eyes glared with the
vindictive and unreflecting rage of the same animal—and his
unarmed fingers were extended, as if endued with an instinct
of their own, to grapple with the foe.

But the eye of the outlaw quelled the inferior, and a pistol
which he drew from his bosom, effectually counselled him to
increase the distance between them. Slowly he sank from
sight into the neighboring woods, from which, however, he did
not then depart. The watch which he had hitherto kept over
the movements of the outlaw, on account of his mistress, was
now maintained on his own account. The malice which is the
fruit of outraged self-esteem, is that which is the last to forgive
its victim; and when Stillyards crept into the woods, it was
with the stealthy mood of the wild beast to which we have
already likened him—the appetite which never knows repose

until it gorges the full feast from the very lifeblood of its prey.

Saxon had some lurking doubts that he had provoked an evil spirit into activity, and though his apprehensions were kept down by that scorn of the feeble and deformed which the strong and proud are very apt to feel, yet a momentary conviction of the necessity of curbing or crushing such a spirit in the beginning, persuaded him, the moment that Stillyards had disappeared from sight, to pursue him.

This he did, but without effect. His search was fruitless. A creature so active as the dwarf, who could crouch with so little effort, and conceal himself in places into which other men could not penetrate, could not well be discovered, unless with his own consent; and hopeless of a search which was no less tiresome than fruitless, he left his unprofitable quest in the prosecution of others far more attractive.

That evening, Saxon, who had sundry agents at work, succeeded in getting Mr. Wilson to the hotel, and safely seating him, with three others, at a game of whist. Without knowing the history of this unfortunate gentleman, which would have given the outlaw a very desirable power over him, the latter had yet been able to discover that leading passion of the other, which had led him from folly to excess, and from excess, by a very common transition, to crime. He saw, in the eager anxiety of the stranger when engaged at cards, in his flushed cheek, fitful eye, and tremulous impatience, the peculiar material out of which the devoted gamester is made. That passion for small risks—that pleasure in a hope of gain that rises up into a feverish sentiment in spite of every defeat, and goes on renewing itself day after day, till the very dregs of moral life are reached, and the carcass becomes a thing of spasmodic and convulsive action, without stability or strength—was there, preying upon and predominant in the soul of Wilson, and renewing those bonds of slavishness and sin, under the coercive trammels of which he had sunk, first into the debtor, and next into the felon—from deep to deep—until but one more gulf— the closing covering gulf of all remained—yielding him refuge and utter ruin at the same moment in its unrelaxing jaws.

It was not long before Wilson surrendered himself up to the

game; and when his tens, twenties, and hundreds lay, upon the board, and when his hands touched the cards with a tremulousness that betrayed all the reviving passions of his feeble nature, leaving him no thought of other objects or relations, Saxon stole away from the company, unseen by any but the lynx-eyed dwarf, who, himself unobserved, was now a far more devoted spy upon the actions of his master than he had ever shown himself before. His own bitter hostility was now his prompter in addition to the jealousy of his mistress; and, he half forgot, in pursuing his own malice, that he had pledged himself to any other service. He followed the outlaw from the threshold, and was the master of all his movements.

But a brief space had elapsed after the departure of Saxon, when a billet was put into the hands of Virginia Wilson. She was sitting, sad and sleepless, keeping a watch doubly lonesome and apprehensive in the absence of her father, to whose errors she could not be altogether blind, in the stillness and silence of her chamber. The younger sister already slept in the couch beside which she sat, and her own loneliness grew more oppressive to her heart as she listened to the sweet, equal respiration from her lips — the breathing of that undisturbed sleep of innocence and youth, ere care has deemed it worthy of a blow, or defeated hope, and anxious affection, brought restlessness and wakefulness to its hours of repose.

How she envied the child that sleep. How she wished she could forget — that she could close her mind as easily as she could close her eyes, to the apprehensions which beset her soul in reference to the fortunes of him, who already occupied so large a place in its interests and being. The billet which was brought her, came from *him.* That assurance aroused her. She seized it with trembling hands and breathless anxiety She carried it to the light and read : —

"I am free, dearest Virginia — but a fugitive. I dare not show myself at your dwelling. I dare not, at this moment, show myself to any but to you. Will you come to me — though for an instant only. Come to me, if you love me — if you have faith in my love — if you believe in my innocence — if you would make me happy at a time when I am most miserable —

meet me by the fallen pine—under those old groves—in the dear sweet walks which have been already consecrated to our hearts by moments which were too blissful to have been so brief. I wait for you, dearest Virginia—my heart trembles with impatient hope. "VERNON."

Vernon would not have written such a letter; but Virginia Wilson was no critic. Her own feelings were too quick, too active, too excited, to suffer her judgment to examine the epistle calmly. Her heart beat with new emotions. What could be his present danger? Why should he be a fugitive? Was he, in truth, a murderer—could he have slain his friend by accident? She had his own assurances that he had not done so, and she believed them. But there was still a mystery, and doubts, to the heart that loves, are agonies.

There was but one mode to escape them; and though not insensible to the awkwardness of a situation which in ordinary cases would seem to be an impropriety, she determined on giving him the meeting which he craved. Leaving or entering her chamber, she had been accustomed to kiss her sister. The custom was a sweet one. They had been almost the all in all, and the only, to each other. Nevertheless, there were circumstances and causes, which, in spite of the real tenderness of the father, made Virginia not unfrequently feel that they were almost fatherless also; and now, when bending over the sleeping girl, and pressing her lips gently upon her cheek, the tears, few but big, fell from her eyes, and trembled upon the forehead of the sleeper, like dew-drops, in a summer moonlight beading the soft crimson of the half-opening flower.

But tears, though not unseemly on the cheeks of so fair a blossom, yet appeared to the mind of Virginia as of evil omen. She kissed them off with the haste of a maternal anxiety, and hurried from the chamber. There was none to obstruct her departure, for the indulgence of her father had left her the complete mistress of his household. She hurried by the garden pale, the forest groves were soon reached—the well known shadows of old trees surrounded her, and now the fallen pine tree appears, and she stands in the presence of—Edward Saxon!

17

CHAPTER XXXIV.

THE BEAGLE CARRIES OFF THE DOVE—HAMLET TIRES OF YORICK—FLIGHT—THE SMILE AND DAGGER.

"The innocency lost,
The bating of affection soon will follow."— BEN JONSON.

THOUGH the shadows were thick around her, and the evening light of the moon imperfect, the keen eyes of love soon discovered the difference between the man she met and him whom she expected. She recoiled with a natural emotion of surprise, but did not feel any suspicions that the appearance of Saxon in that spot was the result of any sinister design. He might be the trusted friend of Vernon on this occasion, as he had always appeared hitherto—but where was Vernon. She looked round anxiously, but without a single doubt of his near neighborhood, until the outlaw approached and addressed her:—

"You look for Mr. Vernon, Miss Wilson—but I come from him. He has told me all—I am his friend—he has sent me to bring you to him.".

"But where is he, sir? He should have met me here—here—it was so written in the note."

"Did not the note also tell you, Miss Wilson, that he is a fugitive? He has need, let me assure you, of every precaution He is in danger—he dare not show himself."

"You alarm me, sir. What may this mean—what is his danger?"

"He has escaped from the officers—they are even now in pursuit of him!"

"Escaped!—Can it be? But why should he escape, if innocent?—Why? But he is here!—Here! At hand—within hearing. You are his friend—and I!—What can he fear from me?—Why should he not come forward? My voice shall re-

assure him—when he hears me, he will know that there is no
danger here. Vernon! Vernon!"

Twice she called aloud, and waited for the answering sounds
that she desired. But her summons was made in vain. A faint
echo of her own accents alone reached her ears. The outlaw
stood patiently and smiled, but did not speak until her eyes
were turned inquiringly upon him again.

"He does not hear you, Miss Wilson—he can not hear you
at this distance; yet it is not far where he hides. I can guide
you to the spot in a few minutes."

"And why should he not come here, Mr. Saxon? Who, beside ourselves, know that he is near us?—But, perhaps, you
can tell me more, but you will not. He has been pursued—he
is hurt—wounded in escaping!—Speak, sir—speak—fear not
my strength—I can listen—I can bear it all."

"You have guessed rightly, Miss Wilson, though I feared to
tell you," replied the outlaw, promptly availing himself of the
suggestion which her fears had made; "he is hurt, but not seriously—he awaits you at a little distance, and I am ready to
guide you to him."

There was a moment's hesitation about the maiden; not that
she doubted as to what should be her duty—not that she had
any doubt of the truth of Saxon's narrative; but the requisition had been so sudden, the event so unexpected, which required her presence, that her sense of propriety had been
startled—her thoughts were all in confusion. The wily outlaw conjectured the true state of her feelings.

"Am I to think you indifferent to his fate, Miss Wilson? His
hurts require—"

"Indifferent! Oh, no! no! no!—but these woods look so
wild—and you, Mr. Saxon, are a stranger."

"But if *he* confides, Miss Wilson."

"It should be—it is enough for me. I will confide also. I
will go with you. Lead me to him, Mr. Saxon, I have no scruples now."

He took her arm within his own, and led her along a little
Indian foot-trail, which carried them over the hill, and still
deeper into the shadows of the forest. The heart of Virginia
Wilson beat with momently rising, but unexpressed emotions

as the way became more intricate, and as she perceived that
every step carried her still farther from the cottage. Still she
went on, anxiously expecting to hear the sounds of that voice
which alone could reassure her. But the woods were silent,
and the only murmur which reached her ears, was that of a
melancholy pilgrim, the wind, pursuing his sleepless way among
the branches. At length they emerged into a little opening
and Saxon paused, as if to listen.

"Is he not here, Mr. Saxon? We are far from the cottage."

"Not here—a few steps farther;" and he would have advanced, as he spoke, to a dark and dense grove in front of them,
but the maiden hung back. There was something in the reserve of Saxon—something in his manner—which made her reluctant to commit herself longer to his charge, and inclined her to
regret that she had already trusted him. Besides, the reflection
was so natural to a mind conscious of its own good faith, why
had he deceived her, when she had declared her willingness to
go with him? They had now been walking full fifteen minutes,
yet saw no signs of the person who had been described as immediately at hand.

"I will go no farther, sir—I dare not. If Mr. Vernon be
not within hearing now, I can advance no farther. I am afraid
I have already erred in leaving home."

"It is too late now to think of this, Virginia, too late to retreat," exclaimed the outlaw, throwing off his disguises, and
grasping her wrist firmly as he spoke—"you must go with me."

"Ha, sir!—will you dare?"

"Ay, much, everything, where I love, where there is a prize
to be won so lovely as yourself. You must go with me—you
must be mine, Virginia."

As he spoke, his arms encircled her waist, and she felt herself lifted from the ground.

"Monster—villain—release me!" screamed the maiden,
with a voice of equal indignation and terror—"Vernon! Vernon! come to me! Save me!"

"You scream in vain, Virginia. I have deceived you. Vernon is not near—not within hearing—the billet which brought
you to my arms was a forged one. But be not angry. You
have found a lover who will be no less true—no less devoted

than himself—one who is no less willing, and far more able to serve you with his love. The life of Vernon is forfeit to the laws."

"God help me! God help him! Villain! I believe you not. He will soon be here. He will follow—he will save me. Beware of his anger and his vengeance!"

"Ah! Virginia, if you but knew how little I regard these threatenings, and of how little value they really are, you would surely forbear them. Why should you thus afflict yourself and me. I suffer only as I see you give yourself fatigue and pain. Your screams are idle. In these pathless forests, there is none to hear you, unless it be the wild cat, who, if the humor suits, will give you scream for scream."

"Yes, villain—there are others nigh to save me. Men are nigh. I hear the tread of a horse—I hear the voices of men. They come—they come! It is Vernon—it is my father. They come to save me. They will avenge this insult. Set me down, and fly! Do this! Release me on the instant, and I will tell them nothing of the outrage."

The outlaw laughed aloud as he listened to this language.

"The men you hear are those whom I have commanded here to assist me. The horses they bring will help to bear us away together. They will carry us, sweet Virginia, to a place of retreat which neither father nor lover can find out. Do you hear that sound?—it is that of the beagle; when I have answered it in like manner, they will be here. Hark!"

And, as he finished, the outlaw replied to the signal in a clear, ringing note, which rose triumphant even above the piercing shriek of despair and terror with which she accompanied it. In a few moments after, the agents of the outlaw, guided by his answer, approached the spot where the maiden, still struggling and shrieking, was held by the firm grasp of the ravisher. His assistants were three in number. One was mounted—the other two on foot.

"Where is the jersey?" demanded the outlaw.

"On the edge of the wood—we couldn't get it through the brush," was the answer.

"Enough—lead the way."

"Shall I help you, captain?"

"No, ..o! Clear the way only!" replied the powerful ruffian, lifting the maiden, while he spoke, as if she were a child, and bearing her forward, indifferent alike to screams and struggles, threats and entreaties, until he reached the spot where the vehicle had been left. Into this she was placed, with all tenderness, but no little difficulty, and leaping in beside her, Saxon secured her within his arms, while one of his emissaries, occupying the front seat, assumed the office of John on the occasion, and drove off with as reckless and rapid a speed as ever did that renowned whip of ancient days.

Their course was for Cane Castle, in the swamp of Chitta-Loosa. They drove round Lucchesa, avoiding the thoroughfare with some caution at the first. After a little while they turned into it, and before midnight the carriage came to a halt with the thickening ooze of the swamp plashing clammily about its wheels. Before this time, exhaustion had come to the relief of the unhappy maiden, and when she was lifted from the vehicle she was in a state of utter unconsciousness and stupor. Jones, the wary coadjutor of the outlaw, was at hand ready to receive him.

"Well, Jones, we are here in safety, and all is as we could wish it. What of Florence? We must have her help here."

"Can you think of it, sir?" demanded the other, with some astonishment. "Can you hope for such a thing from her?"

"Ay, this or anything, as I please, my good fellow. I command her—she is mine—my slave, as thoroughly bound to my service as if the bond were written with her blood. Her love for me—the very passion which works her jealousy to madness—is my best security for her devotion and her service. Think nothing of her grumbling, Jones—I have heard it too often to hearken to it now. A kind word—a soothing entreaty—and all's over. She will forgive the rival, when she can share the conquest."

"I hardly think it, sir, with Florence. There's something I don't like in her eyes, and the way she speaks. She's changed very much these three days."

"Jones, you're a fool. You know nothing of women, my good fellow, or you'd not give yourself such troublesome notions; certainly you would not afflict me with them. Florence is not different from all the rest. She will have her own way if she can, and when she finds that impossible, she will content herself with all that you are willing to allow her."

" But the two in the same house !" said Jones, in a tone of further expostulation.

" And with one man between 'em !" continued the outlaw, with a laugh. " But let this not trouble you, Jones. They shall be kept apart. There's the squatter's cabin by the Little Bend — to that I will carry Virginia. Florence shall see her there — she will need some assistance."

" Better keep them entirely apart. If the young lady needs help — female help — there's Brown Bess, you know."

" What, is she here — and Yarbers ? How's this ?"

" Your orders, I hear. There's a warrant out against John Yarbers from old Badger. Ned Mabry's sworn against him about that horse business."

" True, true — I had forgotten that. Bess is the very person to be with her. Let us have help now, Jones, so that we may carry her safely through the swamp. The river's rising — is it not ?"

" Considerably — there must have been a heavy fall of rain among the 'hills above."

" And wh— did Yarbers arrive ?"

" It's been four days now, and better. He got in on Monday."

" Not pursued ?"

" Not that he told me."

" Cane Castle must look a little livelier than ever ; — and how does your Shaksperean reconcile himself to his bondage ? What of the actor-fellow — have you been able to keep up the ball ?" .

There was some hesitation in the reply of Jones, and his accents were those of a man conscious, perhaps of some fault of commission or neglect.

" I'm sorry to say, sir — he's off."

" Off! How off! You don't mean to say escaped, heh ?"

" Fact, sir — and how. there's no saying at present. I had him well watched, as I thought."

The tidings had the effect of making the outlaw instantly grave. His accents became stern.

"This is a bad business, Jones. Can there be traitors among us?— Another Hurdis affair! This must be.seen to, man. We are not secure an instant if we can not see our prisoner. But you pursued—you have beagles on the track? What have you done? how was it? Speak! By heavens, you are a duller fellow than I counted you."

"I can really say nothing, sir, as to the manner of the escape. The chap was safe enough so late as this morning."

"The d—l, and so he got off in broad daylight?"

Jones gave a mortified assent, and was compelled to submit in silence to the severe upbraidings of his principal, whose reproaches did not lack sarcasm to heighten their severity.

"By heavens, Jones, but I thought you more of a man than this speaks for. With five active fellows in the swamp—all at your summons—with nothing to do but this—you suffer yourself to sleep in your watch, and neglect everything. Did the fellow go off on foot?"

Here Jones was compelled to make another confession, which completed the story of his inefficient watch. Horsey had contrived to resume possession of old Bowline—his worthy father's venerable "Dot-and-go-one."

"Worse and worse!" exclaimed the other. "'...ere's treachery somewhere. We must sift the matter clc...y. Yarbers, you say, is here—his wife and daughter. Ha! Jones—that woman—that wife of his—Brown Bess is at the bottom of it all. She is shameless enough to be more honest than her husband, and will no doubt think it a moral duty to hang us all if she can, and him, for distinction sake, at the head of the string. Well—we must use her now. Away, and let Yarbers bring her to Little Bend at once. I will meet you at Cane-Castle in half an hour. Say nothing to Florence of my arrival—nay, do you avoid seeing her. I will tell her all myself. Away!"

But Florence had not been left uninformed on any of these subjects. She had, as we have seen, her own emissaries at work, and the dwarf had not only beheld the transfer of the captive maiden from the wagon to the squatter's house at Little Bend, but he had listened to every word of the dialogue between the outlaw and his agent, which had accompanied and followed her removal, and which we have endeavored, in the preceding passages, to abridge to our limits. He delivered his information to his jealous mistress some time before Saxon made his appearance.

"She's here," said he to Florence, as he stood suddenly before her where she sat in the gloom and silence of that lonely chamber, looking out upon the solemn swamp. It was in the same chamber that we found her first, when far other thoughts filled her mind, and far other feelings dwelt in her bosom, than those which rule over them now—making the one wild and the other wretched. She started as she heard his accents—she rose from her chair and approached him.

"You do not say it, Richard!" she said, with a solemn tremulousness of accent. "You do not tell me that she is indeed here—that he has dared!"

The dwarf nodded his head ere he spoke, then answered her:—

"At the squatter's old cabin, by the Little Bend."

"So near!" was the exclamation of the unhappy Florence, as she walked to the window and looked out—though, through the dense woods, her eyes could distinguish nothing—in the direction of the designated hovel. She turned again, after lingering a moment, and approached the emissary.

"Richard—you have served me faithfully, and one of the last acts of my life shall be to reward you. But tell me—have you seen her? Is she so very beautiful?"

"Very beautiful, they say—though I don't care much to see beautiful people, and didn't look much at her."

"But you saw her?"

"Couldn't help it—saw her a'most every day since I left you. I always followed *him*, and he went to her every day, and they walked out sometimes in the woods."

"Ha! ha! They walked out in the woods, did they? and she is very fond of him, I suppose? They are well matched—very well matched—a loving couple, Richard? Did you not think them so? But, do not answer me now. Go, Richard—leave me now—I would rather be alone."

"Look you, ma'am—there's one thing," said the dwarf, lingering, "if you think this strange gal's fond of Saxon, you're altogether out. She ain't fond of him, no how. She don't like

17*

him. He put her in the jarsey by main force, and she screamed and made a mighty fuss."

"Ha! Is this true?" demanded Florence, with considerable interest.

"P'int-blank truth. I saw her fighting him, and you might hear her screech for more than a mile — that you might — afore she fainted."

"What! — she fainted?"

"Died off, like 'twas all over with her, and didn't move agin, till they lifted her to carry her to the squatter's house."

"Richard, are you sure of this? Speak nothing but the truth — you know not how much depends on this!" said Florence, with solemnity.

"I'll take bible-oath to it, ma'am! I'll kiss the book to it. There's no mistake in me this time, I tell you."

"Enough!" she said, waving him, with her hand, to depart. "Enough! I thank you, Richard — I will reward you in the morning. Leave me now."

When he had gone, she returned to the window.

"This makes a difference," she said, musingly — "a great difference. If true, she is already a wretched victim, and no blow of mine would do her harm. Yet, even if she be a willing creature of his lust — if he find in her, what he found in me — a weak heart, a yielding nature, a confiding faith — that loved blindly and weakly, and was lost, before it became conscious that there was anything to lose — still, why should she be the victim even then? She knows not that she wrongs another — she *does* not — but he — he who knows all — who wilfully wrongs, and scornfully defies, he — but he is here — it is he who should feel the blow. It is his heart, and his only, which my hand should strike. And it shall strike! I am sworn to this! Lost! — an outcast from all hope, all life, all love — I am not so base, so worthless, or so weak, that I can not strike for vengeance! No! Edward Saxon, you have dared to scorn the heart which you once implored — to insult that womanly pride which you once solicited! — and yet, it lives — it lives to strengthen my arm and resolution — it lives, and will not cease to live, until you are humbled in the dust! For this triumph, and in this hope, I live only! Besides this, what is there in life to live for now;—and when he falls, there is nothing then that I shall even care to hate! God of heaven, how strange it is to me now, that I once should have loved this man—and so loved him—he, who stood over me but a few days ago, and mocked me with the story of his devotion to another, and bade me do her bidding, and commanded me not as a slave only, but as a slave whom he despised! Ha!—it is his foot-step—he comes—he comes to renew his mockery! I should not meet him unprepared!"

She went, as she spoke, to a little dressing-case, and, lifting the upper compartment, drew from beneath it a small silver-hilted dagger, which she concealed in her bosom, then, turning to the entrance of the chamber, encountered her betrayer with a smile.

CHAPTER XXXV.

THE OUTLAW AND HIS VICTIM—A TRAGEDY SCENE—A BLOW —A DISAPPOINTMENT.

"Observe this creature here, my honored lords,
A woman of a most prodigious spirit."—JOHN WEBSTER.

HE also smiled as he appeared in sight, but smiled in such a sort as to add fervor to her resolution. There was a reckless-ness in the scorn which he now betrayed to the woman he had once loved, which was certainly as impolitic as ungenerous; but having discarded his mask, Saxon seemed anxious to show how ill-favored had been the aspect he had concealed beneath it. He was obtuse enough not to see that the feelings he had trampled had risen up in indignation. He was blind enough to mistake the smile upon her lips for a return of her former feelings of devotion. So it is, that the wisest of men will err at those mo-ments when they need all their wisdom. Sagacious beyond most men of his sphere and neighborhood—particularly con-versant, according to his own notion, with women—he was yet deceived without effort, by one with whom his communion had

begun by his own successful deceptions. She had been won in
a moment—by a word!—how idle to think that there were
depths in her mind which he could not sound—that there were
feelings written in her features which he could not read.

Such was the case. The cunning man was at fault. There
was that in the bosom of Florence Marbois, which he could
neither sound nor see; but it was written that he should be
blind in this, as in other matters. *She* had been the victim of
her blindness—it was just, for the sake of retribution, that he
should have his moment of blindness also.

"Perhaps, you believed me not, Florence, when I spoke to
you last; but I spoke nothing but the truth. She is here—
here in the swamp, beside you—the woman whom I now love
—your rival—your successor."

It was thus he spoke, in the language of mockery. Her eyes
met his glance unshrinkingly. Her cheeks were pale—very
pale—for a single instant. In the next moment they were
flushed with a redness which did not depart throughout the
whole of their conference. Her reply was uttered in tones of
calmness which surprised her seducer. He knew not where
she got the strength for such equability—he knew not the
deep, dark sources of her present consolation.

"You mistake, Edward Saxon. I believed you. If I were
a vain woman, it might be some gratification to me to know
that my frequent and previous jealousies—idle as they were in
some respects—were yet not unfounded. I rightly judged
your character. My passions have not been wholly blind--
they were always capable of the task—perhaps, not a difficult
one—of estimating yours. I know you now, in that matter, to
be what I then believed you. If I erred in my conjectures, I
have already borne my punishment. The time for error and
regret, so far as you are interested, is for ever past with me."

"I am glad of it, upon my soul—very glad of it. You
speak now like a reasonable woman, Florence, and I think the
better of you. Now that I find you so calm and sensible, I am
free to speak to you with more confidence. You must have
discovered by this time, as I have done, that these early notions
of love, that so mislead the dreaming girl and the desiring boy,
are only so many masks of passion—masks under which the

considerate nature disguises those tumultuous frenzies which might terrify the young from the paths of pleasure and true enjoyment, much more frequently than they could ever entice or gratify. As the experience grows, the mask ceases to be necessary or even useful. It is then that we cast it aside as an encumbrance which, in fact, impedes possession and qualifies delight. I'm sure, Florence, we shall enjoy ourselves much more by understanding these things correctly."

A faint smile covered her lips as she answered :—

"At least, it is quite as well that we should think so—that I should think so. With the conviction that all is lost, a resignation to one's poverty is no less becoming than necessary. But do you only come to tell me this, Edward Saxon? Have you not some other purpose? I know all this before."

"To say truth, Florence, I came to try you. To see if you had got over that madness that used to possess you in your days of jealousy—"

"And which it gave you pleasure to see?"

"Not so. It vexed—it worried me to bear with your complaints—to listen to your harsh reproaches—to hear your unfounded suspicions."

"But they were not unfounded."

"Till now they were. If I was ever true to woman, Florence, I have been true to you till now. Never had I thought to wander from you, till I met with her."

"And she—she has a name!" exclaimed Florence, with something more of curiosity and interest in her looks and language. "If I am to yield my place to another—if I am to be deprived of that for which I have been so well content hitherto to live, at least—let me know something of her who rises on my ruin? She is beautiful—that I know—that you have told me—but her name? Who is she—what is her family—where did you find her?"

"All in good time, Florence; but you do me wrong, and yourself wrong. She takes no place of yours—she only shares it—and now that you show so calm a temper on the subject, let me tell you that you have risen greatly in my favor. This is the condition of mind to which I would have brought you years ago, if I could. It is the only condition of mind which would make either of us happy. I am one of those men who are always apt to resent and fly from an effort to restrain my liberty. My heart must share the freedom of my limbs, and that sort of exacting love, which suffers no exercise to my eyes, my thoughts, my actions, is, of all others, so tyrannous a bondage, that, to confess a truth to you, Florence, you became hateful to me when you began to exercise it."

"Ha! hateful!"

"It is true — too true. But do not understand me, Florence, as applying to you any such epithet, *now*. This resignation on your part to my will, places you in a very favorable position; and, if you keep in this mood, there can be no good reason, why we should not be to each other as before. Let it be understood that I am to do as I please, and feel as I please, and go where I please, without having that d——d hunchback at my heels, and without being compelled to hearken to the perpetual growlings of suspicion and complaint — and nobody could love you better than myself; and, if you will only promise me to yield to my wishes — to haunt me no more with your jealousy, and pursue me no more with irksome reproaches—"

"Be sure, Edward Saxon, I never will," said the unhappy woman, with solemnity. "Jealousy of you will never more fill the heart of Florence Marbois—reproaches will never reach your ears from her lips. I have seen the folly of such conduct."

"Why, Florence, this is wisdom. We shall do well after this; and you can bear now to behold me in the arms of Virginia."

"Virginia! is that her name?" asked Florence, with a continued effort at calmness, which, had the outlaw been studiously observant, would never have concealed the tremulous curiosity that fill the heart of the speaker.

"It is a sweet name, Florence, but not so sweet as herself. But you shall see her with your own eyes. You shall behold her charms, if you are willing and can keep down your jealousy — if you can still continue unmoved — if you will not hate her."

"Hate her! I hate *her?* Why should I hate *her*, Edward Saxon? In what has she wronged me? No! no! I will not hate her — I can not."

" Well, this is the right temper. By heavens, Florence, but you are wondrously changed for the better within a week. But will you love her, Florence? You should — she is so beautiful, so gentle, and will make you so excellent a companion."

" I can not promise that until I know —"

The speaker stopped abruptly.

" Know what, Florence?"

" Does she love you?"

The more obvious signification of · this question was grateful to the outlaw's vanity. He laughed aloud, as he replied —

" Ah, traitor! what would you have? Suppose I tell you, that she does not love me."

" You jest with me."

" Gad, I know not that, Florence. I don't know whether I can say with safety, that she does love me."

" How then came she here?"

" Hum! — I brought her; and, to tell you the truth, not altogether with her own consent. But I doubt if her opposition was earnest, Florence. Like most women — like yourself, Florence — she probably hides the real sentiment under the disguise of one which she does not truly feel. There was no small portion of this sort of trickery in yourself, Florence, when we first met — when we used to meet by the late — the little lake —"

" Remind me not, I pray you," said the outcast woman, with a sternness of accent that caused the outlaw to gaze at her in suspicious silence for several seconds. With a countenance only half assured, he proceeded : —

" Florence, I half suspect you now. I doubt you are only striving at composure. Your jealousies are returning, and the old reproaches will be renewed —"

" Never! Edward Saxon, never! Before heaven I swear that I can never reproach you again ; and as for jealousy —"

" Enough! I am too willing to believe you to insist upon too many assurances."

The outlaw did not see the contemptuous scorn upon the lips which concluded fitly the unspoken sentence.

" I can be happy with you, Florence — nay, I could have been happy and contented with you all along, but that your

unwise suspicions and goading jealousies drove me from your
side, and made me not only indifferent to your society but anxious to escape it.   Now that you have grown wiser, I trust that
no such necessity will again prevail to make either of us less
happy, than we should and may be.   With Virginia and yourself—"

"But, if she loves you not?" said Florence, coldly.

"I have not said it, Florence; nay—I am not willing to
say, and still less to believe it.   True, I brought her with less
willingness on her part than I could have desired to see; but
now that she is here—in my power—at my mercy—she will
see—her own common sense—"

"Edward Saxon! you surely mean no violence to the girl?"

"Why, Florence!" exclaimed the outlaw, as he read the
horror in her countenance, which was not wanting to the accents
of her voice.   "Do you think it so hard to persuade the maiden,
that I am as proper a man as she could find among a thousand?
She, I doubt not, will be as flexible as yourself, when the
season comes.   Nay, have I not told you already, that I look
upon her reluctance as nothing more than that disguise which
women naturally put on to hide their real sentiments.   She will
love me quite as well as another, when she has paid those due
sacrifices to false delicacy which form a part of the social religion of the sex.   You are all alike, Florence—all alike.
Virginia, like yourself, will go through the various stages of
passion—first, a pretty fear, that woos you to pursue while it
only affects to fly; then a yielding gust of tenderness, that is
all tears for a season—then a glow of greater delight—the
intoxication of new passion, which is all smiles and burning
blushes—then comes the deliberate devotion—then, the jealousy, Florence—the jealousy—which is as certain as the
upward progress of the sparks; and, until this stage is over, no
peace for either party.   Then, as in your case again, and as I
rejoice to behold it now, the quiet calm of love, which is resolved to take it on the easiest terms—to suppose it nothing
but what it should be, and believe, with the poet, in love, as in
the case of higher destinies, that 'whatever is, is right.'   You
can't conceive, my dear Florence, how much I am rejoiced by
the change in you."

"I'm very glad of it!" was the reply.

"We shall be as happy in the swamp as if the world was in our grasp. With Virginia on one hand, and you, Florence, on the other—satisfied as you both should be, that the heart of a man is capacious enough for both—I could pass my days, I think without any sentiment but that of contented enjoyment, and my nights with no other dreams than those of security and bliss. You have read, Florence—nay, you have heard and seen something of those gay rovers of the gulf—that were kings upon its billows, and, fierce in war—as fierce as its own storms —who were yet as peaceful as its hours of calm, when they surrendered themselves, upon the green palm-covered island, to the embraces of beauty—lying beneath the shade of the plantain and the fig, and, with lip to lip, and heart, melting as it were, into the dissolving sweetness of the mutual heart, they gave up life to the sweet delirium—the pleasant repose—the happy confidence of love. Shall we not have these joys again, Florence? No storms, no fear, no scolding, no caprices—nay, turn not away, my girl—forget that there have been words or looks of unkindness between us. Now, that you have come to a right understanding of what should be the condition of our ties, there can be no cause of discontent or strife hereafter. A kiss, a sweet embrace, dear Florence, in token that there is peace between us."

As these words were spoken, he drew nigh to the woman, whose face had been partially averted while he spoke. A tempest was in her heart the while, and a vexing commotion and a burning heat within her brain. Her hand trembled within her bosom, that trembled also with a degree of emotion which shook her whole frame. Meanwhile, the outlaw, utterly deceived by her deportment, and, perhaps, quite as much deceived by his own desires on the subject—pleased to find her so easily reconciled, and beholding her now, in this alteration of her mood, with something like the renewal of an ancient sentiment —intoxicated no less with the warm fancies which he had been breathing in her ears—approached her, and, passing his arm suddenly about her waist, drew her toward his bosom.

"Yes, dear Florence," he continued, "let this embrace renew the pleasures of the past, and this kiss be the token that all

ankindness is forgotten, and there is nothing now but peace
between us."

A shudder passed over her frame as she· felt his arm encircle
her—for a moment she seemed desirous to shrink from his
embrace; but, in another instant, turning as if to requite it,
she suddenly extricated one of her arms, which she threw behind her as she exclaimed:—

"Ay, Edward Saxon, peace it shall be, but it shall be the
peace of death. Take this!—this! Let this be the token of
my forgiveness. This for my wrong. This to the heart that
could not value the sole, the worshipping, devotion of such a
heart as mine."

She struck, as she spoke, with the little dagger which she
had concealed within her bosom. Twice, thrice, she struck,
and for a moment the outlaw spoke not—moved not. Astonishment seemed to possess and overcome his faculties. But
when she had given the third blow, he threw her from his arms
with a violence that sent her against the opposite wall; where
she stood, glaring upon him like a tigress, her eyes starting
from their orbs with an expression of mingled hate and horror.

But Saxon fell not—he seemed not even to be hurt. He
advanced to her without discomposure or irregularity of step,
yet every blow had been planted by the hand of the most
determined hostility upon his heart.

"Your arm is feebler than your soul, Florence Marbois, else
had your hateful purpose been accomplished. Woman, how
have you deceived me!"

She lifted the dagger again as he approached her, but, as it
met her eyes, she flung the worthless weapon from her hand
with a scream that denoted the disappointed fury in her bosom.
The steel, small and slender, having met with the resistance of
a button when she struck, had yielded and curled up at the
contact, without penetrating more deeply than his outer garment. He was utterly unharmed.

"Florence, you are mad," was the remark of Saxon. "This
attempt—"

"Ay, man, monster, villain—I am mad. But who has mad-
dened me—who has driven me to this? I am doubly mad
that I have failed in what I have sought to do. Feeble hand

—worthless steel! But why stand you looking on me, Edward
Saxon?—Will you not kill?—Here, I am ready—my heart
is open—my bosom is bared to .the blow. Strike, and strike
quickly—it is your only chance—for I have sworn, Edward
Saxon—sworn by heaven and by hell—by all powers that
may yield me power for revenge—that the world shall not
contain us both—that one of us must die. I am ready now,
Edward Saxon!—I would not live—I hate you too much to
breathe with you the same atmosphere of life. Strike! strike!
You would have given me peace just now—it is not too late!
I wish no other."

With a desperate hand she tore open the vest which covered
her bosom, and the white realm—still so full of beauty and
sweetness, if not of innocence and love—those heaving hills
on which his head had so often rested in other days—lay bare
before his sight. He turned from them without a word. The
picture reminded even his cold and careless bosom too warmly
of that past, in which his betrayal of her love had so amply justified her present hate.

"I leave you, Florence—I leave you and—forgive you."
He said no more as he parted from her presence, leaving her
where she stood—her hair dishevelled, her bosom bare, her
eyes wild like those of the maniac, but her ear too dull to hear
his last words—her thoughts anywhere but where they should
be, and her whole brain in the wildest commotion.

CHAPTER XXXVI

THE APE CONSOLES THE HEROINE — THE PRICE OF VENGEANCE

"How's this! Let me look better on't: a contract!
A contract sealed and ratified "— BEAUMONT AND FLETCHER.

No sooner had Saxon disappeared from the apartment, than it was entered by the emissary, Stillyards. This indefatigable urchin had maintained beneath the eaves his habitual practices, and his keen senses had suffered nothing to escape him of the scene which has been just described.

Florence beheld not his entrance. Her eyes were open, but, like those of Lady Macbeth, "their sense was shut." He coolly proceeded across the room, and took up the dagger. With a curious grin of equal scorn and merriment, he examined the worthless instrument which had so amusingly failed to serve the purposes of vengeance. While thus engaged, the returning consciousness of the woman apprized her of his presence. She rapidly crossed the intervening boards that separated them. She grasped his arm with one hand, while with the other, she repossessed herself of the ineffective, but handsome weapon. This she hurled from the window, with a laugh of bitterness that seemed a fitting and mocking commentary upon her own unperforming endeavor.

"Ha! ha! ha! So — you have seen it all, Richard? Weak hand, and worthless steel! Ha! ha! ha! did it make you laugh? No! and why not? He laughed? Did he not? Did you not see him laugh? He laughs now — now! Well! he may laugh! What a fool am I — I that am wronged and ruined — dishonored, scorned, abused, and deserted. What a fool am I to dream of justice — to think that there could be vengeance for the lone and feeble woman. To think that a weak arm like mine, should avenge my weaker heart."

And, as she uttered these wild and passionate words, she cast the arm which she reproached, heedless of the pain, with fearful violence down upon the jamb of the window, the blood spirting as she did so, from the ivory-white and soft flesh—a sight to make even the rude but devoted dwarf shudder, and to awaken in him a degree of sympathy which lifted his nature and turned all his better feelings into pity.

"'Twa'n't the arm—'twa'n't the arm, Ma'am Florence—'twas the knife only that wa'n't fit for nothing, with all its shine and silver about it. If it had been this now, ma'am," displaying his own heavy bowie blade, as he spoke—"there's no curl in this!—no mistake!"

"Give it me!" she cried—"this it shall be yet. This feels like vengeance, Richard—there is strength enough in my arm, and resolution still in my heart. I can not fail now—there is still something for which Florence Marbois may live."

She seized the weighty instrument as she spoke, turned it beneath her eye, grasped with one hand the massy blade, which she strove in vain to bend; then, as if satisfied that it was now only necessary to strike the blow, was about to hurry from the apartment, as if in pursuit of her victim; but the cooler dwarf threw himself between her and the door.

Significantly putting his fingers on his lips as if in token of silence—with an audacity which was unusual, and which, at any earlier day, would have found its immediate and unmeasured rebuke from the lips of the haughty woman—he gently grasped her wrist, and led her back into the darker part of the room out of sight and hearing from the window. Once there, he counselled her to the delay of a few moments, while he left the house, and stealthily examined all its approaches which might conceal a lurking spy. His own practices had necessarily made him properly suspicious of all others, and had endowed him with the skill to provide against all detection.

Finding that the coast was clear, and having ascertained that Saxon and Jones, whom he most apprehended, were gone to some distance in the encampment, he hastily returned to his mistress, after the lapse of a few moments. He found her as much excited as ever, and doubly impatient to proceed in consequence of the unwonted constraint which had been put upon her. The reasons for this restraint he proceeded to declare in his own rude language : —

"Why, Ma'am Florence, it's no use for you to go now—Saxon'll never let you try it again. You can't get nigh enough for a single dig at him ; and if you did, he'd be wide awake for you. He'd take the knife from you, 'fore you could say Jack Robinson, and laugh at you more than ever."

A glance of fire—a fierce stare—rewarded the speaker. There could be no enmity at that moment more decided, in the estimation of her anguished heart, than that which seemed to insist upon the impracticability of its hope of vengeance.

"What then? Am I to submit? To bear his scorn, his desertion? Is he to walk with booted footstep across my heart? Wherefore do you stop me? Speak, sir, I command you! Tell me other things than this, or be dumb for ever. I will not hear you—I will hear nothing that takes from me the last hope of my heart—which baffles and denies the only prayer which I am prepared to make in life."

The dwarf was not unwilling to comply. He had no purpose of baffling her vengeance. A bitter smile passed over his squalid cheeks. His mouth widened into a grin, and at another time the malignant fires which darted from his eye, might have awakened in the bosom of his fair companion, a feeling of shuddering disgust. Her own roused and embittered spirit, jaundiced by the passions which inflamed it, sufficed to blind her to the unconcealed malice of his. She saw not the gloating expression of his features—she heard only those accents which promised her the vengeance she desired. He showed her how vain would be her hope to succeed in any renewal of her late attempts, to avenge her wrong in person. He admitted, also, the great difficulty in the way of his succeeding. unless with circumstances greatly in his favor, of a conflict with a man so powerful of frame and so practised in his arms as Saxon; but there was another way, which, while it demanded greater delay, promised to be followed by better results.

"The reg'lators are out, and it's how to hide is the talk among the beagles. There's an old man, a preaching methodist, that's all bite, on t'other side of the 'Big Black,' at a place called Zion's Hill—he's been a mustering more than a week

now, and it's only because he don't know which way to set his
nose, that he ain't on trail after the beagles afore this. He's
got a son that barks with us, and we know from nim how the
cat jumps. Then there's a lad, one Wat Rawlins, that's been
a contriving again us too. Jones is more afraid of him than
t'other, 'cause he don't say much, and Badger always preaches
what he's guine to do; now, it's only to show this here chap,
Rawlins, how to find the track for Cane Castle, and let him
make a start on a sudden, and it's all mush with Saxon. There's
two dogs that barks between us and Rawlins, and it's only to
send 'em off sarching for John Cole's mare; then Rawlins can
bring his men into the swamp unbeknowing to all, and it's a
better knife than yours or mine, Ma'am Florence, that does the
business."

"I see! I see! and you will go to these men, Richard, you
will bring the avenger into the swamp—you will show them
where *he* sleeps—ha!"

To these eager demands and exclamations the answer of the
dwarf was slow. He had his reasons for deliberation—he had
his own bargain to make; and, with the policy of a more cun
ning tradesman, his reluctance to answer the requisitions of the
superior, grew in proportion to the eagerness of her demand
That she might be avenged amply by the means he suggested.
and by his means, he proceeded to reiterate. The particular
process was all shown—his own consent to do the office, which
could evidently be done by no one so well as himself, was the
only point upon which he hesitated to declare himself.

"I will reward you, Richard—you shall have all—every
thing—money, jewels—everything, I repeat—for why," she
added mournfully, as if to herself—"why should I keep aught?
I shall have little need for gold or jewels when that is done—
little need, and oh! how much less desire — speak, Richard,
tell me that I may rely on you for this last service. Be faithful
as you have been before, and take what you will — take all that
I have to bestow."

"You say it, Ma'am Florence—you'll promise me," demanded the dwarf with an eagerness equalling her own, while, in his
gloating eyes an expression of anxious desire, might have been

easily read by any observer less blinded than the woman to whom it was addressed.

"Have I not said? Surely I promise. Why should you doubt—why hesitate? Have I ever failed where I promised, Richard? Have you not ever had your reward from me? I repeat, you shall have, when you have done me this service—when you have brought the officers of justice into this den of thieves—when the chief villain of the band is a captive, and the hope from his heart, like that from my own, is gone for ever —you shall have all the wealth—the money and the jewels— which I have! Nothing shall be withheld of value that you may demand. You shall be my heir, Richard—you inherit all!"

"All in your power to bestow!" slowly spoke the dwarf, repeating a portion of her previous words. "'Twas that you said, Ma'am Florence."

"Yes—again I say it: you shall have all in my power to bestow."

"It's a promise, Ma'am Florence—good as Bible oath."

"As if I had sworn it!" solemnly replied the woman.

He caught her wrist eagerly in his hand, drew her toward him, and, rising on tip-toe, whispered in her ear. As the communication, whatever it was, reached her senses, she recoiled from his contact—shook herself free from his grasp, and, receding a step, regarded him with an expression of countenance in which contempt and scorn were mingled equally.

The eye of the abashed dwarf sank beneath the fire flashing glances of hers; his frame faltered, and an effort which, at the same moment, he made to speak, died away in confused and feeble accents, which were utterly unintelligible and almost unheard.

Meanwhile, various were the thoughts which coursed rapidly through the mind of Florence Marbois. Anger and vexation at first were predominant feelings—so strong in the first moment after his communication had been heard, as almost to obliterate, during the same brief space, all memory of the vengeance which she had sworn against her seducer. But very soon these feelings passed away.

"I must be proud no more," were the words which at length

broke from her lips. "I mock myself with these shadows, Richard," she said, advancing as she spoke, and extending her hand, "it shall be as you say. All that is left me to bestow, shall be yours, when you have accomplished my vengeance."

He grasped the extended hand, and carrying it to his lips, covered it with such caresses as a she-bear might have lavished upon her last cub in licking it into shape. Florence Marbois had sunk wofully in her own estimation. Her pride was gone, and she had nothing to live for; but she withdrew the hand that suffered from the slaver of the deformed, with a strong expression of disgust.

"Enough, Richard. And now to the prosecution of these plans."

It will not need that we follow the dialogue in all its details. It is sufficient for us to say, that Stillyards, being familiar, by reason of his espionage, with all the circumstances of the chief robbers in the swamp, and with all those more prominent sources of danger which they feared, was better prepared, than Saxon or Jones could have believed, to devise an effectual plan for their capture. It was not long before he was despatched by his mistress from her presence.

There were now reasons added to old ones, why she should desire to send him forth as speedily as possible. He was not simply a means of vengeance—he had become a creditor; and the miserable debtor, who, though ruined, had still in her soul some glimpses of the better nature from which she had fallen, began to shudder at the humiliating moral bondage which such a condition always seems to imply. The instrument of her necessity was an object of her disgust. Hitherto, she had been able to reward him with money; now, he felt the large increase of his power, and his demands had grown in proportion. He was become ambitious—money no longer answered his desires; and he, who by reason of his low birth, vulgar life, and deformed person, had never been able to attach the affections of another, now aimed to secure the highest and finest and sweetest of all human affections, as the reward of his ministry.

"And wherefore should I scruple at this?" was the demand which Florence Marbois made of herself, as if in self-justification when she was left alone. "It is at best a word—a pledge

b

which is dissolved in the very hour which brings Edward˙ Saxon
to his doom. She is a fool, a worse than idiot, who survives
life's purposes — and I have but one purpose in life. That satisfied, and I may well assure this vain and miserable game-make
that all shall then be his which is in the power of Florence
Marbois to bestow."

CHAPTER XXXVII

NEW READINGS IN OLD PLAYS — CATASTROPHE OF HAMLET NOT IN ANY FORMER EDITION.

"Good sir, softly : you ha' done me a charitable office."— *Winter's Tale.*

LET us now return to our Thespian in the swamp. We left
him, with Jones, skimming along in a little dug-out over the
turbid waters of the Chitta-Loosa. Jones delighted in fishing,
and found sufficient employment in pursuing this occupation.
Horsey seemed content to be a spectator; but the wily outlaw
very well knew that his content would be of no very long duration, unless the food on which he better fed than anything
besides — the oily applause of the audience — was brought in,
to quiet an appetite that no measure of success could satiate.
Accordingly, he suffered not his own vocation so far to occupy
his attention, as to make him regardless of his companion's
temper.

From the moment when he cast forth his lines, he began to
ply the actor with stage reminiscences, and to challenge his
opinions upon all stage matters. These requisitions were all-
important to the perfection of the proposed establishment at
Benton. Finding deception easy on all kindred subjects, Jones
enlarged his fictions. He suggested a grand scheme of theatrical organization, which was to extend itself over the whole
country, from West Tennessee down to the bay of Biloxi. A
company was to be planned, with corporate powers, in several
of the southwestern states, which was to build theatres in all
eligible places, and divide the year in separate seasons of three

mouths in each of them. The management was to. be conferred on Horsey. Never did the innocent flats of our backwoods suffer the delusion of a mammoth bank, or a mammoth railroad, to take such complete hold of their credulous imaginations. Like the schemes of these great companies, generally, the wily outlaw made it appear, that the plan was not only to be pleasant and profitable, but excessively patriotic.

"At least," said this experienced stockdealer, "at least, my dear Horsey, we shall make, as salaried officers, though the stockholders lose. The profits, if enough to pay us, are enough for the patriotism of the thing."

"But it must be profitable to all parties," said Horsey, whose morality was somewhat less discursive than that of his companion.

"Ay, ay — to be sure it must. The country will be a great gainer in money and morals, and — "

"Certainly, such a diffusion of Shakspere alone, must have that effect."

"It will. That alone should be a sufficient consideration to induce the state to subscribe largely ; and I have no doubt that she will, when her legislators are made to perceive the patriotism of the thing. Then, if we can get a charter for a banking-house with a capital of ten millions, our triumph is complete We can establish houses everywhere — raise companies — issue moneys — do anything. Our labors being for the public good, we can appropriate lands and tenements, I am of opinion, without ever paying for them."

"Impossible!" exclaimed Horsey, who had evidently less legal learning than his companion.

"And why impossible? Ours is a public work. Our charter, it is true, declares it to be private ; but it is admitted that our labors are likely to be productive of public good, and would it not be monstrous if a single citizen, here and there, should resist a measure that is for the good of the whole."

"True, there is something in that," said Horsey ; "but is it so clear that we can take private property at pleasure for the public good ?"

"Certainly — the majority declares what is for the public good, and makes the law accordingly."

"But—the constitution—what does the constitution stand for then—of what use?"

"Nay, I don't know that. For my part I never did see the use of a constitution at all; and it is clear to me, that it could be of no sort of effect against our company, if we can only get a charter for it. That we can do, if we only pay two or three lawyers handsomely, and secure a few of the most famous orators at a fine salary. They'll gull the flats by fine speeches which shall prove to them that they're the most noble, patriotic folks under the sun; and we'll pick their teeth, while their jaws are on the stretch, listening to these fine sayings. Two to one on it, Horsey, that in a year's time, the state will lend us a million to begin with, and take stock in the great Mississippi Shaksperean and Thespian company, to three times that amount."

"I'm not so sanguine, Jones," said the other, "but I'm sure if it would do so, the stock would be a cursed sight better than that of half of these banks and railroads. As for the banks, it's clear, they've swamped all the planters; and as for the railroads, I reckon we shall have to leave them in the swamps, where they'll stick for ever. Your plan, I'm afraid, is almost too grand a one. Something on a smaller scale now, would be more likely to be successful.

"Lord love you, Horsey, my dear fellow, you know nothing about our people when you talk so. It's nothing but grand schemes that go down with them. They can only understand the incomprehensible—they can only admire what is beyond their calibre. Tell them of small schemes which are possible and practicable, and which might yield them moderate profits and be of some service, and they will turn up their noses in disgust. They despise little projects. But get up a grand Religious Steam Association; or a company for connecting Pensacola with San Jacinto by means of chain or floating bridges; or a line of Balloon Stages to the North Star, or a Patent Process for Converting Bad Planters into Great Merchants—propose some such moderate matters to them as these, and they'll take stock directly. They've lately formed a society in New England for keeping the peace among the potentates in Europe, and there's not an old woman in all the villages that don't subscribe a shilling weekly to prevent Louis Philippe from kicking the emperor of Austria, and arrest the czar in his indecorous attempts to void his quid in the face of Sultan Mahmoud. That's a society now that's likely to be profitable."

The outlaw was about to pass, by a very natural transition, trom the consideration of these grand and patriotic modes for picking the pockets of the people, to a short analysis of the half-exploded and vulgar methods of doing the same thing as practised in ancient times. He was prepared to show that the old highway custom of bidding a true man "stand and deliver," was altogether, and happily, abrogated by such small legal processes as are more comprehensively described under the general designation of charters. It would have been very easy, indeed, for one so well versed in the inquiry as himself, to show — what the reader is already prepared to believe — that the "Border Beagles" were, indeed, "chartered libertines" of the same class; yet, as they did not transact business on a scale so magnificent, and as they were rather less ostentatious in their operations, they could not so openly challenge the admiration of mankind.

It caused the worthy outlaw, indeed, a sigh, when he reflected that all that was necessary to enable the company under whose authority he performed his operations, to become shrined in the admiration and estimation of the people from the Tar river to the Colorado, was a simple instrument under the hands of a state legislature, which a fine orator could readily procure, and a docile representation would delight to grant. A change of name might, indeed, be necessary, and, perhaps, a declaration of objects slightly differing from that which were in reality entertained. A people, it seems, who are fitted for self-government, must yet have its expenses concealed from their sight, and its penalties disguised under the name of pleasures. "Border Beagles" was a good name — easily articulated — but to get a charter for far more increased operations, it might be necessary to change it into something of a more imposing, and less vague signification — "The Great Southwestern Transportation and Specie Deposite Company," would be a longer and more specific title — long and loose enough to obtain charters from any six states in the Union

Jones was full to overflowing with these ideas and their trib

ntaries; but Horsey was something less of a moralist and politician than the outlaw; and his undisguised yawns soon apprized his companion of the necessity of returning to the ground
from which they had episodically departed. Even the establishment of great houses for stage-playing, were as nothing to
the play itself, in the imagination of the actor; and when his
attention flagged in considering the former it revived with
double force and interest when the latter topic was resumed.

Jones professed himself tired of law and morality, and begged
that Horsey would restore the tone of his mind by a specimen.
One specimen begat two, two begat three; specimens produced
varieties of readings in favorite passages; and in twenty minutes, with a patient and applauding auditor, Hamlet was "himself again." Never had he read so well before — never had his
action been so flexible and felicitous.

"Cautiously, my dear fellow," said Jones, with a warning
voice — "cautiously, and trim the boat — she dips already, and
it won't take much to cover her bends."

" Yes, yes!" impatiently replied the actor, " I see — I'll take
care;" and then he returned to his theme, which had been the
discussion of one of the readings of a favorite actor.

"Now you see, Mr. Jones, in the reading of that passage,
Forrest is clearly wrong: —

> "'Hang out our banners!'

he says with an exclamatory pause; then adds,

> "'On the outward walls,
> The cry is still they come.'——

Now, why should he depart from the old style of reading, which
is thus: —

> "' Hang out our banners on the outward walls;
> The cry is still they come!'

Why should we suppose that the coming of the enemy is only
announced on the outward walls? The cry is everywhere —
the whole castle hears it. Macbeth himself announces it, he
being *within the castle* at the time. In this reading the passage
is without sense. The truth is, that the intelligence having
reached Macbeth that the enemy is still coming — a fact, which
his previous confidence in the weird sisters has led him to doubt

—he gives those orders which would be given even now by every commander : ' It is time to hang out our defiance — they have come near enough to see it. It will show them that we are prepared for them — it will show our own people that we do not fear the foe.' It was not customary to hang out the banners except on occasions of state and danger. In old times, banners were more costly things than they are now. They were covered with gold and blazonry of a very rich and perishable character. Even now, they are never hung out except in cases of ceremony, or in the expectation of actual conflict They are kept carefully within the castle till the approach of the foe, and then, with the soldiers, advanced to the walls. The same scene in which this passage occurs, describes, as stage directions, the entry of Macbeth, with drums and colors, *within the castle*, followed by Seyton and 'the soldiers. They were then about to go forth to the defence of the walls, the sentinels on the watch having warned them that the time for actual conflict was now at hand, and the hanging the banner on the outward wall, was the only mode by which the proper defiance of the defenders was to be displayed.''

" Clearly you are right," said Jones, whose turn it was now to yawn.

" Now for that famous and much-disputed passage—

" 'She should have died hereafter.' "

" Mind the boat," remonstrated Jones, who felt his little cockleshell becoming momently more and more capricious under the increasing earnestness of the actor.

" Ay, ay !" said the other, reciting—

" ' She should have died hereafter ;—
There would have been a time for such a word,
To-morrow, and to-morrow, and to-morrow——' "

" By Jupiter ! Horsey, we shall be over if you don't be very careful."

" No fear — no fear !" said the actor impatiently, as he hurried with the passage—

" 'And to-morrow, and to-morrow,
Creeps in this petty pace, from day to day,
To the last syllable of recorded time ;——' "

Jones, at this recorded time, was constrained to give all his attention to the trim of his boat.

"'And all our yesterdays,'"

Proceeded the actor with the solemn sententiousness, and gloomy moral reflection of the tyrant at this period, when the last evils of life were accumulating about him, making him "sick at heart." He, Horsey, was as thoroughly blind to the wrigglings of the outlaw, as the outlaw was now become indifferent to the readings of the actor.

"By G—d!" muttered the former, we shall have a capsize.

"'And all our yesterdays have lighted fools
The way to dusky death. Out, out, brief candle!'"

Here the action of Horsey verified the apprehensions of the outlaw. "That putting out of the candle did the business," said Jones, afterward.

"Life's but a——Phew!" The water rushing into Horsey's ears, nose, and mouth at this moment, put an effectual extinguisher upon the sad, moral reflection of Macbeth, and ended the new reading of the much-disputed passage. The boat went over in spite of all the outlaw's efforts to maintain her equilibrium, and Macbeth ended his speech by a puffing, plunging, and blowing, which might have done honor to the wind-bags of a porpoise.

"Phew! Jones—what the devil's the matter?" was his cry, as he rushed to the top of the muddy river.

"'Out, out, brief candle!'" exclaimed Jones, struggling to the banks. "I warned you, Mr. Horsey—I warned you several times."

"Warned me! How warned me?—warned me of what?"

"Of tilting the boat."

"The devil you did—I never heard you."

"'Life's but a walking shadow,'" said Jones, repeating a fragment of the passage; "but, however shadowy, you'll find it difficult to walk where you are. While you have life for it, Mr. Horsey, you must strike out—the water's at least twenty feet over your head."

"So I find," replied the actor, striking for the shore. With some difficulty he scrambled up the oozy elevations, borrowing from the liberal banks as he went, a portion of their capital at every step.

"Good G-d, Jones—my Hamlet!" exclaimed the unfortunate histrion, surveying the ruined garment, which had swallowed up so many goodly bales of his father's cotton. "My Hamlet—a splendid black silk velvet jacket, fly-trunks, and mantle—magnificently bugled—cost me, at Stubb's, three hundred and sixty dollars—and now utterly ruined. D—n the boat—that I should have trusted myself in such a trap as that!"

"Don't be angry, my dear fellow," said Jones, with a grin which conveyed very equivocal consolation. "Once under way, and you will soon be able to replace it, I trust. That scheme of ours—the Grand Mississippi Shaksperean and Thespian Company—"

"Look you, Mr. Jones, don't talk to me of schemes. Let's go back where I can get my bags. I must change. I feel like a drowned rat. I'm as slimy as an eel. It'll take me a week's washing to get this d——d ooze out of my hair."

"No, no! not half so long," said the other, "I was once much longer in the mud, and got clean in three days."

This was said with great gravity. Horsey looked suspiciously upon the speaker, and for the first time, a latent notion seemed to waken in his mind that he had been quizzed a little; but, just at this moment, his eyes were attracted to the opposite banks.

"'Gad, Jones, I must hide—there are women yonder. Who are they?"

The actor stole behind some stunted bushes, from which he peeped out upon the distant cavalcade.

"That's Brown Bess—Bess Yarbers, as I live—and that's my Juliet—my pretty Mary Clayton!—Eh! Jones, am I not right? What the devil do they want here?"

"Hush! Come to join our company, I suspect," replied Jones, with some anxiety in his voice.

"'Gad, I'm glad of it," exclaimed the actor, with a delight which made him quite forget the hurts of his Hamlet. "That Mary will make the loveliest Juliet, the sweetest Ophelia, the dearest Desdemona that ever was smothered when she should have been kissed. I told Bess to make an actress of her- 1 knew what she could do. It's a great acquisition, Jones. I'll go and meet 'em."

" What! in that trim ?"

" Ah, d—n the boat !" was the bitter exclamation of the enthusiastic Actor, as, sinking back into his place of conceal- ment, he suffered the new-comers to pass from sight, and impa- tiently waited the moment when Jones might deem it proper to permit of their return to the encampment.

The latter busied himself in recovering the boat, which had drifted a mile below, and was only kept from the embraces of the Mississippi by the branches of a fallen tree, among which it got entangled. By dint of swimming and wading, the out- law recovered it, and Horsey was with difficulty persuaded to resume his seat in a fabric, in which he could use no action, and accordingly could not speak. To deny him to suit the action to the word, was to make him dumb ; and equally soaked, silent, and sad, the luckless actor suffered himself to be paddled back to the place whence he set forth, only consoled under his mis- fortune by the reflection that he should soon see the lovely little damsel in whose sight, it may be said in this place, he had found quite as much, or even more favor, than she had found in his.

CHAPTER XXXVIII.

JUSTICE IN THE SWAMP — TALL SWEARING — MOLE PRACTICE

"This subtle world, this world
Of plots and close conspiracy."—SHIRLEY

BUT Horsey soon found it was no such easy matter to behold this damsel. The course of true love was not permitted to run smooth in his case, any more than in that of Romeo. It was not the policy of Jones to suffer the actor to come in contact with the Yarbers family. He knew the intimacy which already existed between him and Brown Bess; and, as the reader may have seen, the adherence of John Yarbers to the brotherhood, did not imply any attachment of his wife in the same quarter. Awkward revelations, for which the fraternity were not yet prepared, might have resulted from a meeting of that dame with Horsey; and Jones made his arrangements accordingly to prevent it.

But Jones could not be everywhere, however ubiquitous may have been his desires; and Brown Bess, by some means, found out that Horsey was at Cane Castle. She probably had caught a glimpse of him as he emerged from his oozy bath, in the waters of the Chitta-Loosa; or, as is equally probable, John Yarbers was partially in the habit of serving two masters. He may have shared some of the secrets of the beagles, with his larger, if not his better half. How she arrived at her knowledge, however, is very unimportant to our narrative. It is enough, that, once possessed of this knowledge, all the strategics of feminine policy were put in exercise to defeat the uncharitable designs of Jones.

It was not a mere female curiosity which Bess sought to gratify in once more desiring to see the actor. Far from it. Other and more serious desires filled her mind · and the evi-

dent admiration — however strangely shown — with which
Horsey regarded her daughter, had inspired her with the hope
of connecting Mary Clayton with better fortunes, and less
doubtful family connections, than those to which she had unhappily — and to do her justice — unwittingly bound herself.

Horsey was a wild chap — that she knew; but his heart was
in the right place, and he was the son of one of the most substantial of the small planters in Mississippi. Old John Horsey
had what he possessed of property free from debt, and was,
therefore, more independent than most of his class. As he
owed nothing, he had no favors to ask of the Brandon bank,
and could keep back his cotton till a favorable market. Alas!
for Mississippi — nay, for half the southwest — that his policy
had not been more general among the agriculturists of that region. The debtor is everywhere at the mercy of his creditors,
and we are all debtors.

But a truce to this; and, to sum up in brief, Brown Bess contrived to find a way to the actor. There was a moment when
the outlaw, to whom Cane Castle was given in charge, during
the absence of the master-beagle of the band, was necessarily
withdrawn; and, seizing upon this moment, the persevering
dame sought Horsey with success. At this interview, the poor
actor was utterly overwhelmed by the tidings which he heard.
At first, indignation seized upon him to think how he had been
imposed upon and laughed at; and he was for seeking the outlaw, and punishing him in the midst of the encampment. But
the cooler woman checked these ebullitions of mortified vanity
and impatience. She showed him the danger of this proceeding, and counselled him to a policy as deep and quiet as that of
the beagles. Under her direction, arrangements were made for
his escape; and, wisely leaving all these to her, our actor, now
considerably sobered on the subject of his grand steam company
of theatricals, in which the state was expected to subscribe so
largely, was content to play second fiddle for awhile in this
political duet.

Perhaps, he was the more readily reconciled to this inferior
position by the presence of a third person, who had been judiciously provided to appear at the nick of time by the calculating
Mrs. Yarbers. This was Mary Clayton. After her appearance,

the mother might have made what arrangements she pleased. That nothing should be wanting to her schemes, she made away with herself after awhile, leaving the two children together — the babes in the wood — Horsey being as much a dreaming boy and as full of heart and enthusiasm, as if he never had known any of the world's experience; and Mary — poor Mary — as simple of soul and innocent of mind, as the adhesive, dependent, and docile daughter of Polonius herself.

It was strange with what rapidity the moments flew, when these two were left together. There — in that deep and quiet wood — thickly shaded by the intricate forests, that had never echoed to the dull cleaving blow of the destroying axe — on the edge of that dark, mysterious water, and with no sounds in their ears, but those which seemed to invite them to mutual sensibilities — sounds of birds and insects that hummed beside and above them, without any regular song, and with efforts that seemed to imply wakefulness and not work — life, rather than exertion — the hearts of the twain, in which the fire had been fanned, if not kindled into flame, before, now warmed with a mutual ardor, and gushed freely with the sweet waters of a mutual affection.

" It will do," was the whisper of the mother of the girl, as through the leaves of a copse on one hand, where she had concealed herself, she saw the ardent amateur impress — having not the fear of Ned Mabry in his eyes — his second kiss upon the lips of the trembling and very much frightened damsel; and heard his pledges of love and his promises of marriage. Then the old dame contrived to reappear and separate the parties.

The very day on which Saxon bore away Virginia Wilson to the recesses of Cane Castle, our amorous actor might have been seen on old "dot-and-go-one," his father's steed, with Mary Clayton perched behind him, going as fast as his passions could drive, and his decrepit steed would permit, in the hope of finding a convenient magistrate willing to officiate for love in a hurry, after the fashion of the Gretna blacksmith.

The policy of Dame Bess might be supposed rather censurable by the very staid and starched prudes of a metropolitan city; but let them not bite their thumbs too inveterately. The

. old lady was desirous of getting her lovely daughter out of the swamp, and freeing her from that miserable connection with a clan of robbers, from which, under existing circumstances, she could not free herself. She was anxious to marry her to a man of family and substance, and she knew that she could trust the honor of Horsey, to transact the business of Hymen, according to the state laws on that subject made and provided. She could have wished, it is true, that the affair might have been conducted with more deliberation, and under her own eyes; but as this could not be the case, she was too wise a woman to suffer such matters to stand in the way of primary objects; and, counselling the couple how to keep the narrow road on the swamp, which would lead them, by a short ten miles, to Squire Nawls', she sent them off, with a God-speed, to be happy after a fashion that, however constantly practised for six thousand years, has not yet fallen into disuse.

One incident, which occurred before the departure of Horsey from Cane Castle, should not be unnoted. While yet utterly undreaming of the revelations subsequently made by Brown Bess, and while still perfectly persuaded that he was member only of a brotherhood of Thespians, who, if ignorant, were yet innocent, the enthusiastic amateur found an opportunity of making his way to the presence of Florence Marbois. Regarding her as the prima donna, the great gun, the tragic muse of the company, he could not refrain—though counselled to beware of the weapon of her husband, whom Jones described as, "worse than a Turk for jealousy"—from contriving an interview with one from whose great powers he promised himself no small support in the personation of his loftier characters. The play at cross-purposes between them which followed this interview was as mysterious to both, as it would have been ludicrous to a spectator at all aware of their true history. Horsey addressed her as Lady Macbeth, or Portia, or Constance, and she replied to him in such language as would have suited well the auditories of a conscious knave. The poor actor was utterly confounded, and did not feel at all satisfied with, however much, as an amateur, he might admire, the lofty scorn which looked out from her eyes, and the contemptuous language which rose upon her lips, in reply to all his high-flown speeches. She sooner comprehended his true position than he hers. Perhaps she had some inkling of the truth before.

" You are mistaken, sir, in me, if not in yourself. You have been imposed upon, and are in a den of thieves, from which you had best escape as soon as possible. Leave me, sir."

" But, my dear Mrs. Clifford," was the objurgatory opening of the bewildered actor.

" Clifford! Begone, sir—you are mad. I tell you, you are among knaves and thieves. You are gulled, imposed upon. Go home to your parents." ·

> " 'Was ever woman in such humor wooed !' "

was the slowly-spoken sentence of Horsey, as the haughty Florence, after this scornful counsel, withdrew from his presence.

Two hours after this interview, he was made to comprehend its true meaning and the manner in which he had been played upon, by the more painstaking and common-sense personage whom he was about to select as a mother-in-law. It might not have been so easy for her to subdue the wrath which her revelations excited in his mind, had it not been for her lovely daughter; and that movement of the maternal tactician which left the two children to their own cogitations. The result of these cogitations we have seen, in the departure of the happy pair, riding double on "dot-and-go-one," in search of the country squire.

But one thing qualified the otherwise unmixed joy of the actor in this novel situation. It was the necessity of leaving his saddle-bags behind him, with the best of his theatrical wardrobe. This necessity occasioned some serious fears, but the better baggage which filled its place, soon reconciled him to, if it did not make him absolutely forgetful of, his loss.

Let us now return to Harry Vernon, whom we left, attended by the faithful Jamison and the two constables, on his way to Mr. Justice Nawls, to undergo his examination for the murder of Thomas Horsey, Esquire.

The justice was a plain farmer-looking person, very ignorant of books and refinement, but with some knowledge of men and things, which, on the borders of every country, is by far the better sort of knowledge. He came out of his fields, and in the

same condition in which he used his hoe, he sat down to make
his examination. He was in his shirt-sleeves, which were rolled
up to the elbow ; his bosom was bare, and none of the cleanest ;
and the perspiration, discolored by the dust through which he
had been, stood in dark dots upon his cheeks and forehead.

What a lecture on American jurisprudence would have been
written by that profound spinster, Harriet Martineau, or that
profound sea-attorney, Captain Basil Hall, or that social mar-
tinet, Colonel Hamilton, could they have been present at this
examination. Justice Nawls had no need of books, or statutes,
or authorities, and still less occasion did he seem to have for
tablets and a clerk. The proceedings were summary enough.
There were two sly fellows who swore to several suspicious
circumstances against our hero. It was proved that Horsey
and Vernon were seen together last—that the time of their
separation was unknown—and that, a short time after, poor
Horsey was found in the woods bored through with bullets,
dirked in sundry places, his ribs literally riddled and laid bare
—and his bloody coat and breeches were finally produced in
damning confirmation of this tragedy.

Such was the testimony of Augustus Mortimer and Edward
Montmorenci. The *alias* of a rogue is usually a very ear-
taking concatenation of syllables ; and, *par parenthese*, what an
adroit rascal is Davy Hines, the *celebrated* South Carolina
swindler (all rascals are celebrated in North America, while
great statesmen, orators, poets, and actors, are simply notorious),
in the selection of his temporary *nom de guerre*. He is for the
nonce, an Allston, a Hamilton, a Rutledge, a Berkely, a Single-
ton, or a Livingston. Sometimes he condescends to be a
Hayne, or a Benton, and he has even been known, on trending
farther east, to contract himself into a Webster or an Adams.

Colonel Augustus Mortimer swore with singular precision
and confidence, and Major Marcus Montmorenci followed him.
Vernon examined these two worthies with the utmost care and
vigilance, but they were as impenetrable as they had shown
themselves incorrigible. They just swore to enough to place
the offence at his door, without committing themselves by the
positive asseveration that they had seen him do it. They were
old practitioners, in one form or other, in half the courts of

Mississippi and knew all the quirks of justice, however little they might have really cared about its principles.

Poor Vernon was in a quandary. He saw that Squire Nawls could do no less than commit him, on the strength of the testimony offered ; and though this testimony fell short of convicting him of the offence, he yet could not but feel that the refined rascals whose deposition had been just taken, had wrought him some very troublesome meshes, from which it would not be so easy to extricate himself upon trial. Still the awkwardness, if not the danger, of his own situation troubled him less than his particular arrest at such a moment. There was the affair of Carter, his friend, which he was anxious to bring to a conclusion which might save him as well as the miserable father of the very lovely Virginia. And she—just won, and so soon lost. Ah! reader, if you have a heart at all, and have not forgotten all the love-passages of your boyhood's days, think of the thousand privations involved in that separation.

If Vernon was annoyed, poor Jamison, his Alabama friend, was utterly confounded at the aspect of his affairs. Unwilling to believe the youth guilty, for whom he had taken a liking as extreme as sudden, he was yet staggered by the closeness of the testimony against him — the nice linking together of the circumstances as declared by the joint evidence of Messrs. Mortimer and Mortmorenci, and the grave, deliberate, and very genteel appearance of those worthy witnesses. It was in vain that he added to the cross-examination of Vernon, as many questions as, in his sagacity, he thought might be instrumental in bringing out a difference in their statements. His efforts were more perplexing to himself than to the witnesses, and with a groan that came from the bottom of his heart, and was almost a growl, he gave up all further attempts at examination. So, also, did Vernon himself, and Justice Nawls proceeded to write out and sign the commitment of the prisoner, for further and final trial —a manual performance, not so easy to one whose skill in penmanship was of that "d——d cramp" sort, which bothered Tony Lumpkin.

The deed was done, however, and the constables were just beginning to bustle about for the resumption of their charge, in conveying Vernon to prison, when a hubbub was heard without.

and the accents of a voice which, to the ear of our hero, seemed
no less sweet than familiar.

"Now is the winter of our discontent made glorious summer,"
cried one from without.

"By heavens!" exclaimed Harry Vernon, "that is Mr. Horsey himself."

"So it is, Harry, my boy," cried the actor, rushing in and
bearing on his arm the shrinking form of the half-affrighted
Mary Clayton, whose cheeks, glowing with the deepest tints of
the carnation, betrayed the mingled effects of a ten-mile ride
with her lover, and the not unpleasant novelty which she felt to
exist in such a situation.

"Who else but Horsey," exclaimed the delighted actor—
"who but the young Lochinvar," and he concluded by singing
a stanza from the popular song of that name, by which he
communicated the tenor of his love-adventure, and the reason
of his appearance with his fair companion.

"They'll have fleet steeds that follow, Harry, my boy," he
continued, "though, truth to speak, had they started as soon on
the chase of old Bowline, as they did after Lochinvar, Tom
Horsey would have won no bride to-day. You recollect my
little Juliet, Harry?—Mary Clayton? Come forward, Mary—
don't be shy—don't be scary—it's Mr. Vernon, that came with
me to your house—Mr. Harry Vernon; and there's the squire
that's to make us man and wife—and these gentlemen, why I
take it, they're all friends to a frolic and a good fellow, when
he's about to go off, like a comedy, in a happy ending."

"Mr. Horsey, I was never more rejoiced to see any one in
my life, than I am to see you," said Vernon. "You've come
at the most providential moment for my safety."

"Your safety!"

"Yes—I am here before the magistrate-charged with mur-
dering you."

"The devil you say!"

"However strange, it is no less than truth. Squire Nawls,
let me introduce to you my friend, Mr. Thomas Horsey, of
Raymond, the gentleman with whom I travelled, and whom I
stand suspected of having killed. You see that as he is alive
I can not have murdered him."

Squire Nawls looked bewildered, and turned inquisitively to Messrs Mortimer and Montmorenci. An incredulous and sarcastic smile sat upon the countenance of the first named of these gentlemen. A brief pause followed.

"You see, gentlemen," continued Vernon, turning to them also, "that the body which you found and buried was that of some other person, and the clothes which you have shown—"

"Were those of Mr. Thomas Horsey, and no other," said Mr Augustus Mortimer, with the utmost coolness, and a quiet, imperturbable composure, that absolutely shocked the Alabamian, whom the promise of a change in the color of Vernon's fortunes had provoked to a shouting, cheering, and dancing, which, for several moments, utterly banished silence and stateliness from the hall of justice.

"That is not Mr. Thomas Horsey," continued Mr. Mortimer; "we buried the poor young gentleman with our own hands. Did we not, major?"

Major Montmorenci confirmed this statement, by a conclusive nod to Justice Nawls.

"The devil you did!" exclaimed Horsey, utterly aghast with the reckless hardihood with which the lie was spoken.

"Yes, poor fellow! he lies in the wood, a little way beyond the lower fork that leads to the two ferries."

"The devil he does!" continued the actor, with increasing astonishment, as he listened to the manner in which his body was disposed of.

"Yes, we can show you the grave at any moment. We cut his name, T. H., with the year, in the bark of a beech that stands over the spot."

"You were very good," said Horsey.

"No, no, not at all; it was only common charity!"

"Pray, my good fellow," said Horsey, dropping the arm of Mary Clayton, and crossing over to where Mr. Augustus Mortimer stood, on the left hand of Justice Nawls, and looking him in the face with as much curiosity as astonishment—"pray, my good fellow, who may you be—what may be your name? I am, in truth, very anxious to know."

"Augustus Mortimer, Esq.," was the calm reply, "son of the

Hon. Bannister Mortimer, judge of the United States district-court, in West Tennessee."

"You are, are you?—and you, sir"—-to the other witness —"pray, oblige me with your name and connections?"

The answer was equally prompt and civil.

"Major Marcus Montmorenci, last from Virginia, a late settler in the Choctaw purchase."

"And you are sure, gentlemen, that you buried Thomas Horsey, of Raymond, under a beech-tree on the lower road to the ferry, and it was over his body that you were good enough to mark T. H., with the year—perhaps you put a death's-head and cross-bones above the inscription?"

"No, sir, we put nothing but the initials, and the year; and we did not cut them as well or deeply as we could have wished, owing to the dullness of our knives," said Mr. Mortimer.

"And you are sure that it is my body—that is, the body of Tom Horsey—that you so charitably put from sight in that place?"

"Very certain."

"How do you know that?"

"Oh, my dear sir, these questions are very unnecessary and your manner is somewhat offensive. When I tell you, that my poor friend, Tom Horsey, was seldom out of my sight and company for a spell of four years at least, that we lived together, travelled together, and slept together at different and long periods, you certainly can't doubt that I ought to know him."

"And you, sir, have been equally intimate?"

"Equally," said the more sententious Montmorenci.

It would be difficult to describe the expression of Horsey's face, as he hearkened to these cool asseverations, and marked the stolid composure of the two.

"Really, gentlemen, you must excuse me, if I ask a few more questions. The Horsey, who is dead, and whom you buried —did he look anything like me? There is some mistake— some deception in this, Squire Justice—which I must find out."

"Nothing," said Mortimer.

"Nothing," said Montmorenci.

"And yet," said the former; looking at Montmorenci, with a

grave inquisitiveness, "don't you think there is something in this gentleman's chin that looks like poor Tom's?"

"Why, yes—there is a something—a—

"A sort of split—a—"

"There's no split in my chin, gentlemen," exclaimed Horsey, stroking the misrepresented member—"it's as smooth and round as any chin in company."

"Oh, sir, we don't mean to say that they're alike—but there was a something—"

"Yes, only a something—that is, they were both chins," said Horsey; "for that matter, don't you think that we had other features in common? How about eyes, nose, head, and hair?—pray, gentlemen, oblige me, by answering closely. The question is important, I assure you."

"Well, now, sir, to speak plainly, you are nothing like our poor friend, Tom Horsey. Tom, though an excellent fellow as ever lived, was monstrous ugly; now, if I were asked my opinion, I should say you are a very good-looking sort of person."

"Indeed! I thank you—so Tom Horsey was ugly, was he? Squire Nawls, do me the favor to marry me with Mary here, at once, and while I have some remaining confidence in my own identity. If I talk much longer with these rascals, I shall begin to look upon Tom Horsey as a dead man. I suppose, if she takes me as Tom Horsey, you can have no objection to give me that name till the ceremony's over; and, after that, it's just what you please about the trial. Harry Vernon, don't think I am indifferent to your concerns, my boy; but Mary's here alone with me—a sort of runaway match you see, though we have the mother's consent—and I sha'n't be easy any more than herself, till she has a lawful right to look to me, and I have my lawful rights as well as herself. There may be another Tom Horsey, but I don't believe it, and I know he can't be Tom of Raymond. Those breeches and that coat are mine, though how they came so bloody and holy is past my telling. They were stolen from me in the Big Black swamp, as the newspapers say, by some scoundrel or scoundrels unknown. I don't say you stole 'em, Colonel Mortimer, or you, Major Montmorenci, but I intend to make you show how you got 'em, if there's any justice in Mississippi."

The answer of these worthies was made in high head and
with some show of valor and defiance; but this Horsey, whose
regards were chiefly given to Mary Clayton, at this moment, did
not seem to heed.

"All in good time, gentlemen," he said, "after the ceremony's
over. I invite you to remain till then; though, in your ear,
let me tell you, I look on you to be as arrant a pair of liars as
ever wagged a Munchausen."

Squire Nawls was better skilled in that department of his
business for which Horsey demanded his present aid, than in
any other of its requisitions. He saw no reasonable objection
to giving the actor a wife as Thomas Horsey, though, in the
next moment, he refused his own evidence as such, to prove
himself alive. No assertions that he could make, no proofs that
he could offer, could impair the positive and sweeping testimony
of the two witnesses, or disturb the settled decision which the
justice had made before he came; and, in equal fury, the actor
and the Alabamian listened to the regrets with which he sought
to mollify his resolve, to commit the supposed murderer of Tom
Horsey to prison. Before Nawls came to this conclusion, however—for the dull country-justice had been somewhat confounded by the *contretemps* of the dead man's reappearance—
he was compelled to retire in private conference with Mr.
Augustus Mortimer, a minute's talk with whom was quite
enough to set him on his legs.

"Let him be Tom Horsey, or the d—l, it matters nothing to
you. You have the evidence of two witnesses that Horsey is
dead, and you might go farther and arrest this fellow as an im-
postor. Though we've no instruction to do so, yet it might be
good service to the beagles. Your account is easily squared
with the state's attorney—there's the proof on which you committed Vernon to prison, and that's enough. Send him on his
way, and let Cane Castle do the rest. I'll engage you never
hear of him again from that quarter."

The commitment of Vernon was accordingly made out and
delivered to the two emissaries of Saxon, in whose custody he
had been left before. They had their instructions as well as
Nawls, and they knew if he did not, that the unfortunate youth
was reserved for the sacrifice by those whose secret haunts he

was supposed to have invaded as a spy, and whose practices of crime he had been commissioned to arrest and punish.

Meanwhile, the keen, searching mind of Vernon had discovered the true circumstances and secret of those difficulties by which he was involved. While he was under the impression that Horsey had really been murdered, he had little cause to think himself the object of an organized plan of injustice or detention. But the reappearance of the actor, and the revelations which he made during the random dialogue which took place on the examination, together with the fact that his clothes had been stolen, mutilated, and made bloody, were circumstances of sufficient strength to open the eyes of the lawyer to the whole hidden truth.

The conviction that he was singled out as a victim, and that the persons around him were mostly parties to the conspiracy, strongly impressed him with the necessity of being as cautious, yet seeming as little suspicious as possible. A look, and the significant application of his finger to his lips, at a moment when Horsey was about to blurt out in public the whole burden of his discoveries in the swamp, fortunately served to check the torrent of his speech, and to impose upon him the necessity of a caution like that of Vernon, whose composure had seemed in his eyes very much like the most unmanly tameness. When the resolve of the magistrate was made known, Vernon remarked quietly, without any show of anger or suspicion to the justice :—

" I can not blame you, sir — as a lawyer, I should, perhaps, say that you have done nothing but your duty. There is evidently some mistake in this business; for this I know to be Mr. Thomas Horsey from Raymond, who was the only travelling companion I had from that place. Still, these gentlemen, who have given their evidence, may know another of the same name, who has unfortunately been murdered as they state. I do not gainsay their assertions — I only declare my innocence of the crime. Still,. sir, you are not to know that, and could only do as you have done. One privilege, however, I must pray to be allowed — that of writing to my friends in Raymond and elsewhere, for the necessary evidence to prove my innocence and the identity of this gentleman. If you will suffer me to have a brief private conference with my two friends here, Mr. Horsey and Mr. Jamison, I will provide them with directions for seeing to this business, and procuring all the necessary proofs."

This small favor could not well be denied to a man in such an emergency. The calm, respectful deportment of the prisoner, his forbearance to hint or even look any of the suspicions which he really felt, deceived the witnesses as well as the justice. Looking upon it as certain that any evidence which he might procure from Raymond would come too late to affect a trial which was to take place in Cane Castle, and to be as summary as it was certain to be secret—Mr. Augustus Mortimer, to whom Squire Nawls was wont to refer privately in all cases of especial doubt, recommended that his prayer be granted.

"It will be getting these fellows, Jamison and Horsey, out of the way—they might be troublesome—and before they get back with their witnesses, Cane Castle will have done his business beyond any Horsey's undoing. Let 'em talk together."

"And what are we to do for you, Harry Vernon?" demanded Horsey, the moment they reached the little chamber to which the courtesy of the justice had permitted them to retire. "Say the word, and I'm for you,

"'To the last gasp, with truth and loyalty.'"

In less classical style and language the Alabamian made a like offer of his services and sinews.

"You shall say yourselves what you shall do for me, when I tell you how I stand," said Vernon. "I am in the hands of outlaws—the witnesses who swore against me are outlaws, the constables who guard me are outlaws, and the justice who commits me is their creature."

After this startling preliminary, Vernon proceeded to classify those details of facts—those floating circumstances, which, picked up from sundry quarters, formed the groundwork of the faith that was in him.

"And knowing this, you took it so patiently," was the joint exclamation of Horsey and the Alabamian.

"Had my passions been suffered to play as freely as yours, Horsey, Squire Nawls would never have permitted me this

interview. But, stay, I do not hear their footsteps below —
they have ceased walking — they are watchful. Not a word
now above your breath, gentlemen, for it is now doubly important that we should be secret as the grave. Now, then, hear me.
You are both strong men, and, I am sure, as fearless as you are
strong. I claim your help in a matter, which, were it your
case, should freely command my own. You must help to rescue
me from the clutches of these fellows."

The hands of the two were instantly clasped in frank and
manly assurance upon that of the speaker.

CHAPTER XXXIX.

JUDICIOUS USE OF PERQUISSIONS — HOW TO CURRY A SHORT
HORSE — ECONOMICAL USE OF GREEN MOSS.

> "Come, my good fellow, put thine iron on :—
> If fortune be not ours to-day, it is
> Because we brave her."—SHAKSPERE.

THE reader must not, however, suppose that our three friends
concluded their conference with this vague determination
Vernon was too good a politician, too keen a lawyer, not to
see that, left to their own judgments, Dick Jamison might lose
the game by his rashness, and Horsey by his frivolity. Their
dialogue, which was somewhat further protracted, was carefully
given, on the part of the former, to a consideration of the difficulties surrounding him; and to the necessary steps which were
to be taken by the two in effecting his rescue.

It does not need that we should report these directions in this
place, but leave to time, which usually ripens all projects, even
those which events baffle, to bring about its natural results in
this case as in all others. It will suffice to say that the manner
in which Vernon carried their minds forward, step by step, with
his, confirmed in him that tacit superiority which, from the first,
neither of them had seemed willing to dispute. If Jamison
regarded him as a fine fellow before, he now looked him as a

"mighty wise one;" and the importance and dignity of the new offices, put so suddenly on his hands, seemed to elevate the mind of our actor in his own estimation. He had never been much trusted with matters of importance before; and the idea seemed suddenly, though, perhaps, imperfectly, to open upon him; that, after all, Mr. Aristophanes Bull was not so great a booby, when he denounced tragedies as not "ser'ous things;" certainly, the new task before him of getting Vernon out of his present hobbles, seemed the most serious business of any to which he had ever yet set his hand. Not that Horsey had any scruples or apprehensions. There was no better pluck in Mississippi than that of our amateur. But he had just entered upon a new and exquisitely-delicate condition. He had just formed a new and responsible relationship in life; and when he heard from Vernon that there was no doubt that he should be hurried off that very evening on his way to prison, and that any attempt to rescue him, to be successful, must be made that very night, he could only exclaim with a tribulation in his accents and countenance, which compelled the smile to the lips of his two companions:—

"But, dear me, Harry Vernon, what the deuce am I to do with Mary?"

Vernon had not been inconsiderate on this subject. He had prepared himself to meet this difficulty, and by his counsel, Horsey was persuaded to make application to Squire Nawls for a temporary lodging for his new wife, until he could procure facilities for conveying her home to Raymond. This pretext enabled him to set forth that very evening, and simultaneously with the departure of Vernon under his guard, as if for Lucchesa, where he proposed to find a horse and side-saddle on sale.

Nawls, after some moderate objections, was persuaded by a week's board paid in advance, and the honeyed arguments of the young husband, to accede to the proposed arrangement; and this matter settled, love consented to waive all further objections to the *quasi* warfare which implored his assistance.

Vernon communicated to both his companions the knowledge which he had acquired from his intimacy with Walter Rawlins and the methodist Badger. To the former he recommended

them in the event of their failure to rescue him. As a sanction
for their own proceedings, in a business which promised to involve a great deal that was extra-judicial, he drew from his
bosom the envelope which originally contained the blank commissions of the governor, intending to fill the blanks with their
names, and thus furnish an authority which would not only
assist them in commanding means for acting against the outlaws,
but sustain them in their use. He now, for the first time, discovered the robbery that had taken place upon his person—a
robbery which he could only ascribe to the practised and adroit
hands of Saxon, performed while he was insensible.

A bitter smile passed over the lips of the youth as he made
this discovery, and traced, with rapid thought, the connection
of event with event, and agent with agent, all co-operating to
the same end—his entanglement in present intricacies. But
the resolution of Vernon, his sanguine temper, and great self-
confidence, conspired to make him still hopeful even against the
large odds in favor of the beagle confederacy. Having satisfied
himself, to his great relief, that the other packet, which contained the papers of Carter, remained in its original integrity,
he determined still to keep it in his possession; as it was now
fair to assume that the outlaw, convinced that he had obtained
all that was hidden, and that he had found a sufficient clue to
the progress of Vernon, would never dream of looking in the
same place for a second deposite.

With this conviction, he ceased to feel the loss of the one
packet as a very serious evil. That packet involved none of
his confederates—none of his friends. He alone was singled
out as the victim, and, bating the loss of the commissions,
which might be perverted to evil use by the outlaw, the utmost
extent of his misfortune was already known in his own capture,
and threatened imprisonment, if not murder.

Vernon was not insensible to the risk he incurred among the
outlaws, as one whose supposed endeavor had been to expose
their haunts, detect their doings, and entrap their persons. He
felt that, should his two allies fail him at the fortunate moment,
his blood would probably be poured out in some lone swamp
fastness, while his mangled body would be left uncovered to
yield a midnight repast to the gaunt and famished wolves, that

traversed, at that period, the savage and uncultivated hills of
the Choctaw purchase.

These were annoying convictions, but Harry Vernon was a
man. He spoke none of his apprehensions, and contenting
himself with obtaining from Horsey all that he knew, had seen,
or heard, while in Cane Castle and with renewing his instructions on all matters which he deemed essential to the successful
prosecution of their adventure; he presented himself to the
officers, and declared his readiness to go with them. He had
done all that it was in the power of man to do at that moment
—he had exercised the closest judgment of which his mind
was capable, uninfluenced by his own feelings, and the consciousness of danger, of which he could not entirely divest
himself; and with a cheerful manner, and a resolute spirit, he
left the rest to the courage and conduct of his friends, under the
crowning favor of Providence.

These did not desert him. Though neither of them very
wise men, or solid counsellors, Horsey and Jamison were yet
men of great nerve and composure; strong, as we have shown, of
limb, and of undoubted energy and spirit. In their plans and
schemes, alone, was it likely that they might fail; and in these
respects, the forethought of Vernon had taken every precaution
and made every arrangement that might be done by him under
existing circumstances. His directions, which contemplated
even the particulars of the scuffle with his robber-guardians,
the time, the manner, and the probable place, were ample, if
not copious. But little more was needed, than that their objects
and course should be unsuspected, that their horses should bring
them to the season, and their hearts not fail them in the trying
moment. Of course, it was the assumption of all parties at the
outset, that the strife was to take place with the two outlaws,
and those only, who had served as officers of justice from the
beginning.

One little difficulty, however, started into sight before they
left the presence of the magistrate, and made Vernon tremble,
for an instant, in doubt of all his schemes. The sturdy rogues,
his captors, having no more to say in respect to himself, were
disposed to annoy his friend Jamison, because of his interposi
tion at Lucchesa in cutting the cords which bound their victim

—an act which they had then called a rescue, and which they were still disposed to consider so. They had probably consulted with Nawls on the subject, while Vernon and his comrades were planning his rescue in fact; and, with the sober confidence of veteran knaves, they were resolved to extort a reasonable amount of hush-money from the sturdy Alabamian, while in presence of the justice.

But Jamison's blood, which had been with difficulty restrained by the counsels of Vernon, and the obvious necessity of preserving a large degree of temperance in consideration of his friend's predicament, fired up at the first motion of the rogues. Knowing them, as he now did, to be the most impudent pretenders to official sanction, it was with no small difficulty that he restrained himself from declaring aloud all that he knew, and pouring forth all that he felt. With all his attempts at moderation, his speech was certainly of a character to show but a very limited degree of success in attaining that which he sought.

"Look ye, judge," said he, "these niggers ought to be licked for tying a free white man as they did. I'm the man to lick 'em; let 'em give me the littlest eend of an opportunity. I was a-thinking to bring it afore you myself, because I'm hopeful there's something in the law-books to make 'em sweat for roping a white man, the same as if he was an ingin or a nigger; and, if there ain't, there ought to be, and our *rips* can't put it there a bit too soon. I did take out my bowie-knife, jist as they say, but 'twan't to trouble them; though, Lord bless you! 'twouldn't ha' been so hard a matter neither, to cut 'em up mighty small as they run; but, as I don't altogether like to use a man's weapon upon a chap that shows me nothing but his back, I had no more thought of troubling them with it, than I have of troubling you. I used the knife only to cut loose the rope; and all that was wrong in that business, was in using a weapon that was bigger than was needful, and that made two big men so shameful scary. As for 'resting me for that, squire, why, all that I can say, 'twon't do for them to try it, while I've got the same knife yet, and to the back of it a couple of pair of such bull-mouthed biters as these here *perquissions*. You've seen the new perquission-guns, squire? Well, these pistols are after the same fashion. Here's four of them, and they're a wing

or two quicker in the shot than any race-lightning. One pair
of these pistols, and this here knife, belongs to Mr. Vernon there
—and I'll take care of them for him till he gets out of jail.
I'll drop the rammer down their throats, and you'll see they
all have their bellies full of bullets Now, I'm a peaceable
man, squire, for one that's so well prepared for war; but, if I
was twice as peaceable, and only half so well off in perquissions,
if you was to say the word for these chaps to 'rest me, which I
know you can't do as a gentleman and a righteous justice—
why, I've only to turn one of these perquissions round about
among the company—now here on this one, and now on that
—and as there's no taking aim in such a promisc'us business,
particularly with these mighty quick perquissions, I'm almost
afraid to say, squire, how much risk you'd run yourself; though
I'm hopeful the bullet's far off that'll ever trouble you. 'Twon't
be such a death, squire, as I'd have you die of. As for these
—look at 'em, squire, how they dodge—look at 'em, Harry
Vernon! Ha! ha! ha! That's jist the way they were scared
at Lucchesa—jist the way exactly; they dodged when there
was no sort of call upon 'em for it. Lord love you! my lads, if
it makes you so squammish when I only p'int the thing at you,
it would make you deathly sick, when I come in 'arnest.
Squire, let me go home to my business in a civil manner, and
don't listen to these rediculous fellows. I've done for Vernon
all that I reasonably could; and, by the hocus, I'll be at court
when his trial comes on, and if it's the last picayune in the
pocket of Dick Jamison, or the last blood in his heart, it shall
go to help him out of his troubles. If I hear you say, I'm not
to be 'rested about this business, well, I'll be off at once, before
night, for Lucchesa. If I'm to be 'rested for cutting loose a free
white man, that was tied up wrongfully, say it as soon, and let's
see the eend of it at once. P'int your finger now which way
you please, and I'm ready, any side. If it's civility, well, I'm
all civility—if it's for a close hug, tooth and timber, why
there's not a bear in Loosa-Chitta, that'll come to the scratch
with rougher arms than Dick Jamison."

This interruption consumed some time; and long speeches
for which the western wanderers are rather famous, were as fre
quent and as fine, after a fashion, as half of those listened to with

so much patience by the nation — particularly as they have to pay for them — at every session of Congress. Vernon confirmed the simple statement of Jamison, and insisted that all the violence shown on the occasion was no more than was required to separate the bonds of a prisoner, who made no attempt to escape, and professed his willingness to go freely with the officers. True, this was a rescue in legal acceptation, but, under the circumstances, not such a one as would render a prosecution necessary; and Vernon contended for the point the more readily, as he could perceive that the justice desired nothing more than a loophole by which to escape from the necessity of taking steps against a man who had avowed such levelling principles — we had almost written pistols. The pistols, indeed, were the principles; and no effect could have been more ludicrous than that which Jamison produced upon the company, justice and officers, as with a huge pistol in each hand, both of which he cocked, he made their muzzles describe a slow circuit round the apartment, allowing them to rest for a few awkward seconds whenever the line of sight was brought up to the face of one of the opposite faction. The constables dodged with little shame or scruple on such occasions; and the very justice, it is painful to add, though he did not allow his limbs to yield to such a discreditable weakness, could not keep his eyes from winking with singular frequency; and his cheeks — the Alabamian remarked afterward, with a singular show of satisfaction — grew whiter than any clabber that he ever saw or swallowed. The affair was compromised by the justice bestowing a reproof upon the offender, to which he submitted with the indifference of one who rightly estimated its value.

"You've got to say it, squire," said he, "it's your business, and you can't help it, and that's the reason I let it pass and say nothing. But, look you, Squire Nawls, if you wa'n't a justice, but jist a common man, I'd ha' been on top of you, and through you, afore you'd 'a half-finished what you've been saying. If there's any one thing in this world that I never could like, it's when I'm found fault with, jist at a time when I know that I'm doing the very thing that's right — and then to be spoke to on behalf of such a couple of small-souled sappy-sticks as these — Grim! it makes me all bristles. I feel wolfy in twenty places, and—dang my buttons, judge, if the thing was to be done over agin, 'twouldn't be the rope only that my knife would slit—if I wouldn't cut a juglar or two, there's no snakes in all Alabam."

It was with a feeling of relief that Nawls and his two emissaries beheld this sturdy democrat take his departure. He set out as if for Lucchesa, accompanied by the amateur, whose part ing with his young wife was equally dramatic and characteristic, though still full of genuine feeling. Resolved on having, in this Border chronicle, as little of the lachrymose mood as possible, we refrain from the tears and tenderness shown on the occasion. Our readers of the gentler sex, will please suppose that the omission is ours only;—had they seen the happy couple at the parting moment—had they heard the low but passionate tones and sweet assurances of Horsey, and witnessed the embrace, and seen the face of Mary buried in his bosom, and hearkened to her half-suppressed sobs, which spoke of hope and joy rather than any other emotion—they would have seen that there was no love lacking between the two in this early stage of their matrimonial felicity. Love, however—domestic love in particular—is proverbially a thing of short stages; and the sun which is warm and bright to-day, may be under a very ugly cloud to-morrow;—but this is none of our business—"sufficient for the day is the evil thereof."

Vernon saw his friends depart with some anxiety. His own movements, under the guardianship of the tenacious constables, followed soon after. The evening shades were thickening as the party set forth, and grave thoughts become gloomy ones in the twilight hour. Those of our hero were sad ones, at least, and they restrained his natural vivacity of temper, if they did not subdue and dispirit him. He was without arms, without present friends or succor—accused of crime, and at the mercy of criminals. The increasing gloom of the forest, as they advanced upon their way, served to increase the cheerlessness of his situation, and to give an oppressive weight to those doubts which necessarily came with his very hopes and anxieties. Horsey and Jamison were brave—but might they not miss the route taken by the outlaw—might they not fail at the proper moment? Precipitation might be worse than halting apprehension, and the very levity of the former, with the rough and ready boldness of the latter, might serve to defeat the plans of the most deliberate and thoughtful. To a man of mind, there is nothing so productive of annoying doubts, as the dependence upon mere muscle.

Vernon turned for some sort of relief to his attendants. It was advisable to disarm their watchfulness, and, if possible, to impress them with the conviction that no kind of doubt of their professed character had as yet risen in his mind. To seem to rely upon them, as peace-officers of the country, was the most effectual way to assure them, that he was perfectly resigned to their custody, He, whom they well knew, was guilty of no crime, had nothing to apprehend from the awards of justice ; and the mere temporary detention of his person, however troublesome and unpleasant, was not so great an evil as to make it likely that he would incur those risks to avoid it, which would inevitably follow any violent attempt to shake it off. It was no hard matter to engage them in easy conversation ; and having paved the way for a familiar chit-chat by some good-natured commonplaces, Vernon proceeded to carry out his design in the way that he calculated would be most likely to effect it. He inquired of them, what they knew of the two men who furnished the evidence against him ; and when as he expected they denied all knowledge of the witnesses, he boldly assured them, that they had sworn to utter falsehoods.

"There can be no sort of doubt," he said, "that Mr. Horsey is alive ; and that is he, who came in so unexpectedly, when the case was going on. I never knew any other Horsey, save his father, in my life ; and I am now convinced, that these two persons have uttered what they know to be untrue; and if they dare come to the trial, I shall convict them of a base conspiracy against my life. It will be easy enough for my friends to bring proof of what I say, and of my innocence. Indeed, as soon as Horsey and Jamison go where I have sent them, I shall come out under habeas corpus. But these scoundrels shall suffer for their malice, if there's law in Mississippi.

"I don't know — may be so," returned one of the constables ; "but what should make two men, whom you never saw before swear ag'in the life of another ? and then it seems mighty strange, if so be the man that come to be married was the raal

19*

Horsey — it seems mighty strange he should pop in jist at that minute."

"It was no less strange to me than to you," replied Vernon; 'but the truth is not lessened by the strangeness of the circumstance. That he is the real Horsey, I hope to show, as soon as my friends return from where I've sent them. As for the malice of these two witnesses, that I confess to you, is as singular and surprising to me, as it can be to anybody else I never saw them before — am sure, I never did them any injury and —"

"But why should you call it a conspiracy?"

"It evidently is — here are two men, whom I know nothing of, coming forward most strangely, to swear a crime against me, which I never did commit."

"Yes — but you see, we are not to know that — Squire Nawls ain't to know that."

"True — I don't blame him. He has done nothing more than he was bound to do; but I am speaking of the two who have sworn to this falsehood — why they should — for what reason — with what hope or object — is a wonder of the strangest sort to me."

"You're sure you never had any quarrel with them before?"

"Never saw them in all my life."

"Well, it is strange, if so be you didn't kill Horsey and you never had a quarrel with these gentlemen, that they should swear ag'in you. You ain't made no enemies of anybody? Beca'se these chaps mought be employed by somebody else."

"Not that I know of. I've quarrelled with nobody, and have made no enemies. Stay! — there is one thing!" exclaimed Vernon, with sudden earnestness, correcting himself as he spoke; "now that you put the question, I am reminded of a circumstance which may account for it."

Here he proceeded to relate the event recorded at an earlier stage of our narrative, in which, while rescuing the traveller, Wilson, he shot the outlaw Weston, who was astride his body.

"This robber might have friends and relatives, who have sought in this manner to avenge him."

"I don't think that," said the rogues with one breath. "It would be more apt to scare his friends off, and if they was rogues themselves, they'd know better than to come before a justice. Squire Nawls is a mighty keen man when he's a judging—he'd see through a rascal as clear as a whistle, and pick the crooks out of his story in the twink of an eye. No, no! I reckon there's another way to account for it. We don't want to git you to confess, Mr. Varnon, for nobody's bound in law to tell ag'in themselves, but I reckon you did shoot the poor man, though, I s'pose, 'twas by accident, or else you fou't him fairly, and he got the fling."

Vernon re-asseverated his innocence, with the solemn earnestness of one who was really anxious that they should be convinced—so earnestly, indeed, and with such warm simplicity in his manner, that the rogues burst into a good-humored laugh, and one of them, clapped him civilly upon the back while he expressed the hope, that, even if he did kill the man, he should 'pass under the tree without sticking fast to the limb;" or, as it is sometimes expressed, that he should "graze the timbers, without becoming dead wood."

It was just at this moment that a faint whistle reached the ears of our hero. This was the signal agreed upon between himself and his comrades; and circumstances seemed to be particularly favorable to their project. The road was narrow —a mere wagon-track — through which they were passing; night had set fairly in, and though a bright star-light whitened the wide arch of heaven, but a faint effusion of its rays guided our travellers along the dim and shady paths of the forest. To maintain a more certain power over their prisoner—whom, perhaps, because of the disgrace which had followed their first attempts to cord him, they had not bound — they rode close beside him, on either hand. In consequence of the narrowness of the road, this mode of riding brought the horses of the three in absolute contact. The opportunity was too gratefully tempting to Vernon and his heart bounded with the anxiety which he felt during the brief interval between the first and second signal of his allies. That second signal was the *beagle-note*. With a conviction that the robbers who attacked Wilson's carriage, and those who escorted him belonged to the same gang, Vernon had suggested the employment of this imitation sound, with the hope of misleading his guardians. The whistle

which preceded it, was simply meant to indicate to himself the
certainty of the subsequent signal being given by his friends.
As had been anticipated, an echo from the right hand of the
prisoner threw back an answering voice.

' There somebody's dog in the swamp," said one of the rogues
carelessly, prefacing with these words, his own excellent imitation of the cry. Again more near and more distinct, came the
note of Jamison who proved no unworthy beagle whether in
voice or limb. As if in sheer idleness of mood, did the same
outlaw again respond to it. The third signal from the Alabamian, which immediately followed, was delivered from a bush
almost beside the party ; and at the same instant, the two constables drew up their horses, setting each a hand on the rein of
Vernon's, to arrest his forward movement.

They naturally looked to a meeting with their comrades; but
were surprised in the next moment. as Vernon, yielding his rein
entirely, threw an arm round the waist of each of his attendants,
and by a sudden exertion of all his strength, drew them together before him upon his steed, until their heads clashed with
a stunning concussion. Before they could recover from the
shock, draw knife or pistol, or make the smallest effort, a stout
hand from below had relieved Vernon from his burdens; and
the self-appointed officers of justice found themselves let down
with no gentle ministry upon the earth, which, fortunately,
being on the skirts of the swamp, and sufficiently pliable, manifested no stubborn resistance to the reception of their persons.

The surprise was as successful as it had been sudden; and
while a stout man bestrid each of the prisoners with a heavy
and bright bowie blade pointing down and sometimes painfully
tickling their throats, Vernon, having secured the three horses,
proceeded to divest the rogues of all their weapons. This
done, under the direction of Jamison, who had taken care to
provide the necessary plough-lines, he bound their arms securely
behind them, and thus fastened, they were once more permitted
to rise upon a level with their captors.

"A short horse is mighty soon curried," said Jamison, when
the business was finished. "I know'd all along, Varnon, that
these here chaps hadn't any *perquission* in their guns, and it's
now what we're to do with 'em. That's the question. They're

to be lynched I reckon, of course; but whether to lynch 'em
here where nobody can get any good from seeing it, or to lynch
'em at Lucchesa where it'll be a warning to all rogues, and
gamblers, and abolitionists, that haven't the fear of God in
their eyes, and do large business with the devil — that's what I
ain't yet detarmined about."

To lynching, altogether, Vernon absolutely objected; but he
did not content himself with uttering moral objections only.
With such a man as Jamison, such scruples might not have
been so forcible as those which sprung from mere momentary
policy.

"We have not time for that," said he in a whisper, and when
out of hearing of the captives. "Besides, to go to Lucchesa
with these in company, before we have beaten up the whole
gang and obtained the proper evidence of their villany, will
be only to expose ourselves to discovery, prosecution, and
probably punishment by the laws; not to speak of private
assassination from the hands of some of the numerous outlaws
with whom the whole country seems to be infested. To carry
these fellows with us anywhere, would be to encumber ourselves
with a burden that would be troublesome, and may be dangerous.
No! my counsel is that we bind them to trees in the most secret
places in the swamp — there leave them till we can muster a
sufficient force to secure them, and to pursue their comrades.
We are now in possession of one of their signs, and if we can
keep these fellows from communication with the rest, until we
can penetrate their hiding-places, we may capture a good many
more. I have already told you of friends on the other side of
the river. We must join ourselves to them as soon as possible.
You will set off to-night. You know all that I can tell you
about our friend Rawlins. Horsey and myself, meanwhile, will
ride to Lucchesa, where I will see to some business which I
have with Mr. Wilson, while he procures a horse and saddle
for his wife. With him I will join you to-morrow, and with
Rawlins, who, I doubt not, by this time has got a pretty strong
party together, we will try what we can to capture the master-
spirit of the band. If we take him, we need give ourselves but
little trouble about the rest. He is the chain that binds them
together — and without him, they fall apart without stren

success, or object. We will rope these scoundrels to trees, where they can not see or communicate with each other, and lest they should employ our signals, it will not· be amiss to put a handkerchief in their mouths."

"A handkerchief indeed!" cried Jamison—"that would be a mighty foolish waste, when there's so much fine green moss to be had for the picking."

The economical views of Jamison prevailed, and the mouths of the struggling prisoners were well wadded with green moss in preference to silk bandanas. They were roped to trees in deep and dark recesses of the swamp; but it was not without great reluctance, that Jamison was persuaded to turn away, and forbear the use of a certain bunch of hickories, armed with which, he had prepared himself to requite the rogues for the offensive rebuke under which he had been compelled, after a fashion, to submit in the presence of Mr. Justice Nawls.

Vernon saw that he was dissatisfied with the forbearance of his friends toward the criminals, which he thought as little due to their deserts, as to the cause of justice. They all rode from the place together to the high road, but the Alabamian was very taciturn as they went; his mind seemed to be brooding over some yet undigested purposes. Their parting was evidently hurried on the side of Jamison; and when his two friends had gone from sight on their way to Lucchesa, the matter that troubled him, found expression in words aloud.

"Grim! But I'd sooner sleep in the swamp myself, than let them chaps off without a licking. 'Tain't every day that a rogue gets what he deserves, and 'tain't every month that Dick Jamison cuts a bunch of hickories to throw away. It would be a most monstrous wasting of the wood, to cut a dozen hickories for nothing—besides, it's a mighty great resk to leave the fellows behind, any how: 'spose they get away—then, where's the satisfaction? No, no, that's not my notion—I must write a name on the backs of the critters, so that I may know 'em again, when I see 'em. Then, if they get away, 'twon't be so bad; and one person, that I know of, will be a mighty sight easier in his conscience. I reckon, if I didn't lick 'em, my horse would go mighty rough over the road to-night—I know I shouldn't sit well in the saddle, and my spirits would be a cursed sight heavier than a fat parson's after a bad collection-Sunday."

This soliloquy was made while the speaker took his way back to the spot which he had just left. We need not add, that he carried out in execution, the sentiments and resolutions which it expressed. The hickories were not wasted; and, according to the usual ideas of border justice, in all parts of the world, the rascals met with their deserts. Satisfied with his administration of the border law, the Alabamian found the movement of his horse and conscience equally easy while he rode upon his way that night. He sat as well in his saddle as ever, and a heavy load, for the time-being, was taken from his heart.

CHAPTER XL.

A FUGITIVE ARRESTED — GRAND BEAGLE HUNT IN PREPARATION.

> "Take him to ye,
> And, sirrah, be an honest man ; ye've reason,
> I thank ye, worthy brother: Welcome, child,
> Mine own sweet child." — BEAUMONT AND FLETCHER.

THE impatient Saxon, impatient for his revenge, vainly looked out that night for the coming of his followers, to whom Vernon had been given in charge. His arrangements had been so made as to put his plans, seemingly, beyond the reach of disappointment; and, resolved effectually to arrest the further efforts of an individual, whose courage and conduct gave him some reason for apprehension, he had prepared himself and his accessories in the swamp, for the summary and terrible punishment of one, whom they considered a spy, and had destined to those cruel severities which, under their laws, had been decreed for such an offender. The evils which had followed the successful attempt of Richard Hurdis, had mortified the vanity of Saxon —or Clement Foster—and rendered him unforgiving. From the moment when he became convinced that Vernon was an

enemy, he had solemnly sworn to destroy him. His plot for
this purpose was a good one—his officers were true—the justice was his willing creature; and, Mr. Augustus Mortimer and
Major Marcus Montmorenci, were, he well knew, the most
trustworthy witnesses that were ever yet suborned to carry a
crooked character straight through the sessions. How then
should he account for the delay of his agents in bringing their
prisoner to punishment?

"Should it be that d——d actor, Jones—should he have
spoiled the matter? Would you had put your knife and bullet
through his carcass as well as through his clothes. I fear he
will work us evil."

Such were his muttered doubts, at midnight, to his wily companion, who could say little to relieve them.

"And this proud girl! She, too!—but it can not be very
long. She shall submit, if it be only to save the life of her
lover. I shall obtain my conquest over her, though, as a condition, I am compelled to forego my vengeance upon him."

"But his life is forfeit to the law!" said Jones.

"I am the law!" returned the other, haughtily. Then, softening his tones, he added—"but, I am too feverish, Jones, to
be just or reasonable now. Forgive me if I speak hastily or
harshly. Go you now, and see if there be any tidings of these
fellows."

Meanwhile, Richard Stillyards, the dwarf, was already on
his way to the upper ferry, as fast as he could go; and Vernon
had reached Lucchesa in safety. His purpose in returning to
Lucchesa was to declare himself in private to William Maitland; to reveal his whole connection with Carter; to unfold the
favorable terms which he was commissioned to grant, and,
finally, to crown the work of peace and good-will, by offering
himself in marriage to Virginia, whose own consent, it has been
already seen, he was happy to secure at an early period. But
the misery of the father at the loss of his child, and the deep
feeling of interest which he too had in the matter—which
seemed almost to deprive the former of his reason, struck the
lover dumb:—

"One stupid moment motionless he stood;"

And then his resolution returned to him as he witnessed the old man's despair.

The natural and nobler feelings of old Maitland's heart recovered all their strength at this moment of his greatest privation. Virginia was the apple of his eye—the solace of his bitter cup—the very light that relieved the otherwise groping darkness which had environed his affections. Bitterly did he now accuse himself of neglect, of cruelty, of crime—of all things, and all thoughts evil—while, as the anguished, words poured from his lips, the big, burning tears rolled down his cheeks, on which, the consciousness of evil thoughts and deeds had placed many a premature line and wrinkle. The younger daughter, wild and frightened rather than grieved, as she beheld these ebullitions of a nature which had never shown itself to her under such an aspect before, stood beside the old man, with one hand round his neck, and one resting on his head. He himself sat upon the floor in a state of utter abandonment.

"Cheer up and rouse yourself, sir," exclaimed Vernon, as he looked upon the melancholy spectacle, with a sentiment of pity that became painful—"rouse up, sir, I will give her back to you though I perish!"

"Will you—oh! will you, Mr. Vernon? God bless you if you will!—but I fear—I fear you can not! She's gone—I've looked for her everywhere! It was I that left her for that accursed tavern, and those thrice accursed cards. I am not worthy of my child—my poor child! Oh! where can she be now—in what danger—from what villains! Oh! God, keep me from *that* thought—God in mercy keep her from *that* danger!"

And the miserable father threw himself forward upon the floor—the blood gushing from his nostrils, while his hands tore the scattered white hairs from his venerable head and strewed them around him. The screams of the trembling child mingled with his moans, making a discord which, while it filled the ears of Vernon, did not now so much annoy him. There were some evident fears, not so evidently expressed in the last speech of the father, which made the blood recede from the heart of Vernon, leaving a painful coldness and vacancy behind it.

In what danger was Virginia now? What villain held her in his embraces—scorning her prayers, her tears, her trembling

entreaties—her wild but feeble efforts at release? What brutal
violence, sickening to chaste ears, assailed her gasping innocence—
and none nigh to save by equal violence from that worse violence
that defied the imploring service of every sweet, and soothing, and
pure human affection?"

Vernon felt, as these dreadful doubts and apprehensions rushed
through his mind, that he, too, could throw himself in utter abandonment upon the ground, and mingle his groans also with those of
the miserable father. But other feelings, strengthened by the blood-
giving energies of youth, came to his aid. A fiercer power rose up
in his heart, and with accents of recovered might, he repeated his
assurance to the the old man, that he would rescue and restore his
daughter at the peril of his life. While he made this assurance, the
pitiable prostration of the father struck him as not less discreditable
to manhood, than it was grateful to his paternal love.

Maitland was still a vigorous man—not too old for exertion
—not too feeble at such a time, to seek for his child, and strike
a desperate blow in her behalf. Besides, men were wanting now to
prosecute the enterprise against the robbers in the Chitta-Loosa,
with whom Vernon could not fail to connect the outlaw by whom
Virginia had been torn away from her dwelling. Circumstances
had sufficiently shown the father that her absence arose from an
abduction, which the whole tenor of Virginia's life and virtuous
deportment conclusively convinced all parties, must have been
forcible.

A sudden resolution filled the mind of Vernon. He saw that
no better mode remained of arousing the father to his duty, than by
awakening other fears in his bosom. This was, indeed, the
fitting moment to declare to him the full extent and powers of
his own commission. To ordinary minds it might have seemed
cruel, while the father so keenly suffered, to vex his spirit with
the terrors of discovery and punishment; but the more correct
philosophy of Vernon convinced him that the prostration and
infirmity of Maitland could receive provocation and stimulous from
no other source.

"Mr. Wilson," said he, "rise—send your daughter to her
chamber for awhile, while I unfold to you some business of
great importance. I am the bearer of other evil tidings which

you have not heard, but which sooner or later, must reach your ears. There can be no better season than the present."

The solemnity of these preliminaries had the effect of commanding the attention of the criminal. The daughter was sent from their presence, and the father rose slowly to his chair, with eyes full of a most painful anxiety. Vernon did not delay his communication with any idle formulæ—humanity forbade all such. It will be understood, however, that he omitted nothing which might soften the natural severity of truth, and maintain for himself the proper deportment of a gentleman, and one, too, so closely allied by the tenderest promises to the daughter of the person he addressed.

"You are known to me, sir—you are William Maitland, late cashier of the —— bank."

The miserable old man shrieked in insuppressible terror at the words, while his hands clasped and covered his face, His daughter's fate was in an instant forgotten in his own. The selfishness of his nature preponderated in an instant.

"Spare me, spare me, Mr. Vernon!—for God's sake—for my children's sake—spare me! I am a miserable old man—spare my grey hairs; and I will bless you forever—they will bless you! Spare me!"

Vernon took his hand kindly.

"Be not alarmed, Mr. Maitland—though I come commissioned to recover this money from you, I yet come as your friend, and from one who has ever been your friend."

"Who? who?" exclaimed the wretched man, with as much eagerness of hope in his face as it had lately expressed of fear. But when the lips of Vernon uttered the name of "Carter," his countenance fell—he sunk back in his chair with a deep groan, and again covered his face with his hands.

"Do not doubt the friendship which has ever served you, even when the noble person whom I have mentioned has been suffering most from your injustice. I know your story, and I know his. I know how much you owe to his friendship, and I know how ill you have repaid it. But I am not sent to reproach you, and well I know, were he himself present, his own reproaches would be spared at such a moment as this. My mission brings you safety, Mr. Maitland, though I come as the messenger of

justice. Hear me with patience, then, while I communicate to
you the benevolent designs of my friend—your friend, still, Mr.
Maitland—in behalf of yourself and children."

This communication was soon delivered. The reader is already
familiar with its purport. We need not repeat it here. As little
necessary would it seem to say, that it was listened to by the unde-
serving criminal with some such feelings as those of the culprit
under judicial sentence, suddenly relieved by an unlooked-for
respite from the supreme authority while standing on the very precipice of death.

Vernon did not stop here, though the frequent groans and ejaculations of Maitland, now of remorse and self-reproach, and now of
gratitude and exultation, subjected him to frequent interruptions.
He at once unveiled to the old man the relation in which he stood
to his lovely but lost daughter.

Alas! for the long-diseased heart, and the pampered and prevailing sin which possessed it! Even in that hour of his greatest
privations, and pain, and humiliation—that hour of his partial
relief from the fear of punishment—an hour distinguished alike by
the keen sorrows of the father at the loss of the beloved child, and
the abased feelings of the felon who suddenly finds himself con-
victed before man, without escape, and with his mouth choked with
the bitter dust of his own degradations—in that very hour, the shape
of his old sin once more stood up triumphant and audacious as
ever.

The latter part of Vernon's communication, which declared
the nature of the tie which now united his feelings and interests
with those of Virginia Maitland, suggested to the miserable old
man a new resource for his crime; and he eagerly insinuated
proposals to Vernon that, instead of restoring the vast amount
of moneys which he had purloined, and which he admitted
himself still to have, in great part, in his own possession, to the
rightful owners, they should retain it among themselves, and
by a timely and fair retreat, secure themselves and it from the
grasp of all pursuers. The infatuated gambler, whose moral
sense, by a tendency as certain as death, had gone down, step
by step, with rapid but self-unnoted transitions, to the lowest
sink of depravation, vainly imagined that, to a lover, and one
so young, the charms of a mistress, and the splendid bribe

which formed her dowry, must prove irresistible temptations.
Vernon shrank back with an apparent shudder from the grasp.
which the eager fingers of Maitland had taken upon his arm;
while his eye regarded the stolid criminal with an expression
quite as full of sorrow as of scorn.

"Mr. Maitland, for your daughter's sake, I implore you to
suffer me to respect her father if I can. Let me hear no more
on this subject. I will strive, for my own sake, to forget this
most humiliating offer — an offer no less insulting to me than it
is degrading to yourself. You have heard me state what were
Mr. Carter's propositions. You perceive that he is willing to
provide — that he pledges himself to provide amply — for your
children, on the restoration of the sums in your possession. Circumstances have favored you, and have spared me the necessity
of proceeding harshly. I count myself as singularly fortunate
as yourself in being the messenger of such benevolent intentions
on the part of one upon whom you have no claims of kindness
Carter, indeed, is a ruined man. Having carried out his designs,
and secured your children in the sums specified, he will have
no more left him than will barely suffice to make his friend
Gamage secure against all losses. Let me know at once what
is your resolution ; for we have little time to lose. The safety
of one who is now no less dear to me than to you, requires our
instant pursuit."

Doubly humbled, though, perhaps, not yet contrite, Maitland
acceded to all the requisitions of the youth, and, with a hurried
consent, he would have dismissed the subject, while he proceeded to bustle forward to command the horses. But Vernon
was one of those men who do their work thoroughly.

"Mr. Maitland," said he, "this matter must be settled to-
night, and the money delivered. I have my credentials ready,
and will prepare your guarantee, while you are getting things
in readiness. If you are resolved to go with me in pursuit of
Virginia, it will be your better course to order your barouche,
and take Julia with us. The night is pleasant, and she can be
wrapped up carefully. It will be better than to leave her here,
in the care of servants only, and in a place which has already
proved itself to be so very insecure. You can have no reason
to dread returning now, and at Mr. Badger's she will be in per-

feet safety, while we traverse the swamp in search of her sister
! know no better course either for safety or propriety."

Briefly, Vernon had his own way in all respects. His firmness, mingled with that becoming deference of manner which
youth always owes to age, even when it is criminal and debased,
cowed the spirit, and commanded the respect of Maitland. The
money was restored, and in one hour more the cottage was
deserted The poor Julia, trembling and wondering, confused
at all things, and almost totally inapprehensive of any, was
wrapped away in the barouche, with her father beside her, sad,
ashamed, and silent; while Vernon, mounted on horseback, and
once more armed, after a long interval, with the weapons of
which the sturdy Alabamian had taken such excellent charge
during his arrest and sickness — with spirits unconsciously
heightened by the sense of liberty and strength — rode alongside, and strove to cheer the miserable father, and the innocent
and unconscious child. Though his anxieties and apprehensions
were in no respects lessened in regard to the lost Virginia, yet
the conviction that he was now able to strike in her behalf,
made him sanguine with hope, and rendered him elastic in
movement. He suffered no unnecessary delays to restrain his
progress, and by his voice and example, he urged the driver
of the vehicle to a corresponding action with his own sinewy
steed.

The reader, if he be not more dull —

> "than the fat weed
> That hugs itself at ease at Lethe's wharf,"

will be pleased to spare us some unnecessary narration, and rea
ily imagine a few things in our story which are quite as ea: .
to conceive as to write. He will take it for granted that th.
progress of our night travellers was uninterrupted — and that a
union was safely effected the next morning, at a tolerably early
hour, between themselves and their friends Jamison and Horsey.
He will further learn that, shortly after the meeting of these
with Vernon, they were joined by Walter Rawlins and Master
Edward Mabry. The eyes of the latter, which the adroit fists
of Horsey had sealed up for a season, were now in tolerably
good condition — they wore less of the plethoric form and rais

bow aspect, than they did a week past; but, though restored, they did not seem to regard the actor with any more favor than before.   Some mutual efforts were made by Rawlins and Vernon to bring the parties to friendly offices; but they were partly ineffectual.   Still, there was no open show of hostility between them.   Horsey, certainly, preserved none.   He was a generous fellow at heart; and would have scorned to have fostered any feeling of malice at an enemy.   Besides, he had been success ful, and as those always laugh who win, his good humor was in nowise diminished, because the hand which he offered with frankness to his foe was taken with reluctance.   He disarmed the active rancor of Mabry, by making some concessions—without which it might have been that the operations of the party would have been exposed to conflicting feelings and divided counsels—which he was neither bound by courtesy, nor expected by his opponent to make.

As for Rawlins, his delight at seeing Vernon was excruciating. He hugged him to his breast with what seemed to the latter quite a superfluous degree of affection, and in the same breath, though in a whisper, told him that Rachel had at length yielded to his persuasions, and had consented to name the day.

Another matter of far more gratifying import to Vernon at this moment, was the information which he received of a new ally in the person of Stillyards, the dwarf.   That elegant young person, elated with the boon with which Florence Marbois had consented to reward his industry in promoting her purposes of vengeance, had made his appearance at the door of Rawlins, a little after daylight that very morning; and his communications had quickened the preparations of the latter for the pursuit of that enterprise to which the counsels of Vernon had before impelled him.

He had not been idle, it may be said here, during the interval which had passed.   He had secured the co-operation of nearly twenty men—all stout fellows—good men and true—whom the blast of a horn would bring together in half an hour, from a circuit of five miles.

The revelations of Stillyards had much more effect upon Vernon than they could possibly have had upon Rawlins.   The abduction of Virginia Maitland was now known with certainty:

and it was with no less certainty that he knew where she was
hidden by Saxon. It was no small addition to his desire for
immediate enterprise, when he found that her abductor, and
the consummate chief of the Beagles of the Border, were one
and the same person. These discoveries he kept from the
father. He had come to the conclusion that William Maitland
could be of little service in the adventure—and he counselled
him to proceed at once with Julia to the security of Zion's
Hill. He particularly cautioned him against suffering his own
near neighborhood to be known to the venerable and dogmatical
head of the establishment; still less to suffer it to be suspected
that any enterprise was on foot, by which to rout the outlaws.
To render the old man more cautious in this and every other
respect, the doubtful character of young Badger was revealed
to him, and the danger fully shown of any premature development of a project which could only be successful through perfect secrecy. Having sent the unhappy and criminal father
upon his way, Vernon proceeded to the examination of Stillyards, whom Rawlins had kept under close watch in the neighboring wood.

CHAPTER XLI.

CAMPAIGN BEGINS — THE PIOUS ELDER — THE PICAROON 'SCH
— THE PEERLESS MAIDEN.

"She scorn'd us strangely,
All we could do, or durst do; threatened us
With such a noble anger, and so governed
With such a fiery spirit." — BONDUCA.

THOUGH naturally impatient to commence the war against his
enemies and rescue the fair Virginia from her abductors, Vernon
was too thoughtful and deliberate of character to defeat his
own objects by any premature or precipitate attempts. He
retired as soon as possible into the cover of the forests, and
from sight of any but his own comrades, after sending Maitland
on his way to Zion's Hill. Here he closely examined the
dwarf Stillyards; and this done, he despatched Jamison with
two others for the purpose of bringing in, and more effectually
securing the persons of the two rogues, whom we left fastened
in the swamp the night before. There were two other rogues
to be secured, of whose neighborhood he was now first informed
by the dwarf.

These were fellows, who, in the "Beagle" dialect, went
by the significant name of "smellers." They were, in fact,
advanced sentinels, the keepers of outposts, watching the high-
ways leading to the swamp fastnesses, and conveying the ear-
liest tidings of the approach of any uncongenial or hostile
influences. To divert these watchers from their posts, Stillyards, whom they knew, was immediately sent forward, as if
with instructions from their captain. Being in possession of all
the first signs of the band, there could be little or no difficulty
in deceiving them by means of his agency; and not altogether
prepared to rely wholly upon a rogue, even in the hour of his

20

first conversion, Vernon sent Rawlins, secretly, with two others —all excellent woodmen—to follow the dwarf, and correct his treachery, should he happen to prove faithless to his trust.

But his precautions, though proper, proved unnecessary. Stillyards was now the sworn enemy of the outlaw chief on his own account, even if he were not bound as the agent of Florence Marbois. The humiliating indignity to which his ears had been subjected by the fingers of Saxon had turned all the sweet milk of his nature into gall and bitterness; and he was now prepared, without fee or reward, to prove to his superior the extent of that malignity, which, in the base spirit, never forgives a wrong, and in the weakly, vain heart never forgets a slight. The wish to prove his capacity for vengeance, to him who was to be the object of it, had kept the deformed absolutely sleepless; and it was with the keenest and most suspicious impatience that he heard the resolution of Vernon to make no movement, until night, against the outlaws of Cane Castle.

This resolution was productive of surprise to other minds than his. Rawlins himself wondered, that, with a body of stout, fearless men, which, at mid-day, exceeded in numbers the entire force of the beagles known to be then within their camp, he should forbear instantly proceeding toward their prey. But the determination of the leader was a judicious one; and when explained to the few comrades whom he trusted with his plan, its evident policy overcame all their scruples and disarmed their doubts.

It was not till the evening shadows had fallen that their movements were begun. Before this time, however, the party which had been despatched for the two prisoners had returned with their charge; while, with equal success, the dwarf Stillyards, had beguiled the "Smellers" from their station into the very hands of the attacking party. Before they knew where they were, they encountered a dozen armed men in front, while the three who had been despatched to follow Stillyards, seasonably arriving behind, cut off all chance of retreat.

The four were despatched under an equal party toward Zion's Hill, in time to reach it a few hours after dark. They conveyed a request from Vernon to the venerable elder of that establish ment, that they might be suffered to remain under guard at his retreat, until the return of the party next day. Having several miles the start of the methodist, it was no longer a cause of fear that their plans might be defeated either by the perverse self-esteem and dogmatism of the father, or the treachery of the son ; of whom, by the way, Rawlins had meanwhile gathered such knowledge from Rachel Morrison, as confirmed all his previous suspicions.

These minor matters attended to, Vernon set his party in motion as soon as the darkness was sufficient to conceal their movements, But instead of taking his way down, he advanced up the river, and in a course directly opposite to that where Cane Castle lay. Two miles above the place where he had been concealed through the day, was the ferry which he had that morning crossed, and, while crossing, had scanned curiously, yet in silence, the place where the boat was fastened, and as much of the scene and circumstances around him as he deemed effectual to his purposes.

Having reached the neighborhood, he ordered his party to halt in the woods, while, alighting from their horses, Rawlins, Jamison, and himself, went forward to reconnoitre. Finding the coast clear, they loosened the ferry-boat from its fasts. This boat a huge flat, suited to the transportation of wagons of the largest dimensions across the river—soon received the party without their horses. These were sent to await them, under the charge of a couple of the troop, to a spot on the same side of the river seven miles below, which was described to be directly opposite to that where the outlaws held their abode. Under the guidance of Rawlins, who knew the river, and Stillyards, to whom the upper shore was sufficiently familiar, the flat was suffered noiselessly to fall down with the current; the only toil of the party being to push her off when she touched the shore, and keep her free from the snags and sawyers—a task not so easy to execute in the imperfect starlight, which guided them in their progress.

But they experienced fewer difficulties than Vernon had anticipated, and arrived at the spot already known to the reader by the fishing adventure of Horsey, in perfect secrecy and silence. The flat was now run up, and suffered to rest upon

the oozy plane which skirted the river and lay between it and
Oane Castle; and, through this bog, the most toilsome and unpleasant part of their journey, the little troop were compelled
to scramble—the silence imposed upon Horsey, at this juncture,
being the worst portion of the business to that worthy amateur.
The restraint he found excessively irksome, at a moment and
in a place, which reminded him of some of his strangest experience, and of events which had been sufficiently exciting to himself to make him sure of the dramatic effect which they must
produce in the minds and estimation of all others. It did not
alter the case very materially that he had discoursed over his
experience to several of his present comrades more than once
already. All day he had exercised his tongue in the reminiscences, always pleasant when past, of peril and annoyance:
still, some had not heard—and then, the minutiae!

"It is in the little touches, my dear fellow," he said to Vernon, in a whisper—"the nice and seemingly unimportant features of a subject, that the whole character speaks out. A look,
a nod, a wink, or the slightest gesture in the proper place, makes
all the difference in the world—makes eloquent the commonest
passages of the poet, which the ordinary reader would slur over
in impatience."

"Be a man now, not an actor, Horsey. Everything in season," was the stern response of Vernon, in a like whisper. "He
is neither man nor actor who can not keep his tongue, when the
part actually calls for silence."

"You're right in that, by the ghost of Solomon, Harry Monmouth;" and, as the actor contented himself with this reply, he
sunk back, murmuring from one of his favorites:—

> "This is no world
> To play with mammets, and to tilt with lips:
> We must have bloody noses, and cracked crowns,
> And pass them current too:—"

A reflection, we may add, that only distressed him as he thought
how awkward he should look, appearing a second time with a
bloody nose before Mary Clayton, otherwise Mrs. Horsey.

He was beguiled from his annoyances, however, by finding
that the next person at his side was Master Edward Mabry, his

late rival. This discovery led him to some vague musings about coincidences, from which he was only aroused by the summons, which sent him forward with three others, for the capture of his quondam companion, Jones; a summons which enlivened and gratified him greatly, as it seemed to imply some retributive agency in Providence, which thus left open the door to an atonement for all the indignities of Mr. Aristophanes Bull, and the ruin of his Hamlet.

He followed Rawlins, to whom Stillyards had given particular directions for finding the sleeping-place of that sturdy outlaw, while five others, equally well instructed, were commissioned for the capture of the rest of the gang. Vernon, reserving to himself the dwarf Stillyards only, took his way with a cautious step, but a bounding heart, toward the squatter's hovel, where he had been told by his companion that the maiden was imprisoned. His command to the rest of his party was, that the followers of Saxon should be surprised and captured;—a more sudden, if not more severe doom he purposed for the outlaw himself. For him the sudden shot or stroke was designed, as from him was anticipated the most reckless and resolute resistance

Meanwhile, the commotion at Zion's Hill, inspired by the astounding intelligence brought by those who escorted the captured outlaws, was such as might have been expected from the vexed self-esteem of the venerable veteran. The attempt of Vernon and Rawlins to effect so important a business without his agency, was a source of equal surprise and indignation That Rawlins should be so presumptuous, was monstrous in the extreme; and what made it seem more so, was the fact, that, in all his schemes and counsels, submitted from time to time to the latter, after the departure of Vernon, it seemed to the dictatorial elder, that the woodman was uncommonly obtuse and wretchedly deficient in honorable enterprise. His son, Gideon, on the contrary, by the boldness of his expressions, and the warmth of valor which he displayed whenever the capture of the "Beagles" was the subject, had greatly commended himself to the old man's heart. He even began to think, after making due comparisons between the two on this subject, that it would be only a legitimate right which he had, as the guardian of Rachel Morrison,

and a becoming exercise of his wisdom, to urge his wishes upon
her that she should marry a youth of so much more promise,
and discard one of whom so few expectations could be formed.
He had forborne any attempt hitherto, to bias her affections;
but to one who assumed to himself so large a portion of the
allotted sagacity of mankind, it began to seem perfectly proper
and praiseworthy to employ it in his own way, for the use of
one, who still toiled in a sort of moral darkness and among the
shadows of ignorance. His first attempts at this sort of juris-
diction, were, however, moderate enough. He began by reproaches of Rawlins for his indirection and infirmity of purpose,
and a recommendation, only implied, however, of the worth,
and valiant Gideon.

"What Walter Rawlins can mean," he remarked to Rachel
one morning shortly after the woodman had taken his depart
ure, "by keeping his hands from the good work, I do not understand. Surely he lacks not heart—he hath courage for
strife. There hath been no shrinking, hitherto, on his part, in
the hour of danger."

"He has courage, believe me," was the reply of Rachel, with
the natural and unrestrained warmth of one who loves without
doubt or qualification. "There is no man of more courage on
the river."

"It would please me to think so, Rachel—nay, I have
thought so, but a short while since; yet, to say truth, I have
my misgivings. Why is he backward to stir up the people
when I bid him? Why, when the occasion is so pressing—
when evil men gather with deadly weapons in their hands, and
deadly malice in their hearts, as I may say it, around the holy
places of the Lord; and the innocent traveller is waylaid for
his spoil; and they fear not to smite the unoffending, and the
unprepared, and the innocent—why doth he keep himself
aloof at such a time—how may he justify himself for such
slackness of spirit? Were he feeble of limb, and slight of person, it were, perhaps, to be forgiven him that he is backward;
but he hath strength beyond that of ordinary men, and with a
fitting strength of heart, there would seem to be no justification
for this lukewarmness. Truly, Rachel, it humbleth me much
—this falling off in our friend."

"There is no falling off, dear uncle, believe me. I will answer for Walter, that, when the fitting time shall arrive, he will be ready, and among the first."

"When the fitting time shall arrive!" was the exclamation of the elder. "Have I not said to thee and to him, already, that now is the time and the season? Now! now! Can there be a better hour than the first for the good performances of a man, and those which are so needful for human safety? He hath heard my thought more than once already, in behalf of this necessity."

"But, if he thinks otherwise," was the imprudent reply of the maiden — her anxiety for the justification of her lover, making her forgetful of the mortal stab which such a suggestion must give to the old gentleman's conceit of heart. His hands and eyes were uplifted in unmitigated astonishment.

"Ha! it is so, then, even as I expected. He hath better assurances of wisdom and the truth than older men — nay, than all men around! for all men seem to hold it needful that the outlaw should be arrested, out of hand, in his deeds of evil. He thinks otherwise, doth he? He will tell us when it is the fitting season, will he? He is good and wise, but it is unfortunate that we must do without him. We must conten. ourselves with the strength we have, and only pray to the Lord that it may be equal to the work before us — that we may go forward without faintness of heart or slackness of spirit, and that success may be vouchsafed to us, not because of the strength which we have, but the will for the performance!"

"Oh, my uncle, speak not thus harshly — think not thus unkindly of Walter;" responded the maiden, now fully awake to her indiscretion as she listened to this outpouring of the morbid vanity of age. "You do Walter injustice; I'm sure you do; and he'll be ready to go with the rest, as soon as ever they're ready. He may think it too soon, but I'm sure, when you once set the example, and name the day, he'll be among the first to turn out at your summons."

A reply no less bitter than the former answered this additional speech of Rachel; and was followed up by a sneering comment of Master Gideon Badger, who made his appearance while the controversy was in progress. He muttered some

general remark about the not unfrequent incompetency of the
soul to the frame which enclosed it; and concluded with assu
ring his father that mere bulk or even numbers were not so
necessary as spirit and resolution for the adventure which 'bey
had in view.

"And the sanction of God, my son," said the now approving
father.

The eye of Rachel Morrison turned upon the hypocritical
Gideon, with an expression of fiery scorn which he shrunk to
encounter. Her heart swelled within her with a feeling of
indignant resistance as she replied, addressing herself only to
the son:—

"I can answer equally for the spirit and frame of Walter
Rawlins, Gideon Badger, and will warn you in season how you
provoke either."

"Rachel Morrison!" exclaimed the old man sternly—"would
you threaten Gideon with the violence of a stranger?"

"A stranger, uncle—Walter Rawlins a stranger!—Has it
then come to this?—But if he is a stranger to you, sir, as, indeed, he seems to be, from the manner in which you speak and
think of him, he is yet no stranger to me. I can answer
equally for his strength and courage. As for threatening
Gideon with them, I had no such thought—but I thought it
prudent to warn him against offending either. Walter is patient
enough, but he is young, and he is human; and when human
passions are treated with scorn, they are very apt to rise in
resentment. I respect the courage of Walter sufficiently to
make me think it would not be safe for Gideon to doubt it in
his hearing."

"In a good cause, and with God's blessing," said the devout
young man, "I have little fear of him or of any other person."

"And with such principles, Gideon, my son, you need have
no fear. The gates of hell shall not prevail against him who
goes forth armed by God's favor, and in the prosecution of the
just war of truth. It is even such a war as this, which Walter
Rawlins thinks it not yet a seasonable time to begin; but, as
you have already said, we need not numbers in a righteous
cause. God will provide—God will strengthen—God will see
that numbers even shall not be wanting, in the hour when the

banner is to be raised and the blows are to be struck; and if I have a sorrow because of the absence of Walter Rawlins from this conflict, it is because of his own great loss therefrom."

"He will not be absent!" exclaimed Rachel Morrison— I know he will go in search of these robbers, when the time comes, so far ahead of some others, that even their eyes will not dare to follow him."

This sarcasm was felt by Gideon, but passed the old man without attracting his notice; an escape which no doubt saved the damsel a lecture on presumption of heart, and pride of opinion, and some dozen more of the vital sins of ignorance and youth.

The arrival of the captured outlaws, and the message from Rawlins—events which took place only two days after this dialogue—while they completely justified the warm confidence of the maiden in the manhood of her lover, as completely confounded the stern old methodist, and baffled all his estimates of character. Not that he thought any better of Walter Rawlins than before. If forced to believe him brave and ready now, he was at least thoroughly vexed with the audacity that dared to undertake a business so important without his co-operation. Nay—not only without his co-operation, but actually, with a studious reservation from him of a task in which his own threatened performances were to be the most conspicuous of all human adventures. His self-complacency did not permit him to imagine, for a single instant, the true reason why he should be kept from the knowledge of a scheme, the object of which he had as sincerely and notoriously at heart, as anybody else, and it would have been very difficult to persuade him—the fact is not easy of belief—that a dogmatical old man is of all others the greatest obstacle to the progress of any business, where young men are to be the performers. That Badger would have rejected every plan but his own, for the capture of the robbers, and spoiled any that might be undertaken, the shrewd sense of Vernon perceived in the first hour of their acquaintance; and the doubts which were entertained of the fidelity of the son, naturally combined to strengthen his objections to any participation of the father in the business. His views of the subject have been already given to the reader.

The exultation of Rachel Morrison may be imagined, when
these proofs of the courage of her Walter were produced— an
exultation which spoke in tearful eyes, and a trembling and
l anding heart. Old Badger, as one of the quorum, and one
learned in the law—in all laws—clothed in official authority,
and no less delighted with, than conscious of, the power which
it conferred, was—however angry with the captors—not un
willing to take into custody the captive outlaws. He secured
them under good locks and keys, having first taken the precau
tion, with the assistance of the detachment under whose guard
they came, of roping them to some very heavy articles of fur
niture. The two *soi-disant* constables were bound, with up
ward-looking eyes, on the flats of their backs, *tête-à-tête*, to a
dresser of prolonged dimensions, but not so long, as, when the
rogues were stretched upon it, to admit of a support to their
legs, which were, in consequence, suffered to dangle from it,
only in partial possession of their wonted liberty. They could
kick the wall or each other, at either end of the board, but to
these limited exercises they were unequivocally restrained
If the other two were not equally well-cared for, it was their
misfortune—they were certainly equally well-fastened It
needs not that we should describe the particular privileges of
their situation. Two of the guard were reserved to keep watch
over them until the proper officers of the law could be got in
requisition, while the other two were dismissed, at their own
request, that they might rejoin the attacking party that night,
and before the descent was made upon the camp of the outlaws
  After dismissing them, which he did in no very ceremonious
or friendly manner, old Badger was suddenly seized with the
conviction that he should have gone himself. His *amour propre*
was interested to lead in an expedition for which his past ac
quaintance with the wars, and his present connection with "the
peace," seemed equally to constitute a peculiar justification of
his claim. Besides, had he not been beating up recruits for this
very expedition? Were not some of them in the neighborhood
—could they not be easily mustered? There was Gideon and
himself—Joe Tompkins, the hired ploughboy, Nicodemus Root,
the schoolmaster, who, though a Yankee, was able to ride and
shoot, and had done execution more than once at pigeon-dis-

tance. A timely use of the six or seven hours remaining between that and daylight, would enable him easily to muster up
some half a score; and with these the veteran was not unwilling,
in a fair day, and after due preliminaries of prayer and fasting,
to face all the outlaws between the Alabama and Arkansas.
From the guard that brought in the prisoners, he had been led
to believe that the party of Vernon would not commence the
march before dawn; and as he had no thought of the use which
might be made of the ferry-boat in such an expedition, he took
it for granted that hard riding would bring him to the post of
danger in season for all its honors. This new course of thought
led to instant preparations, which need to be adverted to only.
They do not affect our expedition at this moment.

But when his plans had to be carried out, the venerable elder
discovered that one of his chief agents was reported missing.
This was his own son, the worthy Gideon, who was no less confounded than his father at the developments of the night. If
the old man was vexed and mortified, Gideon was terrified.
The danger was at his very door. The rascals who were taken
knew him as a confederate, and in the very presence of the old
man exhibited those secret signs of intelligence which made the
profligate youth's heart quake within him, though he sufficiently
preserved his equilibrium to return them. The keen eyes of
Rachel Morrison beheld his consternation, and her piercing and
suspicious glance did not fail to perceive that there was some
communion even then going on between the parties.

Gideon, with every additional moment of reflection, fancied
the danger to be increasing. He knew that the outlaws looked
to him for assistance; nay, looked to him to liberate them;—
and also remembered some of the painful conditions which were
coupled with his association with the beagles. He was sworn
to convey the tidings of danger to his comrades in the swamp.
Their arrest almost necessarily led to his own. The discovery
of their secrets involved his safety; and what security could
he have against the revelations of frightened rogues at the foot
of the gallows? He was divided between conflicting fears and
desires. It was important to rescue the outlaws already in custody—it was equally, if not more important, to counsel those
in the swamp of their approaching danger.

A few moments' reflection determined him to address himself exclusively to the latter object. The danger of the prisoners was not immediate. They were yet to be committed for trial, and a considerable stretch of time lay between the present and the period assigned for the county court sessions. If the beagles in the swamp continued free, it would be no very difficult matter to rescue the prisoners at some more favorable moment; and the only evil would be their temporary detention in confinement. He was well assured that such hardy rogues would never make their confessions a moment sooner than was necessary.

That the beagles in the swamp were prepared for their enemies was very probable, and yet a promptness, spirit, and vigilance, such as had already been shown by the assailing party, rendered important every measure of precaution, and demanded the instant activity of every member of the fraternity. Vernon and Rawlins were obviously men to be feared, and the reader has already seen that Gideon Badger was one of those men who are soonest to "despair their charm." He wanted "the natural hue of courage," and his fears on the present occasion, even exaggerated the danger, pressing as it really was. To give a sign to the outlaws in custody, significant of his resolution to serve them, and to slip from the apartment unobserved, even before his father had yet dismissed the two men of Rawlins's party who had brought in the prisoners, were the first steps of Gideon after he had concluded upon his course. The venerable methodist, with eyes shut and hands uplifted, was too busy delivering a searching sermon to the prisoners and their captors alike, to observe the movements of the son. But they were seen by the keen eyes of the damsel, who already knew enough of the truth to comprehend the condition of Gideon's mind, and to anticipate his probable course. She followed him silently from the apartment, and traced his steps to the foot of the garden. She came up with him as he was about to cross the fence, and called him instantly by name.

"Gideon!—Gideon Badger!"

How shrunk his heart in terror at the sound—the sound of his own name uttered by the lips of a woman! But at that moment he knew not whose lips uttered it, and it was a sound of terror. His apprehensions had rendered his senses dull to discriminate, however acute in the appreciation of all sights and accents. The summons seemed full of terror, and it was not till she approached, and he turned full upon her, that he felt relieved. ,

"Gideon," she said, "go not if you would be safe. I warn you, stay where you are—you are in danger if you leave Zion's Hill."

"In danger, Rachel!—in danger, my pretty cousin!" he replied, with some show of recovered impudence, if not courage, in his manner—"why, what should be the danger that I must apprehend, unless it be that to which I have been so long exposed? My danger is from you, Rachel—you only!"

He would have taken her hand as he spoke, with an air of excessive familiarity, but she repulsed him and drew back at his approach, with a manner, the evident aversion of which brought a burning flush upon his cheek

"This is no time," she said coldly, "for these follies; and least of all is it a season for you to indulge in them. Hear me, Gideon; I am in possession of your secrets—I can guess where, even now, you would bend your steps. You go to warn the robbers in the swamp of the danger that awaits them."

"Ha!" It was all he spoke, and his teeth almost chattered in the utterance.

"Yes—it is known to me—the dreadful tie that binds you to these miserable men. I have heard you in speech with their leader, and others of the band. They are in danger—you can not show them this, without involving yourself in their danger, and it is beyond your power to save them. Stay where you are—or, if you leave Zion's Hill, let me counsel you to take a course far different from that you intend to-night. Fly to the eastward; I will keep your secret, and do my best to get the means for you from my uncle."

"Rachel, you must really care for me. This friendly revelation—this pursuit of me—this interest in my fortunes—this care for my safety, sufficiently prove it. Be mine, dear Rachel, and I will do as you counsel—I will fly from this confederacy—I will go with you where you please."

"This is only trifling, Gideon — you should know me better I have already told you that I am pledged to. another."

"But you do not love him — you can not — nay — can I doubt your feeling of preference for me after this proof? It is midnight — the darkness of the night and forest are around us — yet you seek me to counsel me against danger — you —"

"God help you to wiser thoughts, Gideon. Is it not enough that you are the only child of that uncle who has been a father to me? Is this not sufficient reason why I should seek to keep you from danger, and him from misery?"

"I must believe there is yet another and a better reason. I am sure, Rachel, that we can be happy together."

"Never! never!" she exclaimed, with impetuous energy, as. provoked by the insolent self-complaisance of his tone and manner, she wrested from him the hand which he had partially taken in his grasp. "Flatter yourself with no such idle fancies, Gideon Badger. Happiness with you is impossible. Sooner shall the heavy sod lie upon my bosom, and I not feel it, that I yield myself up to the hope, or to the chance of finding happiness in any closer connection with you than now! Even now I pain to look upon you as I must daily, and see you as I do and know you as you are!"

"Rachel Morrison, you have determined your own fate. You know too much for your safety and for mine. My security henceforward must be in securing you. You have been at some pains to pry into my secrets — to follow me here and there, and become a party to those concerns in which you were required to take no part. This proves that you have sufficient interest in my fortunes to justify me in forcing a portion of them upon you. You are right; I am about to join the beagles in the swamp. It is useless now to deny to you that I am one of them. You must go with me. You must be mine from this instant! Your own lips have sealed your doom! Your man, Rawlins is not here to save you now!"

He advanced upon her as he spoke. She retreated a pace and spoke with tones of coolness and deliberation — tones which trembled only from the aroused energies of her spirit.

"You are mistaken, Gideon Badger. I am prepared for this. It is you that have sealed your doom, or will seal it, if you ad-

vance another step toward me! If the man, Walter Rawlins
—he is a man, Gideon Badger!—if he be not here to save me,
he has left me that with which I shall save myself! One of
his pistols is now in my hand—loaded by him, and left at my
request—with a fearful conviction that it might be necessary
at some such moment as the present! Your threats have thus
prepared me; I have learned the use of the weapon; and, as I
hope still to maintain the whiteness of my soul to the last, I am
resolved to use it against yourself, sooner than suffer you to
sully the purity of mine. You know me well enough, Gideon
Badger, to know that I will as solemnly execute the resolution
which I have so solemnly made! Now, approach me with violence, if you dare!"

CHAPTER XLII.

THE WOLF AT BAY—THE APE ON THE SHOULDERS OF THE
TIGER—A COUP-DE-THEATRE, A LA SIDDONS.

"Such a life,
Methinks, had metal in it to survive
An age of men."—GEORGE CHAPMAN.

THE solemn accents, the deliberate, resolved tone of the
maiden, not less than the energetic language which she used,
would have impressed a much bolder person than Gideon Badger with the danger of trifling with such a spirit. It was evident that all was serious and composed earnestness in her mind;
and her words derived no emphasis, or very little, from the exhibition of the pistol, and the click of the lock as it distinctly
sounded under her fingers. To the dastard soul of Gideon Badger it struck a sentiment of fear, which at once disarmed him
of his insolence and arrested his approach. But a moment before he had persuaded himself that he should be able to carry
her in safety to the swamp. He had no sort of doubt that the
beagles would escape the pursuit of Rawlins's party, even if
they remained uncounselled by himself; for, well apprized of

the number less ramifications and resources of the fraternity, he
did not fear but they would be advised of the approach of the
enemy by at least a dozen out-sentries.   How easy to find
shelter with them for Rachel Morrison; and there, secure from
pursuit, and having her entirely in his power and at his mercy,
what should hinder the consummation of any, even of his worst
purposes?

Such was the precious scheme which his mind conceived
from the first moment that night when Rachel appeared upon
the scene.   Such was the scheme which her masculine resolution and her foresight so easily defeated.   Gideon Badger was
not calculated to be a magnificent villain.   He was a petty ras
cal only.   In a city like New York he would have made an
excellent auction-dealer—one of those cunning gentry that sell
baubles by the lot, and bluster when you refuse to keep your
hasty purchases.   Still, base as was his nature, he felt the
meanness of his present position   Incapable of pressing his
villany to the utmost, he would have ascribed his abortive attempt to merriment only.   With a laugh, which did not altogether disguise the tremulous tone of his voice, he said :—

"Why, Rachel, you seem to think that I was serious—at
least, you are grown serious yourself.   And so you actually go
armed?   That, of all things, is the strangest!   Why should
you go armed?   What would you do with a loaded pistol, I
should like to know?"

"Use it for my protection, Gideon, if I found any one seriously bent to assail me," was the cool reply.

"But you could not have supposed that I would do such a
thing, Rachel?"

"I do!—indeed, I know that you would, if you dared!   It
is well for both of us, Gideon, that you are not quite so valiant
as you are wicked!"

"You speak plainly, Rachel," was the hoarse reply.

"It is best," answered the maiden; "it is for your safety
that I have spoken thus plainly.   Hear me, Gideon, while I
speak more plainly yet.   To save you from a great peril, I
have ventured into these woods at this hour of the night, in
spite of the fears and scruples which are so natural to my
sex—"

"And of which your own share seems unaccountably small," was the sneering interruption of her companion.

"That is as you think," was the composed reply. "Small or great, they were sufficient to have kept me back from this interview, but that I was resolved to add one more effort to those I have already made, to save you from the dangers into which you are yet resolved to fall."

"You are very kind — very benignant."

She did not heed the impertinence of this speech, or its equally impertinent manner, as she proceeded :—

"Yet, not because I had care or interest in you, Gideon Badger, did I take these pains, or incur a risk, which your own conduct has just assured me was no small one — but for that good old man, your father, who has been more than a father to me, and whose gray hairs would go down to the grave in wretchedness, did any mishap or dishonor reach his son. I do not seek to save you from the danger so much as I seek to spare him the sorrow and the shame. You have shown yourself too little careful of my feelings, Gideon, during our long acquaintance, to deserve much at my hands, of either respect or kindness. On the contrary, sin e we have reached maturity, I have known you by your persecutions — by your ungenerous persecutions — rather than by any more commendable qualities or conduct. Still, I would save you — from your comrades, from yourself, from the laws which you have outraged, and which you are now about to outrage. I have kept your secret from your father, from Rawlins, from all — I have restrained, though with great difficulty, another from declaring it. I now tell you, Gideon, solemnly here and seriously, that if you go this night into the swamp, you go into unnecessary danger. I have a presentiment, Gideon, that you go never to return."

He would have ridiculed her counsels and her fears. He made an attempt to laugh at her solemnity, but the effort degenerated into a lugubrious chuckle, that died away in a hoarse whisper in his throat.

"Tell me what *you know*," he at length exclaimed, in a tone of emphatic utterance which sufficiently declared his apprehensions — "speak not to me of your presentiments, and all that sort of superstitious nonsense, but tell me what you have heard

—*what you know.* Come—you have it all from your man, Rawlins;—if you really desire to serve my father, and to save me, his dutiful son, to his embraces, let me know what the plan is for the catching of the beagles. A word, Rachel Morrison, a single word of positive assurance will do more than all your conjectures, superstitions, and fancies. Speak that word and I remain at Zion's Hill—I remain with you."

" With me!—But no! I will speak no bitterness, Gideon, in this moment, when your life and my hope may equally rest upon the verge of a dreadful precipice."

" Your hope and my life! What mean you? I do not understand the connection."

" Nor will I explain it, Gideon. The only warning which I am willing that you shall understand is one that I am willing to repeat. Your insolent words, tone, and manner, shall not make me less desirous of your safety; since nothing that you can say or do, can make me lose sight of what I owe to your venerable father."

" Oh this is all talk, Rachel. Can you or will you tell n e nothing of these handsome fellows that are so valiantly resolved to pursue my comrades into the swamp? You see, I admit them to be comrades. You have proved yourself so close a keeper of the secret heretofore, that I can not hesitate in confiding to you my admission of the truth. I tell you, therefore, that I am sworn to go to the swamp to-night—sworn to myself and them—to convey the intelligence of the danger which is supposed to threaten them. I am bound to them for this. My safety—my very life depends upon it. If I fail them, they have their laws and penalties, to which those of society are but toys—the merest trifles that ever yet assumed the features of danger to the eyes of man. Now, Rachel, let me but clearly see that there is an occasion for your caution, and I will not go. I will have an excuse which shall secure me from the penalties of any violated oath."

" Father in heaven! and can it be, Gideon Badger, that you are so fearfully related to these men?"

" Pshaw! Rachel—you waste time with these interjections," replied the youth with tones of dogged impatience. " To the point—to the point. Is there present danger to me, and what is its form—whence comes it—from whom—where? To that—to that, Rachel. Speak to that."

'Have I not said—have you not heard? Surely you do not despise the attempts which Walter Rawlins and Mr. Vernon are now making? You have heard the men that brought in the prisoners?"

"Surely I know all this, Rachel Morrison, but I thought you knew more. Knowing this, I yet resolve to go. As for the danger, set your heart easy on that subject. By the dawn, when your gallant is in motion for the swamp, I shall be at Zion's Hill again, or so near it as to smell the breakfast; and the beagles will be so far on their way from the place of danger that their nests will be cold enough when the hunters arrive. So, Rachel, if you will not think better of it, and go with me—I renew my offer—the best counsel I can give you is, to get to bed as soon as you may, and dream of more evil for Gideon Badger. It will be easy to dream of that which we sincerely wish."

"I wish you nothing but good, Gideon, and once more warn you not to go into the swamp to-night. There is blood upon the path. Something tells me it will be fatal to you if you go."

"Unless you go with me, Rachel. Nay, why will you be so stubborn? You know not what you lose, Rachel! Joys of which you never dreamed, and—"

"Go! evil son of a worthy father—go!" was the stern interruption of the maiden, as she turned from the reprobate. "You obey a written destiny. God will not suffer you to be saved by so feeble an instrument as I."

The solemnity of these tones sounded like a trumpet in the ears of the dissolute youth, and the feeling of awful conviction which lay at the heart of Rachel Morrison, and which impressed her with the faith that no further effort could help him who had been delivered over to his doom by the fiat of Heaven, for a moment impressed itself also upon the soul of the person whom it chiefly interested. But this feeling was not suffered to obtain more than a moment's ascendency. The coward is frequently rash through a consciousness of his own cowardice, and the conviction that he really trembles, leads him to resolve upon a course which shall convince the spectator that he was never

more courageous in his life. He laughed at the omens which
made him shudder, and mocked at the warning which terrified
him. He strove to shroud his apprehensions in his ribaldry,
and his last words to the maiden consisted in a renewal of his
proposition to share with him the licentious life of the swamp;
the freedom from all restraint, which, to his mind, seemed the
very acme of human freedom and felicity. She answered his
proposition by a prayer contained in a single sentence which increased the awe that dwelt within his heart: "Cut him not off
in his sins. Oh, G d! smite him not suddenly in thy anger."

He disappeared in that instant. He had not the spirit to
respond to this.

Meanwhile, the reader must not suppose that the business in
the swamp remained at a stand. On the contrary, never were
men more alert to do execution in an enemy's country, than the
worthy fellows under their several leaders, Rawlins, Jamison
and the amateur. The latter, however, resolute as any of the
rest, when he reached the spot where he had lost his every-day
habiliments, could not resist the temptation of giving to his little band, a brief narrative of those afflicting events and the
other circumstances that followed his arrival in the swamp, and
his connection with that arch-beagle, Jones.

At another moment it might amuse the reader, who is already
familiar with these circumstances. to hear Horsey relate them.
His story would seem a very different one from ours. Nay, the
two would scarce seem identical in any one respect, so completely did he suppress those proofs of mental flexibility—not to
say gullibility—on his part, which rendered it so easy a matter for the cunning outlaw to persuade him that the moon was
a green cheese, and he the best man to cut it. As he told the
tale, it seemed to his hearers, that he had traced the outlaws to
their haunts designedly—that he had cheated the dull dogs into
the belief that he was a simple citizen, ambitious of no fortune more lofty than that of bringing the house down in applauses of his superior merits as an actor—beyond Kemble and
Forrest, Kean and Cooper. How he had concealed his real
purposes, and fathomed theirs; how he had traversed their haunts,
traced their secrets, learned their signs, and read all their mysteries, is a history to itself which might deserve its own volume

Yet, such was the fellow's ingenuity, he told no lie —no actual lie —and certainly meant none. His was one of those active and flexible imaginations that grow ductile at the slightest pressure and catch the slightest change of color from the most casual cloud. His bricks soon became marble, and his fancy never went without its wings.

On the present occasion it almost involved him in a worse difficulty than he had ever been in before. While he related his experience among the beagles, who should he encounter but his old acquaintance, Mr. Bull—Aristophanes Bull—whose headstrong opposition had already been a source of such infinite discomfiture to him; and who, if time had been given him, might very soon have corrected the little mistakes so naturally made in Horsey's narration. Fortunately, Bull had been at his usual potations, and our actor was no less prompt in action than in speech. When Bull struggled forward, with a skin full, thoroughly soaked, and only half conscious of the globe's motion asking in hoarse tones, and with a hiccough: "What the h-ll's the matter here, boys?"—he received in reply, a blow over the skull from Horsey's pistol in such downright good earnest that it would have tasked the powers of all the Bull breed to have kept him well-balanced under it. Down he went, with a thump that fully assured the actor of his intention to await him there.

This occurrence took place not twenty steps from the sleeping-place of Jones; and Horsey —little prudent as he was—began to entertain some misgivings that this cunning outlaw might be alarmed by the noise, and would give him trouble. A clump of shrub trees and one sturdy pine, stood between them and their victim; and here he commanded his men to pause until he should survey the ground alone.

He advanced cautiously, keeping himself under cover of the shrubbery as he went forward, and soon had the satisfaction to find that all was quiet in the sylvan wigwam. He then motioned his fellows to advance , and two at the entrance, and three others conveniently stationed to yield assistance to the active assailants, entirely cut off the outlaw's hope of escape.

Still he might give the alarm, and this it was important to prevent. Handkerchiefs were brought forward and got in readiness, while Horsey led the way and boldly penetrated the tent of poles

and bushes under which the enemy slept. A stout fellow followed and seconded him, and the deep breathing of the outlaw
guided them to the particular place of his repose.

Still! they could see nothing. They had to be guided entirely
by the sense of feeling and the ear. At length, after much
cautious management and some delay, they placed themselves
on each side of his head. This ascertained, a whisper gave the
signal, and while the stout companion of Horsey threw himself
on the outlaw, the latter adroitly passed a slip-noose around
his neck, and awakened the sleeper to consciousness by a pressure of no moderate force. The arms and feet of their captive
were meanwhile secured by the rest of their comrades, and the
power of further harm was taken from him with a promptness
and completeness, that would have been creditable to greater
proficients.

Still, with all their precautions, they could not altogether
prevent his giving some alarm. With the readiness of a veteran
the outlaw, at the first consciousness which he had of the danger
endeavored to shout the signal of the band — a whoop, borrowed
from the Indians, which, with better lungs, they had learned to
endow with a somewhat more terrific energy — but the unre-
lenting fingers of Horsey were as prompt as the beagle's tongue,
and the pressure of the ligature around the jugular, suddenly
cut short the sounds before they had acquired sufficient vigor to
pass beyond the gorge of his throat. A guard was set over him,
with orders to shoot him at the first movement or show of rescue,
while the rest of the captors proceeded in search of other foes.

It will not need that we follow them. It may be necessary,
however, to note one adventure of the party under Jamison.
The worthy Alabamian was a second time fortunate in meeting
with his quondam friend, the Irishman, Dennis O'Dougherty.
His knee was upon the fellow's chest in the dark, when the
brogue of the struggling prisoner declared who he was.

"Ha! Dennis, my boy — is it you?"

"By J-sus, honey, but you're a bit mistaken in the parson.
I'm a very different jontleman, to your liking."

An effort to rise succeeded this speech, which the Alabamian
effectually arrested by tickling the throat of his prisoner with
the point of his bowis.

"Be asy now, will you!—and don't be afther giving your-elf any more throuble. Don't you think I understand plain spaking, my honey?"

"You're no fool, Dennis," said the Alabamian, as he found the Irishman lying quiet. "Had you twisted the lalast inch of your animal, Dennis, after the hint I gave you, I'd ha' been through you with more steel than Dick Smith ever swull wed. I will but run a ploughline under your arms, Dennis, to keep you comfortable, and you may thank me that I du.'t put it about your gullet. Is it easy to your elbow, Dennis?"

"Asy! J-sus, Mr. Jamison, are you a jontleman?'

"Well, anything to make you comfortable; and so I'll let out a little; but, look you, Dennis, be quiet. I'm going from you a bit, and if you're not quiet, the man that watches you won't leave the skin to your teeth. He's a raal Ingin at sculp-ing, and your head will be t his skirts, while your tongue's chattering about it."

But the smaller villains are not our object, and it will suffice to say, that it was not a difficult task, so complete had been the surprise, to capture nearly all the inmates of the swamp. The number at Cane Castle was usually small—the great body of the fraternity, as detailed in our former work, being engaged in active operations while traversing the country. Vernon knew that everything depended on the capture or death of the chief — the master-spirit who had conceived a plan of operations so extensive, so bold, so well detailed, and so sternly carried out. To this labor, as we have seen, he devoted himself. A livelier interest served to stimulate his zeal, and to make him no less anxious and eager than resolute for the conflict. He knew that if he found Saxon awake, the struggle that would probably ensue, must be mortal. For this issue his energies of mind and body were braced to the utmost, and the image of Virginia Maitland, in the power of the ruffian and suffering from his vio-lence, gave a terrible earnestness to his resolve, from the first moment when he embarked upon the adventure. He did find the outlaw awake, and under circumstances to keep alive the in-dignation and resolution of his heart. Conducted by the dwarf, Stillyards, to the wigwam, known among the beagles as the squatter's cabin at Little Bend, he beheld at a single glance, the

object of his affections, and the object of his hate. Virginia Mait
land was before him, and before her was Saxon. The circumstan
ces under which they stood, made the blood boil within the veins
of the inflamed beholder, and he found it difficult so to restrain
his passion, as to look around him with deliberation, and determine calmly what course to pursue. The house in which they
were, was a common fabric of logs such as is universal in the
new countries of the southwest. It stood upon pine blocks,
about four feet from the ground. It consisted of two rooms,
separated from each other by a thin partition, the door of which
opened in the centre. Each room had an entrance from without, independent of the other, and a single window in each sufficed to give it light. On the present occasion the doors and
windows were closed, and the observation of Vernon was made
through crevices between the logs of the building, of which the
number was sufficient for all the purposes of espionage. Conducted by the dwarf, Stillyards, to one of these crevices, which
the urchin seemed to find very readily, the objects that met the
eyes of Vernon increased his emotions. Virginia Maitland was
seated on a rude chair, at the door-way between the two rooms,
her back to the one, which happened to be the sleeping apartment, and her face to Saxon, who strode the room before her.
Her hands were clasped and resting upon her knees. Her
neck and head were bent forward, while her eyes, with a tear-
less anxiety, watched every movement of the outlaw, as keenly
as one would watch the form of the panther crouching in the
tree above him, and in the attitude to spring. It was evident
that as yet no outrage, other than that of her abduction, had
been attempted by the ruffian; but her looks amply testified
her fears, while his as clearly manifested his desires. That the
outlaw had been striving to persuade her to his purposes was
evident enough, and that his persuasions only awakened her
apprehensions, might be inferred from her attitude of mixed
prayer, watchfulness, and terror.

Such was the picture that first met the eye of Vernon. The
words of Saxon a moment after, that met his ears, confirmed
all the first impressions which it made upon his mind; and he
placed the muzzle of his pistol, which was already cocked and
'n his hand, at the opening, which was sufficiently large to

admit of his certain aim at the ruffian. But his cheek glowed
a moment after with a feeling akin to shame. Vernon was not
familiar with the shedding of blood, and no man who is not—
unless he be equally cowardly and malignant—can possibly
take life, except in the whirl and excitement of actual conflict.
He felt that there was something base, from his place of concealment, to shoot down the unconscious man, however deserving he might be of his doom. To fling down from its erect
place and posture an image so noble, made after the form of
God, and filled with such godlike attributes and endowments,
is, at best, and under its most justifiable circumstances, a melancholy performance; and with something of a romantic resolution, such as makes the wisest of men rash at seasons, he determined upon the bolder and more generous measure of giving
the outlaw the benefit of an equal struggle. Such a prize as
Virginia Maitland, seemed to justify every hazard, and Vernon
resolved upon the very last.

He rose from his recumbent position, and was about to proceed toward the doorway, when he felt a hand laid lightly upon
his shoulder. Stillyards, meanwhile, had disappeared. He
turned at the interruption—fancying another enemy at his
elbow—and met the eyes of a woman—one so youthful and
so beautiful as to strike him with wonder at seeing her in so
wild a place. She met his gaze seemingly without emotion.
There was a calm solemnity in her aspect, seen by the serious
starlight, which riveted his attention, commanded his respect,
and would have subdued, even in a far less reverent mind than
his, any ribald thoughts or suspicions.

"Stay!—but a single instant," she whispered, and her uplifted finger gave him like warning. Before he could answer
her, or imagine the object of her intrusion, she was gone from
sight—literally vanished behind an angle of the building.

But her warning was forgotten with her disappearance. Vernon was too much aroused for unnecessary delay, particularly,
too, as he saw not the reason of the woman's injunctions; and,
just then, the pleading tones of Virginia's voice reached his
ears in supplication and alarm. Breathless, he darted upon the
steps of massive pine that led to the door of the building, and
with a single blow of his heel, sent it from its hinges. Another

21

moment found him. within the apartment, and face to face with
the outlaw.

The proceeding was the work of an instant, but it found the
outlaw prepared. He seized his pistols, which lay on a table
near him, and instantly presented them.

Vernon had not seen them before; and had he but waited,
as he had been counselled by Florence Marbois, this danger
would have been-spared him. In the same moment when Saxon
grasped the weapons, the hand of Florence was stretched out
from the inner apartment to which she had penetrated with
noiseless footsteps, for the purpose of securing them.

But, though Saxon grasped and cocked the pistols at his
enemy, he did not dare to use them. With the first appearance
of Vernon, Virginia had started to her feet, and at the sight of
his danger, she rushed between the parties, alternately turning
an imploring face and an uplifted hand to each. She no longer
exhibited the passive attitude of fear. All apprehension for
herself departed when she feared for her lover; and that living
grace of form and movement, which speaks out when the
mother-mood prevails, riveted, at the same moment, with a
sense of equal admiration, the souls of Vernon and the outlaw.

And there, on each side of her, the hostile parties stood —
she, the angel between them, preventing strife, if not securing
peace. Her words, wild, incoherent, impetuous, addressed the
one and then the other; but failed of much effect upon either.
Her position alone controlled the warfare which her presence
was yet calculated to inspire.

Suddenly, the arms of Saxon were grasped by Florence from
behind; a deep imprecation burst from the outlaw's lips as he
distinguished her. Vainly did he strive to shake her off; and
the moment lost in this effort enabled Vernon to grapple with
him at advantage. While they struggled, the dwarf, Stillyards,
dropped upon the shoulders of the outlaw from the scantling
above; and before he could be shaken off or removed, he had
dug with his nails — which had been suffered to grow to an in-
ordinate length — entirely into the ears of his late leader. This
was one of the forms of retribution which consoled him for the
similar indignity to which Saxon had subjected himself. By
this time the house was filled; and the outlaw chief, who had

struggled manfully while any hope remained to him, now yielded quietly to numbers.

"This, then, is your work, Florence," he murmured, as **the** woman he had wronged confronted him.

"Ay, mine! I glory in it—I rejoice, too, that you feel it **to** be mine! You could scorn my love!—perhaps, that was not so great an error as to scorn my power! It glads me to the soul to think that you can feel it and acknowledge it at last!"

"If that will give you pleasure, Florence, be happy. If it can atone for the wrongs which I have done you, to know that you have compassed my doom, you have ample vengeance. I owe my death to your hands."

"Your death atone, Edward Saxon, for my misery!—for the wrong done to my honor—to my hope—to my pride—to my affections—to all things, and thoughts, and feelings, which are dear to woman—which ennoble her to herself and endear her to society! Monstrous vanity! Your death, Edward Saxon, were you thrice to die, could never atone for the wrongs you have inflicted on the frail, fond, foolish heart of Florence Marbois! You have taken from her all that made life precious— and the life which seems so desirable to you, is her scorn! Look, and see what is her value of life, Edward Saxon; and, if you be not utterly base, you will yet learn from her example how to baffle the hangman. She to whom you ascribe your fate, will show you how completely indifferent you have made her to her own."

She advanced closely as she spoke to her betrayer. Her majestic form seemed to tower far above its usual height; and no language could describe the bitter scorn which looked from all her features, as she mocked him with that love of life which she professed to feel no longer. While yet the last words trembled on her lips, she drove a dagger, which till then was concealed within her garments, deep down into her breast. The deed was done before eye could see or hand interpose to prevent it. She was caught, while falling, by Vernon. Her last words, clear and emphatic, though broken, were addressed to the outlaw:—

"Live, Edward Saxon—if life be so precious to you—live!

It has nothing precious now for me!   To you I owe it, at least,
that death is also without pain!   Live!—live!"

Her eyes followed him even in death.   He strove, but vainly,
to avert his own.   He could not—he dared not.   She had conquered, and the spell of her power was upon him in her dying
moments.   Unconsciously, the long breath escaped from him
like a convulsive groan, when the thick glaze passing over her
eyes, rescued him from the fascinating intensity of their glance.
Big drops suddenly started out upon his brow, as if he underwent a fearful agony; and his limbs tottered like one feeble
with a long sickness, as they led him from the apartment under
guard.

CHAPTER XLIII.

FINALE—TWO-FOLD RINGING OF THE BELLS, FOR FATE AND
FELICITY—FUNERAL AND BRIDAL.

"Last scene of all,
That ends this strange, eventful history."—SHAKSPERE.

VERNON bore Virginia Maitland, swooning, from this terrible
scene, the actual performance of which had occupied far less
time than our description of it.   It had passed before the
maiden's eyes, more like some dreadful phantasmagoria of the
magician, than an event of actual life.   He bore her into the
fresh air, which partly revived her; and, under the direction
and with the assistance of Horsey—who affected a better
knowledge of Cane Castle than he really had—succeeded in
finding and conveying her to the little cottage, the mistress of
which had put so fearful a finish to a life of feverish pain and
most unhappy excitement.   The last sacrifice was paid to the
lingering sentiment of that love which still survived jealousy
and anger, and which nothing but death could utterly extin-
guish.   She had obtained the vengeance which she sought; and
the thirst for which, in the first moment of her misery, had overborne the more native feeling of her heart.   That done, the

original passion resumed some portion of its activity, but only to make her feel still more acutely the undesirable and worth-less character of all that remained to life; and the resolution to end it—taken at a moment when her vengeance was yet doubt-ful—seemed more than ever proper to her abased and erring spirit, when its claims were all satisfied. Is it sinful to hope that her crime was softened by her sufferings? There was so much that was bright and noble in her soul amid all its smoke and impurities, that humanity may well be suffered to presume upon the indulgence of mercy, in behalf of one, in whose soul, amid all the cloud, the smoke, and the impurity, there was so much that was really noble in sentiment, and bright and beau-tiful in thought. Florence Marbois, under other auspices, had been one of those lovely lights of society, that guide the hearts which they warm, and hallow the affections which they inspire and requite.

Pass we to the living, no less lovely, and purer woman—to the fair Virginia, who, in the arms of Vernon, was soon re-stored, not less to the consciousness of life, than of those dear emotions that sanctify and sometimes make it heaven! If the past scene of terror, and strife, and death, through which she had been hurried, was not forgotten, its sting at least was taken away by the conviction that all who were dear to her had gone through it in safety, and that all danger to herself and others was *past*. She could now breathe in unrestraint, and yield her-self for a space to that freedom of soul which delights in making its acknowledgments to the beloved one. If ever maiden were justified in speaking freely her happiness to her lover, it is she who has just been rescued by his gallantry from the most evil forms of danger.

Virginia, in the hour of her deliverance, had no reserve. She hung upon the bosom of Vernon, happy in the weakness, which, while it made his valor dear to her, furnished her with the best apology to cling to his embrace.

A moment was given to these raptures—a brief moment; and the lover was recalled by one of his subordinates to a recollec-tion of his further duties. The night was fleeting fast, and it was the counsel of Rawlins, Jamison, and such other of his men, as had a claim to advise in the proceedings, that they

should instantly cross the river, and, with their prisoners, re
trace their steps toward Zion's Hill. But, Vernon thought
otherwise. He knew the difficulty of travelling by night
through unaccustomed swamps along with a daring set of men,
who, though bound, might yet prove troublesome; and who
indeed, might readily find succor from passing bands of their
companions. There was yet another reason which led Vernon
to defer the movement of his party until morning.

"Doubtless," he said, "there are individuals of this gang
going from and coming into the swamp at all hours of the night.
By preserving the utmost silence where we are, placing a guard
in each of their places of watch, and answering after their own
fashion, any signals that we may hear from without, we shall
be able to gather into our fold a few more of these scoundrels.
I would not like to do the work by halves; still less am I willing to risk what has been gained by any precipitation of movement to-night. Our task now is easy; we have only to secure
thoroughly the prisoners."

"That is already done," said Rawlins, interrupting him.

"Then our work is easy. It lacks but three hours to the
dawn. We must keep our eyes open for that space of time,
and our weapons ready, and with the first gleam of light we
can safely cross the river with all our captives. To move now
would be to risk their loss, and, perhaps, our own. It is no
easy matter to keep track in a strange region, and at night,
with prisoners whom we may have to drive before us, and who
might drop us in the darkness without greatly suffering from
our pistols. Have the horses come?—have you heard the signal from the other bank?"

"They are there. Pollard crossed over to them by my order
a bit ago," was the reply.

"It is well! Everything favors us, men. We have lost no
life, but little blood, and have so far succeeded in all our objects
Let us lose nothing by rashness. Coolness now and carefulness
can alone secure our conquests. To you, Rawlins, as you knew
the swamp best of all of us, I must assign the task of placing
guards over the best positions—and—hark! do you hear : th
ing? That surely was a signal."

"A beagle, by the powers! Here's fish for our net!" at

claimed Rawlins, as he started from the thicket where this conference had taken place. Jamison was about to follow, as also Horsey, but Vernon arrested them.

"Rawlins is enough, and you might confuse him. He is equal to any robber of the gang, and will do the business more effectually if let alone. Hark! already he answers. His bay is quite as good as any of the beagles."

Vernon's judgment was correct. The sturdy woodman hurried in the direction of the sound, which still continued to reach his ears at intervals, becoming more and more clear and distinct as the party drew nigh. He stationed himself under cover at a point where he had surprised one of the robbers, and, responding to the signal as he did so, coolly awaited the approach of the intruder. As the latter emerged on horseback from the woods above, he addressed the counterfeit presentment with all the familiarity of an old acquaintance:—

"Ha! that you, Baker, or Chambers, which!"

Rawlins grunted forth a sound which might pass for an affirmative. He feared to trust his own voice till he had the robber in his power; and it was fortunate that the latter had too much himself to say to regret the taciturnity of his companion. As he spoke a chill went through the bones of Rawlins. A few sentences soon assured him that it was Gideon Badger who addressed him. That profligate son of a man whose purism assured him with a chuckle, that he was not like the miserable Pharisees around him, having demanded of the sentinel to lead him to the place where the chief of the outlaws slept, proceeded to develop his great discoveries to his companion, in anticipation of that revelation which he proposed to make to Saxon, and by which, with all the mean spirit of an inferior's servility, he calculated to commend himself to new favor in his sight. Rawlins could only make his responses in a groan.

"What do you groan for, Baker?" demanded the other. "There's no danger now that we know all about it. We've time enough to send and run to-night, and to-morrow we can turn upon that bullhead Rawlins, and dog his heels back to Zion's Hill. Nay, with a little increase of force, we should be able to lather him at his own weapons and at any weapons

188 BORDER BEAGLES.

For my part, I'd rather it should be so. Nothing would give
me half so much pleasure as to try the chance of a little scuffle
with that fellow. If I didn't—"

"Gideon Badger," said Rawlins, in his natural tone of voice,
"you have your wish. I am Wat Rawlins, and we're face to face.
Now, show your manhood — all your manhood, Gideon — for you
fight, let me tell you, for something more than Rachel Morrison —
you fight for life! You fight with a rope round your neck."

"Wat Rawlins!" gasped the confounded youth, as he heard
the words and recognised the voice of one whom in his secret
soul he feared — "can it be!"

"Are you ready?" demanded the woodman. "Be quick,
Gideon; I know I'm not doing right when I give you this
chance for your life; but I want to save your old father from
the shame of having son of his hung up by the neck. If I kill
you, which will be all the better for you, I'll keep the secret.
and bury you in the swamp with my own hands, so that nobody
shall ever know that we met you here to-night. Come!"

"I will not fight with you," was the hoarse but tremulous
response of the youth.

"I'm sorry for you, Gideon Badger," said Rawlins, with an
expression of pity in his accents, not unmingled with disgust.
I would have saved you from something worse than death.
I'm sorry you're not brave as your father. I can do no
more. You must go with me — you're my prisoner."

He grasped the imbecile around his body as he spoke, with a
grasp that would have defied his utmost powers. But these the
unhappy youth did not offer to exercise. His heart seemed to
have turned to water with the first conviction of his mind that
Walter Rawlins really stood before him. His nerves failed
him. His muscles shrunk and seemed to wither. Rawlins carried him into presence of Vernon and the rest with as little
trouble as if he had been an infant.

The victors, having secured their new captive, had no further
interruption in the swamp that night. With the first glimmering of dawn, Vernon made his preparations for crossing the
river to the place where the horses of the party had been carried. This was a task more tedious than difficult. Some of the
men were compelled to swim the river with a rope which h d

been previously fastened to the flat, and which was absolutely necessary in conveying across the river Virginia Maitland, Mrs. Yarbers—who had been an active coadjutor of the assailing party—the prisoners and the inanimate form of Florence Marbois, which the gentler heart of Virginia would not suffer to be buried in the still and gloomy recesses of that swamp forest in which she had dwelt so long. Rawlins ventured to promise that the cemetery at Zion's Hill should yield her a more consecrated place of repose. Her body, stretched out in the bottom of the boat, and completely enveloped in a cloak, was a subject of fearful interest to Saxon, who was compelled from the smallness of the vessel and the number of its passengers, to remain unwillingly contiguous to it. More than once was he seen to shudder as he looked upon the unmeaning and almost shapeless outline, through the thick envelope of which, however, his keen-eyed and conscious spirit, beheld the reproachful expression of that face, and all those glances of love, and those features of beauty, which had once yielded him so much delight, and which his own capricious and unjust passions had obliterated and destroyed. His present situation, mostly to be ascribed to his own injustice to the one who most loved him, gave emphasis to those rebukes of conscience which now, for the first time, were acutely active in the contemplation of her corse. At this moment a persuasion of sentimental softness almost seized his mind—he felt that love would have still preserved him had he still been true to love. Unhappily for him and her, love and conscience equally spoke too late. A desperate resolution succeeded in his mind, and he turned his eyes upon the dark and turbid waters over which he was passing with an expression of anxious desire.

Could he gain the side of the boat, a single plunge would baffle his captors, and defeat all the terrors of a public doom. His hands were bound, but his feet were free. He gave a single glance to the inanimate form of Florence, and made a movement to the opposite side of the flat. Already his foot touched the low gunwale, when the firm grasp of the watchful Vernon upon his shoulder, showed him that his object was discovered, he was led back into the center of the boat and surrounded by those who noted all his movements, with eyes too jealous to leave him any present hope of baffling their observation. Bitter, indeed, was the glance he cast upon Vernon, as the latter withdrew his hand from the shoulder of the felon.

"There was a time, Mr. Vernon, when you were less willing to approach me with so little scruple; — that, however, was when I was better able to approach you. Times change, and he who would have trembled to hear the lion's growl in the desert, takes him boldly by the mane when in the menagerie. Well! courage 'seems to depend very much upon the season. A bright or dark day makes a wonderful difference in the hearts of men. You are in season now, sir, much more so, I think, than when I met you at Lucchesa. Your hand is more ready now "

"It is my good fortune to improve then, sir," replied Vernon, mildly and with a smile. "As for your notion of my courage, let that be as you choose. If you can really persuade yourself that it is not of the proper kind, and the persuasion pleases you, indulge it. My courage is of a sort that will remain perfectly unaffected, whatever course your opinion may take upon it. Another quality of it will be to take every precaution against the exercise of yours. In my custody you are safe enough. I would not forget myself, sir, by using the language of exultation over a prisoner, however small may be the forbearance which he merits at my hands."

"Oh, you are too indulgent!" was the almost fierce reply of the outlaw—"too indulgent! Would I could thank you as I could wish —as you deserve."

A moment after, and Saxon felt the feeble fury of his manner and stopped suddenly, while a burning flush passed over his cheeks. Vernon turned away. They had now reached the opposite bank.

*   *   *   *   *   *   *

An hour after this and the cavalcade encountered a motley party of ten or a dozen men, headed by old William Badger himself. He was dressed up partially in some of the remnants of the ancient uniform which he wore when he followed Andrew Jackson down from Tennessee to his Indian battles in the southwest. The old and ragged cap which covered his grisly locks, the pistol in his holsters, the belt about his waist, and the long rifle in his grasp—were all the same ; and here, it may be added that, though he wore it not on this occasion, he yet, before sallying forth that morning, gave a long and curious examination to the ancient and motley blue wrapper, known in its day as a hunting-shirt—which had been too intimately associated in all the deeds and doings of his prime to be discarded altogether even when the period of its usefulness was past.

The ancient leader, however, made a far less ludicrous appearance than his men, with whom, in the sudden emergency that called them forth, motley seemed indeed to be "the only wear." At another time, the appearance of this regiment would have moved Vernon and all his followers to unrestrained merriment ; but there was a strong feeling in their hearts at this moment which effectually restrained all lighter moods. The thought that the venerable old man was marching forward to behold his own and only son, bound as an outlaw, and destined to all the penalties of such a life, filled them all with a sorrow that was not less deep because it was speechless. The very unconsciousness of the old man as he drew nigh—the rigid and pompous erection of his carriage, and the swelling dignity of his manner—contributed to increase the solemnity of their feelings. Who should convey the truth to the father ? It tasked the boldest heart and the best mind of the troop.

Vernon rode forward as he approached, and giving instructions with Rawlins to keep his prisoners out of sight as long as possible, undertook the painful task of revealing the truth to the venerable elder. The task was rendered more difficult by the self-esteem of Badger. Assuming himself to have been ill-treated, over looked, slighted, and in fact thrust aside from the performance of his proper duties, by beardless boys, still in the gristle, inspired more by presumption than patriotism, he scarcely gave Vernon a civil recognition.

But the latter, at such a time, and to one so much his elder, would have been ashamed to entertain any boyish resentments ; and he bore patiently with the captiousness of the father, and by gradual degrees, brought him step by step to a consciousness of the gulf that was so suddenly to open before him. When the truth was fully shown—when the tale was fully told—there was no more visible emotion in the face of the hearer, beyond a slight quiver of the lips,

than if he had listened to the most ordinary intelligence. His keen
eyes, from under their shaggy brows, narrowly scanned the countenance of the speaker, and there, reading nothing but sincerity and
distinctness, dropped quietly upon the ground. His lips opened but
to exclaim :—

"Son of mine! son of mine! Oh, God! thou hast indeed
stricken me with thy wrath. Verily, thou hast terribly rebuked the
pride that was shooting upward like a rank weed within my
heart."

The exclamation denoted that self-esteem, still strong, still
luxuriant, and still well cultivated in a favorite field, which was
the predominant characteristic of his mind. That Gideon should
be a bad fellow, was an unfortunate thing for Gideon; but it
was something monstrous exceedingly, that Gideon, the son of
William, should become so. "After this"—such was the still
self-complaisant reflection of the elder—"who will believe in
education?"

The stern habits of the soldier, and the pride of the patriotic magistrate, came to the succor of the old man.

"These wretched people must be committed for trial, Mr.
Vernon, and though you have heretofore found yourself sufficient
to do without my help, as a man, it is probable that you will
require my assistance as a magistrate. Let them be brought before
me, sir, as soon as you please, that I may examine them for
commitment."

"All, sir?" said Vernon.

"Ay, sir, all! God will sustain me, I trust, as he hath ever
done, so that I shall be able to perform the trusts which have
been confided to me, without fear or favor. I trust in his mercy to
have no feeling with one more than another of these unhappy
wretches."

The reader need not ask to know how such a man went through
such a trial. William Badger's proceedings on the present occasion,
would have gained for him, in Roman ages, a column of enduring
fame.

Our story is nearly ended. That very day Horsey was made
a special deputy, with two others, to arrest Mr. Justice Nawls;
but the bird had flown. He had received from some secret
quarter a warning of his danger, and had disappeared on a fleet

horse an hour before the appearance of the party sent to arrest. The return to the magistrate was one which is said to have assumed the official dignity in some of the states—G. T. T.—which, rendered into the vernacular, signifies "Gone to Texas." There is a report current at this time on the Big Black, that Nawls has become a great patriot in Texas, and has distinguished himself by several military achievements of no common order. He is not the first citizen who has lived a scoundrel to die a patriot. It was fortunate for the amateur that he did not take Mrs. Horsey with him to texas, and make her a patriot too. Perhaps he would have done so, had time been allowed him. How many good deeds are defeated through a want of time.

When the roving husband and his lovely wife returned to Zion's Hill, who should they encounter there but the venerable sire of the former, limping as much as ever, quite as rash and boisterous, and full of storms and cataracts at the sight of the fugitive. He had come, in obedience to Vernon's letters, along with Ben Carter, and was confounded to meet a living son, where he thought it might be difficult to find even a dead one. His very joy—such was the force of habit—took the features, and indulged in the language of anger and abuse.

"You ungrateful spendthrift—you—"

He was silenced by a very summary proceeding. He little knew the sort of answer his son had in store for him.

"Make you acquainted with Mrs. Tom Horsey, dad," said he, with a swagger admirably theatrical, as he strutted full up to the old man, with the shrinking Mary hanging on his arm.

"Mrs. Tom Horsey! Why, Tom, it can't be possible. I expected to find you dead, and here you're only married. But are you married, Tom?"

"Ay, dad, if the ceremony performed by such a scoundrel as Squire Nawls is worth a fig."

"Well, God bless you, Tom—you're born to be an actor after all. And you, my gal—who are you—what's your name? And, since you are Tom's wife, give's a smack. Another! another! Well, Tom, to a young man, marrying's not so bad after all. But where's Ben Carter?"

This is a question which we may also ask. In another apartment, to themselves, Carter and his unfaithful friend, Maitland communed for a lengthened hour. They came·forth reconciled. Maitland frankly confessed his offences equally against friendship and good morals; and in making every atonement which had been left, he found Carter as he had ever found him, an indulgent benefactor.

The relation in which Vernon stood to Virginia contributed greatly to this end. They also, to themselves, had their own explanations to make, and their several adventures to relate; the day promised fair, amid all the clouds that overcast the horizon at the beginning, to terminate in equal calm and brightness. To the three happy sets, whom we have conducted with persevering industry through the groves to the temple—from love to marriage—such, indeed, was its termination; but there was one storm that passed through the forest about this time which filled even their hearts with solemn shudderings, and for a long season after maintained a heavy weight upon their memories. Rawlins, who, with a select party, had the charge of the prisoners, returned at midnight, alone, to Zion's Hill, and brought with him a terrible narrative of outrage and bloodshed. The mob had risen upon his little party, and rescued the prisoners from his hands. But they did not rescue them to save. Goaded to madness by the long-repeated crimes of the outlaws, they had resolved not to wait the tardy proceedings of justice; and in equal defiance of the entreaties and the efforts of the little guard, the unhappy criminals were dragged to death from their custody and. protection. Another moment precipitated their doom. They were drawn up by the ropes which bound them, to the swinging branches over head, and hurried into eternity without a moment's grace—their prayers drowned—their convulsions mocked in the frantic joy and the exulting shouts of the populace.

The unlawfulness of their punishment suggests the only occasion for sympathy in their behalf. They died on a spot which they themselves had deprived of all the securities of law, and had shadowed with every sort of crime. They perished by a reckless rage, for which a partial sanction may be found in the wantonness and brutality of their own deeds—in their unscrupulous robberies, their frequent cruelties, and most unfeelng murders. Saxon died as he had lived, a brave, fearless man. Perhaps, the compunctious writhings which troubled him at the death of Florence Marbois, had made him better prepared to die. In his death perished the spirit, the energy, and the capacity of the Border Beagles He had made them what they were—resolute, compact—one and indivisible. Scattered at his death, they lost the faculties which had made them powerful, and have generally given up the more daring profession for others of a like but less dangerous character. Some, like Nawls, have gone to Texas, filled with a sudden desire of becoming patriots—others have taken to shaving, speculating, and banking; and a few, it is reported, have formed a new confederacy which bears the innocent, if not unmeaning title of "The Hypothecators." What is the particular occupation which, under this head, they intend pursuing, is only conjectural. The more knowing seem to think that their purpose is nothing worse than the invention of fancy stocks; the designs of which they will dispose of to the numberless associations of humbug, which cover this scheming nation as with an eighth plague. The locusts of the Egyptian never diminished his crops with half the success with which our locusts, the progeny of that fruitful Scotchman, John Law, have devastated the fields of Mississippi. The Border Beagles were nothing to them, public enemies.

www.ingramcontent.com/pod-product-compliance
Lightning Source LLC
Chambersburg PA
CBHW032014110726
47901CB00004B/1087